Dragon's (

Rap
Rocky Mountain Sanctuary
Zombie Plagues

RAPTURE's AFTERMATH

7 YEAR GREAT TRIBULATION

> TWO WITNESSES & FALSE PRESIDENT (BEAST)
> TIMELINE COMMENCES 1040 - 2300 T/D

2300 Days "until the Sanctuary is Cleansed"

TIME OF REFINEMENT 1260 DAYS	TIME OF REDEMPTION 1260 DAYS
REFINED CHILDREN OF GOD MARTYRS OF UNDERSTANDING CHRISTIAN MARTYRS OF CHRIST	**REDEEMED - REPENTED - SAVED 7 SPIRITS 7 THUNDERS 2 WITNESSES OF GOD FLYING HELL MONSTERS**

1260 T/D
- WAR IN HEAVEN
- DRAGON HURLED TO EARTH
- WOMEN FLEES
- WILDERNESS SANCTUARY
- DRAGON'S HUGE SERGE FLOOD WAVES
- GREAT DOMED CITY
- RISE OF THE "UNHOLY TRINITY"
- DRAGON'S TATTOO 666, 3-COLOR
- CHRISTIANS PERSECUTED
- FLEE TO THE HILLS
- ROCKY MOUNTAIN SANCTUARY
- TWO WITNESSES @ 1040 T/D BEGIN
- ZOMBIE PLAGUES @ 1040 T/D BEGIN
- BEAST ATTACKS @ 1040 T/D BEGIN
- POWER OF THE HOLY PEOPLE SHATTERED
- GOD'S WILDERNESS CHILDREN "REFINED"
- MARTYRS OF UNDERSTANDING "REFINED"
- DRAGON BREAKS PEACE TREATY

1290 T/D
- DRAGON'S IMAGE IDOL CRAFTED
- DRAGON'S TEMPLE DEDICATION CEREMONY
- ABOMINATION OF DESOLATION ACTIVATED
- DRAGON'S IMAGE IDOLS WORLDWIDE
- DRAGON'S TATTOO 666, 1-COLOR
- GET ITS MARK ON RIGHT HAND, OR DIE

1335 T/D
- TIME OF HOLPEN
- MARTYRS RECEIVE: HOLPEN
- CHRISTIAN MARTYRS OF CHRIST "REFINED"
- MARTYRS GATHERED SKY GREAT TRUMPET
- BLESSED IS COMES TO THE 1335 DAYS.
- WEDDING IN HEAVEN. @ 1335 T/D

DRAGON'S TATTOO 666 Trilogy © 2011 RICHARD VANDERPLOEG

1040 T/D
- TEMPLE OF GOD, people worshiping there, but no Ark of God's Covenant present.

1290 T/D
- REDEEMED ISRAELITES
  "PRIOR TO SEEING" the abomination of desolation" in the Dragons temple 1290 T/d certain Israelites went to the Two Witnesses of God and accepted their Testimony "IN FAITH" they go to the "Wilderness Sanctuary" as the "Temple Priests"

1290-1400 T/D
- REPENTED ISRAELITES
  "AFTER SEEING" "abomination of desolation" 1290 T/d. Jesus said those in Judea flee to the hills. Certain Israelites flee and accepted their Testimony; 1290-1400 T/d., and go to the "Wilderness Sanctuary" as the "Repented Congregation".

1400-2300 T/D
- REPENTED SAVED NATIONS
  Lands of the 10 kings. They accepted the Two Witnesses "Baptism unto Repentance," received and kept their salvation garments. 1400-2300 T/D. God says; "Go and gather them" & then "Come out of her, my people, lest you share in her sins, and lest you receive of her plagues". "Blessed are those who are called to the marriage supper of the Lamb!"

2300 T/D
- SANCTUARY IS CLEANSED, now the Temple of God is seen having the Ark of His Covenant.
- GREAT RED DRAGON RELEASED
- TWO WITNESSES KILLED
- JERUSALEM DESTROYED BY FIRE
  UNWORTHY ISRAELITES, flee to the hills and repent only out of fear. God says; go and gather these "BAD" so His wedding hall may be filled. These are the Evil Seeds, in the Kingdom of Peace.
- ARMAGEDDON COUNTDOWN BEGINS
- ARMAGEDDON

Dragon's Tattoo 666 Trilogy
Rapture's Aftermath
Rocky Mountain Sanctuary
Zombie Plagues

Richard D. VanderPloeg

Copyright © 2014 Richard D. VanderPloeg.

All rights reserved. No part of this book may be used or reproduced by any means, graphic, electronic, or mechanical, including photocopying, recording, taping or by any information storage retrieval system without the written permission of the publisher except in the case of brief quotations embodied in critical articles and reviews.

Abbott Press books may be ordered through booksellers or by contacting:

Abbott Press
1663 Liberty Drive
Bloomington, IN 47403
www.abbottpress.com
Phone: 1-866-697-5310

Scripture taken from the New King James Version. Copyright © 1979, 1980, 1982 by Thomas Nelson, inc. Used by permission. All rights reserved.

This novel is a work of fiction. With the exception of historical persons and facts as noted on the Web site, names, characters, places, and incidents are either the product of the authors' imaginations or are used fictitiously. Any resemblance to actual events, locales, organizations, or persons in the present day is entirely coincidental and beyond the intent of either the authors or the publisher.

Editor: Ursula VanderPloeg
Contributor: Danielle Vann
Contact Information:
www.dragonstattoo666.com
Art graphics Design, X Agency Inc.
Kristopher Hadfield, klhadfield@gmail.com

Because of the dynamic nature of the Internet, any web addresses or links contained in this book may have changed since publication and may no longer be valid. The views expressed in this work are solely those of the author and do not necessarily reflect the views of the publisher, and the publisher hereby disclaims any responsibility for them.

ISBN: 978-1-4582-1510-9 (sc)
ISBN: 978-1-4582-1512-3 (hc)
ISBN: 978-1-4582-1511-6 (e)

Library of Congress Control Number: 2014905653

Printed in the United States of America.

Abbott Press rev. date: 04/14/2014

abbott press®
A DIVISION OF WRITER'S DIGEST

DEDICATION

Praise **God**. God said,
"For many are called, but few are chosen."

PROLOGUE

Dragon's Tattoo 666 will redefine how the masses of Christians and others seek and find the mysteries of God's Plan of Salvation. Deceived world-wide populations open their hearts and souls to a galactic imposter posing as their messiah returned. Those seeing through his masquerade are targeted for slaughter by the hundreds of millions.

If, during your life you only read and dissect one book cover to cover, this is it. What you need to know is not only exposed for the first time, the book also lays down a route through hell leading souls to God, for only a select few sparkle, vanish and are taken directly to God in Heaven. God Himself said; 'this earth was created for many, Heaven only a few'.

Discoveries are unearthed that have stymied scholars for past millennia, now brought to light by the ushering in of a most unconventional thinking process that some say only dyslexia can achieve. A search for the truth and reality with penetrating insight into the 'end of days'.

Dragon's Tattoo 666 contains Biblical facts from millenniums past predicting horrific futuristic events. The events morph into real time flowing in the readers mind like a motion picture and not just static references.

Dragon's Tattoo 666 commences with the Rapture Event soon to take place, followed by the Rapture's Aftermath Events that take place during the 7 year Great Tribulation Time called the "Time of Sorrows". The conclusion of these days culminates with the "Cull of the Damned": Armageddon.

Dragon's Tattoo 666 was inspired by the book of Revelation written by the Apostle John and the Biblical prophet Daniel and his vision of the; 2300 days "until the sanctuary is cleansed". The riddle of this Biblical conundrum prophecy has now been solved and fully documented within the book.

We live in the present, however, as recorded in Daniel 12:4 "But you, Daniel, shut up the words, and seal the book until the time of the end; <u>many shall run to and fro</u>, and <u>knowledge shall increase</u>."

Today, people are so preoccupied with their day to day lives they 'can't see the forest for the trees'.

Bible verses used as references are identified by chapter and verse along with their corresponding end note numbers and to the best of the author's ability some are paraphrased when used within the main body of the book.

Also included is a flow chart reference guideline. Please refer to this often to keep your bearings.

RAPTURE:
The 'Rapture' will take place unannounced; some will be participants, unfortunately most only witnesses, suffering its aftermath.

THREE SACRAMENTS:
If by chance the 'Rapture' has not occurred prior to your reading date of *Dragon's Tattoo 666*, seek out the Christian religious institutions that have been offering the 'three Sacraments' for a very long time.

If you just asked yourself the question, "What are these 'three Sacraments'?", most likely, you don't have them. Seek them out.

BRIDE OF CHRIST:
"Who are they? Am I one of them?" They are discovered and discussed in detail and the answers will indeed, amaze you. If you just asked yourself the question who is the 'Bride of Christ' and the Rapture has already taken place, one thing is certain... you weren't.

THE SEVEN RAPTURE REWARDS:
Read in the book what the Son of God, our Lord, has to say about them, they're fantastic and only given to a few!

RAPTURES AFTERMATH:
This is day one that commences the 'Time of Sorrows' of the *Dragon's Tattoo 666*. To those who read this book after the 'Rapture' has taken place, take heart, it does not matter to which religion upon earth you belong, the 'God of heaven' is the 'God of all'. You are greatly loved. The Son of God said "I have other sheep in other folds".

FIRE BREATHING SUPERNATURAL BEINGS FROM GOD:
They are sent to earth by God and commissioned to offer God's salvation or plagues to everyone across the entire world prior to Armageddon. This religious conundrum has been solved as to how it takes place. These beings are active mainly during the second half of the 'Time of Sorrows'. Their daunting task will be gargantuan. How can only two beings testify unto billions of people in only 1260 days? You will discover how they accomplish this along with their helpers, the 7 Spirits and 7 Thunders of God. Oh yes, I almost forgot, they are followed by the 'Flying Hell Monsters' who unleash the 'Zombie Plagues'. Ok, laugh now, however, once you've read what the Bible has to say about this topic, your laughter will turn into horror.

FURTIVE DISCOVERIES:
The events of *Dragon's Tattoo 666* contain over 50 furtive discoveries hiding in plain sight but oblivious to the casual reader. These fascinating discoveries unfold as you delve deeper.

MARTYR OF THE CHRISTIANS:
The events portrayed can only be described as horrific as the antichrist will slaughter everyone not in accordance with their agenda who will not bow to Satan, the Great Red Dragon, god of earth, and get his mark that the Bible calls 'the mark of the beast' and that I call the 'Dragon's Tattoo 666' shown on the front cover of the book. Notice his mark it's not frightening or evil looking, rather unique to behold however those wearing it are numbered to the 'cull of the damned', the antichrist.

MATURE CONTENT:
This book, the product of nearly three years' intensive research, is intended for mature readers only. There are no precedence baselines past, present or future that offer comparisons as to the author's knowledge.

During the 7 Year Great Tribulation 'Time of Sorrows' billions elect to be willing participants and join the 'unholy trinity' and become the antichrist culminating with the end of this world: ARMAGEDDON.

AM I GOING TO HELL?
That depends. Over 90% are! One thing you should know, God has not forsaken you. Your faith is going to be put to the test. You will either side with God or the 'unholy trinity', the antichrist.

So you ask yourself the big question, "Why me?" It's simple. You didn't see the forest for the trees because you were so preoccupied with earthly trinkets. Remember, 'all that glistens is not gold'.

God is giving you another chance, although you're going to have to do it the hard way.

7 CATEGORIES OF GOD'S PLAN OF SALVATION[1]
During the 7 year great tribulation 'time of sorrows' 7 categories of people emerge during these two 3½ year time periods. God's plan is complicated, yet glorious.

The 'Time of Refinement' produces three groups during the first half of the 'Time of Sorrows'. The Children of God 'refined', the Martyrs of understanding 'refined' and a vast number of Martyrs of Christ 'refined' Revelation 7:9-17[2]. Perhaps you may be one of them. If so you're blessed.

The 'Time of Redemption' produces three groups during the second half of the 'Time of Sorrows' a vast number of people become Redeemed, Repented and Saved.

The seventh group are the 'Evil Seeds', they're in the book and you will never guess who they are.

Dragon's Tattoo 666 contains Biblical facts along with conjecture. Many fascinating discoveries were made along the way and now brought to light in a unique manner.

There is a great deal of newly introduced to the world information about God's Plan of Salvation so go slowly and absorb it. This is one book you do not want to speed read as your soul salvation may depend upon it. Subsequent readings uncover furtive subtleties triggering the "I get it" thought.

To the unfortunates who will live during the Rapture's Aftermath, you are being given a second chance to prove to God you deserve His mercy. Like I previously said, this time it's the hard way.

There will be two main groups during these days; those who choose God or those who sadly choose Satan and become the antichrist.

Remember, God has not abandoned you and those who become 'Martyrs' will receive what the prophet Daniel referred to as 'Holpen'. This is 'Divine Help' from God. 'Holpen' is another of the discoveries made and we will discuss this marvelous miracle in great detail later.

Dragon's Tattoo 666 takes a futuristic Biblical look at the Rapture's Aftermath events, you will either be reading this book pre or post Rapture. To those who do not believe in the Rapture soon to take place, Tom, Maria and Joe say hello, get yourself a short wave radio, the BSW type, so you can communicate, you're going to need it.

Keep the faith, whatever faith you belong to. Maria, Joe and Tom will be seeing you soon, and perhaps even their strange friend, Mel.

𝔇ragon's 𝔗attoo 666 𝔗rilogy

CONTENTS

BOOK ONE
RAPTURE'S AFTERMATH

1. Blown Away ... 19
2. Along Came Tom ... 31
3. Get Out of Dodge ... 39
4. Cabin Talks ... 65
5. Taboo Tattoo ... 91
6. Woman Clothed With the Sun ... 95
7. Wilderness Sanctuary ... 97
8. Rise of the Unholy Trinity ... 105
9. Dragon's Temple Construction ... 125
10. Mark of the Beast ... 129
11. False Messiah's Agenda ... 137
12. Christians Persecuted Worldwide ... 143
13. Get Out of Dodge 'Again' ... 147
14. Cabin Exodus: Flee to the Cave ... 151

BOOK TWO
ROCKY MOUNTAIN SANCTUARY

15. Arrival at the Cave ... 163
16. Summit Cave Living ... 169
17. Rise of the National Guard ... 175
18. Invisible to the World ... 181
19. Nomads Coming Our Way ... 189
20. Abram, First Temple Priest ... 193
21. Prelude to the 1040 T/D ... 197

22.	Martyrs of Understanding	199
23.	Daniel's Prophecy: End of Days	205
24.	Gentiles Tread the Holy City	209
25.	Mathematical Biblical Conundrum	211
26.	God's Temple Partially Opens	217
27.	7 Year Great Tribulation Overview	219
28.	Do the Math, Israel Year One 1040-1400 T/D	223
29.	Do the Math, Nations of the 10 Kings, 1400-2300 T/D	227
30.	Heavenly Monkey Wrenches 1040-2300 T/D	233
31.	Supernatural Powers 7-7-2 FHM	235
32.	Salvation of the Nations	243
33.	Supernatural Abilities of the Two Entities	245
34.	Kings Highway	249
35.	Flying Hell Monsters	253
36.	Zombies & Vampires in the Bible	255

BOOK THREE
ZOMBIE PLAGUES

37.	Zombie Plagues	267
38.	Entities of Death Slaughter 200 Million	281
39.	Biblical Support for Zombies	297
40.	How the Events Unfold	307
41.	Thunder Message One 1040 T/D	317
42.	Thunder Message Two 1260 T/D	343
43.	Thunder Message Three 1290 T/D	363
44.	Martyrdom: Maria and Joe	375
45.	The Last Martyr: Tom	385
46.	Mel, Supernatural Guide	389
47.	Thunder Message Four 1400 T/D	417
48.	Thunder Message Five 2260 T/D	455
49.	Thunder Message Six 2300 T/D A/C@-220	471
50.	Thunder Message Seven A/C@-216.5 T/D	481
51.	Armageddon Countdown A/C@-66.5	495
52.	Great Babylon	509
53.	Great Babylon Remembered Before God A/C@-33.0	519
54.	Marshalling the Troops at Mount of Megiddo	525
55.	Armageddon A/C@-00.00	527

56.	Christ on a White Horse & Heavenly Army	531
57.	The Beast and His Armies Defeated	533
58.	Book of Life	537
59.	Lamb's Book of Life	541
60.	Bride, Marriage, Wife of God's Son	543
61.	Hierarchy of the Bride	545
62.	New Jerusalem	547
63.	Functions of the Hierarchy	549
64.	Blessed is He Who Waits and Comes to the 1335	555
65.	Sanctuary is Now Cleansed	557
66.	The Order of Melchizedek	561
	Epilogue	563
	Endnotes	567

Dragon's Tattoo 666 Trilogy

Rapture's Aftermath

Synopsis
Humanity, backs turned to God, running to and fro are caught off guard by the Rapture's galactic war events played out in the Heavens. Satan loses and is hurled down to the earth by supernatural forces crashing into the Gulf of Aqaba. Along his downward spiral come the Raptures Aftermath, complete with its tragic consequences. Catastrophic destructions, now triggered causing great joy or sorrow depending on which side is served. You are either with God, or against God- there is no room for complacency. Forces of evil antichrist now pitted against good compete for domination, with the winner takes all. Three unlikely heroes, Tom, Maria and Joe arise, challenging and confronting the unholy trinity. At the best of times, they are only one heartbeat ahead of death. They flee across America playing 'cat and mouse' with the forces of evil hot on their trail. Will they arrive at the ultimate safe house nestled high up and in the Rocky Mountains? Will they 'get out of dodge', or be caught by the evil Tom spent years trying to escape?

CHAPTER ONE

BLOWN AWAY

Pentecost Sunday: time/date 'T/D' current year

7am comes too early on a Sunday, even with the sound of Louis Armstrong's "It's a Beautiful Life", birds singing in the trees, and a gentle breeze flowing in through Joe and Maria's half opened bedroom window. It's already a lazy morning in the city.

Maria, mumbling to herself for forgetting to turn off her alarm the night before, fumbled with her cell phone's snooze alarm, pressing it just as the announcer voice instructs to "Take shelter immedia—" With the announcers urgent warning cut off by Maria's drowsy actions, Joe, her husband, turns to ask,

"What did he say?"

"Something about shelter?" Immediately trailing her words, a loud roar much like a diesel locomotive, erupts straight through their bedroom.

A series of tremendous booms shook them to their bones. Shock waves began pounding their heads so severely one would think their heads were splitting in two. Rifling debris now screeching past their partially opened window, did little to distract them as the ground beneath their bed began shaking vehemently.

After what seemed like an eternity of ear shattering sound the roof of their home began peeling away, layer after layer and disintegrated before their eyes in what seemed slow motion. Splinters and fragmentation shards, as from grenades, began exploding in rapid succession. Seconds later their roof's superstructure no longer existed and was gone. Both were mesmerised by these destructive happenings.

Transfixed they stare up at what a mere few seconds ago was their bedroom ceiling, now turned into a darkened chaotic sky. Astonished, they watched as patio chairs, lawn ornaments, shingles and large flying debris flew by just above their heads.

Both, now completely bewildered and engulfed in total calmness, hoped that whatever happened was over as quickly as it began. However, the sound of silence was shattered when several wall ornaments intermittently began dropping and crashing to the floor.

They look at each other with a combination of fear and relief as they were unscathed by this occurrence. After sitting up in bed and shaking dust and debris from their heads Joe exclaimed, "Whoa, that was close!" Immediately, as if on cue, upon uttering these words, their large floor to ceiling wall unit began to sway and toppled crashing onto their bed. They were saved from injury only due to their bed's large foot board.

"Whoa!" Joe yelled out and immediately, as if on cue again, they looked up at the exposed brick chimney that now reached twenty feet above their heads, and cringed as it started making strange sounds. Bricks and mortar began to fracture and crack, creating roars best described like mini machine gun explosions spitting out brick shrapnel in all directions. The chimney's foundation, having been severely fractured during the devastation, now began crumbling. As the towering column began teetering to and fro in slow motion they scrambled out of bed, stumbling over debris and escaping out through the opening where their large window used to be. They tumbled out onto the grass just as the chimney fell crashing onto their bed driving it through the floor and what was left of their house crumbled into the basement.

"Whoa." murmured Joe.

Maria rolled onto him shouting, "What's with you and your, 'Whoa, Whoa, Whoa's?' Stop saying them. You're going to get us killed!" (Revelation 8:13) Maria rolled off of Joe only to join him in staring up into the sky. Both become mesmerized by what they are witnessing.

"Maria, what do you see?"

"Whoa!" she exclaimed, raising her eyebrows and rolling her eyes at him teasingly. "It looks like the 4th of July in outer space! What do you think it is? An explosion? Or meteorite or something? Whatever it is seems to be far away, like lightning way up high in space. This is intense, and almost thrilling other than our house being destroyed and that we were almost killed." She pauses, then in a softer voice says "I wonder how long the fireworks will last."

Joe takes her hand in his, comforting both her and himself and uses his other hand to point,

"Look, over there it seems like sun spots all over the place. If I didn't know better, I'd say they look like nuclear explosions far out in space."

"I thought nukes made mushrooms. Those look like balls out in space and wouldn't we be blind if we looked at a nuke explosion?" Maria asked.

"What am I, Mr. Know-it-all? If this were at night we could probably see it better. Even in daylight it's amazing. It looks like a meteor shower, actually, really big meteors. See over there, some are burning out as they enter the atmosphere and some look like they're exploding. They almost look like mini suns to me."

"Whatever they are, I hope there are no really big ones."

Upon rising to their feet they slowly rotated their heads and viewed the carnage. At first they did not fully absorb their surroundings, but as reality set in, a look of astonishment came over them as they beheld a path of destruction about a mile wide and extending its wrath far in front of and behind them.

"Now that's something I never expected to see. Everything's flattened, just like I've seen in news broadcasts when communities were hit by tornados. Do you think it's over?" Maria turned to Joe.

"Yea once a tornado extinguishes itself that's it, game over. Our neighbourhood is wrecked, and I bet thousands of houses were destroyed." Joe answered.

"We're lucky to be alive and unhurt."

Joe snorted, "Unhurt? You're kidding! Just look at me! I've got scratch marks all over my arms!"

Maria looked at him sheepishly and said,

"Actually, I think they're from me trying to shut you up from saying those whoa words again! Suck it up buttercup.", and she smiled teasingly.

"Maria, give me a break! Only you would be that superstitious as to think my words Whoa-Whoa-Whoa were doing us in!" But suddenly, in the same breath he said, "Look at that explosion way up there! It's so bright, brighter than the sun. I can't see I'm blind, can you see?"

"Ugh! I don't know yet, I was looking slightly away from it but I'm seeing lights dancing in my head, that's for sure. What is happening?"

Joe, now on his hands and knees, took deep breaths. "My eyesight's starting to come back but I'm seeing stars in my head from that explosion. It was like looking into a million flash bulbs right in front of your face!" Maria agreed her eyesight was slowly starting to focus but still not right. Joe attempting to calm her down, half-heartedly asked "Do you want to wish upon a falling star?"

"Don't make me hurt you".

Joe noticed a flash of light high above them.

"What was that? I've never seen such a massive lightning bolt like that before. I'm guessing it came from high up in space travelling to the east somewhere."

"Joe, I don't like this! We need to find shelter or make shelter with what's left of our house."

Suddenly, Maria cried out,

"Where is that screaming in my ears coming from? Joe! The ground is shaking again!" A crack of lightning struck so close, it almost knocked them off their feet.

Things were getting too close for any sense of comfort Joe and Maria might have had left.

In a panic Joe yelled,

"There's something heading our way—fast!"

"Can we make it into our basement yelled Maria?"

However, in a heartbeat Joe realized that action would be futile as he saw from the corner of his eye some type of shock wave obliterating everything in its path mere seconds away. He grabbed

Maria, hurling them both into the drainage gulley by the side of the road a few feet from where they were standing.

They tumbled into it, dazed and confused as to whether it was the fall that knocked the wind from out of them, or whatever it was that came their way. Flying glass shards and splinter debris filled the rushing air mere inches above their heads shredding everything in its path. And after what seemed like an eternity of gasping for air they warily began trying to talk.

"What just happened?" Maria whimpered. They both stared at each other in bewilderment as Joe silently tried to explain to Maria that the sound of the destruction had probably affected their hearing and to calm down. As Joe struggled to gain volume and composure with ears still ringing, he knew he had to take action for him and his wife who after a few minutes said,

"I seem to be ok, but I hurt all over. No blood, I think we're ok. What was it this time?"

"To be honest, I'm not sure. I think it was some kind of subsonic boom that seemed to shake my bones more so than my body."

"Yah! Like something just took a hold of me from the inside out. This is getting really spooky. It felt like when you stood in front of an enormous boom box used in rock concerts. The subsonic sound wave could almost knock you over. What just happened was a thousand times greater." Maria could not see how such a thing was possible and let out a huge frustrated sigh.

Joe lifted his wife into his arms and carrying her said, "Let's get into what's left of our house for safety and supplies."

"Good idea, you rummage around. I've got a headache. Ha, ha. Oh it hurts to laugh. At least we can hide there to regain our composure."

They huddled for a few minutes then Joe asked

"Does your cell phone still work?"

"I must have lost it during the chaos."

Joe smiled and pointed to her hand still holding her phone. After they pried it loose from what seemed like a death grip she began fumbling with it for a few seconds, trying to get a news channel to look for a report on this disaster.

"I can't believe what just happened! One minute it's a beautiful day, everything's fine and the following second we're flat on our backs lucky to be alive."

Maria yelled "You're not going to believe this! My News App is still working and they're tweeting updates about people 'sparking'."

"What do you mean 'sparking'?"

"I don't know, look for yourself. They're here one second and gone the next. Looks like a big spark and the person disappears, people are texting videos showing them and everything! Right now all I want to know is this; are these explosions over? Are we safe or what?"

Joe said he thought it seemed as if they were over in their area at least from what the announcer was saying.

"Did those explosions cause spontaneous human combustion, or were they vaporized by the debris striking them?" Maria wondered out loud.

"Well, all I know is that we're safe. We weren't vaporized."

"No! Not us! I mean those people getting sparked! I don't think those explosions and debris would travel that far to burn them up — it's got to be something else."

Joe turned on the radio App on Maria's phone and found one of the only clear stations had a preacher talking and ranting about this being the 'Rapture'.

Another station had a 'Reverend Bob' who was calling it the 'Wrath of God' and the 'end of time.'

"What did he mean by the 'Wrath of God'?" Joe asked.

"I don't know. But, I bet that Tom would. You know that brother of yours. The one who is always talking about doomsday? Remember how he wrote that book called *Dragon's Tattoo 666*? At Christmas, he even signed it for us . . . and then went native."

"Oh, I forgot to tell you he left a voice message on our phone the other day saying he's dropping by this Sunday, Maria. That's today, I think. I'm so confused! He said sometime today on his way back home, wherever that is, he'll drop by and that he has a surprise for us."

"Great that's all we need to top off the day. Where's his book?"

"It was in our wall unit library. Now it's in the junk pile somewhere in our bedroom."

"You mean what's now our basement bedroom."

"Yea that's a scary thing. Now may be a good time to find it. I'll go and search through the debris and try to find it. You keep watching the news."

"Joe, I don't think this is a good idea. The remaining structure is very unstable."

"What structure?" murmured Joe. "I have a feeling we need it. I'll be careful."

"Just don't use any more of those little four letter words."

He carefully slid down the debris into what was left of their entertainment room.

"It's got to be here somewhere. Where is anything when you really need it?" Talking to himself, he muttered, "Now where can you be little book? Nope not there."

As minor debris cascaded down around him, Maria yelled out, "Are you ok?"

"No problem. Let's see. Ah, there you are. Strange, it was just lying there out in the open. A little spooky, if you ask me." He muttered again as he climbed up out of the basement and rejoined Maria. "There's lots of reading here, well over three inches of pages. Do I have to read this whole thing to figure out what this 'Rapture' thing is?"

"Of course not." Maria said. "Just look in the index for the part concerning the Rapture."

"I knew that. Ok, here it is, there are two listings, the 'Rapture' and the 'Rapture's Aftermath.'"

"Start with the first one." Maria said, so, Joe read out loud:

"The Rapture is an event that occurs during another event called the 'First Resurrection'.

"Oh great, a riddle within a riddle! This is all Greek to me."

Joe replied, "How about I read the first paragraph as follows: 'the First Resurrection is a plurality of linked events having commencement and conclusion events occurring over a time span consisting of a generation of like-minded people.'"

"That's a mouthful of double talk, if you ask me."

Joe kept reading, "During this time span a 'Singularity Event' known as the 'Rapture' takes place whereby certain predestined 'holy' people are caught up to God in Heaven. Should I read more?"

"No," replied Maria.

"Good," he sighed, "as I can't understand a word that I just spoke."

She replied, "No need. The announcer is already talking about it."

"This breaking news! Some reverend was discussing this thing called the 'Rapture'. For all of you out there wondering what's going on, you're not alone. It appears that a special event has just happened worldwide as foretold in the Bible. The Bible predicted that God would send His Son to return and take from this earth His elect who were chosen to be His Bride."

Maria interjected rhetorically, "His Bride?"

The reverend went on to say, "I must confess that I am perplexed. It appears that I was not one of them and if you're watching me then you, too, were not one of them and this means that we are all living in the 'Rapture's Aftermath'."

The news channel now switched to another somewhat weird looking person who was challenging his views. He was saying that it had nothing to do with the so called 'Rapture' or the 'Rapture's Aftermath' and that this entire event can be logically and scientifically justified.

Maria said, "Get a look at his suit jacket. It's navy blue having a v-cut neck line and blackish type T-shirt under it. Look at his colorful armband logo. My screen is too small to make it out clearly. What does your brother's book have to say about all of this?"

Joe mutters, as he read out loud, "Something about billions of people will witness these supernatural events and that they were in fact the result of a great war fought in the heavens by the devil and the forces of God. The devil loses and was hurled down to earth by the Archangel Michael."

Maria interjected, "The news channel guy is talking about these events. They're saying some sort of a natural phenomenon. Whatever it is, they're all very excited."

"Turn up the volume. How can you say exciting? We could have been killed!"

"I didn't say exciting. They're saying it." Maria whimpered. I still can't hear very well. My ears are ringing. They're calling it some type of galactic fireworks about 10,000 miles out in space. It sure looks closer than that to me. If it's so far out then what knocked us on our asses and how did we hear it so loudly? I thought sound can't travel in space maybe it's not in space."

Joe exclaimed, "What a science question that would make. If a nuclear explosion occurs in space, will it make a sound when it strikes our earth and would we hear it?"

"Stop talking like that! Who cares about your science question?"

"Right now I just want to be safe from those things blowing up in the sky. That last bang that hit us was from a massive and very bright lightning bolt!"

"Joe, could this be something like the northern lights, just much more powerful?"

"Maria, are you asking me another science question?"

"Whatever. I don't know, they seemed awfully bright to me and I don't think the northern lights make any noise or can knock down skyscrapers."

"You know Joe, in college, I did some research on the Northern Lights. They were also called the 'Finger of God' when they touched the ground. For what it's worth, we were definitely touched, more like hammered. Is it just me? I can feel the ground pulsating even in here. Are they still happening?

Joe replied, "No, I think it's only aftershocks of some type. The whole thing is like the ending to the movie Independence Day when the alien mother ship blows up shooting all those burning debris with their fire contrails to earth."

Maria was still shaking so he held her even closer. "I'm so far passed frightened, it's scary", she said. "This is too unreal. I'm just thankful we're still alive."

"Listen! You won't believe this! They're saying that the sparking is affecting even cars."

"What do you mean? Are they 'sparking' too?"

Chapter Two
ALONG CAME TOM

"Hello, can I come in?"

"I don't believe it! It's your brother, Tom, asking permission to come in, to what I'll never know."

"I thought things couldn't get worse, and what do you mean 'It's your brother, Tom'? Like I've forgotten who he is?"

"Have you missed me?" Tom asked.

"Actually, no!"

"Oh don't listen to him," said Maria. "We're happy to see you."

"Guys, I overheard your neighbours yelling at you. I think I know what they meant. We should head for the hills, "get out of Dodge" to my country cabin."

"Told you he was nuts.

"Joe be nice. Tom's just different."

"I was referring to 'the 'Dutchman', he's a little nuts. I can't remember his wife's name, I do recall she was kind, and gave me some banana bread once. He was always giving me books about religion, seems like it didn't do him any good either. But speaking of nuts, Tom's a close second, he marches to the beat of a loony drum."

"Listen up, both of you," Maria gently commanded.

The emergency broadcast standby signal that was flashing on the screen of Maria's cell phone came alive. "This is an emergency. The President will be making an announcement within the next few minutes."

"Finally we're getting somewhere! I feel safer knowing that our government is taking action."

"Maria," Tom replied in an ominous tone, "Be careful what you wish for," emanating an aura of wisdom and assuredness that sent shivers up and down the spines of the young couple.

"Tom, you always did worry too much."

"We'll see soon enough." Tom almost whispered, taking a pause to breathe in slowly and assess the situation around them.

Joe replied, "The fireworks are over so we can all relax."

Tom looked at both of them and said, "I have something to tell you. Remember the book I wrote, *Dragon's Tattoo 666*? I gave you a copy of it for Christmas a few years ago? Don't roll your eyes. Everything that I predicted *started happening today*. That cosmic light show witnessed by the whole world was not solar flares and nuke explosions; I believe that it was in fact the 'Raptures Aftermath'."

"Tom, we love you, you're my brother but what you're saying very farfetched. Maria, what do you have to say about all this?"

"Well, now, I think we all have to take a deep breath and review the events that just occurred. Remember Joe, only a few minutes ago we were in a panic and started to get all religious"

"Yea, I hear you." Joe sighed.

"We need to try and find some clothes to put on, these pyjamas make me look like a mud wrestler: and don't even think about using my phone to make a video of me either." Maria chuckled.

"Really," Joe muttered, "what kind of person you think I am?" grumbling to himself about not knowing he could even make videos with it. Carefully, he climbed back down into the debris. Wondering where their dresser had gone, he stumbled into their storage closet and retrieved some track pants, tops and hiking boots. As he climbed back up and out of the debris he said, "It's a little over the top but this should work for now."

"Guys, Tom said, "there's a mini plaza less than twenty minutes from here and hopefully you can get some clothing there at the hiking store and there's that coffee and donut place, you know the new one from Canada, hopefully it's still standing. I'm sure we could all use a sense of normalcy."

"How about we go there and for the first time in our lives listen to Tom when he talks to us. He came to find us in this chaos, and gave us a better plan within minutes of being here. So far, he's got the right idea." Maria said.

"Ok, we all need to settle down," Joe replied. "That sounds good. We all could use a coffee and a donut to boot, Maria just loves their Boston creamers or whatever they're called."

"Look! All the debris seems as if a tornado just screamed through only our section of town." Maria said. "I'm somewhat relieved just to be out of all that destruction and they even have power out here."

Soon they were at the plaza, got some clothes, hit the coffee shop and in a few minutes were deep in conversation.

Joe said, "Ah, the coffee, smelled and tasted divine, the aroma was fantastic. You know they make fresh coffee every 15 minutes."

Maria asked, "Joe what's with you and your compliments about this Canadian coffee shop. Sounds like your 'donut-Joe', their spokesperson."

Joe replied, "I wonder if I could turn this into a gig and make some money, you know 'here's Joey'."

Maria whispered, "You're shameless. We're almost killed and now you want an endorsement. What could you do for them anyway except tell everyone you ate a dozen for supper last week when I was away."

Tom added, "You actually ate a dozen of them? Joe, you're a real man, but didn't you get sick of them?"

"My secret to this feat," he leaned towards Tom and whispered, "I ordered them assorted. This way every donut was a new experience. You know Maria maybe you're on to something. I could promote the slogan. Like Tom says, 'It takes a man to eat a dozen'."

"More like a pig" she retorted.

Joe said, "I seem to remember you eating three of them one night."

"If I did, it was just to spare you from gorging yourself," she replied.

Maria placed her cell phone in the middle of the table. They listened to the news man who said very soon the President will be making an announcement.

Joe returned to the table with three fresh coffees saying, "You know I find the second cup better than the first. You know that's also a great name for a coffee shop.

"It's already taken, Joe."

Now with second cups in hand, Maria said to Tom, "You have our attention, so speak your mind. Just go slow."

"Ok, here it goes." he replied. "What you saw was not a solar flare explosion. The Son of God has removed his Bride from this earth during the 'Rapture' and what we just experienced was the 'Rapture's Aftermath'. We are now living in day one of the seven year great tribulation 'Time of Sorrows'."

"Tom, what? What are you talking about? You're going to have go even slower with all of this religious stuff. You're saying that there is a biblical aspect to these past happenings?"

"Let's start at the beginning shall we. Joe, Maria, can you explain all these unexplained happenings across the planet? People of all walks of life having diverse occupations just started sparking. From the news reports this sparking occurred simultaneously worldwide and preliminary reports suggest that many millions of people just 'sparked'. I wonder how the President will cover this up.

People vanishing in plain sight; this was not some type of publicity stunt. Cars actually rolled along the roads unattended, not just a few but thousands of them. People on planes, buses, schools, businesses and many more places, while talking to each other 'sparked' and vanished."

This phenomenon referred to by thousands of people as 'sparking' is mentioned in the Bible and resulted when our Lord Jesus was told by His Father, God to go and get His Bride from earth."

"That's the second time today I heard about people being called the 'Bride' of the Son of God. Who are they?" Maria asked.

"Certain 'Holy' human beings were taken up to God" Tom stops as Joe interrupts asking, "Like a resurrection? I remember hearing about that in church."

"No, Joe, not like that. The resurrections you're referring to would be the examples in the Bible about Jesus resurrecting the dead, or himself being resurrected after his crucifixion. These sparking events are a living transportation or teleportation, not quite sure what word to use."

"More like 'beamed' up," added Joe.

"People are taken up in their living, breathing bodies. That is to say that they did not need to die to leave the earth and enter into the Heavenly realms. They were taken just as they were."

"That's heavy stuff, Tom." Joe replied.

"It is, but, you can't possibly believe that these happenings so high above us, like the bright flashes, appearing as a great cosmic fireworks display are man-made.

Hundreds of millions of people, including us, witnessed a brilliant lightning bolt streaking to earth and scientists say that it struck earth somewhere far away from us and to the east."

"Guys, not so fast. Look at the TV up there."

"That's cool!" Joe said. "The store manager has made all the flat screen monitors to now show the announcer as he said that the president was about to begin his address to the nation."

They all turned towards these monitors to hear what their government, the earthly law, had to say about what was happening.

"Good afternoon everyone. I know you're all worried about the cosmic fireworks in space. You don't have to worry. As you can see all the fireworks have ended and we're all still living and breathing.

Our NASA scientists are reviewing the data and preliminary findings indicate that this event was caused by some type of anomaly, perhaps a solar flare of enormous proportions that detonated our Earth Defence Array 'EDA' in low earth orbit. Twenty, one hundred megaton nukes went off simultaneously and, I must admit, made one hell of a bang and the largest fireworks display in history. Now let me be clear, luckily for us the solar flare only sideswiped our planet and the main blast of these nukes and its radio activity continued into space far away from us.

Now everyone should be aware there may be some side effects, like atmospheric anomalies, as everything comes back to normal. There will be tidal waves along with earthquakes, however, we will address each issue as it occurs.

But, all in all, we escaped the so called 'wrath of God' as some say. So relax, take a deep breath, and get back to whatever it was you were doing. The lightshow outside has gone and everything is getting back to normal."

"Why are they trying to explain future events they call anomalies, that haven't even happened yet?" Joe wondered aloud.

Tom answered, "You mean like tidal waves and earthquakes? Seems like they're setting the stage for more weird happenings. Seems like they know more than they're letting on."

Maria said, "One thing the President said seemed off to me. If this solar flare detonated twenty nuclear bombs, then why did we witness hundreds and hundreds of these explosions?"

"Good catch! Most people would simply have overlooked that." Tom gave her a thumbs up and Joe rolled his eyes.

"Talk about weird. What about our home being obliterated along with perhaps thousands of others? Maria and I have been trying to figure out how explosions out in space could cause so much destruction here on Earth."

Tom replied, "The government is not interested in what just happened. Seems like they're busy with other things. Everything they're saying sounds plausible. However, when you dig deeper, I'm telling you, it's all lies. I wonder if other cities were targeted like ours was."

"What do you mean targeted?" asked Joe.

Tom's answer was right to the point, as usual. "Someone wanted us out of the way." He hesitated for a second, then continued. "I was so careful to keep my whereabouts secret and was under the radar. I made a mistake."

Maria said, "Explain!"

"When I called you, someone must have been monitoring your phone and it seems that they knew I was coming to see you this morning and that I was in your area. That blast that almost killed the two of you only missed me by a few minutes."

Joe responded, "I think you're being paranoid. This disaster was just a natural happening, how could those explosions from space have included the targeting of you?"

"What if you're wrong Joe, I know it's a stretch to think that during the Rapture's Aftermath we were targeted during the ensuing chaos?" queried Maria. "I'm not a conspiracy type person, however, if someone wanted us dead, what a cover up that would have been."

"The President is lying." Tom replied. "The tidal waves that he is alluding to will be the result of Satan being cast down into a large body of water and the earthquakes are when God opens the earth to swallow this water."

Joe retorted, "You're saying the earth opens and swallows a flood of water? I think your reaching a little too far Tom."

"All this is very interesting, but, if what you're saying is correct then what?" Maria asked.

"Well, in my opinion, your neighbours were doing the right thing by 'getting the hell out of Dodge' and we should do just as your neighbours advised as they left in what was left of their minivan. By any chance were they religious, Joe?"

"Don't know. What about you Maria?"

"I know that they went to church on Sundays but I never paid much attention to them, until now."

Joe cheekily replied, "Seems not to have done them much good since they're still here."

"Speaking of 'getting out of Dodge', finish your coffee and buy a couple thermoses filled with coffee for the trip along with a few dozen donuts, muffins and other stuff. We have a long way to go."

Tom continued in a more sinister tone, "I'll explain later but right now let's jump in the Expedition and put lots of distance between us and here, before all hell breaks loose. Remember when I said that the President is lying through his teeth? Trust me! He is!"

"Then, let's 'get out of Dodge'" Maria said. This was becoming their slogan when events surrounding them were deemed to be dangerous to their lives and to leave immediately, evacuate, or scram or simply put, 'get out of Dodge'.

Joe said, "This is actually a reference to Dodge City, Kansas, which was a favorite location for westerns in the early to mid-20th century. Most memorably, the phrase was made famous by the TV show 'Gunsmoke', in which villains were often commanded to 'get the hell out of Dodge'. The phrase took on its current meaning in the 1960's and 70's."

Maria just rolled her eyes upon hearing him recite trivia, saying, "Some things never change."

Chapter Three

GET OUT OF DODGE

"Tom, slow down! You're going to get us killed! Where are we going?" Joe's hands on the dashboard left sweaty imprints as he became more nervous.

"Not back to your house." he replied. "Remember it's gone! You two are coming with me to my log cabin. It's a cozy little cabin far out in the country."

"Thanks for the offer, but we couldn't impose upon you for that long." Maria said.

"It's fine with me. I don't mind mooching off my rich brother for a while. Besides, don't forget, we're now homeless."

Tom responded, "Then it's settled you're staying with me. I will explain everything to you soon but for now, please let me concentrate on my driving."

"Yes, yes, please do" whispered Maria, as she grabbed the head rest on the seat in front of her.

"Hey that's my shoulder you're clawing!"

"Oops sorry, Joe."

"I've got more cuts and scrapes from you than from the explosions!"

"Let's change the subject for now." Maria said. "For such a large truck, why am I so cramped back here?"

Tom began by saying, "My plan was to get to my log cabin and arrange my final trip up to my cave, high up in the Rockies, well before the end of summer to beat winter because the snow would be a great obstacle when climbing up to it.

It took me some time to make my list and assemble all the items you're complaining about and sitting on. I just finished purchasing everything and this was my final buying trip. That's why I wanted to drop by and say goodbye."

Maria replied, "Ok, let's try this again. What list? What items? And what's this goodbye talk? What are you up to?"

"Suffice it to say I'm saving your lives."

"What's that funny smell?" asked Maria. Both guys gave each other a glancing smirk but neither responded.

"At least we still have our sense of humor." she sighed.

Tom then caught on and chuckled, "My Expedition runs on diesel fuel and there is a jerry can of diesel for good luck behind you."

"I wondered what that smell was." she muttered.

Tom, now slightly amused, said, "I'm starting to get the feel of the road now, even at this high rate of speed."

"What's with all these rations from that survival outlet in town?" Joe asked.

"Sounds like someone knew the future." piped in Maria. "Great! I'm finding a hard time finding a comfortable place to sit."

"I was not intending having company on this trip and never gave it a second thought that you both would be with me."

Joe commented, "Good thing you dropped by. Exactly how much junk did you cram into this thing?"

Tom replied, "This is only one of many such loads. I've made many trips like this to the cabin with my trailer which is much bigger than my truck."

"Tom, how do you explain all those huge explosions that destroyed our home, knocked us off our feet and that enormously huge lightning bolt from way out in space that almost killed us?"

"For now, at least, how about I just give you the quick answers and save the details until we're safely in the log cabin. The quick answer is that this was the grand finale of the 'Rapture's Aftermath' when the Great Red Dragon, 'Satan', after losing the war in the Heavens, was being hurled down and crashed into the water here on earth."

Maria exclaimed, "What? That's the quick answer?"

Tom chuckled and continued saying that it is written in the Bible that "Jesus saw Satan falling to earth as lightning" and before anyone could react he said, "How about you park your questions, at least for a while, so we can travel safely. I have a strange feeling in the pit of my stomach that we should be moving away from here even faster than our current 100 mph."

"What about getting a speeding ticket?" Joe asked.

Tom gave a quick smirk and said, "Look in the glove box."

"Whoa!" Joe said as he pulled out a 44 long barrel magnum. "Now that's power!" Joe exclaimed, "And that's putting it mildly."

Maria asked somewhat timidly, "Exactly what would be your intentions if we are pulled over by the police?"

"I would be nice and accept the ticket, unless the officer offers something different. For now, the police are not the ones we should be worried about. It's the National Guard (NG). If they get their hands on us we would be either killed or arrested and sent to a detainment camp for processing."

"Processing for what?" asked Joe.

"Death!" Tom replied.

Simultaneously, both Maria and Joe shouted, "What? Ok, now you really have our attention!"

Tom went on to explain that the NG form part of the emerging antichrist whose first mission is to capture, convert or kill all Christians.

Maria asked, "Why us Christians?"

Tom replied, "Satan hates us the most so we're his first target and then all others also are targeted by him and his antichrist. So, if we're pulled over, it's either them or us."

"How long will it take to get to your country cabin, Tom?" asked Joe.

"I reckon about three days."

"Make it two!" replied Maria.

"And before the end of summer, when we leave, it will take up to another 4 days to get to my hideout in the Rockies."

Joe said, "Explain 'hideout in the Rockies'."

"This is starting to sound like one of those movies that has a double entendre plot that keeps getting worse and worse." Maria added.

"When we reach my cabin we can discuss this topic and many others. All this is going to take some time, folks. How about, for now, let's just concentrate on getting out of here in one piece. Look at the destruction. It extends much further than first appearances. It seems like we're heading back into it again."

Joe said, "Go slow around all the debris" as Tom's Expedition was moving at a snail's pace through it.

"People are just wandering about the streets. Look over there, some are by that super-store and they're looting it. Amazing! It only takes a few minutes for people to turn into animals and for hive mentality to kick in. Where are the store employees?" wondered Maria.

Joe laughed and said, "Many of them are wearing store uniforms."

"Why are those guys looking at us? Oh great, here they come." Maria yelled. "Are they going to attack us?"

"Actually, I think they want to attack my Expedition. Must be Chevy lovers, the bastards!" Tom hit the vehicle's accelerator propelling tons of metal into motion. As a result, the attackers hastily tumbled out of its way. "I've got over twenty thousand dollars' worth of supplies on board and they're not getting their hands on it."

"I can't believe all the crap in our way. It looks like some kind of war zone and to think just a little while ago everything was normal." Joe said, looking back in the direction of their home. "It looks as if the destruction carved a pathway all the way to here."

Maria interjected, "Tom, calm down and focus on your driving and the road! I thought Joe was a crazy driver."

After another 30 minutes of tense driving they saw country and lots of it.

Maria softly said, "Thankfully we're out of the city. Seems like they didn't get much damage out here. One minute you're being attacked by crazies—"

In the middle of her sentence, Tom started laughing, saying, "Don't get me started on the topic of the 'crazies' or as I refer to them in my book as the 'ZOMBIES'."

Joe jumped into the conversation saying, "I love zombie movies. Tell me more."

Tom's response, again, was, "Wait till we get to the log cabin because this is a huge topic that will take days to explain." He knew that to digest all of the information he wanted to share with the young couple, he would have to give his full attention and have theirs. But he was filling with anxiety to get the truth out to them. It was his brother and sister-in-law! He wanted them to know how serious this all was going to get! Tom remembered to take a breath, and center himself. This was too important to rush.

Maria said rhetorically, "You're serious, aren't you? How can you talk about the Rapture and include 'ZOMBIES' in the same sentence?"

Tom took another deep breath. "We will discuss this topic later. Right now you wouldn't have the stamina to absorb the full scope of it."

Joe piped in, "What highway are you going to take?"

"For now, we're going to take the express to put lots of distance between us and them to get far out into the country."

"Turn the radio on to the traffic channel. You know, they're not saying much about traffic. Seems people are not fleeing out of the city." Maria chimed in.

"Well, they're being informed that the cosmic fireworks are over, so relax and take it easy."

For what seemed an eternity, they almost flew along the highway making good time.

"How long has it been since I had that coffee?" Maria asked.

Joe commented, "About 4 hours ago, why?"

"I don't know about you guys, but I've got to go pee. How about you look for the next pit stop. I can hold it for a little while."

"At the next convenience store we can pull in for a few minutes. Can you hold it that long or do you want us to stop and you can squat by the truck?"

"Yea right, I'll hold it." replied Maria.

Joe started laughing recalling years ago when all three of them were travelling together and Maria had to pee. Tom stopped the vehicle and Maria squatted beside it along the highway. During the middle of her pee Tom gently pulled the car about 10 feet forward exposing Maria in the squat position. Every car passing them honked their horns. Maria was not impressed to say the least.

"Joe, I know why you're smirking. It wasn't funny back then, either!" her words coming out in a snarl.

"Ok, there's the service station. I'm going to stretch my legs a bit while Maria makes her pit stop."

"Me, too!" added Joe, "and maybe I'll find a tree."

"Make it two." said Tom.

Moments later, Maria hustled out of the store and in a stage whisper said, "Let's 'get out of Dodge'." their new code word for don't ask just do. They made a straight line for the truck and took off posthaste without squealing the tires or making a scene of it.
"Ok, Maria explain yourself!"

"There were some people inside. I could hear them talking in a back room. They were getting rowdy and were waiting for some orders to begin a mission of some type."

"Who were they? Could you see them?"

"No, but they seemed organized, not your typical country bumpkins. Their voices had serious tone to it, sort of like when soldiers are planning an assault for war."

Joe said, "While you were inside the store, I noticed a strange military type vehicle, partially concealed by the trees. It was a dark green colour, with some kind of camouflage colours."

Tom inputted that the military use Humvees, a type of tough ATV whose capabilities are superior to his when used off road. It is only used in war conditions and mostly overseas, so why was it being used here and for what mission?

"This is very strange. It's only been hours, not days or weeks following the fireworks and already people, very likely that the NG are starting to gather."

"Seems like you weren't the only one prepared for the fireworks."

Maria asked, "How can that be? How could anyone be prepared these happenings?"

"If I was prepared, why not those on the dark side?"

Maria asked how was it that they could have been mentally and scientifically prepared for the Rapture?

Tom replied that a long time ago he watched a scientific documentary about German rocket technology during the Second World War. Their lead scientist was asked a direct question as to how they could have advanced in technology so quickly. The scientist said that they had help and simply pointed with his finger towards the heavens.

Maria asked, "You mean aliens?" and Tom's reply was yes.

"How could this be possible? Scientists have searched the heavens for signs of extra-terrestrial life and to date have found none."

Toms reply was, "Are you sure?"

Curiosity now peaked, Joe jumped into the conversation saying, "And here comes one of Tom's furtive discoveries."

Tom's ambiguous reply was, "How about I give you a scenario and let you decide. Let's say that aliens gave certain technology insight to humans. They would have to water down their information so that humans could understand and then build it. What's the good of giving them plans for a light speed star craft powered by dark matter, energy matter from a black hole, when the raw materials and manufacturing capabilities did not exist on earth? It would be like giving a cave man plans to build a car. It might look and be impressive but useless to him as he can't read or write. It would be better to simply show him how to rub two sticks together and make fire. Remember, there are aliens out there that have perhaps existed for millions of years. So these aliens simply gave the Germans suitable technology for their time period."

Joe asked, "Where did these aliens come from and why have we never seen them?"

Tom sort of chuckled. "You have seen them thousands of times. Since 1960 there have been over 10,000 UFO sightings along with 3,000 near misses."

Joe said, "The government has always said they're just the over imagination of people." He paused and continued, "Why am I not surprised. They have always debunked all these sightings."

Tom said, "Of course. They could never cover them up so why not just ridicule those claiming sightings. It worked fabulously. If you were to tell someone that you saw a UFO, they would think printed memories, animal mutilations and a host of ungodly happenings.

"Exactly!" replied Maria. "Their intent would only be to frighten people so they would not want to believe in aliens."

Tom continued to say that he had heard of a UFO sighting in Mexico where thousands of people witnessed a huge space ship that appeared to be only hundreds of feet above the ground and travelling very slowly. Slow enough for all on the ground to be able to see human like people waving at them from the many porthole windows. This, he believes, is how Godly visitors would, if allowed, present themselves.

"Remember God said, 'Behold, the days come, that I will begin to draw nigh, and to visit them that dwell upon the earth.' This most likely was one of those Godly visits."

Maria persisted with her belief that we were the people that Jesus came to redeem.

Tom gave a strange reply. "What if there are aliens created by God in His image that did not sin like Adam and Eve did. They would then not have needed Jesus to be martyred on the cross in order for people to be reconciled back to Him. Strange as it seems, Adam and Eve may have been the latest to be created in God's image and that's why the Rapture and Armageddon are taking place now."

Joe said, "Perhaps it's only us humans that screwed up making it necessary for Jesus to allow Himself to be martyred in order for us to be able to return to God."

Maria said, "This may be a stretch. We know that God created Angels having different status. What if there are other beings created by God. It then may be possible that they are being allowed to view us because we're created in God's image, and are maturing hopefully into a Godly state."

Joe added, "Or perhaps we're missing the obvious. We know that Satan and his angels lose the Rapture war and were hurled down to earth. Those who defeated him were also Angels of God, so maybe their observing us."

Maria commented, "That seems logical because, according to you, Tom, they've been monitoring and assisting us for millennia."

"Enough of this UFO stuff." replied Tom.

Maria said, "OK. Let's get back to when we were talking about the NG or some agency tracking you."

"As a matter of fact, I suspected that in the past they were following me and bugging my house." said Tom.

"How do you know they didn't keep following you, even snooping on you right now?"

"I had a special alarm system from Israel installed a while back. Nobody could get into my truck without setting off one of the alarms. Also, I have this frequency scanner and use it to check my truck every now and then. The trucks clean. No bugs.

Each time I left my house, I sprayed a special chemical in front of the door. If someone walks on it, this light from my key chain tells me. I even sprayed the floor inside the door way. From what I can tell it's still private inside. Each time I'm in town, I slip in during the night to check things out and so far so good. From what I could tell the only thing they did was to bug my home phone in the city and evidently yours too. That's why I had no land phone, just these throw away, pay as you go type cell phones called 'burners'.

Before I left my city house, I told the neighbours that I was going on an around the world vacation and would be sightseeing for the next year. I entrusted my house keys with a neighbour's son who was prepaid to look after the grass, snow, mail and general maintenance. I think that whoever was starting to watch me, lost interest and thought that I was just vacationing around the world or they perhaps had other priorities, for now.

We've made it this long, so far so good. I have no doubt they'll be looking for me at some point in time. They're most likely just waiting for me to surface, then kill me. That's why when your house was obliterated, it may have been targeted. Perhaps I'm just paranoid."

Joe stuttered and sighed, "Just great! People are chasing you and want you dead and you come to visit us!"

Tom wearily replied, "Perhaps it was a bad idea for me to announce my intentions to visit you today. Perhaps it almost got us all killed."

"Well now." said Maria. "We can't let that happen to any of us! Right?"

Tom yawned. "Guys, I'm tired. How about we call it a day. We've been motoring fast for over 10 hours and I need some sleep. We can't maintain this pace in the dark anyhow. It's safer to continue this speed in daylight."

He picked a secluded spot, slightly off the road and killed the engine. Sleep came to all of them within seconds.

Sunrise came quickly on day two and in minutes they had made any necessary nature calls, gathered everything that somehow made it out of the truck, and were on their way. Tom pushed his vehicle over 100 mph although the Expedition just loved this speed as it was fully loaded and designed for this type of extended highway driving. They made good time for the next seven hours, soaring past the legal speed limit with such ease that one could say the trio considered what was once an enforced speed, a mere suggestion, given their circumstances.

They made the decision to get off at the next exit before trouble found them, exiting at some obscure turn off. By this time they had the GPS on and were looking for secondary roads only.

Now they had to think smart and become invisible because who knows what could be coming their way. Tom said he knew this general route and Joe inputted data to find a route that would not take them through towns and draw attention to them. These secondary roads were not too bad, actually more like the scenic routes people take when they're not in a hurry to go somewhere. In fact, if it hadn't been for the urgency and anxiety to get to safety, they all could have taken more time to enjoy the gorgeous greens and scenery around them. They were pushing their luck but could still make pretty good time.

After several more hours everyone was becoming a little bored. Maria started up the conversation again, saying, "It seems not many people are heading for the hills."

Joe turned on the radio just as the news network was reporting that some type of massive surge waves were occurring in the Middle East.

Tom almost yelled, "Here it comes! I told you so!" in a somewhat triumphant tone. "The announcer just said that its epicenter is in the middle of the Gulf of Aqaba."

Maria piped in, "What do you mean, 'I told you so'?"

Tom replied, "In my book, I described these exact happenings. The Gulf of Aqaba is about 165 miles south of the Dead Sea and these surge waves will be travelling out of it, northwards along the Dead Sea fault line heading towards the hills just outside of Jerusalem."

Joe said, "Listen to what they're saying. These waves are well over 2,000 feet high and travelling around 200 miles per hour."

Maria murmured, "Wow! Just as you predicted the announcer is saying that these waves are travelling northward along the old Dead Sea river bed fault lines. Talk about timing. We were just talking about this, like yesterday? And now it's actually happening."

Tom replied, "Now if that fault line becomes active and the earth opens up into another grand canyon and swallows these surging waves then not only are we 'getting out of Dodge', but we're staying out of it for good."

They all remained quiet as the announcer continued, "Earth focused satellites are tracking these surge waves as they advance in a northerly direction just to the east of Jerusalem. This wall of water is being contained somehow in the valley between the 2500 feet high mountains on either side of the fault lines."

The announcer, now even more excited, said, "Satellite imagery is showing something unbelievable! It appears that these monstrous surge waves are heading straight towards some type of a huge dome. It looks like a great city with a brilliant dome of huge proportions covering it. But that's impossible! No such structure could be that large and just appear out of thin air."

Tom said, "I don't know its actual size, but that's really immaterial. I imagine if there was a great dome covering the Metropolitan City of New York, and having over ten million people living within its boundaries, that's what it would look like."

The announcer continued, "This huge dome, situated at the north end of the Dead Sea and less than 20 miles east of Jerusalem, is in the direct pathway of these gigantic surge waves which still measure well over 2,500 feet high, racing and frothing between the mountain walls on both sides. Imagine seeing the water flowing over Niagara Falls. That's only about 300 feet high. Now increase this to 2500 feet travelling at 200 mph and then turn this mental picture so that the water is rushing horizontally. This is truly a scary sight to behold. At this rate, this huge domed city will be leveled momentarily."

Tom said, "This is the 'Wilderness Sanctuary' to which the 'woman' who was given the 'wings of a great eagle' flew."

Maria and Joe both piped in almost simultaneously, "Who flew? What and where?"

Before Tom could reply, the announcer, in hysterics, yelled, "I don't believe it! A great earthquake is occurring and a huge crevice is opening at the north end of the Dead Sea! A great chasm is now opening and all the existing water in the Dead Sea, like an enormous Niagara Falls, is crashing downwards into it."

Tom interjected, "This action is actually flushing all the accumulated salt sediment on the floor of the Dead Sea into the abyss."

With great excitement, the announcer said, "The crevice between the mountains is now so huge, you can easily see it from space. This series of gigantic billowing surge waves, well over 2,500 feet high, extending all the way back to the Gulf of Aqaba, one after the other are cascading down into the Dead Sea basin.

Will you look at that! The earth actually opened and swallowed the old dead salt water. The Dead Sea has now been filled back to its ancient water level and its new shoreline is beautiful."

The announcer went on to say, "From space we are able to see what all this fault activity has caused. Fresh water is now flowing from the Sea of Galilee southward down to that city sized dome. The Dead Sea is now filled with living ocean waters on its south end and living fresh waters are entering it from the north."

Tom said, "We will now be calling the Dead Sea the 'Living Sea'."

The announcer, as if on cue, commented, "Looks like the Dead Sea has now become the 'Living Sea', filled with living waters."

Maria exclaimed, "I just got shivers when he said 'living waters'."

Joe added, "You know Tom, you're smarter than you look!"

The announcer continued, "These waters now look to flow along its new river banks all the way down to the Gulf of Aqaba that is connected to the Red Sea and out to the Indian Ocean."

Tom exclaimed, "That's exactly what's recorded in the Bible. It says that the earth would open and swallow the water, the announcer's exact words. This entire area has filled up with living water."

Maria questioned, "What is this Dome thing?"

Tom answered, "It's the Wilderness Sanctuary where certain holy Christians not taken in the Rapture were transported to for the next 3½ years."

Joe interrupted, "Transported? How?"

"The details are complicated. Let's discuss it later when we've stopped fleeing at 110 mph. Suffice it to say that it's a place prepared by God that protects special people from all the coming atrocities."

Maria said, "That sounds great. Can we get to it?

Toms abruptly replied, "No!"

"That's not the answer I expected to hear."

"Once we have safely reached the log cabin I will explain everything in great detail."

Maria said, "Sounds like we're going to hear stuff we don't like, Joe."

The President's emergency broadcast cut in. "Citizens of our great country, due to the unstable worldwide events and recent terrorist attacks we have called up the National Guard."

"What's all this talk about terrorist attacks?" Joe asked.

"What terrorist attacks and that was quick calling up of the NG. This seems contrived to me," said Maria, "especially since these disturbances have taken place on the other side of the world. Is he now saying that our home was destroyed by terrorists?"

Tom answered, "When you spread lies upon lies you get a confused nation and that's exactly what the President wants. Like I said, others have also been prepared for this event."

The news people commented that the President appeared different but they just chalked it up to the stress of the situation.

Maria turned off the radio since it was now just rehashing the latest events.

Joe said, "Describe your hole in the wall cave to me in further detail and why don't we just go there now?"

"Firstly, it's much more than just a cave. In fact it's a mini command center and well stocked for an event like this. I think it's wiser for us to get half way there and lay low at the cabin for a little while to get a handle on what's up."

"Tom, if you knew about this a long time ago, why didn't you make sure to belong to those who were taken in the Rapture?"

"Truth be told, I wrote about it, but didn't fully believe it. I deemed it too good to be true, especially for a bum like me. I didn't search for a religion that offered the <u>Three Sacraments</u> because my time was limited and there are thousands of Christian denominations out there. In hind sight, I should have tried harder and perhaps even told you about it."

Joe replied, "We most likely would have not taken you seriously anyway. People have their own opinions about the Bible and most opinions are not based upon Biblical facts."

Maria asked, "What are the Three Sacraments?"

Tom replied, "That's a huge topic, better suited for when we reach the log cabin."

"Great, my question is once again 'parked' for 'cabin talks'."

"Shut down again." smirked Joe.

Tom replied, "I'm trying to get us to the cabin safely. I can't drive at this speed and concentrate on anything else. I'll explain everything in detail when we get there."

Maria continued, "Do you think that people will come looking for us again?"

"For sure! I'm the author of the book called, *Dragon's Tattoo 666*, that's making all these accusations about people, powers and religions. And many events that I've written about have now started to come true! For now we're ok. There are no immediate concerns. But I don't know how long that will last."

Joe said, "Famous last words."

"The Bible says that we have entered into what I believe is the beginning of the first 1260 days of the seven year Great Tribulation time. Just for the record the Bible refers to these events in different ways. It could be 1260 days, 3½ years, 42 months, a 'Time, Times and half a Time'. These all equate to the same thing."

Joe asked, "Why describe them four different ways?"

Tom answered, "By doing so, it differentiates between the events."

"I'm still confused." said Joe.

Tom replied, "It takes a while to get a handle on it all."

"What happens after these 1260 days?" asked Maria.

"You don't want to know!"

"Yes, I do!"

"Ok. We're murdered."

"You mean the end result of all of this is that we still get murdered?"

"Yes, but on our terms. We will actually long for it."

Exasperated, Maria sighed, "Life sucks! I can't even get comfortable back here and what's this long box cramping my feet?"

Tom said, "It's my new over and under shotgun."

Maria responded, "I'm not even going to ask what you intend to do with it."

Joe asked, "Will other people be doing what we're doing?"

"Those in the know, who have read my book or followed the warnings in the Bible and taken it seriously, may. However, bear in mind, I've known about this possibility and have been preparing for it for several years now."

Maria responded, "You seem to have prepared for the wrong event."

"Hindsight is 20/20."

"How many copies of your book were sold?"

"I think within the first six months over 25 million."

"So perhaps that many people may do what we're doing. Seems like things are going to get a lot more hectic soon. Tom, step on it. All of a sudden, I want to get as far away from 'Dodge' as possible. I feel betrayed by my own complacency and ignorance."

"Mighty big words Maria!"

"Actually, they're from a movie I once watched. This is the first time I'm reading your book's introduction. Talk about melodrama.

'The 'Rapture' will take place, all people will witness it, most will be caught off guard by it and now you're in it.'

"Oh this really sucks!" Maria let out a large, defeated-sounding sigh.

Tom replied, "I never thought that my own words would bite me in the ass either."

"Well Tom, try not to hit any bumps, for now I've got lots of time for reading, so here it goes."

Maria began reading aloud: "Now that you're alive and in this time period here's what you need to know" and then became silent as she read on. Later in the afternoon they stopped and stretched their legs for a few minutes. It was peaceful out in the country.

"You only miss these things when you've lost them." Maria commented.

Back into the truck they climbed and continued.

As Maria was once again reading she started talking out loud saying, "The Great Tribulation is divided into two 3½ year time segments that together will last 7 years and together are called the "Time of Sorrows". <u>You will hear and see calamities worldwide and there will be many sad happenings</u>.

In your book you talk of the Great Red Dragon, the Beast from the sea and the Beast from the earth. What are these creatures?"

At second thought, Maria answered her own question reluctantly, "Oh, I know, 'cabin talks'."

Tom replied, "All your questions will be answered. However, it will take time for me to show you how all the interconnecting parts fit like the pieces of a puzzle. The quick answer to your question is these three evil forces comprise what I call the 'unholy trinity'."

They continued travelling until darkness fell and found a secluded spot to turn in for the night. The next day dawned and with no formalities such as shaving, washing and grooming, they were driving within minutes.

Maria was fascinated by Tom's book and while skimming through commented, "Tom, you know I was an English major in university correct?"

"Yes. What's your point?"

"Well now, who proofed and edited your book?"

"Nobody."

"Looks like it." she replied cheekily.

"Your content is explosive. However, if you had taken the time to refine and polish the final product, it would have been much slicker."

Tom chuckled, "True, but then I would be dead."

"Dead! Explain dead!" said Joe.

Tom snorted, "What part of dead don't you get? I had a friend at the publishing house that was going to do all the finessing and editorial details but then the publisher received strange calls from people claiming to be from the National Security Network. I never even heard of that one. They intimidated him with legal and then death threats. My friend took what I had and ran with it. Since my manuscript was electronic, he exported it to one of their printers they didn't use very often who was appreciative for any business sent his way. My book has a cover design that immediately mesmerized the person's attention. It's the Great Red Dragon's Eyes as described by God in the Bible. <u>His eyes are like the eyelids of the morning</u>. They're haunting and scary. Also, on the back cover is a drawing of the 'Flying Hell Monster', a scary but true 'Zombie Plague' monster, a terrifying thing to behold."

Maria interjects, "In your book it gives a brief description actually given by God in the Bible as to the Great Red Dragon's true appearance. In Job 41:1-34[7] it describes the monster as having:

Burning lights flash and flames go out from his mouth;

Smoke goes out of his nostrils.

God says; will he speak softly to you? Will he make a covenant with you?

He has terrible teeth all around, his rows of scales are his pride that are shut up tightly as with a seal, his sneezing's flash forth light, and his eyes are like the eyelids of the morning. Out of his mouth go burning lights; sparks of fire shoot out.

He makes the sea like a pot of ointment, he leaves a shining wake behind him; one would think the deep had white hair.

On earth there is nothing like him, which is made without fear. He beholds every high thing; <u>he is king over all the children of pride</u>."

Tom replied, "This is only a partial description of him and I believe that on his forehead is his mark which is the 'Dragon's Tattoo 666'. It's made up of the three colors, RED-YELLOW-BLUE as described in the book of Revelation."

Maria answered, "The 'Dragon's Tattoo 666' design on your book cover is striking to look at and sort of mesmerizes me. His eyes are scary."

Tom said, "We didn't even publicize the book for fear of some type of governmental injunction citing national security or some other trumped up charge.

The book, *Dragon's Tattoo 666* hit the book stands as a sleeper and within one week grew into a best seller and sales are still rocketing. The publishing company couldn't keep up with the demand and brokered out the next batch to three large printing companies and their combined volume propelled the numbers into orbit. The E-BOOK on line sales of the book also went wild and matched the printed copies sold."

"So what's the total sold to date?" asked Joe.

"Beats me." replied Tom. "My publisher died in a very strange traffic accident. I believe, in retribution for the publishing of my book. That's my take on it. I'm too frightened to contact the other publishers for my royalty monies as this could very well lead the 'antichrist' to me. What good is money if I'm dead?"

Joe said, "I never thought people would actually be called 'antichrist'."

"I do know that my book was still on the top ten best-selling list since its release. That's where my money comes from. I just used my debit cards when I purchased anything and for my last big purchases I withdrew twenty five thousand dollars."

"Do they know about your cave or country cabin?"

"No, I made sure of this and since I always feel somewhat paranoid I even left my old truck in the garage back home. Six months ago I bought my new Expedition with cash. Isn't she a beauty?"

"Boys and their toys! Some things don't change—even in a crisis!" quipped Maria.

"I used a fictitious name and address. As far as I can tell, this truck is off the radar."

Several hours later they spotted a country greasy spoon diner that they were grateful for. They ordered the largest portion serving on the menu. Now, with full stomachs, they once again continued their trek.

After travelling on country back roads for what seemed like forever, Joe said, "Look over there. What's that way down in the valley?" Looking through his binoculars, he said "They are vehicles! The same type as those we saw at that convenience store. Seems like the NG has blocked the highway and are turning cars around, sending them back to where they came from. Get real! One car is making a run for it! I can't believe it. They're shooting at the tires. Those people are so busted. Wait! Now they're shooting at them in their car. What are they doing? They can't do that! What's going on? They didn't even have a chance to surrender! They've killed them all. They murdered them! There were kids in that car!"

"They're supposed to protect us, not kill us." yelled Maria. "Why are they doing that?"

Tom, in a low, sad voice, said, "May they rest in peace. It looks like this is starting sooner than I expected. The NG has already started setting up road blocks to keep people contained."

"Do you think they spotted us this far away?"

"No, they were too interested in killing those poor souls and we're hidden by all these trees."

As a cautionary measure, they turned around and back tracked twenty minutes to an exit that would take them even higher into the hills and remote roads. This suited them just fine. It meant their progress would be slower but much safer.

They were now travelling on truly country roads that alternated between something that resembled asphalt and gravel.

"Thank goodness for four wheel drive." Joe whispered.

Maria asked, "What do you mean?"

Tom said, "Certain trucks have special transmissions and traction control."

Maria cut him off saying, "What did you mean when you said that it's starting sooner than you expected?"

"I thought there would be more time for people to flee to the countryside, perhaps up to a month, not just a few days. Turn the radio back on. Let's listen for any news updates. You can read my book and ask all the questions you like later."

"They're saying that for the protection of its citizens, the President has ordered everyone to remain within their primary residences. Also, under the new terrorist act, he has activated and empowered the National Guard who are setting up security posts across the country to combat the terrorists."

"What terrorists are they talking about?" Joe asked.

Tom replied, "There are no terrorists. He just wants to control everyone, the same as those poor folks who we just saw gunned down by the NG".

Maria asked, "Where do all these evil people come from and why are they already trying to kill us?"

Tom replied, "In the Bible in <u>Revelation 12:3</u>[8] <u>it says 'and another sign appeared in heaven: behold, a great, fiery red dragon.</u>' Many people on earth don't acknowledge the God of the Christians or any other religious group's name of their deity. When I searched how many Satanists there are in the United States, I found numbers ranging from 100,000 to 200,000 and these people live a life out of the public's view for the most part."

Joe asked, "How many NG are there in the States?"

"The National Guard have in excess of 500,000 citizen soldiers in over 3000 communities across our country."

Maria commented, "If these people sided knowingly or unknowingly with the 'unholy trinity' and turned into the antichrist no place will be safe as they have boots on the ground everywhere."

Tom replied, "If you go online and look at their logo, it actually shows the three colors of the 'Dragon's Tattoo 666', <u>RED-YEL-</u>

LOW-BLUE. It seems that they're not too concerned about people seeing their 'true colors' you might say. Even if some of them should side with or somehow become demoniacs then there would be hundreds of thousands and possibly millions of people waiting for Satan to return and reward them.

Just look around today, do you feel safe walking the streets in your neighbourhood at night or even in the daytime for that matter? Today there are hundreds of thousands of people in prisons who if given the opportunity would repeat their crimes if they could escape. There are gangs across the USA who sell drugs that kill the souls of people. These people are evil and have no regard for human life, just money and power, perfect for the Dragon.

Look at the hate crimes, bullying crimes, rape and more. There are many other types of people devoid of a conscience."

Maria said, "Look at our schools. They have taken the Lord's Prayer out, the bibles out and they teach the children that there is no God and that we all came from monkeys. When an antichrist crazy goes and kills the school children and teachers, people all of a sudden blame God."

Joe added, "Even look at the divorce rates, now over 50%. Every imaginable vice now seems to be the norm."

Tom replied, "There are probably millions of people in the USA who are Satanists and don't know it and when the Dragon appears they will flock to him like the sands of the seashore.

Today research shows hundreds of millions of so called Christians do not believe in God. This earth is loaded with 'antichrists' in the waiting. The antichrist have been preparing for what's to come."

Maria sighed and said, "I'm not even going to ask about this until the cabin. How's our fuel situation guys?"

"A little less than ½ tank."

Joe asked, "Is that bad?"

"No with this truck we're still good for at least 700 miles. Hard to estimate using the 4 wheel drive and these hills. I know of a gas station about 200 miles ahead. I normally tank up there. It's the last fuel stop before reaching my country cabin. The owners name is Bob, a really nice guy."

They played cat and mouse for the next 6 hours, keeping an ever watchful eye for the NG or anything else for that matter. Tension and nerves were high.

"Good thing your head's on straight, Tom, or else we would be screwed back there."

"Yea, it's very important to remain inconspicuous. If the NG spots us, we're cooked. Just over the next hill will be the gas station. They stay open late so we can refuel and buy some junk food for the remainder of the trip."

Several miles before the service station Tom pulled the Expedition off to the side of the road and asked Joe to take the binoculars, climb up a little way to view the station to make sure the coast was clear. A few minutes later Joe was back talking in a controlled but close-to-panic whisper, "We've got problems folks. The NG have already taken over his station."

Tom and Joe climbed back up to see what was happening. "Looks like their refuelling themselves. Must be 10 or more of them. That's odd. They're not even paying him. They're...they're... They just shot him! They shot Bob! I think he's dead! Now what do we do? Let's hunker down and see what gives."

A while later Joe said, "They're getting ready to leave. It looks like they're throwing balls into the store."

As the army vehicles roar away, several explosions ripped the store apart.

"They're gone. Do you think we can still get fuel?"

"I think so. I looks like the pumps are ok. They didn't blow them up so maybe they're planning to come back. We don't want to wait for that so let's get going. Joe, would you climb up that TV tower to make sure we're safe?"

"Thanks, but no thanks. I don't like heights."

"Ok, sissy. I'll do it."

"I'll fill up the truck." volunteered Joe.

"Maria, how about you carefully rummage throughout what's left of the store and gather everything and I mean everything, all the junk food you find and anything else that looks worth taking."

Fifteen minutes later, with the truck fueled and more junk added inside, Maria found another jerry can that Joe filled and strapped to the roof of Tom's SUV.

"Let's leave and make it look like we were never here."

Tom drove the truck a little distance on the main road and then back onto the secondary road, stopped and got out of the truck.

Maria asked "What's he up to?"

"He's using a tree branch to erase our tire marks leading onto this back road since not many vehicles use it."

"Guess you can't be too careful now."

"Ok. Let's put some distance between this place and us." said Tom as he put the Expedition back into gear and got going.

After several hours of continuous driving, they could see in the far off distance, black smoke ascending into the sky.

"I wonder what that is or what it was." Maria said.

They looked at their map and guessed it was some type of rural community building.

"Whatever was in it made a lot of smoke." said Joe, looking through his binoculars for a better view. He was surprised to see helicopters circling the site.

"Does it look like the news channel helicopter?" Maria asked Joe.

Before he could answer, Tom said, "Most likely, they are a dark mottled green color having some type of camouflage."

"You're right." replied Joe. Camouflage indicated they were Apache Gun Ships. The question that needed an answer was why was that building destroyed? None of them knew anything other than assuming that the military wanted it gone.

Tom said, "I bet the news channels blame terrorists for this act so the military can spin the situation unfolding itself to their advantage."

They made good time as daylight faded into night time. Tom was pushing hard to get to his country cabin.

The rest of their journey was uneventful. They had now been travelling North-West, far out in no man's land since they left home. They travelled throughout the night taking turns at the wheel.

As dawn approached, Tom said, "This is my exit." They followed a gravel road that seemed to go nowhere for about an hour. It then turned into a dirt lane that seemed to go on forever and leading nowhere. At some point Tom said, "My turn off is just up ahead."

"Where?" asked Joe.

"See that dead tree up there? That's it." Tom stopped the Expedition, got out and went to an old tree trunk and moved it, sort of like a gate, then drove onto a grassy trail, stopped and put the old trunk back to where they found it and continued.

"Talk about secrecy!" Maria sombrely spoke.

Joe said, "I saw this same trick once in a 'B-Class' movie."

"You talk a lot, darling." Maria was exhausted but secretly loved how well her husband was keeping it together under all the pressure and uproar. He was still relating back to their life before this chaos. She longed to wake up from this nightmare and go back to their simple and peaceful life. But she realized now that their simple life was also one of ignorance to warnings of impending doom that were open to them to recognize, if only they had taken the time to listen and find room for God in their life.

For a while, they travelled over flat but uneven fields that were at best old farmer trails, and then continued over rolling hills for about another ten minutes until they came to a thicket of trees.

Tom told them that his property backed into a provincial park but the name escaped him. "It seems like there's thousands of acres of hundred year old first generation very tall trees."

Maria commented on how dense the forest was and that you certainly would not want to get lost out here. They travelled another ten minutes over what could only be described as a pathway, just barely wide enough for the Expedition, which ended alongside a stream. Tom carefully drove along the rocky embankment for about one hundred yards. As they rounded a bend, finally, Joe and Maria saw their destination. There was Tom's small cabin, quietly nestled within the enormity of the forest around them.

Chapter Four

CABIN TALKS

The garage was actually a car port enclosed on three sides. Joe said, "When you said it was small that was an understatement. No one would look twice at it."

Maria piped in, "Actually, there's no one around for hundreds of miles to even look at it, even if you could see it."

Inside, it was nicely furnished with all the toys and was surprisingly well built using the old style log method. Joe said, "This is really a turn of the century log cabin, not a country home."

Tom smirked and said, "I lied. I had to get you two here somehow."

Maria said that it was charming, like one of those cottages you see on greeting cards with a winding stream flowing alongside of it and mature trees protecting it.

They all agreed that sleep was next on their agenda. They slept until noon the next day.

Tom turned on the TV. Impressed, Joe asked, "How can we watch TV way out here without electricity?"

Tom did that smirk thing of his, that only an older brother could pull off so well, and said, "Later, my friend" and turned to the TV. The news commentator was discussing the usual stuff as they started watching.

Joe said, "Nothing new. They're just rehashing the same things."

Tom said, "How about we all get comfortable and begin discussing my book, beginning with the background information necessary for you to come up to speed."

When they agreed, Tom said, "Until now, the Great Red Dragon, Satan, has had the ability to change certain times and laws."

Maria questioned what he meant.

"I believe that he could sort of time travel by suspending or twisting the laws of the universe."

Joe said, "Do you mean, maybe something like being able to use wormholes, black holes and stars for travel throughout the universe?"

"Yes and until now, as far as I know, he's had the ability to roam space doing whatever he desired.

Now he has lost the war in the heavens and been cast down, bound in the 'pit' within this planet and wants to make the best of it."

Maria asked, "What did you mean by time travel? Isn't that impossible?"

Tom answered that in the Bible in the book written by the prophet Esdras, Esdras asked God to tell him more of His plan and the Archangel Uriel said to him that if he could answer three questions he would be told more.

"In fact we can look it up. In II Esdras IV 4-9[9], The Archangel Uriel asked Esdras the following:

<u>Weigh me the weight of fire.</u>
<u>Measure me the blast of the wind.</u>
<u>Call me again the day that is past.</u>

Esdras responded "How is this possible?" and the angel replied "I asked you <u>but only</u> of the fire, and wind, and of the day where through thou hast passed."

Tom eagerly awaited to see how his brother and sister-in-law would respond to the information.

Maria exclaimed, "That's so amazing! Who would think things like this are in the Bible?"

"These wonders are just a few of what's in the Bible. Now, because these seem to be three of the simplest wonders recorded in the Bible, then Satan the Great Red Dragon, may have been capable to a certain degree to do such things."

Maria asked, "Why is he called the Great Red Dragon?"

Tom replied, "I don't know. Perhaps this was the physical appearance given to him by God as recorded in the Bible due to all the blood he sheds. Perhaps red is either the actual or the symbolic color of evil.

Now back to our topic. In my book, in addition to the standard index I have also included a flow chart index, beginning with the Rapture's Aftermath and concluding seven years later with Armageddon.

Have a look at my '7 year great tribulation' flow chart index."

Maria said, "It looks convoluted."

Tom replied that it took him over fifty revisions to get it this far.

"So, basically it's a flow chart that starts with the 'Raptures Aftermath' and ends 7 years later with 'Armageddon', sort of our personal 'road map index'." Maria said.

Tom answered, pointing to the 'Rapture's Aftermath' shown on the left side of the chart, "And this is what we have been experiencing. However, let's backtrack a little and see what events preceded it during the last half century or so.

This could be called the 'pre rapture'. Certain events took place that culminated in the 'Rapture'. Next followed the 'Rapture's Aftermath' that we just experienced.

To understand the unique relationship of the 'pre Rapture', 'Rapture' and 'Rapture's Aftermath' happenings, we have to delve into what's called 'The First Resurrection' and I will paraphrase it for you." Joe piped in, "What does that mean?"

Tom smiled and said, "I'm going to give you the condensed version detailing only the highlights. It was very confusing to me also and after many thousands of hours of research the details started to become clearer, finally culminating into my article titled, THE FIRST RESURRECTION: TITLE, TOPIC OR COINED PHRASE[10]. I wrote this article about it and you can read the entire article in my 'reference end notes' in your quiet time.

Now what people don't know is that the Bible gives extremely detailed descriptions concerning what the future is going to be like. People were always talking about the 'Rapture' meaning when the Son of God comes to take His Bride to Heaven. However, when you look into the timeline we find that the 'Rapture' is a singularity that happens during the 'First Resurrection' which itself is a plurality."

Joe said, "Wow! Sounds like science fiction terminology to me."

Maria agreed. "Sounds 'trekie' to me. I vaguely recall reading these few words just after our house was destroyed prior to your arrival."

Tom continued, "The 'First Resurrection' is a 'plurality of linked events' that I believe commenced some time ago with a great religious happening of some type.

When doing some basic internet research into 'religious predictions' one in particular jumped out called the 'Fatima Prophecies' that was scheduled to be revealed by the Vatican to the world in the year 1960.

Three children saw a vision and over time millions of people have learned about them. These children were given three visions. The third vision was kept secret and later in life one of these children, now a nun, wrote down the events on one sheet of paper decades ago. This single sheet of paper was sealed and given to a Vatican representative. The nun's instructions were that the contents of her vision were only to be opened and declared to the world in the year 1960.

Thousands of people knew of this letter and awaited its reading. However, 1960 came and the Vatican, after reading it, declared that the world was not ready to receive its contents. This caused an outcry of 'foul play'. The Vatican, under pressure, introduced to the world a three page typed document published on 26 June 2000. Those claiming 'foul' said that her letter was only one page and was hand written. A high level Vatican source also confirmed this fact and said he had actually read her one page letter but he was forbidden to disclose its contents.

Many people speculated that the prophecy depicted nuclear war or some type of spiritual happening that would shock the world. Since there was no nuclear war and no earth shattering calamities then it must have referred to a great spiritual happening of some type that was to occur in 1960."

Tom said that he researched the book of Revelation searching for such a unique event. After much research there was one and only one such happening that supported his search parameters.

He continued, "The Bible mentions a unique group of Martyrs of Christ known as <u>under the altar Martyrs</u> who cried out for our Lord to avenge them.

The Son of God then gave them all 'white garments of salvation' and since they already had the 'Holy Baptism of Water', obtained while alive on earth, these garments of salvation meant that they were now 'sealed with the Holy Spirit' by the Son of God."

Maria asked, "How do you know it was the Son of God sealing them?"

Tom replied, "Because they referred to him as 'Lord'. I believe this event describes the 'first group of Martyrs of Christ' who were killed for their faith during the dark middle ages. In Revelation 6:9–11 it talks about the Fifth Seal and The Cry of the Martyrs[11].

The Apostle John saw a vast number of souls martyred for their belief in Christ 'under the altar' crying "How long, O Lord, holy and true, until You judge and avenge our blood on those who dwell on the earth?" The Son of God then gave each one a white robe saying to them that they should be patient for a little while longer until both the number of their <u>fellow servants</u> and <u>their brethren</u>, who would be killed as they were, was completed. The 'white robes' signifies them receiving the 'Holy Spirit', receiving the 'mark of the Lamb' upon their foreheads and being 'sealed'."

Tom took a sip of his coffee to let the two absorb the incredible amount of information and enlightening evidence that he was telling them before continuing to say, "When the Son of God said that they had to wait a while longer until '<u>both the number of their fellow servants</u>' and '<u>their brethren</u>' was completed, it may also indicate that the first 'under the altar' Martyrs and the last 'Great Tribulation' Martyrs both initially only had the 'Baptism of Water' so both groups could be referred to as, 'fellow servants'. During the 'Great Tribulation' there will also come the 'Martyrs of Understanding'. I'll tell you about them later. They already have the 'Holy

Baptism of Water' and the 'sealing with the Holy Spirit' so this also makes them 'their brethren'.

I believe the two groups are distinguished when the Son of God says, 'both the number of their fellow servants' and 'their brethren'. Remember, the last group of Martyrs of Christ only receive the 'sealing with the Holy Spirit, upon their martyrdom. The Bible says that their works follow them.

I also believe that this great spiritual happening took place in the year 1960 and this was the Commencement event of 'The First Resurrection'. Oh and one last tidbit of information. When the Vatican did publish, what many believe to be their edited version, they let one thing slip out and that was the last sentence. "

Tom began reading this sentence. 'Beneath the two arms of the Cross there were two Angels each with a crystal aspersorium in his hand, in which they gathered up the blood of the Martyrs and with it sprinkled the souls that were making their way to God'.

Maria said, "That supports your theory about the 'under the cross Martyrs' who were given 'white robes' of salvation of their God."

Joe said, "Maybe they didn't let it slip out. Maybe they had no choice in the matter and had to do so as commanded by higher powers."

"Never thought of it that way." Tom replied. "I like it."

"The next event to occur was the 'Rapture', which just happened when all those people 'sparked' and vanished. Now we are experiencing the 'Rapture's Aftermath' that followed and soon will be the conclusion event of 'The First Resurrection' which takes place about 3½ years from now when the 'second group of Martyrs of Christ' are called unto God and His Son."

Maria said, "You mean us?"

"Yes." came the reply. "In Revelation 7:9-17 you can read about The Multitude from the Great Tribulation[12]. Here it shows seemingly millions of people consisting of all peoples of the earth clothed with white robes and with palm branches in their hands. The Apostle John was told that they came from the Great Tribulation and that they will serve God in His Temple.

Later, almost at the end of the Bible in Revelation 20: 4-6[13], it says that at the Conclusion of the First Resurrection their Heavenly reward will be that they shall be priests of God and of Christ. It says that they did not worship the beast or his image nor get his mark. They are blessed and holy and partake in the first resurrection."

Maria said, "So what you're saying is that even though we will be 'martyred' for our belief and faith in Christ, God has not abandoned us and is refining us for our future which is definitely worth the effort. But, we're going to die."

Joe wrapped his arms around his wife. This was all very heavy and hard to take in.

Tom agreed. "Those who kill us will in like manner also be killed with the sword of Christ. We read about this in the Bible in <u>Revelation 13:9-10</u>.

If anyone has an ear, let him hear. He who leads into captivity shall go into captivity; <u>he who kills with the sword must be killed with the sword</u>. Here is the patience and the faith of the saints.

So there we have it, the <u>First Resurrection commences</u> and <u>concludes</u> with these <u>two groups of Martyrs of Christ</u>."

Tom paused, saying with sincerity, "When you can understand and comprehend these facts, then the book of Revelations comes into focus and God's Plan of Salvation becomes clear. You are now also part of the top 1% of knowledgeable humans upon earth who know about the Rapture taking place between the First Resurrection Commencement and Conclusion events."

Tom summed up everything with his own theory based upon his research and offered the following scenario. "What if the prophecy slated to be introduced to the Christian World in 1960 indicated the occurrence of a most spectacular event, and if so, how would the Vatican then contend with such a message that didn't include them? If this is the case, then the vision's true contents as recorded by the nun pertaining to the third and final prophecy that was sealed and not to be opened and proclaimed to the Christian World until 1960 still remains a closely guarded secret kept within the Vatican vault.

Imagine the media headline if this nun's message read:

SON OF GOD RETURNED
UNDER THE ALTAR MARTYRS REDEEMED
FIRST RESURRECTION COMMENCED
RAPTURE, NEXT

Maria said, "One would think such a prophecy would generate great excitement and renewed faith upon earth for Christians and possibly the entire world."

"The Bible refers to this first group of Martyrs of Christ along with two other groups. Look in

1 Thessalonians 4. It tells us about the different groups. It says:

<u>The dead in Christ will rise first;</u>

These are the 'Under the Altar' Martyrs sealed by our Lord Jesus Himself in 1960 when He returned and the First Resurrected commenced. They are the first group of Martyrs.

<u>Then we, who are alive and remain, shall be caught up together</u>.

These were those 'sparkers', the Holy ones who are the Bride of Christ having the 'three sacraments' and taken to God during the 'Rapture'. They are the second group.

When it says '<u>With them in the clouds,</u>' I think it means they are also these 'Holy' ones, the Bride of Christ having the 'three sacraments' who died in faith during the early years of the first Apostles until John, the last Apostle, died around the year 100 A.D.

Also included with them are those having the 'Three Sacraments' who died in faith prior to the Rapture. They received the 'Holy Sealing' either by 'living Apostles' or by some other method authorized by God. They come from the earth commencing around the early eighteen hundreds when the second outpouring of the Holy Spirit took place. They come with our Lord and God in the 'clouds' and are the third group."

Maria spoke, "If I understand correctly, we are not part of these three groups. However, we will be numbered to the final group of Martyrs who are described as 'The Multitude from the Great Tribulation'. We're these Martyrs. We make up the Conclusion Event of the First Resurrection."

"I think we could take a leap of faith and could call ourselves the fourth and final group that makes up the 'Bride of Christ'. In the Bible it also talks about <u>trumpet Martyrs</u>. It says: 'Who at the sound of the great trumpet will be taken up to our Lord and God.'"

"Our reward will be great but what did we do that was so bad as to warrant all this?" Joe asked quietly.

"That's a good question," replied Tom. "Perhaps nothing or perhaps we could have been more diligent in our faith or more specifically to the correct faith."

Maria asked, "What do you mean by, 'the correct faith'"?

"Remember the 'Sparkers' that the world witnessed a little while ago? These were instances of certain chosen 'Holy' Christians being transported up to God in Heaven. The question is who were they? That is a religious conundrum and I don't think we will ever get the exact answer. The news channel went off the air before saying so. My best guess is that these chosen 'Holy' Christians who 'sparked', either belonged to one or more specific Christian churches that were preparing their members for the 'Rapture' event. During the thousands of hours of research for my book, I came across information in the Bible that referred to them as the 'Bride of Christ'."

Maria asked, "What do you mean by the 'Bride of Christ'?"

Tom said, "They must have the three 'holy acts'. From my research, these were the 'three sacraments' granting them the highest religious designation possible that a person could obtain."

Joe asked, "What are they?"

Maria despairingly sighed, "If we don't know of them, we surely don't have them."

"So then we could not have been part of this group anyway." said Joe.

Tom replied, "I don't have all the answers but that's a good question. I do know that it says, in Revelations, that this group, whoever they are, is caught up to God in Heaven as Royal Kings and Priests or Firstlings, whatever that means, when the Great Red Dragon is hurled down to earth.

This group was special. They were designated as 'Holy'."

Maria asked, "What does that mean, specifically?"

Tom replied, "When I looked up this word 'holy' it meant 'of divine origin' and 'consecrated to God'."

Maria replied, "So these people were truly special. Too bad we're not part of them."

"This group[14] went directly to God and the Dragon had no opportunity to get to them. My research indicated that they apparently had the 'Three Sacraments' consisting of the Holy Baptism of Water, Holy Communion and Holy Sealing."

Maria said, "I know of the first two but what exactly is this 'third sacrament'?"

"We read in the New Testament that it's when the believer receives the Holy Spirit of God from one of those 'living apostles' commissioned by Jesus."

Tom went on showing them several more references to the Holy Sealing in the Bible where it says: You were <u>sealed with the Holy Spirit</u> of promise.[15]

Maria commented, "How come we never knew about it?"

Tom replied, "One thing is for sure, we do not have this 'Holy Sealing', the last of the 'Three Sacraments".

Joe piped in, "Not only do we not have it, we never even heard of it."

Maria, now reacting with controlled vexation as to her loss said, "I realize we don't have it. However, what does it mean to be 'sealed with the holy spirit'? Perhaps if the internet was still active we could easily type in 'churches offering the holy sealing' and then check every one of them. That would be a no brainer."

Tom agreed saying, "Hindsight is 20/20. Do you want to continue hearing more about the 'holy spirit'?"

They both replied, "Why not? Better late than never."

"OK," said Tom, "Let's read a few references given in the Bible about those 'sealed' with the 'holy spirit'.[16] It says that, the Apostle Paul, while in Ephesus, after learning that some disciples there had been baptized with water, asked them if they had received the Holy Spirit. When they replied that they had never heard of it, the Apostle laid hands on them and the Holy Spirit came upon them."

Maria said, "So you're saying that when the Apostle Paul places his hands on them, they received the Holy Spirit?"

And Joe asked "What's so special about this 'holy sealing'?"

Tom replied "Jesus himself referred to the two baptisms when he said, "unless one is born of water and the spirit, he cannot enter the kingdom of God."

Maria, puzzled, said, "If I understand this correctly, it appears if we do not have the last of the 'Three Sacraments', the 'Holy Sealing', then we don't get into God's kingdom."

"Seems so." answered Tom.

Maria said, "The Bible actually has a lot to say about the 'Three Sacraments' and the 'Holy Sealing'. Once again, if the internet was still active I could easily type in these two phrases to see what religious denominations offer them."

Joe replied, "Too little, too late, darling'."

Maria said, "I now understand about the 'Three Sacraments' and that the Apostle Paul dispensed the 'Holy Sealing'. But what exactly is an 'Apostle'?

Tom replied, "In Luke 6:13, the Bible says Jesus called twelve Apostles."

Maria questioned "How did these twelve Apostles themselves get the Holy Spirit."

Tom said "We read that after Jesus was crucified and resurrected He appeared back on earth in the midst of His disciples for 40 days and then He ascended into Heaven to His Father. During one of these days we can read how He commissioned His Apostles[17]. In John 19:23 Jesus came and stood in the midst, and said to them, "Peace be with you." And when He had said this, He breathed on them, and said to them, "Receive the Holy Spirit.

Tom continued, "So we see that during these 40 days Jesus himself breathed on those whom he had previously commissioned as Apostles and gave them the Holy Spirit. He then commissioned them to forgive sins.

Jesus also commissioned them to baptize with the Holy Spirit,[18] and to be witnesses to Him in Jerusalem, and in all Judea and Samaria, and to the end of the earth."

Tom said "Now these 12 Apostles received power when the Holy Spirit of God came upon them and became witnesses of the Son of God unto the end of the earth. If we look at Acts 1 in verses

9-11[19] and read excerpts from these verses it says that the Son of God was taken up into a cloud as they watched and two men stood by them in white apparel saying, "This same Jesus, who was taken up from you into heaven, will so come in like manner as you saw Him go into heaven."

Tom told Maria and Joe that he believed that this meant when Jesus returns from Heaven during the Rapture, His Apostles must be active and living on earth at this time, dispensing the 'holy sealing'.

Maria pointed out that this message was given by two men in white garments.

Tom said that these two men were Two Witnesses of God and he would bring them up to speed concerning them later.

Joe asked, "Were there other ways to get this 'sealing'?"

Tom replied, "I don't know but some people said that they received the Holy Spirit during their church services when they raised their hands to God and accepted Christ as their personal Savior. One thing is for sure, though. It's God Plan, so who knows?"

Maria said, "If only we had known this information sooner, we might have been able to be part of these holy people, the Bride of Christ."

Tom agreed saying, "Now we must endure the Raptures Aftermath that we just experienced and that segues into the '7 year great tribulation, time of sorrows' with all its various components."

Joe said, "This is heavy reading."

Maria answered, "I don't think a person can grasp all this during one attempt."

Tom responded, "Let's look at our 'road map index' again. We can use it as a guideline to see where we're going and what's coming our way."

Maria scanned the chart again and almost cried at its complexity.

"Don't be overwhelmed. It took me thousands of hours to compile this information and I have revised it over five times. We'll take lots of time to go over it in great detail now that we are relatively safe out here in no man's land. Let's just get comfortable and keep the coffee pot going."

Tom began their tutorial saying, "The day your house blew away was actually day one of the Rapture's Aftermath."

Maria said, "There it is on the left side of the chart and as you said, day one of the Great 7 Year Tribulation time period."

Tom continued, "It came unannounced to all upon earth and the fortunate ones were caught up to God in Heaven in the Rapture while the vast majority were oblivious to it and have to experience the sorrows that follow."

Maria asked whether there was even a remote chance at all of still being one of those taken up to God in the Rapture and was told no but there still was a window of opportunity for them to take part of phase two.

"Tell me how." Maria gently whispered. "I need some uplifting."

"During the 7 Years and more specifically a little past the 3½ year point we will be taken up to God in Heaven."

"Great," replied Maria. "So all we have to do is wait it out?"

The answer she received was not going to be an easy task, to say the least. Tom went on to say, "We will have to be martyred for our belief in the Son of God."

Maria in frustration cried out, "That's not very uplifting, Tom. You mean we have to go through who knows what and after it's all done, we have to be killed in order to go to Heaven? Something's very wrong with this picture, Tom!"

Joe asked, "Why would God allow His people to suffer such torment for remaining faithful to Him." Tom said, "God's giving us a second chance to come to Him and the reward of our belief and faith will be fantastic.

Now, one more thing. A miracle will be given to each one of us. God will give us 'Holpen' at the time of our martyrdom."

Maria asked, "What's that?"

The answer was what she needed to hear even though she didn't understand it. Tom said, "This will make your day, Maria. Holpen is 'Divine Help' from God. It's something beautiful. How about I save this beauty for a little later on. Sort of gives you something to look forward to."

"Remember," Tom continued, "our God has not abandoned us. He's just refining us and I believe that God's angels are right beside us as we speak."

Joe turned to Maria and said that he would take care of her until then and gave her a big hug.

In the background the radio announcer was commenting about the sparking incidents so they turned up the volume to listen to him. By this time, there were now hundreds of thousands of worldwide sightings that were captured on cell phone videos by bystanders and security cameras in buildings capturing scenes of people in lecture halls, hospitals, at work. You name it. There were reports of this happening everywhere.

After many hours of videos showing these events, no one could deny their existence. The media started to dig into the significances of these happenings.

The news channel now had religious experts discussing the events of the recent days and their meanings. These experts were still divided in the responses. Some were saying they were a natural phenomenon, while others were saying it was the wrath of God, a truly divine happening.

The news network had some scientists now discussing these events. They were from the National Weather Department, which among other things monitors the earth's static discharges. They have computers stationed at key locations around the earth and can actually record the lightning strikes per second that occur globally. They claim that the earth has a frequency of 8 cycles per second (cps) and by tuning into this frequency they can record all static discharges across the planet that take place each and every second. A computer then compiles this data from the remote sensors and then equates this to the actual number of static discharges per second. Their computers, on 24/7, captured and recorded these spikes created when people 'sparked'. The scientists then filtered out the normal earth background lightning static discharges of 3 million each day and then they were able to calculate these spikes. They have totalled them and the number of sparkings is around 10 million spikes. Their computers were limited in data collection as they were not intended to isolate such large numbers so the tally is only an estimate.

The news people were all over this figure as that many people having 'sparked' was in fact very alarming. The question now being bantered about was if there was a common denominator linking these people? As more details started becoming available the initial results were that the sparkings were concentrated where Christians lived. This news drove the media into a frenzy. They wanted to know more personal details concerning these 'vanished people'. Everyone wanted to know whether this 'sparking' was a good thing or a bad thing.

One news channel had previously commented that some 'conspiracy theorists' were saying that it was a deliberate attack intended to remove certain groups from earth, an ethnic cleansing.

Another news channel reported that, during the past days, millions of people worldwide had not shown up for work or appointments. The media delved into this and examined what they had in common. Certain people who sparked were Christians who lived in the same towns and made up the majority of the population in those towns.

The next information was perplexing as the announcer started with the words "You're not going to believe this! These so called 'sparkers' belonged to ... hiss-hiss." The airways went silent.

This news channel, as well as all channels, went off the air and a bulletin appeared on the screen that read "Due to matters of national security the following content has been censored. Please stand by as our programming will continue shortly."

Tom's elevated voice said, "There's something really scary going on. Someone or some group doesn't want the people to know who this group was."

Maria asked, "Why is this fact so important?"

Tom answered that he didn't know but because they chopped it out it must be significant and he would try to figure out why. "One thing is for sure," he continued. "These 'sparkers' were special, 'Holy' people who fulfilled God's dictates and who were fashioned into the 'Bride of Christ'. Perhaps they also lived in large groups in these cities and in a spark all disappeared."

Maria said, "It would be easy then to check out the religion or religions they belonged to. We would only have to compare several large groups of 'sparkers' to establish if they, in fact, were from one or more religious groups."

Joe interjected that he was starting to smell a rat. "It seems that the government does not want anyone to know to whom they belonged. The internet would then have thousands of references to them and their beliefs."

Tom said, "Look how easy it would have been if the internet was still functioning."

Joe asked, "Do you think it will come back online?"

"I doubt it as this would give too much power back to all the people."

"We know that their total was around 10 million." Joe responded.

Maria said, "Just by entering these search parameters, it would most likely produce accurate results. If we could have tracked their religion, we could then have known what they predicted."

Tom said, "You know, in the Bible[20] it tells us their number."

Maria said, "Yes, these 144,000 people."

Tom, sidestepping her answer for a moment, replied, "The Apostle John heard the number and then wrote it down."

Puzzled, Maria said, "So the total sealed with the Holy Spirit was only 144,000 not 10 million or so?"

Tom replied, "No. This, once again, seems to be a furtive discovery."

Joe commented, "What do you mean?"

Tom opened the *Dragon's Tattoo 666* to the corresponding end note reference, Revelation 7:4, and asked her to read the words that the Apostle John heard the angel of the east having the seal of God tell to him. He further asked to write down, on a piece of paper, her answer and she wrote, 144,000.

"Look again." he replied.

Now she began to get perplexed and after a few seconds Tom said, "Now read the printed words exactly, word for word, as you see it"

Maria replied, "144,000."

"Wrong answer again." said Tom. Nowhere in the Bible does it state 144,000. Here's the secret to understanding what the Apostle John meant. The Apostle John does not claim that he saw this ritual of sealing in his vision, only that he heard the number of those who were sealed, one hundred and forty-four thousand, from all the tribes of Israel.

Now, read the printed words as the Apostle John heard and wrote and this time write their corresponding numerical values omitting the commas."

Maria wrote the following numbers: 100 44000.

"Now put them together and you get 10044000. Now, add the comas and look what you get: 10,044,000.

"That's amazing!" she said. "This closely matches the number of 'sparkers' who were taken during the Rapture."

Tom said, "Here's another way of looking at how many I believe are actually saved during God's Plan of Salvation. Once again write down what you see." as he moved his hand over the words. They appeared, one at a time: One hundred and forty-four thousand. "Ok, here we go: 100 40 4000. Now squeeze them together and add the comas: 100,404,000."

"Wow! That's over 100 million!" Maria said. "That's amazing. You can get three answers and they are all correct: 144,000 - 10,044,000 - 100,404,000."

Maria continued, "Sometimes our brains interpret the written words differently as originally intended."

Joe commented, "I fell for this once when I took my clothes to be dry-cleaned because the sign offered free dry-cleaning. When I went back to pick them up the man wanted money. I said, but your sign says: My name is Fink and what do you think, I press clothes for nothing. So that means it's free. The little man then read his sign slightly differently: My name is Fink and what do you think, I press clothes for nothing? I laughed so hard for falling for this gimmick that I actually gave the man a little tip. We sometimes see what we want to see."

"I remember your story and I also remember I gave you the ten dollars for him. Shame on you for trying to chisel that old man." said Maria.

Joe laughed saying, "No harm, no foul."

Tom then said, "Getting back to our topic at hand, even 100 million is not that many as compared to the billions of people on earth. And what about the 100 billion plus that have died since Adam. Somewhere in the Bible it says something like this earth was made for many but Heaven only for a few."

Maria began reading in 1 Corinthians 15:52 and asked, "Listen to this, Tom.

In a moment, in the <u>twinkling of an eye</u>, at the last trump: for the trumpet shall sound, and the dead shall be raised incorruptible, and we shall be changed.

Does this 'twinkling' and 'sparking' mean the same thing?"

"Yes." replied Tom. "If you look up the word 'twinkle' in the dictionary it says: light reflected from the eye. This 'sparking' is similar to a lightning flash. In a flash of lightning the children of God, fully matured in their faith, were taken up to Him in Heaven as the 'Bride of Christ'. In the twinkling of an eye, remember 'twinkle, twinkle little star', this twinkling is a 'sparking' like a lightning bolt. That's possibly why people coined the term, 'sparkers'

Jesus said as lightning shall the coming of the Son of God be, so in a flash of light it shall take place.

Just to give us a reference as to how fast this is, the twinkling of an eye happens at the speed of light. This means the flash could travel around the world 20 times in one second."

"That's fast." said Joe.

"You're right," said Tom. "There are three portions of time to consider here, the wink, the blink and the twink."

Maria, laughing, said, "Here they come, winky, blinky and twinky."

Tom, with a hint of indignation, then answered, "A wink is about half a second and is a controlled movement of the eye. A blink is about a quarter of a second and is a reflex action of the eye. A twink is a billionth of a second and is a reflected particle of light seen in the eye and since we all know how fast the speed of light is, this equates to an infinitesimally small fraction of a second."

Maria, still laughing, said, "Tom, where do you find all this stuff?"

Tom asked, "Was that a compliment or what? On last night's news, the one commentator labeled this 'sparking' to be intentional ethnic cleansing."

Maria said, "Such dark comments." She paused and then asked, "Is that even remotely possible?"

Tom replied, "In theory, this would not be too difficult to accomplish for a government or a group of diabolical others."

He continued to say that some time ago he devised how it could be done.

Maria piped in saying, "So you devised a weapon of mass destruction that could cause people to 'spark'?"

Tom's answer was right to the point. "No! I was theorizing on how to calculate the world's population of the different races. As I delved into it further, I decided to abandon this quest as it could be then used for ethnic cleansing."

"Fascinating!" she said, insisting that he elaborate further.

"Every so often, when you're just lying around you experience an electrical body jolt whereby a part of your body actually jumps. This lasts only for a fraction of a second but it's quite shocking to the person. What just happened is that one and only one of your nervous system electrical cells shorted out and jolted you, sort of a micro sparking you might say.

Now, imagine your body having trillions of such cells, all short circuiting and jolting you in a billionth of a second. The result would be catastrophic to the body. It's called 'spontaneous human combustion'.

Up to now, these events have happened naturally and have been limited to a specific body area without burning the surrounding area or mattress it was lying upon.

This shows us that a unique energy was at play that consumed them but not their surroundings. The difference now being since a trillion or trillions of these cells were triggered simultaneously the 'spontaneous human combustion' effect would be that the entire body becomes vaporized and most likely there would not even be any ashes left due to the enormous cellular flash of energy.

I reckon that the entire event is over in a fraction of a second and that there would be no heat generated as this is a different type of energy.

If you wanted to have this happen at the push of a button you have to have three components: identification, targeting and a delivery system.

The identification system is based upon the DNA of humans and their respective races. It is obvious that at the DNA level certain genes are different between the races. So you just have to identify the race DNA marker specific to the group you want to kill off.

Next, you have to target the specific gene's DNA frequency that controls their central nervous system, sort of an off and on switch.

Finally you establish a delivery system by creating an electronic signal that targets this on/off switch and either broadcast it similar to a short wave radio signal that can travel around the world in a fraction of a second to large groups or you could focus the signal using a space satellite to target smaller groups or individuals.

This signal when activated by the push of the enter key of a lap top computer, activates a power source and broadcasts this specific signal targeting a specific gene to switch off and on in rapid succession. They 'spark' and they're gone."

Maria said softly, "Tom, it's a good thing that you're on our side. You actually make it sound plausible . . . and that's scary."

Tom answered, "Even if it could be done, the 'unholy trinity' would be forbidden to use this weapon. They are not allowed to mass slaughter, just yet, but must test everyone's loyalties, and tempt them to turn away from God to the dark side."

Maria turned up the volume after seeing the bulletin sign flash on and off.

Their attention was trained upon the loud voice of a news announcer. He and his showroom were now different. This new announcer was taking an entirely different approach to this 'sparking' topic. He just rambled on that it could all be explained by their panel of experts on science and religion.

Tom remarked, "Well look at that!"

The news channel now featured people wearing uniforms having some type of a suit jacket with no lapels only a 'V' cut design. Their attire was black with three diagonal stripes of red, yellow and blue across their chest. They also had armbands displaying a color logo of some type in the same three colours but it was too small to get a good look at it. These strange people were now discussing the 'sparking' reports. They were now claiming them to be the result of natural incidents that occurred during the solar wave incident. They believed that the number of incidents was much less than people were maintaining.

They were calling the vast majority of the videos absolute fakes, similar to the crop circles that were appearing all over the planet.

They were also saying that these images were mostly all electronic copies and variations and went on to say that even the media networks, desiring higher ratings, were part of this subversive trickery.

Joe brought up a good point saying, the explosions that almost destroyed them were concentrated over North America but the sparkers were worldwide. This proves the so called solar storm or nukes going off would not have affected people on the other side of the earth.

Maria said, "Listen, these people were referring to themselves as the scientific religious panel. However, they are not acting very scientific or religious and are themselves propagating their own version of a hoax. They said that people who propagated these lies and hoaxes with the aim to create anarchy should be arrested as terrorists for their subversive activities."

Tom nearly jumped out of his chair saying, "This has now gone from scary to dangerous!"

Joe asked, "What do you mean?"

"Not only have they censured the truth about the 'sparking' but now they are debunking it and going after anyone who witnessed these events. They're trying to erase history. This so called religious panel is a witch hunt targeting Christians. They're trying to confuse the people and take them in another direction, from a 'Rapture Event' to that of a 'natural event' or even 'hoaxes' and tying it to terrorists." replied Tom.

"I wonder what they're going to say next." said Maria.

"Whatever it is, it's going to be bad for us Christians and I guarantee you it will all be lies."

Tom went on saying, "Everything you experienced were not natural explosions but rather some type of sonic boom explosions of epic proportions created by some type of disintegrating star ship entering earth's atmosphere. Just like it says in the Bible, Jesus saw Satan falling to earth as lightning."

Maria said, "Like lightning sounds pretty fast to me."

Tom replied that Satan's star ship appeared to fall as lightning and we know that lightning is powerful and deadly. The star ships of his followers were also hurled down to earth with such velocity that they created not only massive sonic booms but also atmospheric abnormalities of epic proportions as their star ships also disintegrated.

Joe commented that these explosions blew their home and neighbourhood apart and nearly killed them.

Tom, then reflecting on the President's last address to the nation, said that he found it strange. "The President normally concludes his address with the words, "So goodnight and God bless all". This time he didn't say it."

"I've had enough of this doomsday scenario for now. How about we play some cards and relax, have a drink or two. Speaking of that, do you have any booze stashed in here somewhere?"

"Got lots of scotch but nothing else."

Maria said, "I don't like that burnt tasting stuff."

"Great." Tom replied. "More for Joe and for me."

Maria retorted, "But I'll grow to love it."

Both guys remonstrated.

Joe just couldn't leave the subject alone and commented, "You say that massive lightning bolt that millions of people saw streaking from outer space and across the sky to whereabouts unknown was a contrail of a star ship?"

Tom answered, "That star ship from somewhere in the universe was hurled down to earth like a lightning bolt and impacted in the Gulf of Aqaba and there's more.

Their captain or whatever they called him is Biblically referred to as the Great Red Dragon, Satan, Devil or any other names given to him. He was cast down to earth by Michael, the archangel of God.

That star ship just didn't come to earth. It was engaged in a celestial battle. Upon being defeated, it was hurled down to earth with sort of a controlled crash."

"I like the President's fireworks version better." commented Maria.

"Me too." said Joe. "I guess we'll know soon enough. Tom, you're really starting to terrify us."

"How about we take a little break and I give you the grand tour of my log cabin? I bought this place online. It was an estate auction sale. The surviving family just wanted it sold so I bought it for peanuts, sight unseen. One of its main attractions for me was that it didn't have hydro, phone, or cable. Out here, we're invisible to the rest of the world."

Joe said that it would be impossible to get hydro lines out to such a remote place even if you wanted it and then enquired, "How come the lights are on?"

Tom smirked again and Maria caught it. "OK, what's up?" she said.

Tom said, "Follow me." He went outside to what he called his back mini deck.

"Not much of a view." said Joe.

"That's the way I like it. I can't see them, and they can't see me."

Tom proceeded to walk to the dock projecting about 15 feet into the stream. "See how it narrows and forms rapids. This means the current is stronger. I have a small submerged electric turbine secured under the water at the end of the dock. It produces just enough electricity to allow my house electronics to work."

Joe asked, "How's the fishing out here?"

"Good trout and pickerel." was the reply.

"Is there a toilet or outhouse or would that be too much to hope for?"

"You're in luck. It's a flush toilet with a rudimentary septic system."

Tom and Joe got the fire place going to remove the smell of dampness, typical of an unoccupied dwelling. In short order, the cabin was to their liking. Tom unpacked a new thirty inch flat screen TV and said, "Now isn't that better than using our cell phones?"

They were once again glued to it, catching up on what was happening worldwide.

Maria said, "I can't believe all that has happened during the past week. Our house disintegrates before our eyes."

"Almost including us, don't forget." interjected Joe. "We almost got blinded, deafened, blown away, attacked, heard military people conspiring, experienced Rapture's Aftermath stuff, explosions in space, and aliens. Oh, and don't forget, we're going to get martyred."

Tom piped in, "What a day!"

Maria said, "Seems like we may be safe here for the time being. No time like the present for you to continue tutoring us concerning the contents of your book."

Tom replied that he was up to the cause but cautioned them that from here on it gets worse as the events that he would be discussing were extremely disturbing.

Both Joe and Maria looked at each other and gave their nods of approval and said, "We're all going to die anyway."

Maria said she was plowing her way through the book but there were so many pages of detailed references that she was getting bogged down.

In reply to this, Tom said, "How about we start fresh in the morning!"

All nodded in favor and after listening to the news station for a few more minutes, since there was nothing new, just a rehashing of the day's events, exhausted, they called it a day. Bed time brought sleep and escape from reality, at least until sunrise.

Upon awaking the next morning and having their coffee, Maria's first question was, "What exactly do you mean by the 'Great Tribulation'?"

Tom replied, "For now, I will just give you a quick overview of things to come because very soon we'll be experiencing them." He said, "Remember that saying 'hell on earth'? It's more than just a saying. We're now living in it and it's called the 'Time of Sorrows'. This tribulation time is going to last seven years and concludes with Armageddon. During these seven years the Great Red Dragon uses his 'unholy trinity'."

Maria said, "Stop right there! What is this 'unholy trinity' you keep talking about?"

Tom replied, "Another name would be 'false messiah', 'false president', 'false prophet'.

The 'unholy trinity's' agenda is to deceive all the people on earth. The false messiah will gather all nations as his people under his umbrella and make a seven year covenant of peace and prosperity with them, offering them all the luxuries sin can buy. After all, he is portraying himself as their 'messiah' returned.

The 'unholy trinity' will now start to systematically subvert the foundations of Christianity. The first tactic is to claim that Christians are gathering in secret places to conspire against the government and are to be deemed terrorists.

The so called 'messiah' says that all shall only worship him as he is their 'messiah' returned. As time goes on, no formal worshiping in any religion's church, temple or any other such structure is required or allowed. People should keep their money and spend it on pleasures that please them. They should buy gifts for one another, gifts of gold and precious gems as he doesn't require these offerings to prove their faith since he has returned to them.

The 'unholy trinity', along with the antichrist, will begin to intimidate people to join with them in accepting their messiah's three color insignia as a sign of acceptance and honor to him. The now empty religious buildings will be reassigned for other functions of a more sinister nature.

Although the majority of people will buy into this scheme, large numbers of Christians will not buy into this diabolical plan. They will not spend what little they have, but rather, they will share everything with the less fortunate, sort of an indirect offering to God, along with good deeds and prayers.

The 'false messiah' will again be enraged as this is not what he wants. His plan to get people desiring pleasures for themselves needs to take a different approach. Using clandestine measures he will establish security groups of people loyal to his cause.

Secretly, the 'unholy trinity' will persecute anyone who does not believe in their goals. In other words, we're looking at total annihilation of anyone who dares to not follow them."

And with these last words, they all went to bed

. . . but no one slept soundly because each knew that every day they awoke, was one day closer to the last day of their lives.

Chapter Five

TABOO TATTOO

Tom said, "The 'mark of the beast', mentioned in the Bible, is what I call 'Dragon's Tattoo 666', the title of my book. It consists of three sixes, $^6_6 6$ arranged to form his mark. When you put them together it makes a logo image as shown on the front cover of my book. Sometimes I will refer to this as the Taboo Tattoo."

Maria said, "We get the picture."

"May I continue?" replied Tom. "There is a lot more to what's going on than people know, such as the 'unholy trinity' that is made up of these three monsters, the false president, false prophet, and false messiah. They put on a fantastic dog and pony show that for the most part works like a charm.

The false messiah being the 'Great Red Dragon' has had eons of time to prepare for this time period and knows the eventual outcome of it. Talk about misery loves company, this takes the cake.

I believe God has intended that the first half of the Great Tribulation time is the 'Time of Refinement' when the Martyrs of Christ become refined. And the second half is the 'Time of Redemption' when God places two supernatural beings on earth who offer redemption to all people, tongues, nationalities, nations and tribes regardless of their chosen religion."

Tom said, "Are you still with me?" When Joe and Maria nodded, he continued, "The false messiah has three strikes against him already. STRIKE 1: The Great Red Dragon a.k.a. the false messiah, loses the war in the heavens and is hurled down to the earth.

STRIKE 2: He failed on his attack on the 'sparkers' taken up to God."

Maria sighed, "You're talking about those special 'Rapture Christians', right?"

"Yes. And STRIKE 3: He failed on his attempt to kill those in the 'Wilderness Sanctuary' when he created those huge surge waves that the earth opened up and swallowed.

This caused him to go crazy with wrath. His first encounters end in defeat and embarrassment. Here he is, the great and powerful so called 'messiah' returned. He's cast down to earth and he cannot kill these two groups of Christians. He now targets those Christians living throughout the world.

The 'unholy trinity' will move on to begin their plan of deception of the billions of others still out there. They will soon begin many different tactics of persecution, domination and deception to deceive the people into turning away from their true God."

The TV station now interrupted their discussions with the beeping sound used to get ones attention to get ready for a bulletin.

The President appeared to be nervous while giving another speech intended to calm people down. His tie was knotted in a single knot, not in his customary Windsor double knot.

"Well folks, the past week has been quite exciting. For the past 50 years CETI has been trying to communicate with extra-terrestrial intelligence and has been searching the heavens for proof. Now we have the answer: yes.

That enormous lightning bolt that streaked across half the planet was caused by their entry down to earth. On behalf of the citizens of the United States of America, Canada, Mexico and South America and the entire world for that matter the following: Last Sunday @ 7:00 AM, EST will go into the annuls of history.

'FIRST CONTACT'. We are not alone.

Star Beings have now returned to earth, that's right, have now returned. Their return has been prophesied and foretold in many religious books. Now the prophecies have been fulfilled. They are now with us on our planet. What a marvellous happening!

They plan to address the United Nations General Assembly next week and give their formal introductions. I expect that the entire civilized world will be watching and listening. Our visitors would like to assure everyone that they plan to usher in a wonderful seven year peace and prosperity time period. They will be offering all inhabitants of our planet the opportunity to participate in their unification society whereby we will have the opportunity to advance in all walks of understanding, science, and education. Imagine having the cure for all diseases and much more.

I, and one other, have now had personal discussions with them. I now know for a fact that their global peace initiative will be offered to everyone, regardless of race, color, creed, rich or poor. Everyone will be treated equally."

"You mean targeted!" piped in Tom.

"They plan to offer this for free. Now that's something you don't hear very often. Our friends have travelled an extremely long distance. We can't even imagine such distances. They said to give an example from here to the Milky Way would be for them like us going to one of our corner stores for food. Absolutely amazing, isn't it. Up to now we have had limited contact with our new friends.

I was informed that the name of their star craft using our language is: 'Eyelids of the morning'. Kind of sounds romantic, doesn't it. We all love sunrises and sunsets.

That's all for today. We plan to give updates to these momentous events on a daily basis, so stay tuned for updates as they happen."

Maria spoke first and said, "Tom, a little earlier on you said your book's cover had the Dragon's eyes and that in the Bible God refers to them as "eyelids of the morning" correct?"

Tom responded, "Yes, so it's no coincidence that the name of the Great Red Dragon's star craft is called 'Eyelids of the Morning'."

"The President said this was a beautiful thing which means he is already under their control." said Maria. "Tom, your paranoia is rubbing off on me and I'm the most well balanced one of us all. I now see why you say that he is full of lies."

The next day, more scientists appeared on the news channel dressed in the same strange RED-YELLOW-BLUE uniforms. Now on the larger flat screen TV one could see their armbands were made up of these same three colors forming some type of colorful logo. They started to address the so called 'fireworks' that happened recently. They claimed that it was caused by some type of a massive solar flare energy spike, similar to the northern lights but vastly more powerful. This solar energy they're now saying caused the malfunction of many low earth satellites of which many had nuclear power plants inside of them. These power plants exploded when the solar flare energy travelling at the speed of light impacted them and this was the cause of everything.

During the next few days other groups offered their opinions as to what they believed happened. Tom said they were confusing the people with logical scenarios so after a while the truth would fade away into darkness.

Joe turned the volume down and they continued their conversation. Tom reiterated that the star ship belonged to the Great Red Dragon who was hurled down to earth along with his fallen angels, by Michael, the archangel, after losing the war that broke out in heaven.

Chapter Six

WOMAN CLOTHED WITH THE SUN

Tom, continued on, "Now I need to tell you about 'the Woman Clothed with the Sun'. In Revelation: 12:1-17[21] it gives us a description of this woman. It says that she is <u>clothed with the sun</u> with the <u>moon under her feet,</u> and on her head a garland of twelve stars.

"What do you mean, clothed with the sun?" asked Joe.

"Did you ever try to look directly at the sun? You can't for more than a fraction of a second, it's too brilliant. Her garment resembles the sun with all its radiance and glory.

When it says she has the moon under her feet, the light of the moon being a reflection of the sun, it indicates that she is above all that is ungodly.

The garland of twelve stars that is talked about is a wreath of some type, a sign of honor. These stars in fact are suns and we refer to them as stars because they're far away from us. Nevertheless, they are suns, too. There can be no doubt the number twelve here is significant.

The 12 stars may represent the 12 tribes of Israel. I believe that over time the Israelites have migrated to all countries of the globe, who I believe are today, Christians. These people are the ones taken during the 'Rapture'. They are Christians belonging to a special group on earth and in eternity. These are referred to as the 'Royal Kings and Priests of God'.

These people, I believe, are the scattered people of God. One source did DNA research into two groups, the Israelites of today and the Christians of today. DNA was taken in from old tombs where the scientists believe Adam may have been buried and dating back as close to Adam's time as possible. The findings were very strange. It appears that there is more Adam DNA in Christians living today than in Israelites living in Israel today. So the 144,000 Firstlings, these Royal Kings and Priests are Christian descendants of Adam. It is very possible that these Christians are in fact the DNA offspring of Adam."

Maria asked, "Does that make them all Jewish?"

Tom responded, "They have Adam as their forefather. The term Jewish just means a certain group of people from the tribe of Judah".

Joe interjected, "God's plan seems very complicated."

Tom continued, "This woman represented special Christians who had the three sacraments but required a little more time for their faith to fully mature.

Even though they were not taken up to God during the Rapture, they are still protected from the Dragon. Even in a natural harvest not all fruits mature and ripen at the same time.

When the dragon saw that he had been cast down to the earth after failing to kill those Rapture sparkers he went to kill the rest of the Children of God but they were transported to the 'Wilderness Sanctuary', out of his reach."

Maria said, "Tell us about the woman fleeing to the 'Wilderness Sanctuary'."

Continuing Tom replied, "They will remain there for 1260 days protected from the presence of the serpent. They are provided with food and necessities of life during which time they will finish their spiritual maturing.

Because the dragon failed to kill them once again, he will now go after and persecute the rest of Christianity, the righteous Christians, which includes us, who are scattered all around the world."

Maria said, "So to sum up what you said, the 'holy' children of God not taken in the Rapture, go to this 'Wilderness Sanctuary' that is within what you call the 'Great Domed City'. The dragon tries and fails to kill them using those surge waves. Now, he is furious and makes war with those who keep the commandments of God, the 'righteous Christians' living on earth world-wide, in other words, us. How am I doing so far?"

Tom replied, "Right on."

Chapter Seven

WILDERNESS SANCTUARY

Maria replied, "Tell me more about this 'Wilderness Sanctuary'."

Tom answered, "In the Bible, it says that God has prepared a place in the wilderness and they should be there one thousand two hundred and sixty days which equals 3½ years. The occupants are protected from the Dragon, the unholy trinity or antichrist followers, by what I think is some type of barrier shielding them, similar to a Force Field that may look like a dome. We could call this group 'the wilderness Christians', children of God now in the 'Wilderness Sanctuary' requiring a little more time to fully mature spiritually.

Those in the 'Wilderness Sanctuary' cannot see out. They are there to fully ripen so the events going on upon the earth are of no concern to them and their spiritual ripening. They require a little more time to mature."

"So, where is this sanctuary located and what is this place they flee to?" asked Joe.

Tom replied, "My research tells me that the 'Wilderness Sanctuary' is close to the Mount of Olives, about 16 miles to the east of Jerusalem, at the north end of the Dead Sea which now is the 'Living Sea'. I had to locate an area that was relatively close to the Mount of Olives that had level land. This area also had to have a connection with water due to the fact that the Great Red Dragon targets it with a vast amount of water. This area, to a certain degree, is void of people. There are not many suitable areas for such a large group of people in Israel.

My research pointed to one suitable location as mentioned at the northern area of the 'Living Sea'. There is flat land in this area that can accommodate a large group of people. This area can be seen from the Mount of Olives.

Those who are transported to this place in the wilderness are kept from the presence of Satan and are protected from his physical and supernatural influence."

Tom saw that both Joe and Maria were struggling to understand this overload of information coming at them but continued, trying to answer their questions to the best of his ability. "As to what this place is, it is a self-contained city requiring no outside support. Its area has to be large enough to handle millions of people for 1260 days. This requires an infrastructure to be able to accommodate these people with food, water, clothing and sundry items. The area is referred to as a wilderness. The dictionary describes this as a natural environment on earth that has not been significantly modified by human activity."

Joe then asked, "Why call it a 'wilderness sanctuary'?"

"Well," said Tom, "The dictionary definition of the word: sanctuary: is a holy place, within the Temple building that is used as a place of worship being the area around the altar in a Christian church. There will be an altar and souls worshiping during these days. This means that the GREAT DOMED CITY may be visible to the antichrist followers, but it's off limits.

The Bible states that this place was prepared for these people for 1260 days. They are nourished, are supplied with the substances they require to live, grow, keep healthy and grow and develop spiritually. This Great Domed City gets its living ocean water from the Gulf of Aqaba to its south and it fresh water flowing into it from the Sea of Galilee to the North. The Living Sea has mountains on either side of it that are about 2500 feet high. As I said before, I believe that this dome, has some type of force field over it so those inside are sort of in their own little world."

Joe asked, "Are they allowed out to come and help us?"

"Excellent question, but I don't think so since they are protected from the serpent. However, it's God's plan."

"I'm really confused, Tom." Maria said. "I thought you didn't know who the Bride of Christ was."

"Correct. The 'Rapture Event' threw a monkey wrench into my plans to write more books. If I could have applied another hundred hours of internet research looking into all Christian beliefs, prophesies and predictions concerning the year 1960 I should have been able to figure out who they were."

Maria softly sighed, "So I guess we'll never know."

He looked at her quizzically and smirked, "Trust me. You will, and sooner that you think."

Maria, bewildered, chirped rhetorically to Joe, "How does he know these things?"

Joe responded, "Beats me. How do you think I feel? He's *my* brother."

Maria smiled and gently shook her head in disbelief saying, "Joe that was a rhetorical comment and didn't require a reply." Chuckling to herself, she said, "Thank goodness I married you for your body, not your brains".

After several minutes of much needed tension release, Tom continued, "On the eastern slope of the Mount of Olives, located just outside Jerusalem, is a small town called Bethany. It was associated with important events in scriptural history. Luke 24:50 tells us that this is where the Ascension of the Son of God took place. Bethany is also the home to "THE 3 MARYS"[22] and Martha, Lazarus, and of Simon the leper. It was called also the house of misery on account of the invalids who congregated there and its isolated location."

Maria said that she vaguely remembers hearing about Marys from her Sunday school days.

Tom gave her that cheeky smirk of his and said that there were actually three Marys, the one everyone wanted to stone, the other who poured oil on Jesus feet and the one who poured oil over Jesus head. "As a matter of fact, they're all the same Mary."

Maria exclaimed, "I don't follow you."

Tom replied, when you have time, look in the reference index of my book and you will see how I discovered this. I originally intended to publish more books with the next one titled 'The 3 Marys'.

Anyway, we're off topic. Getting back to what we were talking about. I believe it is from Bethany that Jesus saw Satan fall to earth like lightning. On a clear day when you look out from the Mount of Olives towards the east you can easily see the Dead Sea."

Cheekily, Maria said, "Don't you mean the Living Sea?"

Tom continued, "The Living Sea is about 15 miles away to the east with high mountains behind it. The town of Bethany is about 1.5 miles to the east of Jerusalem on the south-eastern slope of the Mount of Olives. From this vantage point one could only look to the south-east because to the east would be mountain ranges. To the west more mountain ranges so your view would be restricted to that of south-east.

When Jesus said that He saw Satan fall as like lightning, I think this means that his fall was very fast and brilliant. Lightning is energy, and the Great Red Dragon being a fallen angel is also comprised of energy; energy that was hurled down to earth by non-earthly means.

With respect to the dragon's fall, we know that his starting point was high in the heavens and his ending point was on earth somewhere because in the Bible it says that the Archangel Michael 'hurled Satan to earth'. Jesus saw Satan's fall to earth and to keep it simple let's say that this lightning bolt struck the earth within a distance of several hundred miles south-east of Bethany.

Due to the curvature of the earth anything farther away would be impossible to see the touchdown site."

Joe commented, "You mean the super brilliant lightning bolt, that almost killed us, came from space, streaked across the sky and struck south-east of Bethany?"

Maria said, "That's the gulf of . . . what did you call it? I forget."

"Yes, I believe that Satan's impact site was in the Gulf of Aqaba, 165 miles to the south of Bethany." said Tom. "My theory is that the dragon impacted into water and that's why he issued 'out of his mouth water', not fire, or other types of energy. He used his powers to push huge surge waves from the Gulf of Aqaba northward along the Dead Sea Fault Line to the Living Sea."

Tom continued, "People today, are planning what they call the 'Red-Dead'. They plan to direct sea water from the Gulf of Aqaba situated on the Red Sea and then along the Dead Sea Fault Line using large pipes, canals, and tunnels to bring the water about 165 miles from the Gulf of Aqaba to the 'Living Sea'. This would create new marine life over time and water from the Sea of Galilee would flow down through the 'Living Sea' into the Gulf of Aqaba and out into the Indian Ocean."

Joe commented, "Seems like this is now a reality."

"From the Gulf of Aqaba there is a drop of 1400 feet to get it there so gravity is actually helping. The 'Living Sea' is actually in the Jordan Rift Valley, and it's surrounded by mountains on both sides from Israel and Jordan. In total, the sea covers about 250 miles of area and because its surface is 1,300 feet below sea level, the shore is actually the lowest, driest place on Earth.

The 'Living Sea' could hold a lot of water if its shore line was brought back to ancient levels. This influx of new sea water would also increase its overall shoreline. This new northern shoreline of the once Dead Sea is where the Wilderness Sanctuary is located."

Both Maria and Joe were mesmerised by all this added information. They listened intently as Tom continued. "Now it gets even more interesting. Consider this. If the Dragon's impact site was upon the surface of the earth, he most likely would have issued fire, air or some other land based projectiles from his mouth. He then would have tried to incinerate or blast away, 'the woman clothed with the sun'. However, he landed in water. Targeting the woman in the 'Wilderness Sanctuary' at the northern end of the former Dead Sea that is surrounded by mountains on both sides, his power was great enough to generate giant surge waves, which were probably manipulated by force fields.

Now, let's run the following scenario. The Gulf of Aqaba gets it water from the Red Sea. Next, the former Dead Sea is part of the Dead Sea Rift Fault Line that runs south about 165 miles south down to the Gulf of Aqaba. The Gulf of Aqaba is itself about 100 miles long and about 16 miles wide and reaches a maximum depth of about 3,000 feet. This gulf contains a lot of available water, more than enough for the dragon's purpose.

Remember the Dragon issues out of his mouth billowing surge waves from the center of the Gulf of Aqaba using force fields to target the 'Great Domed City' that houses the 'Wilderness Sanctuary'.

The former Dead Sea has fault lines running north to south and others east to west such as the Amazyahu Fault Line. One or more of these faults opens and the water came crashing down into it. As the Bible says 'the earth opened and swallowed the water'. In addition there are mountains on both sides that are over 2,000 feet high.

As long as the dragon kept these surge waves around 2,000 feet high and with a sufficient push of water, these huge waves could easily generate massive destruction with severe flooding and truly at Biblical levels.

With such an enormous torrent of rushing water, I believe it may be that this actually could cause the existing salt deposits built up upon the floor of the former Dead Sea begin to be dislodged, dissolved or disintegrated in a matter of seconds and go crashing down into the depths of the earth. The resulting body of water is now healthy living sea water from the Gulf of Aqaba and as their water levels equalize and their sea levels adjust to allow fresh water from the Sea of Galilee from the north to flow south down through the Dead Sea and then to the Gulf of Aqaba, into the Red Sea and into the Indian Ocean, it will allow marine life to migrate into the Dead Sea that now can be called the 'Living Sea'.

The Great Domed City has fresh water from Galilee flowing into it on its northern border and sea water teeming with marine life on its southern border and all this is the after effect of the Great Red Dragon.

The effects of the flood are localized within the valley areas. There are over 5 fault lines under the Living Sea that run both East to West and North to South. These fault lines are more than sufficient, when opened, to swallow this huge amount of water. So now the Dead Sea is the 'Living Sea' full of marine life. So those in the Great Domed City now have all the essentials of life."

Joe said, "Wow! You are so knowledgeable on this subject. You really did a lot of research. Earlier on you said that these surge waves were controlled by force fields of some type. Can you elaborate further?"

"Back in the days of the Exodus, in the Red Sea Crossing[23], God caused the waters of the Gulf of Aqaba to be held back by some type of force that created a wall of water on both sides and a great wind from the east that dried the ground. Today, we would say that this wall of water being held back was due to force fields in play. When the Great Red Dragon was hurled down to earth, he impacted in the water and that's why he issued water out of his mouth. This water is much more than huge waves, rather a colossal series of billowing surge waves, that the Great Red Dragon used force fields to control, push and direct through about 160 miles of old river beds that are surrounded by high mountains on each side to the Dead Sea and more specifically to the north end of the sea where the 'woman' is being protected in the 'great domed city'."

Joe asked, "Where exactly in the Gulf of Aqaba did the Great Red Dragon splash down?"

"The splashdown is exactly in the center of the Gulf of Aqaba."

"Is there any significance to it being in the center of the Gulf of Aqaba?" asked Maria.

"You're going to love this. In order for such a volume of water to be generated and pushed out of it, the site had to be at least in the center. This is also the exact site where Moses led the Israelites across on dry land while force fields pushed the waters back on both sides of them and where Pharaoh's army of 600 chariots, and who knows what else, died when the waters crashed back together.

Even to this day, there are two large pillars having inscriptions on them that state the crossing and landing sites of the Israelites during their Exodus. They are referred to as the 'Israelites crossing pillars'[24] on both sides of the Gulf of Aqaba."

Maria exclaimed, "That's incredible! Water and force fields were in play *back then* to control and separate the waters and *now* to control all the flood surge waves!"

Joe said, "This seems very uncanny that these two events share the same place on earth, sort of a *'then and now'* scenario.

Maria added, "God's plan is so intricate and fascinating".

Chapter Eight
RISE OF THE UNHOLY TRINITY

"Talk about being complex. Now the Great Red Dragon or Satan will introduce his son and false prophet and together they form what I call the 'unholy trinity'. This is the phrase that I have given to describe the false messiah, the false president and the false prophet.

Spiritually speaking, they are the Great Red Dragon, the Sea Beast, and the Land Beast that are described in the Bible. Initially, they take on human appearances and will deceive billions with their lying wonders and deceptions.

During the war in the Heavens, there is only mention of the Great Red Dragon and his angels being cast out with him. However, it does not specifically mention the sea beast or land beast. Either they were included, but not specifically noted in the Bible, when his angels were cast down or they may be some type of concoction he puts together to copy God's holy trinity by forming his own unholy trinity.

RISE OF THE SEA BEAST
Now, let's look at what the Bible says about the rise of the sea beast[25]. In Revelations, the Apostle John sees a beast rising up out of the sea, having seven heads and ten horns, and on his horns, ten crowns, and on his heads a blasphemous name. This beast looks something like a leopard, has feet of a bear, and the mouth of a lion. The Great Red Dragon gives this beast his power, his throne and great authority. The whole world will marvel and follow this beast. They will worship him and the Great Red Dragon.

The Bible also says that the people said that this beast is so powerful, who is able to make war with him? This may be a two edged reference whereby the antichrist with gladness will join the beast while others out of fear obey him. According to the Bible, this beast was given authority to continue for forty-two months. He blasphemed God, His tabernacle and those who dwell in Heaven. He made war with the saints, subdued them and was given authority over every tribe, tongue, and nation. All who dwell on the earth will worship him except those whose names are written in the Lamb's Book of Life.

"Who's the Lamb?" asked Maria. "Do you mean Jesus?"

"Yes." answered Tom. "The sea beast is the antichrist leader and the Great Red Dragon's son that he calls LEO. We know that this Beast has various names and will soon use demonic powers to take possession of our current president. His title then may be more grandiose, perhaps, the 'president of earth'. He will be absolute dictator to all the people on earth. For the first 3½ years, he will not show his true appearance as this would terrify everyone. How then could his father, the so called 'messiah' returned, then proclaim peace and prosperity to all with such a monster at his side?

As I said, during the first 3½ years, he disguises his hideous appearance as the president. He looks human but that man does not exist anymore. The Beast has taken possession of him and soon will eradicate all existence of him."

Just then, in the midst of his explanation of the beast, the Emergency Broadcast System declared a special bulletin from the President would be forthcoming.

The 'false president' made a broadcast to the people of the USA and the world that was going to signal a total change in the way people lived up to now, a 'game changer' as it is called.

The 'false president' started out calmly for the first few minutes with the standard rhetoric and then the bombshell. "Folks, I would like for everyone to sit down. What I'm going to tell you is either going to make your day or mess it up. Our new messiah had a private meeting with me and our Global Religious Prophet. I have been given a new perspective concerning his goals. We both whole heartedly concur with his agenda."

The President went on addressing the people. "We will be increasing our home land security measures to new levels in order to better serve our messiah. This means that we will be implementing extremely strict control measures to protect everyone as there are terrorists out there who are against our cause. In order to curtail terrorists from entering and leaving our country I have grounded all international air flights as well as all other modes of travel. We have all witnessed curfew measures during times of lawlessness. As of tomorrow, a new nationwide and very soon a total global curfew will be introduced whereby 8 p.m. will be the maximum time allowed for anyone other than authorized personnel to be out of their residence. This may seem a little drastic, but look at the positive side. You can now spend more time at home with your loved ones. I am sure that these measures will, after a while, be welcomed by all of us. I have authorized the NATIONAL GUARD to oversee, implement and enforce these new measures between all homeland security agencies, law enforcement agencies and bureaus. During these times we have to take a strong stand against all the sleeper cells now being activated within our borders."

He went on the say that by now all the NG has been outfitted with their new uniforms, arm bands and headgear designating their status.

"Look at him carefully." said Tom. "His mannerisms are changing." and in an unintentional whisper said, "Our President is changing. The Beast is taking him over."

Moving forward Tom said, "We now look deeper into the Leopard aspects of the beast. The Bible says '<u>now the beast which I saw was like a leopard</u>'."

Tom said that the word leopard consists of two words: LEO and PARD, LEO being a large cat and PARD being a legendary creature. When he entered the word LEO into the search engine it pulled up the names of 14 popes, perhaps a harbinger of things to come.

He continued, "We also have <u>Leo, the lion of the zodiac.</u> So here we have the Devil's son referred to as a lion (LEO the Lion)."

Tom said, "The next event totally shocked me, for when I entered the word: 'LEO' into a search engine, it pulled up www.LEO.

GOV[26]. Immediately, you are given a threat! To paraphrase, it said, 'Warning, you are accessing a U.S. Government information system, which includes this computer, this computer network, all computers connected to this network. This site is a virtual command center used for tracking, displaying, and disseminating intelligence and tactical information. LEO supports the FBI's TEN priorities by providing time-critical national alerts and information sharing for law enforcement, antiterrorism and intelligence agencies in support of the Global War on Terrorism.

LEO also supports antiterrorism, intelligence, law enforcement, criminal justice, and public safety communities worldwide.

Users anywhere in the world can communicate securely using LEO.'"

Maria exclaimed, "You've got to be kidding me!" now exhibiting exasperation in her voice. "You mean the FBI, and who knows how many other clandestine agencies worldwide already have this system in place and they are using it, targeting terrorism or us?"

Tom replied, "Yes and look at their colors: RED, YELLOW, BLUE with a picture of the Lion (see the end note) and with the word LEO beside it, and count the sulphur yellow main tips. You get 10 of them, just like the 10 horns of the Beast.

To me this points to the fact that the Beast, Leo, Dragon's son, false president, call him what you like, will be in charge of all the military on earth that includes persecuting Christians worldwide.

The designated color of the Beast, Leo, is Blue and is at the top of the Dragon's Tattoo 666. Blue at the top indicates that they belong to a certain group known as government military forces and if my theory is correct they will first wear his insignia on their uniforms, armbands headgear proudly displaying the 'Dragon's Tattoo 666' with blue at the top. Very soon thereafter many will start wearing this mark on their foreheads having the blue portion at the top."

This was scary, as it was an Online Law Enforcement Government Restricted Site that all agencies and bureaus worldwide collaborated with for the searching and tracking of people or groups.

Even prior to the Rapture this 'BEAST' site was already being activated by the 'antichrist' in the guise of law enforcement including the NG.

Maria asked, "Why does the false messiah need this SEA BEAST?"

Tom replied, "He is copying the Holy Trinity of God and therefore has created his son and named him LEO, the 'antichrist' leader. Bear in mind that at this time the Great Red Dragon or Satan if you want, is confined to the pit and remains there until the 2300 days (time/date T/D) are up at which time he will come up out of it and kill the Two Witnesses of God. Until that time he can only manifest himself through his projected image, the false messiah."

Maria, with a deep frown on her face, asked, "Could he actually be manifested within a human being?"

Tom sighed and answered, "Quite possibly. Either way works as it's still him masquerading as their messiah returned. He gives authority to his son, LEO, the beast, to carry out his wishes to conquer every nation and their people using violent methods."

Tom took out his book and showed Maria and Joe a quick overview guide that highlighted the rise of the Sea Beast along with his title.

SEA BEAST: CONQUEROR OF SOULS
COLOR: BLUE
NAME: LEO, Dragon's Son
TITLE: PRESIDENT of EARTH
FUNCTION: MILITARY LEADER of the Antichrist who persecutes the Christians worldwide along with many others and ushers in the new world order. Those who voluntarily accept and are loyal to him have on their foreheads the 'Dragon's Tattoo 666' with 'Blue' at the top. <u>And remember current polls indicate that Christians alone account for over 300 million people who do not believe in God.</u>

These will be easy pickings for him. He will, in the guise of anti-terrorism, reach out across the entire world during the first 3½ years

APPEARANCE: First 3½ YEARS: From 1-1260 days this demon possesses, inhabits and controls the human being, the current President of the USA and with his new title, president of earth, manipulates and deceives the nations on earth to side with him.

APPEARANCE: Second 3½ YEARS: From 1260-2520 days this False President now morphs from his human appearance into the Sea Beast, a fierce looking demonic leopard beast and begins making war and subjugating the people on earth to worship their messiah. Christians having the Baptism unto Repentance and displaying the mark of God upon their foreheads will with patience and faith be martyred. They will not fight with the sword. Their names are recorded in the Lamb's Book of Life.

The Sea Beast, the leader of the antichrist who conquers all world powers and subdues the people on earth for his father's new world order, establishes a one world government and has all military and law agencies in plain sight or clandestine in nature serving him.

His colour, blue, is the color of government agencies, police, law enforcement, Clandestine Agencies, CIA and others.

He will deceive and give flattery, riches and promises of diverse types. He will give gifts and other tokens to those who in return offer their loyalty to the 'unholy trinity'.

HIS END: Captured and thrown into the lake of fire."

"Oh, wow!" exclaimed Maria. "This is really scaring me."
"You said 'unholy trinity'. I suppose you also have descriptions of the other two." added Joe.
"You got it." said Tom and continued to show them the next section of his book.

RISE OF THE LAND BEAST[27]
In Revelation 13:11-18 the Apostle John wrote about the land beast. This beast comes up out of the earth, has two horns like a lamb and speaks like a dragon. In the presence of the Sea Beast he exercises great power and causes the earth and those who dwell in it

to worship the first beast. It seems that they are a tag team and once the people have been conquered by the Sea Beast, the mission of the Land Beast is to convert them to accept and vow their allegiance to their new messiah returned.

The Bible continues to say: He causes all, both small and great, rich and poor, free and slave, <u>to receive a mark on their right hand or on their foreheads, and that no one may buy or sell except one who has the mark of the beast or the name of the beast, or the number of his name.</u>

Here is wisdom. <u>Let him who has understanding calculate the number of the beast, for it is the number of a man it is; six hundred and sixty six."</u>

"666! That's the number in the title of your book." said Maria.

"You're right. Park that thought for a minute. I'll get to it later. Let me continue. It's my belief that this land beast will take possession of the earth's then current 'global religious icon'. He is the false prophet. This takes place during his United Nations introduction ceremony when the sparkling mist envelopes him and the president.

Even the prophet Daniel wrote about this beast[28] and said that he this beast with a horn waged war against the saints, defeating them, until God intervened.

I believe this little horn is a tiara worn by the Global Religious Icon. He shall speak pompous words against God and shall persecute His saints for 3½ years. He will become extremely powerful and muster a large army. This is the beginning of BABYLON THE GREAT, and it will expand and encompass all the lands surrounding Rome, the Mediterranean Sea and Jerusalem. The nations of the 10 kings will establish their cities here, along with their command centers.

This beast will even exalt himself as high as God and abolish the daily sacrifices in Israel and all offerings to God throughout the entire world."

Joe exclaimed, "This is getting weirder and more terrifying by the minute. You're saying that this is what's going to happen in the next 3½ years, aren't you."

"You're right." said Tom. "Not only that, but this satanic entity makes promises to the world that their messiah now returned will usher in a time of peace and prosperity never before experienced by human beings and all that he asks is for everyone to worship and vow loyalty to their messiah. He stops the religious custom of the daily sacrifices and in their place introduces his own. In his new temple, he will place an abomination of desolation. This is his idol that has life and kills those who will not bow to it.

Now, Maria, I'll get back to the '666'. The Global Religious Prophet has 666 jewels in his tiara. This is a headdress consisting of three coronets with an orb and a cross on top and was also worn by ancient Persian kings. When you look at the False Prophet's coat of ARMS it displays the colors RED, YELLOW, BLUE with the color YELLOW being it's predominate color. This is the color of commerce. You won't be able to buy or sell without the 'Dragon's Tattoo 666'. It's interesting to note that the great seal of the United States of America also displays these same three colors and on the back of this seal is a pyramid having a circle that has an eye in its center. It's my belief that this is the Devil's Eye. It's black and also is the center of the 'Dragon's Tattoo 666'.

The false prophet desperately wants his followers to voluntarily worship their new messiah. Multitudes will be swayed by his charm, power and offers of riches. However, there will still be millions of people who will refuse to worship the so called messiah. This will embarrass the false prophet, infuriate the false messiah and false president who will take out their anger on the Christians.

Many people will still secretly worship their true God in Heaven. All this will take place during the days prior to the 'abomination of desolation' being set up and activated in the Dragon's temple around the middle of the seven year Great Tribulation time.

The 'false prophet' will be busy making alliances and bestowing riches, power and every imaginable luxury possible to those who give their loyalty to him. 'Dragon's Tattoo 666', during the early days will be optional and only those who desire to become part of the antichrist will be given it. The person vowing allegiance to the 'unholy trinity' will then receive the 'Dragon's Tattoo 666' on their forehead and be proud of this mark. The color on top will signify their function. This will give the person an immediate status symbol that carries with it authority and powers over life and death. The 'unholy trinity's' deception revolves around deceiving the people to voluntarily follow and worship the false messiah. Those with his mark will do his bidding by persecuting the Christians in order to break their will power. He will deceive those who dwell on the earth because of the signs which were given him to perform in the presence of the sea beast and induces by way of riches, power, bribes and more to get as many people on earth as possible to voluntarily receive their messiah's mark. Initially the Global Religious Icon, the false prophet, will conduct church services that will be attended by record numbers of people. Some will be elated, others terrified, by what will be going on. Nevertheless, they will go to church. Never in the history of the planet did such happenings take place. Satan, the false messiah, has now been hurled down to earth with his fallen angels by Michael the Archangel and will be communicating with political and religious officials.

Some religious leaders will advise their adherents to rejoice and attend services with great joy. Some leaders will say to remain calm and let the dust settle. Others will proclaim the end of the world and say to flee from this demonic occurrence. The problem with that advice is where do they to flee too? Some will take to the roads, resulting in traffic jams and accidents, and as we saw, the NG will slaughter them.

Some religious leaders will pray for guidance and want to be with these star people as soon as possible to find out first-hand what their intentions are. Then the Global Religious Icon, the false prophet will start to have his sermons televised to the world through the national media."

"Tom, this is getting to be way too much to bear. I'm really not understanding all this." said Maria. "I don't remember hearing about any of this before."

Tom only smiled at her and said, "In Daniel 19 and 20, the Prophet Daniel wrote about the little horn, in the middle of the beast that plucks out 3 horns and has eyes of a man and a mouth speaking pompous words. This again refers to the false prophet. Even today he wears on his head a cone shaped horn or tiara."

Tom told them that over the next little while, the human race would be in a state of flux. The people will be either ecstatic or devastated by the events of the recent past. The false prophet will gather together a great army of devotees, all willing to carry out his intentions to either convert or kill those not committed to his cause. He will expand his area of control from Rome to Israel and use great signs to deceive the people and to prove to his devotees that his calling is divine. However, some will not be deceived and will begin to see through his ruse.

Tom continued on, quietly saying, "The false prophet, this land beast will persecute the Christians until his time has been fulfilled, just like it says in Daniel but he will eventually be captured and cast into the lake of fire. This little horn having eyes represents the false prophet, the land beast. The 10 horns represent the nations of the ten kings who give their loyalty to him. The false prophet gets his power from the sea beast. He can call forth great fire from the sky including lying wonders."

Tom went on to say that at the 1290 T/D he now shows his true demonic appearance.

"What does T/D mean again?" asked Maria.

"It means which day within the seven year tribulation period has been reached." answered Tom.

"So you were going to tell us what he looks like." said Joe.

"In my Bible research he is shown to have two horns like a lamb and speaks like the dragon. He gets his authority from Leo, the beast. Daniel said that as he watched, this horn was waging war against the saints and defeating them, until the God pronounced judgment against him.

Again if you take a look in my book, this is an overview of the land beast.

LAND BEAST: CONVERTER OF SOULS
COLOR: YELLOW at the top of their logo
NAME: GLOBAL RELIGIOUS PROPHET
TITLE: FALSE PROPHET

FUNCTION: COMMERCE: Leader of the Antichrist globally. Deceives the conquered with lying wonders convincing them to serve their new Messiah.

His color represents greed. Merchants, vendors, traders, those who desired to buy and sell will have to wear this color at the top of their Dragon's Tattoo 666 engraved upon their foreheads and distinguishes them as part of the elite, increasing their stature immensely.

APPEARANCE: FIRST 3½ YEARS, 1-1260 T/D the Global Religious Leader, looks like a human being although he is demonically possessed.

APPEARANCE: SECOND 3½ YEARS, 1290 T/D the False Prophet now morphs from his human appearance into the Land Beast. Upon the 'abomination of desolation' in the Temple and all places of worship on earth, he mandates all people worship, bow and get the mark of the beast on their right hand or die. After the 'abomination of desolation' is activated and the evil mark is made mandatory it then is only one color: BLACK, indicating that the person only took the mark out of fear and not loyalty to the 'unholy trinity'.

HIS END: Captured and cast into the lake of fire.

Are you still with me? Do you want me to stop and take a break?" asked Tom.

"No way!" said Maria. "Let's get this over with. You've told us about two. Tell us about the third one."

"OK. Let's look at my book again." said Tom. "The third beast is called the False Messiah. So let's read what it says about him.

RISE OF THE FALSE MESSIAH[29]
The Apostle John says that another sign appeared in heaven and he saw a great, fiery red dragon having seven heads and ten horns, and seven diadems on his heads. His tail drew a third of the stars of heaven and threw them to the earth.

Also, in Daniel, it says that Daniel sees a fourth beast, dreadful and terrible, exceedingly strong having huge iron teeth, devouring, breaking in pieces, and trampling the residue with its feet. It was different from all the beasts that were before it, and it had ten horns.

The ten horns are the ten kings who shall arise from this kingdom.

The Arch angel Michael and his angels fought against the dragon and his angels who lost and were cast down from the heavens to earth.

This event commences the 'Raptures Aftermath'.

The false messiah will proclaim that for the next 7 years there will be peace and prosperity, however, in the middle of the week, 1260 T/D, he shall bring an end to sacrifice and offering.

Every country now shall no longer fight against each other and all should work together towards their collective common goal.

Unbeknownst to all, this is actually the Beginning of the 7 year Great Tribulation that is anything else but.

The people accept this offer in a heartbeat. Now prosperity can take place. They can live, have fun, marry, and do whatever they like.

Under the allusion of freedom, the Dragon starts his systematic approach to get all people to worship him as their god. The Dragon, from what I can tell, copies God, and since God has a son, then he too must have one. He is proud to give his son, the beast, great powers and gives unto him a secret name, Leo. All this seems reminiscent of the structure of God's Holy Trinity.

He is the ultimate deceiver. He says to the rulers and people of each nation exactly what they want to hear. He will have the Israelites construct his temple to his specifications that will copy the original temple. He will have his temple on the site of the former dome of the rock. This building along with other religious places of power were destroyed when he and his demons were cast down to earth.

The false messiah will blame those rebel terrorists, Christians, for this act of violence as this will incite all others to hate them.

Joe asked, "Is that why we have to remain hidden, because everyone will begin looking for us to kill us?"

"Right." replied Tom, and then continued. "The false messiah will say to the nations and religions of the world that he is their messiah returned.

His new temple will cater to the religions of the nations of the 10 kings and this will be their seat of power on earth. There are currently within the old city walls of Jerusalem groups of Israelis, Christians, Muslims and Orthodox Christians.

The false messiah's image displays a regal exterior appearance at the beginning of the 7 year Great Tribulation Period in order to deceive the whole earth.

During the first 3½ years the people will worship him but never actually see his true appearance, that of the Great Red Dragon. This would tip his hand that he was not the true 'Messiah' prophesized in the Bible. They worship their new false messiah and this is exactly what the Dragon's pride dictates. However, their worship was not based upon love but rather on lust, power, riches and fear.

In 2 Thessalonians 2:9-11 it says that there will come the lawless Satan, with all power, signs, and lying wonders, and with all unrighteous deception.

The false messiah will deceive the people. He calls for the reconstruction of the Third Temple along with the re-instituting of Old Testament sacrifices that will be dedicated unto him for the first 3½ years. He will appear as the 'god of earth' and will appeal to all people. He will fulfil their hearts' desires and win them over using flattery and deceit."

"In my studies at university," Maria said, "I learned that many religions are awaiting the return of their deity."

"There will only be one way to differentiate the lawless one who is the 'god of earth' from the true 'God of Heaven'. The false messiah will speak pompous words that contradict the words of God. He will blend lies with truth. A small amount of poison added to food results in poisonous food. His first mission is to try and deceive everyone into accepting him as their savior. Christians worldwide will be a hard sell for this false god who due to their doctrine are taught about his lying wonders and deceptions.

His next mission is to deceive and convert the worldwide Jewish population. One source estimates about 100 million Jews scattered worldwide. The reference that I found estimates about 14 million Jews. One possibility for such a great numerical difference may be that the larger estimate includes Israelites scattered by God in times past. They are today's Christians. Someone once said, this may be the golden thread of lineage. Remember as we have read previously, the DNA of North American Christians has more of Adam's DNA then the current Israelites living in Israel. Is that weird or what?"

Both Maria and Joe nodded.

"Anyway, let's continue. Upon the arrival of the false messiah about 9 million Israelis live out of Israel and 5 million live in Israel. The population of the city of Jerusalem is over 600,000. The false messiah is going to have lots of people to deceive. Knowledge of him will fill the world. His next plan is to deceive the nations of the 10 kings. These are the non-Christian nations of the world.

From my past internet research, 52% of Israelis do not believe in God? This is 7 million people who may immediately gravitate to the false messiah as he gives them all the desires of their hearts. 10% of Protestants do NOT believe in God. This equates to 100 million people. 21% of Roman Catholics do not believe in God. That's 210 million people. This means the false messiah will very quickly have hundreds of millions of people worshiping him.

This being has many names and is referred to as the Great Red Dragon, devil, Satan, the great deceiver, Sataniel and more. This being is the former archangel of light who rebelled and took with him one third of the angels of God, who were cast out of Heaven. He is depicted as the Great Red Dragon and is given 42 months by God to test the people on earth by deception. The result is various groups. Some don't fall for these tactics and remain loyal to God while others join this 'unholy trinity'.

Up to the Rapture, he, and his fallen angels, whom we refer to as demons, have been at liberty in the heavens, doing who knows what. However, one thing is for sure. It was not good. It appears that as the time drew close to the Rapture Event when God would visit earth and instruct His Son to fetch His Bride, this Rapture Event was no secret in the heavenly realms or on earth.

I knew about it. So did hundreds of thousands of Christians and many other evil people having loyalty to the Dragon. We call them the Antichrist. All were waiting for their deity to return to them."

"If the dragon knows he's going to lose the war, why would he want to come to earth?" asked Joe.

Tom said, "I doubt that the Great Red Dragon would voluntarily come to earth knowing what his fate soon will be. One explanation, using our vernacular, is that he was teleported into our solar system and somehow confined to it.

He and his demons were gathered and waiting in the proximity of earth for the Rapture to take place. How long they remained in our solar system is unknown by me but it would explain many mysterious encounters by nasty aliens.

No matter what, the Rapture event was absolutely no secret to the powers to be. Only the exact day and time was not known to anyone except God."

Joe said, "It sounds like the false messiah will look very regal and impressive but when does he change into the Great Red Dragon?"

Tom answered, "In two stages. First, when his temple is dedicated, he transforms into a demonic looking beast. Towards the end of the 7 year Great Tribulation, with only 220 days of this time period remaining, he is released from the pit in which he was confined. At this time his true appearance is shown, now the Great Red Dragon emerges and he is absolutely huge. Then Armageddon takes place, he is defeated and cast into the bottomless pit or some type of confinement sphere for 1,000 years."

Maria said, "Hold on just a minute. I'm confused. You're saying that the Dragon knows full well his fate and that he is going to lose the battle."

"Uh-huh" replied Tom.

Joe piped in, "Then why go through all of this just to lose?"

"Well now, he doesn't lose."

Joe said, "Make up your mind. Either he wins or he loses. You can't have it both ways."

"Listen, you guys, have you ever heard the expression 'misery loves company'?"

"Sure, who hasn't?"

"Well then, yes, the Dragon knows full well that in the end he loses the war. However, he takes with him billions of souls and to him this is a win."

"You mean that God has made billions and billions of people for the 'unholy trinity' to kill?"

"No, actually these people voluntarily side with this 'unholy trinity'. They go against God. Therefore their fate is that of the 'unholy trinity'. The Bible says: This earth was made for many but Heaven only for a few."

Joe said, "This is scary stuff and this plot couldn't be written any better if it were for a Hollywood movie."

Maria started to ask about the particulars Dragon's Temple.

Tom answered by saying, "The Dragon will use the area called the old Jerusalem. I believe that the Vatican either owns or controls this area that encompasses the Dome of the Rock, destroyed by Satan when he and his demons were cast down to earth and then blamed the destruction on the Christians. This area is now to be the site for the construction of his new temple. The false messiah will manipulate all religions of the world into believing that their new temple is for their new era and all people will now be unified and he will be their messiah. Who knows just what lies, promises or bribes he will softly speak to all of them. Suffice it to say, they all will buy into his scheme and start to work together in the construction of it.

If we turn to my book again, I've got a good description of the false messiah, the Great Red Dragon's projected image. Take a look at this."

All three of them huddled around the kitchen table and looked at the description in Tom's book.

GREAT RED DRAGON: COLLECTOR OF SOULS
COLOR: RED
NAME: FALSE MESSIAH
TITLE GOD OF THE EARTH
FUNCTION: RELIGION
MISSION: Deceives people that he is their 'MESSIAH' returned. He has law enforcement agencies of the new world order, both in plain sight or clandestine, serving him.

APPEARANCE: FIRST 3½ YEARS: 1-1260 T/D His image manifests in human form having regal features. Those who voluntarily accept and are loyal to him have his 'Dragon's Tattoo 666' on their foreheads with Red at the top.

APPEARANCE: SECOND 3½ YEARS: 1260-2520 T/D
At the 1290 T/D, his idol image, the 'abomination of desolation' is dedicated unto himself and activated in his newly finished temple in Jerusalem.

The False Messiah now morphs from his regal human appearance into a fierce demonic looking human being and along with his antichrist followers slaughter all Christians and those who will not bow to him. This genocide takes place between the 1290-1335 days T/D.

At the 2300 T/D with only 220 days remaining unto Armageddon, the Great Red Dragon is released from his confinement pit. He surfaces as a huge monster, makes war with and kills The Two Witnesses of God."

"Again, the Two Witnesses . . ." interjects Maria.
"Sh! Maria. Let Tom finish." said Joe.
"He has eyes like fire, terrible teeth, and fire shooting out of his mouth. Nothing on earth is like him. He is king over all the children of pride, those who follow Satan. He can even travel under water. He seems to have some type of force field covering him and can travel by supernatural means. The antichrist followers will be

amazed at his powers and believe that he is a god and do whatever he commands.

His true appearance is not shown until he kills the Two Witnesses of God only 220 days until Armageddon. If he was to actually show his true form, the entire world would obey him only out of fear and not voluntarily worship him as their god which is what he desires most of all. By this time, most of the people on earth will have his mark so he is not concerned about them seeing him as they are damned anyway.

HIS END: He is captured in the battle of Armageddon and bound during the 1000 year Kingdom of Peace. At the end of this time, he is released out of the pit for 15 months and goes to gather those, as many as the sands of the sea, who still have his evil in their hearts. He, and some other beasts of his who had their lives spared for the final 15 months, gather these people for the CULL OF THE DAMNED."

Tom turned to Maria and said, "Perhaps, I could call this Armageddon Two, the final event."

He turned back to his book and continue reading. "This is called Judgement Day and is the spiritual death for humans who sided with Satan. They are cast into the river of fire along with the Great Red Dragon and his fallen demonic angels."

Maria said, "Enough already. I can't assimilate any more information today. Let's call it a day."

They all agreed and within short order were sound asleep.

Minutes later they were jolted awake by the sound of a jet screaming by only a few miles from them.

Maria jumped out of bed yelling, "That was close." as she ran to the living room. The blackout curtain was fully drawn. "For a few seconds I couldn't remember if I had drawn them closed."

"You didn't." replied Tom. "You were so tired you just got up and went to bed, Joe actually spotted it and motioned for me to close them. That's why we have these fail safes. We always double-check each other constantly." They had previously instituted the plan that all window curtains at night must be closed, all non-essential lights were turned off and the fire place was only on at night so the smoke couldn't be seen.

Joe's job was to only stoke the fire place with enough wood so that well before dawn the fire was out and the smoke debris thinned to nothingness. This was a most critical function since a smoke trail could be seen for many miles. The light escaping from an unclosed curtain would only be able to be seen if a flying object flew directly over them.

They went back to their rooms and tried to get some sleep, however, this was proving difficult as their blood pressure was high and pulses were racing.

As the next day dawned, they all rose groggily. Tom, after their breakfast, started to explain that the new world order will have various color coded uniforms, hats, headgear, vehicles, insignias and more.

The colors of the antichrist, RED-YELLOW-BLUE, will be seen everywhere and are very important. The color at the top of the Dragon's Tattoo 666 logo designates which of the three unholy trinity beasts the person serves. The color of their uniforms and the top color on their logos will also reflect their choice.

The color of the CONQUEROR OF SOULS is BLUE. It is the color of the FALSE PRESIDENT, the Sea Beast, and the Military.

The color of the CONVERTER OF SOULS is YELLOW and is the color of the FALSE PROPHET, the Land Beast, and Commerce.

The color of the COLLECTOR OF SOULS is RED. It is the color of the FALSE MESSIAH, Satan, and Religion.

Chapter Nine

DRAGON'S TEMPLE CONSTRUCTION

"OK, Tom. You said that a new temple would be built for the Dragon. You probably researched that for your book, too, didn't you?" asked Joe.

"Yah. Can you tell us about it?" Maria asked.

"His new temple will be built in the 'old Jerusalem' section that has high walls surrounding it. These stone walls were constructed thousands of years ago to keep out enemies. Now, their function will be to keep people in. However, those inside will, in the beginning, be oblivious to this fact.

In the Bible, Daniel 9:26 it tells us that 'he who comes will destroy the city and the sanctuary. The end of it shall be with a flood.'

From this, we see that the Great Red Dragon, Satan, will destroy the city and the sanctuary. This, I believe took place when he and his forces were cast down to earth after losing the war in the heavens. There were explosions all over the earth and some of the falling debris obliterated the Dome of the Rock, leveling the surface in that area, thereby paving the way for the building of his temple. The part dealing with the flood is when he issued those surge waves from the Gulf of Aqaba along the Dead Sea Fault lines leading to the Wilderness Sanctuary at its north end of the Living Sea.

The south east portion of Jerusalem will be destroyed and I believe that the Dragon will incite everyone to blame the Christians.

The Israelites are even now preparing this area for the construction of this new temple, even though it will really be Satan's temple. Because his massive entity is confined to the pit for now, he must use a human appearance to achieve his goals. This masquerade claiming to be their messiah is working like a charm.

Maria said, "I can sort of picture this false messiah, but from what you have told us so far, nobody's really seen him right?"

Tom replied, "The false president and prophet have seen him, other than these two, you're correct."

Maria asked, "So when will we and the world actually see him?"

"Soon." was Toms reply, "and you don't really want to see him. Why look at the beast if you don't have to?"

Tom continued, "The Prophet Ezekiel, in the Bible, says that God will place His Temple on earth[30] and that His sanctuary will be in their midst forevermore.

I believe that this prophecy will be used by the false messiah to deceive the Israelites along with the entire world. When we analyse these Bible verses, we can see how the false messiah will easily be able to deceive the Israelites and others by stepping into the shoes of these prophecies and pretending to be the one destined to fulfill them. The Israelites have been waiting for their version of their messiah for thousands of years."

Joe asked, "What do you mean by their version?"

Tom answered, "They're waiting for a messiah to come in great power and promote them to the highest status. They want exactly what the false messiah is offering. Remember 'be careful what you wish for'.

He will make a 7 year covenant of peace and prosperity with the Israelites and others. He will give them great power. He will place his temple and sanctuary with them. He will rule all nations. He will gather all Jews back to the land of Israel. He will spread his version of universal knowledge to unite all humanity as one. He will be King over all the world and once he is King, leaders of other nations will look to him for guidance. The whole world will worship the god of the earth."

"But tell us about the temple." said Maria.

Tom continued as if he hadn't been interrupted. "The Temple will immediately begin to be rebuilt using the exact same plans as Solomon used."

Joe asked, "Why doesn't he make it different, sort of his way?"

Tom answered him, "The false messiah only knows how to copy his God and whatever has been created in the past he just copies it. The false messiah will claim one universal religion with him and will orchestrate that the Israelites are the architects of the construction of the new temple since they know the dimensions exactly."

Joe asked, when you say the exact specs, where does this come from?"

Tom replied, "These specs are given in the Bible, right down to the minutest details.

Now with respect to the nations of the 10 kings, they will supply the materials used in construction since it was also their Dome of the Rock that the so called Christian Terrorists destroyed.

This new temple will create some form of alliance between the Israelites and the people of the 10 kings who make up the non-Christian nations. The Israelites will again have a temple in Jerusalem during the Great Tribulation and those who also have in times past laid claim to it. All now merge into one mindset, as all have the same messiah.

The temple will be built in the first half of the Great Tribulation and the Israelites will offer sacrifices there to their new messiah. Jerusalem will be occupied by the Israelites. Most will be truly deceived by the false messiah. They gladly buy into his scheme and are involved in the building and management of the new temple with open arms for they have been waiting for their messiah for millennia. These Israelites, good and bad, live in Jerusalem, but unbeknownst to them, they are prisoners. The antichrist followers of the unholy trinity live in the area surrounding Jerusalem and eventually will occupy all of Israel. The antichrist[31] followers will take over Jerusalem and desecrate it for forty-two months (1260 days).

These antichrist followers will occupy Jerusalem during the time of the Two Witnesses of God whose time of testimony is also 1,260 days, but I digress. I will discuss these two fire breathing supernatural beings later."

Maria said, "Quit teasing us about them."

Tom, chuckling, replied, "Soon, Maria. The false messiah will, in the beginning of the second half of the Great Tribulation, set up his image in his temple during its dedication and proclaim himself as god[32].

You know, the Bible foretells that Satan will be revealed. Up to now he has had to conceal his true appearance and work through humans. Soon his secret will be made known when he proclaims himself as god and sits in the reconstructed original temple plans drafted by the God of Heaven."

Chapter Ten

MARK OF THE BEAST

Tom continued to explain that during the entire Great Tribulation, the plan of the unholy trinity is to turn as many people as possible away from God. There will be two main groups living upon the earth, those who have or will get the 'Mark of God' and those who have or will get the 'mark of the beast'.

He went on to say, "People have read or heard about the 'mark of the beast', but, until now, no one has ever created it in full color and design."

"People, in general, talk about this mark as looking like something evil, sinister or scary but what if it looks anything but.

I started to envisage the basic design of the mark by overlapping three sixes as shown on the cover of my book: RED 6 BLUE 6 and YELLOW 6, arranged to form what you could refer to as a 'logo' or 'tattoo'. When you put them together in a certain way the tails of each of the three sixes touch. Upon their tails overlapping their combined colors produced a black circle.

In effect you have a black inner circle representing death, surrounded by three colors of red, yellow and blue and that produces a striking mark that represents the logo of the 'unholy trinity'. These three colors form the 'Dragon's Tattoo 666' and the Bible calls it the 'mark of the beast'.

The color at the top of the person's forehead indicates which of the three unholy trinity entities they serve under. This is very eye catching to look upon as it displays the insignia and colours of the Great Red Dragon: RED-YELLOW-BLUE. The colors along with their positioning have a very definite meaning."

Maria interjected, "So if I understand this correctly, the 'Dragon's Tattoo 666' indicates to the world that they belong to the messiah returned to earth. Their top color designates whom they serve and their antichrist function. They will all have the identical 'Dragon's Tattoo 666' on their foreheads and just the top colour rotated to indicate their status."

Tom nodded and said, "And one other thing. These people took the dragon's mark out of pride. They wanted the power and status and flocked to him."

He continued, "Each group will also have different colored uniforms indicating the group to which the follower is assigned. For example, those who follow the false prophet wear YELLOW, a sulphur yellow, the colour of commerce at the top of their 'Dragon's Tattoo 666' and their clothing will also reflect a predominant sulphur yellow with red and blue being minor.

Those who follow the false president wear the color of military, BLUE, at the top of their Taboo Tattoo, with predominately blue uniforms, with red and yellow accents.

Those who follow the false messiah wear the color RED at the top of their Taboo Tattoo, with red robes having yellow and blue stripes."

Tom continued, "This 'mark of the beast' is a numerical number that is also the number of a man. The title of my book is: *Dragon's Tattoo 666*. When you read this phrase, it always represents evil. The Bible has lots to say about the number of the beast "666"[33]."

In fact, it says that he causes all, both small and great, rich and poor, free and slave, to receive a mark on their right hand or on their foreheads, <u>and that no one may buy or sell</u> except one who has the <u>mark</u> or <u>the name of the beast,</u> or <u>the number of his name.</u>

Here is wisdom. Let him who has understanding <u>calculate the number of the beast, for it is the number of a man: Six hundred three-score and six</u> (666)."

"How come we didn't know about any of this? Why didn't you tell us, Tom?" asked Maria.

"I sent you my book. You didn't read any of it, did you?" answered Tom. "And the bible has been around a long time. Anyway, I'm explaining it now.

With respect to his evil number, we find references such as, if you count the number of jewels in the false prophet's tiara you get 666 jewels. The Roman Numerals DCLXVI=666 are 'carved into his altar' that is now perpetually covered with an altar cloth so no one can see it. I saw it many years ago on a postcard. It seems people are getting wiser so they now have it covered."

Tom looked at Maria and Joe and said, "Let's have a little fun with figures again. One additional meaning may be as follows: Six hundred and sixty and six

If we look at the words, we can get a different number: 600 and 60 and 6

600 60 6 = 600,606 this sum may mean something.

Let's say this figure represents hours.

Divide 600,606 hours by 24 hours. That's 25,025.25 days. Divide these days by 360 to convert to years and we get = 69.51483 years and this is 69½ years."

Maria said, "So the number of the name of the false prophet equates in your example to 69½ years. OK, so what?"

Tom replied, "In the Book of Daniel, with respect to his vision of the 70 weeks[34] that many scholars say represent years, it says, 'Know therefore and understand, that from the going forth of the command To restore and build Jerusalem until Messiah the Prince, There shall be <u>seven weeks</u> and <u>sixty-two weeks</u>; Then he shall confirm a covenant with many for one week; <u>But in the middle of the week</u> He shall bring an end to sacrifice and offering.

Here we have two figures: The seven weeks and sixty-two weeks that total 69 weeks. But in the middle of the week, being one half week, this seems to indicate 69 + ½ = 69½ weeks. Scholars suggest this represents 69½ years.

As we already have calculated the number of his name, six hundred and sixty and six = 69½ years, in addition this may also refer to these 69½ years prophesized by Daniel. Mind you, this is just a guess on my part. Perhaps others can devote the time to fully work the figures. Anyhow, they both total 69½ years. So, when we calculate his number, perhaps the Prophet Daniel's words may reflect my findings. If I'm wrong in my thinking, then I had fun playing with the figures."

Joe commented, "The thing I noticed was that you said, in the middle of the week and this could be the middle of the seven years. If this were the case then as we already have discussed, Satan ceases all daily sacrifices in the middle of the week or at the 1260 T/D. This makes sense to me."

Maria said, "I'm so confused."

Tom simply continued. "The bible also says, it is possible to calculate his number and we know it's 666. You want to know something weird? If one were to take the evil number being #6 and then take the alphabet ABCD etc. And assign values to the letters like A=6, B=12, C=18, D=24 and so on and then if you were to take the word COMPUTER C=18, and do the same for the rest of its letters and then add them up, it would total 666. This is the calculated number of his name."

Maria and Joe were totally astounded by what they heard. Maria asked, "What do you mean?"

Tom answered, "It has something to do with the 'Dragon's Tattoo 666'. This mark of the beast is more than just a tattoo. I believe it also is some type of visible tracking and identification device. Even today, we can insert microchips or bar codes on or in products and people to track them. This may explain how he communicates worldwide with his people using this futuristic sensor. The tattoo's black center may be what's referred to as the 'devil's eye'. Perhaps the 'unholy trinity' can even hear or see through this. No matter what, the 'Dragon's Tattoo 666' is evil. At first glance people may not understand the full significance of this. Black is the color of death. It is also the color of the pupil portion of the Great Red Dragon's eye."

Maria commented, "So you're saying that this 'Black Eye' or the 'Devil's Eye' is what people often refer to as the 'Evil Eye'."

Tom replied, "You could be right. The 'unholy trinity' may actually see what the person with the mark is seeing. This 'devil's eye' may somehow be connected to the person's brain and this allows the 'unholy trinity' access to everything going on across the earth in real time. Perhaps I'm reaching a little about what the 'Dragon's Tattoo 666' can actually be capable of, but, bear in mind, this being may have been around for millions of years so who knows what capabilities he has.

After the 'abomination of desolation' has been activated at the 1290 T/D everyone must bow to his image or die. Then the 'Dragon's Tattoo 666' will only consist of one color: BLACK. This, black only version, will differentiate between those who voluntarily accepted his 3 color RED-YELLOW-BLUE mark upon their foreheads with pride and those who were forced to receive his 'black mark' upon their hands in order to live.

During the first 3½ years, the 'Dragon's Tattoo 666' will be voluntary: 1-1260 T/D people will have the option to vow allegiance to their messiah returned along with his 'global president' and 'global prophet' who make up the 'unholy trinity'.

Those of the military, get and proudly wear the 3 color version of it on their foreheads. They receive great status and power and conquer the people of the earth. They will have the color blue, the colour of the sea beast, at the top of their 'Dragon's Tattoo 666'. This indicates they serve the 'president of earth'. Their uniforms are predominantly blue. I know that I've said this before but these color identifiers are really important for you to memorize.

Joe said he did already. "Think of a stop light. It's RED-YELLOW and now BLUE. Works for me." He said.

"During the early days the NG will wear his colors on their arm bands, uniforms and other paraphernalia. Soon the mark of the beast, the 'Dragon's Tattoo 666', in full color is offered to those vowing loyalty to the beast. Those who only wear his colors will not receive as elevated a status as those wearing it on their foreheads.

They will be under constant pressure to get his mark on their foreheads as a sign of great loyalty.

<u>During the second 3½ years</u> the BLACK 'Dragon's Tattoo 666' is now MANDATORY. Even though I mentioned this earlier, it is a very important issue, so a little more clarification is warranted. We discussed how at the 1290 T/D the 'abomination of desolation' the Dragon's Image is placed and activated in his temple along with tens of thousands of smaller sized 'mini-me' monsters around the world in all places of gathering or worship. At this time, all must bow and get the mark of the beast on their right hand or die. The mark now will only be offered in BLACK. It indicates that those wearing it are second class and did so only in fear for their lives."

"This is getting more and more complicated. How can you keep all this straight in your mind?" asked Maria.

"Don't forget, I've put thousands of hours of research into this." replied Tom. "The antichrist followers will be easy to identify in the beginning as they will proudly display the 'Dragon's Tattoo 666' on their armbands, headgear, and uniforms. Following the introduction of the 'unholy trinity' at the United Nations, they will line up to get the tattoo on their foreheads. This will indicate a position of power."

Maria exclaimed, "The logo on the people on TV looked very striking, as a matter of fact."

Tom interjected, "Yah, sort of 'hell's beauty mark', you might say."

Joe said, "It seems strange that these arm bands were made well in advance of the Rapture event. They must have been prepared for this event, just like those people who were participants in the sparking events."

"These NG soldiers," said Tom, "are the ones responsible for all our problems up to now. They have been waiting for just this event to be able to kill with impunity."

Maria said, "Those NG back in that convenience store were fully prepared and waiting for orders from someone, but who's that someone?"

Joe commented, "Were beings from UFO's supplying them with these orders?"

Maria quipped, "That's crazy and you know it Joe. Why would such beings do this?"

"To win the war." said Joe.

"You know," Maria said, "at this time anything is possible. Not long ago my world was stable. Now it's all turned upside-down. Sorry for calling you crazy, hon."

Joe replied, "I caught that you know. First you called my theory crazy, then you called me crazy. I think it's spanking time."

"Come on children," inputted Tom, "let's keep focused and move forward. You can spank her later."

Maria added, "Please don't encourage him, Tom. Continue, please."

"From my research, this mark shows up in various other country emblems and flags. Look at the British emblem[35] and count the number of sixes: 6 strings in the harp, 6 Heraldic figures of walking lions and 6 black areas in the visor, but no actual face."

Joe asked, "What do you mean by heraldic figures?"

"For example England's heraldry depicts the image of a lion viewed from the side facing left, with its head turned toward the viewer and one front leg raised. You can go on and on looking for sixes throughout it."

Joe said, "Look at the colors of its crest: red-yellow-blue with six black openings in its eye visor. The entity is depicted as black, devoid of an actual face. I think this represents, among other things, death."

Tom said, "Yes, and we know that the unholy trinity somehow sees and hears through the black center of the 'Dragon's Tattoo 666'."

Maria yawned and said that she was tired of everything and wished that their lives were back like it used to be. However, all knew that she was just venting.

"You know," Tom said, "Joe was correct when he said that it seems strange that these arm bands were made well in advance of the Rapture event. When you look at the colors red-yellow-blue of the NG they already have been wearing the colors of the beast, sort of hiding in plain sight. Just like the LEO website. Same colors."

Chapter Eleven
FALSE MESSIAH'S AGENDA

"The false messiah's agenda will begin with the 'unholy trinity' deceiving the news media. Tomorrow they will need to address the United Nations delegates in New York City." said Tom. "It's going to be a strange day. We'll actually see the 'unholy trinity' in their physical appearances."

The balance of that evening was low key and as nightfall arrived, sleep came their way.

The next day, Maria arranged their chairs around the flat screen TV so they could view these beings. The proceedings started when all the members of the United Nations General Assembly were seated and awaiting the commencement of the proceedings.

As of yet, the people on earth have not seen the star people since their arrival. They communicated through the President and Religious leader. There was great excitement and anticipation of actually seeing and hearing the 'star people' on television, as they were starting to be called. The meeting time, slated to commence 10:30 a.m. EST, was almost at hand. Rumours were abounding that the 'star people' were on site and coming to the podium. The side door to the stage opened. All present, immediately, were silent. A sphere, about 8 feet in diameter, floated in about 1 foot above the floor and came to rest in the center of the stage. This sphere appeared to be black but not like something painted black, rather as if one were looking into a black hole that captured light, giving off no reflection. Everyone looked a little dumbfounded by what they were witnessing. The assembly started murmuring and became uneasy.

As if on cue, their President emerged or materialized in front the sphere with a glowing three color emblem on his forehead with blue at the top of the emblem.

Next, there materialized in front of the sphere, a most recognizable Global Religious, leader clothed in a white robe with a tiara headdress with a cross on top. He also had this glowing emblem on his forehead with yellow on top.

The two of them remained silent and motionless, one on the left and the other on the right side of the sphere.

Something weird began to take place. A <u>sparkling energy mist</u> emanated from the sphere positioned slightly behind them. This strange mist slowly and gracefully enveloped their President and the Religious Global Leader.

The assembly murmured in awe at what they witnessed. These two figure heads now remained motionless and silent.

Now there appeared what seemed to look like a brilliant burst of light and then, a regal king. His black flowing robe was majestic and beautiful to behold in colors of red, yellow and blue. His robe consisted of a red wrap-a-round covering his shoulders with two vertical side panels flowing to the floor. The effect of these three colors on a black background proved very striking indeed. The side panel on his right side was blue and on his left side, yellow. Upon his head, he had a crown of some type having 10 cones or perhaps horns with insignias like Egyptian hieroglyphics in an unknown foreign language.

His most striking feature was a glowing emblem on his forehead, a circle about two inches in diameter consisting of a phosphorescent red at the top, and on each side were blue and yellow. The center was black, very black, just like his black sphere.

Now it was Joe's turn to shine when he said, "It's not the color black at all, but rather the 'Devil's Eye' as Maria said."

For a brief second, the camera operator zoomed in on this emblem. Even though they physically could not see it, they all somehow perceived that it was an eye looking at them.

Joe said, "In the movie, Godzilla, there was a scene when the people were in a cave and at the far end there was only black but it was actually the black pupil of Godzilla's eye looking at them and it was scary to behold."

Maria said, "It's also like when you look at a large portrait of someone as you move from side to side it seems like the eyes of the person are always watching you. Just this time it actually is."

This entity, after gazing over the assembled delegates, introduced himself as their long awaited and prophesied messiah, now returned to earth for the salvation of his people. To the amazement of everyone, they heard his soft and gentle voice in their own language without the requirement of the translation interpreters. They started whispering that this was a miracle for each to hear in their own mother tongue. Without prompting they started to applaud, some even raised their hands in praise to him, so far so good for his plan.

This self-proclaimed messiah proceeded to address every individual with a uniquely personalized message, its contents being exactly what each wanted to hear. He conveyed the message that he was their messiah returned to them and that their religion that they adhered to was authorized by him. This immediately validated all beliefs. Everyone had a feeling of amazement and respect mixed with fear that is often coupled with a feeling of personal insignificance or powerlessness or simply stated, awe.

This self-proclaimed messiah said that he would be offering a new 7 year plan that offered 'peace and prosperity'. All prior hostilities will now cease as his global religious prophet will merge the constantly fighting thousands of religions into his one peaceful and united world religion. He further stated that all were correct and he would usher in a time of peace and harmony. He further stated that his global religious prophet would be in charge of commerce for this earth. This royal looking messiah then proceeded to elaborate by saying that his galactic appearance consisting of energy greater than the sun would be too brilliant and powerful for humans to gaze upon and to do so would instantly vaporize the individual. This statement immediately had the religious groups recalling that in their holy books it was stated that no human could look at God directly or they would die. The false messiah capitalized upon their thoughts by saying that if someone looked directly upon his entity they would 'spark' and die. He said that's why his entity must be shielded from humans as this protects them.

Maria once again said, "He could just as easily project himself into some well-known human just like the other two."

If this were the case, then three global icons would have materialized in front of the sphere and then his energy mist would then have entered this person also.

Tom replied, "Either way works for him. Either he uses a projected human image to deceive everyone or projects into a human being known to all. Personally I believe his vanity is so great he would never manifest in a puny human since a god should be able to do whatever he wishes."

Their new messiah said, "The recent 'sparking' events were not supernatural occurrences. It was the effect of my star craft emitting rays of energy that unfortunately struck people causing them to 'spark' upon my star craft's arrival. The great explosions, a while ago, that people thought were from a solar flare, were actually from my star ship coming down from the heavens and entering earth's atmosphere. It was only logical for your scientists to describe it as a great solar flare that triggered the space missile defence array. This was the cause of all the fireworks recently experienced on earth."

This vindicated the words of the President and those of the religious panel who all claimed these events were not the 'Rapture', just an unfortunate result of natural occurrences.

The false messiah had now masterfully segued into another topic saying that his entity was within the sphere and what they were seeing was only a manifestation of his being because to behold his presence would cause certain death. This was the truth. His true appearance, being the Great Red Dragon, along with his great power would have frightened people to death. He conveniently omitted the fact that he was currently confined to the pit in the Gulf of Aqaba, and that the sphere itself was an only a manifestation.

He personally went on to introduce the two people, on his right, the President of the United States of America and on his left, earth's Global Religious Icon. He continued communicating with all present and to those connected by transmission saying that during the past days he has been working with these two highly revered world leaders to establish his new world order.

He went on to elaborate and explain that the <u>sparking energy mist</u> enveloping these two were for their own protection. Their new messiah then said the President of the United States of America now embodied the energy of his son Leo and Earth's Global Religious Leader now embodied the energy of his religious prophet. Their appearances for the most part remained unchanged save and except for the similar glowing emblem now upon their foreheads. The only difference was that the president's emblem had blue at its top and the religious prophet's emblem had yellow at its top.

Their new messiah continued by saying they had meetings concerning the best way for humans to comprehend and view their omnipotence. They all agreed that it would be best for *his son* and *his prophet* to work in harmony within these two highly respected earth beings as their appearances and reputations were well known to all upon earth. These two dignitaries would convey and fulfill the wishes of their new messiah. Those in attendance agreed that this seemed an excellent method and in unison stood up and applauded their newly arrived messiah. Christians, knowing their Bible, were skeptical and alarmed.

All in all, the introduction of the 'star people' went exactly as planned and now the 'unholy trinity' could get down to business and the countdown to the 'cull of the damned' drew one deception closer.

The assembled members of the United Nations, including those connected by global transmission, were deceived by the generosity and promises of the camouflaged Great Red Dragon. His manifestation as their messiah, along with the Sea Beast, his demon son, Leo, manifesting as their president, and the Land Beast, his religious demon, manifesting as their religious prophet, worked like a charm.

Maria commented, "Tom you just said that there are two demons possessing these people. Somewhere in your book I read about three demons. Is the third one the false messiah?"

Tom replied, "That brings us back to your other question. Does he possess a well-known human with this third demon?"

Joe said, "I think his ego is, as you said Tom, too great for him to promote himself within a human."

Tom commented, "I think you're right Joe. Most likely what the people are seeing is an actual demon looking like a human being."

Maria added, "Seems like my theory was just overruled by the two of you."

Tom answered, "Not really because we're just guessing at this. Your explanation is just as valid as ours. Time will tell."

Unbeknownst to the majority of people on earth, they had just unwittingly embraced the unholy trinity who offered only deceit, lies and more lies.

The people of earth now had two new demonically possessed global leaders; the false president, leader of the antichrist armies, and the false prophet, leader of the antichrist of commerce.

The stage was now set for the implementation of a new world order.

The unholy trinity would be very successful at deceiving all the nations on earth. The Bible says that[36] Satan will gather all Jews back to the Land of Israel. He will usher in an era of world peace, and end all hatred, oppression, suffering and disease. He will spread universal knowledge and unite humanity as one.

These attributes were meant for the God of the Heavens, however, the god of this earth was making claim to them, for now. Next on the unholy trinity's agenda would be the systematic annihilation of Christianity. He is given a designated number of days to test those during the 'Time of Refinement' and later during the 'Time of Redemption'.

Chapter Twelve
CHRISTIANS PERSECUTED WORLDWIDE

Tom said "Remember when we talked about the bible passages that said the dragon was enraged with the woman, and he went to make war with the rest of her offspring, who keep the commandments of God and have the testimony of Jesus Christ."

Maria said, "That's us again, unfortunately, isn't it?"

Tom nodded and reflecting said, "Remember, the <u>dragon gets strike one</u> when he can't kill the woman's male child, those Sparkers, caught up to God in Heaven. <u>He gets strike two</u> when he can't kill God's children who fled to the 'Wilderness Sanctuary' requiring a little more time to fully mature spiritually.

The Dragon is now filled with great anger and will focus on his next victims, the rest of Christianity, over two billion souls, and then all others.

Currently, the Great Red Dragon has been cast down to earth by the Archangel Michael and lies at the bottom of the Gulf of Aqaba or even lower. He is confined to the 'pit' which is some type of containment prison. He must work through his manifested messiah image, his false president demon and false prophet demon, collectively speaking, the 'unholy trinity'. By the use of these three, he intends to deceive all nations, tribes, peoples, and tongues. Trust me, he's great at what he does."

The Dragon's unholy trinity and his antichrist followers systematically persecuted Christians and non-Christians worldwide. It seems the unholy trinity are not allowed to mass slaughter the people for now. They must try and deceive all people on earth to join with them and turn away from their God of Heaven.

All people must be tested and tried by Satan and overcome his deceptions. They will be given the opportunity to stand up for their faith in Christ and receive a great reward or to abandon their faith and be a participant in the 'cull of the damned'. Billions of people will worship the unholy trinity and partake in this cull.

Sometime later, Joe asked Tom to explain all the names of the Great Red Dragon.

Tom replied, "He is called the Devil, Satan, Lucifer and other names and through his projected human image masquerades as messiah of earth, now returned.

From now on the Great Red Dragon will be referred to as the 'false messiah' until the last 220 days prior to Armageddon at which time he comes up from the 'pit' in his Great Red Dragon form.

The sea beast, the Dragon's son, Leo, masquerades as the President of Earth. He is the antichrist leader that from now on I will only refer to him as the 'false president'. Upon the 'abomination of desolation' being set up and activated at his father's temple at the 1290 T/D, his appearance morphs into a fierce looking being. Towards the end of the 7 Year Great Tribulation with only 220 days remaining he now shows his true appearance as the Sea Beast, sort of a mini-me version of his father. In the Bible it says that he is given 42 months 1040-2300 to conquer almost everyone on earth and systematically targets any one or any group that stands in his pathway.

The Land Beast, the Dragon's Religious entity, masquerades as the Global Religious Leader subjecting Christians to worship their new god of earth. From now on, I will only refer to him as the false prophet to limit confusion. Towards the end of the 7 Year Great Tribulation with only 220 days remaining, he will also show his true appearance as the Land Beast with two horns."

Tom continued discussing the book saying, "Chaos and panic will soon start to spread across the world as the antichrist begins persecuting Christians and anyone they consider a threat. This is what the unholy trinity wants. He will have his followers, who include those at the highest levels of government, start to implement measures designed to weed out the good from the evil, as only the evil interests him. During this time there will be two groups of people, those who believe in God and those who believe in the unholy trinity."

Tom again takes out his Bible and shows Joe and Maria a description of the false messiah as recorded in Daniel 8:23-25 where it states 'and in the latter time of their kingdom, when the transgressors have reached their fullness a king shall arise, having <u>fierce features</u>, who understands sinister schemes. His power shall be mighty, <u>but not by his own power</u>.'

This means the Great Red Dragon who is currently confined to the pit manifests through his projected image, the false messiah. This image or entity has great power. However, as said above, 'His power shall be mighty, but not by his own power.' The Great Red Dragon gives power to his projected image, the false messiah. And in turn his son, LEO, gives power to the Land Beast, the false prophet. Seems like it's a pecking order of some type. The false messiah, false president, false prophet and the antichrist shall destroy fearfully. The Bible also says, they shall prosper, thrive and destroy the mighty, and holy people. Through his cunning, he shall cause deceit to prosper under his rule; and he shall exalt himself in his heart. He shall even rise against the Prince of princes; but he shall be broken without human means.

I believe that the false messiah's fierce features become fully evident upon the 'Abomination of desolation' event at the 1290 T/D, when he morphs from his regal appearance to this fierce looking being that one could say looks somewhat like a demon depicted in movies, minus the horns and tail, perhaps. This happens just past the middle of the Great Tribulation Time.

His true appearance, being the Great Red Dragon, does not emerge until the 2300 T/D when he comes up from the pit and makes war with and kills the Two Witnesses of God."

Chapter Thirteen
GET OUT OF DODGE 'AGAIN'

As days turned to weeks, they noticed more sky activity on the horizon than usual. Jets, rarely seen, were now almost a daily event, and even several helicopters were seen in the far off distance.

Maria said, "At the speed those jets travel, they could be over us in less than 10 minutes if they were alerted to us."

Tom said, "This could only mean that the NG are starting to tighten the noose with respect to people attempting to flee to safer areas in the country."

Joe asked if the jets could see them.

Tom replied, "We're pretty well camouflaged here having 100 foot trees all around us."

Joe said, "I think it's the helicopters that move slowly that could spot us."

All agreed that they were living on borrowed time the longer they remained. They felt safe where they were up to now, however they thought that it was only a matter of time until they were spotted.

Joe said, "If we are still here in the cold weather, the smoke from our chimney will linger in the air above us, and will give our position away."

Maria said, "It's then only a matter of a few months before someone spots our cabin."

So once again they decided the better part of valor was to 'get out of Dodge'.

During the next week they began to make exit preparations. They methodically started to load up the Expedition cramming as much stuff into and onto it as possible. In a few days the vehicle was loaded to the max.

Joe asked, "How long will it take to drive to our cave?"

Tom chuckled to himself as now it was 'our cave'. He replied, "About 3 days or so depending on the roads we take and how much travelling is done in daylight hours playing hide-and-go-seek with the NG. We will have to head north-west towards the Rocky Mountain range.

Our cave is about the size of a large house, about 2,000 square feet. I have all the necessities of life, solar powered electricity, and good water from a stream that passes through the back lower section of the cave."

"Why am I not surprised." said Maria.

"How secluded is it?" asked Joe.

Tom answered, "It's even difficult for me to find each time. You cannot see it from above. You have to go up and then down and tucked in under an overhang is my entrance. It took me a dozen trips to lug everything into it. I have it plotted on my GPS or I probably couldn't find it. You'll see soon enough."

"You know, I never thought I would team up with a loony, even if he's my brother."

"We only have enough fuel to get about part way there so we will have to tank up once or twice along the way. Just don't mention anything about our cave and its location. People will try to follow sooner or later."

Joe said, "If you're so concerned about security, then you should disable your vehicle's GPS tracking device."

"I didn't know it even had one."

"What do you think you're GPS option does?"

"How do we disable the tracking portion of it?"

"Leave that to me. I'm the electronics expert."

"At least you're good for something, love." Maria teased.

In a matter of minutes, Joe had the thing made dead.

"How did you kill it?"

"With a screwdriver and hammer. I lobotomized it."

They finished loading the expedition with small items. This vehicle was oversized to begin with. Now with all Tom's extra supplies all loaded in and on it, seating space was limited to say the least.

Tom surveyed the cabin one final time and then said to Joe and Maria, "Everything considered, we're leaving some good memories here."

Tom drove about 100 yards until the first bend and said, "How about take one last look at our cabin for old time sake." They looked back for a minute of silence.

Joe said, "In another time, this would be a place we would never want to leave as it is so peaceful and secluded."

Maria broke the silence saying, "Let's go."

They drove along the river bed and laneway, retracing their prior route. Joe commented, "You know, I liked that cabin and Maria's post card description of it, a picturesque country cabin with its winding stream."

Once on the road, they traveled as fast as possible to put distance between them and the cabin. Their new goal was, as Tom called it, their 'Rocky Mountain Sanctuary'. With the log cabin and its site sterilized of their presence, they felt reassured that any future occupants would just clutter it even further and this would be a good thing. They commented on Maria's wipe down technique of fingerprints including reversing the vacuum cleaner and blowing dust over everything. The interior now looked uninhabited. The boys had removed anything that would indicate someone was there within the past 10 years or so, such as the mini turbine and some computer cables. All windows and doors were left open for the elements and wildlife to do their thing. One last thing, they brushed away the tire marks in the sand. The elements would do the rest.

Chapter Fourteen
CABIN EXODUS: FLEE TO THE CAVE

They made good time travelling along relatively smooth roads. After about 9 hours of travel, in the latter part of the afternoon, they saw, far off in the distance, sunlight reflecting off the wings of jets and assumed they were looking for unauthorized travellers like themselves. Immediately they decided to pull off the road and hide. Tom unfolded some type of rolled up blanket and covered the Expedition with it. They hustled back inside and made sure all the blanket straps were tied closed. Now sitting in total darkness they listened as the roar of the jets drew ever closer. Finally after 30 minutes of a very tense nerve-racking waiting game, the sounds of the jets drifted away and were no longer heard. They had survived their first encounter.

The trio continued driving as fast as possible during the afternoon into the evening.

Joe said, "It's getting dark so what should we do, stop or go on? If we go on, our lights will be able to be seen for miles away and that would be bad."

Maria pipes up, "I can fix that."

"How?"

"Watch me." She said and she took one roll from the package of the two inch duct tape that she had been sitting on for the first hours until she looked into what was causing the problem. Maria proceeded to tape about 90% of the trucks head light so only a very little light from its bottom could escape, just barely enough to light the road immediately in front of them.

Joe laughingly said, "Now where did you learn that trick?"

Maria, showing a flash of pride, said, "Old war movie trick."

"Joe, how about you take over driving. My eyes need a rest."

After some time Joe said, "Tom, where do you think we are in relation to the cave?"

"I think that we should arrive there in about 2 or 3 days, if all goes well."

At about midnight, Joe called it quits and pulled over saying, "Let's sleep."

At dawn they continued travelling and soon Maria complained, "This is really rough country guys. Remember, I'm stuck back here and it's not very nice!"

Not long after that, Joe said for them to look far off in the distance. "I think I see jets of some type flying in formation, right?"

"Here we go again. Let's hide for a while in these trees."

"What do you think they're up to?"

"I know exactly what they're looking for! Us, or people like us, that are getting out of dodge and got through their blockades."

The jets were crisscrossing the expanse of land and started slowly coming ever closer to their position.

"What do we do now? Seems that they'll be upon us in a little while. Do you think they'll be able to see us?" asked Maria.

"Not if we hide in those trees." replied Joe.

Tom piped in, "If they have infrared vision, and most likely they do, they will see our heat signature. It looks like 'blanket time' again. This is one of the main reasons I came back your way. I bought this cover for the truck so no one from the air could see it. Seems we have to test it earlier than I imagined."

"How does this blanket work?" asked Maria.

"This is no ordinary blanket, it's a solar block. It works by keeping heat in and blocking infrared signatures. Basically I bought it to be able to drive or travel at night by looking out through those pop up panels without being seen by satellites. I never considered jets but it works the same way. We cover the entire truck with it and get back inside and wait them out."

What seemed like hours, was only 30 minutes until the unmistakable roar of jet engines were heard. It was extremely nerve racking. Even Tom was visibly nervous this time. Joe picked up on this fact and enquired as to why, and got his answer.

"If there is a flaw in the blanket, the jets would see a hot spot and who knows what they would then do. Any hot spot indicates a live animal, person or thing."

Fortunately after another 30 minutes all was quiet. During this period they all just talked about nothing to pass the time away. They continued driving for what seemed like an eternity at a good speed.

Finally Tom said, "See way up ahead, you can barely make out something grey on the horizon? It's a hilly range."

Maria corrected his grammar, "You mean rolling hills. Looks small to me guys."

"Yah, but wait till we get closer. You'll change your mind fast enough."

During the rest of the day, they made pretty good time considering that they had been on back roads.

Tom said, "Back roads may be slower in speed but they have the benefit of going over ranges and not the long way around them like tourists take. Fortunately, we have not come across anymore NG, or anyone really. I told you both that the cave was really in no man's land."

Joe said, "How did you ever manage to buy such a hide-a-way?"

"Who said anything about buying it? I just adopted it for a while. This way there is no record of me being here. Even when I got fuel, the man never asked and I never said more than the basic pleasantries and when I left his place, I always took the main road, then veered off for the back roads for a while in case anyone was curious."

Maria said, "You're smarter than you look."

Joe chuckled and said, "Thank goodness for that."

Tom smiled and said, "Joe, you're just jealous that mom loved me more that you."

"Maybe, but I got all the good looks."

By the end of the day Maria said, "You're right. They do look a little higher now."

"We're approaching the foothills of the Rockies. However, they still are about over 500 miles further. Wait until we seriously start climbing in another day or so.

About 200 miles ahead is our last gas station, just a hole in the wall actually, at the cross roads of some highway and our 'sort of road'. We will have to pretend were travelling on the main road to throw them off, you never know."

They cautiously approached the gas station. Everything looked normal so they pulled in for fuel. The boy filling their truck was friendly and spoke openly to Joe. Tom and Maria used the facilities and purchased some much needed junk food and beverages. Finally, cold beer. They couldn't resist buying a case. However, jamming it into the truck was an experience.

The boy asked where they were headed and Tom lied. "About 1,500 miles due south towards Texas."

The boy informed them that they had heard of reports of terrorists looting and destroying important places. They thanked him saying they would be cautious and left.

They headed due south for a while and pulled off on some obscure logging road that would sooner or later cross paths with their north-west route. They now had sufficient fuel to make it to the cave, providing nothing interfered with their route. The extra fuel they were carrying provided an added insurance bonus. After another 20 minutes, this logging road started to climb in elevation, up and down an unending series of hills and valleys.

Tom commented how good the traction was with the truck and he tried to maintain 50 mph but this was taxing on his nerves considering the terrain.

Later in the day the NG arrived at this fuel station where one of the soldier's kid brother worked and when they asked if any other vehicles had come for fuel he said just the Expedition headed south to Texas.

The NG had been coming from that direction for the past 4 hours and did not see such a vehicle. Now curious, they decided to investigate. They figured since they didn't see them that they must have exited using one of the logging roads that were all on the west side of the road. They had a description of the Expedition and occupants.

The NG began to investigate the logging road exits and later that day spotted fresh tire marks exiting from the main road to a logging road. They started to pursue their quarry unbeknownst to the three. After some hours in these hills, the NG, towards dusk, spotted a reflection from Tom's truck and were now closing the gap. When the NG rounded a curve, they prematurely took pot shots that missed. This was foolish on their part since now the three were alerted to their presence.

Tom accelerated to dangerous speeds considering the terrain and almost slid over the cliff's edge several times.

Joe asked, "Where in the world did they come from?"

"The only possible explanation is that kid back at the gas station. He must have talked."

"Even so," Joe asked, "how's that possible? We were moving as fast as possible, considering the rough road."

Tom hesitated, then confessed that on a highway his expedition was very fast but in off road conditions the military Humvee with its extra wide body and tires was king.

Tom tried to gain more speed but it was impossible as they had been climbing then descending in cyclical fashion with trees on their right and bad ass cliffs on their left. He was pushing the vehicle well past its traction limits and each time it rounded a bend they started to slide dangerously close to the cliff edges of the road. They were becoming very nervous and for the first time showed extreme fear.

"If they catch us, we're dead." he said to Joe. "I can see them at the bend we just passed. They're about three football fields back and gaining."

Maria, who was pondering their next move, took control of the situation and said, "Well if we can't out run them, then we have to out think them. Here's what we're going to do. Joe you take that shotgun Tom was bragging about a while ago."

Joe opened the case and took out the Remington over and under 12 gauge long barrel. He popped in two sabot slugs, the ones having a muzzle velocity of one mile per second which meant it would instantly kill a bear or whatever upon impact.

"The shotgun is for Tom." she said. "Now, Joe you take that dirty Harry gun!"

Joe loaded both weapons and said, "Now what?"

Maria took charge and orchestrated the ambush attack. "Firstly," she said, "Since there is no signal for our radio, this also applies to the NG, so they are the only ones that know they are chasing us. Radio transmissions are useless in these hills that go high and low hundreds of times."

Maria looked at Tom and said, "Tom, just around that bend up there you will slam-break to a stop. Joe you rush towards the Humvee about 20 feet and hide along the side of the road in the bushes.

Tom you wait until the Humvee starts coming around the bend. The road's very narrow with a cliff on one side and Joe on the other. As soon as they round the bend and come into your line of sight, fire at the driver and then the front passenger and reload and keep shooting.

Joe you start firing at the people in the back seat and don't stop shooting until your gun is empty, reload and if necessary continue shooting. Remember, we have the element of surprise but they have automatic rifles."

The Expedition rounded the bend. Tom hammered the brakes using two feet and tons of metal slid to a stop. The gear selector was thrown into park even before the truck came to a full stop. Tom grabbed the loaded shotgun and like a mad man, in seconds got into a shooting stance and took aim.

Joe made his frantic dash and actually dove into the bushes in wait.

Tom had a pocket full of nasty sabot slugs in his jacket, and two in his mouth like cigars, just in case. Two barrels of death with safety off, triggers cocked and finger on the trigger, he was more than ready to kill, morality not an option. He could hear the Humvee charging up the road. His heart was pounding fiercely and then he heard Maria's calm voice, "We're here for a reason Tom. Make me proud."

At this point, it was only a matter of seconds before the Humvee came into view. Tom steadied and aimed the big brute of a weapon into its final head shot position. As the Humvee rounded the bend, Tom aimed his sights on the drivers head. He prepared to fire, applied pressure and slowly started to squeeze the trigger. The driver of the Humvee fixated on two barrels of imminent death and knew he was going to die. Instinctively, he swerved the vehicle to his left in order to dodge the hell fire coming his way, just like when you automatically swerve to avoid hitting an animal in the road.

The Humvee responded lurching violently to the left, went out of control and in one fluid motion took flight. It sailed over the edge of the cliff in what appeared to be slow motion. Next, it began tumbling, end over end, down the steep cliff mountain side. Now, doors flew off and windows exploded due to centrifugal forces. After what seemed to be an endless descent into oblivion, it merged with a huge old tree, resulting in its final and abrupt halt.

Tom and Joe were dumfounded. They had not even fired a single shot. Maria ran to the edge of the cliff and yelled out, "They've got to be dead."

All three looked around and saw no other vehicles or air craft in sight.

Joe uttered the words of his favourite song, "You won't come back from dead man's curve". They all sort of nodded in unison not realizing it and not looking at each other.

Tom and Joe carefully scaled down the embankment to the demolished Humvee that surprisingly was not on fire. Tom explained that was due to it having a diesel engine as they didn't catch fire easily. You didn't have to be a rocket scientist to see they were all dead. Tom spotted another intact jerry can of diesel fuel and commented that this would be good insurance in getting them to his cave. There was a box of automatic rifles that lay scattered throughout the truck, so they decided to take two of them and an ammo box of shells. Joe spotted a sophisticated hand held transmitter of some type and threw it over his shoulder.

They were just about to leave to go back up the embankment when Tom froze. Joe yelled, "What's the matter now?

Tom only said, "Look!" and pointed to an arm of one of the soldiers. On it was a black arm band with a 3 color logo. It was distinctive and consisted of the three colors, blue, yellow and red and looked like swirls of some type. Tom said, "Look closer. It's the logo on my book."

Joe slipped the arm band off the dead man and shoved it into his pocket. They started the steep climb back up to the road. After resting several times to get their strength, the two completed lugging their stash up to the top.

Laboriously, they refuelled their truck and decided to smash in the sides of the empty container and toss it back over the cliff. They watched as it tumbled right back down to where the other debris was. Tom said that should others discover the truck and the empty jerry can, this would not raise any alarms. The three then scampered back to their truck and slowly drove away.

Maria started laughing hysterically a few minutes later saying, "Do you realize that we just executed the perfect crime? We killed four NG soldiers without firing a single shot. We scared them to death."

No one laughed, no one spoke and for the next while they just drove in absolute silence absorbing the entire event.

After several hours, Joe traded places with Tom at the wheel and within seconds Tom was out for the count. Maria got her second wind and started gabbing almost nonstop. This annoyance helped Joe stay awake.

They travelled on until midnight without further incident and were able to put on another 200 miles. Joe said he was totaled and pulled the truck to the side of the road and changed places with Tom who after his catnap was good to go. He started to drive and as sunrise came he was still pumped up and alert.

The Rockies were now an impressive sight in front of them, stretching from north to the south along the horizon. The boys took turns at the wheel while Maria kept reading Tom's book with ever increasing questions. As they travelled along the secondary roads leading into the foot hills of the Rockies it seemed to take forever for their massiveness to gain prominence.

They made good time and around midday Tom changed the Expedition from all wheel drive into 4 wheel high as they were now entering the foot hills that were consistently climbing in elevation.

The next 6 hours were bumpy. "Talk about a rough ride. My bum's numb." Maria complained.

Tom handed her a sleeping bag and said, "Here, sit on this."

"Now you offer it to me. Now? Why not days ago?"

"Well you only said your bum's numb right now, and why didn't that husband of yours think about your poor bum earlier on?"

"Please, let's leave my bum out of this conversation."

Joe asked, "I wonder how high up we are? Do you have any idea?"

"Look at the gauge over there. It's an altimeter. What's its reading?"

"1,500 feet. It's amazing that this truck has such features."

"Like I said before, it's fully loaded."

"Yah, it's a fully loaded, fully loaded truck all right." Maria chuckled.

Joe said, "Was that a joke or something?"

They kept travelling and dared not stop. Finally, Maria spoke again. "Those mountains are becoming very impressive now."

Tom checked their GPS and said they were officially in the Rockies and steadily climbing. They had exited the country road some time ago and were on what could be called a glorified trail.

Tom now put their Expedition in 4 Wheel Low. Their truck pushed onward and upwards, seemingly with ease, but it seemed one could get out and walk faster. They pulled over along a small stream that crossed their pathway, drank and splashed water on their faces. Maria commented on its coldness. Tom replied that it's always cooler at higher altitudes. Several minutes were spent stretching and then, back into the truck they went. After what seemed like forever, they reached 5,000 feet and Joe commented that they are now part of the mile high club. It was only 6 p.m. but it seemed to be getting darker faster now. They found a small clearing and called it a night.

Dragon's Tattoo 666 Trilogy

Rocky Mountain Sanctuary

Synopsis
Perched high in their self-sequestered cave atop the Rocky Mountains, Tom, Maria and Joe challenge evil by bouncing electronic signals off the ionosphere to millions of terrified people worldwide with access to short wave radios. Our heroes have discovered hidden Biblical treasures now brought to life within Tom's book, *Dragon's Tattoo 666*, and now offer to all interested in what to look out for and what to run from. Furiously, the antichrist seek their elusive whereabouts, who coming close never find their elusive quarry, except for one time, Holpen. Events are viewed through the eyes of our three heroes, who never lose their individuality or idiosyncrasies- which prove to be their greatest assets. Blood-virus plagues will soon begin at the 1040 T/D., in Israel, then in Judea for the first year. Then during the next 900 days, globally with those infected referred to as 'Zombies' who run and scream like wolves on a full moon. Plagues, turn water sources to blood, not metaphorically, actually real human red blood. Those infected, God will not allow death to save them, and however, they are in unimaginable pain and have an insatiable appetite for blood. Our three heroes' lives take a supernatural twist upon their Martyrdom as they are sent back from Heaven to Earth for one last quest. Through their eyes and senses the reader views events, Hollywood could never imagine. Global pandemics create 200 million zombies of the 1-color tattoo and

200 million of the 3-color tattoo. Soon come 200 million demonic angels depicted in the Bible as demonic 'Hell Horses' who flee to the waiting 200 million 3-color tattoo 'riders of death', who then combine into the Entities of Death. Next comes the Biblical "third of the people on earth killed". The slaughter is watched by Satan standing in Ancient Babylon as their blood flows in the dried Euphrates River to the depth of 6 feet and flows south for 200 miles. During all of this two Supernatural Godly Beings constantly confront evil and in the process many are 'saved', many more are not.

Chapter Fifteen

ARRIVAL AT THE CAVE

As dawn came, they again started their travels. By noon, their altimeter indicated they were at the 7,000 feet level. They continued to 2 p.m. and were now at 8,000 feet and by 3 p.m. at 9,000 feet.

"Do you still think we'll be there before nightfall?"

Tom said, "I think so. We've crested the mountain ridge. Now we have to go back down to around 8,000 feet and come up to where the caves are. Ours has an overhang. We will actually have to drive up and into it."

Joe responded. "This cave sounds like a cloak and dagger Fort Knox to me."

After another hour or so they were back down to 8,500 feet.

"We were almost two miles up at one point." commented Joe.

"You have to be careful around here. There are many cliffs and dangerous areas, no second chances."

"How close can we get the SUV to the cave?"

"Pretty close, I'd say. We're almost there."

"You've got to be kidding. "Where is there"?

"Another few minutes and you'll see."

Maria exclaimed, "You better never get lost out here. Everything looks the same to me."

"Very dangerous too." replied Tom.

It was late afternoon when they arrived at the cave high up in the Rocky Mountains.

"We're here."

"I give up." said Maria. "I don't see a cave."

"I told you it's hard to spot."

Joe piped in, "Hard isn't the word for it. It's impossible."

"This is your captain speaking. We're here and we're even going to drive into it."

For the past few hours they had been riding over soil, rocks, dirt and fields with some type of wild growth.

"Here we go." Tom said and with that he made a hard left turn, went up some type of incline and brought his massive truck to an abrupt stop. "OK, we're here! We're actually in."

"I now see what you mean. Even knowing where it is, you still can easily miss it. That's also good to remember if you decide to venture outside. Always keep this marker visible."

"What marker is that?"

"This broken stick. It looks like it's meant to be there but it's our marker and without it even I would have a harder time spotting the exact entrance."

Joe asked, "Why all the cloak and dagger secrecy?"

"When you bet your life on something you don't want to leave anything to chance."

Facetiously, Joe asked, "Where's the front door bell? It's dark in here. How do you see?"

"Let there be light." said Tom, as he flicked a switch to his porch light.

"Oh, you've got solar lights in here." said Joe. "How do you make them work inside a cave?"

Tom replied, "I have a solar collector grid hidden out there and a wire brings electricity to batteries in the cave. They supply the electricity to these low wattage LED lamps when I flip the switch."

"I can just make out some type of door." Joe said.

Tom replied, "Actually, it's an insulated garage roll up door that I painted to blend in with the surrounding rocks."

Maria commented, "Your artistic flare looks good. The wall really looks like solid rock with debris here and there."

Joe added, "It looks like one of those hundreds of overhangs we passed, having no caves."

Tom unlocked the bottom padlock and lifted up the door.

Joe commented, "Hey, that's neat. There's a patio door behind it."

"A thermal pane patio door to be exact. This lets in lots of indirect light, keeps the cold out and weighs a ton. I had to dismember it and use hand dollies to maneuver it into position. The reassembly and installation took me 3 days of back breaking work. Come on in and get the grand tour."

"We thought you'd never ask."

"I've been waiting a long time to show her off. Flip the switch and 'Voila!' There she be!"

"Tom, how on earth did you ever get all this up here?" asked Maria.

"I've been busy these past years, partly getting ready for some natural or supernatural catastrophic event or just for my own peace of mind. All the comforts of home, even two bedrooms."

"Why two?" asked Maria.

"It never hurts to be prepared for the expected."

"Don't you mean the unexpected?"

"No, I was expecting something like this."

"Tom, how camouflaged are we from the air?" asked Joe.

"100%, I think. I've taken great care not to be seen from any angle, or satellite. What's the sense of all of this if I can be spotted? Let's unload part of the SUV and start getting settled in. It's been a long trip."

"How did our lives go from normal to running from our government, which is now called the Antichrist? What next?" Maria asked.

"Tomorrow, I'll start telling you everything else and I have the feeling it's not going to be a fun day. Joe how are you doing?"

"Fine just now, but I was thinking. Have you ever seen anyone up here?"

"Never. I scouted this area for an entire summer first until I found the perfect site. It had to be hidden, and very difficult to get to. Only a high clearance SUV can make the climb and it has to be a powerful engine with off road type knobby tires because the roads are nonexistent and the grade is very steep. You both found that out today."

"Tom, what about food and water? You said something about an underground stream?"

"Yah, at the back of the cave and I should mention that so far I have not been able to find its end, just a myriad of tunnels with streams of water coming down the walls. In one area, there's even a nice water fall."

"Great, a natural shower!"

"Nope, it's ice cold. For showers I have a small 5 gallon solar heated hot water tank. It's not really hot but as long as you get in and get out fast you're fine. If you dilly dally around it's going to get cold really fast.

For food I have years' worth of vacuum sealed stuff. It may not taste great, but it works. For fresh meat, I go hunting with my cross bow. I've gotten pretty good at it actually. There's deer all over the place but every now and then you can hear wolves or large wild cats, cougars, I think, that weigh hundreds of pounds so don't go wandering around without a weapon of some type."

"What do you do for entertainment way up here?"

"Other than fleeing for our lives, not much. For starters, I never have bonfires. That would make me too visible. My short wave radio allows me to listen to everything going on in the world. We can watch TV on the two laptop computers, and also the big flat screen TV that we took from the cabin. I have a small antenna outside. The signals are not that strong but being up so high I can pull in 24 good TV channels."

"Will cell phones work here?"

"Nope, too far out of range. Actually cell phones stopped working at least a day ago, Maria. We are very isolated here. Over 500 miles from nowhere."

"So what will we do during the coming years?"

"Firstly, we must keep fit and have no accidents. No doctors around here although I managed to buy some black market antibiotic pills, just in case we need them. I have a large supply of basic vitamins and herbs, mostly pills or the dried type. For fresh greens we will hike down to the slopes of the smaller valleys where we can find wild natural herbs. During the last two years, I did some rudimentary sowing, mostly small items so as not to make them obvious to planes possibly passing overhead. The soil is rich, not too deep, but it's more than adequate for our needs."

Joe said, "This is actually amazing. Almost all the comforts of home. Speaking of home, we don't have one. I wonder what is going to happen when they look for us and don't find us."

"I really don't think they're going to do much searching because your entire neighbourhood was mostly levelled. From what I can tell you're not the exception to the rule as hundreds of areas were hit by the concussion waves from all those exploding things and from that lightning bolt or star ship, whatever you want to call it."

"Sounds trekie to me." Maria commented. "Can we listen to the radio for a while to get caught up on the day's events?"

"We can pick up skip channels or even short wave radio transmission from all around the world. Night time is always best for these. For some reason there seems to be less static interference."

After listening for a while, Tom said, "They're just reiterating the events of the past weeks."

"I'm still having difficulty imagining that so many people were waiting and prepared for this event." Joe replied.

"Why not?" Tom said. "You're already forgetting about that arm band on those NG killers. Show Maria the one you took from the dead NG guy.

It takes time to design, order and circulate them. Christians have been preparing for this event for centuries so it is entirely possible that the antichrist have also been preparing for this event for centuries."

"Not to change topics," Maria said, "but how often can I shower here?"

"It takes the system about 3 hours to reheat the tank providing there's sunlight and luckily there's almost always sunshine up here. To answer your question I would say 1 for sure each day and during sunshine periods. If you and Joe both take only a few minutes each and then me, we should be fine for tonight."

A little while later Tom remonstrated, "I just made it and the hot water ran out. So next time I go first."

"How about a toast to celebrate the fact that we're alive and made it this far. That means something doesn't it?" said Joe.

"Let's go outside for the toast. It's about 11 p.m., and the stars are absolutely beautiful out here. A toast! We're alive and well!"

"Now off to bed I go." said Maria.

Tongue-in-cheek, Joe asked, "Is it a queen or king size?"

"You've got to be kidding me. Separate twins, I'm afraid. You try and lug this stuff up here." said Tom.

"I was kidding, Tom. Do we have to take turns on sentry duty or something like it?"

"No, the patio door locks are good. But since you're a little paranoid, we can lower the metal roll- up door and lock it from the inside. Also the SUV has a proximity alarm surrounding it. Should anything come near it, my alarm will go off. If you will notice, there's a handgun above your bed on a shelf."

Joe asked, "Do you have one, too?"

"Not just one. I have many, the long barrel 44 magnum, the over/under shotgun and the two NG rifles. We're good to go. Help yourself to them."

Joe picked up one of the NG semi-automatics and said, "Sweet."

Maria laughed and said, "Boys and their toys."

There was absolute stillness and silence outside, no cars, horns, sirens, planes or lawnmowers and the likes thereof. And so ended day one of their new existence that had produced more adrenalin rush than during their entire past life.

Joe asked if there were any fruit trees in his backyard, and received the reply, "Yes, lots of berry bushes."

"Great!" Joe replied. "We can build a still and make hooch."

"How about we have a talk about all your toys, tomorrow? Good night! Go to sleep."

Sleep came within seconds as all crashed out fast and for the first time in days they felt somewhat secure.

Chapter Sixteen

SUMMIT CAVE LIVING

The next morning came early. Maria sat up looking at Joe and commented, "It's been a little over one month now since our home was blown away and our lives inexplicably changed."

Joe acknowledged this with, "Thanks to Tom, our destiny turned on a dime. All in all, we're blessed in a strange way. It could have been worse."

Maria remonstrated, "Seems strange to say blessed when we're going to be martyred, but I hear you."

Today there was a sense of excitement and trepidation as they started discussing their plan of action.

"Before going outside, we have to put on some special clothes." said Tom.

Maria looked at them and said, "Excuse me, but that looks like a deer skin, complete with antlers. You must be kidding!"

"Nope. Let me explain. First of all, it's not real. Many hunters use them to lure deer. We have to use them just in case there are eyes in the sky or a plane way up high. We don't want to give our position away."

"Seems a little paranoid to me."

Tom chuckled and said, "And who wanted the steel door lowered last night? But what the heck, see I said heck."

Maria gave him the nod of approval. "You've been right about everything else, so let's play deer. This way if for some unknown reasons we're spotted, they will only be spotting deer."

"I realize I'm being paranoid, but for now just appease me until we get a better handle on everything. Let's boogie."

Joe asked, "Do you really think someone may be looking for people in the Rockies?"

"Let's put it this way. They may not be specifically searching for us but we must be careful not to create reflections. A reflection of light from our binoculars, sunglasses, or equipment, can be spotted by planes or drones hundreds of miles away and from space thousands of miles away. A reflection means people in hiding and that triggers a drone or even something worse to come our way."

The trio made their way out of the cave and followed Tom as he wandered about for about thirty minutes. They took a break and in the stillness could hear the sound of running water. A few minutes later they were dipping their hands into it, helping themselves to a refreshing drink.

"Ah! Pure water." commented Joe.

"This is like paradise, and were living in our Rocky Mountain Sanctuary." said Maria.

"Don't get too comfortable. Remember, we're now living in the seven year great tribulation time that is referred to as the 'time of sorrows'. It's what I call the time of 'hell on earth'."

"Mood spoiler." Maria said. "How about we just refer to it as cave living."

"Look around. Can you see the entrance to the cave?"

Maria and Joe shook their heads.

"Thought not. Look for the stick leaning against that rock way over to your right."

"I see it!" replied Maria.

"When we're inside, the stick comes in with us." said Tom.

"Look over there." whispered Maria.

"Where?"

"About two football fields away. It looks like deer or something."

"You're correct. It is. I told you there's lots of potential food around here if needed."

Maria was basking in the morning sun when in the distance a faint droning sound could be heard. Even this minor change to the absolute quietness up here was cause for alarm. She quietly called to the guys to help her look for the plane or whatever it was. Tom listened for a few seconds and said to turn their deer skins over and cover themselves with it and sit cross-legged on the ground.

Maria commented, "We look like rocks now."

Tom replied, "Now we're camouflaged, so even if a plane was looking our way they'd see nothing."

They sat motionless and listened as the sound came closer. Joe said, "I think I'm going to sneeze." And proceeded to do so. "Sorry guys." It was still many miles away with respect to their location.

Tom said that sometimes bush pilots skirt the Rockies and travel this way when flying to cities. He carefully used his binoculars looking out through the slit in his cover, and could faintly see a plane with pontoons on it. Wherever it was heading, it must have water to land on and there was no water around their hideout. Even though this plane was far off in the distance, they all agreed that if this type of sound was heard or any sound out of the ordinary for that matter, they would immediately get back into the cave, or hide or find refuge. The only way a pilot could have permission to be flying around was to be in favour with the NG.

Tom said, "Rule number one: Never hide under your deer skin cloak under these conditions as people in the plane may take pot shots for fun at the animals. No sense getting shot due to dumb luck. Rule number two: Only use the binoculars when the sun is at your back like it is now and never if the sun is in your eyes. If the sun was behind that plane, your binoculars would act like a mirror and the pilot would immediately see a mirror flash and we would be exposed."

Maria commented, "Up to now, I thought you were just paranoid. Now I get it. If he saw a flash and radioed it in, they would come for us and the game would be over."

"If you're too far away from the cave, just turn the deer skin over like we just did and use the camouflage pattern and make like a rock. It totally blends in with the terrain."

The rest of the day offered no more surprises and they concentrated on getting their new cave home in order.

Tom positioned the flat screen TV on a table, proceeded to hookup some wires and they started to watch TV. This was now a novelty to them, being so far removed from civilization.

Joe said, "Our cell phones don't work because there's no signal, so how can the TV work?"

"Remember at 8,000 feet in elevation we can pick up many signals though they sometimes drift in and out. Using the mini-tube antenna, we can watch TV pretty much distortion-free. I just had to camouflage the tube so that it was not visible from up above. Today I have it aimed towards Washington DC. I can aim it elsewhere but it takes a little trial and error to get it just right."

The TV came to life and who should appear but the false president.

"Aha! The beast, in human clothing." adlibbed Maria.

Not to be outdone Joe added, "Leo, Satan's son. By the way, is Leo his real name?"

Tom replied, "Leo is the short form, sort of a nick name. The long form is unpronounceable to us. We don't have the vocabulary to pronounce his galactic name."

He was sitting behind his desk in the White House in Washington.

Tom said, "Remember that for the first 3½ years the 'unholy trinity' does not show their true appearances as this would stampede all the people on earth into panic and a great number would then never turn their backs on their true God. They've disguised themselves by taking over, by demonic possession, certain well known human beings. Right now we're looking at the false president."

Joe said, "And who knows how many other so called religious teachers are out there in the wings."

Tom jumped in saying, "Do you know what Jesus said in the Bible concerning false Christ's and false prophets[37]? 'Then if anyone says to you, 'Look, here is the Christ!' or 'There!' do not believe it. <u>For false Christ's and false prophets will rise and show great signs and wonders to deceive, if possible, even the elect.</u>' This warning is actually another furtive discovery. The antichrist will announce for people to come out into the desert or in the inner rooms. Jesus said not to believe such things."

Maria said, "Perhaps this means those Israelites or others who have fled to the wilderness to escape the antichrist may be tempted to return to their former homes."

Joe added, "It seems to me that this also applies to us."

"You might be right. The Bible passage I just quoted also says, false Christ's and false prophets will rise and show great signs and wonders to deceive, if possible, even the elect. I believe that this means that they will create great signs and wonders to entreat those in hiding to come out and back to them. These people in hiding may be the Israelites, Christians or Saved Nations people. If they come out of their hiding, they will be turned or slaughtered."

Joe said, "Do you think these false beings could create lying wonders so that those in hiding could see and possibly hear. This would give the allusion that perhaps Jesus was calling them."

Maria said to them, "You know, back in the days of these prophesies, they would have interpreted seeing this false teacher on TV would qualify as a 'lying wonder'. I wonder if we will see, from up here, some of their evil wonders? "

Tom replied, "If we do, they sure won't appear to be evil, more like, whoa."

"Joe, I think that you're also absolutely right as to the number of false teachers. The 'unholy trinity' will possess perhaps hundreds of false religious beings who will go out and deceive many. People will be totally confused after a while and not know to whom they should turn."

Maria said, she has a feeling there were be tens of thousands of false teachers of religion worldwide.

Tom went on saying, "I predict, according to my research that now, secretly, the unholy trinity will start to persecute anyone who does not believe in their goals. They may or will plant false evidence in the homes of many people. Then someone close to that person would supposedly call the police and lodge a complaint about certain things going on behind closed doors. The police will then come and arrest these people along with any trumped up evidence. Those arrested will be taken away to camps and will never be heard of again. This tactic will cause many to second guess their commitment level towards God. Families will start to turn on themselves, brother will inform upon brother, child against parents and after many months of this everyone will be agitated, except those enjoying the moment. Some of the antichrist will spread false information concerning certain Christians claiming that they are terrorists. These will also be rounded up and disappear."

Maria commented, "Talk about diabolical."

Chapter Seventeen
RISE OF THE NATIONAL GUARD

The following day, during the next address that the false president gave, he seemed strangely different. His eyes appeared fiercer looking, more sinister, and the three of them were convinced that the Beast, Leo, had not only taken possession of, but now had completely consumed their former President.

This false president, the antichrist military leader, was now starting to sway the entire world. His mission is to conquer all nations during the first 3½ years as he deceives them with power, flattery, riches and promises of diverse types. Gifts and other tokens would be given to those who in return offer their loyalty, with great pride, to the 'unholy trinity'. He was implementing conditions that pleased his father.

"That's scary." said Maria.

Tom replied, "Everything he says is a lie or has some truth mixed with lies, but the end result is poison. His intentions are to subjugate the entire world to worship his father's image, an event coming down the pipeline that will take place around the middle of the great tribulation period.

In contrast, during the second 3½ years, he is going to use brute force, dark secrets, and all evil tricks to accomplish his means for everyone on earth to now bow and WORSHIP his father's image, that the Bible refers to as the 'abomination of desolation'.

He will use the NG in the USA to carry out many of his plans and will use other forces throughout the world in like fashion."

"I'm really not liking what I'm hearing." Maria mumbled.

"I did a little research in the past with respect to the National Guard of the United States. It is a joint reserve component of the United States Army and the United States Air Force that maintains two subcomponents: the Army National Guard of the United States for the Army and the Air Force's Air National Guard of the United States." said Tom.

"We witnessed both during our travels." said Maria.

National Guard units can be mobilized for active duty to supplement regular armed forces during times of war or national emergency when declared by the president. During the next little while, upon authorization by the President, the NG began persecuting and killing Christians and many others under the pretence of national security. The NG soldiers displayed the 'Dragon's Tattoo 666' on their arm bands during early days but soon millions volunteered to have the 'Dragon's Tattoo 666' actually placed on their foreheads.

∞

As time progressed, and days turned to months, during one of their conversations in their cave, Joe commented, "From early times certain types of people considered tattooing a form of body art and a culture has developed over the years that has a following of millions of people. This body tattooing was a projection of the person's persona and proclaimed to the world a personal statement of the wearer."

Maria added, "Seems like this new group of NG all have this same persona. They were making a statement and that statement was one of power and contempt for the old ways. It used to be said that such people had the cowboy syndrome, meaning they never really grew up and wanted to wear a gun. The gun established them as a figure of power that the average person had to give respect to. Having this strange 'Dragon's Tattoo 666' on their forehead accomplished exactly what they wanted, respect. However, this type of respect comes only from fear and is not earned."

Tom continues, "It didn't take long for millions of people to get this colorful mark of authority. Once the 'Dragon's Tattoo 666' is placed on a person, they have the authority over life and death, should they choose to use it. From what we have seen on TV and reports we have heard, it is obvious that many have abused their new found authority and have started persecuting everyone without the voluntary mark on their forehead."

Maria asked, "Is it mandatory to have the 'Dragon's Tattoo 666' on your forehead?"

Tom replied, "From my research, the Bible tells us that it was totally voluntary up to a certain time when the 'abomination of desolation' is unveiled in the dragon's temple. It was a sign of great respect to the governments in power who followed the 'unholy trinity'."

Joe said, "I think that one would immediately look at this 3-color mark of the beast upon meeting them."

Tom continued, "Yah, how could you miss this beastly thing. During these times of sorrows, his soldiers, puppets, or whatever one wants to call them, have been persecuting Christians by arresting them for some national security trumped up violation. From our reports, it's always the same. Once a person is arrested, that person disappears and is never seen again. Satan implements a system of rewards for those who hate the one or the other,

Joe asked, "Do you think parents, children or relatives for that matter will turn on each other?"

"Yes," Tom replied, "these traitors of humanity bear false witness against others to gain favor and rewards. The Bible says families will turn on each other as the love bonds disintegrate." The NG, under the control of the false president have blue at the top of their 'Dragon's Tattoo 666' identifying them as military of the false president. Although he is an extremely powerful, supernatural being and could easily kill millions of people on earth, he is restricted and must first allow the people to be tested to see if they will be loyal to God of Heaven or to him, god of earth. He must rely on his servants, the antichrist, to do his bidding. As the months pass, under the guise of national security, the false president issues executive orders curtailing all types of freedoms, especially of the religious type. His ego demands that the antichrists, who want his favors, worship him which they do gladly. He has no love within him as he is evil personified. He offers power to those who follow him. As the months dragged on the crazies grew in numbers.

While watching a news report on TV, Tom said, "Up to now the crazies were held in check by the rule of law, but imagine them being free to carry out their evil inclinations. You know, the crazies also include the police and law enforcement agencies, who are now free to fulfill all their sick fantasies. They'll start ordering people to surrender their arms and to trust the new government."

Joe asked, "I wonder if the people will just surrender their weapons because up to now it seems that the President has tried and failed to achieve such results."

Maria joined in saying, "I think you're right. Many of these survivalist groups, or gun association members will buck at giving up their weapons."

Joe added, "I can just picture thousands of encounters of such conflicts."

Maria said, "Conflicts? How about skirmishes or all out battles."

"You know, Maria, remember when we were travelling . . . correction fleeing, through the mountains, we saw far off in the distance those helicopters that had destroyed some buildings?"

"Yes, and Tom saw through his binoculars that they were cobra choppers." replied Maria.

Joe said, "Seems like these battles had started way back then. Tom was right when he said, 'let's get out of Dodge'."

Maria and Joe are visibly shaken by all that has transpired and by what they have heard on the news broadcasts.

After a much needed break from all the gloom and doom and a scotch or two later, Tom said, "OK guys, you wanted to know more. This is what I believe is going to take place."

Maria interjected, "It doesn't take a leap of faith as we're seeing so many things happening already."

Tom smiled and continued, "I believe that the 'unholy trinity' is meeting with the world leaders of both governments and religions be it Christian or whatever because he wants their obedience and devotion; actually unknown to them, their souls."

Tom asked' "Are you with me?'

Joe and Maria nodded, so he continued with, "They are in the process of implementing their version of a 7 year treaty of peace and prosperity whereby under their control there will be good times for all who are loyal to them."

Maria asked, "What is the state of the Christians like now?"

Tom replied, "According to our reports, at present, things are not going well. Many of the Christians have not been fooled by his masquerading as their messiah returned. He is becoming frustrated with their staunch faith in Christ. In response to this, the NG are becoming vicious and resorting to extreme acts of violence."

Joe commented, "Hey guys, I think, at this point, one error on our part would be disastrous to us."

The three of them agreed that their actions now must make them 100% invisible to the NG.

Chapter Eighteen
INVISIBLE TO THE WORLD

Tom spoke to Maria and Joe saying, "We are currently in the first 3½ year time period. From the safety of our cave, we can monitor events worldwide using the short wave radio."

Joe said, "If it's a short wave radio, then we can send out messages, right?"

"That's correct," replied Tom, "just that the old method will take several minutes or longer to tap out the message using Morse Code. The new state of the art unit that we have is called a burst short wave or for short BSW. This short wave radio that we have been listening to can also transmit and uses a laptop. You type in your message using normal words and a software program translates this message into an electronic data file, compresses it and then when I hit enter it's transmitted in a fraction of a second. Then the recipient downloads this burst and their compatible BSW turns the short wave electronic message back into typewritten words displayed on a laptop screen. Many such radio devices have a small one line screen that can display up to 10 words. Some even older short wave radios receive the message into their radio's memory and then hear it as a Morse code message. This prevents the NG or other people intent on snooping and locating them from getting a fix on our locations. The micro burst transmission message is over in less than a fraction of a second. This makes triangulating next to impossible. It's over before anyone can get a fix on it."

Joe asked, "Why all the hype about this radio?"

Tom replied, "From this elevation, we can not only listen but also transmit and communicate with anyone in the world without being blocked. Our transmission sort of bounces off the upper ionosphere and circles the earth."

Maria said, "This may prove valuable someday."

As things go, it did not take long for them to receive their first BSW message.

Maria said, "I understand the BSW but how does it work?"

"Using the BSW we can communicate with people on the other side of the world because short wave radio signals are different than regular long wave signals. Ours reflects off the top ionosphere and back to earth with little interference. So we can just listen and reply, should we wish to do so."

Maria asked, "Is there a best time to listen to what's out there?"

Tom replied, "In the night, when interferences settle down, is best for us. When other people send out messages, our unit will record them and when we hit the play key, the unit will display the messages in normal printed words. It's not as refined as listening to someone talk but it's just fine for our purposes. This BSW will come in handy for us to know what's going on around the world."

The short wave radio was always set to the scan setting which continuously jumped from one frequency to the other in search of a data stream at which time it would lock on and record the information. They all took turns checking for messages. This gave them up to date information concerning the events happening worldwide.

At the same time they were also listening to the TV for events happening in New York City. Apparently people were becoming increasingly uneasy as rumours were floating around that the 'star people' were not what they claimed to be. More and more people were using short wave radios to hear the truth regarding the persecutions and atrocities worldwide that no true messiah would ever stoop to. Those with the BSW were chattering saying that sales of the BSW were phenomenal and now illegal under penalty of death in the USA and other countries. The homeland security agencies were calling them the choice of terrorists and started offering rewards to anyone informing of their whereabouts.

People were seeking a religious take on the events of the past month. Even thousands of miles away from the big cities, the three of them could sense that people were terrified of the events happening.

The infrastructure of families started to crumble. Localized fighting began over trivial matters which some called the descent into madness. The Dragon loved all this misery.

Unknown to everyone, the Dragon was not authorized to effect mass extermination that would be easy for a being having his capabilities. He had to give them the 'Biblical Job Test'. The 'unholy trinity' wanted all to turn away from their true God of Heaven and to worship him, or in the alternative, give them pain and suffering as they languished in these conditions.

As daybreak came again one day, Maria, looking out, said, "I can't see the sun, just its reflection off those mountain sides over there in the distance."

"That's because we're protected by mountain ranges with many layers of valleys. The morning sun is more like morning reflected sun. Later in the morning it will be shining on us so until later in the day we're golden. It's also perfect for the solar generating system as we get great peak sun exposure."

"Don't tell me you picked this site because of it."

"No, actually, just luck on this one."

"Coffee's on everyone. Its aroma is comforting, isn't it?"

"Yah, just like home."

"Don't remind me. Our home's gone."

"Okay, what's for breakfast?"

"How about something that looks like bacon and eggs with toast and hash browns?"

Maria made survival ration eggs that resemble poached eggs, Joe's on toast and Tom's on something that resembled potato bits. After lots of coffee and food, they ventured out exploring more of the countryside, continuously getting a better handle on their enforced terrain.

"I must confess," said Joe, "the view is spectacular from here. You can see for many miles, especially through the valley passages. It reminds me of that movie 'Shangri-La' whereby once you were inside the mountains it was a different world."

Maria piped in, "For some reason, I feel secure and at home here."

Tom chuckled and asked, "Maria, do you think it could possibly be the quarter million I've spent to make it that way?"

"I didn't know you were that well off or I would have been nicer to you."

Maria said, "Behave, Joe."

"My book deal made me millions of cash, brother, and I invested part of it here."

"Luckily for us, Tom's your benevolent brother."

Maria said.

Joe replied, "Yah, I always thought highly of you."

"You're so full of it." piped Tom. "So do we want to go exploring or listen to the news?"

"Well, the news is always getting worse, so let's go trekking."

Maria was now starting to mentally adjust to the fact that they were going to have to live through tough and tougher times and to make decisions as to their future, spiritually speaking.

Maria said, "You've brought us up to speed, Tom, but how long until the antichrist targets us?"

"The Bible says that he is given a little over 1260 days to try and deceive all people on earth to worship him as their god and after that he clobbers everyone. To answer your question more specifically, I don't know when our turn comes."

They grew accustomed to their new environment and became adept at being invisible to all eyes in the sky. The days seemed to fly by. During the day, they hunted for berries and herbs and by night, they listened to their electronic instruments. After a while, they had a good handle on what was transpiring worldwide.

As the months turned into a year, there were ever increasing amounts of people exiting or trying to exit from the cities. Now, well into the 'time of sorrows' of the Great Tribulation Time, lawlessness abounded. The rule of democratic law and order and the current infrastructure had long since collapsed and crumbled into oblivion. People had become terrified and resorted to violence to get their way. The antichrist's one world government of power had now expanded the scope of Marshal Law for the entire world for the so called good of the people. This was just a ruse for atrocities to follow.

During these days it had become ever increasingly difficult to make a living and buy necessities of life. More and more measures were put into place intended to destroy the hope and future of all those on earth who opposed the 'unholy trinity'. One would think that people would flee and hide when they heard of the mark of the beast that millions were now calling the 'Dragon's Tattoo 666'.

Great numbers of people actually desired his mark, especially those who already had a predisposition towards evil. These people flocked to the antichrist, who designated them for positions of power over the people of earth who were reluctant or refused to get his mark.

The Dragon had anticipated that people would receive his mark on their forehead and for a large part he was correct. Those who displayed the 'Dragon's Tattoo 666' on their forehead were in fact proud of his mark. They were evil anyway and this prominent designation was a status symbol to them. His army of souls started to increase at an alarming rate. However, in contrast, people were also sneaking away from the cities during the night in ever increasing numbers.

Underground systems started to pop up and just like in the days of slavery when people were helping people escape. At first, it was easy to escape to the country side but as time went on the local police and then the NG tightened the noose around all cities. After some time, escaping was no easy matter.

Everyone that had the 'Dragon's Tattoo 666' were issued weapons and had orders to shoot and kill anyone that dared to offer resistance to their cause, now deemed terrorists against the new order.

As time went on, Tom, Joe and Maria developed excellent survival skills. Several times they had narrowly escaped being spotted by flying drones; these little things did not make much noise. Fortunately for them, they were at such a high altitude, this made the drones sound louder due to the mountains all around and if you saw a flash or the sun's reflection bouncing off an object, they would 'make like a rock' until the object disappeared and then some. At first they could not figure out why these drones were even out this far. After a few more months they found out. One day Joe was listening to the radio that he had taken from the NG crashed Humvee a long time ago. This military device rarely picked up any chatter due to its limited transmission range of about 300 miles, but today was different. Whoever was talking on it considered their conversation private and secure.

Joe called to Maria to turn down the short wave radio and listen to this. They intently listened and were soon riveted to its sounds. It seemed like the terrorists, as they were called by the NG, were migrating their way, not necessarily directly towards their cave hide out, but rather, people were fleeing to the hills and figured that if they could make it to the Rocky Mountains then they would have a better chance of survival. Good thinking on their part, but bad news for the three.

Maria asked, "The Christians know that they will soon be martyred for their faith, so why flee?"

Joe laughed and said, "Ask yourself that question, Maria. We fled."

Tom now took over the conversation, saying, "Remember Christians living at the time of the Rapture really didn't have a clear understanding of what was going to take place. That's why I wrote the book, sort of a guideline for them."

Maria added, "Unfortunately, for us too."

The NG had commenced drone operations during the daytime hours but fortunately not at night due to the difficulty in landing them for their range of sight using infrared vision was limited.

Joe said, it would only be a matter of time until these nomads came into their domain. They started to plan a course of action for this eventual happening.

The first and second year flew by and now only seemed like a distant memory. Now many Christians were migrating their way who formerly were being held captive in their houses or cities due to marshal law restrictions. Those not having a plan of escape remained in their homes while others, out of desperation, fled to the countryside. They began to migrate further away from the cities and most had the idea to 'flee to the hills'. Slowly but surely, the radio chatter increased and indicated that groups were now heading for the Rockies and in the general direction of their cave.

Maria asked, "Is our plan for this in place?"

Tom replied, "I'm working on it."

Joe was fiddling with that weird radio thing that he took from the Humvee debris. He wanted to reassure himself that it didn't have a concealed GPS locator of any type. It didn't.

Maria asked, "Could they track us?"

Joe proceeded to say, "As long as we just listened and did not try to broadcast no one could track us. This unit was not that sophisticated."

Tom said, "We would never do that since it would be our downfall."

Chapter Nineteen
NOMADS COMING OUR WAY

Month after month their main topic of conversation following breakfast was always the same. The nomads are advancing steadily closer in their direction.

Joe said, "Our plan better be a good one. There's going to be hundreds of them coming soon."

Quite a few days later their plan was finished. They were prepared for the fleeing people.

Joe said, "What do we do now?"

"Sit tight." replied Maria.

About one month later, the chatter on the NG radio started much earlier in the day, about 6 a.m. This was before dawn for them and indicated that something was up.

Joe reported the drones were spotting nomads about 100 miles to the east of them. This seems far enough away but for drones that can fly at 100 mph that meant they could be overtop of them in a little over an hour. This fact now limited their excursions.

They had mastered the art of being invisible with their camouflaged costumes when planes could be seen many miles away and most of the time they even put the head antlers on with the rest of the hide just trailing to the ground. They thought that if a satellite was viewing the mountains, their costume should fool the automated scanners. The drones, however, were another matter because the live controller could pilot the drone in for a real good look and their deer costumes would most likely not fool them.

The NG were saying to each other that some terrorists were visible in clearings and called for the weaponized drones to come in for the kill. They were distraught but couldn't do anything but sit there and pray. After a while the drones were in position and the order was given to commence firing. After several minutes, fire control reported no movement and the NG could be heard cheering in the background.

The NG reported that about 15 were killed but their previous reports indicated around 40 people in the group. The NG were discussing their strategy for tomorrow. The three knew what was going to happen but what could they do about it? From that day forward the chatter on the NG radio increased greatly. From the safety of their cave they listened but there was no chatter indicating any activities to the north of them, mostly from the south.

Maria said, "The months have flown by and have turned into years. The antichrist is now dominating the earth. They're becoming extremely powerful and demanding, their numbers are so huge. The Christians are being unmercifully persecuted and chased from place to place. Nowhere seems safe for them any longer. They are for the most part remaining faithful, yet they're now totally exhausted spiritually and naturally. The traitors within their midst are increasing as many are simply giving up."

One day while outside their cave and getting some sunlight, the trio spotted the reflection of a mirror like object way down around the 4,000 foot mark. Since there was no NG chatter, they presumed it might be fleeing nomads.

The three had previously made the decision that if and when this event occurred they would begin their plan and offer help to as many as possible.

Tom asked what the date was. They had no reason to remember what day of the week it was. Even the months were replaced by the seasons.

"900 days." answered Maria who kept track of the 'Time of Sorrows' by numbering the days, not months. Now a milestone occurred. They had now passed the 2½ year mark and as Joe commented, were still living.

During the past and after numerous discussions of faith, they knew that when the time came, they would stand for their belief in Christ and be martyred.

Life up there in the cave had its ups and downs. They were surviving, in style actually, but they never lost sight of their goal, martyrdom.

Maria asked Tom the big question, "What do we do if they stumble upon us?"

Tom's reply was, "Follow the plan that we all agreed on."

"And if we don't," said Maria, "we, too, are cowards of the cause."

Joe piped in, "Now she gets religion."

They now started to discuss their tactics on how to best help the nomads.

They agreed that when the time came they would rise to the event and stand fast in their faith in their Lord.

Their expectations were that some fleeing Christians would sooner or later stumble upon them and if so, they would be helped.

"You know, " said Tom, "the Bible states in Daniel 12, that after the Dragon has been persecuting the Christians for 3½ years, which by the way is rapidly approaching, he succeeds in shattering their way of life. The NG have been making life very miserable for the Christians."

At this point, the Dragon realizes that he is never going to actually break the Christians of their belief in Christ, just like when he couldn't break the Biblical Job or his faith in his God. The 'unholy trinity' realizes they are rapidly running out of time and now change to another strategy. They begin killing any person that seems to be a leader of these Christians. During these days, while listening to the BSW, they began hearing reports of certain Christians who did not flee, did not hide, rather they boldly stood their ground and testified to other Christians about God's plan. They were instructing them to stand fast in their faith for the reward was going to be so fantastic. They moved from place to place during these days and it seemed that before the NG could arrive they had proclaimed their message and moved elsewhere, almost as if someone from above was guiding their efforts. These special testifiers were creating renewed faith in the Christians and frustration among the antichrist. The Christians started to call these special testifiers the 'enlightened ones' who had a very in-depth knowledge of God's plan.

Maria asked, "Tom, do you know of them?"

Tom replied, "Yes, they're really special people. For now, let's just call them the 'prodigal children' testifiers."

Maria pushed slightly, "That doesn't make sense, Tom."

"During the next few days, I'll tell you about them in much greater detail. They really are a very special group." Tom replied.

He continued, "Due to their high profile, the antichrist will be extremely vexed since they won't be able to capture them. The 'unholy trinity' will be enraged and frustrated with their inability to capture them."

These 'enlightened ones' were doing a great job during these days now coming ever closer to the 1000 T/D.

Tom, Maria and Joe were sitting at their table when they received a BSW message from someone in Israel.

"Now it begins." Tom said. "We've been expecting this for some time."

Maria asked Joe, "What do they want?"

"More information about what's going on and who was this Jesus person many were talking about," replied Joe.

The sender requested that the responder, transmit their message at 12 midnight his time. His request was honoured.

Chapter Twenty

ABRAM, FIRST TEMPLE PRIEST

Abram, was his name, however, this was never given out over the air waves. The people around him said that he just roamed from place to place as a small child, and now at 16, everyone just looked upon him as a youngster, the shepherd boy. Abram lived in a secluded cave nestled within the numerous mountains throughout Israel. His only possession, his prized short wave radio. Throughout this region there were thousands of caves created mainly by natural forces over time.

During these years, all that Abram understood was that their long awaited messiah had returned. All religions made claims that his return was for their benefit and was the one they had been waiting for. He appears to them with supernatural powers and says that anyone against his new world order will be killed as they are terrorists.

Many Israelites in the land of Israel flocked unto him. He was saying exactly the words they wanted to hear.

Some Israelites, including Abram, living in Judea, have been listening to short wave broadcasts on their BSW radios or even the older short wave radios that have been in use for decades were already suspicious of this being and had a gut feeling that he seemed much too proud and pompous to be divine.

Abram lived in the remote area, somewhere in the vicinity of the Sea of Galilee. Lately, being a shepherd was becoming an ever increasingly risky occupation due to poachers with guns who would not hesitate in killing him for one of his sheep.

Abram had a crank powered short wave radio BSW type transmitter that served him well in his cave that of course had no electricity. He intently listened to as much world news as he could find. He put on a good act when around others by pretending to have a speech impediment. This afforded him some level of security as the military were always searching for the so called terrorists with radio transmitters. Abram's night time activities were his secret and he stashed and concealed his unit cleverly in one of the thousands of caves in the countryside, for to be caught with it meant certain death. Abram once received good advice; keep your mouth shut and ears open. This he did with great efficiency.

At 12 midnight his unit picked up a 'beep-beep'. This indicated that someone, somewhere in the world, had just transmitted a BSW message to him. He pressed a button on his unit that opened the compressed message and started reading words on the small LED display screen of his unit. The message concerned the activities of a false messiah who was deceiving the Israelites and all people on earth.

Abram's radio was not as sophisticated as some of the laptop BSW later models like Tom's. He could only read a single sentence at a time on his little screen. Typing responses was always tedious as he had only a little mini key board interface, the size of those on cell phones.

Abram read their message and was confused. It was saying his messiah was a false god and in fact was Satan deceiving the people. The message stated that Satan wanted everyone to take his mark on their foreheads as a sign of honor to him. The last part of the message hit home when he read that his messiah was persecuting millions of people and this is something a true messiah would never stoop to. Abram had even seen this peculiar mark on some rather mean looking people.

People never gave out their real names over the air so when he asked to whom he was communicating with the response was; #1, #2 and #3. Abram responded saying his name was #4 and indicated #5, his strange friend Mel would hopefully be joining them soon.

They soon began communicating almost every day at a mutually prearranged times. Even though they were half a world away the events surrounding them were by and large the same; persecution of those deemed terrorists.

Certain people who already were the rich elite on earth gravitated to the 'unholy trinity' in a heartbeat. Their 'god' was money and power. They became the leaders of commerce, seemingly overnight. However, in reality, they and their ancestors had been preparing for these days for centuries.

During these days, virtually all of Israel worshiped their new messiah and wore his mark with pride. Abram was brought up to speed during the following months but all they could do was watch and report what was taking place.

Maria questioned Tom saying, "Our fellow Christians must have a super strong faith to resist Satan."

"True," replied Tom. "The dragon underestimated the resolve of Christians. He had success in converting millions of them but the majority still resist his efforts and instead of their faith becoming weaker, it is becoming more resolved.

The Dragon is succeeding in shattering their peace and infrastructures and has the Christians on the run. Our reports indicate that they can only meet in the safety of 'safe houses' and only in limited numbers to limit exposure as numbers means Christians worshiping."

Joe asked, several times you said the word 'shattered'. What do you mean?

Maria answered this, "I think it means they became exhausted over time, like when one's peace has been shattered. It doesn't mean their faith was broken and destroyed."

Tom nodded and continued, "During these days some family members are siding with the antichrist for various reasons. They turn against their loved ones and by doing so wish to garner favors from the NG and others."

Tom told Joe and Maria that in the Bible, specifically in Matthew 24:10 it says that many will betray one another, and will hate one another.

Just as Jesus predicted, families were turning against and hating each other. In fact, children and parents were conspiring against each other and aligning themselves with the antichrist to gain the upper hand.

Maria added, "This is common during times of war when families take sides and become enemies."

Each week as Tom tutored them they gained valuable insight into God's great plan of salvation.

Joe motioned for all to be quiet. Many times from within their Rocky Mountain Sanctuary, as they loved to call it, they heard the roar of military jets.

Joe kept the official tally that soon topped 50 times. It was at this time he called it quits, saying "That's enough."

Maria commented, "Now that was a really loud one." She said, "You know last week, when that other jet flew over us, it was a close call."

Tom replied, "And that's why we always wear out deer costume, right guys?"

"Why are you two looking at me?" lamented Joe, who then quickly added, "OK, I get the message. I just get so hot in them."

Maria chided him, "Better hot than dead."

Tom said, "When that jet last week flew past us, we had no advanced warning."

Maria agreed saying, "By the time we heard it, the jet was long gone. I don't even know how a pilot could have seen us at that speed."

"Sometimes they are video recording their flights and someone may be scanning their results using a 'face recognition' program tweaked to spot human shapes." said Joe.

Maria agreeing, then said, "It's very important now with these jet flybys becoming more frequent that we remain camouflaged. Our lives depend upon it.

Joe again said, "OK, OK, I get the picture."

Chapter Twenty-One
PRELUDE to the 1040 T/D

The days of sorrows were passing and the time was drawing close to the 1040 T/D. By this time Abram had been tutored wisely by his distant friends including one closer by and had prepared himself for the arrival of the 'Two Witnesses of God' that would happen soon. They communicated now, on a daily basis, about current and coming events. The topic always revolved around the antics and the lies and deceitfulness of the 'unholy trinity' that were becoming more and more obvious. They said one thing and did another.

Rumors started floating around the world, via the thousands of short wave radios hidden by people, that their 'religious prophet' was having his people make a statue in honor of their messiah. This statue's appearance was kept totally secret and only certain antichrists knew what it looks like.

In addition, rumors abounded that there were thousands of his mini-me statues of his likeness also being made in his honor that were being stored in secret places. Nobody knew where they would be placed or when, for that matter. During these days the antichrist were persecuting and tormenting anyone deemed a threat to their agenda.

Tom gathered Maria and Joe after they had finished their supper meal.

"What's up?" they asked.

"The time is at hand." replied Tom, who then asked Maria, "What is tomorrow's time date?"

She looked at her chart on the wall and replied, "It will be the 1040 T/D."

Tom said, "Tomorrow begins the time of 'Redemption' of the Two Witnesses of God."

Chapter Twenty-Two

MARTYRS OF UNDERSTANDING

The morning dawned, coffee aroma and a few cups got them going.

Tom began by saying, "Yesterday we established that today marks the 1040 T/D. Now, the 220 day overlap period begins, of the Time of Refinement and the Time of Redemption. During these days there will be many events taking place.

These 'Martyrs of Understanding' have for a while now been testifying to the Christians across the world."

Maria asked, "What about Christians living in Israel? Do you think they're still alive or were they the first to be killed off?"

"Don't know if there will be any surviving the earlier persecutions or the new ones coming," Tom replied and visibly shivered.

"What was that all about?" she said.

"Don't know," replied Tom. "It felt like something touched my face."

Joe added, "Wasn't me."

Tom said, "Whatever it was, it felt like a caress."

"Definitely not me." added Joe.

Tom said, "On a moving forward basis, the 'Martyrs of Understanding', that some called the 'Enlightened Ones' are going from being a nuisance to being a threat to the 'unholy trinity'. They are now ramping up their defiance to the antichrist and are creating major problems.

The Prophet Daniel refers to them as, the people who know their God. I believe this is another furtive discovery reference because you would think that all Christians know their God. This sentence, to me, indicates a deeper meaning. They know their God because He is their Heavenly Father and they are His Children.

These righteous people lived a God fearing life and are a very special people who already had the 'three sacraments' but they drifted away from the faithful 'children of God' who were caught up to God during the Rapture and those who were transported into the 'Wilderness Sanctuary'.

You know, I believe the Biblical 'Prodigal Son' parable may apply to them. I refer to them as the Prodigal Children who come home. Remember they are still the Children of God and have a great deal of intimate knowledge about their Heavenly Father's plan of salvation. During the past months they have been making up for lost time, the Bible says about them 'for it is still prior to the appointed time'."

Joe asked, "Explain what you mean by 'prodigal son'."

Maria piped in saying, "I got this one. In the Bible, Jesus told a parable to illustrate that His Father never gives up on His people and always welcomes them back into his arms should they return to Him. Remember Joe, when the younger son, no reference to you, wanted his inheritance, got it, spent it and then came back to his father who gladly took him back and even made a celebration feast for him? The father said that he who was lost was now found."

Joe squirmed slightly, "I didn't squander it and how was I to know it was swamp land that I bought."

Tom looked at Maria, Maria looked at Tom, and both rolled their eyes yet said nothing.

Maria asked, "What does it mean when the Bible says 'for it is still prior to the appointed time'?"

Tom answered, "God has designated specific time dates for certain events to take place."

Maria added, "I get it. As long as they came back before it's too late, the time of grace still exists."

Tom said, "Yes, you're correct and I believe that the Prophet Daniel makes phenomenal reference to them. Maria, get the Bible and let's look up Daniel 11:32- 33. Read what it says."

Maria did as she was asked and read: "but <u>the people who know their God shall be strong</u>, and <u>carry out great exploits.</u> And <u>those of the people who understand shall instruct many</u>; yet for <u>many days they shall fall by sword and flame, by captivity and plundering.</u>"

"Thanks, Maria. To me, this is another furtive discovery reference. Within Christianity, during these days, there are two groups of Christians, those having three Sacraments and those having two Sacraments."

Joe added, "Are there any one Sacrament Christians?"

"Don't know." replied Tom. "I do know that the prodigal children have the three Sacraments that we have talked about. They have deeper insight into God's plan of salvation than their two Sacrament brethren. They fortify the Christians to muster their faith and to prepare for martyrdom.

This group of bold testifiers of Christ will stand out and directly challenge the antichrist with the result being, they are targeted by the antichrist and for many days they shall fall by sword and flame, by captivity and plundering, just as Maria read."

Joe asked, "It is obvious that some are killed by a sword or flame, but what does it mean by captivity and plundering?"

Tom responded, "By captivity it means imprisonment. They are locked in a cell and the key is thrown away. Since it is impossible to escape, they die of starvation and who knows what else.

And plundering means, they are killed when the antichrist make hostile raids and instead of arresting them, they kill them. Today we would call them bandits, robbers, living in mountain or forest regions. Our friend Abram is always on the lookout for them. Remember he said, they would not hesitate in killing him for just one of his sheep.

I believe when it says; '<u>for many days</u>', this means 'many days' not 'years', so we can say this time may be less than one year and this fits into the 1040 T/D to 1260 T/D. These are the days when I believe they are martyred."

Maria said, "If they're being martyred between day 1040 and day 1260, it is 220 days, well shy of one year."

"You're right, Maria. Now if you look up in Daniel again, Chapter 11:34, it says: Now when they fall, they shall be 'aided with a little help'. I believe this is another furtive discovery reference. When I read this verse, the thought immediately came to mind, what does 'a little help' mean. The prophet Daniel once again did not disappoint me as he would not use such a word without knowing what it meant. Their great exploits will cause them to be targeted and killed in various ways. When they are being martyred, God will help them.

I did some research into this by reading in older Bible translations and found they used the word 'Holpen'[38] instead of 'a little help'. 'Holpen' in older dictionaries means to furnish with strength and the means of deliverance from trouble as the evil approaches. [1913 Webster] Therefore, in my way of thinking, this is the 'Time of Holpen' or 'divine help', just like in the Bible, when Deacon Stephen was being stoned to death, he looked up and saw God and Jesus in Heaven. He then pleaded for God to have mercy on those who were stoning him. The Bible then says; 'he fell asleep'.

It is my belief that all Christians being martyred, will during the final moments of their lives, actually see God, Jesus and perhaps much more.

Their faith will be rewarded as their God will protect them and they will, like the Deacon Stephen, fall asleep. I think this is a wonderful furtive discovery reference, don't you?"

Joe said, "So what I'm hearing you say, as far as you can tell, God will not allow His people to feel pain upon their martyrdom. Am I right?"

"That you are, Joe."

"Well that's a relief." Maria chimed in. "So there is something to look forward to."

Tom just smiled at them and continued. "Now another 'weird or what' happening, as we read further in Daniel 11:34, it says, <u>But many shall join with them by intrigue.</u> The Martyrs conviction of faith is so spectacular, I believe that during 'Holpen', they will witness the Heavens opening and they will see God, Jesus and perhaps the faithful, just like Deacon Stephen. The overall aspects of 'Holpen' are so intriguing that some of the antichrist doing the killing are so fascinated, they actually join them and are slaughtered as well. However, because they have taken the 'Dragon's Tattoo 666' they are damned and their death is futile."

"You're scaring me again, Tom." said Maria.

"It gets even weirder." Tom answered. "If we continue to read in Daniel it says in chapter 11:35: And <u>some</u> of those of <u>understanding</u> shall fall, to refine them, purify them, and make them white, until the time of the end, because it is still before the appointed time.

It says 'some' of those of understanding shall fall, not 'all' of them. Even though this group has the understanding, not all have the heart's attitude to rejoin their fellow brethren. Perhaps they have drifted too far away."

Maria interjected, "What do you mean drifted away?"

Tom answered, "They separated themselves and left the company of their former brethren in faith.

To continue, these Martyrs of understanding due to their great courage become; <u>refined</u>, <u>purified</u> and <u>made white</u> because the time of grace still exists and they have now proven their loyalty to God and Jesus.

Their heroic actions may allow them to regain part of their lost status as 'Children of God' as priests of some type. Ergo, 'the Prodigal Children' come home."

Tom paused trying to regain his composure and said, "These 'prodigal sons' come back to their Heavenly Father with the right heart's attitude and were refined, purified, and made white, because it was still prior to the appointed time."

This brought tears to Maria's eyes, such marvelous grace of God.

Joe said, "God never gives up on His people and wants everyone to be saved, that's for sure, as someone once said, 'Come home children, it's time.'"

Joe then asked the question, "What about the rest of <u>those of understanding</u> who do not fall by this method? What is their outcome?"

"They will have the opportunity to be martyred along with their Christian brethren prior to the 1335 T/D. They may not have been stand-out testifiers and leaders. Instead, they were followers."

Joe asked, "What if they are neither? What if their faith is insufficient and they fall to the deceptions of the unholy trinity? Then what?"

Tom again shuddered.

"Don't look at me." Joe said. "Tom did you get caressed again?"

"Yes." was his reply.

Maria said, "We've had enough for today, especially Tom. Let's call it a night and get some sleep."

"Good call." Tom replied. "Tomorrow we'll talk about the Prophet Daniel's prophecy concerning 'the end of days'."

Chapter Twenty-Three

DANIEL'S PROPHECY: END OF DAYS

"Daniel's Chapter 12 is very strange and powerful and I believe is once again a furtive discovery." commented Tom, the following day, as they sat around the table.

"The Prophet Daniel begins by describing an entity in verse one that during the time of the 'end of days' is called Michael. Daniel sees this entity and describes him in chapter 12:1[39] it says: At that time Michael shall stand up. <u>The great prince</u> who stands watch over <u>the sons of your people</u>. <u>And there shall be a time of trouble, such as never was since there was a nation, even to that time.</u>

I've always wondered about this 'end of days' verse that says: Michael the great prince will stand and watch over God's people. Who was this being referred to as a prince? Due to our fast paced lives, however, this thought migrated to the back of my mind and became parked for a future time.

Sometime later, while visiting a Catholic School, I noticed a large old Bible prominently featured on a bible stand in the entrance lobby. Being somewhat curious, due to an inner prompting, I looked up the Book of Daniel 12:1 to see what it had to say about 'Michael the great prince' and was shocked to read: 'At that time Michael shall stand up, <u>The Great Firstling</u> who stands watch over the sons of your people... The first translation states 'The great prince', the second translation states 'The great firstling'.

There is a vast difference in their meanings. 'The great prince' can be attributed to either Michael, the Archangel or to a human prince, whereas the second translation, 'the great firstling', can only

| 205

be attributed to a human being due to the fact and with great respect, an Angel cannot be a firstling. After a little digging, I found some information concerning this.

The Hebrew word 'firstling' denotes the firstborn of human beings, the first of a kind or category. Abel also offered of the firstlings of his flock.

Only a human who has overcome Satan and who has the 'three sacraments' can become a 'firstling' and furthermore it states 'the great firstling'. We could say, a 'superior firstling'. Back then, I didn't comprehend its meaning. However, now it is very important as it points to a superior man of God living in the twentieth century. Daniel 12: 4,9,13 says this time refers to the time of 'the end of the days'. Daniel is also instructed to shut up the words, and seal the book until the time of the end; many shall run to and fro, and knowledge shall increase, your inheritance at the end of the days.'

I believe this means that people in the 'end of days' will be very busy running around doing every conceivable thing. During these days the knowledge and advances of humanity will increase at phenomenal rates."

Tom began summing up the above. "I believe that this 'Michael, the Superior Firstling' who fights for the 'Children of God' must be a human being of great spiritual stature who before the 'end of days' stands watch over God's people."

Maria asked, "Who is this 'Superior Firstling'?"

Tom replied, "Other than that his first name was Michael, I don't know."

Joe asked, "When did this 'Michael' live?"

Tom could only say, "He must have lived and stood watch over the 'Children of God' prior to the Rapture Event taking place."

Tom concluded, "This 'Superior Firstling', Michael, was a unique person and must have been a remarkable and unstoppable, global testifier of God."

Maria vexed, began gently chastising Tom saying, "You had all the pieces of the puzzle at your fingertips and for some reason couldn't see the forest for the trees. You're like a sign post for others to see and get directions. However, you failed to see them yourself."

Joe commented, "He's here for us now."

Maria acquiesced. "I know, I know, I'm just venting. Sorry Tom."

Tom replied, "And how do you think I feel, I wrote all about it and still missed the Rapture."

Tom said, "Moving on, the Prophet Daniel overheard two beings talking about how long it would be to the end of this time.[40] Their answer was it would be for a time, times, and half a time. When the power of the holy people has been completely shattered, all these things shall be finished.

I believe the reference to a time, times, and half a time refers to the first 3½ years of the Great Tribulation Time being days 1-1260 T/D.

During this time, the Christians are greatly persecuted and become devastated, yet their faith in their God and Saviour remains intact. At the conclusion of these days, this portion of the prophecy will be fulfilled.

Daniel said, even though he heard, he didn't understand, but when he asked what the end of these things would be, he was told the explanation is sealed until the time of the end.

I believe when he was told: 'Many shall be purified, made white, and refined', it refers to those, who during the 'end of days', remain faithful and are the Martyrs of Christ.

I just love Daniel's futuristic prophecies. In Chapter 11:11, he goes on to explain that from the time the daily sacrifice is taken away, and the 'abomination of desolation' is set up, there shall be 1290 days."

Tom went on, "Now when we reach the 1290 T/D, the 'abomination of desolation', Satan's idol image that looks like the Great Red Dragon, will be activated in the dragon's temple, and this portion of the prophecy will then be fulfilled.

At this point comes the gruesome slaughter of the Martyrs when 'Holpen' comes into play. From day 1290 to day 1335, Christians who refused to bow and get the mark of the beast, 'Dragon's Tattoo 666', will be martyred globally.

Daniel says in Chapter 11:12, <u>Blessed is he who waits, and comes to the one thousand three hundred and thirty-five days. (1335 T/D)</u> I believe that this concludes what the Bible refers to as 'it is still prior the appointed time'. The people who come to the 1335 T/D partake in various ways, in the marriage ceremony of the Son of God."

"Who makes up the Bride of Christ?" asked Maria.

"I think the Bride of Christ are made up of 'Firstlings'.

Who are these 'Firstlings' she said.

Tom replied, "The answers will be forthcoming further into this book."

"You mean your book, don't you? Aren't you the author?"

Tom said, "I'm beginning to wonder this myself. I just had that 'shivering' again and have a feeling that many secrets are going to be given to us, as this book takes on a life of its own." Maria told Joe to get the thermometer. "I think Tom's got a fever or something."

Tom just replied, "I need a scotch!" and all agreed.

CHAPTER TWENTY-FOUR
GENTILES TREAD THE HOLY CITY

Later Tom continued, "Now also at this 1040 T/D, and for these last 220 days of the first 3½ years, according to our reports, the antichrist followers have been migrating into 'Babylon the Great', a conurbation consisting of all the nations of the 10 kings surrounding the Mediterranean Sea with Israel to the east.

During these days, they are busy getting their master's temple built. They dominate all people and as we previously discussed, those whom they cannot convert or control are either killed or arrested and shipped to other countries to be dealt with.

The 'unholy trinity' and the antichrist, in ever increasing numbers, are now converging upon their messiah's almost completed new temple in Jerusalem. It is being constructed on the south east corner of the old City of Jerusalem where the previous temple once stood."

Tom continued, "According to the news broadcasts we have heard, they are surrounding Jerusalem, forming large camps, knowing that their messiah will in the near future dedicate it. These antichrist who are, physically and in loyalty, the closest to their messiah, have the 3 color 'Dragon's Tattoo 666' with RED at the top on their foreheads signifying, with pride, their absolute loyalty to their messiah.

They gain even more favor in the eyes of their messiah when they trample and desecrate everything having previous religious history.

In Luke 21:20 Jesus said that when you see Jerusalem surrounded by armies, then know that its desolation is near.

This again is a furtive discovery. One might think that when we read of Jerusalem being surrounded by armies, they would be the cause of the destruction. Actually these armies are loyal to the 'unholy trinity' and consist of the antichrist. This event starts at day 1040 T/D and parallels the time of the testimony of the Two Witnesses of God.

Jesus says the word 'desolation' means Jerusalem is totally ruined and destroyed and the word 'near' means it will not happen immediately, but it will take place soon.

It seems, up to now, the 'unholy trinity', along with their antichrist followers, have had their own way. They have tried and tested the Christians. Many Christians have fallen to the deceptions of the 'unholy trinity' for various reasons and the rest have had their faith tested to the max.

The Christians globally are being persecuted and driven out of their places of worship. Their faith has been sorely tested during this time, but many still remain steadfast in the belief in their saviour, Jesus Christ."

Joe commented, "The times are getting even rougher now."

Maria spoke to Tom saying, "A while ago, you talked about two time periods. They have now overlapped by 220 days. What's the importance of this?"

Tom answered, "This is very important but let's leave that until tomorrow. It's late."

Joe piped in, "Right now it's time for scotch."

Chapter Twenty-Five
MATHEMATICAL BIBLICAL CONUNDRUM

Tom began the next day discussions following Maria's Morning Prayer. "As you are well aware, the Great Tribulation Time of Sorrows lasts for seven years or 2520 days. We have two 3½ year time periods, each being 1260 days.

Now the mathematical conundrum; how can these two time periods that total 2520 days be fit into Daniel's Prophecy of 2300 days until the sanctuary is cleansed.

This impossibility has defied the logic of scholars for centuries. However implausible, this biblical conundrum is, it is now solved by overlapping the two 1260 day time periods. The first 1260 days or the first half of the Great Tribulation Time of Sorrows is the 'TIME OF REFINEMENT'. The second half of the Great Tribulation 'Time of Sorrows' is the 'TIME OF REDEMPTION'. Together they total 2520 days.

Now make your hands into the shape of a finger gun with your thumb being the trigger just like you did as a child and overlap your fingers of each hand to the first digit. Look at the picture in my book. Can you see the two finger guns pointed at each other?

"I almost need reading glasses to see them." Joe added.
"Perhaps they could have been a tad larger." agreed Tom.
Joe added, "A 'tad' larger? I'd say a 'smidge' larger."

Maria, knowing better, yet now amused, asked, "What's a 'smidge'?

Joe answered, "A 'smidge' is a tad bigger than a touch, but less than an ikkle bit."

Maria now losing it, began to howl.

Tom was getting annoyed, but rather than fight, he joined in saying, "You two remind me of Abbot and Costello, and their comedy act of 'Who's on first?'"

"'What's on first?" asked Maria.

"'Who's on first," Joe replied, "'what's on second."

"'I don't know', I just asked you," she replied.

Tom responded, "'I don't know's on third."

"'Who's on third?" she asked.

Joe said, "'Who's on first."

Maria said, "I didn't ask you 'what's on third."

Tom replied, "'What's on second. I didn't ask you 'who's on second, 'Who's on first." replied Tom.

"I asked you first." she howled.

"'I don't know's on third," replied Tom.

Maria looked at Joe for help, "Joe, 'who's on third'?"

"'I don't know'." came his reply.

Laughing, Maria looked at Tom for help, saying, "You're smarter than Joe. 'Who's' on third? 'I don't know', 'what's' on second and 'who's' on first."

Maria laughed, sighed, and closed her eyes. With a deep breath, she paused to process everything. Understanding the severity of the extremes around them did not diminish her appreciation for having her family together.

The three of them had had a brief start to their award-winning banter when Maria and Joe started dating back in high school. Maria had grown up with an unloving stepmother, and while Joe begrudged his older brother for always trying to be a part of his business, Maria loved having Tom's brotherly concern and protection around her and Joe when their relationship started out- she had never had any siblings that cared enough to be involved. However,

Joe never let that protection and concern get close enough for Tom and Maria to really get to know each other.

When Maria and Joe were nearing their high school graduation, the men's parents were taken in a terrible car crash that left both brothers devastated. Understandably, nothing felt the same after their loss. And as time passed, the brothers grew up and grew apart. Regardless of the present day situation and doom- Maria was grateful that she could learn more about her estranged brother-in-law and that her husband could, too.

They went outside for a breath of fresh air. Their solitude soon was interrupted by the sound of a plane that could be heard but not seen. They scrambled back inside and Tom continued.

"Now," Tom said, "by overlapping these two 1260 time periods to your first knuckle, this represents a 220 day overlap. Due to the overlapping of the time periods 2520 days can now be fulfilled as per Daniel's 2300 days prophecy.

Maria added, "So that's how two time periods can

be reconciled and merged, and all the events in each time period still take place. That's brilliant Tom."

Joe added, "perhaps we should call this Tom's Knuckle Theory'?

Maria quipped, "Or 'Joe's Knucklehead Theory'."

"Hey, that's not funny." he replied. "OK, I 'knuckle under'."

Maria got in the last word, "Joe, behave or I'll knuckle you."

Tom knew better than to try and limit their teasing so he just said, "Let's look at the chart at the front of my book, the one that shows '2300 Days 'until the Sanctuary is Cleansed', chart."

Tom asked Maria to look for it in the front index. She interrupted him saying, "You mean this thing?"

"Yes, when we look at this index, we see the Time of Refinement and how the Time of Redemption overlaps into it by 220 days."

Joe asked, "Where exactly does it show the overlap of 220 days?"

Tom replied, "Look just under the title, '7 Year Great Tribulation'. See that box under it?"

Maria answered, "Got it."

Tom then added, "This overlapping also allows for the time of the 'Gentiles 1260 days, to tread the holy city' as read in Revelation

11:2 and for the Time of Testimony of the Two Witnesses of God, 1260 days, to begin and end on the same dates.

Joe said, "So they begin at the 1040 T/D and end 1260 days later at the 2300 T/D."

"Right." said Tom. "I believe this is once again a furtive discovery. Jerusalem is surrounded by armies consisting of the antichrist who encamp around Jerusalem and the dragon's temple so this is definitely not a 'holy city'.

The question then is where is the 'holy city' and I believe this means the 'Great Domed City' that houses the 'Wilderness Sanctuary' located at the north end of the 'Living Sea'. This would definitely fulfill the dictates of a 'holy city'."

Joe asked, "Was Jerusalem ever a holy city?"

Tom answered, "Good question. I think when the Temple in Jerusalem was completed by Solomon, it was holy, but as to the rest of Jerusalem, perhaps isolated areas. I really don't know the full answer."

Maria said, "Tom, this is a lot of information to absorb."

Tom continued, "You're right, but it's important. Between fleeing from people trying to kill me before the Rapture and trying to get this book published, I've got over 6000 hours of research into it and I'm trying to give you a quick overview of the information."

Maria said, "What do you mean, trying to kill you? Do you mean when our house was blown away?"

"No. Many times in the years prior to that while researching articles for my book, attempts on my life were made. Each time the attempt was made to look accidental such as when a dump truck came out of its lane and almost creamed me and then just kept going. That's why I'm so paranoid. That's why I didn't come visit, for fear of involving you two."

Joe jumped in and said, "I'd be paranoid too if all this was happening to me, Tom. This is unbelievable. I guess I should thank you for making yourself scarce."

In an aside, he whispered to Maria, "He drops by once and our house is destroyed."

"Just bear with me. I know it's taxing but let's back to the chart, the 7 year great tribulation chart, OK?"

Both Joe and Maria nodded.

Tom continued, "You can see how these time periods overlap each other by 220 days. The reason for this is that the Prophet Daniel in chapter 8:13-14 heard two holy ones saying that it will take 2300 days until the sanctuary is cleansed. So, this now solves this riddle of the centuries as to how 2520 days or 7 years can be fulfilled in 2300 days."

Maria then asked, "How is it that you alone have solved this dilemma?"

Tom replied, "To my knowledge, nobody else has ever delved into it like I did."

Joe chuckled, "You don't look that smart.

Tom grinned at him and replied, "I got all the good looks and brains in the family."

"That's not what Mom once told me in confidence."

"Spill it." Maria said.

Joe caved and spilled it. "Once when I was only 7 years old, I asked Mom where we came from and she said we were made by God in His image. Then when dad came home I also asked him the same question, and he replied that we come from monkeys. When I went back to mom, she merely said, 'Joe my darling, you now know where my side of the family comes from and now you know where your father's side comes from.'"

Maria, howling, said, "But that doesn't mean Tom came from monkeys."

Joe replied, "Sure it does. Dad always said that Tom was the spitting image of him, and I agree, monkey-face."

Maria, now in total hysterics, said to Tom, "I think you're losing this round, bubba. Come to think of it, Tom, let's have another look at your side profile. You know Joe, you may have a valid point."

Tom acquiesced. "Tomorrow is another day guys. Let's stop for today. Maria, please don't encourage him further. If my profile is monkey-like, then so is your brain Joe."

"Wrong again my friend." said Joe. "Everything I got came from Mom's side of the family."

They needed and took a break. Their custom was to go outside for fresh air, more of a mental break since all the air up there was pure.

Maria said, "It seems like this 1040 T/D. is pivotal. It sort of initiates different elements."

Tom replied, "You're right, Maria. When we go back inside do you want me to get into how God's temple 'partially' opens?"

Chapter Twenty-Six
GOD'S TEMPLE PARTIALLY OPENS

Maria looked at Tom and said, "Sure Tom. I really want to know what else we can expect to happen."

Going back inside after their break, Tom replied, "As I mentioned, at the 1040 T/D, God's temple 'partially' opens and is located within the 'Great Domed City' that houses the 'Wilderness Sanctuary'. This is where the Christian 'Children of God', who needed a little more time of grace to fully mature, are. They will be taken up to God at the 1260 T/D."

Joe said, "You mean where the 'woman' fled to escape the Great Red Dragon."

"Right." replied Tom."

Tom continued, "That portion, the 'Holy of Holies', the 'sanctuary' where God's presence is manifested, remains closed and not on earth until the death and resurrection of the Two Witnesses.

To the best of my knowledge, according to all my research, it was not a Christian custom to bring physical offerings into God's Temple. This was an Israelite custom."

Maria countered, "Not so. We bring our physical offerings into God's Temple, the difference is that ours is monetary."

Tom now revised his thinking. "Maria, you're absolutely right."

Joe added, "Plot flaw. There is no money in the Great Domed City, currency does not exist any longer."

Maria said, "Joe's right, Tom. I believe the Christians and later the Israelites would most likely carry out some type of worshiping around it, similar to church services in houses of worship. Like you said Tom, these Christians only needed a little more time to get their spiritual house in order, so what better way than worshiping at God's altar."

Joe added, "And the Israelites will carry out their style of worshiping less their daily sacrifices".

"Perhaps there are different types of daily sacrifices, like worshiping or praying or singing." Tom added.

Maria said, in university she had to sacrifice her time, Joe said when he got engaged he had to sacrifice his freedom.

"Me too." Maria smirked.

"Not funny!" he said.

"Seriously Joe," Maria said, "I did some translating in university and the word 'sacrifice' means the same as 'offering' and in German it is called, 'opfer' and spellcheck says its 'offer'. My version of the meaning of 'sacrifice', is to freely and out of love, zealously serve God. There are many methods of sacrifice. It could be such as, monetarily, charitable services, services of labors, prayers, one's will or opinions, visiting the sick and the list goes on. Strictly speaking, however, an offering does not become a sacrifice until a real change has been effected".

Joe said, "I got it. Give, give till it hurts."

Maria continued, "Those in the wilderness sanctuary, now worship before the altar of God. God's altar stands in front of His unopened Temple. They sacrifice their, opinions along with everything that caused them to drift away in the first place and submit their will and worship God. In effect, they become refined, ergo, the 'Time of Refinement'."

"Excellent!", Tom replied, "We read in Revelation 11:1-2, that there is an altar in God's Temple with people worshiping at it and this supports your theory Maria."

Joe said, "I know you already told us but when does God's Temple fully open?"

Tom continued, "When Daniel's 8:14 prophecy '2300 days until the 'Sanctuary is Cleansed' has been fulfilled, then God will fully open His Temple and the Ark of His Covenant will be seen.

Now I will begin to explain in more detail the Time of Sorrows which is also called the 7 Year Great Tribulation Time."

Chapter Twenty-Seven
7 YEAR GREAT TRIBULATION OVERVIEW

Tom continued, "You know Maria, when you just talked about the Time of Refinement, you are absolutely right on. The first 3½ years (1-1060 T/D) of the Time of Sorrows are the Time of Refinement. There are three groups that emerge during these days.

The first group are those from the 'Wilderness Sanctuary'. Like I said before, these are those children of God who require a little more time to fully ripen who are taken up to God by His Son at the end of the 1260 days and are now 'Refined'. They had the 3 sacraments.

The second group are the 'Martyrs of Understanding'. These are those children of God that it speaks about in Daniel 11: 33-35. They are martyred and taken up to God by His Son before the end of the 1260 days and are now 'refined'. These Martyrs previously had the 3 Sacraments.

The third group are the 'Martyrs of Christ'. They are from all over the world and have the 'Baptism unto Repentance' that gave them the 'mark of God' upon their foreheads. This was done at some stage of their lives by Christian ministers. They had the first two sacraments. This righteous group will not bow and worship the Dragon. During these days they become refined and martyred en masse, between 1290-1335 T/D. They become Priests in God's Temple."

Joe asked, "You mean even these 'Johnny come lately' get the same reward as those Christians who were faithful for many years prior?"

Tom replied, "Yes, the 'workers parable' applies again to them. Also Joe, the long term Christians will not look at it your way, rather they will rejoice in the fact that God has spirited away from Satan, these 'Johnny-come-latelies'."

Maria responded, "Talk about grace."

Tom went on saying, "You're absolutely right, Maria. So after this, is the Time of Redemption commencing at the start of the overlap days, from 1040-2300 T/D, the second 3½ years. According to my research, God now introduces a 'game changer' one might say. The Christians who are still loyal to God in this time period, get to witness many supernatural events before they are martyred. The combined efforts of the 7 Spirits of God, the 7 Thunders of God, the 2 Witnesses of God produce another three groups; the Redeemed Israelites, the Repented Israelites and the Saved Nations."

Maria interjected, "Tom, you're really confusing me! I'm trying hard to understand, but I'm on information overload."

"What's confusing you, Maria?" Asked Tom.

"There are so many groups. How do you keep them all straight?"

Joe added, "Go slow, Tom, and explain each one clearly for us because Maria's right. This is a lot of information to absorb."

"Basically, that's why there are two 3½ year time periods. The first 3½ years are for the refinement of the Christians and the second 3½ years are for the redemption of the Israelites and Saved Nations. In each time period there are categories."

Maria chimed in, "OK, I'm starting to see where you're going with this."

"Good," said Tom. Now let's go on to the groups. <u>The first group</u>, The Redeemed Israelites, during 1040-1290 T/D, accept the Testimony of the Two Witnesses of God prior to the 'abomination of desolation' being displayed and activated in the false messiah's temple. They form the 'Temple Priests'. In fact, their first convert was Abram.

The second group, The Repented Israelites, during 1290-1400 T/D, after seeing the 'abomination of desolation', flee to the hills surrounding the Dead Sea, now the Living Sea, and then accept the Testimony of the Two Witnesses, receive the 'Baptism unto Repentance' and then receive the 'Mark of God'. They form the 'Repented Congregation'. The Two Witnesses of God have for the past year been in Israel and now move on.

The third group, the Saved Nations, during 1400-2300 T/D, come from the non-Christian nations of the 10 Kings. They form the Repented Saved Nations."

Maria asked, "That's your version of a quick overview?"

Tom responded, "You ain't seen nothing yet. Now the heavy action begins."

Chapter Twenty-Eight
DO THE MATH, ISRAEL YEAR ONE

1040-1400 T/D

Tom continued to tell them that during the first year of the Time of Redemption, the Israelites will receive special attention from God as He sends two supernatural beings to teach his people about His plan of salvation.

Maria asked, "How do you know this?"

Tom said, "You won't believe the answer."

Joe then said, "Try us."

"OK," Tom said, "while fiddling with a short wave radio that I purchased a way back when, and unsure of how to talk properly, I said, "Hello! Is anyone out there listing?"

"I received a very strange reply."

"I am here."

"I then transmitted, "Who are you?" and received an even stranger reply."

"It is I."

"I thought someone was jerking me around until I heard, "Tom how are you?"

"Now this really frightened me since I never gave out my name, so I said, "How do you know my name?"

"The person replied, "I've been watching over you for some time. Who do you think has been whispering all those tidbits of information in the back of your mind as you were writing your book?"

"I then said, "Give me some specifics.""

"The response was, "In time my friend. You are the last of many.""

"I must confess. Now I was perplexed to say the least. I didn't have a clue what that meant. I asked him what his name was and he replied that it was Mel.

I asked him, if I knew him and is reply of 'soon', only confused me more."

"That's fantastic!" Maria replied, "So there's some overseer watching over you."

Tom commented, "Maria, I know you mean well but your answer almost terrifies me. How can someone I've never met say he knows me? Let's just move on. I don't even want to think about it."

But Joe, being Joe, just had to ask one more question, "What did he mean by 'soon' and 'you're the last one'?"

Tom said he was now 'out of sorts' and wanted to continue discussing their current topic.

He continued with, "Right from the beginning of the Bible God desired His people to obey, love and walk in His ways. Unfortunately, they chose poorly. Now, rather than cast them aside, He still desires them to repent and return to Him. I believe that the Israelites have over time been misled by their religious leaders and now, with them all out of the way, God's two supernatural teachers can set the record straight."

Tom answered, "Let's go slowly because you will be blown away by the answers."

Maria piped in, "Blown away! Bad choice of words Tom."

"Ok guys. Here comes some more good stuff. While I was researching the Two Witnesses of God, it was mentioned in the Bible that their time of Testimony was 1260 days. It is easy to say that they testify to the Israelites and then to everyone person on earth. The problem is when you do the math, weird things happen. Let's say they testify to each person individually and let's say that they spend 5 minutes explaining to each person about God's plan of salvation and that they have the commission to offer each person the 'Baptism unto Repentance' with water, similar to the baptism of John the Baptist.

Now, do the simple math. To testify to 14 million people living in Israel at 5 minutes each, it would take over 135 years and that's only the people in Israel."

Maria said, "Well it looks like some other system will have to be implemented."

"OK, for example, to testify to everyone in Israel, you would have to gather about 40,000 people once a day and repeat it every day for one year. This means that their message could be heard by over 14,000,000 Israelites in Israel."

Maria said, "40,000 people each day is not such a tall order as there have been recent concerts and sporting events that draw up to 100,000 people."

"OK, then let us, for the moment, hypothesize they cover an area of land about 5 miles by 5 miles square being 25 square miles. The total land mass area of Israel is about 8,000 square miles divided by the 25 square miles this would then take almost a year for the Two Witnesses of God to somehow testify to everyone in Israel. To recap then, if they testified daily to a group of 40,000 people each time, they could easily cover the land of Israel within one year.

Remember that today only 50% of Israelites believe in God. Who knows how many of them will remain faithful to him."

Joe added, "So then the other 50% who do not believe, have either joined or will most likely join the 'unholy trinity'. If so, they have sealed their fate which will be to participate in the 'cull of the damned, right Tom?

Tom nodded.

Maria said, "You've really put a lot of thought into this, haven't you?"

"You bet! Like I said, over 6000 hours of research have gone into my book. To continue, we have established they must broadcast their message over an area of land about 25 square miles that I refer to as the 'Zone'. I believe that only the people within the 25 square mile 'Zone' can actually hear what's going on. Similar to the conversion of Saul[41] to Paul, only he could hear Jesus talking to him. Those with him, heard nothing."

Joe asked, "Will those in adjacent zones be able to see what's going on?"

"I'm not sure, but I think so," replied Tom.

"Now we come to the next conundrum. How can they possibly testify to hundreds of millions or even billions during the next two and one half years?"

Chapter Twenty-Nine

DO THE MATH, NATIONS OF THE 10 KINGS

1400- 2300 T/D.

Maria asked, "If just testifying to the people in Israel is such a great daunting task, how can they fulfill such vast numbers as to testify to the rest of the world that may have up to 6 billion people upon it?"

"Once again, Maria, do the simple math. To testify to all the people on earth, using the same formula as used in Israel, would take them well over 5 million years, and even if you cut this figure in half and divided by two, as the saying goes, it's still way over a million years."

Maria said, "There must be a solution to this conundrum since they are only given 3½ years to do all this and they have already used up one year of it in Israel so now they only have 2½ years left of their Time of Testimony."

Tom said, "To begin, I believe that the continents have by this time recombined to form one large super continent. Scientists believe that prior to Noah's flood, the continents were all one large mass and they were split and pushed apart by the pressure under the crust of the earth. They say that the continents separated at around 60 mph. With water being under so much pressure, it actually was ejected into the upper atmosphere. This water came back to earth as freezing pellets and evidence of this is found in the mastiffs in the USSR. There are pictures of these creatures sitting down and having their large ears covering and protecting their faces. These poor animals were frozen to death in a matter of minutes by these freezing ice pellets. Scientists found them perfectly preserved with undigested food still in their stomachs. This fact demonstrates that it was not a slow evolutionary process that killed off the animals, but rather a catastrophic quick event. These scientists claim that the mastiffs died as a result of Noah's flood.

Continents and climates can change quickly. It would only take several days to take place, as far as these scientists are concerned. In my opinion, other scientists, who claim belief in only evolution and cannot believe that worldly catastrophic events can alter the earth, do not believe in God and are therefore the antichrist, unless they repent."

Maria asked, "So in your opinion, do science and religion fight or do they complement each other?"

Tom answered, "I believe that the wise scientists complement my theory and the foolish, challenge it. The irony is that God created the very science that some scientists try to use to disprove him."

Maria commented, "Hmm, how do you think that they view the false messiah then?"

Joe added, "It doesn't take faith now to believe in him, so they will most likely accept him with all his scientific trinkets."

Tom brought them back on topic saying, "This being the case, it then stands to reason that the continents could recombine within several days once again. There are many verses in the Bible about tectonic movements, earthquakes and more, like when the Prophet Jeremiah says in chapter 4:24; I looked at the mountains, and they were quaking; all the hills were swaying. To me, this indicates that there will be great movements. It is possible that they recombine into one large mass and if so the Two Witnesses can easily travel to this new global land mass that houses the 10 nations that will exist at that time.

Even if the continents do not recombine the Two Witnesses will travel throughout the entire world by some supernatural means and testify to all people as it says in the Bible in Revelation 11:10. When the Two Witnesses are killed, the people rejoice and send gifts to each other because these two prophets tormented them constantly with their plagues. But I'm getting a head of myself. Let's, just stick to the current time frame."

Tom continued, "They travel to all the 'peoples, tribes, tongues, and nations who dwell on the earth'. This is very specific and indicates that the scope of their travels will be vast.

They testify to the nations who were not allowed to join Christianity due to past domination by their religious leaders, traditions or geographical limitations."

Maria asked, "Will we see these Two Witnesses?"

Tom replied, "We know during the first year they will testify only in the land of Israel. However, I am sure we'll hear about them as there will be lots of chatter on the BSW radio."

Joe commented, "Perhaps we'll see pictures of them on TV."

Tom shuddered, and then said, "We will most definitely see them when they start their time of testimony and many times during it."

Maria asked, "When and how?"

Tom replied, "What are you talking about?"

"You just said to us that we will see the Two Witnesses many times."

"I don't recall saying that." he replied.

"Moving forward, after they have testified to those in Israel, they will for the next 2½ years, travel to all nations on earth prophesying and offering salvation. However, we will be long gone by then."

Joe asked, "How do you know that they testify in Israel for the first year?"

"Good question! I felt as though the answer was given to me, it just popped into my head. I believe that the majority of people living in the northern half of Israel will be the people of the 10 kings who migrate to Israel. When they see the pillar of fire from afar the smart ones flee to be close to the 'unholy trinity'. This being the case, the Two Witnesses will encounter continuous hostilities as they travel from zone to zone, as the dumb ones remained.

"The Bible says they <u>can turn water to blood</u> and strike the earth with all plagues, as often as they desire."

Tom repeated the last line saying, "They cause plagues upon the earth. Notice that the word 'plagues' is plural. This supports the fact that during their time of testimony there will be many plagues. <u>There will be no rain, water will turn to blood so if that's all you have to drink, they will drink blood.</u> You'll be astonished when we read what the Bible has to say about this."

Maria said, "You know, Joe's 'Zombie Plagues' are starting to make scary sense to me and you say the Bible refers to it?"

Joe commented, "Can't wait!"

Maria asked, "Why does God send Two Witnesses?"

Tom replied, "The Bible says that it takes two to form a witness so this may be the reason. These Two Witnesses of God see and record everything so no person can ever claim they were not testified to.

During these days, Christians have been so persecuted that they have either caved in to the 'unholy trinity', been captured, killed, placed into detainment camps or they are in hiding just like us."

Maria asked, "Is there any difference in the 'Holy Baptism of Water' that we have and the 'Baptism unto Repentance' as offered by the Two Witnesses of God to the Israelites and then others?"

Tom replied, "As far as I can tell, they're the same. Both groups receive the Mark of God. The only thing that I can see as being different is that the Christians received the Mark of God from the act of Holy Baptism being one of the three sacraments from duly authorized Christian ministers.

In olden times Israelites were 'Baptised unto Repentance' by John the Baptist. In either case, both groups get the Mark of God on their foreheads. I believe for all intent and purpose they are the same.

So, to further answer your question as to whether we will see the Two Witnesses of God, no, I believe that we will not, as we already have the Mark of God on our foreheads. If we were to see them, that would mean we were not martyred. We will hear about them but not actually see them because our martyrdom takes place months before they come to North America. If we weren't martyred, that would mean that we were cowards who would not stand up for our faith in our Lord."

Both Joe and Maria jumped up simultaneously saying, "Hold on there, Tom." They looked at each other in amazement as they both had said the exact same words at the same time.

Maria continued, "Tom, you just finished saying to us that we will definitely see them and many times at that, and now you just said if we see them, we're cowards. This, this doesn't make sense."

Tom once again shuddered and then replied, "You're right Maria, we will."

"Now I'm really confused." she said.

"About what?" Tom replied.

"About seeing them." she said.

"Seeing whom?" Tom questioned.

Joe interjected, "Maria, just give up. He's hearing voices again or is on cheap drugs."

Joe asked, "Will the flying hell monster plagues come our way?"

He was given the answer, "Yes. After Israel has been purged during year one, they will come at some point in time during the next two and a half years and fulfill their mission, attacking everyone not having the Mark of God."

Joe couldn't resist the jab, "Who just answered me, was it you Tom or Mr. Spooky?"

Maria didn't take the bait this time. She said, "As long as we become faithful Martyrs of Christ we will be in Heaven by then."

Joe remarked, "You know, it would be cool to see them."

Tom replied, "Be careful what you wish for. Aren't you the one who can't remember if he's baptised or not?"

"Not funny." Joe said.

Tom smiled and continued, "The Israelites up to this point are experiencing prosperity and good times due to their belief that their long awaited messiah has returned to them. This 'false messiah' has been busy deceiving and seducing them with his flatteries, riches and power.

The Christians, on the other hand, are being taught by a unique group as it says in the book of Daniel, 'those of understanding'.

These are those 'Children of God' whom I call the 'Prodigal Children' who have come home, those with the 3 Holy Sacraments. Due to their more in-depth knowledge of God's Plan of Salvation, they continue to teach and bolster the Christians' faith and bring them up to speed concerning the function of the Two Witnesses.

They teach everyone saying that this so called messiah is actually the devil along with his false prophet and false president who are hell bent on destroying them and all people on earth."

After a short break, Tom continued, "You know, during these days many Israelites resent anyone calling or referring to their messiah as being false and persecute them. Their actions fan the flames of evil and the 'unholy trinity' will take advantage of every such opportunity because they want the loyalty of these deceived Israelites and others to help with the destruction of the Christians who are faithful to God.

Many Israelites gladly followed and worship the Dragon impersonating as their 'messiah' returned. They're building a new temple for their 'false messiah' to dwell in. It will take about 3½ years to build this replica of the first temple built by Solomon.

I really believe, in the beginning, the Dragon will not have to force them to get his mark because these Israeli people gladly open their arms and hearts to him. They willingly follow and serve him in his temple and in Jerusalem and this plays to his vanity.

Others around the world also have taken his mark for power and status while the Israelites simply worship him as their god. He wants everyone on earth to turn away from their God of Heaven and to worship him as their god."

Chapter Thirty

HEAVENLY MONKEY WRENCHES

1040 T/D

Maria said, "You know, Tom, I've heard some TV reports of people saying that God has abandoned them."

Tom answered, "Yes, I've heard the same reports but God has not abandoned His people on earth. Let me explain. The overlapping of the two time periods is now taking place. As the first time period, the Time of Refinement, is winding down, the second time period, the Time of Redemption, is ramping up. If you look at the 'road map index', in my book, as Maria calls it, you will see that these two time period overlap each other by 220 days."

"Been there, done that." she replied.

What now takes place is so fascinating that it seems like way over the top science fiction. Chaos is now being introduced into the plans of the 'unholy trinity'. God introduces the 7 SPIRITS, 7 THUNDERS, 2 WITNESSES and FLYING HELL MONSTERS.

I couldn't come up with a suitable acronym for them and just refer to them as the '7-7-2-FHM'."

Joe commented, "How about the Four Musketeers?"

Both Maria and Tom just stared at him.

"It was just a thought." he said.

"The '7-7-2-FHM' are special supernatural entities, mostly from Heaven."

Maria asked, "What do you mean by mostly?"

Tom's replied, "The Flying Hell Monsters or FHM, are also supernatural and carry out God's instructions but as to where they come from, it seems, to me at least, from down below.

The '7-7-2-FHM' are far superior to the powers of the 'unholy trinity' and antichrist on earth. And at this time, they begin to trump the deceiving actions of the unholy trinity who are using great and powerful, signs, lying wonders, and unrighteous deceptions to deceive the people."

Tom, looking a little perplexed, said, "With respect to what I refer to as the 'heavenly monkey wrenches', there was a better phrase. The thought in the back of my mind told me to use another phrase, but for the life of me when I awoke from my dream, I couldn't remember it. I think Mel was speaking to me again."

Continuing he said, "They wreak havoc wherever they go. In Luke 21:11 it describes some events that have and will take place. It says that 'there will be great earthquakes in various places, and famines and pestilences; <u>and there will be fearful sights and great signs from heaven.</u>'

These 'fearful sights' are the events that started with the Rapture's Aftermath' that caused tremendous destruction and loss of life. We've all watched on TV in the past when fearful storms occurred, such as category 5 tornados and other fearful storms like hurricanes.

We can also read about the great miraculous signs from Heaven. In one Bible version, in Joel 2:30, we read, 'I will show wonders in the heavens and on the earth, <u>blood</u> and fire and billows of smoke.'

These great and miraculous signs from Heaven are wonders. When I looked up this word in the dictionary one meaning was to be filled with amazement or awe.

When we look at the words: earth, blood, fire and smoke, they will all come into play in the time that will now follow."

Chapter Thirty-One

SUPERNATURAL POWERS OF THE 7-7-2-FHM

Tom continued, "Like I said, the 7-7-2-FHM have massive supernatural abilities which is good because in order to trump the 'unholy trinity's' evil deceptive tactics, something massive must now take place in order for the people on earth to be totally awestruck so that there is no question that what they are witnessing is from the God of Heaven.

First on the scene come the, 7 SPIRITS OF GOD[42]. The Bible makes reference to them four times in the Book of Revelation."

Maria interjected, "Who are they?"

Tom replied, "A little Biblical background is necessary to introduce them. The Apostle John, while looking at God's throne, sees and says, 'there comes flashes of lightning, rumblings and peals of thunder, seven lamps were blazing. These are the <u>seven spirits of God</u>.

Can you imagine what these events must look and sound like? Flashes of lightning? Rumblings? Peals of thunder? Seven lamps blazing?

Try to picture this. Seven spirits, each as brilliant and blazing as the desert sun. They emit scintillating lightning along with booming reverberating rumblings of sustained thunder.

Each of the 7 Spirits are phenomenally greater than our most severe electrical storms.

During electrical storms people watch from the safety of their homes as lightning flashes overhead and strikes the ground."

Maria commented that every time such a storm passed over their home she became very frightened and counted the seconds between the flash and thunder and when the seconds increased she started to calm down.

Tom said, "These are 7 Spirits of God and even though it is impossible for us to comprehend them and their purpose, I will try to give an example of what might take place."

Joe said, "How do you know so much about them?"

Tom replied, "I had a dream one night and someone was speaking to me telling me of such matters."

Maria spoke up, "Was it Mel again?"

Tom's quiet reply was, "I think so. The 7 Spirits of God position themselves into 7 strategic areas around the world. Each area can be called an 'Angel Halo'; one Angel Halo for each of the 7 continents or designated area: Europe, Africa, North America, South America, Australia, Asia and Greenland. These areas cover most of the world's population. Places like the Antarctica are either covered off by one of the above or perhaps at this time none are alive there.

The function of these 7 Spirits is to create global atmospheric wonders by creating a tremendous and unique blending of lightning and fire for all the people within to look up and see.

This supernatural scintillating lightning fire is called 'fire lightning'. Imagine, combining 'ball lightning' and the 'Northern Lights' into one element. Now, again imagine, this entity many millions of times more powerful. Now, if you can, imagine 7 of these domed shaped continent sized things that I call the 7 'Angel Halos'. When a person looks up into it they see this fire lightning that seems to have a ripple effect and its movement resembles that of sea waves."

Maria commented, "I know a good deal about the Northern Lights. I've written an article concerning them while in university. They come in the form of draperies, ovals, beams and arcs. The solar wind can cause interference with radio, television and satellite communications. If you were in space unprotected and were to touch them, then their energy would kill you."

Maria looked at Tom and said, "You're going to love this! Some theorists claim that if you could touch the Northern Lights in space and somehow not die, you'll open up an 'aurora portal'. You could end up being transported to another place or time. It seems very dangerous! Scientists today even sometimes see the arc of fire on the surface of the sun and perhaps this description may help describe the immense energies of an 'Angel Halo'."

Joe asked, "Can they actually touch the earth?"

Maria answered, "Yes, the Northern Lights can extend up to 600 miles above the earth and viewed from outer space, there are pictures of them surrounding continent size areas like Antarctica, the North Pole, Canada and other huge land masses. These phenomenon would most certainly look like vast continent size halos of fire that we could call 'Angel Halos'.

Early Arctic explorers, recorded close encounters with the Northern Lights in their journals. Reports from Norway often described how the Northern Lights appeared to touch the earth itself, producing a wind like effect on the faces of mountain travellers. In 1882 a Norwegian government official wrote in his journal about the Northern Lights actually coming down to the surface of the earth and they walked through it. It created a tingling sensation that they described as walking through electrical light. People have also reported hearing hissing and cracking sounds."

Joe said, "Can you imagine bathing in this light? It would be a phenomenal experience."

Maria chimed in that she remembered from her research that the Northern Lights were also referred to as the 'dance of the spirits'.

Tom answered saying, "I believe Maria's description is strangely appropriate due to the scintillating effect of the fire lightning within the 'Angel Halos'."

Maria remarked, "It seems surreal that all these descriptors that were taken for granted are now real."

Tom said, "I believe that the 'Angel Halos' touch the ground and if one would touch this energy field, they would die. This is necessary to contain the antichrist so they all can be testified to and to prevent them from fleeing to another continent to escape the Flying Hell Monsters that terrify them the most."

Maria said, "Tom, can you backtrack and summarize the 7 Angel Halos for us?"

"Sure thing, Maria. First, each Angel Halo is huge and covers a very large land mass and possibly an entire continent. These 7 Angel Halos will cover the entire planet where people are living.

Second, each Angel Halo looks like a great dome, its top perhaps a hundred miles high or more. The underside looks like that of an umbrella.

Third, each Angel Halo dome arcs out, perhaps a thousand miles or more, and extends down and touches the earth.

Fourth, each Angel Halo extending from space down to the earth is made of some type of force field that restricts those within its enormous dome. It has a circumference large enough to circle entire continents, effectively restricting all people within it from leaving.

Fifth, in each Angel Halo, if one were to stand on the ground and look up, one would see, from its central hub, 10 scintillating and massive lightning rays called fire lightning radiating outwards that follow the dome's outer surface down to the surface of the earth.

Sixth, the area within each Angel Halo is made up of hundreds or thousands of zones, each being about 5 miles square, approximately the size of a typical city."

Joe said, "That's way too much information. Could you describe all this in one sentence for me?"

Tom looked at him and said, "I can give it a try. Here goes; an Angel Halo is a continent sized energy dome consisting of ten scintillating lightning rays called fire lightning radiating outwards from its top, down to the earth."

"Not bad!" commented Maria, "but you missed, 'dance of the spirits'."

Joe finished the thought, saying, "Works for me."

"OK, so next on the scene, and in conjunction with the 7 Spirits of God, come the 7 Thunders of God[43]."

"The Bible says that the Apostle John saw a mighty angel coming down from heaven with a rainbow on his head, his face like the sun, his feet like pillars of fire and his voice like the roar of a lion.

When he roared seven thunders responded but the mighty angel said not to write what they were saying.

I believe they proclaim 7 different global messages in unison. All people on earth will hear their thunder messages simultaneously and in their own language. Their messages will make sense to those listening and their intensity is so great that everyone on earth within these 7 Angel Halo domes are in awe. Even today with thunder boomers people watch from the safety of their homes as lightning flashes and windows rattle from the thunders."

Tom continued "God has allowed us to know of these 7 Thunders and that they will proclaim messages. The Apostle John actually heard their thunder messages and understood them, but <u>their identity and message contents were sealed</u>."

Maria asked, "Who might they be?"

Tom replied, "They are Seven Heavenly entities of God that God is using to proclaim His messages of salvation, sort of person to person you might say."

Joe said, "This gives a new definition to the term, 'rolling thunder'."

Tom said, "Next come the two fire breathing supernatural beings of God that prophesy to every person on earth."

"Finally," sounded Maria, "let's get into them!"

Tom agreed saying, "OK, here we go. They are the 'Two Witnesses of God' who bear witness to the word of God, and to the testimony of Jesus Christ."

Tom began paraphrasing a few verses from Revelation 11:3-6 about the Two Witnesses of God[44].

"God says He will give power to His Two Witnesses, and they will prophesy one thousand two hundred and sixty days. And if anyone wants to harm them, fire will come out of their mouths to devour their enemies. They have power to shut heaven so that no rain falls, they have the power to turn the water to blood, and the power to strike the earth with all plagues, as often as they desire."

Tom continued, "The Two Witnesses can be considered the Heavenly quarter backs orchestrating spectacular Godly events for the next 3½ years commencing at the 1040 T/D, and concluding at the 2300 T/D, of the '7 year great tribulation'.

God wants all people to be saved even during the Time of Sorrows. There are Bible references where the Apostle John gives us more information about these Two Witnesses[45]."

The Apostle John said he <u>bore witness</u> to the <u>Word of God</u>, and to the <u>Testimony of Jesus Christ,</u> to all things that he saw.

I believe that the 'Word of God' and the 'Testimony of Jesus Christ' can also refer to the Two Witnesses."

Maria said, "Do they have names?"

Tom replied during one dream he heard someone talking about them saying Moses the great teacher of the law and Elijah the great defender of the law. However, they may have other names also.

Tom then said he heard another voice saying make him understand.

Maria asked, "Did you?"

Tom shrugged his shoulders and said, "Maybe."

Maria commented, "So what you're trying to say is that it was this Mel person again."

Tom replied, "I never said he was a person."

Joe jumped in saying, "Some years ago I remember watching a movie called 'The Book of Eli'. It took place in apocalyptic times about someone called Eli who carried the Bible in his mind and perhaps this was like one of the Two Witnesses of God as Eli could be the nickname of Elijah."

"I'm impressed!" commented Maria.

Joe had to ruin a good thing by saying, "I'm more than a pretty face you know."

Tom, trying to get them back on track continued by saying, "Both in the Bible and the Israeli Torah we read of these Two Witnesses. As I said before, The Bible requires at least Two Witnesses to establish any important truth.

Roughly speaking, the second half of the 7 Year Great Tribulation is for the Israelites and Saved Nations and is called the 'Time of Redemption'.

The Israelites will relate to the Two Witnesses of God and their 'Testimony unto Repentance'. This infuriates the 'unholy trinity' who will go from protecting Israel to now persecuting her."

Tom continued, "We read in the Old Testament the Prophet Zechariah wrote in chapter 4: 1-14[46] about <u>one</u> lampstand and <u>two</u> olive trees. Many Israelites know of this Bible passage and some of the people refer to them as Moses and Elijah, great people of the Old Testament. In the New Testament we have references in Revelation chapter 11:4 these are the two olive trees and two lampstands standing before God.

I believe this means that there is one olive tree designated for the Old Testament and one olive tree for the New Testament, so in our time the Book of Revelation shows Two Olive Trees representing the past and future times. We see that these Two Witnesses have their roots going back many thousands of years during the times of the Israelites. With the linking of the Two Witness to the Old and New Testaments, we see how easily it will be for the Israelites to relate to them.

Also the Bible says that just prior to Jesus starting his time of testimony, John the Baptist, himself an Israelite, was preaching and Baptizing unto Repentance to many Israelites. So the term Baptism unto Repentance is known to them already.

Therefore, the Two Witnesses of God will have immediate credibility with the Israelites. John the Baptist[47] told the Israelites to repent and be baptized with water unto Repentance but that someone mightier than he would come and <u>baptize them with the Holy Spirit and fire.</u>

I believe that the Two Witnesses of God will testify to all people on earth during the 'Time of Redemption' offering them the 'Baptism unto Repentance' not with water necessarily rather through the 'spoken word'."

Chapter Thirty-Two

SALVATION UNTO THE NATIONS

Maria said, "Tom, you've mentioned the nations of the 10 Kings, several times. Who are these 10 kings?"

Tom replied, "This refers to the non-Christian world leaders that have forbidden the gospel of the Kingdom to be preached to their people. Their citizens most likely are aware of the Christians but don't know much concerning their belief. They have been fed propaganda denouncing it as evil. These people would be harassed or even killed if they turned away from their faith and became Christian.

In order for the prophecy to be fulfilled that everyone will be testified to, God has arranged for fantastic supernatural beings and happenings to occur.

In Revelation 10:11, the Apostle John says that the gospel of the kingdom will be preached in all the world <u>as a witness</u> to all the nations and then the end will come."

Maria interjected, "Tom, I think this is another one of your furtive discoveries hiding in plain sight. Am I right?"

Tom replied' "Right you are."

Joe piped in, "Do you mean 'as a witness' refers to the Two Witnesses?"

"Once again, right you are." replied Tom. "The Two Witnesses of God will prophesy of God's plan of salvation. They offer the '<u>Baptism unto Repentance</u>' to all people on earth desiring salvation. This conveys the 'Mark of God' upon their foreheads which in turn gives them their '<u>Wedding Garments</u>' for the 'Kings Feast' as dictated by God. Now they become a 'friend of God', no longer heathens. Providing they remain faithful, they will make up the people of the 'Saved Nations'. Once all have been testified to, the end will come."

Joe said, "I get the picture of what the wedding garments are all about but tell me more about the wedding and who's going to be there."

"I believe the forces of God will gather these people who will be brought into the 'Wedding Hall' within 3½ days following the 2300 T/D. In Matthew 22:8-10 God is talking to his servants about a Wedding Feast. To me, this is another beautiful furtive discovery in the form of a parable.

In this parable, God told His servants that the wedding was ready, but those who were invited weren't worthy. He then told them to go into the highways and invite as many as they could find to the wedding. So they went out into the highways and gathered together as many as they could find, both bad and good and filled the wedding hall guests."

Joe said, "That still doesn't tell me who's going to be there."

"There will be many groups present. All will have wedding garments, so basically, I think, it will be everybody except the antichrist and the unholy trinity."

Chapter Thirty-Three

SUPERNATURAL ABILITIES OF THE TWO ENTITIES

"Tell me more about the Two Witnesses." Maria chimed in.

"Well," said Tom, "They have fantastic abilities that are described in the Bible. They are not human flesh and blood, rather supernatural beings of some type. They have the ability to travel at will, using some type of locomotion unknown to us, to be able to testify to the hundreds or thousands of 'Zones' within each 'Angel Halo'.

They initially travel throughout the land of Israel for the first year and for the next 2½ years to all the nations on earth, the 'Nations of the 10 Kings', testifying of God's Plan to of Salvation to every person for 1260 days so the prophecies may be fulfilled. This is just another way of saying 3½ years.

The Two Witnesses' voices resonate like 'rolling thunder' intertwined with 'scintillating fire lightning' within the 7 domed 'Angel Halos'.

This 'scintillating fire/thunder message' of the Two Witnesses of God will be heard worldwide, simultaneously in their mother tongue, due to the actions of the 7 Spirits and 7 Thunders of God.

All will hear, however, only those in the vicinity of the Two Witnesses will be able to receive the offer of their 'Baptism unto Repentance'. The rest of the world will be given their opportunity in due course.

Wherever the Two Witnesses of God are testifying there will also be a huge 'pillar of fire' over 5 miles high with 10 rays of pulsating light extending outwards and doming down to the earth forming a circle about 20 miles in diameter creating a most awesome, Heavenly sight."

Maria asked, "Again, how do you know all this? Let me guess. Was it Mel or research, or both?"

Tom answered, "Both, I think."

"OK, so what significance do these 10 rays, that you were talking about, have?"

Tom said, "Maybe they represented the 10 Commandments of God. They are very striking to behold. The 'pillar of fire' and its mini-dome move in tandem with the Two Witnesses as they travel throughout the country side from one zone to another. They continue their travels in this Angel Halo until every person good or bad has heard or received their testimony."

Maria asked, "Will they do the same in each Angel Halo or is this one unique because it's in Israel?"

Tom replied, "This is the template for them all. When the Two Witnesses have completed their testimony in each zone, the people who accept their Testimony and desire the 'Baptism unto Repentance' of their true God of Heaven are instructed to raise their hands. Perhaps they hear a gentle whisper or a thunder voice in their ears telling them to raise their hands in praise and supplication to God. Immediately, upon the people raising their hands to God, there will appear, out of the 'pillar of fire', some type of lightning and fire blended together, resembling 'fingers of God' radiating outwards and touching all of them simultaneously."

Maria piped in, "That sounds just like when God's finger wrote the 10 Commandments onto the stone tablet and gave them to Moses."

"Exactly!" replied Tom. "Upon being touched by these 'fingers of God', there will appear what seems to be tongues of fire upon their foreheads."

Maria said, "I remember that from my Sunday School days when we learned about Pentecost."

"Absolutely." said Tom. "The 'Mark of God', His seal, will now be upon them, just like when tongues of fire touched the first Christians on the day of Pentecost. These people are saved from Armageddon, provided they keep their spiritual garments clean."

Looking perplexed, Joe asked, "What does that mean, Tom? You're really going way above my pay grade."

Tom replied, "It means they can't fall back in league with the antichrist."

He continued, "With respect to the supernatural powers of these Two Witnesses, if anyone wants to harm them, fire comes from their mouths and devours their enemies. The Bible says that they have power to shut heaven, <u>so that no rain falls</u> in the days of their prophecy. They have power to turn <u>waters into blood.</u> They have power to strike the earth with <u>all plagues,</u> as often as they desire."

Joe commented, "That's really intense. People need water to drink."

Tom said, "You're right, Joe. When the water turns to blood, no matter how repulsive, they will then drink blood. And there will be a great number of plagues during the 3½ years of their time of testimony."

These horrific events easily segue into your 'Zombie Virus' and 'Zombie Plagues', Joe.

As to their travels within this continent size 'Angel Halo', the Two Witnesses will travel methodically throughout the country side from one zone to another. Each zone contains thousands of people.

This gigantic 'pillar of fire' moving in tandem with the Two Witnesses appears, at times, to fully engulf them. Since thousands of people surround them, it appears that they sort of rotate around or through the fire so all could see them. Even when inside the fire they remain clearly visible and appear much larger in size to those in the zone.

This pillar of fire has no effect upon the Two Witnesses of God just like the Biblical three men, Shadrach, Meshach, and Abednego who refused to turn their backs on their God of Heaven and were thrown into the fiery furnace[48] as recorded by the Prophet Daniel."

Joe said' "In the back of my mind I kind of remember singing about them."

Maria then commented, "See that means you were baptised because you were taught this song in Sunday school."

There appeared a sigh of relief on Joe's face who now became convinced he was a Christian.

Tom continued, "The Two Witnesses are also like these three men. The pillar of fire will have no effect upon them. They testify to all the people living in the country of Israel during the first year of their mission."

Chapter Thirty-Four

KINGS HIGHWAY

Both Joe and Maria looked at Tom with furrowed brows trying to make sense of everything they have been told.

Tom asked, "Are you still with me?"

Joe said, "We're hanging on, barely, but keep going."

Maria interjected, "It's a lot to digest!"

Tom nodded and continued, "There are two groups of Israelites. The first group are 'Redeemed'. They accepted the Testimony of the Two Witnesses of God in faith prior to the abomination of desolation being set up and activated in the dragons newly built and now dedicated temple at the 1290 T/D.

The second group are 'Repented' Israelites who accepted the Testimony of the Two Witnesses of God after seeing the abomination of desolation set up and activated in the false messiah's temple that now demands they all to bow to it, get its mark, or die.

Upon each group receiving their Baptism unto Repentance, they are instructed to travel upon the King's Highway to and into the Great Domed City housing the 'Wilderness Sanctuary' of God."

Maria asked, "What is this King's Highway to which you keep referring?"

Tom answered, "OK, let's get into this topic. The Biblical Prophet Isaiah refers to the King's Highway[49] as a highway called The Holy Way. He tells about a voice saying to walk along this way and no evil, wicked or unclean can travel on it."

Maria said, "This seems like the Holy Spirit of God somehow leads the redeemed along a supernatural route that only they are allowed to travel upon".

Joe asked, "When you spoke of the Holy Spirit of God, is this one of those 7 Spirits that are the fire lightning in the dome?"

Tom replied, "You caught me off guard on this one. However, I think you're correct."

He then said, "Maria, you're right, the repented Israelites travel upon this protected route into the great domed city that contains the Wilderness Sanctuary where the partially opened Temple of God is and where they are allowed to worship safely. They remain there until the 2300 T/D, at which time more fantastic miracles take place. I'll tell you about them later."

Joe commented, "This great domed city is about 15 miles to the east of the Mount of Olives and at the north end of the now called Living Sea, where they are protected, right?"

"That's correct," replied Tom, "and don't forget this was the same place to which the Woman fled and where she is provided for and nourished for the 1260 days during the first half of the 7 years Great Tribulation."

Joe asked, "Won't the antichrist, in the same zone where the Two Witnesses of God are testifying, try to kill them and those newly baptized?"

Tom replied, "Yes they will, but as the antichrist fire their weapons, bad mistake on their part as it has no effect upon the Two Witnesses. They, meaning the antichrist, are consumed by fire issuing out of the Two Witnesses' mouths."

Joe further asked, "What about the antichrist that did not fire weapons at the Two Witnesses? Won't they try to kill the newly baptized."

Tom replied, "There are three reasons that I don't think so. Firstly, they have just witnessed fire coming out of the mouths of the Two Witnesses consuming soldiers from their group. This in itself would be terrifying to behold.

Secondly, these antichrist would be terrified with what they were seeing. Imagine beholding a huge continent sized Angel Halo, its underside all covered in flaming lightning that's even talking like rolling thunder. This being the case, many would flee as far away as possible in their zone, desperately trying to escape from the pathway of the pillar of fire and the plagues of Two Witnesses of God.

In contrast those desiring to accept God's offer would seek to get as close to His Two Witnesses as possible which in turn positions them very close to the pillar of fire.

And thirdly, as the Two Witnesses depart that zone, the fourth group of the 7-7-2-FHM, or as Joe called them the four musketeers, start their onslaught. These are the Flying Hell Monsters that immediately follow upon the heels of the Two Witnesses as they travel throughout the many zones within that Angel Halo."

Chapter Thirty-Five
FLYING HELL MONSTERS

Maria said, "I don't believe it! What next!"
Tom said, "Buckle your seat belts now as we enter into Joe's movie genre, apocalyptical horror with the FHM or 'Zombies' and 'Vampires'.

As Joe's eyes beamed, Maria's dimmed. Her expression shouted louder than her words. "I had hoped you were just leading us on when you said <u>zombies and vampires in the Bible</u>. Looks like I was wrong."

Tom began, "We read in the Bible[50] that when the bottomless pit was opened smoke came out like smoke from a great furnace. The volume and intensity of this smoke darkened the sky and effectively blocked all sunlight resulting in darkness. Now out of this smoke come monstrous flying locust aberrations.

They can fly and sting like scorpions. They were commanded not to harm the grass of the earth, or any green thing, or any tree. Now comes the weird part. They were specifically ordered to attack only men who did not have the seal of God on their foreheads.

When this time comes there are three categories of people on earth, those with the seal or mark of God, the antichrist wearing the three color 'Dragon's Tattoo 666' and some still without any mark."

"I know this!" interjected Joe, "The Taboo Tattoo!"

"Just great," Maria muttered, "Now even he's saying it."

Tom chuckled as he started to describe these not so little monsters saying, "So out of this blackness come flying locusts having strange characteristics and abilities."

Joe exclaimed, "These locusts must be supernatural if they're given tails of scorpions to sting people. This in itself would look and be terrifying. Imagine if six inch <u>flying scorpions</u> existed on earth today."

Tom said, "When they fly upon the winds of the earth creating a sky of blackness, they also make a horrible deafening chattering sound. Talk about shock and awe.

It gets even weirder. They were commanded to <u>attack</u> only people not having the seal or mark of God on their foreheads."

Maria said, "Tom, you already told us that a couple of minutes ago."

"Just checking to see if you were listening. Moving on, when I looked up this word attack in the dictionary one meaning said; to cause an <u>infection</u>, illness, or damage in somebody. I was astonished by the word <u>infection.</u> This indicated to me that their sting would actually impart a virus of some type.

These Flying Hell Monsters must have intelligence to be able to visually differentiate between the Mark of God and as Joe just said, that Taboo Tattoo."

Maria asked, "Will these Flying Hell Monsters attack the people of the nations of the 10 kings who are not Christians?"

Tom's quick answer was, "Yes and no. The people will be testified to by the Two Witnesses of God and only those who do not accept their offer of salvation will be attacked. So here we see, some will and some won't be attacked depending upon whose side you're on."

Joe asked, "Will some evil people take the Mark of God just to escape these monsters?"

Tom replied, "I don't believe they can as the evil inside of them creates fear and hatred, and even if they attempted this ruse, the finger of God would kill them instead.

Now we come to the time that Joe has been waiting for."

Chapter Thirty-Six

ZOMBIES & VAMPIRES IN THE BIBLE

Tom looked over at Joe and said, "Joe, you're going to love this. At first, I couldn't believe that there were zombies and vampires in the Bible. However, the more research I compiled, it seemed there will come a time, and not far off in the future, I might say, when these events actually take place.

We just read in the Bible that these Flying Hell Monsters were not given authority to kill people, they were commanded to <u>torture</u> them for <u>150 days</u>. Their torture was like the torment of a scorpion when it strikes a man.

When I researched scorpion stings they normally subside in a few days or so, but some are deadly. The sting and infection of these Flying Hell Monsters was entirely different. Now the type of sting that could infect a person with some type of virus and make them deathly sick for 150 days, which is a very long time, nearly half a year, is today still unknown to scientists."

Joe said, "That may be an understatement. I believe scientists are already experimenting on ways to reanimate dead tissue or zombie flesh as some call it."

Tom replied, "I've researched some of the effects of the scorpion sting tormenting the infected person and unleashing in Joe's words the, 'Zombie Virus'. Their skin turns blue due to lack of oxygen. Severe pain racks their bodies. They have bouts of unconsciousness and can have abhorrent brain disorders resulting in cannibalism. They can have involuntary muscular convulsions and spasms and primitive base instincts having no conscience. It's unbelievable!

Every person not having the Baptism unto Repentance resulting in God's Mark on their foreheads will be attacked. These Flying Hell Monsters sting and infect the people with the Zombie Virus from which there is no escaping.

We can read in the Bible about foul and loathsome sores[51] that come upon the men who had the Taboo Tattoo mark of the beast and those who worshiped his image.

In the dictionary 'foul' means disgusting to the senses, contaminated by impurities, <u>decaying and rotten especially by defecation</u> and loathsome means repulsive, abhorrent, detestable, and vile."

Joe said, "So you're saying that the Zombies will stink due to their rotting and decaying flesh caused by the Zombie Virus and by the toxic feces of these Flying Hell Monsters. They will also look repulsive and vile, absolutely abhorrent to behold. It's easy to see how they fit the description of a Zombie."

Maria asked, "Are there any references in the Bible about the walking dead?"

Joe's attention now sparked to a fever peak.

Tom replied, "This is for you Joe. This is what the Prophet Isaiah has to say in his chapter 26: 19...20[52]. I'll just paraphrase it. It says your dead will live, and their bodies rise. Enter your rooms, shut the doors behind you and hide yourselves for a little while until his wrath has passed by."

Maria commented, "So in modern day language the good people are being told to stay in their homes, lock or barricade their doors, and hide themselves for a little while until God's fierce punishment for the crimes committed by the antichrist have passed by."

Joe said, "So, here we see several things. They must remain indoors and hidden for just a little while until those who were bitten and infected finish flopping around, get up and leave. These events are extreme punishment given by God."

Tom said, "And here's another. Isaiah says in 28: 18-19[53]. It seems during this event death is removed from the equation. The antichrist will receive overwhelming severe punishment that drives them into temporary insanity at least. And look, it says that this sweeps by, a swift and strong force, sort of in one huge wave, they are inflected by the Flying Hell Monsters. Just like when the Two Witnesses of God moved from zone to zone, this is also like a sweeping action."

Maria said, "Yah, we can refer to this as the global epidemic pattern that begins with thousands and turns into hundreds of millions."

Tom said, "Do you want more Bible references?"

Maria said, "No!" but Joe said, "Oh yeah!" Joe won.

Tom continued, "In chapter 14:12-13[54] the Prophet Zechariah does not say that they die. Instead, it says that their flesh dissolves. One definition of 'dissolve' is a transition from one form to another, so perhaps their flesh changes and begins rotting away. They will be like walking corpses. It also says their eyes will shrivel in their sockets, and their tongues will decay in their mouths."

Maria said, "Oh, gross! Remember Joe, that movie where the infected turned into zombies within 10 seconds? Perhaps their eyes turn and shrivel within a few seconds also. On that day, they'll be so terrified, and panic stricken that they'll fight against each other in hand-to-hand combat, just like the Prophet Zechariah said."

Joe said, "See, once again they don't die. They're rotting away and fighting each other. When it says that their tongues will decay in their mouths, they won't be able to speak. We said earlier that they will howl and scream. Now we know why."

Tom replied, "Yes, the walking dead and notice their eyes change becoming shriveled little things."

Maria said, "So there are many reasons why these zombies don't go after the good people. First, they now have the Mark of God. Second, the zombies can't even see them and third, their eyes may only see the pillar of fire that attracts them to follow it."

Tom replied, "This zombie stuff just keeps getting weirder and weirder. They devolve into a pitiful state with no hope of recovery in sight. It's one thing to be sick and you hope for a full recovery and it's another thing to be sick and actually cry out and want to die. In Revelation 9:6 it says that <u>men will seek death</u> and <u>will not find it</u>; they will <u>desire to die</u>, and <u>death will flee from them.</u>

This seems impossible that those <u>infected will seek death</u> but <u>can't die</u>. They are so despicable one could easily refer to those infected with the Zombie Virus as the walking dead or in this case, the undead. They want death but to no avail because it is so deemed by God for them to suffer beyond comprehension for their actions. When they took the Taboo Tattoo, their fate was sealed. Their previous nature was extreme violence towards Christians and others who did not agree with their agenda. Talk about payback being you know what."

Maria just shook her head and said, "This is scary stuff, Tom. I'm really not liking it."

Joe finished this conversation by describing the zombie in his normal gory way. "So what you're saying is that the infection of the Zombie Virus makes them go crazy, they fall to the ground and become soiled. They roll and flop on the ground for at least three days. Just imagine how someone would look after doing this. Their eyes have changed and shrunk down to pea size and they can't see clearly, just follow the pillar of light. They can smell or sense blood and then rush to it for feeding. Their skin has changed in color to dark blue and is beginning to rot, similar to leprosy. Their tongues have after several days been bitten in half and either eaten or spit out. The rest of their tongue is infected and is rotting. Due to all their flesh rotting, they stink, although they themselves don't comprehend this fact. They are all loners and just migrate, following the light. There may be fighting among themselves as they vie for a better placement within their group. Closer to the front means closer to blood. During their travels their column gets larger every passing hour as hundreds of thousands are added each day."

Maria said, "Imagine the stench when millions of rotting zombies pass by your home."

Joe said, "It only takes the aroma of one skunk to make people run for cover."

Tom said he recalled the Bible story of Lazarus who after only three days was brought to life by Jesus and the people said that by now he would be stinking.

Maria said, "You know, after 1260 days of this, one would think that the entire earth may be stinking."

Tom answered, "You know, by them diving into blood pools, their clothes would not last long either. They would soon rot and disintegrate, so they would be naked and rotting zombies."

Maria added, "They would not even think to find clothing, even if it still existed."

Tom also added, "Since the climate is controlled within each angel halo, they would not even need clothes for warmth.".

Joe said, "Forget their clothes. Remember, "that after the initial 150 days of the Zombie Virus, they could be attacking and eating each other."

Maria piped in saying, "Remember a while ago we talked about the good people not reverting back to their old ways? Well, it just occurred to me that during the migration of zombies, some having the 3-color taboo tattoo will not turn from stage one into stage two so they will revert back to some state of normalcy. So then, isn't it entirely possible that these recovered zombies will try to regain their status and dominate the people using riches, incentives or brute force?"

Tom said, "Maybe they actually will travel to safer areas, like you said Maria, and live in colonies or compounds."

Joe interjected, "That brings up a good thought. Since they did not follow the pillar of fire, then they must have stayed put for the 150 days."

Tom shivered. Both, both Maria and Joe were getting used to this by now and asked, "Mel again?"

"I think so." Tom shrugged and then said, "There is another answer to what the 3-color do after getting attacked and turn into Zombies."

Joe asked, "OK, what did he say?"?

Tom's answer was cryptic, "Soon my friends."

"What kind of an answer is that?" Joe said.

Tom shook his head and said, "I really don't know."

Maria said, "What did they eat to stay alive?"

Both guys just looked at each other, sort of smirking and Maria caught on saying, "Oh my goodness! Each other!"

Joe, once again, just couldn't help himself saying, "Why do zombies eat all races, colors and nationalities? Because they wanted a balanced diet."

Tom was actually so tired, he even snickered. Maria left the room, disgusted.

Joe whispered to Tom, "Perhaps we should have just said that 'they drink blood'. I think she's in the bathroom vomiting. I think I'm sleeping on the couch tonight."

After a well-deserved break, they once again gathered together. Maria said, "No more Zombie talk for a while."

Joe led the conversation by saying, "Tell us more about these darling little flying things." Maria tried, but failed, to poke him.

"Try to visualize this." Tom looked at Maria and Joe and then continued. "These never before seen on Earth Flying Hell Monsters looked like horses prepared for battle. Their size is like a small bird. In the Bible it say their headwear is some type of golden crown. They have the face of a man and long hair like a woman. They have the teeth of lions. Their breast plates were an impenetrable iron-like material. They even have head protection plates. Their wings make tremendous clattering noises that will instill panic and fear to the hearer. These flying locust monsters have tails of a scorpion with a stinger that increases their horrific appearance by another four inches. This means as they attack and lock on to a person biting them, they also sting them with their tails. So all together they're about ten inches in length."

"So much for your darling little flying things." Maria chided Joe.

"Now," Tom continued, "they do not just attack, infect and leave. Their mission is to <u>torment</u> and <u>torture</u> their helpless victims who during that initial day may be attacked repeatedly by these Flying Hell Monsters. Their severe pain lasts for 150 days, almost half a year, and that's just the beginning.

When I looked up the definition of torment and torture it said; <u>infliction</u> (punishment, extreme bodily pain, great mental suffering, and torture from their lion's fang teeth biting and their tails stinging from repeated attacks."

Joe said, "Imagine a flying hornet or wasp that is about one inch now being six inches with a tail about four inches long having a huge one inch stinger and fanged teeth like a lion. They are truly gruesome little monsters."

Maria muttered, "I wouldn't refer to them as 'little' monsters. I'll continue calling them the, Flying Hell Monsters."

Tom said, "Swarms by the billions of these Flying Hell Monsters will fly over the land creating darkness and causing panic in most, and awe in some.

Locusts are yellow and one scientist doing experiments on them injected them with a dye called 'Lucifer Yellow'. When I read this article, immediately it seemed strange that the color Lucifer Yellow was identified with these Flying Hell Monsters from hell. It seems fitting somehow. I believe that the feet of these locusts will be claws, perhaps like a lion's, that can grip and attach themselves to their victims. This will allow them to clamp and lock on to people when biting and stinging them.

The infected, unlike zombies that movies are made of, are still living people who have been infected by the Zombie Virus, causing loss of higher brain functions such as speech, communication and self-awareness. They will have no control over their motor functioning and stagger aimlessly in short uncoordinated steps."

Maria said, "It seems we've gone back to zombies again."

Joe paying no heed continued, "Tom, your book says, all will at first be crawling in the streets. Then several days later, they'll start staggering around as drunkards not knowing where or even who they are. After about a week, they will migrate. So, Tom, when they begin their migration, will that be the beginning of the Zombie Plagues?"

"Nobody really knows, Joe."

Maria commented, "Here's another 'weird or what' question. What's the purpose of their lion's teeth? We know that they're forbidden to eat anything green of this earth. And, as a matter of fact, lion's teeth would be useless for eating grass anyhow."

Tom replied, "My research indicates that they attack and torment the people, chunking out pieces of flesh like black flies and sucking out their blood for sustenance or mere torment until they move on to the next zone.

Their lion's teeth have the typical four large canine teeth used for piercing and ripping out flesh and are up to a hundred times larger than the black fly's teeth."

Joe commented, "I didn't even know that black flies have teeth, but I certainly know that vampire bats have fangs and suck blood."

Maria glanced over at Joe and said, "Joe, you're good at sketching caricatures and faces. If you were to draw a Flying Hell Monster, what would it look like?"

Joe said he had already formed a mental picture and began to describe it. "First, their most notable facial characteristic is their teeth. They have lion's teeth meaning they have canine teeth or fangs. Imagine four one inch fangs coming at you. It's going to be a fearsome sight. Have you ever seen a dog showing its fangs? Tom, you read that the face was that of a man having long hair like a woman, perhaps like a horse's mane that is thick and coarse covering the neck. This man-faced monster has four fangs that will be used to bite, chunk out flesh and suck blood. Now comes the scary part. Maria, what does this mental picture remind you of?"

Maria said, "That's easy. I've seen many movies with a man's face having fangs. It's called a vampire."

Joe replied, "These fangs may also be hollow like snakes' fangs are, so they will be able to suck blood."

"That's gross!" Maria yelled. "Tom, I think you're reaching now."

Tom's reply was short and to the point. "Hollow or not, they suck blood. Would you change your mind if the Bible says you're wrong?"

Joe asked, "Is blood drinking actually in the Bible?"

Tom replied, "I'll keep you in suspense for a little while longer before I answer your question."

Maria said, "Oh, I hate it when he quips!"

Tom, smirking, went on, "Just as certain mosquitos transmit the malaria virus, and these monsters will transmit the Zombie Virus, causing the Zombie Plagues worldwide."

Tom, wondering out loud why these monsters have the face of a man, asked Joe, "Joe, what's your take on this?"

Joe, using his artistic flair, said, "Perhaps they take on the appearance of the person they're attacking."

Maria said, "Now that would be eerie to see. Imagine these Flying Hell Monsters with vampire-like fangs having your face attacking you."

Joe replied, "Or perhaps they look kind and gentle and at the last second morph into a monstrous appearance like that of my mother-in-law."

Maria was silent, her jab wasn't.

"OK guys," Tom continued, "Using their four canine teeth they are easily capable of chunking out a nasty piece of flesh. They will attack, grip, bite and chunk out flesh in one continuous action and even remain sucking out blood."

Maria asked, "Can people kill them?"

Joe answered before Tom saying, "They can't be hurt by people swatting at them as they are armour clad and supernatural.

These Flying Hell Monsters have the mindset that causes them to repeatedly use their lion's teeth to attack, chunk out flesh, infect and torment the antichrist people.

They may attack in groups like other vampire type insects do, similar to mosquitos, deer fly, black flies and more. So a person may, during their attacks, have many bites over their body until these monsters move on to their next victims in another zone.

What's more, locust droppings are toxic, and this may be a source of reinfections or even some other type of infection unknown to us.

They'll infect millions and this produces loathsome sores in addition to their stinging tails that make the people deathly sick for 150 days."

Maria concluded, "It's not going to be pretty."

Joe bewildering said, "What about the blood drinking in the Bible? What happened to that answer?"

"Rightly so," replied Tom, "You'll get it soon but I want to talk about another important topic."

Joe grumbled, "I hate it when he quibbled my question."

Maria laughed, "You know Joe, quibbled is actually a word meaning to evade the truth of an issue by raising another trivial issue."

"I knew that." he replied and added "Maria you look very lovely today."

Maria smelled a rat but decided the compliment took precedence for now, although she couldn't comprehend how Joe could have possibly known that word and even more so how to correctly use it. Her fumbled attempt at some type of response was cut off when, Tom interjected saying, "Enough of this banter. Let's move on."

𝔇ragon's 𝔗attoo 666 𝔗rilogy

Zombie Plagues

Synopsis
Most who begin this journey will come to the end having their life profoundly changed. A call to arms resonates within one's soul created by the awesome 'shock and awe' produced by the events now at hand. Our three spirit heroes, along with a very unique but strange supernatural guide and mentor, take the reader by the hand through the events as they are far to horrific to wander through unattended. Through our heroes' eyes, we will all witness humanities disintegration and the devolving of modern life into its most base form. Now, come the 7 Spirits of God, the 7 Thunders of God, and the 2 Ambassadors of God testifying to every soul on earth, in continents recombined after exiting Judea. From hell's pit again come Flying Hell Monsters attacking, infecting all save and except a few with the blood-virus plagues resulting now in a global pandemic of zombies. Those infected, have their eyes turn red within seconds, shriveling to the size of peas, their vision now restricted, as moths attracted to a flame. For the next few days they attack others also now infected with the blood-virus, thus fulfilling what God had commanded; that people will eat each other even fathers will eat their loved ones and friends. Those infected will gorge upon others while being gorged upon themselves because they feel no pain, a very horrific sight indeed. During their first 150 days of the blood-virus plague, stage one, they cannot die, rather the opposite, their wounds scab

over quickly. In short order, they rise up, begin to stagger, walk then run, all the while howling and screaming as wolves to the full moon, chasing the pillar of fire that can be seen in the distance yet never obtained.. The infected are not reanimated like Hollywood movies, and they did not transform into some grotesque monster having sharp teeth. They do, however, become filthy, wretched, naked and stink. They do, however, also have a keen sense of smell and are attracted to blood as camels to water. They plunge head first into these sources in the vain attempt to quench their insatiable desire for their lust of blood. People with God's Mark, safely, from the security of their homes and tents hear, and later smell them, coming and passing by, yet nothing harms those who are 'saved' as they are invisible to these hordes. 200 million 1-color disgustingly loathsome things, mowed down by 200 million 3-color zombies that causes the dried up Great Euphrates River to rise six feet deep in blood, flowing 200 miles southwards. Who is looking and cheering them on? The, Great Read Dragon standing in the ancient city of Babylon. Now come the destruction sequences of Babylon the Great along with even more destruction including that of thermo nuclear releases of energy and soon, **ARMAGEDDON.**

Further, never before discovered information surfaces concerning the New Jerusalem and of the Bride, the Lamb's Wife, and how you can become her.

Chapter Thirty-Seven

ZOMBIE PLAGUES

"The plagues that you have called, the Zombie Plagues, Joe, will start exactly on the 1040 T/D. Today," Tom said, "more and more people, institutions, agencies other entities are relating to the word 'zombie'. Various definitions can be found like a type of monster representing undead beings.

Zombies currently are fictional undead beings, regularly encountered in horror themed works and typically shown as mindless human flesh-eating beings. How is it that science fiction sooner or later turns into science fact? If you want more information about them, look up what one government source has to say about the subject of zombies.

One may ponder as to why Zombies, Zombie Apocalypse, and Zombie Preparedness can be found on the CDC web site. As it turns out, what first began as a tongue in cheek campaign to engage new audiences with preparedness messages has proven to be a very effective platform. They say we continue to reach and engage a wide variety of audiences on all hazards preparedness via Zombie Preparedness and as our director, notes, if you are generally well equipped to deal with a zombie apocalypse you will be prepared for a hurricane, pandemic, earthquake, or terrorist attack.

I realize they're spinning information to suit their purposes, but the fact remains they are talking about zombies.

One person actually informed me that the government of the USA is training certain special soldiers on how to cope with zombies in case fiction turns into fact and they're doing it now."

Maria corrected him saying, "Not in case, but rather when fiction turns into fact."

Joe added, "It seems like military, perhaps even the NG and other countries, may be involved in these zombie preparations or experiments."

Tom said that he believes the skin color of those infected is a deathly blue due to a lack of oxygen, which makes them very weak with bouts of unconsciousness following.

Tom continued, "Those having the 'Mark of God' are protected from the actions of the zombies. They do not have to travel anywhere and may just remain where they are because in short order the zombies will be walking away from them."

Maria said, "The zombies may very well walk away from them but what happens to those with the Mark of God in the next zones, along the route of the zombies?"

Tom replied, "They may just sit tight or form groups and stay indoors until the zombies all have passed."

Joe added, "There will be lots of food for the 'saved' to eat since the zombies can't eat food any longer as they only desire flesh and drinking the blood of humans."

Maria commented, "Quit talking about zombies drinking blood."

"Sorry about that, Maria. It was quite unintentional."

"Right." she muttered and then said, "Let's move on. I like this last scenario better. When Joe and I travelled overseas to Africa for a safari, people from the United States lived together in a mini-city. This mini-city offered most of the amenities of home and security that we were accustomed to. It seems logical that those with the Mark of God in each zone may band together within the dwellings of their own or those abandoned by the antichrist. They most likely will not have to stock up on food, clothing and other necessities of life because the millions of zombies will have abandoned everything. They have been taught of the events coming their way and soon at the 2300 T/D., God will come for them and until such time they are to remain faithful. Or, it may be that they gather great amounts of food and other items and then make a journey to some designated areas. Am I right, so far in my thinking, Tom?"

Tom nodded in response as Joe wondered out loud, "Do you think once the zombies have left and only those with the Mark of God remain, will they all remain faithful to God?"

Tom replied, "That's a great question!" and all three started to try and answer it.

Joe said, "I think even though the zombies have moved, the unholy trinity still exists and will continue their lying deceptions."

Maria asked, "What kind of deceptions do you think they will do to deceive the remaining people?"

Tom replied, "People are creatures of habit. Perhaps they will be influenced by greed or power. Remember, to remain faithful to God, certain requirements are in order. Also remember at the time of the Rapture, about 50% of Christians had turned away from God. It is possible that many of the newly Baptised unto Repentance people may also backslide and turn away from God."

Joe said, "When it comes to salvation, nothing is a given. They, they and us included, must work for it. We have to live by God's 'rules of conduct'."

Maria said, "That's a strange way to say it, but I hear you. All saved must be, God fearing, oh yeah, and follow the golden rule to be kind unto others and love God above all."

Tom said, "The Bible does say for them 'not to lose their garments of salvation'."

Maria said, "We know about these garments or wedding garments that you told us about some time ago. Is there more significance to them?"

Tom replied, "Yes, but I don't want to get ahead of myself."

Joe said, "From what you have been telling us, after the antichrist are attacked and infected they will go from normal to some form of insanity. At first both the 1 and 3 color zombies will crawl or stagger around eating anything that they can sink their teeth into, human or animal. In short order, they rise up, become mobile, and by that I mean, they start racing towards the light or the smell, depending if you're in the first or second group," Joe said, "and the chase is on."

"That's one way to describe it, Joe." Maria said. "I don't even want to think about what you just said about eating humans or animals. It really saddens and scares me."

Joe commented, "So zombies eating people are OK but not animals?"

Maria said rhetorically, "Why do the poor animals always have to take a hit because of human screw ups."

She continued, "So the zombies travel from their zone to the next adjacent and infected zone thereby accumulating in massive numbers, only separated by mere days?"

Joe said, "From what Tom told us, and what's in his book about this, the 1-color zombies, after 3 days, rise up, become mobile, and begin following the pillar of fire, and the 3-color, take another 3 days of flopping around, then rise up and become mobile, and then the chase is on."

"You're right and wrong." Tom said.

Maria replied, "I'm confused. Make up your mind."

"I don't know if there will be much of a chase." Tom commented. "Remember at the 1040 T/D., the mark of the beast is still optional. For sure, the vast majority of people who have drawn close to their new messiah have also taken his 3-color mark of pride. I think the balance that have not taken his mark will either run towards the Two Witnesses or flee to the open arms of the antichrist within that zone."

Maria said "Right, just like Abram, so there must be many others, so what happens next?"

Joe added, "It may even be possible that a third group exists, those who did not want salvation and who hid in caves or crevices."

Tom said, "Remember, those saved, who accept the testimony of the Two Witnesses, immediately travel upon the King's highway, to the Great Domed City. They're no longer there. They're long gone, sort of like 'vanished'. I wonder if we could say they, 'sparked' like those during the Rapture."

Maria replied, "That makes sense, and now the vast majority of people remaining are the 3-color along with a lesser amount of 1-color antichrist, right?"

Joe answered, "Yah, that makes sense, because you said, Tom, that they would eat each other, remember?"

Tom added, "Yah, it may even be that the 3-color attack themselves during their initial 6 days."

Joe, getting right into it, commented, "Maybe they lie comatose for a period of time, then begin flopping around and attacking other infected. Come to think of it, the 1-color will rise up sooner so they could bite others lying on the ground."

"You're right." Maria said. "The curse is that fathers will eat their daughters, sons their fathers, friends their friends, you get the picture?"

Joe commented, "I like a challenge" and continued her thought process saying, "Imagine how this will really look, zombies attacking and eating other zombies. Cool!"

Maria said, "Really, Joe? Cool? It's going to be a horrific series of events, definitely not cool."

Tom agreed and said, "When we look at the bigger picture, we see the Zombie Plagues spreading across the entire land of Israel one zone at a time. Each day their numbers multiply and the Zombie Plagues increase exponentially."

Maria said, "In the past, when we watched virus epidemic outbreak type movies, the officials always showed a virus progression map that indicated how long the epidemic would take to cover the entire country."

Tom said, "The Zombie Plagues will start and spread across all remaining Angel Halos during the 1260 days of plagues upon earth. Only those zombies having the 1-color tattoo will after 3 days of being infected get up and follow the pillar of fire as it meanders across Israel."

Joe brought up another weird or what scenario. "Even when these zombies finish their 150 days of death, crying and howling, exactly what state of normalcy can they attain? Remember, they have for about half a year been eating flesh that they had tripped over, and drinking blood!"

Tom agreed. "For sure they will look horrible, possibly looking like people having leprosy with skin falling off their bodies. If their tongues rotted or were bitten off, so they can't talk, being unable to communicate would most likely make them furious."

Joe said, "Imagine those who are in the military and now these soldiers cannot talk, only scream and howl. It seems to me, this alone could make them go insane."

Maria commented, "So back to the 1-color zombies. In Israel, there will be less of them because the 3-color dominated the scene. Between them, there will be, at first, thousands afflicted during day one, then about a quarter million within the first week, then it will grow into the hundreds of thousands, and then millions. By the end of the first year in Israel and Judea there will be over 15 million of them.

When this plague leaps to the rest of the world, beginning in year two, the number rises from thousands to millions each. This process keeps repeating itself until the plagues have occurred in all 'Angel Halos'.

Towards the end of days, their numbers will be in the hundreds of millions of zombies travelling from zone to zone within that last 'Angel Halo'."

Tom said, "Right you are, Maria. Remember, it's only a one way access. Once in that Angel Halo, all zombies must follow the pillar of fire as it travels from zone to zone and when all zones have been testified to, then the pillar of fire moves on to the next Angel Halo. This process repeats itself from angel halo to angel halo until all pass through the 7th and final one, the Middle East countries."

Joe said, "You told us, only the 1-color zombies can mutate and during their 150 days they are mobile but constantly screaming and crying out for death. Once their 150 days have expired, they turn into stage two zombies, and for the balance of the 1260 days remain infected, and still screaming zombies. Imagine thousands . . . no millions . . . no hundreds of millions of insane zombies roaming earth, walking, running, screaming and swarming over blood sources uncountable number of times. You know, many zombie movies show a global epidemic of zombies, and now we can understand how it could actually happen."

Tom jumped on this bandwagon saying, "Imagine the following. Throughout the remaining six Angel Halos and for the remainder of the time of the Two Witnesses which equates to two and a half years or 900 days, the people either receive salvation or torment. Talk about black and white choices.

The remaining Angel halos cover the balance of the inhabited areas where people live. We know the Two Witnesses of God follow a specific pre-designated pattern so by the end of their time of testimony at the 2300 T/D., all of these zombies have followed them and are congregated on the eastern side of the Great Euphrates River numbering in the hundreds of millions or more."

Joe, getting on the band wagon, answered, "Now, imagine hundreds of millions of them running after the pillar of fire that has just crossed over the dried up Great Euphrates River and into an invisible wall. That's going to get messy."

Maria interjected, "It seems like the journey of the zombies takes them all over the globe. I would think that the recovered 3-color zombies witness these events happening and stay clear of the 1-color, stage two zombies during these days."

Tom looked at Joe, saying, "Are you ready grasshopper? Here we go down the garden path."

Joe just chuckled. "OK, master."

Tom said, "First, we have to remember that in the land of Israel and Judea where the false president and false messiah are, the Zombie Plagues have at this time finished and those 3-color zombies stay put. They do not migrate anywhere."

Joe asked, "What happens to any 1-color zombies remaining there?"

Tom answered, "I think the recovered 3-color will kill them after their 150 days are over."

Joe piped in, "Or they will eat them for supper. Whatever the case, these zombies are insane so they have to be dealt with, that's for sure. I think the same holds true for the rest of Babylon the Great, all 1-colors will have to be killed or eaten."

Maria added, "And remember, all water sources have been turned to blood. This establishes the fact that even the 3-color, must drink this blood to survive."

Joe commented, "Since they drink blood, it's logical that they also eat flesh."

Tom said, "Remember those 3-color zombies stay put within their lands. They do not migrate anywhere."

Maria asked, "What then happens to the good people living there?"

Tom smiled, "Ain't none, just like in Judea after those wanting salvation fled, all remaining were antichrist."

Joe said, "I see where you're going with this. So the same scenario happens in Great Babylon, with respect to the good people; ain't none."

Maria said, "Firstly, your grammar sucks and secondly what happens to the other people living elsewhere in the world?"

Tom said "That's a different story. A while back we discussed how the good people perhaps had to remain in their homes until the 3-color zombies became mobile and began following the 1-color zombies. We thought once they had recovered they may attack the good people since they would have to leave their homes searching for food. But, now, it gets weird or what again. These 3-color zombies, in the next and all subsequent angel halos, don't have any place to go. They must, after 6 days of flopping around, begin following the 1-color horde who are maybe hundreds of miles ahead of them."

Maria said, she thinks that God puts this thought into their minds to do this.

Tom now teased them slightly saying, "Remember back when we were discussing how vast the 200 million army must be and asking where did they come from? Now we have the answer. They are made up of the 3-color zombies who have been mindlessly following behind the 200 million 1-color zombies as they travelled throughout the angel halo domes. As they arrive into the last angel halo dome, they are now all congregated in the land of the 10 kings of the east."

Joe commented, "So are you saying that throughout their travels, their kings went with them?"

Tom's reply was, "I don't know. Either during the final days of the zombie migration, they get infected and join the ranks of the 3-color zombies or they are all living in India, get infected and after their 150 days are up become somewhat normal again, taking charge and organizing their armies."

Tom continued, "So now, the recovered 3-color zombies are in the lands of the 10 kings of the east. There they assemble into vast camps."

Maria asked, "Do you think these camps will be close together?"

Tom replied, "They could be many hundreds of miles apart but all will be within that angel halo."

Joe said, "Yah, perhaps one dome encompasses more than one country, all depending upon size and boundaries."

Tom said, "Getting back to our discussion as to the good people and their safety, they just have to wait, until the 1-color and 3-color zombies become mobile and join the migration."

Joe said, "This makes perfect sense to me. That means they will only have to remain faithful to God, keep their spiritual garments clean and not revert back to their former ways. You don't think that they would revert back knowing what's coming down the pipeline, do you?"

Tom replied, "The Israelites, in the Bible, reverted back to idols and turned their backs on God over 20 times, so who knows."

Maria said, "Remember, the band of Korah, during the Exodus out of Egypt, went against Moses, God's chosen leader. So it doesn't take long for people to revert back to their former ways.

I wonder what hundreds of millions of zombies would look like all converging on one location."

Tom said, "One thing is for sure, they don't have any manners, sense of order, or rule of law. They will just do what their base instincts tell them."

Joe commented, "Rule of law! I haven't heard that one for a long time."

Tom replied, "Very soon it will be called God's Law."

Maria sighed saying again, "It's definitely not going to be pretty."

Tom shrugged and continued, "As to what this vast amount will look like, I think they follow the leader when travelling, just like in Africa when a column of ants travelling for many miles encounter a stream crossing their pathway. The ants just go into this stream and drown. Eventually their dead bodies pile up, forming a bridge for the rest to travel over. They resemble an automated following of some type as they travel, not knowing why, they just do."

Joe commented, "Something like the blue-eyed Pied Piper in his red and yellow who leads all the rats to the river to drown or in this case all the zombies. The Piper also said something about getting rid of huge swarms of gnats and monstrous broods of vampire-bats."

Maria said to Joe, "How you know all this stuff, I will never know. Only you could turn the Pied Piper into a zombie thing, but you do make some valid points."

Joe said, "Oh yah, I almost forgot. The Piper also said that in Transylvania there's a tribe of alien people having risen out of a subterraneous prison who wear strange dress."

"Great!" replied Maria. "Now you've also got aliens from the pit involved. Weird or what! Now you got me saying it too!"

Tom, trying to get everyone back on topic said, "When these events take place, then the antichrist will consist of all the zombies from all the remaining Angel Halos that will then congregate on the eastern side of the Great Euphrates River."

Joe asked, "What would be the significance in having perhaps hundreds of millions of antichrist zombies parked on the east side of the Great Euphrates River?"

Tom's answer, "Good question. For now, just keep this phrase in mind. The Entities of Death will dispose of them soon."

Maria said, "No way bubba! This time you have to keep the thought train going. Joe can wait for his blood drinkers, but not me."

Tom relented. "Fine. First we'll discuss how the 1-color zombies come into the picture and how the armies of the 10 kings slaughter them. The newly infected zombies, as usual, had the thought instilled into them to follow the pillar of fire that constantly moved from zone to zone."

Maria asked, "Wouldn't they re-encounter the Flying Hell Monsters?"

Tom answered, "No, because after 3 days they regain consciousness, begin crawling, staggering and soon running after the pillar of fire. They still are in great pain and desire death for the remainder of their 150 days but now they have the ability to walk, and then run with explosive rapid movements faster than an Olympic sprinter, and craving mostly blood."

"Now we're talking!" said Joe. "The more they drinky, the more they stinky like a skunky."

Maria stopped him saying, "Are you really trying to make a rap song? If so, I'm going to seriously hurt you, Joe."

Tom almost lost control but stayed the course. He continued, "The Two Witnesses are always ahead of the zombies moving from zone to zone. This means that the Flying Hell Monsters have also moved on, so the coast is clear, for these other zombies, we might say. They never again catch up to the Two Witnesses or the Flying Hell Monsters.

The effect created by these events produces epidemic cycles of more and more zombies migrating across the globe. At this time, the Two Witnesses are moving from zone to zone on an hourly basis. Remember when we discussed 'do the math'. In Israel they moved every day, but now they move every hour."

Maria just shook her head as Tom continued. "The route of the 1-color zombies brings them into contact with other newly attacked and infected 1-color zombies. They may attack each other but more likely they are driven to source out water which has now turned to blood. And remember they still can't die for 150 days."

Joe said, "Sort of like wild animals fighting over a fresh kill."

"The plagues of each zone form a ripple pattern across the earth. The plagues of the zombies starts in Israel, Judea and then meanders throughout Africa, the Americas that have by now along with all the other islands drifted back forming one massive global new land mass and don't ask me just now to explain how I know this, just trust me."

Joe merely grunted, "Mel, again, right? Are we ever going to meet him?"

Toms reply was pointed, "We better hope not. I'll explain later."

"Now the Zombie Plagues continue through the northern countries, USSR, China then India. They have during these 900 days made a huge global loop that eventually heads them westward back towards the Great Euphrates River and Israel."

Joe commented, "If I understand you correctly, the oceans have turned to 'dead-man's blood'. However, within the remaining 6 angel halos, the water sources only turn to blood after the Two Witnesses make it happen. So there is always fresh water for the people who have not yet been attacked by the flying hell monster to drink from."

"Good thinking Joe. I never thought that far ahead on the matter. I was always on the run hiding from the antichrist prior to the Rapture event."

One strange characteristic of these 1-color zombies is that they can move very quickly at times, their actions similar to piranha that are either docile or ferocious when stimulated. Only after their 150 days are up will their pain stop, but for all other intents and purposes they are still insane zombies in every detail who are insanely fast runners."

Maria asked, "What's to stop this ever increasing horde of zombies from simply running into those who have just been infected on their day one, we might say? If this were to happen they may devour those now flopping on the ground before they can after three days get back on their feet and join their ranks."

Joe answered, "I think I can answer that. They are not interested in these floppers because the floppers are sick so their blood doesn't taste good, only healthy blood attracts them."

Maria said, "But there's no healthy blood, only those with the Mark of God in their homes."

Tom took over saying, "After 150 days, the virus mutates them into stage two zombies. Now they become like piranhas travelling in large groups. At this time, the desire to attack their own, virtually ceases. However, the smell of blood whips them into a frenzy causing them to stampede and producing a horrific scene. Little wonder why the Bible says, people will hiss at them as they are so detestable."

Tom continued, "Remember, due to the actions of the Two Witnesses, as these 1-color zombies followed the pillar of fire, there was always lots of blood to drink as all the rivers and springs of water had turned to blood[55] due to the plagues created by the Two Witnesses during their zone to zone travels.

This blood was their sole means of survival and somehow they can sense the smell of blood in the air causing them to swarm at a high rate of speed, ferociously seeking it out. You might say that they are addicted to blood and should it become scarce their pain would increase. It would be similar to withdrawal symptoms suffered by drug addicts. This blood drought would not kill them but as their pain increases so does their howling.

Their howling, strange as it seems, also increases upon sensing a new source of blood to drink or when their withdrawal symptoms come back. Either way, they make lots of noise."

Joe said, "Unbelievable!"

Tom responded, "They are going to be faster than any race sprinter in the past because they will never become winded and their muscles never ache. Their pain is of a different nature, more mentally perhaps. They won't be affected by heat or cold and only long for blood. They don't have the reasoning faculties to understand why they are attracted to and have to follow the pillar of fire."

Joe stared at Tom and frowning, said, "I hear you. Even though they all follow the moving pillar of fire, itself always visible in the far distance, they never seem to catch up to it and should they get too close, their attention is then directed to a body of blood, which provides a feeding frenzy for them and causes them to slow down, allowing the pillar of fire to always stay ahead of them."

Joe said that he thought these zombies could see or perceive the pillar of fire hundreds of miles ahead of them because it was so high in the sky and was always visible to them especially at night. Once zombies began their trek, they travelled ceaselessly day and night, similar to how moths are attracted to light or fire, save and except those that got lost due to various reasons, who then became target practise for a later time.

Maria now spoke. "Just to summarize, if I understand everything correctly, they get attacked by the Flying Hell Monsters, contract the Zombie Virus turning them into zombies. Then, three days later these 1-color zombies begin crawling around, stand up and begin staggering towards the pillar of fire in the distance. The 1-color zombies are called type or stage one zombies and are in great pain for their first 150 days. Then their desire to die subsides and they turn into stage two zombies for the remainder of the 1260 days.

During these days, their numbers are constantly growing and they congregate into massive colonies numbering in the hundreds of millions. These colonies can sense blood and then move at high rates of speed to its source swarming and drinking until their gorging has been temporarily satisfied. They continue their trek and as Joe said, they followed the Pied Piper."

"You're right, Maria. Now just to confuse you even more," said Tom, "let's talk about the 3-color zombies whose virus did not mutate them into stage two zombies.

Their main areas of concentration are initially in lands controlled by the land and sea beasts, the false prophet being in Rome and the countries surrounding the Mediterranean Sea and the false president in Israel."

Tom continued, "Save and except the 3-color zombies in Babylon the Great, all other 1 and 3-color zombies will eventually end up in the Far East, in the land of India, controlled by 10 kings.

During the latter portion of these days, just prior to these zombies being released to enter Pakistan, the 200 million soldiers are organized into columns of zombie soldiers, who by this time have all recovered from their plagues."

Tom continued saying, "The 200 million fallen angel horses, once released from their confinement at the Great Euphrates River, travel on the winds of the earth."

Joe commented, "You mean like the song 'Ghost riders in the sky'?"

Maria, this time, agreed and Joe responded, "You do?"

Tom didn't answer but continued, saying, "Three demons went east to the ten kings at the 2260 T/D. doing their deceiving wonders."

Joe again said, "But what about the blood drinkers in the Bible?"

Tom replied, "Soon, Joe. I'm getting there. Right now I want to tell you about the slaughter of the zombies when one third of the people on earth are exterminated. Did that get your attention, Joe?"

"Yep!" he replied.

Chapter Thirty-Eight
ENTITIES OF DEATH SLAUGHTER 200 MILLION

Tom continued saying, "Let's jump ahead to the time that immediately follows after the Two Witnesses have finished their testimony of 1260 days.

Now it gets totally 'weird or what' again. I believe, the 200 million 3-color zombie antichrist soldiers mount these 200 million Hell Horses that when combined form the Entities of Death and for the next 150 days will travel westwards towards the Great Euphrates River.

When mobile, their massive numbers will bring them into constant encounters with straggler zombies of both colors. They are all over the place due to the numerous mountains and valleys so it is easily possible for them to lose sight of the pillar of fire that is always on the move. They only have to find a suitable source of blood and then linger there feasting. Also as they draw closer to the dried up Great Euphrates River there are a great many stragglers. Their numbers total in the millions and make good slaughter practice for the Entities of Death."

Maria shook her head and said, "I wonder if the two groups of zombies would fight over the blood reserves."

"Good point!" replied Tom. "We know that wild animals will guard their food sources, so these two groups may also fight each other."

Joe commented, "It may also be that when they gorged themselves drinking fresh blood they became unconscious for a period of time." He looked at Tom for a reaction to his blood drinking segue but Tom simply did not acknowledge this tidbit of bait. Joe continued, "This would also cause them to lose sight of the pillar of fire."

"Right you are." commented Tom. "These lost meanders, no matter whether 1 or 3-color, will be hated by and considered despicable by the Entities of Death who with delight slaughter them along their travels. By this method, millions will be relieved of their plight.

Don't forget, those on foot are of no value to them. They just get in their way and would slow them down."

Maria commented, "Once again evil cleaning up evil."

"As their journeys bring them closer to the Great Euphrates River, the long columns of the Entities of Death change in formation as they begin their pincer movement in preparation for the great slaughter.

Now, getting back to these 1-color zombies, it gets so far past 'weird or what', I don't know what to call it. As these zombies come into view of the ancient city of Babylon in Iraq and approach the now dried up Great Euphrates River, something seemingly impossible takes place. As they rush forward and enter this dried up river bed, they impact and plow into an invisible wall that blocks their exit. This barrier was created I believe, by the 4 angels positioned who in the past and using a Biblical term of 'a time and half a time' ago, were commissioned to restrain the 200 million Hell Horses."

Maria did some quick math excitedly saying, "I get it. The Bible says that these 4 angels were prepared for the 391 days. You told us that they were prepared for one year, one month, one day and one hour. What happened to the 'hour'?"

Tom replied, "OK, grasshopper, the month is when the 3 demons were released and allowed out of the barrier to travel to the kings of the east.

The day is the time it takes to kill the 200 million 1-color zombies. The hour is reserved for the nuking of Rome."

Maria began laughing, "Caught you, Mr. Math fudge master."

Joe quizzed, "Hey, what did I miss now?"

Tom chuckled, "I know, I know, I said the demons go out 40 days prior to the end of the 2300 days."

Maria, now in hysterics said, "What is it 40 or 30 days?"

Tom replied, "You have my answer."

Joe just couldn't help himself "But is that your final answer?"

Maria jumped in, "Tom, you just can't leave it like this."

Tom replied, "Look, I was just about to talk about these 1-color zombies that sort of hit a brick wall and couldn't cross the dried up river bed. Don't you want me to get into this?"

Maria still laughing said, "No, we want to see how you wiggle out of this one. Right, Joe?"

"Fine!" responded Tom. "Remember the 40 days was just an arbitrary figure, and yes, 30 days is a better fit to tie into this equation."

Joe said, "Why didn't you just go back in your book and change the dates?"

Tom answered, "Remember when I said people were trying to kill me and my publisher got those death threats if he printed my book? I never had the opportunity to do a final proofing. And, if I remember correctly, even you, Maria commented that my book didn't make it to a wordsmith. Back then, I made my exit plans, grabbed up oodles of money, and as we now say, 'got out of Dodge'."

Joe commented, "Makes perfect sense to me."

Maria, jokingly said, "Joe, you still believe in Santa Claus."

The expression on Joe's face indicated he didn't know if that was a dig or compliment. With a what-ever expression of her own, Maria turned her attention to Tom and said, "If I buy your rationale, which by the way I don't, what's correct 40 or 30?"

Tom looked at her and said, "Beats me."

Before Maria could respond, Joe said, "Maybe it was a scriptural misprint."

Immediately, Maria and Tom burst into laughter saying, "Joe, it's me that's incorrect, not the scriptures."

"Just a thought." replied Joe.

Maria, now with tears in her eyes, said, "Joe, 'park that thought'."

Tom finished this topic by saying, "That's my story and I'm sticking to it."

"Now", he said, "moving on, these zombies could not exit to the other side the dried up river bed and they couldn't go backwards due to the Entities of death on their heels."

Joe commented that these zombies wouldn't even have the intelligence to retreat and what about this brick wall.

Maria said, "Joe, that's only Tom's failed attempt of humor. It's a wall all right only not made of bricks. It's a force field."

Joe's imagination now peaked. He said, "How high is it?"

Maria said, "Why is the height so important to you? It's a wall like any other, say 50 feet high."

Tom replied, "Actually, Joe's right on this one. I'll give you the answer in one minute."

Tom continued. "Picture this. It's similar to the olden days when cowboys herded horses into a coral. These zombies were corralled at this location. Now just like that column of travelling ants we discussed a while back, these zombies tried to scale the invisible force field wall. Their living bodies piled higher and higher upon each other vainly trying to reach the top and get over."

Joe grabbed his calculator and punched in some numbers. "Two hundred miles wide equals about one million lineal feet. Assuming two feet per zombie, you get about 500,000 on row one lying in the dried up river bed. When you divide 200 million by 500 thousand you get 400 rows high. Now assuming their bodies are just one foot thick this make a wall of zombies 400 feet high."

Tom replied, "And that's assuming this wall of zombies is a constant height."

Maria piped in saying, "If you look at the ants, they don't spread out at first. They just keep on trampling over other ants until they have created a bridge that is higher in bodies at its center. Then the rest of these ants are able to climb over."

Joe said, "Look at this picture. As up to 200 million zombies approach, they attempt to cross over at the middle section of this invisible wall. From this point, they begin to smack into it and bodies begin to pile upwards and outwards. Picture a triangle of bodies, highest in the middle, fanning outwards one hundred miles on each side."

Tom replied, "The two hundred miles is what the Bible says that the amount of blood flows at around six feet deep."

Maria said, "So it's possible that the middle height of these zombies could reach very high into the sky."

Joe, again with his calculator, figured out that this height could be 1600 hundred feet high and 50 miles wide.

Maria supported Joe saying, "If you go back to your triangle assumption, then the triangle's peak would not be feet but miles high, sloping down 25 miles northwards and 25 miles southwards."

Joe said that he thought they just kept coming and coming, oblivious to the fact a barrier of bodies was growing before and under them. He thought this sight alone would be beyond imagination as the ever increasing numbers could be well into the hundreds of thousands and eventually reaching hundreds of millions. Because they were alive, they would be wiggling about like a pile of maggots.

Maria wigged out and said this was too much for her to cope with.

Joe, giving her a big reassuring hug, said, "You did a good job of describing the picture, Maria. I never thought you would get so zombie involved."

"I'm scared." she said.

Tom had trouble describing his mental picture of what was going to take place.

Joe came to his rescue saying, "Picture this. When the 200 million Entities of Death approach, in order for there to be blood and lots of it, these Entities of Death' cannot unleash weapons of fire. Rather they use impulse weapons similar to Gatling guns. You know, the new type that can unleash a million rounds per minute."

Tom continued, "You're right. This blood bath carnage will be of Biblical proportions. As the slaughter progresses, the blood from the zombies is so great it flows into the dried up river in ever increasing amounts soon reaching up to the horses' bridles of the Entities of Death. These Entities of Death are right in the middle of this streaming blood and they rejoice in this. The blood volume will be so massive, it flows over 200 hundred miles south in length[56]."

Maria asked, "Does the 200 miles represent any other Biblical significance?"

Tom then replied, "This 200 mile section of the Great Euphrates River has history attached to it. I believe this is also where the 200 million Hell Horses originally confined by the 4 angels were released."

Joe said, "What are the odds that 200 miles and 200 million are related to this area? These are not coincidences."

Tom replied, "It gets even better. This is also where the 2 Ambassadors of God, His witnesses, cross over at the end of their time of testimony."

Maria commented, "As you said Tom, this is also from where the 3 demons were released."

Tom added, "And remember, this river bed is also the promised border of ancient Israel."

Joe said, "There's probably more history. We just don't know it yet."

Tom said, "You're right, Joe. There's much we have no clue about. We do know that the Entities of Death, these 200 million passed by the ancient city of Babylon in Iraq on their final days as they headed for the Great Euphrates River."

Maria posed the following. "Perhaps they didn't just pass by this ancient city. Maybe they fulfilled some prophecy we don't know about."

Tom said, "In ancient times, Babylon was evil. These Entities of Death travel through this same area. There's a correlation there somewhere."

Maria asked, "Do you think that the Great Red Dragon is there watching with pride as his armies pass by?"

Joe said, "If so, it would be like when the President or leader of a country stands and watches his soldiers passing by him during a parade or in this case on their way to the slaughter of one third of earth's population."

Tom said, "Talking about pride, this is also the area where the Tower of Babel was located or one could say the tower of pride."

Tom further said, "Also in this area, there's another 'weird or what' event. It is from Ur in Babylonia that God called Abraham to go into a land that he would show him. I'm not sure of the correlation but it's there somewhere."

Maria commented, "Perhaps the Great Red Dragon sets up camp for a while where the ancient city Babylon once stood after his temple in Jerusalem crumbled into oblivion"

Joe commented, "I seem to recall, from my Sunday School days, that the Tower of Babel was about one third the height of the Empire State Building. God stopped its construction well before it was completed so its final height is not known. We know that the Great Red Dragon is very huge. Perhaps he is the same size as the old Tower of Babel."

Maria elaborated saying, "I picture him standing there just as God described him in the Bible in the book of Job. I remember that light flashes out of his nostrils, his eyes look eerie like when you see a morning sunrise over the ocean, fire comes out of his mouth and here's the part I'm leading up to, 'sorrow dances before him'. His heart is hard as stone and he is king over all the children of pride. He delights in watching as up to 200 million 1-color zombies in their pathetic misery come screaming and howling by. In his twisted thinking, he has succeeded in stealing them away from God and this is a great victory for him. Next, come the 200 million 3-color zombies, the children of pride, his Entities of Death that he is king over."

Joe said, "I can just picture him flashing energy light rays and fire overtop of his Entities of Death. This would spur them on even more so."

Tom said, "Ancient Babylon was located straddling the Great Euphrates River. In the Bible, God said that 'sorrow dances before him.' From Satan's location, the site of ancient Babylon, he delights in the slaughtering of one third of the people on earth. They never worshiped him out of love anyway, only out of fear of death."

Joe said, "I think that every human death counts as a victory for the dragon as far as he's concerned."

Maria asked, "Following this horrific slaughter, what happens next?"

Tom answered, "I think that Satan then moves to the Mount of Megiddo and begins making preparations for the final battle of Armageddon which is looming soon.

During my research, I once drew a line from the ancient city of Babylon to Jerusalem. You know the saying, the shortest distance between two points is a straight line? It was. After I drew the line I noticed they were both on the same latitude directly in line with each other."

Joe said, "Then when these Entities of Death that have combined into one unrealistically large army cross over the Great Euphrates River of blood, as you said, what happens next?"

Tom held up his hand indicating for Joe to pause. "Park you're thought for now, as Mel has once again intervened. God of Heaven places the thought into their minds to first do some house cleaning using the fire and brimstone as their tools."

"You mean nuking, don't you?" replied Joe.

Maria said, "Joe, you have such a way with words!" and just left it at that since by his expression she could see that he thought it was a compliment. She finished her thought asking, "House cleaning?"

Tom commented, "I guess everything will be told to us sooner or later by Mel."

Tom moved forward saying, "Joe, you're going to love this. 200 million Entities of Death slaughter 200 million zombies and their blood will travel southwards 200 miles as gravity assists in the flow."

Joe said, "If the mile portion were stretched to 266 then the three above numbers would total 666. Another 'weird or what' incident."

Maria commented, "It's a bit of a stretch Joe, but sometimes you make sense."

Joe rebutted saying, "I always make sense. You're just not at my level."

"Thank goodness," came her muted reply.

Tom continued, "Maria, Joe's right."

Joe replied, somewhat bewilderingly, "I knew it, but just for Maria's sake, please inform her how right I am."

Tom continued, "When Joe said that if the miles were stretched to 266 then the three above numbers would total 666. Maria, your input gave me the answer to be able to understand Joe's comment. The zombie pyramid along with its trail of blood could easily reach 266 miles in length."

Maria, somewhat perplexed by Joe's grasp said, "You said that by the time the slaughter of the zombies was completed the total body count would be one third of the population on earth just as foretold in the Bible."

Joe said, "There are about 2 gallons of blood in a large man and multiply this amount by 200 million people you get, 400 million gallons of blood. Put another way, enough blood to fill up all the cars in the USA."

Maria tossed in her own zinger saying, "Does that also include Canada?" and before Joe could answer, sighed and said, "I can't even imagine such gross things and who talks like that? You're both weird."

Both Joe and Tom complimented each other and agreed the analogy was perfect.

All three were now rambling about so many Entities of Death heading on their westward trek across the Middle East and killing great numbers of lost 1-color zombies. Tom was about to say something when he went silent.

Maria poked him slightly but he was unresponsive and for the next several minutes he was transfixed.

Tom snapped out of his trance mid-stream of a sentence saying, "We got it wrong."

Joe said, "Got what wrong?"

Maria said, "Give him some space Joe. He's not quite right. He's 'out of sorts'."

Tom said that Mel had just spoken to him.

Maria said this was the first time that they actually witnessed Mel in action manifesting through Tom.

Joe asked again, "What did you mean that we got it wrong?"

Tom replied, "A little while ago we were discussing how these Entities of Death travel across the Middle East killing everything in their sight. Mel just told me how they all come to be there and how they do it."

Maria said, "I'm not quite following you Tom. What do you mean?"

Tom continued saying that Mel sort of gave him a recap or overview of things to come.

Excitedly, Joe said, "Can you remember them?"

Tom replied, "I will never be able to forget them. They're indelibly inscribed in my mind."

"So just calm down and recite them." said Maria.

Tom said, "OK. Maria, get a pen and paper.

I.   Those with the 3-color tattoos are the people of pride having his mark on their foreheads and are as you say the 3-color zombies.

II. Those who rejected the offer of salvation of the Two Witnesses and voluntarily turned to Satan then automatically received his 3-color tattoo.

III. After the 1290 T/D., the 1-color tattoos come into existence, when only out of fear of death people took the mark of the beast but only on their right hand. They had no conviction of any faith.

IV. Now listen closely, after the 1400 T/D has been reached, this concludes year one. Next comes the 900 days granted to the rest of the people on earth that produces the 'saved' people. Those who accepted the testimony of the Two Witnesses are Baptized unto Repentance.

V.   Mel said they don't get their Baptism, spark and go into the pillar of fire. Remember, they still have to prove their loyalty to their God of Heaven.

VI. They will be tempted by the deceiving prophets and spirits calling, "Look here is the Christ". Do not believe it. False Christ's and false prophets will rise and show great signs and wonders to deceive you. They will say to some "Look he is in the desert" or "He is in the inner room". Do not believe them when they call out unto you. It will be no easy matter to remain faithful. Remember, salvation is no easy matter. The people still have their earthly lusts for riches and power. Remember, God said in the book of Job, "Will he make supplications to you? Will he speak softly to you?" Remember, Satan never quits trying for more trophies.

VII. Many of these people soil their garments of salvation, forfeiting eternal life. You ask how they accomplish this. Remember the band of Korah? Even in the midst of a miracle, they challenged God's will. Perhaps I will dwell on this in greater detail later.

VIII. After 3 days the 1-color zombies, get up from slithering on their bellies and follow the pillar of fire no matter where they are on earth.

IX. The 3-color zombies, in Israel (the area of the sea beast, or as you say, the false president) and in the lands surrounding the conurbation of Rome (in the lands of the land beast) or as you say the False Prophet, also stay put.

X. Now pay close attention, the 3-color zombies, everywhere else on earth, also rise up after exactly 6 days (I shouldn't have to explain the significance of this number) and follow on the heels of the 1-color zombies who are themselves following the pillar of fire. This delay prevents them from running into the first group who are only a bit ahead of them.

XI. The three of you had the story partially correct. The people stay indoors, they do not flee to the hills, and they just wait out the two groups of hordes as they pass by after which only they remain.

XII. When the 1-color zombies become mobile, their ever increasing vast hordes will take over a week to pass by the saved people sequestered within their homes.

XIII. Their homes are safe havens from the screaming hordes due to the mark of blood applied by angels to the doors of their homes. This mark is actually the blood from the Martyrs of Christ. The infected stay clear of this blood mark. Trust me, this scenario is very complicated but this rationale is good enough for you.

XIV. After the horde of 1-color zombies have passed by, come the 3-color zombies who again can take up to another week. As they pass by, the newly infected join their ranks and move on.

XV. So after a while the horde of the 1-color zombies can take at least a week for them to pass by the saved within their homes in the zone just attacked by the Flying Hell Monsters. Also, on their heels come the horde of the 3-color zombies that after a while will also take at least another week to pass by. As their numbers grow so does the speed of their travel. Finally, in India, there will be 200 million 1-color followed by 200 million 3-color zombies.

XVI. All the saved will remain within their dwellings during the migration of these hordes as they come rushing by, screaming and howling. The effects of their pain can be heard a great distance away as when a thunderstorm is approaching. The stench of the 1-color zombies after a while is so great it causes those in their dwellings to involuntarily shiver and make a hissing sound as words cannot express their reactions.

XVII. The hatred of the Entities of Death will cause them to also hiss as they kill everything in their path, leaving only death behind. Their hissing comes from their tails like that of a snake.

XVIII. There is an order that must be followed, first the Thunder/Fire Lightning Messages, then the Two Witnesses in tandem with the pillar of fire, on their heels come the Flying Hell Monsters using your vernacular after which come the hordes of the damned.

XIX. You may wonder how the saved will be fed in the 6 angel halos. Remember how Jesus with only a few loaves of bread and some fish fed thousands. Don't worry, they won't run out of food or water and besides there is plenty of food abandoned by the two groups of zombies.

XX. The pillar of fire migration will take zombies across all populated areas on earth. Remember how the Israelites had to follow the pillar of fire for almost 40 years? After the areas previously known as Africa, and North and South America have been dispensed with, the pillar of fire travels through the northern lands of the bear, dragon and tiger and adjacent areas. All are drawn like moths to light, the pillar of fire. By the end of the 1260 days of Testimony of the Two Witnesses there will only be three categories of people, the saved, the 1-color and the 3-color zombies. Except for those within the lands of the sea beast and land beast, everyone else will congregate in the land of India.

XXI. As both groups of zombies enter India, we have the 1-color zombies following the pillar of fire and the 3-color zombies following them. The 1-color zombies are allowed to exit into and through Pakistan which is the last angel halo. They still follow the pillar of fire only a few days ahead of them for the next 150 days.

XXII. The 3-color zombies must stay put. They remain within India congregating along the border of Pakistan for these same 150 days allowing for the recently infected to recover and join their ranks.

XXIII. All 3-color then merge with and are bound to the fallen angels now Hell Horses and once combined become the Entities of Death as you called them.

XXIV. Your thinking was correct that their tongues rotted in their mouths. This caused them to scream, howl and hiss. Once merged with the Hell Horses, their minds became as one and that's why your description Entities of Death is most appropriate.

XXV. These armies are bound at the border separating India and Pakistan and only begin their path of destruction when released after the 150 days have expired at the 2300 T/D. One should take note that also at this time the Two Witnesses of God have now exited this last dome and have crossed over the dried up Great Euphrates River. Other than the obvious that they have moved on, now there is no more pillar of fire.

XXVI. Those 1-color zombies that were allowed 150 days ago to enter and pass through Pakistan when they were following the pillar of fire by now have ended their migration at the Great Euphrates River now dried up. Upon their arrival, they become estopped.

XXVII. Now, these 1-color zombies, having no point of direction since the pillar of fire is now gone, begin meandering in search of blood to drink. Not far away they find lots of it in Lake Tharthar about 100 miles north east of the ancient city of Babylon in Iraq.

XXVIII. Upon the release of the 3-color zombies at the 2300 T/D., they now cross into and through Pakistan and form many single lines of riders stretching 666 miles from north to south. From space, as you like to say, this line would be from the northern border limits of Pakistan down to its most southern portion, the Arabian Sea. The appearance of this army viewed from the heavens appears as a dark shadow moving across the Middle East.

XXIX. They will form hundreds of such north to south columns, miles deep and truly a sight not to be seen.

XXX. These Entities of Death sweep across the lands of Pakistan, Afghanistan, Iran, and Iraq, killing anything and everything in their path of slaughter. Truly no life exists behind them.

XXXI. All humans now only exist in front of them and are made up of the 1-color they are pursuing along with wandering 3-colors who having no horse to ride were considered expendable. The remaining 3-colors were on the other side of the dried up Great Euphrates River living in the lands of the sea and land beast that you call the false president and false prophet.

XXXII. The roar of their insanity and weapons will be heard hundreds of miles away.

XXXIII. The column of 'riders of death' will travel a serpentine route. Even though it is less than 2,000 miles to the dried river bank of the Great Euphrates River their distance of travel is much greater. The route of Entities of Death will take them, as in the days of Moses, when 40 days turned into 40 years. So in the past what took only minutes to accomplish now will take them 150 days as they are also now earthbound.

XXXIV. The 1-color and 2-color zombies will hear these Entities of Death coming from a far off distance and this drives them into a frenzy. The approaching Entities of Death now begin their final assault by corralling and driving them to the ancient city of Babylon. They will, in vain, attempt to climb the invisible wall miles high, their efforts futile. The next event is witnessed by their god the Great Red Dragon who is enjoying every minute of the action.

XXXV. Tom, as to what happens next your assumptions were for the most part accurate.

Tom, after speaking the last sentence, slumped into his chair and immediately fell asleep.

Maria covered him will a blanket saying, "Perhaps we too should get some rest."

Joe said, "Maybe we should review all these pointers from Mel to be helpful when Tom wakes up."

"Right," she said. However, only minutes later, they too were sleeping.

Chapter Thirty-Nine
BIBLICAL SUPPORT FOR ZOMBIES

After some well-deserved rest, they once again began discussing the prior events.

Tom, now refreshed, began by saying, "That was the longest dream that I have had in which Mel was talking to me."

Maria asked, "Tom, do you know what you dictated to me?"

"Not a clue," he replied. "It seems like Mel is keeping the facts straight for some reason."

"Rightly so," she commented. "Too bad many didn't read your book before the Rapture came and went, sort of like us." she muttered.

"Exactly so," replied Tom.

Joe asked, "Could you see him?"

Tom's reply was, "Thank goodness, no." and left it at that.

Maria asked Tom if he was up to continuing their topic about these zombies.

Tom said, "Let's get on with it. There's lots to cover."

Joe replied, "Great." and asked, "What does the Bible have to say about them?"

Tom answered, "More than you ever thought possible."

Maria commented, "I don't think we're going to like what we hear next about these 'zombie flesh eaters', and before Joe says it, 'blood drinkers'."

Tom began by saying, "Let's read what the Prophet Jeremiah recorded about what God has to say in chapter 19:8-9. He says: I will make this city desolate and a <u>hissing</u>, <u>everyone who passes by it</u>

will be astonished and hiss because of all its plagues.[57]" He further says they will eat the flesh of people.

During my limited research of 'Cannibalism in the Bible', I came across about 10 instances of the Israelites doing such gross things. They only did these abominations out of desperation that they brought on themselves because they always turned away from their God.

Now the Prophet Ezekiel writes in chapter 5:9-12 that God is angry due to their abominations as we just read and now we read[58].

God says, 'and I will do among you what I have never done, and the like of which I will never do again,' because of all your abominations.

Therefore fathers shall eat their sons in your midst, and sons shall eat their fathers.

This shows us that God is going to do to the Israelites and others a onetime and only a onetime horrific event."

Tom said, "The Bible further says, even the most gentle and sensitive man among you will have no compassion on his own brother or the wife he loves or his surviving children, and he will not give to one of them any of the flesh of his children that he is eating."

Joe commented, "That's even gorier than I thought."

Maria said, "It's easy to grasp the meaning. This isn't referring to the past instances of cannibalism in the Bible when the Israelites brought upon themselves such calamities, is it? This will be a one-time future event."

"Exactly," Tom said. "God continues his judgement saying[59], 'Therefore, as I live,' says the Lord God, 'surely, because you have defiled My sanctuary with all your detestable things and with all your abominations, therefore I will also diminish you; My eye will not spare, nor will I have any pity.

One-third of you shall die of the pestilence, and be consumed with famine in your midst."

Tom paused for a moment to let this sink in and then said, "When I looked into the meaning of the word 'pestilence', I found it to mean; one of the four Horsemen of the Apocalypse in Revelations symbolizing plague (contagious and infectious disease). This third are the 1-color zombies slaughtered by the Entities of Death.

God further said, <u>One-third</u> shall fall by the sword all around you. I believe this third are the people living in Babylon the Great, the areas surrounding the Mediterranean Sea, the areas controlled by the false prophet. They are killed by the Entities of Death because God has put this thought into their minds to do so."

Tom further stated that God then said, "<u>One-third</u> I will scatter to all the winds, and I will draw out a sword after them."

"I believe that this third will be destroyed by the Son of God during the battle of Armageddon.

Are you OK with one more passage?"

As Joe and Maria nodded, Tom continued, "In Joel 1:6 we read: 'For a nation has come up against my land, powerful and beyond number; its teeth are lions' teeth, and it has the fangs of a lioness."

Maria said, "I really didn't think that there would be so many passages in the Bible dealing this topic."

Tom agreed saying, "OK, so let's summarize this information."

Joe snickered saying, "Now, like Mel, Tom's doing the numbers thing."

1. Tom, appeasing him, said, "But I only have eight points.
2. Fathers shall eat the flesh of their sons.
3. They shall eat the flesh of their daughters.
4. Everyone shall eat the flesh of their friends.
5. Sons shall eat their fathers.
6. They shall be driven to despair as the circumstances are too much to cope with.
7. There is a furious struggle for survival with utter disregard of consequences.
8. And <u>I will do among you</u> what I have never done because of all your abominations, <u>and the like of which I will never do again.</u> Never will this plague be repeated as it is so horrific.
9. People who see these zombies will hiss utter contempt by making this sound. These possibly are the people having the Mark of God and/or the Entities of Death hissing at the black tattoo zombies."

Tom continued, "It's clear to me that soon zombies will be on the earth. This plague will be a one-time event and we know it will last 1260 days."

Maria commented, "Tom, just a minute ago you said that fathers shall eat their sons and sons shall eat their fathers <u>in your midst</u>. Then you said <u>one-third of you shall die of the pestilence</u>, and be <u>consumed</u> with <u>famine in your midst</u>. Did you understand what you just said?"

Tom looked somewhat perplexed saying, "What are you getting at? What did I miss?"

Maria answered, "Twice God says 'in your midst'. This means that the good people will see the zombies eating the flesh of people in their midst. Just picture this! They sort of look out their windows and witness these atrocities and soon these zombies will be slaughtered at the invisible wall at the Great Euphrates River."

"The next time when God said 'in your midst', you said one-third of you shall die of the pestilence, and be consumed with famine in your midst. The good people will see the Zombie Virus <u>pestilence</u> resulting in the zombies, <u>consumed</u> with <u>famine</u>.

Tom, I think pestilence means that they will die from an infectious epidemic disease that is virulent and devastating. Joe has been calling it the Zombie Blood-Virus resulting in the Zombie Plagues.

When you said consumed, I think that it means to take in as food, eat or drink as in cannibalism when the zombies attack humans for meat and blood drinking.

About famine, I think zombies will experience an extreme, fierce and savage, devouring hunger. A comparison is like ravenous, wild, ravening wolves craving and eating a great deal of food in the attempt to satisfy an insatiable hunger lust."

Tom said, "That's exactly what's going to happen. The final person attacked and infected with the Zombie Virus and who turns into a zombie will take place at the 2300 T/D when the Two Witnesses have left the seventh and last angel halo and cross over the dried up Great Euphrates River and back into Israel to where they first started their mission 1260 days earlier."

Joe, out of left field, jumped in saying, "Speaking of the river of blood, what about the drinking of blood."

Tom started laughing and said, "We haven't come to this section just yet. It's still a little way ahead."

Joe smiled saying, "Too bad. I know you've got the Biblical support because you keep snickering every time I mention blood drinking. I know from watching 'zombie' and 'vampire' movies about these so called flesh eaters. The act of eating blood is more common than people know. For example, vampire bats and cannibals drink blood. European butchers drink blood when making blood sausage which is used as a thickener for sauces.

Reference material states that in the past, during executions in continental Europe, where the axe fell routinely on the necks of criminals, blood was the medicine of choice for many epileptics.

In Denmark, the young Hans Christian Andersen saw parents getting their sick child to drink blood at the scaffold. So popular was this treatment that hangmen routinely had their assistants catch the blood in cups as it spurted from the necks of dying felons."

Maria interjected, "Ugh! That's gross!"

Joe continued, "Some vampire cult followers have been sucking over two quarts of blood a month straight from human donors for decades. I've even heard of a mother who says she is part of a huge underground sub-culture of other blood drinkers around the world, and doctors say the craze is gaining momentum."

Joe looked over at Maria and even though she was turning green, he continued, "Haematologists have reported that a variety of cultures have been drinking blood for thousands of years but it could be due to deficiencies in the body.

There has been a resurgence of cult drinking blood vampirism in this country and throughout the world, possibly due to all the cult TV shows and movies that have become so popular."

Joe further talked about a girl who started drinking blood with a vampire cult in a cemetery. On returning home <u>she hissed at her mother and stepfather</u>, calling them 'humans', <u>as well as hissing at the family dog.</u> He continued, "What seems strange about this is the fact the word '<u>hissed</u>' is used in connection with blood sucking. The Bible says that people will look at the 'zombies' <u>and hiss at them</u>, weird or what?"

Maria commented, "It's so gory that people were, and still are today, blood thirsty, sort of a harbinger of things to come."

Maria once again said she was amazed at all this 'weird or what' information in Joe's head that she was unaware of.

Tom acquiesced saying, "OK Joe, since you're so persistent would you care to read what the Bible has to say about blood drinking?"

Joe not missing a beat replied, "How about we do this after lunch."

Maria gave him that 'I'm going to hurt you expression' and snickering, he changed his mind.

Tom said, "I promised to get back to this subject and here we go. Joe, you take over now."

Joe began reading in Revelation 16:4-6, "Then the third angel poured out his bowl on <u>the rivers and springs of water, and they became blood.</u> And I heard the angel of the waters saying: "You are righteous, O Lord, The One who is and who was and who is to be, Because You have judged these things. For they have shed the blood of saints and prophets, <u>and You have given them blood to drink.</u> For it is their just due."

Joe continued, "You've got to be kidding! I knew you would have some references but this is amazing. The Bible actually says, the 'waters turn to blood' and it says 'give them blood to drink'. It doesn't get any clearer than this."

Maria said, "It seems like since there is only blood to drink, then they must drink it to survive."

Tom nodded and continued, "In addition, don't forget that the plagues of the Two Witnesses of God will include controlling the rain, <u>turning water to blood</u> and to <u>strike the earth with all plagues,</u> as often as they desire as they travel to all nations.

The Bible makes many references whereby waters were turned to blood, cannibalism and blood drinkers."

Joe said, "So there you have it. The Bible says they will eat the flesh of people and they will be blood drinkers, and by this I mean zombies and vampires, not the Hollywood zombies and vampires but these will be actual cursed people. What more can be said!"

Maria asked, "Can you explain in more detail the sound they make?"

For some reason Tom had drifted once again into the 'weird or what' zone and was jolted back to reality by her words. He replied, "Due to their extreme pain, mental insanity and the fact that their tongues have rotted and fallen off, the zombies will make very strange sounds when moving. A type of sound that depicts a crazy person, perhaps screaming like a siren sound that can be heard a great distance away."

Joe commented, "You know that last thing you said, that they have no tongues, that's a real humdinger. They can't talk so they scream, and their pain causes them to scream extremely loudly. A long time ago, I read that it was possible for a person to make a siren sound as loud as a police siren that can be heard from a good distance. The howl of wolves can also be heard for miles creating great fear in people."

Maria replied, "Those with God's mark, even though they're protected, would still be alarmed just like when we hear a siren and it concerns us."

Joe added, "Forget the siren. Remember a few years ago when we were camping and heard the howling of wolves far off in the distance?"

Maria added, "And even though we were in our camper we were still frightened by their howling."

Joe asked, "Hey, do you think that both the stage one and stage two zombies will make this horrible sound?"

Maria thought, then said, "You know, I think both the 1 and 2-color zombies initially scream and howl during their first 150 days. This is their death screaming."

Joe piped in saying, "Remember when we heard, during one of our camping trips, an animal being attacked and killed during the night?"

Maria said, "How can I forget it? The sound of its screaming seemed to go on for ever. It was terrifying to listen to."

Joe said, "You know Maria, when I asked our neighbor in the next campsite about it, he said it was a rabbit that got killed by a coyote or something."

Maria shivered saying, "You mean all that screeching came from such a small animal? Imagine the sound a zombie could make. It could frighten a wolf. Just talking about it makes me feel creepy."

Joe said, "After their 150 days of Maria's 'death screaming'. . . "

"Hey! Don't say it like that Joe! Say 'after the zombies finish their 150 days of 'death screaming'. Now, what were you saying?"

Joe continued, "I stand corrected. Now, as I was saying before being rudely interrupted, only the 1-color zombies will continue their 'death screaming' after their 150 days are over because then they devolve into stage two zombies and continue until the end of their days."

Maria added, "Yah, the Entities of Death will for sure hear them but this may be music to their ears and this sounds leads them directly to them during their travels across the Middle East."

Tom said, "Remember, we talked about the good people staying in their dwellings as the hordes pass them by."

Maria replied, "But they will hear the screaming and howling for some time. Imagine, as the column of zombies grows in numbers and let's say one hundred thousand of these screaming and howling things rush by their dwellings, it's going to be nerve racking to say the least."

Joe said, "Can you imagine when you say a million or millions pass by them screaming and howling, they won't be just scared, they'll be terrified by their howling."

Tom said, "If that many howling wolves rushing by your house, their volume would be deafening."

Maria said, "I'm already scared and glad we won't be around when they come this way. Right Tom?"

Tom smiled, nervously saying, "Absolutely 100% correct!"

Joe said to Maria, "Well your animals won't be sticking around. When they hear this sound they take to the hills."

Maria said, changing topics for a while, "Tom, from what you've told us, the continents will all be rejoined like in times past. So when will this happen?"

Tom answered, "When the first thunder message takes place, very soon now. This is the start of their recombining."

Maria asked, "Will we notice this happening?"

Tom said, "Trust me. It may knock us to the ground because the earth will be shaking so much it will seem to last forever."

Joe agreed and commented, "I think that when entire continents move, the effect won't be as violent as when earthquakes hit but it will definitely be a weird sensation."

Maria said, "Maybe it may feel like being on an escalator at an air terminal, you know the type that can move you many football fields to another location. You just stand there, but you know you're moving."

Joe said, "Imagine having a view from space during and after this happens. The earth must look like one large land mass surrounded by water. I wonder if the pole caps are still there."

"Good question," replied Tom, "because I even wonder if the earth had pole caps in the time of Noah before the continents split apart?"

Joe quipped, "Ask Mel the next time he shudders you Tom."

Maria added, "You mean when he shivers because to shudder means to shiver convulsively and this we certainly do not want Tom to do."

Maria said she was becoming really confused again. "Tom, could you do a little recapping so I can wrap my thoughts around everything?"

Tom agreed saying, "OK, so I believe that the continents will recombine during the first thunder message and Joe's 'Zombie Plagues' will begin at the 1040 T/D, and conclude upon the 2300 T/D. These are the beginning and ending dates of the Time of Testimony of the Two Witnesses of God. I've also referred to this time period as the 'Time of Redemption' that will begin in Israel, then the entire world, and then end back in Israel."

Joe added, "Yah, and as you said, the plagues also start and end with these dates."

"Yes, Joe, so I believe. To continue, towards the end of their first year of testimony the Two Witnesses' travels will bring them to the outskirts of the area known as Judea, the southern half of Israel. They will hopscotch over this area because it's filled with the antichrist. Certain Israelites will flee to the hills and will be saved by the Two Witnesses of God. Following on their heels, in Judea, come the Flying Hell Monsters. The 3-color tattoo antichrist who upon being attacked and infected with the Zombie Virus do not follow the pillar of fire of God. They will simply stay put. After 150 days they will revert back to some type of normalcy, whatever that may be. The same will be true of their counterparts in northern Israel. Their fate is already sealed. They're part of the 'cull of the damned'.

Maria commented, "Wow, it's a really intricate plan."

"You're right," said Tom, "and that's not all. After year one has passed and Israel and Judea have received the testimony of the Two Witnesses of God, they will now travel to the remaining six Angel Halos that blanket the planet and for the next 900 days, until their Time of Testimony will be completed, they testify to all. This allows them to remain in each Angel Halo for 150 days and then move on to the next one.

The Flying Hell Monsters always follow on the heels of the Two Witnesses as they move from zone to zone. The antichrist has no protection from them. It doesn't matter if people lock themselves into rooms, since these Flying Hell Monsters just go through walls like they aren't there. Nothing can hinder their mission.

As the Two Witnesses of God testify to the people, some will accept, but most will reject their offer of salvation."

Maria asked, "Why wouldn't everyone want to be saved?"

Tom replied, "Remember most people fall for the deceiving tactics of the unholy trinity."

Maria said, "Oh, like when we talked about hundreds of false Christ's going out to deceive the people and Jesus cautioned the people not to fall for their tricks."

Joe commented that Satan has up to now been in charge and his deceivers have done a great job to sway people into accepting him as their returned messiah.

Tom said, "You're right. OK, now back to reality. I've jumped ahead and have to backtrack on our time line. We're almost at the 1040 T/D at which time a game changer takes place, you might say."

"You've said that before. What do you mean by a game changer?" asked Maria.

Both guys rolled their eyes.

Tom replied, "You'll see."

Chapter Forty

HOW THE EVENTS UNFOLD

Tom said, "We've been discussing the 7 Spirits, 7 Thunders, Two Witnesses of God, Flying Hell Monsters and the Zombies. All this begins at the 1040 T/D and lasts 1260 days."

Maria asked, "Why did you use 1260 days instead of 3½ years?"

Tom smiled and commented, "Just to see if you were paying attention."

Joe said he felt slighted that he was not included in the conversation.

Tom said, "OK, Joe's Zombie Plagues last for a time, times and half a time."

Joe replied, "I thought they lasted for 42 months."

Tom, slightly amused, ignored Joe's statement and decided to brain tease him by saying, "Joe let's unite these events forming the mosaic of the matrix showing how they are interconnected."

Before Joe could say, "What?", Maria countered, saying, "Joe, he's just teasing you. Tom means how the pieces of the puzzle form the picture."

"OK, I got carried away on that one." grinned Tom.

"What picture?" was Joe's response.

"Joe, are you kidding me?" replied Maria.

"Guess so, I think." came the reply.

Tom said, "Can we please move forward? For Joe's benefit, the events we just discussed, begin on the 1040 T/D., and continue for the next 3½ years until the 2300 T/D, until the Sanctuary has been cleansed of Satan. This period is referred to in my book's 'road map index', flow chart or whatever Maria calls it."

Tom continued, "During the 'Time of Redemption', you'll see these events begin. You'll experience the 7 SPIRITS OF GOD, the 7 THUNDERS OF GOD, the 2 WITNESSES OF GOD, ANGEL HALO FIRE LIGHTNINGS, ROLLING THUNDER MESSAGES, FLYING HELL MONSTERS, GLOBAL PLAGUES OF ZOMBIES, during the TIME OF REDEMPTION."

Tom now began speaking in a more somber and serious tone saying, "During the 6,000 plus hours it took me to reference and write the book, *Dragon's Tattoo 666*, I think this is how it all takes place."

"Hey," Joe added, "and all the times the antichrist were trying to kill you and you somehow outsmarted them each time?"

"I didn't ever say I outsmarted them Joe," he replied, "I had help."

"Oh no," said Joe, "here comes Mel again. Did you shiver each time back then, too?"

Maria said to Tom, "Don't mind him. He's just jealous."

"Now moving on, Joe, I've been waiting for this information about how all this takes place for some time now."

And Joe nodded approvingly.

Tom commented, "It's complicated, so pay close attention and no joking around Joe."

Maria said, "Yah Joe. Behave yourself."

Tom, losing control again, said, "OK children here we go. The function of the 7 Spirits and 7 Thunders is to herald the coming of the Two Witnesses of God.

People across the earth look up within their respective continent size Angel Halos which are seemingly hundreds of miles high and have a massive great center dome that looks like the underside of an umbrella. Its center has 10 light rays, miles wide, coming out of its hub radiating outwards thousands of miles in all directions. These golden light rays follow the dome's curved surface down to the earth somewhere in the far distance. As I said, these are continent sized domes.

When a person stares upwards, the dome appears as pulsating northern lights, consisting of fire lightning that some call the dance of the spirits.

These global atmospheric wonders are used to get the attention of everyone on earth simultaneously.

Now, with all the people gazing up into the heavens seeing this fire lightning that's filling in the entire undersurface of the dome, they all hear a tremendous voice from the 7 thunders of God proclaiming their first of seven messages. This message is spoken worldwide and in unison in the mother tongue to everyone on earth, which in itself is a wonder.

The fire lightning and thunder message combine, producing a magnificent Heavenly Wonder that all on earth see, hear and feel simultaneously and they have no echoes which in itself is unique as their message is truly global and simultaneous."

Tom looked at Maria and Joe and asked, "Are you still with me?"

When they nodded, he continued, "Unique to the Angel Halo where the Two Witnesses of God are active, is the pillar of fire. During the first 12 months this takes place only in the land of Israel and then for the next two and a half years in the remaining six continent size Angel Halos across the earth.

This pillar of fire[60] in Israel appears like in the day of Moses when God looked through the pillar of fire or the 'Eyes of God', as Maria called it, to see what was going on.

The Bible also says, 'God led them by day with a cloudy pillar, And by night with a pillar of fire, to give them light on the road which they should travel.'"

Maria said, "Maybe this pillar of fire also guides the Two Witnesses."

Tom replied, "Good thought, and with respect to the pillar of fire, just to be clear, it extends about 5 miles or so upwards with its top projecting out about 20 miles in diameter forming a mini-dome that from the ground looked like the underside of a giant mushroom as well as reaching outwards and downwards touching the earth and covering everyone within its radius. It is about the size of a large city."

Joe asked, "When it touches the earth are there sparks or flames?"

Tom replied, "I don't know. What I do know is that if one touches it, one would receive a strong shock but not die as that would be too easy. No matter what, you cannot pass through it. This ensures that everyone within the dome hears the testimony of the Two Witnesses."

Maria said, "OK, to be clear on this, there are 7 continent sized angel halos and only one mini-dome that has the pillar of fire in it, right?"

"Correct," replied Tom.

Joe added, "You know no one would want to jump into the next angel halo as they would be attacked by the Flying Hell Monsters all over again."

Maria said, "What about those who hear and desire salvation offered by the Two Witnesses."

Tom replied, "They are instructed to raise their hands to their God of Heaven. Immediately, out of the pillar of fire comes fire lightning called the 'Fingers of God' and touches them. They receive the 'Baptism unto Repentance' and the Mark of God upon their foreheads and as the Finger of God touches them, they appear to sparkle.

The work of the Two Witnesses is now completed for those in this zone. Those newly Baptised unto Repentance are instructed to remain behind closed doors for the next while until the plagues pass them by."

Tom repeated the time table for Joe saying, "Remember, the first year, is for the Israelites. They are told to listen to the gentle voice talking within them (the Holy Spirit), telling them which way to travel upon the 'King's (God's) Highway'. This is a supernatural route that only those Baptised unto Repentance can see and travel upon and are protected by God. This route will safely lead them to the location into the Wilderness Sanctuary where they can worship at the altar of God in His partially opened Temple.

The second two and a half years, is for the nations of the 10 kings. The saved are instructed to keep their garments and remain faithful to the God of Heaven.

They are instructed to wait for a while until the forces of God come, gather and bring them to the Wedding Feast.

OK, so moving on, in each zone being testified to, the pillar of fire is the only light source. This zone has a mini-dome covering it, good for some, and bad for others. Natural sunlight is blocked out with the light source only coming from the pillar of fire, failing which there would only be a thick darkness within it."

Joe said, "It seems like the pillar of fire continues throughout the Angel Halo on a predetermined route."

Tom answered, "The pillar of fire within the mini-dome not only touches the ground but its roots extend deep down into the bottomless pit where the Flying Hell Monsters are being restrained. As the pillar of fire moves to the next zone a different type of light comes back, similar to natural sunlight, from the upper regions of the continent angel halo, but only fleetingly.

It's my belief that from the base of the pillar of fire comes smoke out of the bottomless pit that darkens this light. Out of the ensuing darkness comes the clatter of beating wings as chariots of war. This must be a horrific sound and remember, because there are millions or billions of these things the people can't see because of the darkness caused when they block all light. Once released, these Flying Hell Monsters attack everyone not having the Mark of God in that zone and then move on to the next zones in succession."

Maria said, "I'm on information overload, Tom."

Tom replied, "Do you want me to stop?"

Maria shook her head saying to please continue but looked very confused. "Perhaps take it even slower."

Tom continued, "These Flying Hell Monsters will keep attacking in this fashion from zone to zone within this continent sized Angel Halo and in all subsequent Angel Halos across the earth until the time of the Two Witnesses of God has been completed at the end of their 1260 days of testimony."

Maria said, "Now I'm lost. Is the pillar of fire dome the same thing as the angel halo dome?"

Joe replied, "I don't think so, Maria. I think I heard that they're two different domes. One covers an entire continent so that the antichrist can't flee and not hear the testimony of the Two Witnesses. Remember many reject. The mini- dome has within it, the pillar of fire and the Two Witnesses."

"Got it now," she said, "a big and a little dome."

"Good job!" replied Tom. "Now as the Two Witnesses finish testifying and along with the pillar of fire move to another zone, the Flying Hell Monsters carry out their attacks following on their heels. As these Flying Hell Monsters also exit, in their wake, this strange light returns. However, this is of little comfort to those remaining in that zone as they have all been attacked and infected with the Zombie Virus. They, by now, are all lying on the ground flopping and crying out in great pain. They long for death which eludes them."

Maria said, "When you just said that normal light returns but this is of little help because they have all been attacked. What about those who accepted? What about them?"

Tom clarified his thoughts, "OK, in the land of Israel you're correct because they travel upon this supernatural highway. In the land of the 10 kings this light would be necessary for the saved. Yes, the zombies wouldn't need it but the saved need it. Thanks, Maria."

Joe said, "As you were saying Tom, this must be really scary. Imagine such torment, wanting to die but death is denied, truly hell on earth. Does the Bible use the word Zombie?"

Maria couldn't help herself, her mouth beating her brain, saying, "Yes, they're called, Joes."

Tom replied, "Please children. As to Joe's question, the answer is no because the word zombie didn't exist back then. It's a modern term for the undead."

Joe jumped in saying, "Even Mel calls them zombies, right Tom?"

"I really can't remember, Joe. Nevertheless, call it what you will, there will come the 'Plague of the Zombies'."

Maria replied in one breath, "You know what they say about payback. I think I need a scotch."

Someone muttered, "What a waste."

Someone got elbowed.

After a break and with minds refreshed Tom continued. "Now during the first year in Israel, the Pillar of Fire will move on a daily basis from zone to zone. The Two Witnesses testify to perhaps 50,000 people each day. During the balance of the two and a half years or 900 days, they testify to perhaps 50,000 each hour on the hour of each day. This 50,000 each hour was only based upon 1 billion people. Imagine if there were say 3-5 billion."

Maria said, "I can't. Even at one billion, its mind boggling."

Joe commented, "You know, if there were billions that would create more zombies and more of everything. Maria's right, its mind boggling."

Tom continued as if he had not been interrupted. "You know, those outside of Israel see and hear wondrous Thunder Messages happening within their specific Angel Halo. However, their time is yet to come as the time of the saved nations will start at the beginning of year two when the Two Witnesses will come to them."

Maria said, "So they are being encouraged throughout the entire time of the Two Witnesses by these thunder/lightning messages to not be deceived."

Joe asked, "Who are these 7 Thunders?"

Tom replied, "Their identity and messages are currently sealed as recorded in Revelation 10:1-4[61]. It says that "The seven thunders uttered their voices. I (Apostle John) was about to write, but I heard a voice from heaven saying to me, 'Seal up the things which the seven thunders uttered, and do not write them.'

It seems like the Apostle John heard and understood their messages but he was not permitted to write them down verbatim. I did not read anywhere that he was forbidden to perhaps indirectly refer to them so perhaps in the book of Revelations and elsewhere there may be furtive discovery passages."

Maria commented, "That's really a stretch, Tom."

Tom agreed commenting, "At first that's what I thought until I came across another reference that peaked my imagination. Maria, what do you think of this passage recorded at the end of the book of Revelation 22:10 and he said to me, 'Do not seal the words of the prophecy of this book, for the time is at hand.'

Perhaps this is a furtive discovery message in itself because we are the end of days. This verse indicates to me that if one were to look deep enough one might be able to find their seven messages."

Joe asked, "Just out of curiosity, how long did it take for the Apostle John to write everything that is recorded in the Book of Revelation?"

Tom's answered, "Some say it took from the year 70 -100 A.D. Why do you ask, Joe?"

Joe replied, "Well, since it possibly took him 30 years to record everything, it stands to reason that over time that which was 'first sealed became unsealed'. So your idea of finding hidden furtive references in the Bible seems to be well founded."

Maria almost fell out of her chair. She said, "Joe, that's amazing, what you just said about 'first sealed became unsealed' makes perfect sense." and gave him a big hug and kiss.

Joe's ruse worked until later in the day when Maria, scanning Tom's book, came across these exact words 'first sealed became unsealed'.

Maria grunted knowing she had been conned but saw Joe's 'weird or what humor' at its best and began laughing. It then dawned on her that Tom was also in on the ruse, and her laugh changed to a roar. She thought, "It's good to see that even in times like this, humor still abounds."

Tom gathered them together and segued back to the topic and said "Following our little detour, after researching, I've picked out seven proclamations from Revelations, Matthew and Daniel that may serve as humble examples. Each of the 7 Thunders of God have a specific message that corresponds to a specific time and to a specific people."

"That's a mouthful." added Maria.

Tom said, "OK so this is my best attempt to find these elusive, thunder booming, fire lightning messages."

Maria asked, "Did you have help again?"

Tom replied, "Yes, Mel once again sort of tutored me."

Joe asked, "Can you contact Mel at will?"

Tom replied off handily, "It's more like I seem to sense something and then hear him speaking to me, sometimes when sleeping and at times when awake. Seems to me that whenever something 'weird or what' is going to happen, he's there."

Maria said, "Tom, it seems like Mel is your guardian angel."

Joe responded, "Either that or you're nuts."

Tom said, "Thanks for the vote of confidence Joe, but let's get back to our topic. Here are the dates, and I'll try to explain them at the appropriate times.

THUNDER MESSAGE ONE:	1040 T/D
THUNDER MESSAGE TWO:	1260 T/D
THUNDER MESSAGE THREE:	1290 T/D
THUNDER MESSAGE FOUR:	1400 T/D
THUNDER MESSAGE FIVE:	2260 T/D
THUNDER MESSAGE SIX:	2300 T/D (220 days to Armageddon)
THUNDER MESSAGE SEVEN:	2303.5 T/D (216.5 days to Armageddon)

CHAPTER FORTY-ONE

THUNDER MESSAGE ONE 1040 T/D

Fear God and give glory to Him, for the hour of his judgment has come, and worship Him who made heaven and earth, the sea and springs of water.

Revelation 14:6-7

Maria was reminiscing about her past life that now seemed like a vague and foggy memory.

Joe interrupted her thoughts when he said, "Today is that special day." She looked up at Joe holding their official calendar in his hands.

Tom joined saying, "That's right. It's been 1040 days and we're still alive."

Joe was counting the number of times they had played cat and mouse with flying air planes or unidentified flying objects. That number now reached over 40 times. All encounters had the same common denominator, the NG were on the prowl and they eluded them each time.

Those camouflaged deer and rock getups had always kept them out of harm's way. Maria commented that in the early days she hadn't fully appreciated their 'get-ups' full potential, saying, "We could never have made it without them."

Joe added, "You know, after a while, even though each close encounter was nerve racking, the outcome was always predictable. We survived."

Tom doing some reminiscing of his own commented that they had now transmitted slightly over one thousand BSW messages.

Joe said, "It seems like this has become our daily routine to randomly transmit our global news update to thousands of people scattered around the world."

Maria, now fully back to reality, said, "I wonder how many hours of TV watching we've done up to now. I can't believe I even said that. Here I'm talking about watching TV during these days while the unholy trinity has been steadily persecuting the Christians as well as those of other religions who had the guts to say something was drastically wrong with the so called time of peace and the self-proclaimed messiah returned."

Tom added that yes, they were surviving very well in their cave hideaway but the tension they suffered watching their fellow brethren being systematically targeted, killed, captured and who simply disappeared, was mentally exhausting.

Maria spoke, "We've been eagerly waiting for this date and now it's here."

Joe turned on the TV to see what was happening throughout the world. They were surprised by the fact that the religious prophets of the false messiah were issuing bulletins of national and global security. They were informing all, that Christians were in the process of committing terrorist attacks in Israel and possibly in other countries as well. Reports were being released that a newly conjured up virus was going to be secretly added to lakes, rivers and all drinking waters that will be turning them red. This virus they claimed would affect the person's brain similar to malaria mixed with meningitis. They said it will cause people to have hallucinations and imagining all sorts of things such of which nightmares are made of. One report even said it could be fire breathing monsters. One medical doctor commented that he had just been given information taken from captured Christians that indicated that the virus would make people sick for about half a year but not kill them. He continued saying that its effects were worse than death as the infected would, as indicated in the report, make people into zombies along with other weird things.

Maria asked Tom why the unholy trinity along with their followers were talking about these things?

Tom replied that the antichrist were preparing for what was to come next in hopes of minimising their effects. The authorities had begun these vigorous campaigns in the attempt to conceal the true nature of these events with propaganda, lies and more lies.

Maria commented, "They can't hide the truth so they're trying to distort it by supplying misinformation and all the while claiming to the world that the Christians are responsible."

Joe said, "It seems strange that the so called messiah of earth has nothing to say as to how he let this catastrophe take place."

Tom replied, "Give him time. He will very soon declare all-out war and instruct everyone on earth to capture these Christians and place them in detention centers. The false prophet will intervene, claiming that these Christians have been deceived by their leaders and only they should be charged with terrorism and executed. The false prophet will also declare that the rest of the Christians scattered across the world will be given the opportunity to repent and accept in faith their messiah who loves them."

Joe said, "It's amazing how the unholy trinity can weasel out of everything."

Tom said, "He will most likely also claim that the angel halo domes are of his doing to contain the plagues caused by these Christians."

Tom continued, "We've been waiting for this day and we're not being disappointed. A great many events will now being at 5 p.m."

Maria asked, "For some time now, you have predicted that today at 5 p.m. the first Thunder Message will take place. How do you know this?"

Tom merely commented that Mel had informed him.

"Oh him again!" she said.

Joe was the official time keeper for the countdown and began giving a 10 second countdown, saying, "Here we go folks.

Joe was the first to spot the Heavenly wonder out of the corner of his eye exactly when Tom/Mel had predicted. "There's something high up in space, just like when at night you stare up into the stars and see a reflection from a passing satellite."

Tom pointed towards it saying, "Look, it's like a mini 4th of July fireworks explosion."

They all watched as this small sparkle grew in intensity and very quickly formed lines.

Tom now yelled, "Here we go. We're actually looking at the underside of the angel halo as it develops."

Maria, excitedly said, "You were right when you said it would resemble the underside of an umbrella and those lines are beginning to glow."

Joe replied, "Never thought anything could look and actually be so huge."

Tom excitedly said, "See those rays of light? They're extending outwards thousands of miles and even though we can't see it, these light rays actually dome down to the earth. Remember, we talked about them."

All by now were mesmerized as they gazed into the heavens and in a matter of minutes the entire sky looked like the underside of an umbrella. The light rays, now fully sparkling, grew in intensity.

Maria said, "I can feel their presence. Remember when we talked about the Northern Lights and explorers reported they were in the midst of electrical light? That's how I feel, and strangely enough, it's reassuring."

Joe remarked, "It's like when the hairs on the back of your neck stand up."

Tom commented, "Have you ever had a premonition? That's how I feel."

Maria said, "It's not a premonition Tom. We know what's going to happen next."

No sooner had her words finished when the air filled with visibly electrical light that sparked all around them, as if they were in the middle of millions of fire flies. Now this electrical light began to make a tingling sensation upon their faces that felt soothing but weird.

Joe said, "Imagine everyone on earth experiencing the same thing."

Tom said, "Whether they're indoors or outside like us, they would all be seeing and feeling the same thing."

As they basked in the calmness of this light for a minute or so, a massive sub-sonic boom knocked them to the ground, and definitely got their attention. It was like thunder, but hundreds of times more powerful; you could feel it pounding your body.

Tom exclaimed, "Here we go guys! The continents are now recombining and Joe's right. What a beautiful view this must look like from space."

Maria said, I'm frightened. Tom! How long are these trembling's going to last?"

Tom said, "Hours or days, possibly."

Joe said, "The distance between New York City and London is about 3500 miles. If the continents recombine at the rate of 100 mph, then it would only take about a day and a half for all this to take place."

Maria said, "It seems to feel more like a cruise ship in rough waves."

Joe said, "If you didn't know what was going on, you would be terrified."

"Look at my face Joe! Does it look happy?"

"More like your mother's." And before Maria could respond, a booming thunder now started to resonate, making a low growling sound that didn't seem to end, and in fact would go on for a day and a half. The electrical pulsating light was now growing in intensity. These enormous pulsating light rays seemed hundreds of mile wide and thousands of miles away, reaching up from earth's surface to the center hub of the angel halo way up in space.

Maria pointed up and said, "Look!"

The electrical mist surrounding them now began moving upwards into the sky. Soon it began filling in the spaces between the 10 massive light rays. The air was charged and all knew instinctively that something was about to happen, sort of like when the hair on your neck goes up and lightning strikes nearby.

Joe looked at the sky and said, "The electrical mist has now completely filled in between the light rays and the natural light from the sun is no more."

Maria said, "We're looking at something resembling the Northern Lights, just millions of times more powerful." She continued, "I can see why they called it the dance of the spirits."

The entire undersurface of the angel halo's dome was made up of a scintillating fire and lightning show, complete with that low thundering sound. At times it even seemed as if voices were also being heard, and that was another 'weird or what' occurrence.

Joe said, "We can't see the clouds any more. Will we be able to see the stars tonight?"

Tom answered, "No. For the next 1260 days, all people on earth will look up and see this sky fire that at times thunder-talks to them."

Joe said, "Is that why the false prophet also draws fire from the sky?"

Tom was actually impressed with Joe's question and said, "You know, I never thought of it like that but it seems logical that the false prophet, in plain view of the false president, will also call forth fire from the sky in his attempt to deceive the people. He will claim the sky fire dome is his doing but the thunder messages will undermine his credibility."

Joe asked, "Why did you say that the false prophet, in plain view of the false president, when he commands fire from the sky?"

Tom replied, "The false prophet himself is a human possessed by a deceiving demon that has limited powers. The false president is actually Satan's son, who even though possessing a human being, has been given great powers by his father, Satan."

Joe replied, "It's sort of a demonic dog and pony show that has, up to now, been working."

All three were huddled together, the hair on the back of their necks now standing fully on end just like when in school when you came too close to a giant high voltage tesla coil. This effect grew from being somewhat entertaining to that of an irritation that became close to unbearable.

Tom in a stage whisper said, "Yes! Yes! Here we go. The first Thunder Message is now taking place, as recorded in Revelation 14:6-7"

Fear God and give glory to Him, for the hour of his judgment has come, and worship Him who made heaven and earth, the sea and springs of water.

The words spoken were so loud and thunderous their physical impact almost knocked them to the ground. For the next several minutes they were awestruck and just stood, or more correctly wobbled there, motionless. They had just experienced their first encounter with the 7 Thunder-Spirits of God.

Tom said, "We're high up in the Rockies and these mountains are still quaking."

Joe added, "The higher up you go in a building during an earthquake, the more the building sways."

Tom replied, "Seems like the mountains are moving. It's hard to tell because we have no reference points."

Maria said, "That was totally awesome! What a fantastic Heavenly Wonder!" She had goose bumps to prove it. She had unknowingly latched on to Joe's arm, who had the scratch marks to prove it.

Tom, trying to talk calmly, said, "What we just experienced was heard worldwide, in all the continent sized Angel Halos."

Joe responded, "All the people on earth also must have also looked to the heavens, just like we did, to see this Heavenly Wonder. The entire underside of the angel halo dome was fully engulfed with this thunderous pulsating fire lightning when God's message was being spoken."

Tom pointed and replied, "See it's still raging with pulsating fire and lightning."

Maria said, "Remember when we said some may refer to this as the dance of the spirits. Now I can relate to how they must have felt. The entire sky was, as you said Tom, scintillating."

"Amen." Joe replied.

Maria was impressed by Joe's one word sentence.

Tom now said, "You know, everyone, worldwide, would have heard, simultaneously and in their own language, these enormous Heavenly thundering and pulsating lightning wonders."

Joe commented, "Imagine how massive it must have been for everyone around the world to witness this event."

Tom replied, "Remember for the first year, even though all can hear and see what's going on, only the Land of Israel actually has the pillar of fire and the Two Witnesses testifying."

Joe added, "Don't forget the Flying Hell Monsters and zombies."

Maria said, "Who could forget them, Joe?"

Tom continued, "Now begins the time of repentance in Israel for one year."

As he was speaking, Maria cut him off saying, "How about we go inside?" She felt nauseated and out-of-sorts and needed to sit down for a while.

Joe said, "You know, just looking at the dance of the spirits is really mesmerizing and overwhelming."

This wondrous event high up in the sky seemed so close that you felt you could reach up and touch it.

Once they were settled in, Tom continued, "The Two Witnesses of God must now be testifying and offering everyone in the first zone their Baptism unto Repentance of God."

Maria said, "Tom, from what you have told us, those desiring salvation were instructed to raise their hands to the God of Heaven."

Joe, not to be out done, said, "And immediately out of the pillar of fire came the fingers of God touching them. God's Mark, now sparkling upon their foreheads, and they are saved."

"Not bad," replied Tom, "and now they will be further instructed to follow the King's supernatural highway that only they could see that will lead them to the Wilderness Sanctuary at the north end of the now Living Sea."

Joe commented, "And this is located within the Great Domed City, right?"

Maria smiled, rolling her eyes, and said, "That's correct, Joe."

Tom went on saying that the people in the countryside adjacent to this zone being testified to could possibly see the pillar of fire and the fingers of God but they most likely won't know that salvation is being offered, at least not in the early days.

Most were fearful and furious after witnessing these events and didn't understand what was going on. Some in ignorance and some with knowledge fired weapons at the Two Witnesses. Wrong choice, as the witnesses countered by having fire issue out of their mouths. They were consumed which caused even more panic in the rest.

Joe asked, "Do you know if the source of the fire originates from the pillar of fire, and then exits through their mouths?"

Tom said he didn't know but that it was a good thought.

"Perhaps we'll get some details later from the BSW transmissions," Tom commented. "The remaining antichrist that did not fire any weapons aren't off the hook, you know. As the Two Witnesses move on to the next zone, they will see the sky darkening and hear tremendous sounds like chariots going into battle."

Tom looked at Joe and said, "Joe, you take over."

Without missing a beat, Joe continued, "From what I've read in your book, it must be billions of Flying Hell Monsters making a tremendous clattering sound, most likely from their wings clapping together. They're attacking, chunking out flesh, sucking blood and then adding insult to injury, stinging and infecting them with the Zombie Virus."

Maria looked at them both saying, "The light source in each continent sized dome is from the pulsating fire lightning similar to the northern lights only hundreds of times greater, right?"

Joe said, "Since there is no natural daylight, it must be that the number of Flying Hell Monsters is so great that their numbers are also blocking out the light from high up within the angel halo dome. This black cloud of plague can then been seen from a distance by the antichrist."

Maria brought up a good question saying, "What's to stop the antichrist in all adjacent zones from fleeing to the remote areas of Israel?"

Tom thought about it and answered. "Two things. First, they never know where the Two Witnesses will show up next since they don't travel in a predictable pattern. It may be possible that the antichrist actually do flee to areas as far away as possible from the pillar of fire but still within that continent size dome.

Or, the only other thing I can think of is that wherever the Two Witnesses are testifying, surrounding the pillar of fire there is also a mini-dome."

Maria signed, "I'm really confused."

Joe commented, "A mini-dome. That's a simple answer and would easily solve Maria's question."

Maria agreed saying that it would have to be something like that or else the antichrist would just flee as far away in Israel as possible.

Tom again went blank and just sat there motionless.

Maria whispered to Joe, "Seems like Mel again."

Tom came back to them quickly this time saying that Mel just spoke to him. "Remember how God led the Israelites in the desert for 40 years following their exodus out of Egypt. The Israelites had to meander all over the place and never in a straight line following the pillar of fire. The path of the Two Witnesses also meanders all throughout the countryside along with the pillar of fire until the 1260 T/D., at which time everyone in the northern half of Israel will either be given direct Testimony by the Two Witnesses or hear from a distance. Those in the zone being testified to are contained and restrained within it until the Zombie Plagues come and after that their desire to flee will be removed from their thoughts."

Tom then said something strange, "Some of the antichrist, who see and hear from outside the zone being testified to, may indeed flee from Israel into Judea."

Maria asked, "What would this accomplish?

Tom only replied, "Soon Maria, you will supply the answer."

"Really?" she said, "Those who can't flee are attacked while others at a distance may hear, see and flee most likely southwards. That's interesting but not the answer we're looking for."

Joe said, "Patience, Maria. All this information is being taught to us by Mel. It seems like he is actually tutoring us and if Mel said you would give the answer you will in due time."

Tom said, they could use all the help possible.

Maria wished that Mel would also talk more to them.

Tom continued his topic saying, "This Thunder Message was understood by Christians and Israelites. Others also around the globe heard what they believed was the God of Heaven, talking to them, and not that imposter."

Joe asked, "Did they also understand the meaning of the message?"

Tom replied, "Why not? We're almost half way through the great tribulation time of sorrows."

"You know guys, it makes sense, by now millions or billions of people either outright know, or have a bad feeling, that this so called messiah is not genuine."

Maria said, "By this time the people of the nations of the ten kings should be aware of persecutions taking place everywhere and may even have seen those with the color tattoos on their foreheads forcefully demanding them to submit to their strange god that offered only riches and power but nothing lasting for their afterlife. This doesn't bode well with them as in the past they were taught the exact opposite."

Tom commented to Maria, "You know this is the first time I've ever thought of it. The false messiah never once offered eternal life to his followers. He offers everything else. I wonder why not this lie, also."

Maria added, "Is this a 'furtive discovery', Tom?"

"I think so," he replied, "and perhaps Satan is not allowed to offer eternal promises."

Joe commented, "When they heard the first thunder message they could very well have understood that something was not right. Is this a furtive discovery like Maria's?"

Both retorted, "No!"

Maria said, "Remember the message said 'Fear God and give glory and worship Him'. The people now at least have seen and heard thunder fire in the sky talking to them and now they will be on guard and frightened."

Tom said, "I wonder how this message was understood by the Christians and the Israelites."

"The Thunder Message enormously bolstered *our* faith and I would think that of all the Christians around the globe," Maria said "and even those of other faiths now have an option to only worship the God of the Heavens and not this other one that wants them to wear his colors and is extremely violent and bloodthirsty."

Tom said, "Since the days following the Rapture, Christians primarily have been horribly persecuted, captured and tortured by the forces of the unholy trinity. They know that they have less than a year remaining before their Martyrdom.

Christians already had the Holy Baptism of Water and the Mark of God so they don't need the Baptism of the Two Witnesses but it's comforting to know of their activities and that their God will avenge the persecutions inflicted on them by the antichrist."

Maria asked, "What about the prodigal children testifiers? You called them the Martyrs of understanding or something like that."

Tom replied, "Right you are, and now they're going to get into high gear and begin creating waves. Up to now they have been active secretly in small groups but now something twigs in them. According to Mel, they are going to organize the Christians into groups and testify to them concerning what's going to happen very soon. These initial groups will then begin relaying their knowledge to others and so on until virtually everyone knows what's coming down the pipeline. They will become very bold testifiers of God and Jesus knowing full well they will be targeted by the antichrist who are everywhere."

Joe asked, "So why don't these antichrist just kill them, and be done with them?"

Tom replied, "They would like nothing better but the Christians have become very adept at smuggling people from house to house."

Maria commented, "And most likely the Angels and Heavenly Powers of God have a function assisting them." Maria went silent for a few seconds and then perked back up saying, "Hey! Mel just spoke to me! He said 'And who do you think I am? Who do you think changed the alarm setting on your cell phone to play 'It's a wonderful life', and that specific channel was the first to be interrupted by the warning bulletin, that saved your lives, as seconds counted. And think Maria, you actually turned off your alarm the night before because you had a headache. Now you know who turned it back on and adjusted it to a radio news channel, and by the way upped the volume'."

Joe added, "I remember, you said to me before we went to bed that the alarm was off so we could sleep in."

Maria began shuddering. Joe had to hug her for several minutes to calm her down. Finally she spoke, "I remember now. Something stirred within me when that song came on. I shivered, but only thought it was a cool breeze from the window."

Tom said, "Now you know how it feels when he communicates."

Joe said, "What about me, Maria makes a furtive discovery, Mel talks to her and even manipulated her cell phone. When will it be my turn?"

"Soon."

"What do you mean, Tom?"

"I didn't say anything."

Maria added, "Maybe next time, it's your turn Joe."

"I think next time just happened." Joe shivered.

Maria spoke softly saying, "I don't feel abandoned anymore. Seems like God has been keeping his eyes on us. I wonder why?"

"We seem to have a function," commented Tom, "so anyway, to continue, these bold Christians are extremely dedicated and loyal and would risk their lives in a heartbeat to help other Christians. They shuttled these testifiers from one location to the next. Remember," Tom said, "the antichrist up to now were not allowed to mass slaughter Christians. They had to first attempt to turn them away from their God to that of the false god, their god. The unholy trinity knows full well that the 1290 T/D., is drawing near at which time they will be allowed to carry out their evil inclinations of global genocide."

"So, have you heard what the Israelites also think of this first Thunder Message?" asked Joe.

Tom continued, "Well, the Two Witnesses of God start their Time of Testimony around the north end of the Living Sea and from there travel throughout the Northern half of Israel. During these days those Israelites who accept the Baptism unto Repentance from the Two Witnesses of God, do so in faith, prior to the abomination of desolation being set up and activated in the false messiah's new temple. That will take place soon, at the 1290 T/D."

Tom said he selected some Bible verses that address Joe's question. "I'll try to paraphrase them for easier understanding[62]. Israelites saw and heard the first Thunder Message and then received testimony from the Two Witnesses of God. Some heard, accepted, and received the Baptism unto Repentance thereby receiving the Mark of God. Abram, was the first who realized that his former way was wrong and accepted what he heard."

Tom continued, "They are the 'Redeemed'.

Maria added, "I remember, now. They form the first group, the 'Redeemed' who accepted before the abomination unveiling ceremony."

"Right. They are described as the priests who weep before the altar of God in the Wilderness Sanctuary that we can read a little about here and in the end notes of my book."

"The people who are being assembled perhaps refers to the elders. God says, "Yet I have reserved 7,000 in Israel, all whose knees have not bowed to Baal. This I believe can also be a futuristic prophecy about that abomination thing.

It is interesting to note as recorded in Ezekiel 9; 1-11 in the vision of slaughter, the LORD said to him, "Go through the midst of the city, even through the midst of Jerusalem, <u>and put a mark on the foreheads</u> of the men who sigh and groan over all the <u>abominations which are being committed in its midst.</u>"

Maria spoke to Tom saying, "Sorry for the interruption but now I'm really confused. Please explain 'and put a mark on the foreheads of the men who sigh and groan over all the abominations'. Is this the same mark given by the Two Witnesses?"

Tom replied, "First of all, you never have to be sorry for any interruptions. Like I said before, I don't have all the answers, so your input is always appreciated."

He continued, "Now to answer your question. It's the same mark, as far as I can tell, because they now have the Mark of God upon their foreheads."

Joe asked, "Is this the same mark that we have?"

Tom replied, "Yes Joe, it's the same mark. They are the temple priests in the Wilderness Sanctuary until Daniel's prophecy of '2300 Days until the Sanctuary is cleansed' concludes at the 2300 T/D."

Tom began to further elaborate, "God says, 'I will make them one nation'. I believe this means that at this time God will make one nation in the land, on the mountains of Israel, and in one day a new nation will come into fruition.

In the Bible God said, "<u>My tabernacle also shall be with them</u>, I will be their God and they shall be My people. The nations also will know that I, the Lord, sanctify Israel, when <u>My sanctuary is in their midst forevermore.</u>"

Tom continued, "This also shows that God's Temple and His Sanctuary will then also be in their midst. Furthermore, he said this event happens just after the death of the Two Witnesses during the earthquake that I will refer to as the 'Resurrection Earthquake' from now on."

Maria concluded, "So God's plan will include these Redeemed Israelites?" Her comment was more of a statement then question.

Tom continued talking about the Two Witnesses and how they do not necessarily move in a predictable pattern, thereby keeping the antichrist off balance not knowing where they are going to show up next. He said, "Then, the false messiah will attempt to counter the effects of the Two Witnesses by having his false prophet draw fire from the sky and do lying wonders, desperately trying to deceive and confuse the people who must decide whom to believe. He will have his false prophet send out many deceiving prophets to the people to create confusion in the minds of the people because there are many groups out there saying that their way is best. This will come into play in a major way during their last 900 days when the saved people are tempted by the forces of evil to turn away from their God."

The time drifted into the late afternoon and the three of them gathered around their BSW radio for the latest updates from around the earth. The news broadcast said that the unholy trinity blames the Flying Hell Monsters and the plagues they cause on the Christians and declares to the world that all Christians worldwide must be killed to end these events.

Maria said, "You know, one thing is clear. The Heavenly Wonders of our God are dwarfing the lying wonders of the false prophet."

Joe replied, "Back to my monsters. We already know that as the Two Witnesses leave that zone, the Flying Hell Monsters will begin attacking and stinging all people not having the Mark of God."

Tom took over saying, "We must remember that immediately upon the start of the Two Witnesses of God at the 1040 T/D, chaos ensued within the unholy trinity. People were witnessing unprecedented worldwide supernatural events. These fire lightning thunders were admonishing them to only worship the God of Heaven."

Joe added, "And water sources started becoming blood."

The unholy trinity and the antichrist became furious due to these events challenging their authority but they never give up fighting.

Tom continued, "The unholy trinity are now losing their hold on the people. The 'cats out of the bag' as many of the people are beginning to see through them.

Various groups are now attempting to influence those listening around the world and try to put a spin on other events to diffuse the situation. There is global hype that make people excited and get them talking about their messiah's temple in the process of being completed. They're saying that it is being constructed exactly as their first temple was right down to the minutest detail concerning the sanctuary and the holy of holies."

Joe said, "Listen to this. People are also spreading rumours of something bad coming as word has leaked out that the religious prophet was not what he appeared to be and that he is in fact evil. They're now starting to call him the false prophet. You've told us that this is his name recorded in the Bible and what we've been calling him all along. They're also saying that he was in the process of creating something monstrous that was being kept secret. This is making some happy and others terrified."

Reports of atrocities went from weekly to daily to hourly as the days passed by. Those with the 3-color tattoos on their foreheads were becoming very domineering, demanding all to worship their messiah and those who refused were not worthy of his benevolence. Many refused to voluntarily have his mark tattooed on their foreheads, especially since other strange happenings were now appearing in the heavens. Someone else was now talking to them claiming to be their true God as well as punishing those who took the mark of the beast.

Joe enquired, "This taboo tattoo, how exactly does it get put on the person's forehead?"

Tom said that it was not just ink, like people have been getting during the past decades. The dragon's tattoo is very advanced and is a futuristic sensor of some type that can track the person's whereabouts and allows the unholy trinity to hear and possibly see through its center black portion. By some scientific means the 3-color tattoo is branded onto the forehead of the person vowing loyalty to the beast.

Maria commented, "Their 'soul is marked'."

Joe said, "One things for sure. It's not ink of some type, and I agree it's rather a futuristic mark and may even have some depth to it."

Maria said, "The pertinent fact is they went against the command of God. They turned their backs on Him and vowed their loyalty and, many unwittingly, their souls to Satan."

Tom said that all the misinformation being propagandized globally in the attempt to minimize the efforts of the 7-7-2-FHM did little. Nothing they could do lessened the notoriety of the Flying Hell Monster Vampires that created the Zombie Plagues of stage one and two zombies. These detestable abominations were unstoppable, and ever increasing in numbers.

Many people around the globe did not know what to make of all this, having two beings each claiming to be their God. The foundations of their faiths were being tested and for many it was more than shaken.

Global chatter confirmed many of the antichrist were justifiably disconcerted. Behind the scenes the actions of the 7-7-2-FHM were creating chaos in the unholy trinity's plans.

Joe heard the familiar beep-beep from their BSW radio indicating a burst message had just been received.

The three of them again gathered for they knew it was intended for them because they had conceived of the plan with Abram that all communications only took place at a very specific time, right down to the minute, and in this case the exact second.

Joe said, "Talk about timing." And he then electronically uncompressed and displayed the communication on their mini-screen. They were very curious now because their friend Abram was Redeemed and left the scene some time ago. Now #5 entered the picture.

He, was reporting on what was being referred to as 'Flying Vampires' that have been attacking and infecting thousands of people, as predicted in the book. The attacked and infected fell to the ground and appeared to be dead but about three days later rose up and began staggering around making blood curdling sounds. They now were able to walk haphazardly. Their pain increased exponentially and their crying intensity increased to a cross between crying and howling. He said they began following the pillar of fire, like moths to the light. Those infected all had one thing in common, the 3-color mark of the beast. People began to refer to them as 'zombies' as they appeared to die and then reanimate as Joe predicted, the Zombie Plagues.

Joe shuddered saying, "It's one thing to predict the Zombie Plagues and zombies but when it actually happens and people call it that, it's freaky."

Tom looking perplexed said, "Joe, you once asked if we would ever meet Mel. Well, we all just received a BSW message from him and that's about as close as I ever want to come to him on this time plane."

Joe said, "He even used my phrase 'Zombie Plagues'. We never mentioned this to Abram."

Maria spoke to Joe saying, "I don't want to alarm you, but how did he know your name. We only used our numbers? Mel seems to know more than he is letting on."

Joe said, "Tom, who is this guy Mel who talks to you, and now in a strange way to us too? Also, how did he know about your book?"

Tom said, "Remember Abram once called him his strange friend who seemed to have just materialized out of thin air walking towards him. Abram thought he must have been dozing off and that's why he didn't see him coming which could have proven disastrous since there were many murderers in these lands. Abram said this man introduced himself as Mel and when asked where did he come from, he only said from the past."

Joe said, "I remember hearing about him in Sunday school, you know when the guy who materialized out of thin air and came to that Bible person."

Maria said, "I think you're talking about the three angels who appeared as men to Abraham."

"Three or one. Close enough." commented Joe. "So that's how Mel came on the scene."

Maria acquiesced, "OK, as long as it makes sense to you."

Tom said, "It seems like the cat's out of the bag regarding the virus, plagues and zombies."

They decided to ramp up their global presence and began broadcasting everything that they knew concerning these matters. In their next BSW broadcast, they brought the world up to speed about how the zombies are following the pillar of fire throughout Israel and soon the entire world.

They also condensed and paraphrased the highlights of Tom's book as much as possible. This task took them many hours but thankfully Tom had an electronic version on his laptop. They began transmitting in BSW to the world and then within only hours their message went viral thanks to there being tens of thousands of the BSW type radios with an internal central processing unit that could save and display the information in a readable format in many electronic display devices including EBooks. Everyone who heard also retransmitted their message contents either by electronic format or in their own words. Within the week, the entire world was brought up to speed on what they knew. The chatter was endless as people all wanted more information on these flying hell vampire monsters, the Zombie Virus and the 3-color zombies.

The three huddled in their usual fashion and agreed to be silent for the next week. They had done enough damage for now and the last thing they needed was to have the NG knocking on their door.

Joe, not thinking, began rapping, "I hear you knocking but you can't come in."

Maria had her hand over his mouth in a flash saying, "Really?"

"Just trying to break the tension." he replied.

"You're the main cause of my tension right now," she said.

"OK children!" came Tom's exasperated reply. He now continued, "The false prophet during these days is busy having his followers make an image of the Great Red Dragon for all to worship and by this time it's almost completed. The long-time antichrist followers of the false prophet have no problem in this as they are used to having images and idols in their churches for thousands of years.

This inanimate object when completed will be very large and rumours report it's even larger than the idols of Greek gods that were very tall and that still exist throughout the world today.

The dragon's idol image is slated to be placed in and not outside, of his new temple in Jerusalem. This fact hasn't been made public to the world."

Long before this date, the false president had instructed the false prophet to also make many smaller images. He wanted an image of his father to be placed in every religious house of worship worldwide. Hundreds of thousands of mini-me statues were being created and were secretly being distributed worldwide by the antichrist and at the designated time would be activated. In the USA, the NG had their hit list of targets and were awaiting orders to place them in every house of worship, irrespective of denomination.

Tom said, "The first half of the Great Tribulation Time of Sorrows is slowly drawing to a close. The 1260 T/D will soon be at hand."

Maria said, "We know that. You have already told us about all of this. What does the Bible have to say about it?"

Tom opened his book to the corresponding page and handed it to Joe asking him to read what the Prophet Daniel says about it.

Joe began reading in Daniel 12:7, "It shall be for a time, times, and half a time and when the power of the holy people has been completely shattered, all these things shall be finished."

Tom said, "These words of Daniel illustrate how time can be referred to in various ways, for example, a time, times, and half a time, 3½ years, 1260 days and 42 months. All contain 1260 days.

The dragon's wrath of the first half of the 7 Year Great Tribulation time was targeted mainly towards the Christians and their eradication and now, unknown to the Israelites, the second half will be targeted at them and the rest of the world."

Maria said, "So here we are, closing in on the first half and there will be another two events that happen on or prior to that date also. The Martyrs of understanding are slaughtered by the antichrist on or prior to that date and then those in the Wilderness Sanctuary are taken by the Son of God into Heaven exactly on that date. Right, Tom?"

"Well done." replied Tom, "Even though we discussed them a while ago, I'm impressed you remembered. I referred to them as the 'refined Martyrs of understanding', who know their God."

Joe commented, "I remember them. They had drifted away from their main group and were scattered around the world. They are children of God, you called them the 'Prodigal Children' come home."

Tom continued, "I'm doubly impressed."

Maria said, "Joe, are you reading ahead in the book again?"

Joe's feelings were hurt, not so much from reading ahead but rather from being caught. He said, "Maria, don't you trust me?" They both began laughing for some reason.

Tom, trying to hold it together, continued, "The Martyrs of understanding carry out great exploits over and above the general Christians, who themselves also demonstrate great exploits of faith. They do not flee. Rather at the appointed time they stand up and rally all Christians to stand fast and not to cave in as their God has His eyes on them.

They may all be martyred prior to the next thunder at the 1260 T/D. This allows them to be with their 3 sacrament contemporaries who altogether then await the next group of 1335 T/D. Martyrs, meaning us."

Joe said, "Three-color tattoo and three sacraments. I wonder if they have any connected meanings."

Tom said, "The three sacraments may depict God, His Son and His Holy Spirit. And the three-color tattoo depicts the unholy trinity, Satan, His Son and His False Prophet."

Maria said, "That's a great topic for some other time. It looks like everyone is 'getting out of Dodge.' Welcome to another day 'not' in paradise."

"The false messiah's temple at this time is in its final stages of completion. He is also making elaborate plans to soon dedicate his newly built temple unto himself along with a few more surprises, like when his idol comes to life."

Tom said that one day a while back when he was out in the meadow he had another Mel thought.

Maria chuckled, "First Joe's 'Zombie Plagues' and now Tom's 'Mel thoughts'. What's next?"

"Funny," he replied saying while contemplating how this idol comes to life he sensed the presence of Mel and heard the answer.

"Satan allows the false prophet once again to deceive the people. Foreign words are spoken by him and then this monstrous idol apparently comes to life. The key word is 'apparently'. This Great Red Dragon abomination seems to come alive, but it's only a use of higher technology, bewildering people. Remember, just like when you said the black center of the mark of the beast might have some type of communication aspects? You are correct. It's only higher technology being used. Satan will then communicate world-wide using tens of thousands of smaller abomination statues of himself and through his many devotees wearing his 3-color tattoo on their foreheads."

Joe said, "I'm really starting to like this Mel person or whatever he is." Joe then slyly looked at Maria and said "I knew Tom was not that smart."

Tom, hearing, pretended not to, and continued speaking, "Enough for now about Mel. Now as we have been discussing when the 1260 T/D arrives in the near future, not only will the Refined Martyrs of Understanding have been removed from earth, but also the Children of God will have been harvested from the wilderness sanctuary by the Son of God and taken to His Father."

Maria asked, "Why don't they get martyred like everyone else?"

"Fair question," replied Tom. "We can read about reaping the earth's harvest in Revelation 14:15-16."

Tom paraphrased saying, "The Son of God thrust in His sickle for the time had come for him to gather the harvest of the earth now fully ripe."

Tom said, "This group was in the Wilderness Sanctuary and only required a little more time to fully mature."

Maria said, "So these Children of God already had the three Holy Sacraments that we discussed. They, in effect, have all the Heavenly Documents and only needed a little more time to be refined, as you said. Will they also be part of the Bride of Christ?

"Sounds about right to me." commented Tom and continued, "As the '7-7-2-FHM' approach the land of Judea, the southern half of Israel, once again as we come to the 1260 T/D., strange events happen. They change their strategy and rather than going into this land they bypass it.

The reason being, there may be millions of antichrist along with thousands of undecided Israelites concentrated in the land of Judea. Those undecided are highly visible to the antichrist 3-color tattoo Israelites. Satan knows this and is giving them lots of leeway."

Maria asked, "Why would the antichrist unholy trinity, especially Satan, allow them to exist right under his nose. Wouldn't that anger him?"

Tom replied, "You would think so. Consider this. Satan has plans for them."

Joe said, "And don't forget, God has plans for them as well. I think that some of these are the people, who after seeing Satan's monster image unveiled in his temple, flee to the hills."

Maria said, "I know about those who flee to the hills but what about those that Satan desires?"

Tom confessed he didn't exactly understand his comment himself and was mulling it over in his thoughts. He said in time it would come to him.

Joe said, "Maria, Tom needs another M&M."

"What's that supposed to mean?" she asked, even though she knew better.

"A Mel moment," he replied.

All three actually burst out laughing, however, it was short lived when they perceived Mel saying, "It is not for you to know of them. I will supply this answer perhaps when you're not here."

Maria said, "What did he mean?

Tom said, "I think it means that the answer may only be given to those reading the book after we've been martyred."

Joe said, "Why don't we just read in your book what he says?"

Maria answered, "Joe, because Tom doesn't know the answer. This means that in our timeline it's not written in his book."

Tom then said, "And that's scary. It means that certain information in my book doesn't come from me."

Joe said, "You mean Mel sort of whispered it to you and you sort of just verbatenly wrote it?"

Tom said, "No, it wasn't even in my book but somehow it will be and don't ask me how this happens."

"I know," replied Joe.

Maria was waiting for one of his sly comments but Joe said, "Remember Tom, you once said that if the Prophet Esdras could answer the question 'call me the day that has past' the mysteries of God would be explained to him?"

Tom said, "I do recall this, but how does it factor in to our discussion?"

Joe then said, "I think that Mel is a time dimension being, so he can maneuver up and down the time line, meaning he can place words in your book even after they are already printed."

Maria looked at Tom. Both were stunned by Joe's answer and dared not challenge it because for some reason they knew he was correct. However, none of them fully comprehended Joe's answer, especially Joe.

Maria asked, "I thought you said we would never meet Mel and if we did that would not be good?"

"I know, I know," replied Tom. "Luckily for us, we only get messages from him."

They paused for a moment to gather their thoughts and then went on with the previous discussion.

Joe said, "If I understand you correctly, the Two Witnesses of God didn't actually have to testify to those in Judea. Once all people in Judea have taken the mark of the beast there will be no possibility of salvation."

"That's right," Tom said. "The plan of God was for His Son to simply set the stage so those in Judea still loyal to their God of Heaven can flee to the hills when they see Satan's abomination in his temple. That is going to happen in the near future. Remember 'finger on the trigger' and these are the 'repented' who form the congregation worshiping at the altar of God in the Wilderness Sanctuary. They're the second group of Redeemed."

Maria laughingly said to Tom, "A few minutes ago you told us that they changed their strategy and rather than going into this land they bypass it. How could you have possibly known about their strategy change?" and then said, "Mel?"

By the expression on Tom's face she knew that she was correct. Maria continued, "Tom, how many of your so called furtive discoveries actually came from Mel?"

Tom, chuckling, uttered, "For me to know, you to find out and that's my story and I'm sticking to it."

Maria said, "Tom, your eyes said it all. Sooner or later you'll spill the beans. Joe, work on him."

Joe, not missing the opportunity to bug his older brother, said, "Mel loves me better, you know."

Maria chimed in, expressing her opinion. "That's not what I mean and you know it."

Tom continued, "I know they changed their strategy for the reasons I just said, but where they now go is still a mystery to me."

Maria continued, "I know the answer. The 7-7-2-FHM, instead of moving into the land of Judea, hopscotch over it. They go into the Judean Mountains and all the lands adjoining the Living Sea to the Israelites or Israelite descendants from the lands of, Moab, Edom and Ammon, countries formerly included in the promised land of Israel. After the Two Witnesses finish testifying to them they now await those Israelites who will very soon be fleeing their way at the 1290 T/D."

Tom replied, "Maria, remember a while back Mel informed you that soon you would say the answer? It just happened."

"Cool!" Maria said.

"When is it my turn?" added Joe.

They ignored him.

"Your answer solves a lot of concerns I had as to why they hopscotched over Judea and where they went, but we're getting a little ahead of ourselves."

They took a break from their discussions for a while and talked with the many others using their BSW radio.

Days and months passed by during which they felt secure because they had learned to keep themselves invisible to the world. Unfortunately for the Christians and the rest of the world, the actions of the antichrist were becoming intolerable.

Maria listened to their BSW all the time now when the men went out looking for fresh vegies and fruit. There were literally thousands of reports of Zombies numbering in the tens of millions throughout the land of Israel. As Tom had predicted, they did not migrate anywhere, they simply stayed put. During the next 150 days the Zombie Virus subsided. However, they were still of the stage one, the 3-color zombies. They never returned to normal and their eyes and skin still showed the evidence of 'zombieness'. They could eat regular food, or for that fact, any food that came their way. This was only possible in Israel and not the rest of the world.

Tom said, "I don't know if 'zombieness' is actually a word, Maria."

She commented, "It is now."

Joe pondered a while and said, "So those who were first attacked at the beginning of the testimony of the Two Witnesses are by now recovered and this still leaves 70 days until the second thunder message."

Tom added, and "That's a lot of them, however, even if allowed to do so, they wouldn't come into Judea since the Flying Hell Monsters would soon be attacking everyone who didn't flee to the hills."

Joe said, "And remember the 3-color zombies stay put and don't migrate, so those who previously fled to Judea could not go back into the northern half because millions of hungry blood thirsty zombies are there."

Time passed by and as the days counted down, they grew anxious and at night as their usual custom they read from the book of Psalms and then sang the words using the melody of nursery rhymes because they didn't know many church songs. They concluded every night with a little prayer spoken by Maria who for some reason began this custom on the very same night after reaching their cave. It came easy for her to do so and was very reassuring to all three of them.

Chapter Forty-Two

THUNDER MESSAGE TWO 1260 T/D

Maria rounded up the boys and began the conversation. "Here we go again. It's almost 5 p.m. again. Let's see if the next Thunder Message takes place at this time once more."

Joe said he thinks it will be right on time and in the middle of his sentence was cut off by a thunderous sound.

Precisely at 5 p.m. Thunder Message Two was seen, heard and felt by all the people on earth and it was once again understood by both Christians and Israelites, alike.

"When you see the abomination of desolation spoken of by Daniel the prophet, standing in the holy place anyone who worships this beast and his image, and receives his mark on his forehead or on his hand, will suffer the wrath of God. When you see this, those in Judea, flee to the mountains."

Tom spoke, "The obvious and main focus of this Thunder Message is three-fold.

Firstly, do not worship the beast, get its mark or you will suffer the wrath of God.

Secondly, when the abomination of desolation stands in the holy place.

Thirdly, then those in Judea, flee to the mountains.

This Thunder Message combines three Bible passages. Even though the first part relates to the Christians and the second and third parts relate to the Israelites. When they are combined they create this Thunder Message, and both Christians and Israelites understand it."

Maria asked, "Why does it take three passages to make this message?"

Tom said, "The Bible doesn't necessarily make it easy. That's why it's called furtive, you know hiding in plain sight."

Joe commented, "Then why not just say it, plain and clear?"

"Let's just say," Replied Tom, "that knowledge of the Bible without wisdom gets you nowhere."

Joe said, what in the world does that mean?

"Exactly," quipped Maria.

Tom continued, "Both the Christians and Israelites immediately understand this furtive discovery message. The combining of the three Bible passages was necessary for the Israelites so they could relate to the message of Jesus even though they didn't believe in Him, just yet. By linking their Prophet Daniel to this Thunder Message, it allows the Israelites to comprehend the scope of the message."

Tom asked Maria to read the three Bible passages to see why it was necessary to combine them.

Maria began, "Revelation 14:9 says <u>if anyone worships the beast and his image</u>, and <u>receives his mark</u> on his forehead or on his hand, he <u>himself shall also drink of the wine of the wrath of God</u>."

Maria continued, "Daniel 11:31 says, and forces shall be mustered by him, <u>and they shall defile the sanctuary fortress; then they shall take away the daily sacrifices</u>, <u>and place there the abomination of desolation.</u>

Maria continued once more, "Matthew 24:15-16 says "Therefore when you <u>see</u> the <u>'abomination of desolation'</u>, spoken of by <u>Daniel the prophet</u>, <u>standing in the holy place</u> (whoever reads, let him understand) <u>then let those who are in Judea flee to the mountains</u>."

Maria commented, "That's a lot of blending but I see what you are getting at and when you combine them the message is clear."

Tom said, "At this time the false messiah will also stop the Israelites from offering sacrifices. This indicates that something has gone wrong because why would the false messiah stop them from offering to him?"

Maria said, "Perhaps they weren't offering to him. Maybe they secretly were offering to the God of Heaven."

Joe said, "It's because they smelled a rat."

"Not very eloquent Joe, but we get your drift."

Joe asked, "Please explain again about those who are in Judea and why will only they be commanded to flee to the mountains upon seeing the abomination."

Tom replied, "This is another Biblical furtive discovery message to the Israelites in Judea. This command has always concerned me as to why only those in Judea are commanded to flee. Judea was the southern half and Israel was the northern half in the time of Jesus.

During a church service one Sunday the answer was given, even though the minister was unaware he did so. Whatever he said triggered this answer. Simply stated, the only people living north of the land of Judea in Israel at this time were the antichrist."

Maria said, "Do you think Mel was in church with you?"

Tom replied, "If so, that would make him some type of Holy Messenger of God, but at this point your guess is as good as mine and please can we get back to my topic before I completely lose my train of thought?"

Joe said, "I can help you out there, Tom. Remember we discussed that those in the upper half of present day Israel, were suffering the effects of the Zombie Virus since the beginning of the testimony of the Two Witnesses. Many of the population that were infected will still take months to recover. There are going to be possibly millions of them wandering around looking for a hot meal or blood."

Maria almost yelled, "Hey, that's why Mel gave the answer. Remember, a while back Tom, you said that the antichrist in adjacent zones, upon seeing the pillar of fire in the distance, may flee to the farthest areas to get away from them. They did. The only direction open to them was to go south, to Judea."

Maria continued, "And even though we call them zones, the people living in Israel didn't know about this. They were just out in the countryside, maybe living in tents so they could easily have moved around to avoid them."

Joe then spoke, "So it is possible that many did move southwards for another reason, to avoid the plagues. This means that many, and by that I mean many millions, could have moved into Judea."

Tom said, "So that means, everyone in Judea had already taken the 3-color taboo tattoo, as Maria says. They either got Satan's mark a long time ago or they are those with his mark who just migrated there to avoid the zombies."

Maria said, "They all are wearing the 3-color taboo tattoo. Don't you just love that alliteration? At this time, if someone did not have the 3-color mark of the beast, they would stand out easily. The Two Witnesses then could not testify to them without the antichrist immediately killing these people."

Joe said, "The overall effect is like a good 'pied piper' drawing them out Judea and the clutches of Satan and to the hills. And another thing, those antichrist living in Judea could not flee northwards since that area was swarming with millions of zombies who would attack them for their blood. They could not flee westward as the Mediterranean Sea was there and possibly this also is the outer barrier of the continent dome, or because the ocean had turned to blood. Either way they were contained."

Tom added, "When oceans turn to blood everything in them dies. However, out of death come new plagues such as maggots, flies, bugs, diseases of many types and so on."

Maria commented, "They also could not flee into Egypt because it is on the other side of the barrier, in the next angel halo dome, number two."

Tom nodded and replied, "And they for sure would not flee eastward towards the pillar of fire far off in the distance, as the blood virus plagues could have been out there in their wake."

"And they would not dare flee towards the Great Domed City. They were terrified of it." said Maria. "They had no options, they were restrained and just remained in Judea."

Joe said, "Once the Israelites flee out of Judea and into the mountains, it's fair to conclude that those remaining must be the antichrist."

"Ya think," Tom replied, "Included within the fleeing group will also be Israelites who will become part of the evil seeds. There will also be some more evil seeds when Satan's temple crumbles. Mel told me that we will discuss them later."

"Wow!" Maria said, "The analogy that the Two Witnesses hop-scotched over Judea and then for the next while testified until all in the lands surrounding the Living Sea of Moab, Edom, and Ammon, as I mentioned a while ago, is a good one, even if I say so myself."

Joe doing the math said, "When the 7-7-2-FHM have finished in these lands, the Flying Hell Monsters go back to Judea for a while and finish attacking the antichrist. If their attacks begin when the Christians have all been martyred by the 1335 T/D., their attacks could then also start on this same day and then end at the 1400 T/D."

Tom jumped in saying, "Now that's going to be one scary sight. Imagine all of Judea being one large zone, no pillar of fire, just billions of Flying Hell Monsters. This time they don't just attack thousands of people but rather millions of them.

Joe added, "However, those infected still cry out for death for 150 days following. By this time the Two Witnesses have been in Egypt for some time along with their plagues."

Maria smiled, "Joe, you never cease to amaze me. I can't quite figure you out, and either you're a diamond in the rough or lump of coal."

Tom interjected, "Getting back to why the command to flee was only directed to those in Judea. The area north of Judea is the seat of power of the Sea Beast whom we call the false president. This area is home to the elite armies loyal to the false president. There were no redeemable people in the Northern half of Israel, as only the antichrist lived there now."

Joe added his two cents worth saying, "Those who repented had long ago 'gotten out of Dodge', to the King's Highway."

Tom then said, "The command to 'flee' specifically concerns the Israelites. It instructs them what to do when they see this 'abomination of desolation'."

Joe said, "You might say, it's like the starter person of a race having his 'finger on the trigger' and when these Israelites in Judea see the 'abomination of desolation' during the dedication of the dragon's temple, the 'trigger is pulled' and 'bang', off they 'flee to the mountains'.

The command to flee is urgent and means don't gather goods, don't pack clothes and those on their roof tops don't go back inside, just flee to the mountains, 'get out of Dodge'."

Joe continued, "Another rationale is that if you packed your goods, you then became a target as the antichrist would see that you were going somewhere and that meant you were fleeing, whereas, if you had nothing on you but your clothes, you blended in and would not be spotted."

Maria said, "That means that those who took goods were still earthly minded and their greed did them in."

Many were killed and their possession looted by the antichrist.

Joe said, "OK, now comes the 'exodus out of Judea'. Seems like those who take heed and 'flee' out of Judea make it out alive to the mountains where their salvation awaits them."

Joe continued, "It also seems like the window of opportunity for the Israelites to be able to flee was very narrow, perhaps days certainly less than one month."

Tom said, "It may be that during these days the antichrist were focused on getting their messiah's temple completed."

Maria commented, "And don't forget these antichrist were also engaged in rounding up all the Christians for the soon-to-be slaughter."

Joe said, "Right, that's their main focus because they're going to slaughter millions."

Maria said, "Let's not forget, many Israelites by this time have noticed their 'messiah' was doing things inconsistent with the teachings of their prophets of old."

Tom took over saying, "They also have, during the recent past, seen and heard the Thunder Message to fear God from the Angel Halo high above their heads. This Heavenly Wonder must have had some effect upon them. Those of strong faith believed that their

God talked to them and that something evil is going to take place soon, upon the dedication of the temple."

Maria commented, "This second Thunder Message must have startled the Israelites when it talked about some 'abomination' beast that's going to be seen standing in the holy place, meaning their new temple. If you worship it, get its mark on your forehead or on your hand, you will suffer the wrath of God."

Maria continued, "I think that God's plan is so intricate. The people hear Heavenly messages and the wise around the world understand the meaning, no matter what their religion is."

Tom said, "Certain Israelites, knowing their scriptures, immediately began reading what their Prophet Daniel had to say concerning this. They read that in the end of days one will come who will defile their temple and place some abomination in it. They read how their Holy Scriptures have foretold of this and how a false messiah will after 3½ years stop their sacrifice and offerings. By now they have heard that their messiah will not allow any daily sacrifices in his new temple and this disturbs them to no end. Now the Thunder Message made complete sense to them even though it shattered their belief that their messiah had returned to them. They realize they have been deceived and their messiah is actually Satan and very soon this abomination thing will be seen. They may not have known exactly what this evil thing is but now at least they are prepared for something bad coming their way."

Now certain 'Israelites of understanding' were prepared using Joe's 'finger on the trigger' analogy and were waiting for the 'bang' to flee to the hills. Currently, it was not possible to do directly as the area was teeming with antichrist so any travel had to be covert.

Joe asked, "How do these Israelites physically 'get out of Dodge'? How does this actually take place?"

Tom said, "Good question. There will be hundreds of thousands, perhaps millions surrounding the dragon's temple, especially as the time draws near to its dedication."

Maria said, "Maybe many Israelites will see the 'abomination of desolation' event on TV. Millions will also view this event worldwide on some form of electronic devices. This means that there is at least some distance between the temple and the local Israelites unless they happened to be inside of it."

Tom said, "Park that thought, Maria. We'll discuss those inside the Dragon's temple later on. They are those most loyal to him and are the 'evil seeds'. Remember this phrase."

Tom continued, "Soon upon the temple dedication when the 'trigger is pulled' and 'bang' so to speak occurs, the Israelites of understanding will flee to the mountains east of Jerusalem. Remember to the east and less than 20 miles away is the Great Domed City that houses the 'Wilderness Sanctuary'."

Maria asked, "Will this Domed City be visible to everyone?"

Tom answered that he believes so but the false messiah will have some rationale for it.

Joe said, "He may even claim it to be his and reserved for those loyal to him."

Maria said, "And why not, since he is the great liar."

Joe asked, "Do you think they will try to destroy it using rockets or other explosives?"

"Now that would be very foolish of them, if Two Witnesses can overwhelm their best weapons, imagine what the power of the Great Domed City could do. I think the unholy trinity stays clear of it."

Tom said, "The Israelites will have a month to prepare and some will travel towards Jerusalem under the pretense of wanting to be close to their temple for its dedication. Some may even position themselves on the east side of Jerusalem awaiting this event so they can flee more easily, while others are simply clueless."

Joe asked, "What's to stop them after hearing this 'Thunder Message' to just immediately flee?"

Tom answered, "Some may do so and secretly escape, but if they pack all their belongings into cars or trucks or whatever and head out, this would be too obvious. The antichrist controls every inch of the country, stopping and questioning everyone as their roundup of Christians is reaching a fever pitch. Those with no valid reason for travel will be arrested, as travel by this time will be highly restricted. As to their disposition, most likely they would simply vanish and some may be exiled as captives to other lands."

Tom began to say something else and went silent mid-sentence. The both watched him and said nothing.

Moments later Tom continued his sentence mid-stream and immediately cut himself off saying that Mel was just talking to him. Tom said, "We were just discussing those Israelites living in Judea who had not as of yet taken the mark of the beast upon their foreheads. Mel told me in order to help people in their timeline he decided to give the reason why Satan allowed them to exist, under his nose as you said. One may ask the question why Satan would allow so many close to his temple who were not forced to take his mark and who would soon be fleeing to the hills. The reason is that he was counting on it."

Maria said, "This doesn't make sense to me."

Tom replied, "Mel just told me that thousands will flee to the hills and remember that 'many are called but few are chosen'."

Maria asked, "What does that mean?"

Tom said, "Those in Judea not having the dragon's tattoo consist of three groups.

First, are those 'finger on the trigger' Israelites who fled to the hills and become the repented Israelites.

Second, those of the evil seeds who 'fled to the hills' but are not aware that they are evil, but their loyalties could be bought. Remember the band of Korah? They only went along for the ride and soon showed their true colors by attempting a revolt and we all know that was a poor choice.

Third, are those of the evil seeds who stayed within the Dragon's temple but flee when it crumbles. They are really Satan's spies."

Joe said, "Both of these fleeing groups get the Baptism unto Repentance of the Two Witnesses, right?"

Tom agreed.

Maria said, "Even those covert evil seeds? It still doesn't make sense to me."

Tom agreed and said they would have to wait for Mel to elaborate.

"Just great," replied Joe, "now even Mel is getting in on the action."

Maria chastised Joe tenderly saying, "Don't even joke like that."

Tom said, "Remember, when those in Judea 'flee to the hills', this includes all of the lands surrounding the Living Sea.

Then the 7-7-2-FHM come to the southern portion of Israel called Judea. They hopscotched over this area and went to the lands of Moab, Edom and Ammon as these three areas escaped the hand of Satan. That's recorded in scriptures. This tells us why they escaped. When this text is viewed as a future reference it means in addition to certain Israelites living in Judea, others shall also escape the unholy trinity's hand.

Looking at a map during the time of Jesus, one would see the area of Judea as very large having an area of about half of Israel, the southern half. Today, this also includes the area known as the west bank. In total it's estimated that the Jewish population living in the west bank is about 325,000 along with about 160,000 Christians."

Maria said, "So that's where a lot of the Christians come from that are martyred in the Dragon's temple."

Tom said, "Makes sense since they're in the unholy trinity's backyard, so to speak, and they don't flee, but rather they confront Satan."

Maria also said, "And that's another reason many Israelites escaped. The antichrist had their hands full capturing the Christians."

Tom then continues, "Now, when you take the areas of Edom, Moab, Ammon and their mountains, all have the Living Sea as part of their borders. These three areas have history attached to them, one might say 'the golden thread of lineage'. Some say this phrase was attributed to an Apostle of Christ. Some of their forefathers did notable deeds or for other reasons for which God in His grace spares them. Remember Ruth who said to Naomi, her Israeli mother-in-law, 'Entreat me not to leave you, Or to turn back from following after you; For wherever you go, I will go and wherever you lodge, I will lodge; Your people shall be my people, And your God, my God. Where you die, I will die, and there will I be buried. The Lord do so to me, and more also, if anything but death parts you and me.' The legitimacy of David came from the lineage of Ruth, the Moabite who I believe was not an Israelite. Ruth, was the great-grandmother of David, and, according to the Gospel of Matthew, an ancestress of Jesus."

Tom concluded saying, "I mentioned before that these three lands were originally included within the promised lands given to Israel. There are maps called the 'Southern Kingdom of Judah' that show them connected."

Maria commented, "You know it seems that God is always reaching out to people who appear not to be Israelites. We know of Abraham and now Ruth. Or is there more to the story than we know?"

Joe added, "And us too."

Tom said, "Moving along, the people are beginning to resist the unholy trinity. At this time the false prophet is under great pressure from the false president as the people are not willingly bowing in reverence to them and receiving his 3-color mark of pride like they used to. They are now starting to call it the Taboo Tattoo. The false prophet has succeeded remarkably in deceiving the people to worship the unholy trinity, however, the majority of Christians do not abandon their God and are eluding their combined efforts."

During these days, these Israelites received through the Thunder Message indirect testimony of the Son of God. They also had a gut feeling that something was wrong in Jerusalem as rumors abounded that craftsman were making a weird statue of their messiah and this was exactly opposite to what God had commanded of them in the past. They all remembered the band of Korah who made a golden idol and that the earth opened up and swallowed them.

Certain Israelites were becoming leery of their messiah and were beginning to see through him. He was severely persecuting the Christians and this went against their general beliefs as this did not support what the Holy Scriptures had to say about their messiah who would return to them and establish peace on earth.

During the beginning of the second 3½ years the false prophet became extremely frustrated. The people are worshiping his master but many refused to voluntarily get his mark. Word has leaked out that their messiah's religious prophet and president are all part of some evil trio that was now being called the unholy trinity.

Many people who were deceived by the antics of the false prophet still did not voluntarily take the evil mark as it was not mandatory to get it.

As Tom, Joe and Maria were conversing about the passing events, Tom said, "Remember that the unholy trinity has terminated the so called time of peace at the beginning of this month. Up to know the Israelites believing that their messiah was legitimate were enjoying good times."

He continued, "There is great distress in the northern land, mental suffering, hardships, and even physical pain resulting in part from the Zombie Plagues. Furthermore, the unholy trinity angered by the people's stubbornness will seek revenge and punish the people."

Tom went on saying, "Now the unholy trinity is starting to kill even the Israelites and anyone voicing an opinion contrary to theirs is targeted."

Following the latest Thunder Message telling everyone on earth 'not to bow and get his mark' word spread. In Israel, certain people had the gut feeling that something was terribly wrong. They spread this message to many others how their messiah would desecrate their newly completed temple. They read how he would dedicate it to himself and at the same time unveil his monstrous idol. What they did not know was that it would soon come to life.

Their so called religious prophet was saying that at the end of the month the Temple will be dedicated to their messiah. Rumours were now floating around that at that time, all must out of respect bow and worship their messiah. In the past, they never were forced to worship him and never had to bow. Some were secretly saying that those who refuse to bow and get his mark would be killed.

It now was no secret that something bad was beginning to take place. However, it was still so mind boggling that their messiah could be false and actually be Satan that they had not connected the dots because they were paralyzed with fear.

Maria commented, "What a difference from the early days when the false messiah's temple was being constructed by the Israelites and friends who wholeheartedly jumped into this temple building plan with great enthusiasm and joy."

Joe said, "From Tom's book, we know that the construction takes 1260 days and during this time the Dragon has been busy orchestrating the persecution of the Christians worldwide. Upon completion of his temple, he plans to inaugurate it with the unveiling of his image to be placed strategically in his temple and then dedicated to himself."

Tom continued, "And the false messiah is losing his control. He has promised good times to the people of earth but that's not happening. There are countless persecutions and atrocities. The evil gladly follow him but these, he does not care about. He desperately wants the Christians to give their loyalty to him, and their trophies. However, most refuse to do so.

In addition, even Israelites are jumping ship as they repented and he lost them to those Two Witnesses of God. This infuriates him to no end."

The efforts of the unholy trinity have deceived all nations, including those of the 10 kings, that he is their 'messiah'. They have fed propaganda saying that the Christians are responsible for the horrific plagues and they had to go. Somehow, they even tried to say the Two Witnesses were Christian engineered monsters.

The plagues created by the Two Witnesses are creating mass hysteria for everyone as word spreads that they will sooner or later be at their doorsteps.

Maria said, "It seems like the unholy trinity is setting the stage to stir the antichrist to such a degree that they all want to slaughter the Christians."

Tom replied, "The false messiah becomes furious as the Christians, even though decimated, still remain loyal to Jesus. The Dragon is enraged at his inability to get his own way with them. He is becoming more and more frustrated with the lack of success of his false prophet who, even by doing great wonders, has not been able to convince and sway tens of millions of Christians to change loyalties. The effects of the 7-7-2-FHM are undermining his efforts so severely even some of his prominent followers are beginning to complain.

Each Christian not having his mark is a pain in Satan's side. Christians are now actually mocking him as he has grossly underestimated their resolve and great faith in their Lord and God."

Joe added, "From what you have taught us, by this time, the power of the Christians has been shattered. They have been tormented, had their peace robbed and have become exhausted with nowhere to run or hide. The fact has eluded the unholy trinity that if you have nowhere to run and hide, then martyrdom is almost a welcomed event."

The Dragon during these past years has made it impossible for Christians to worship anywhere. The Christians were relegated to hide and not antagonize the antichrist. As their persecutions increased, their resolve in their faith in Christ actually became stronger. The respect and loyalty of the Christians still eluded the false messiah.

Up to now the merchants of commerce wore golden yellow uniforms, headbands and hats. This was also the same color displayed at the top of their 'Dragon's Tattoo 666'.

Maria said, "They voluntarily elected to receive this mark upon their foreheads as a sign of respect that identified their status and power."

Tom continued, "The thunder messages heard worldwide have had a tremendous effect on everyone. People either desired or loathed what the messages offered."

He continued saying, "The time is rapidly drawing close to the 1290 T/D. and now another Biblical furtive discovery are taking place. Remember when we read in Matthew 24:15 "Therefore when you see the 'abomination of desolation,' spoken of by Daniel the prophet, 'standing in the holy place' (whoever reads, let him understand)?"

Maria said, "Tom you have now used the phrases 'Abomination of desolation'[63]' **and** 'standing in the holy place' quite a few times. Tell us what you mean."

"Great minds think alike." he said. "When you carefully read this sentence, the meaning of these two phrases 'abomination of desolation' and 'standing in the holy place' are diametrically opposed."

Joe asked, "What do you mean?"

Tom answered, "In direct opposition or being at opposite extremes."

Maria said, "Hold that thought." and asked, "How can these two phrases be in the same sentence? There's absolutely no holy place in his temple."

Tom agreed saying this also completely eluded him for a long time and then one day the answer was given to him.

Joe said, "Did Mel communicate with you again, telling you the answer?"

Tom only made a 'weird or what' expression and sidestepped his question saying, "Whatever. The important thing is that the answer was given."

Maria pushed saying, "So how can they both be in the same sentence?"

Tom began by saying, "You're going to love this. Let's begin with a little background information." and using his hand in an expressive way said, "So you can fully appreciate my answer."

Maria cutting him off now made the 'weird or what' expression and jokingly said, "Tom you're not some prophet, you know."

Tom hesitated for a moment letting that remark sink in and thought to himself, "Maybe I am and Mel's my guide."

Now jolted back, he said, "OK, let's get moving. As promised, a little history. The Temple Mount used to be located on the south-east corner of the Old City of Jerusalem which features significantly in the Bible. The Kidron Valley runs along the eastern wall of the Old City of Jerusalem, separating the Temple Mount from the Mount of Olives. It then continues east through the Judean Desert towards the Living Sea descending thousands of feet along its 20 mile course.

The Old City of Jerusalem was made up of about 200 acres and had large walls surrounding it which were built originally to protect the borders of the city against intruders. The false messiah uses these walls now to contain many people, especially the Israelites."

Tom said, "Now the dragon will have his new temple constructed on the south-east corner of the city of Old Jerusalem. The size of the grounds of the temple in this corner is about 20 acres.

The Bible says that during the great earthquake a tenth of it (Old Jerusalem) falls.

This also is about 20 acres and is the same south-east corner of Old Jerusalem where the current Temple Mount is situated. This I believe was the site of Solomon's Temple known as the First Temple, in ancient Jerusalem."

Maria said, "So both the first and now Satan's temple is on the same south-east corner of this old walled city. Why is this so significant to you?"

Tom continued, "This Temple Mount location is the holiest site in Judaism and is the place Israelites turn towards during prayer. Due to its extreme sanctity, even today many Jews will not walk on the Mount itself, to avoid unintentionally entering the area where the Holy of Holies formerly stood in times past that contained the Ark of the Covenant of God. According to Rabbinical law, some aspect of the Divine Presence is still present at the site."

Maria reiterated, "Just to be clear, up until the Rapture, certain Jews won't even walk around on this site for fear that they may set foot onto the ground where God in times past had His Ark of the Covenant. That's amazing."

Joe commented, "So they didn't want to offend their God inadvertently."

Tom then said, "During the next 30 days the finishing work will be done upon this abomination along with the tens of thousands of mini-me idols. Currently it is now standing in a certain spot in the Dragon's temple. The Prophet Daniel sees the abomination being a monstrous image of the Great Red Dragon that seems to come to life. This, their Prophet Daniel said, takes place 30 days after the daily sacrifices of the Israelites have been terminated."

Maria asked, "So during thirty days from the 1260 + 30 = 1290 T/D. the abomination of desolation will be set up?"

Tom continuing, said, "Maria, with respect to your comment that there's absolutely no holy place in his temple, I agree and had wondered about this for some time. How can the two phrases stand side by side "Abomination of desolation" and "Standing in the Holy Place? The answer to this conundrum was given brilliantly in the caption (whoever reads, let him understand). This is a brain teaser. It prompts the reader to dig deeper for the answer."

Maria asked, "What does it mean (whoever reads, let him understand)?"

Tom replied, "It's a religious conundrum. Even though it seems to be impossible, it happens and Apostle John using this furtive reference to push us to further delve into this matter. Then let's dig deeper shall we. The first Temple has centuries ago been destroyed. There is no physical temple anymore. At best, just pieces of it where it used to be. There now only stands Satan's temple on this site."

Tom paused for a few seconds to gather his thoughts and then said, "In a humble way, <u>this religious conundrum will now be solved."</u>

Joe almost choking on his drink said, "Hey what happened to Mel? I thought he told you the answer."

Maria said, "Hush up, Joe. I want to hear the answer."

Tom somberly replied, "One must take a deep breath and ponder very carefully the following two things.

<u>FIRSTLY,</u> The Old (first) Temple was constructed by King Solomon, using plans that were given by God through the prophet Nathan. King David had too much blood on his hands to build the temple and was told that his son would build it.

In 833 BC, King Solomon began the construction of the Temple. The site chosen by King David was on the top of Mount Moriah. It took seven years to complete the Temple.

King Solomon dedicated the Temple and all its contents to God."

Tom continued, "<u>The Ark of the Covenant was brought into the Temple</u> amidst inaugural celebrations that lasted for seven days. For 410 years, the Jewish people would bring their daily offerings into God's Temple. <u>The Israelites would gather three times a year to witness the Divine Presence of God in His Temple and</u> despite the wind, the column of smoke from the altar always rose straight up and the wind never extinguished the fire on the altar.

SECONDLY, Satan has his temple replicated exactly to the first temple dimensions. It is constructed and positioned exactly on the spot where the first Temple stood."

Tom continued, "Now picture this. Using a computer, we overlay the dragon's temple floor plan over the Temple floor plans built by Solomon in times past, God's Temple we might say. Both are exactly the same, right down to the smallest detail."

Joe, due to his artistic abilities spotted the correlation saying, "This means the false messiah's so called 'holy of holies' lines up with and is positioned geographically directly over God's former 'Holy of Holies' that was located within the first Hebrew Temple of centuries past."

Maria said, "We just read how the Israelites would gather three times a year to witness the Divine Presence of God in His Temple. And you said they did this for 410 years, so this totals 1230 times."

Tom said from his research there seems to be a discrepancy between scholars as to the exact amount of years.

Joe then calculated, "If we say it continued for 420 years @ 3 times each year we get 1260. This figure then represents the 1260 days and this is the same as saying 3½ years."

Maria said, "Joe, what did you base your figures on?"

Joe replied, "Upon nothing."

She howled saying, "At least you're honest. 'Based on nothing'. I don't think anyone could argue with that logic."

Tom said, "I didn't think it was that funny. It's probably more factual then we know. Let's get back to solving this religious conundrum. The furtive discovery clue given here is 'whoever reads, let him understand'.

We know that God is past, present and future, meaning that this invisible spot of land may still be considered 'Holy' because God's presence was manifested on this very 'spot' of land in the past.

So we now understand the abomination of desolation happens when the Great Red Dragon's beast image is physically placed in his temple within his holy of holies on the exact same 'invisible spot' of land where 'God's Holy of Holies' was situated in times past and where His 1260 manifestations were shown."

Maria said to both of them, "You know I can't argue with that."

Tom said, "This now becomes a 'desecration' to that which in the past and perhaps even presently is sacred and is a great offence to God.

This is what it means when Jesus said, 'Therefore when you see the abomination of desolation, spoken of by Daniel the prophet, standing in the holy place (whoever reads, let him understand)'.

So now this bible passage becomes clear when the 'abomination of desolation', Satan's idol image, is placed on that exact spot of land where God previously manifested his Glory unto the Israelites. This is an abomination unto God.

This will take place during the dedication of the false messiah's temple unto himself, very soon now, on the 1290 T/D."

Tom continued, "As a side note, this desecration will continue until the 2300 T/D. The Prophet Daniel heard the angels talking about this number of days as to how long it will take 'until the Sanctuary is cleansed'. When the 2300 days have been fulfilled a great earthquake takes place and the dragon's temple crumbles into oblivion taking with it the 'abomination of desolation' that formerly stood on that 'invisible spot of holy land' where 'God's Holy of Holies' was in times past. The dragon's temple will be no more.

The Temple now will have been cleansed spiritually and physically of the Great Red Dragon, Satan, the devil or whatever you care to call him".

Joe asked, "What does it mean when the Bible says 'holy'?

Tom said, "How about you read about the 'holy' aspects. Joe began reading in Exodus 3:5 "Then He (God) said, "Do not draw near this place. Take your sandals off your feet, for the place where you stand is holy ground." Then in Acts 7:33 'Then the Lord said to him, "Take your sandals off your feet, for the place where you stand is holy ground."

Maria said she now understands what God meant back in the time of Moses when He said, take off your sandals for you are on Holy Ground.

"So there we have it, the religious conundrum solved. The abomination of desolation standing upon God's prior Holy ground was an abomination unto God.

The dragon and his antichrist must loathe God to be so blasphemous. I once thought if Satan could be redeemed and now I fully understand that there is nothing in him redeemable."

Chapter Forty-Three
THUNDER MESSAGE THREE 1290 T/D

'Blessed are the dead who die in the Lord from now on.' "Yes," says the spirit, "that they may rest from their labors, and their works follow them."

Blessed is he who waits, and comes to the one thousand three hundred and thirty-five days.

Maria asked, "When will this next Thunder Message take place?"

Tom answered, "Soon, very soon. From my research I know that the first half will be for the Christians and the latter half is for the Israelites. This thunder message comes from Revelation 14:13 and Daniel 12:12 The above Bible passages are intertwined. "That they may rest from their labors, this is a 'past tense' sentence, their labors occurred prior to this time period. And the Prophet Daniel makes reference to the 'blessed' that come to the 1335 T/D. This is the 'marriage celebration' when the Bride and Bridegroom are married by God.

During these last 45 days 1290-1335 T/D. Two massive events will take place. Blessed are the dead who come to the 1335 T/D. They are firstly the Christians who were martyred and received receiving Holpen and secondly the Israelites who repented and fled to the hills.

<u>First</u> let's talk about these Christians who for their faith and trust in the Son of God are martyred.

During these 45 days, Christians carry out great exploits of faith and become 'refined'. These Christians scattered across the entire earth will be martyred for their belief and faith in Christ. There will be maybe hundreds of millions of them. The slaughter will be horrific. However, no bad deed goes unpunished in the long run.

Starting at this Thunder Message and for the duration of the next 45 days, the first order of business of the 'unholy trinity' will be to bring the Christians before this living monster in the Dragon's temple in Jerusalem as well as in front of the thousands of other mini-me monsters placed worldwide in other places of worship. The majority of steadfast Christians will refuse to bow before this satanic beast and as a result they will be killed by the sword right there and then or dragged out into the court yard, the streets, detention camps and locations worldwide, and killed. They will be carted away in trucks to many mass grave pits where their bodies will be heaped up into an ever increasing bloody mass.

The more Christians that are killed, the more furious become the 'unholy trinity' as these Christians are absolutely loyal to their God and Jesus. Although it will be a bloody event, they somehow will muster such faith that they will actually be smiling and gazing heavenward as they are slaughtered.

The 'unholy trinity' will become very furious because they will look bad. Christians will not be bowing to them. There are millions of deceived Israelites who are actually viewing or listening via BSW to these events that are going on day and night, for a month and a half."

Tom continued, "Maria and Joe, you're going to appreciate what the Bible has to say about these Martyrs. In Revelation 7:9-17[64] it says that <u>They sing the song of the Lamb</u>, saying: "Great and marvelous are Your works, Lord God Almighty! Just and true are Your ways, O King of the saints! Who shall not fear You, O Lord, and glorify Your name? For You alone are holy. For all nations shall come and worship before You, for Your judgments have been manifested."

Tom said, "The Bible references them in three groups that have overcome the unholy trinity. I'll paraphrase what it says in Revelation 15:2-4.

It says: And I saw something like a sea of glass mingled with fire, and those who have the Victory over, the beast, (Satan), the Apostle John then elaborates further about them. He said that they have the victory over his image, his mark and his name's number.

Maria said, "Tom, what you just said identified three evil designations of Satan. What else can you tell us?"

Tom replied, "During my research, I found that the Bible mentioned <u>three martyr victory groups</u>.

The 'FIRST' group, have gained the victory over the beast (Satan) and his abomination of desolation image idol. Those who worship him or his idol wear the 'Dragon's Tattoo 666' having the 'RED' six at its top. I call Satan, the false messiah. He's the 'collector of souls'.

The 'SECOND' group' have gained the victory over the Sea Beast and his mark, those who worship him wear the 'Dragon's Tattoo 666' having the 'BLUE' six at its top. I call the Sea Beast the false president. He's the 'conquer of souls'.

The 'THIRD' group, have gained the victory over the Land Beast and his number. Those who worship him wear the 'Dragon's Tattoo 666' having the 'YELLOW' six at its top. I call the Land Beast the false prophet. He's the 'converter of souls'."

Joe said, "I think the proper order would be, the 'conqueror of souls' (Sea Beast), the 'converter of souls' (false prophet) and the 'collector of souls' (false messiah)."

"You're right," Tom replied. "They all do their dog and pony show to deceive billions."

Maria said, "If my thinking is correct, all antichrist wear this evil insignia, you call the 'Dragon's Tattoo 666', on their foreheads and the only variation is the color at its top that designates which group they belong to."

"Right again," replied Tom.

Joe commented, "Sounds like you're describing us Tom. Which group of overcomers are we in?"

Tom answered, "I think we are in the second group because sooner or later the antichrist NG will come our way."

Maria said, "They're the military forces having blue at the top of their dragon's tattoo, just like that armband Joe removed from one of them a long time ago."

Tom smiled saying, "You guys are really learning fast."

Maria asked, "What becomes of them, or rather us for that matter?"

Tom said, "These three martyr groups from the Great Tribulation are taken into the Marriage Ceremony by our Lord as recorded in the Bible in Revelation 7:9-17. It says: They are before the throne of God, and will serve Him day and night in His temple[65]."

Tom continued, "I'm going to paraphrase as it's a long Bible passage."

Maria stopped him saying, "Read all verses Tom. This is extremely important to us and those who may read your book later on, especially during the Rapture's aftermath."

"OK," he replied and began reading.

'After these things I looked, and behold, <u>a great multitude which no one could number</u>, of all nations, tribes, peoples, and tongues, standing before the throne and before the Lamb, <u>clothed with white robes</u>, <u>with palm branches in their hands</u>, and crying out with a loud voice, saying, <u>"Salvation belongs to our God who sits on the throne, and to the Lamb!"</u>

"Ok, pause there for a moment," Maria said. "It says our number will be massive. That means Christians will stand firm. Next it says, we will be clothed with white robes. I get this, but next it says, we have palm branches in our hands. What does this mean?"

Tom replied, "Palm branches symbolize we're at peace. We're not angry or mad at those who killed, we're reconciled. We are giving praises to our God and our Savior Jesus Christ."

Maria asked, "I think we are shown with palm branches symbolizing we're at peace because we received Holpen during our Martyrdom."

Tom replied, "I think you have just made another furtive discovery Maria. I often wondered why the first group of Martyr's depicted as 'under the altar souls' did not have palm branches in their hands. Now I know why."

Maria said, "OK, explain yourself."

Tom replied, "It's so simple. The first Martyrs did not receive Holpen upon their Martyrdom and as a result they're restless and crying to our Lord that He avenges their blood."

Joe commented, "They're looking for payback, that's why. Most likely the first group looking for payback, will then do just that. They will work on earth and perhaps even in the realms giving testimony to people. When I say payback, I don't mean with violence rather they're energetic and anxious to begin testifying to everyone."

Tom added, "What you two have just brought to light is fantastic. Now, let's keep reading about us again. 'All the angels stood around the throne and the elders and the four living creatures, and fell on their faces before the throne and worshiped God, saying: "Amen! Blessing and glory and wisdom, Thanksgiving and honor and power and might, Be to our God forever and ever. Amen."

Then one of the elders answered, saying to me, "Who are these arrayed in white robes, and where did they come from?" And I said to him, "Sir, you know." So he said to me,

"These are the ones who come out of the great tribulation, <u>and washed their robes</u> and <u>made them white in the blood of the Lamb</u>."

Joe commented, "Does this washing of our robes in Jesus blood mean that our sins have been forgiven? If so, this seems to me to represent one of the three Holy Sacraments. And then our robes are white, this again seems to be one of the three Holy Sacraments. Where's the third one?"

Tom replied, "Remember we already have the Holy Baptism of Water. We got it when we were young."

Maria said, "Maybe we get the Holy Sealing when we receive 'Holpen' when we're martyred."

Tom replied, "I like your answer. It's either then or later when we meet Jesus. I don't know." And then he continued reading.

"<u>Therefore they are before the throne of God, and serve Him day and night in His temple</u>. And He who sits on the throne will dwell among them. They shall neither hunger anymore nor thirst anymore; the sun shall not strike them, nor any heat; for the Lamb who is in the midst of the throne will shepherd them and lead them to living fountains of waters. <u>And God will wipe away every tear from their eyes</u>."

Maria said, "Why are we referred to as those before the throne of God who serve Him?"

Tom answered, "I don't really have a good answer for you, Maria, however, I do know that we're the second group of Martyrs, and I think we will be Temple Priests."

Joe asked, "Really? Priests?" and Tom replied, "That's the feeling I'm getting. Maybe it's Mel again, I don't know."

Maria said to both of them, "It actually says that God Himself will wipe all our tears away. I can't even imagine such a beautiful time."

Joe said, "We must remain absolutely faithful to our Lord and God."

"Well said," Maria gently whispered.

Tom, continuing, said, "Now along with our group of Martyrs we also have another group of Martyrs from centuries past. This group has already received their Holy Sealing in eternity by our Lord Jesus and they are waiting for us."

Joe asked, "Really? They're waiting for us? How do you know this?"

Tom said, "It tells us about them in Revelation 6:9-11," and then then began reading.

"When He opened the fifth seal <u>I saw under the altar the souls of those who had been slain for the word of God and for the testimony which they held.</u> And they cried with a loud voice, saying, "How long, O Lord, holy and true, until You judge and <u>avenge our blood</u> on those who dwell on the earth?" <u>Then a white robe was given to each of them</u>; and it was said to them that <u>they should rest a little while longer, until both the number of their fellow servants and their brethren, who would be killed as they were, was completed</u>."

Joe asked, "Why were they under the altar?"

Tom answered, "From my research, these Martyrs were just like us. They had the Holy Baptism of Water."

Maria said, "And from what we just discovered, they are given white robes but they don't have palm branches in their hands and now we know why they were not reconciled."

Joe said, "They, like us, have the Holy Baptism of Water but lacked Baptism of the Holy Spirit, again like us."

Tom replied, "Yes and then Jesus gave them their white robes. This seems to indicate that Jesus himself gave them this last holy sacrament, the Baptism with the Holy Spirit."

Maria said, "It says that Jesus told them to rest a little while longer, until we come along."

Joe said, "Too bad we didn't read all this stuff before the Rapture took place."

Maria said, "Again, hindsight is 20/20."

Tom said to them, "All this killing happens during the 1290 – 1335 T/D. At the conclusion of these 45 days everyone that God desired for the <u>Wedding Ceremony of His Son</u> at the 1335 T/D, have been removed from earth."

Maria said, "It seems like our time is almost at hand and I never thought I would say this, but I'm looking forward to 'Holpen'."

Joe said, "I wonder if all Christians will replace the words, killed, slaughtered, martyred with 'Holpen'."

Tom said, "Christians, thousands of years ago, greeted each other saying, 'Maranatha' an expression of greeting meaning, 'O Lord, come'. Now they may use the greeting 'Holpen'. They encourage each other to stay the course, keep the faith, for our Lord comes to take us home and we will receive a great miracle, 'Holpen'."

Tom said, "As these Christians, meaning us, are being Martyred, many of the antichrist will actually join with us by intrigue. As strange as it seems, this 'Holpen' is so awe inspiring to behold, some of the antichrist, mourned the fact that they had chosen poorly. Some allow themselves to be killed alongside hoping to achieve what we are experiencing but to no avail as their fate was already sealed because they wore the Taboo Tattoo and thus numbered to the 'cull of the damned'."

"From what you're saying, Tom, this now concludes the time of the Christians as we have now reached the, 1335 T/D," said Maria.

"You're right, Maria. The 'Time of Refinement" of the Christians is completed. This is the First Resurrection, its conclusion event."

"We now turn our attention and focus on a special group, the 'Israelites of Understanding' who from the 1040 T/D to the 1290 T/D accepted the Testimony of the Two Witnesses of God and received the Baptism unto Repentance <u>before</u> the "Abomination of desolation" was activated at the 1290 T/D. They did so in faith, were redeemed and go into the Wilderness Sanctuary, Temple Priests who minister unto the next group. The time of the redeemed Israelites is completed between 1040-1290 T/D."

Maria said, "I'm impressed how the puzzle is coming together."

Tom continued, "People around the world begin to sense some type of a strange event is going to happen. Rumours will be rampant during the weeks that their messiah's newly constructed temple will be officially dedicated along with a statue of him on the 1290 T/D.

So now we turn our attention to the time following the 1290 T/D. I believe that during the dedication many Israelites will be nervous as this will not be your typical type of ceremony. All will be watching as 10 beings in black hooded robes appear to just float in procession. Across their chests are hieroglyphics of some type in red, yellow and blue. On their backs is a large version of the 'Dragon's Tattoo 666'. The faces of the black robed beings are hidden like that same type of blackness of their messiah's sphere, eerie to say the least. They bow to the veiled huge statue. Their 3-color Taboo Tattoo begins to glow brilliantly and appear to be fiery like the sun, yet their robes do not burn."

Maria interjected, "Is all this in the Bible or is this your theory?"

Tom answered, "This is all conjecture. It's how I think it will happen based on many hours of research. To continue, next comes the sound of trumpets, very disharmonic and irritating. Then the false president and false prophet will come forward from somewhere behind and stand, one to the right and one to the left of this covered thing. Hundreds of high echelon devotees in red robes but no hoods will come next. Their 3-color Taboo Tattoos on their foreheads appear to glow most brilliantly."

Joe asked, "In your book, what's the purpose of the glowing tattoos?"

"The evil energy from the evil beings is being transferred to them," said Tom.

"To get back to what I was saying, it's all in my book, you know. Now the 10 black hooded beings each take hold of a single tassel attached to the veil. Upon the audible voice command of the false prophet, they will simultaneously pull, and the veil is rent asunder, falling in two pieces to the ground as if to signify some event. As the pieces touch the floor they burst into flames and disappear. When they look up to what was previously hidden by the veil, they will see some type of dragon with its mouth open displaying large teeth all around. This idol, well over 25' high, looks extremely ferocious. Those in attendance and those connected by video transmission will be transfixed by this thing. After a few moments the false prophet, taking a cue from the false president, speaks very loud words in a language unknown to most in attendance. Upon the utterance of this sentence, the 10 raise their arms upwards and those in the red robes kneel down on both knees with their arms also raised upwards. The false president then speaks loudly in this same strange language and the eyes of the beast become a glowing red. The false prophet then utters more strange words and the idol begins to take on life. The appearance of this monster goes from a solid granite, stone-like object to an appearance resembling a liquid metal capable of movement."

Tom continued, "Try to imagine it being a silvery mercury colored metal of some type that is able to move as if it were alive. This huge dragon now morphs into a blood thirsty red beast with eyes that look like the morning sun, sort of slits and behind these slits fiery red eyes that moved scanning everyone and everywhere. The skin of this beast is made up of many shimmering reddish shields of some type of battle plating. These shields are not normal but are all covered with what appears to be undulating force fields having a scintillating pattern making him look like some type of science fiction monster. This monster does not speak, yet it communicates with those around it.

The false prophet now commands that all people on earth must bow to their god and get his mark on their hands or die. Those in attendance will cheer and give praises to their god for they already have his 3-color mark. Those watching from a distance either rejoice or are terrified by what they have just witnessed."

Maria said, "There must have be many thousands of people living in Judea that have fallen for the deceiving tactics of the false messiah."

Joe responded, "Those so close to him would have taken his 3-color mark, wouldn't they?"

Maria said, "For sure they had to have taken his mark by now since they are living in Jerusalem and perhaps even had certain religious functions as the temple was being constructed."

Tom went silent for a moment then said, "Those Israelites living in the walled portion of Jerusalem who served their messiah wore garments of red only. They took his mark, not outwardly but inwardly."

Joe asked, "Was Mel talking to you again?"

Tom nonchalantly replied, "Uh huh."

Maria said, "What did he mean by that answer?"

Tom, somewhat perplexed, only said, "I don't know. Sometimes Mel seems to tease us."

He continued, "In my book, my research indicates that the Israelites who in their minds and hearts decided not to bow to this beast recall what their friends had told them some time ago about an abomination that would stand in their temple. As they witness this first hand and take to heart what they were told to do, they 'get out of Dodge' and flee to the hills, more precisely the mountains."

Maria said, "Maybe the Israelites fleeing out of Judea now witness some type of Heavenly Wonder such as seeing the brilliance of the pillar of fire off in the distance and they instinctively head towards it. They possibly remembered this from millennia's past during the exodus out of Egypt. You told us that the Two Witnesses and the '7-7' have been for the past month been testifying to the people living in the lands of Moab, Edom and Ammon."

Tom continued, "Yes, but now at this 1290 T/D., the Israelites begin 'fleeing' out of Judea into the mountains surrounding the Living Sea and for the next 110 days will have opportunity to once again accept God's mercy. I find it interesting to note that Noah completed the ark in 110 years. Strange how these numbers repeat, don't you think?"

Maria said, "Those fleeing out of Judea would be able to see this pillar of fire and flee towards it. Everyone would be able to see it but only those fleeing would dare travel towards it."

Tom replied, "Your scenario is fantastic, one could easily write a book called 'The Third Thunder' that would include events such as, 'abomination of desolation', 'global genocide', 'finger on the trigger', 'bang, get out Dodge', 'exodus', 'pillar of fire', 'sparkling' 'salvation' and entrance into the 'Wilderness Sanctuary'.

Maria said, "Or one might say, the "Ark of Salvation"."

Tom chuckled, "There will come the time of the 'six arks of salvation' that I refer to as 'star crafts'."

Joe said, "You mean space ships?"

Tom's answer was, "They could easily travel to the stars but for now they shuttle the 'saved' people from the nations of the 10 kings."

Maria said, "When will we see them?"

Tom replied, "This will take place between the 2300-2303.5 T/D. We'll be long gone by then."

Joe commented, "The size of these star crafts must be huge."

Tom replied, "Perhaps they're a mile or more in height."

"Back to basics," said Maria. "I believe that all of those who flee to the hills will accept the Baptism unto Repentance by the Two Witnesses of God, but who really knows. They'd be crazy not to."

Tom replied, "The Two Witnesses have been waiting for this last group of Israelites to come to them. In my book, they are made up of the 'repented congregation' and are referred to as the 'repented Israelites' worshiping in the Great Domed City where the partially opened Temple of God exists. They repent not through 'faith' but through 'sight' after witnessing the 'abomination of desolation'. They have come to the realization that their messiah was false and was actually Satan. Once this final group of Israelites has been testified to the repented Israelites taken into the pillar of fire are now safely deposited into the 'Wilderness Sanctuary'."

Tom continued, "These final days of the first year of testimony of the Two Witnesses of God conclude at the 1400 T/D.

The Flying Hell Monsters also create wide spread terror in the hearts of the antichrist living in the land of Judea along with some future 'evil seeds'."

Maria said, "So for the antichrist living in Judea, it is now their turn as here come the Flying Hell Monsters."

Joe said, "Could we call them 'holy terrors'?"

Tom and Maria were silent. Nobody voiced an audible opinion, however, silently they thought there's nothing 'holy' about them.

Tom continued, "Their time in Israel and Judea including the lands of Moab, Edom and Ammon now completed, at this 1400 T/D. Now the pillar of fire with the Two Witnesses move on in tandem with the fire/thunders to the next 'Angel Halo', beginning in Egypt."

Maria commented, "And hot on their heels will come the Flying Hell Monsters, fresh out of Judea and the areas they just exited."

Joe said, "And once again the Zombie Plagues begin in the lands of the 10 kings. Angel halo number two, here we come."

Tom had to remind him, "We are dead by then."

"Are we?" shivered Joe.

Chapter Forty-Four

MARTYRDOM MARIA AND JOE

Not long after the 1290 T/D, Maria and Joe were outside tending to some chores and were discussing how their end may come about for they knew their time was very near at hand and were somewhat perplexed due to the fact that no one had come to round them up, arrest them or kill them. They both were mentally prepared to become Martyrs of Christ as they wished to obtain the goal of their faith.

While they were walking around looking at the scenery, all of a sudden high above them they noticed a reflection and upon closer inspection saw that it was from a disc drone that was slowly moving from east to west. Joe uttered, "I wonder how long it's been observing us?"

They gazed up intently at this thing and were not afraid of it and wondered if it would start shooting at them. This flying disc silently drew closer and then emitted some sort of brilliantly energy burst. Joe and Maria were no more as they disappeared from their location.

Unknown to anyone, they were in a flash teleported into this disc. This moving craft travelled for some time and made frequent stops, each time depositing more people into the containment area where they were. After what seemed like an eternity it landed somewhere. Large doors opened and they found themselves staring at soldiers pointing weapons at them. They were marshalled along a fenced corridor to a holding area.

Joe and Maria looked around and then at each other, they were surrounded by thousands of others. There were no blankets, food or water, just earth under their feet. Throughout the rest of the day and night other flying crafts constantly deposited their cargo of Christians into their camp.

Joe and Maria were not afraid and began to testify to those present and to their amazement many knew of them and their great exploits. Throughout the night more and more people spoke with them saying how much they relied on their BSW transmissions. They were thankful to learn of what was happening and the events that would soon take place.

Maria and Joe testified to all to bolster their faith. Everyone had mixed emotions. They were afraid of what was coming their way, yet they were also looking forward to 'Holpen'.

Maria whispered to Joe, "It's so gratifying to see how the people are clinging to their anticipated time of Holpen."

At some point during the night many began singing and praying. The shouts of the guards did little to quell their devotion their Lord.

The next day dawned, and a tractor pulled in something on a float. Whatever it was had a canopy covering the object. People with the 3-color 'Dragon's Tattoo 666' mark were surrounding it and they had rifles pointed at their captives to keep them at bay. Soon an announcement was loudly spoken without the means of any speakers. Whatever was under that canopy was doing the talking. This thing kept talking for what seemed to be days on end. It was speaking blasphemies towards their God and Savior. Joe said it was some type of brainwashing. Both Maria and Joe took advantage of this time to encourage their fellow captives about what to expect next. Most agreed with them, some did not.

The detainees consisted of Christians and non-Christians. They seemed to have one thing in common, all were those that had fled the cities and migrated to the remote areas. During these days all prisoners lost track of time. They could have been there for a week or more. Confusion abounded.

At sunrise, they heard a siren and soon many soldiers were marshalling them into a very large circle with this veiled thing in their center. The antichrist themselves had formed a smaller circle around this thing and seemed anxious. Their leader gave a command to remove its veil and upon so doing there appeared a beast about the size of a person. The image of this beast looked like what Tom had described in his book, a red dragon horrible to behold with fierce glowing eyes and huge teeth. It was speaking but its mouth was not moving. It was commanding all to bow, worship him and get his mark or die. Those who did, received a black mark upon their right hands to be able to buy and sell. This mark also meant that they worshiped and swore allegiance to their 'messiah', the god of earth. Upon getting the mark they were immediately escorted through the fenced in corridor, were released and free to depart, cheered on by the antichrist.

Those who refused and defied the offer of the beast, and who would rather die than betray their faith in Christ, remained.

Maria pointed and said, "Look over there."

Another group of soldiers were coming their way. They had in their hands what appeared to be light saber swords that up to now were only seen in science fiction movies. They moved towards the Christians and with great malice and without speaking, began to slaughter them. As they were being martyred, the Christians all looked up towards Heaven and started smiling and singing, for some reason known only to them. As they stared into Heaven, they saw God, Jesus and what appeared to be an uncountable multitude in white robes all cheering them on to victory. It was as if each martyr was being spoken to by God and Jesus.

As they watched others being martyred, they saw as Tom had predicted that even some of the antichrist that were doing the slaughtering were so impressed that they too wanted to be killed. They too raised their hands to God. They desired what these Christians were getting but to no avail. To them 'HOLPEN' was not offered and their death was meaningless but this fact alone bolstered the faith of those being martyred and those awaiting martyrdom. Their actions angered the antichrist to see their own turning away from their messiah.

When Maria and Joe saw these antichrist with some type of light swords only a few feet away, fear was not present. They fully embraced each other, shared one last kiss, looked up into Heaven, smiled and received 'Holpen'.

Tom had decided about an hour before on the day of Maria and Joe's abduction that it would be good to move his Expedition to another area further away from their cave. They needed the room as more and more nomads were arriving on a daily basis.

There were many overhangs carved by water erosion over time. During this time he had asked Maria and Joe to find some vegetables for their supper meal.

He was a mile or so away which may seem far but the gentle slope of the valley actually enhanced his panoramic view of their cave making its appearance much closer.

He selected an appropriate cave large enough to hide his vehicle and had been gone a little over one hour. He decided to put the tarp blanket on his Explorer to be on the safe side. Even though he could see Joe and Maria in the distance, he was not too concerned about them as they knew the safety drill.

He was reflecting upon the events of the last week and pondering what next would be coming down the pipeline. As he was securing the tarp, he glanced over in their direction and smiled to himself to see them in the vegetable field. Flash, and in a blink of an eye he couldn't see and only after several minutes did his sight and balance begin to return. Then slowly focusing, he looked towards where he last saw Joe and Maria. He was astonished. They were gone.

He ran outside the cave into the sunlight and with difficulty scanned the skies for anything that could have caused this event. The sky appeared clear.

Then he saw it, or rather a reflection of sunlight from it, in the far off distance rapidly vanishing and then nothing.

He felt as if he had been punched in the gut but this didn't stop him as he ran back to where he last saw them standing. Frantically, he began searching and yelling as loud as he could. Everything happened so quickly, there was no forewarning just a flash and they were gone.

Although he knew what to expect, he was perplexed as to what just happened. Were they martyred? Incinerated? Or was it something else? He too was waiting and wanted to be martyred.

Tom moved wearily towards the cave, then went inside, overcome with sorrow at the loss of his loved ones. He felt abandoned and collapsed on the sofa.

Several hours later when he regained consciousness, he tried to comprehend what had happened. He frantically turned on his BSW with the hopes of getting more information as to what just transpired and was not disappointed. The air waves were teeming with people openly talking as to what was happening to everyone during these last week's just prior to the 1335 T/D. Tens of millions of Christians already had been martyred and now the false messiah, president and prophet along with the antichrist followers were mopping up loose ends. The straggler Christians from the more remote areas, and this included Maria and Joe, were now on his list but for some reason they missed him and those of his flock.

The NG were now in absolute control and using non- terrestrial discs that could travel, remain motionless and could emit some type of what trekie fans would call a tractor beam, locked on to them and teleported them up to their ship or to another location.

He rationalized that this must have happened to Maria and Joe. They were not vaporized. They were teleported to some other area on earth, most likely some type of containment area. Tom theorized that wherever they were taken their fate would be certain martyrdom. He was extremely sad that he was not with them to the end. From what he was hearing, the appearances of the unholy trinity were changing. The false messiah now took on a demonic, sinister and fierce appearance. The false president transformed into some type of leopard-looking beast speaking blasphemous words.

And the false prophet transformed into a beast with two horns and spoke like a dragon. They were all scary to behold and the people now either rejoiced or were mortified.

During these days from 1290-1335 T/D., the antichrist killed almost all of the Christians worldwide and within short order only a few stragglers remained hidden, out of sight and hoping for various reasons, to make it through this time alive.

For the next several hours all that Tom could think about is why did this happen without taking him. He desperately wanted to go when the antichrist came.

Now, alone in his cave, and knowing what the future had in store for him, he picked up his book and it opened to the section entitled 'Martyrs Gathered from the Sky'. The thought occurred to him that he could fulfill one last mission. The three of them had already offered guidance and a safe refuge for those fleeing to the mountains. Now, with little time still remaining, he prepared to be martyred for his faith in the Son of God.

For some reason his martyrdom was being postponed but he knew full well that as long as he was martyred before the 1335 T/D., that was now very close at hand that, he could still go and be with his loved ones.

After pondering his predicament, he formulated a plan to be of service to God. Tom decided to go on the offensive and attack. The best way to do this was by using his BSW radio to inform the nations of the 10 kings what to expect during the balance of the 'Time of Sorrows' for approximately the next 2½ years.

Tom theorized that since he wanted to be martyred along with Maria and Joe and this did not happen, then God had another purpose for him, for now.

Now with a purpose and goal in sight, Tom started to broadcast his messages out to the world and not just at the predetermined times like he did in the past with Abram. Instead, he recorded his message to the world and set the BSW to transmit every 5 minutes in an attempt to reach as many people around the world as possible. He transmitted detailed 'burst' messages along with a simple message. He proclaimed to the nations of the 10 kings that they should not worship, bow or get the mark of the 'false messiah' who actually the devil was pretending to be their god.

He went on saying in his broadcast that the God of Heaven was responsible for the global wonders of the fire lightning and thunder messages that everyone was witnessing in the skies.

Included in Tom's transmission was a message that the Two Witnesses from the God of Heaven would soon be coming to them.

Tom also informed them that there will be another four fire/thunder messages from God. Tom repeatedly said for all to remain faithful and that the Two Witnesses of God will be soon offering them the Baptism unto Repentance. Those who accept will be saved from the great destruction that would come upon the earth soon and referred to it as 'Armageddon'.

He remembered his friend Abram who had been redeemed a long time ago and was now safe in the Wilderness Sanctuary and most likely a Temple Priest.

He reminisced about his friend's last few messages to all of them saying he was not frightened anymore and thanked them for their guidance and testimony concerning these Two Witnesses of God and their helper, and only now did Tom comprehend what Abram had meant by 'helper'; his friend Mel.

Abram had said that he believed but please pray for him as the Christian doctrine was so new to him and to accept meant he had to cast aside centuries of tradition where they never even mentioned the Son of God in any type of worshiping.

Abram shortly thereafter had communicated one final time. Tom now was reflecting and pondering Abram's message to the three of them about seeing the Fire Lightning and hearing the Thunder Messages. His final words were the 'fingers of God are so beautiful' along with a one word comment from his strange friend Mel, 'soon'. Abram's finger seemingly having a mind of its own released the transmit button. He was gone.

They all knew instinctively what he meant by 'Fingers of God"! All three had been speechless as they too awaited their turn. As to his message, time will tell.

Tom shook the cobwebs out of his head realizing that he had been reminiscing about past events when Maria and Joe were still with him and even their friend Abram and for some reason he once again drifted into reminiscing mode thinking about the 'nomads', as they were called, who were hiding in the mountain caves in the surrounding area.

Tom, during these final months, intuitively had the feeling that someone has been leading them subconsciously. Perhaps it was his friend Mel again. He had become the father figure to many nomad Christians who up to now had eluded the NG. They did not have the 'Dragon's Tattoo 666'. They were just frightened. Many of them previously lived in mobile campers. They were all in one mind that the best place to hide from all the killing that was going on was to flee to the mountains and the Rocky Mountains seemed to be a logical refuge.

During these waning days, hundreds found their way to the general area of their cave. The three of them had come to the conclusion that those who were coming their way were now their responsibility. From their lofty height of 8,000 feet, using binoculars they could see them, perhaps a hundred miles away. Many of them were now walking as their vehicles had run out of gas or broken down along the way.

They could not transmit a message to them as this would have been a sure give-a-way. Joe had come up with a novel idea to simply use a mirror to signal each little group as they approached him in the distance.

As long as the sun was in a favourable position, he signaled to them. In short order, they could see them climbing and moving towards him. The people were actually making a beeline to them.

The cave soon became a command center of sorts, offering food and information. There seemed to be hundreds of caves scattered throughout the mountain sides and valleys and they knew many of them from their daily excursions.

As each group reached him, they were confused, scared and did not know what to do. Food from the cave was shared and the people organized into little groups who were taught how to be invisible from the sky.

Soon they were good at foraging and gathering wild berries, herbs, water, and food of any kind. Almost immediately they started asking questions and fortunately for them, they were given answers which resulted in teaching sessions.

As each new little group came into their midst the existing groups would offer general information as to the circumstances surrounding them.

In short order, these Christian nomads had come to the understanding that their God had not abandoned them. The people rejoiced upon hearing that there still was hope for them.

Tom was smiling to himself and once again jolted from his quiet reminiscing mode by the shouts of hundreds of people who had converged in the valley outside of his cave. Tom went out. The sight of them humbled him, and he knew now why his mission was to stay a little longer and offered comforting words that even impressed him as they were well above his pay grade and wondered how such wisdom came from his lips. He muttered to himself, "Mel's here."

Tom explained how Maria and Joe had been taken by some flying disc that in a flash took them.

Tom brought them up to speed saying that their time would now happen within days, not weeks. Tom said that if he were fortunate enough to have the same opportunity as Maria and Joe, he was going to take it.

This was somewhat difficult for them to initially digest. However, in short order, they agreed that God must have been guiding them and for such a special purpose.

He now informed them that he was transmitting a special bulletin every five minutes to the people on earth advising them about what was going to take place. Tom told them that the antichrist would soon be able to triangulate his position and for those who wanted this all to end, to be martyred for their Lord and to receive His reward, get prepared.

They had a signal, a series of bell ringing. When the bell was rung three times, it meant come to the meeting for discussing. Tom said that he would ring the bell 5 times when the time was at hand for their martyrdom and they should then rush to his cave for the event.

Those who did not want this were advised to move on to even more remote areas in the mountains and try and wait it out until the Two Witnesses of God came to testify to them. The only difference would be that they would then be numbered unto the saved people and not Priests of Christ. The choice was theirs.

Most had already decided that they wanted to go the route of the Martyrs to be with their Lord and were ready for the 5 bells.

Chapter Forty-Five

THE LAST MARTYR, TOM

As things turned out, it was on the 1335 T/D., the very last day, last hour and last minute. Tom was fully prepared to be martyred for his faith in Christ and actually was longing for this day to be gathered with his loved ones. Finally it came, although not in a way that he had contemplated.

As Tom and a few others were outside sitting on the grass and finishing their supper, unknown to them their 'Last Supper', Tom saw in the far off distance a reflection from some type of disc shaped craft. Immediately upon sighting it, he instinctively knew that it was the NG looking for him due to his incessantly repeating global BSW bulletins.

Tom rang the bell 5 times signalling that "it was time". This meant that the NG were approaching and those who had decided to stand up for their faith in Christ should now do so or in the alternative hide until the time that the 7-7-2-FHM would come to them and they could be numbered unto the 'saved' nations if they accepted their testimony and remained faithful.

Upon hearing the 5 bells toll, the old and the young, fathers holding children and some mothers with babies in their arms came running. All were watching this large flying disc approaching them.

Tom, along with all gathered, were filled with some type of serenity and heard voices gently whispering to them. Now something inexplicable took place. These Christians, as if given some silent command, started raising their hands in praise to God. Their actions guaranteed that the NG would see them. This disc came closer and closer towards them and when it seemed almost upon them, it stopped and hovered several hundred feet above the ground.

There was an eerie silence for the next several minutes, possibly due to the fact that the NG were not accustomed to seeing a group of Christians actually waiving their hands and drawing attention to themselves. Within minutes, there somehow appeared on the ground many NG dressed in uniforms displaying the colors RED-YELLOW-BLUE, all with some type of light saber sword in their hands. They started to approach Tom and his flock who stood firm in total silence, including some children, who did not panic or run. This caused a very unnerving situation for the NG who in the past were used to instilling fear and sometimes panic before they slaughtered their victims.

Tom had promised that they would all receive 'Holpen' from God prior to being martyred and they were not disappointed. Seconds before these antichrist NG reached them, and still with their hands raised, all simultaneously looked directly straight up, not to the sky but somehow through it, into Heaven. They saw into the eyes of God and Jesus and then witnessed a vast number of souls encouraging them.

Those who were about to be martyred could somehow feel the power of their prayers and along with something else, a gently whispering voice that they perceived in their souls saying, "Your Time of Refinement is over. Come home children. It's time." And they experienced 'Holpen'.

Tom, as he steadfastly looked into the eyes of God only seconds before becoming the last martyr of His Son, spotted two familiar faces. Yes, it was them!

He smiled, hearing Mel's uniquely comforting voice one last time whispering, "Well done my true and loyal servant. Come home, it's time." And he experienced 'Holpen'.

The NG could not comprehend what was happening and again a few of them actually threw their weapons to the ground with the hope of attaining what these Christians were getting, but to no avail as they had already received the 'Dragon's Tattoo 666'.

The rest of the NG scoffed at them and merely slaughtered them as well. The majority of antichrist noticed the blood of the

Martyrs flowing down the rocks and mocked their sacrifice, saying "Where's your God now?"

They were laughing but all looked up into the sky upon hearing a great trumpet sound that seemed to originate from all directions as if it encircled the entire world. Unknown to them, it did exactly that. It is written in the Bible[66] in Matthew 24:31, "And He will send His angels with a <u>great sound of a trumpet,</u> and <u>they will gather together His elect from the four winds, from one end of heaven to the other.</u>"

The antichrist murderers were all terrified by this enormous trumpet sounding in the Heavens that knocked them to the ground. They had to cover their ears and had no clue what was going to happen next.

The sky turned to thick darkness, lightning scintillated, thunders peeled, fire issued and a thunderous voice said, "Vengeance is mine." Those NG murderers were no more. So ends the time of the Christians upon earth with Tom, the last martyr, at the 1335 T/D.

The Prophet Daniel said in Chapter 12:12, "Blessed is he who waits, and comes to the one thousand three hundred and thirty-five days."

All Christians loyal to the Son of God at this date have been martyred and removed from earth. As prophesised, with a great sound of a trumpet, the Martyrs were gathered by our Lord and taken to God in Heaven. Apostle Paul even said in 1 Thessalonians 4:16, "For the Lord Himself will descend from heaven with a shout, with the voice of an archangel, <u>and with the trumpet of God.</u>"

All the martyred are now in the sky and upon the sound of a great trumpet that is heard worldwide the angels of our Lord gather together His elect from the four winds, from one end of heaven to the other and then all the tribes of the earth will mourn because they were not partakers of this great event. Those of the nations of the 10 kings, of which many had BSW radios, were foretold by Tom that the Two Witnesses would be coming their way soon. One could not say in words how this infuriated the unholy trinity and their antichrist followers. The cat's now out of the bag. Those remaining on earth had salvation coming their way.

Christians not desiring martyrdom, if any still remaining upon earth, have fled to very remote areas and remain in hiding. In the past, from his research Tom had said that some Christian religions taught their membership that they will survive during the great tribulation and go into the 1000 year Kingdom of Peace still in their earthly body as citizens.

Now, if this is the case, then these people come under the Baptism of Repentance of the Two Witnesses of God and become part of the saved nations and are gathered by the forces of God for the 'wedding feast' of His Son, in His wedding hall around the 2303.5 T/D. Some people insist on doing it the hard way.

Tom, the last Martyr of Christ, has been transported into Heaven for the Wedding of the Bride and Bridegroom. The time of Tom, Joe and Maria has been completed and this now concludes phase one of God's Plan of Salvation called the 'Time of Refinement'.

Chapter Forty-Six

MEL, SUPERNATURAL GUIDE 1335 T/D

In the past, I counselled Tom, Maria and Joe, and now you. What you didn't know was that Joe and Maria were the last of their group to be martyred and immediately following them, was you Tom. It has been decided that you, 'Last Three Martyrs of Christ' return to this time plane for a little while. They serve a special purpose. Through my guidance and their eyes you will witness many spectacular events. Some may ask, who am I? Those conversant with the Holy Scriptures know of John the Baptist and how they foretold of him in the Book of Malachi 3:1, "Behold, I will send my messenger, and he shall prepare the way before me." As the spirit of Elijah was manifested in the person of John the Baptist, in these 'end of days', I communicated through Tom. Until the appointed time of the end, I will continue communicating through Tom, Maria and Joe, now in spirit, yet human in appearance. Together they will travel with me, observing the events, past, present and future.

Even though the time date is now at 1335 I am going to recall some of the days that have passed by reversing the time line to the 1040 T/D.

Maria looked at Mel and asked, "Because we were transported back to be with you do we miss the Wedding Ceremony taking place right now?"

Mel answered, "No, you don't."

Maria queried further, "Please explain."

Mel's answer was, "Trust me."

They trusted. Mel thought, "They're just like Daniel. They believed." Mel, impressed, answered, them. "Remember time can be moved forward or backwards in its plane." They did not fully comprehend, but they believed.

"It is at this time the Two Witnesses of God or as I call them 'God's 2 Ambassadors' commenced their 'Time of Redemption'. These events were only touched upon by Tom, Maria and Joe, but now we will actually witness them in real time.

What now takes place may be called 'beauty and the beast'. The 'beauty' is the time of redemption and the 'beast' is the consequences of bowing to the beast and getting his mark.

Now come the 7 SPIRITS, 7 THUNDERS, 2 WITNESSES and FLYING HELL MONSTERS as Tom, Maria and Joe used to say and speaking of them, here they come."

Maria, looked around at Joe, then Tom saying, "What happened? Why are we back on earth?" Maria, eyes now riveted and penetrating into Joe's, said to Mel, "Did we, or more specifically Joe, screw up again?"

Mel actually laughed and said, "No, we have another mission for you, 'Last Martyrs of Christ'."

Maria said, "You mean Joe, Tom and I were actually the last three?"

"Yes," Mel replied.

Tom asked, "We're back on earth, right?"

"Correct," Replied Mel, "and the time line has been reset to 1040 T/D."

Maria gasped, "Oh no! Do we have to be martyred again? Once was enough!"

Mel, sensing human confusion, said, "Relax. You're back in time to assist me. Look at your bodies. You're now in spirit form. And Maria did you feel pain upon martyrdom or 'Holpen'?"

"You've made your point," she said.

Tom said, "How come we still look the same?"

Joe offhandedly said, as for his looks 'one cannot improve upon perfection'.

Maria almost punched him, if that were now possible.

Mel continued, "Actually that's one reason the three of you are back. It seems like my tutorial may be somewhat point-blank lacking in your strange sense of humor that humans can relate to, complete with your idiosyncrasies. Since we want the human race to become worthier, it was decided to have you accompany me for a while, including Joe," who smiled at the compliment, he assumed.

Tom asked, "Why are we back at the 1040 T/D?"

Mel answered, "You talked about and described the events that would take place and you actually lived in, but did not experience most of them. Now, Joe's coining of the word 'Zombies' will take on life of its own. We will soon see this happening in what you call 'real time', sort of like a movie picture unfolding before the viewer's eyes."

Maria asked, "Who exactly will be the audience watching this strange movie of sorts?"

"Billions prior to and billions after the Rapture Event," said Mel.

"Wow, talk about pressure!" commented Maria.

Joe asked, "What type of camera will we be using?"

"Camera?" asked Mel. "Oh, I get it. The camera will consist of each of your five senses." Mel again sort of chuckled, "When the 'action' begins you will be able to reach out and touch the zombies should you desire to do so. As for me, I don't touch abominations."

Maria asked, "Will the zombies be able to see us?"

Mel said, "No, we're on a different time plane. However, Joe, if you touched one of them they would receive an energy jolt. This would cause them to panic and this in turn would create havoc, as you say, creating the 'butterfly effect'."

Maria asked, "Are you using our terminology or yours?" Before Mel could answer, she again spouted, "Are you sure we're not back here because of Joe?"

Joe stammered, "Hey, that's not fair Maria!" and from somewhere in the background a voice was heard, "Make them understand."

Mel commented, "Poor Joe. Always getting the 'short end of the stick'. Someday, I'll tell you the story about where that saying really originated.

Now, the three of you, listen up. You're here as a reward for the great work you did during the time of sorrows you found yourselves in."

Maria sighed, "Thank goodness!"

Joe laughed. "I knew it! Nobody gets kicked out of Heaven."

Mel, looking somewhat perplexed, said, "Joe evidently 200 million did, remember?"

Joe's expression jolted to that of somberness.

"OK, now that we're all on the same page," Mel said, "let's move forward." With the wave of his hand, they were flying through the air yet there was no feeling of rushing air. In what could be only be expressed by saying, 'in the twinkling of an eye' they were standing upon the ground back in the USA.

"See," said Tom as he pointed to the Statue of Liberty.

Maria spoke saying, "I never thought I'd ever see that again."

Mel looked at them and immediately they were standing in Central Park.

It was Joe's turn to comment. "Look at that. There are thousands of Christians gathered around someone speaking to them using a megaphone." All moved closer to a make-shift platform.

Mel's next comment riveted them, "Listen to his words." The speaker was calling on all present to 'stay the course' and 'keep the faith' for their Lord and Savior will be coming for them soon. "Listen to what he says next," whispered Mel, although only the three could hear his words. The speaker as if on cue said something. All three were astounded by his next words. He said, "Soon, at the 1290 T/D, the Beast will dedicate his temple and then the antichrist will slaughter all Christians and although we have been sorely persecuted during this time, we are standing firm in our faith. Now, during the next 45 days, we will be taken up to our God and our Savior." Before any of the three could comment the speaker concluded saying, "and don't fear, for when the time comes we will all receive 'Holpen'," and again as if on cue they began raising their hands to God in praise and started singing a song.

The three were astonished and could not speak.

Mel had to break the silence saying, "See, how your book and the three of you impacted upon the people on earth. That's why I kept you cloaked, as you say, from the eyes of the evil one and his followers."

Tom, regaining his composure, looked at Maria and Joe, saying, "We never in our wildest dreams thought our transmissions from our cave would have such benefits."

Maria said, "And don't forget your book *Dragon's Tattoo 666*. It seems the content was or is right on the mark." Maria was mesmerized by these Christians and said, "Who is their leader?"

Mel, with great emotion said, "They're the Prodigal Children of God, the Martyrs of Understanding."

Joe commented, "They are not intimidated by the antichrist lurking around the outer edges of the park."

Mel said, "Soon the antichrist will begin killing those of understanding. "However, this is only allowed at the appointed time."

Maria, listening to them singing, said, "The song they are singing is beautiful but I don't know it nor its words."

Mel, smiled this time saying, "Think hard, for you know the answer."

"It's the 'Song of the Martyrs'", replied Joe. "Somewhere in my thoughts I remember something about 'they sang a new song'."

Mel said, "This new song is not memorized, rather their souls are singing praises to Heaven."

Tom said, "I don't understand what you mean by their 'souls are singing'.

Mel responded, looking at them and saying, "Just prior to your martyrdom what did you hear?"

"I heard a soft whispering in my ear, something about 'come home children, it's time'."

"That's right," said the other two.

"That was the last line of their song. Remember, you were protected for the most part high up in your cave. These Christians had no such protection."

Maria asked, "Did our cave protection hinder us from anything?"

"No," Mel said, "each soul is refined individually. Your mission was what it was, and still is. You are, were and will be."

Joe said, "He's riddling us again."

Actually Joe, he's absolutely right," said Maria. "I'll explain it to you later."

Tom said, "Look at the antichrist. The song is driving them into a frenzy."

Mel added, "Certain things, like the Martyr's Song, blood, and sounds drive them crazy."

Joe asked, "What is the Martyr's Sound?"

Mel said, "It's the 'pillar of fire's thunder roaring'."

Upon hearing this, all three in unison said, "What?"

Mel said he would explain this later and with the wave of his hand, they were in South America.

"Look," Maria said, "that large statue of Jesus still stands and below it people are gathered in mass numbers."

Mel said, "Evil was not allowed to topple this statue. For these Christians, this statue of the Son of God gave them hope although the unholy trinity claimed it was their messiah. This deceived some, not all."

Tom pointed and said, "Look over there. A woman is testifying to them just like that man back in Central Park."

Mel responded, "I have but shown you two of thousands of such great exploits of faith. Soon they will receive 'Holpen'."

Now, waiving his hand as this was becoming his method of choice of moving them forward, they found themselves high up and looking downwards to earth. For some reason they were just there, motionless.

Mel said to Joe, "Are you going to ask your question?"

Joe, looking perplexed, as only now did his question awaken within him, asked, "When do the continents recombine because that would be a fantastic sight to behold."

"How about now?" Mel commented and immediately time was manipulated and as they stared at the earth, it began to move.

Maria was the first to comment. "There is no catastrophic happening, no earthquakes, no tsunamis, and no volcanoes erupting, only the land masses are moving. How can this be possible?"

Joe, side stepping her question, said, "Look at the water. It's sort of vibrating but not swishing around, like in a bucket being moved."

Mel said, "Just as in olden times, water was held at bay by higher power energy."

Joe smiled saying, "That's his way of saying 'force fields'." Then he asked, "Mel, will you teach me how this is done?"

Mel sort of smiled and said, "Ask me again, a million years from now."

Maria commented, "You asked for that one, Joe."

Tom said, "See, these continents simply rejoined like pieces of a puzzle. They actual fit perfectly, even Australia slid in gently."

Joe asked, "Where did the islands go?"

"What islands?" Mel replied.

"That's not an answer, Mel."

"Perhaps, but that's all you're getting," was his reply.

Now as quickly as it started it ended with the waive of Mel's hand, and then his words, "We come to the 1040th day and by this time the Martyrs of Understanding have all received 'Holpen'."

They found themselves at the north end of the Living Sea where the Great Domed City was situated.

Tom was the first to speak, "Look at the size of that dome. We knew it was massive but this is unimaginably huge."

Joe looked up and had difficulty seeing the top of the dome.

Mel commented, "Joe, think it, and it happens." In a heartbeat all four were ten thousand feet high in the sky looking down at this huge glistening dome.

"I never knew it glistened," said Tom.

"Me either," commented Maria.

Joe was too preoccupied with its splendor to comment.

Mel said, "Inside are the Children of God who required a little more time to mature and then they will also be caught up to Heaven. That is how they gain more intimate knowledge of God's Plan of Salvation."

Maria said, "First to come in are the Redeemed Israelites and then the Repented Israelites, if memory serves me right."

Tom, remembering the information in his book, thought, "So they have up to 220 days for such fellowship depending when they came into contact with the Two Witnesses."

All three nodded in agreement, though saying nothing audibly.

Now, Mel did his waive thing, and they were swooped several miles further north of the dome and back onto the ground. After looking around for a few seconds at the numerous groups of people who were mostly wearing the dragon's mark, a massive light exited the dome and between them and it stood two motionless beings.

Maria began to describe them and Mel immediately intervened saying, "Maria, the people will all be seeing through your eyes when you speak as well as Joe's and Tom's. Remember your five senses will be doing the recording."

Tom said, "Look at their massive size! How tall do you think they are, Joe?"

His reply, "One hundred feet?"

Maria looked at their eyes which were glowing like fire.

Mel said, "Wait till you hear them speak."

Joe asked, "Why don't they move or say something?"

Mel said, "They're waiting for the 7 Spirits and Thunders to announce them and their 7 Thunder Messages of God."

The three looked at each other sort of smiling as they recalled that these thunder messages were also in Tom's book.

Tom began saying that the 7 great domes would soon be activated and no sooner did he say it, and it happened.

Mel began saying, "See these domes forming. They're not round, rather their sides align like when children blow soap bubbles. Their perimeters all follow predesigated pathways, not geographical boundaries." After what seemed like only minutes, these giant domes began to sparkle from their epicenters.

Maria was amazed by their intensity as the sparkle grew to that of what they had referred to a pulsating fire lightning. Viewed from space Joe said it reminded him of the word 'scintillating' and both agreed this was a great word to describe this growing fire lightning.

After what again seemed like only minutes, all seven domes were completely covered with what could be described as the 'Northern

Lights' having undulating waves of light that pulsated seemingly at random.

Mel said, "These are the seven Spirits of God. Now see another seven Angels are joining them. These are the seven Thunders of God.'

Joe said, "You know, looking from space, one would get the message, 'Do not enter'."

Mel agreed saying, "That's one way to express it."

Mel sort of waived his hand and all were now back looking at these two huge beings standing in front of the great domed city.

Tom said, "You know, from when the land masses began to recombine to right now, didn't take much time."

Mel then said, "Speaking of time, here they go." Immediately God's two Ambassadors began to move. If they had legs, they could not been seen for their brown robes that looked like hooded kimonos seemed to touch the earth. Their movement was more like a gliding across the earth, not jerky like when walking.

Maria said, "Remember when we heard the First Thunder Message? It knocked us to the ground. When does this take place, Mel?"

"Soon."

The epicenters of the domes began to really sparkle, even brighter than the fire lightning, like a fourth of July sparkler, only vastly larger and brighter. Its intensity was so bright that humans on earth did not dare to look directly at it. The three of them though, thought it looked most heavenly.

As the enormity of the sparkling grew, during the next few minutes all three knew what would now happen.

When the combination of fire lightning and thunderous sound reached an unheard of intensity and volume it happened. This time they did not tumble to the ground, this time they knelt, raised their hands and gave praise to God for His mercy.

Tom admitted, "I never pictured myself doing and speaking like this," and the other two agreed.

Mel had been observing them and later began speaking, "I now fully understand humanities love for their God. Some must be forced to bow while you three automatically did so, in love, and that's the secret. Heaven once said to Daniel, 'thou art greatly beloved of God' for you Daniel 'believed'. You three are also 'greatly beloved of God' for you also 'believed'."

Mel continued, "In contrast, the evil one desperately seeks such acts of devotion but evil can never obtain such loyalty because it only knows pride."

Immediately following Mel's words, God's two Ambassadors began gliding across the surface of the earth and making a strange sound.

Mel said that this sound was that of the Martyrs of Christ stirring who were awaiting their fellow Martyrs that soon would be coming their way.

Joe said that this sound was like that of a very low subsonic rumbling and words could not describe it.

Mel added, "I thought I just did, Joe."

"Right you are," said Maria and whispered to Joe, "Think before you speak."

"Agreed." said Mel, displaying a slight hint of dry humor.

Joe whispered to Maria, "He only told us what it was. I described its actual sound as perceived by humans."

Maria looked at Mel, then Joe, and said, "I think he can read our thoughts."

"Scary," thought Joe to himself. "I have trouble reading my own. Poor Mel", he thought, who then appeared to shake his head and gave a whimsical smile.

Now from out of nowhere came a most magnificent pillar of fire. It seemed to just explode out of nothing and was there. This fire was actually swirling and enfolding upon itself, a most glorious sight to behold and engulfed the two testifiers.

Mel and the three were about a mile behind God's two Ambassadors when they began to speak. Their voices resonated and made a thunderous, low subsonic rumbling sound just as Joe had thought. Mel, looking at both Joe and Maria, had a twinkle in his right eye.

Mel said to the listen to the sound produced by their words, not their words and asked "What don't you hear?"

Tom replied, "I give up."

Mel replied, "No echoes from the hills over there."

Joe commented, "Now that you mentioned it, even the Thunder Message had no echo to it. Why is that?"

Mel answered, "What we are hearing is not a human voice, rather the unified voices of the Martyrs that were formerly depicted as the 'under the altar souls' crying out for God to avenge their deaths."

"They're a rowdy lot," Mel thought to himself yet they somehow perceived his thought as a low whisper. The message of the two testifiers was slow and deliberate. No one had to say, "Pardon, could you please repeat what you just said."

"Look," shouted Tom. "Some people are raising their hands to God in acceptance of what they are hearing but most are not. Those who accept are then touched by the finger of God and immediately they just vanish."

Maria said, "Now that's something you don't see very often," and then corrected herself saying, "I mean not ever."

Tom joined in saying, "Remember, they are instructed to travel upon the King's Highway and this is a supernatural route for them. So I think that they are there but we can't see them."

Joe said to Mel, "Why can't we see them?"

The answer came, "They're now invisible, correct? So what's the sense of invisibility if you can still see them?"

"Just great. Now he's talking like Tom used to, in riddles."

Mel again seemed to look perplexed and said, "Joe, if everyone is looking through your eyes and if they could still see them travelling on the King's Highway, it would then be an oxymoron."

"I get it," replied Joe, "but I don't like the connotation of the last word. I thought heavenly beings didn't revert to name calling."

Maria saw the bewilderment on Mel's face and with an angelic face howled. Tom immediately caught on and joined in.

Mel merely said, "Ah, Maria, patience of the saints. Seems that Joe, even in a heavenly body, still doesn't have the IQ to match."

Joe's only comment was, "Funny, very funny! But I still don't get it."

Mel had the last word saying, "Maria, was your vow for 'until death do us part' or for 'all eternity'?"

Maria, losing it, replied, "I chose poorly, but I love him dearly," and, gave him a big hug and whispered what the word meant into his ear. His reply was, "Really?"

Mel said, "Look at all those people who rejected their offer of salvation. They're waiving their fists and shouting at them in great anger and now some are actually shooting at them with rifles."

Joe said, "Look over there. Some are firing rockets at them." No matter what they did, their actions had no effect on the testifiers.

Tom said, "We all know what comes next," as fire issued out of their mouths consuming those shooting at them.

Joe said, "And now come the Flying Hell Monsters. We had a mental picture of them but now we will actually witness their arrival."

The two testifiers sort of waved and moved to the next zone and were gone. The pillar of fire could be seen in the distance along with the roaring sound it made.

Maria asked, "Why didn't we hear this roaring sound when the pillar of fire was right in front of us."

Mel replied, "You did."

Maria gestured to Joe to remain quiet as she knew he was about to say, "Great, a riddle again."

Joe thought, "This telepathy stuff really sucks. I wonder if I can block it?"

Mel commented, "No Joe. Either you hear the sound of the two testifiers or the sound of the pillar of fire. They're both the same. They're the sound of the Martyrs of Christ talking or moving. Remember they're stirring in anticipation of their fellow brethren that are soon coming their way."

Maria was about to ask what "No Joe" had to do with this answer, but Mel continued. "Get ready for what comes next. It's more fearsome than you described in your book, Tom."

From where the pillar of fire once stood came a low rumbling sound. The earth trembled as if some portal had just been opened. Out of this portal in the earth, hundreds of feet wide, came firstly a weird sound of clattering and screeching and seconds later not millions but billions of the Flying Hell Monsters. People remaining, being only the antichrist now, panicked and began fleeing from this sound that was soon followed by the flying monsters for they had no name as yet, for them.

The light from the dome far above their heads turned to grey, then dark, then to thick blackness. People deprived of light were now blind and stumbled over each other and everything in their path, their futile race to safety being non-existent.

The sound of these Flying Hell Monsters was, for humans, most deafening for they could not even yell to each other let alone hear their own thoughts.

Now, in the presence of the three, Mel did something unexpected. He held up his right hand with palm extended and immediately one of these flying monsters alighted.

The three of them drew close and looked at it. In real life this flying monster was vastly more horrendous looking then they imagined and they had a good imagination. This little monster was actually not that little, for along with its wing span and long scorpion tail it was larger than Mel's palm.

Its eyes were glowing red, first the pupils, then the irises, until finally nothing white was left. Its tail and stinger was constantly moving as if searching for something to penetrate.

Tom said, "Look! Its plating is like a steel of some type."

Joe commented, "More like some type of advanced Kevlar, you know the material bullet proof vests are made of."

Their cladding was flexible and Mel said that nothing on earth could penetrate it.

Maria looked at its four lion like-fangs and was shocked by their ferociousness for the monster was snapping at her.

Mel said, "Don't fret. They won't attack. They're just showing off. Mind you, they have a nasty temper. Look at their stingers. That's where the blood-virus comes out of."

Tom said, "Why is it flapping its wings so violently?"

Mel replied, "It wants to get back in on the action. Remember, it has only one command and that is to attack those not having the mark of God."

Mel also told them that even if people could hide in caves or shelters, this menace could penetrate anything and to remember, they're supernatural.

Joe asked if he could hold it and Mel, by just looking at the beasty thing, caused it to hop and light on Joe's hand. This thing tried, with it claws, to dig into his hand, either for stability or wrath, but to no avail because Joe, even though manifested in human form, was a spiritual being.

Mel said, "Listen to the sound it makes when released."

The monster now began to clatter its wings and then began emitting a screeching sound. As its eyes glowed even brighter, it leaped off of Joe's hand and rejoined its horde of flying monsters.

Maria commented, "In the thick darkness out there, their eyes must look even more menacing. Imagine being in total darkness stumbling around and the only thing you can see are their eerie eyes."

Mel said, "Only we are allowed to hold one of them because all others are targets."

Joe asked, "Do they see the saved people?"

Mel said, "The answer is two-fold. In Israel, those who were saved sparkled and become invisible to the antichrist. These critters can see them but they are not allowed to attack them. Later, in the time of the saved nations, the people are visible to the critters and the zombies but both are forbidden to attack them. By having the mark of God, these flying monsters will pass them by and the zombies will flee from them."

Joe whispered to Maria, "Hey, we're even following the pillar of fire."

As the Two Witnesses moved from zone to zone, the number of infected grew enormously.

Mel commented, "See, this group consists of those who took the mark of the beast in pride. They have the 3-color tattoo on their foreheads."

Tom now said, "We were correct when we said that the 3-color do not migrate. They stay put and after their 150 days of infection return to some state of normalcy."

Mel quickly said, "Their bodies heal, scars remain. Their mental state never goes back to where it was previously. They retain their base instincts and continue drinking blood since that's all there is to drink. As to whether they still are cannibals, remember they have no moral compass."

Maria commented, "And after 150 days, they can be killed or just die and if so, others could eat them quite easily."

Joe whispered to her, "They love a hot meal."

Mel looked puzzled at Maria. She thought, "Please don't ask."

Mel agreed, saying that while eating flesh gave them a little blood, all preferred the numerous blood pools for their sustenance.

Joe's quip, whatever it was intended to be, was cut off by Maria's hand before its first syllable was uttered.

The three found it amazing that the antichrist were so determined to look good in the eyes of their god.

"During the commencement of the plagues only rumors of the Two Witnesses floated around in the land of Israel, then Judea, then the world, thanks to you three," said Mel.

Tom, on behalf of them said, "We never thought our broadcasts would be that successful."

Mel said, "You may have had a little help from me by keeping those attempting to trace your signal somewhat confused as to the location of your mountain cave."

Mel said, "The unholy trinity tried to cover up and spread their own propaganda that worked for a while claiming the plagues were caused by Christians contaminating the water supplies. Your transmissions were a constant pain to them."

The three meandered across Israel during the first half of year one, watching and seeing firsthand the plagues and its consequences. They never ceased to be amazed by what they witnessed. By this time there were millions of infected zombies who during their first 150 days roamed aimlessly crying for death. During these days their wounds from the flying monsters scabbed over but infections of other types were ramped. Leprosy, hepatitis and many other diseases began infecting thousands. There were no drugs available for them.

Joe caught on first and the others listened as he spoke to Mel. "It seems that when the Two Witnesses first started their testimony in the northern areas, each day produced more and more zombies and now for the last several months each day produced less and less of them. Why is this?"

Mel looked at Joe and them saying, "So you caught that did you? I thought I would have to explain this to you. Remember when you were talking about the antichrist who from far away saw and heard the pillar of fire and fled south into Judea. That's why there were less and less because tens of millions of them all jammed into Judea."

Joe said, "I get it now. So many antichrist fled into Judea, there were fewer numbers of them in Israel to be attacked, resulting in fewer zombies."

Tom said, "So some of the antichrist flee while others try to kill the Two Witnesses and that explains these occurrences. Those who did not flee were infected and turned into the zombies and there were less and less of them in the remaining zones."

Joe said, "I thought the Two Witnesses would have hop-scotched and traveled from zone to zone along the ancient border between Israel and Judea. By doing so it would have placed a barrier of zombies that those antichrist fleeing out of Israel into Judea could not get past, right?"

Maria asked, "I thought that the zombies were restrained from crossing into Judea?"

"One of you two is correct," replied Mel.

"Now I'm confused," said Maria, "Help someone!"

"Don't look at me," said Tom.

Mel then proceeded saying, "Maria is correct the zombies are restrained from going into Judea. There is no physical barrier halting their migration."

"So what stopped them?" she asked.

"Simple," Mel replied, "what did the zombies like?"

Joe immediately answered, "Blood!"

And Mel said, "Were there any blood sources at this time in Judea?"

They all mused and seconds later Joe shook his head and said, "None."

Mel agreed. "The zombies in Israel just stayed put. Why migrate if all the blood they desired was right in their midst."

Maria caught on to why everything happened in that order and said, "God's plan is fantastically complex, yet somehow also simple."

Both Joe and Tom now far out of the loop had to say, "Explain."

Mel looked at Maria and said, "Please continue to educate them further."

Maria said, "It's simple. The first few days, when the Two Witnesses began testifying, resulted in many not accepting. This paved the way for zombies in Israel. Soon news of what was happening leaked out to the world. Many then fled during the next months out of Israel."

Mel refined her answer saying, "The unholy trinity knew full well what was taking place. They communicated with their higher echelon to flee and come to Judea. Those now remaining were of lower caste and when their turn came, they either fired weapons or merely fled in the wrong directions and were attacked."

Joe and Tom now saw the big picture. They discussed what was happening. As each person raised their hands to God and received His mark, they traveled along the King's Highway to the Great Domed City. The infected at this time were lying on the ground withering in pain. Even when they, after a few days, got up on their feet, the only thing they were fixated on was 'blood'. Should those with God's Mark pass by zombies, the zombies would flee in terror from them.

Mel said, "I hear what you're saying but I'm going to refine your answer. The zombies would indeed flee in terror if they saw the Mark of God on a person. However, in this case, the saved people become invisible to them and once upon the King's Highway the zombies, even unintentionally, could not walk on or cross this highway of God."

Maria said, "It looks like God used evil to chase evil away from His people."

Joe ended her thought, "Yes! God's plan is so amazing."

These events became a daily happening and continued throughout the land of Israel until the two testifiers came to the border of Judea. It is at this time that they hopscotched over Judea and into the lands surrounding the Living Sea.

Tom said to Maria and Joe, "Look at that. The pillar of fire did not hopscotch anywhere. It made a bee line cutting across Judea leaving in its fiery wake smoldering ashes."

Mel said, "Even though the Two Witnesses are now in the lands adjacent to the Living Sea, we will remain here until the Christians have been martyred between the 1290-1335 T/D."

Maria said, "I'm beginning to get the hang of this time dimension jumping thing."

Joe said, "Cool, we're back at the 1290 again."

"Correction," commented Mel. "We're actually about a week prior to it."

Mel continued, "Just look at the people in Judea, Satan's back yard. His elite are there. Most have already taken his 3-color mark of pride."

Maria commented, "There are also some who even though they serve the false messiah, have not taken his mark. He is saving them as his evil seeds."

Tom asked if his representation of the mark of the beast was accurate. Mel commented, "Yes, and your thinking was also correct. The mark itself does not instill fear, but what it signifies only gives death."

Mel continued, "Look at those Israelites in Judea. Some of them, along with the evil seeds, will soon flee to the hills when they see the abomination in their temple."

Maria asked, "Were the Christians by this time all in some type of concentration camps?"

Mel said, "For the most part, yes, although some were still hiding here and there like you three were doing in the Rocky Mountains."

Joe said, "Mel, what about Christians who were hiding in places that escaped the mass slaughter from 1290-1335?"

Mel's answer was simple. "Christians not martyred will be treated the same as those of the saved nations, providing they also keep their garments clean and pure. They have the mark of God so when the zombies come they will just remain in their dwellings. They will be gathered by the forces of God while still in their physical bodies and, as you said, go into the star crafts at the 2300 T/D., then, a little later, into the Kingdom of Peace."

Maria asked, "What if they were hiding so well that no antichrist could find them, so they did not get martyred? Should they be penalized for that?"

Mel answered, "Maria, where are you currently standing?"

She said, "Here in Judea."

"Now look to China," Mel said and pointed towards the east. "Tell me what you see."

She looked and said, "Mass amounts of people."

"Look more closely and what do you see now?"

She said, "Individual people."

Mel replied, "You can see every person in China, if you so desire. What does this tell you of Satan's view?"

She replied, "He can see everyone too?"

"Right," said Mel, "so he sees all and only at certain times is he allowed to kill them."

Tom interjected, "So that's why you sort of kept us under some type of 'cloaking device' so Satan couldn't locate us in our cave."

Mel responded by saying, "You could call it a cloaking device. In the Bible it says in John 8:59 Then they took up stones to throw at Him; but Jesus hid Himself and went out of the temple, going through the midst of them, and so passed by. See this is another furtive discovery added as of today for your book published years ago."

Maria said, "How does Mel do that time dimension thing? What about when we were being hunted by the NG? Were you sort of hiding us then too?"

Mel replied, "I was keeping tabs on you, and by the way Maria, do you think you three were capable of pulling of the 'perfect crime' as you so eloquently said when that NG vehicle veered off the road?"

All were silent.

Joe asked, "How far back were you watching over us?"

Mel answered, "Oh I'd say, a long way back. A really long way back. Now Maria, to answer your question, if other Christians can hide and avoid him seeing them, the answer is no. However, he leaves many alone. They form part of the saved people and out of them many become his evil seeds."

"One final comment," said Maria. "Why did they not elect to stand up for their faith when, from their hiding places, they saw the antichrist who were always around?"

Mel only commented, "They had faith, but their teaching dictated their actions and yes many will go into the Kingdom of Peace still in their human bodies and yes there is a function for them."

"Now," Mel said, "we will take a look at the dragon's temple that is almost fully built. See, it looks identical to the former temple built by Solomon.

Tom, your theory was correct about the dragon's abomination standing where God, in times past, revealed Himself at certain times. This spot of earth is truly identified as the Holy place. Satan has no conscience. He is pure evil and spiteful."

Mel continued, "During these last days, until his temple is completed, the false prophet is busy finishing the creation of an abomination. By this I mean what is being created is pure evil and represents absolutely everything that is revolting in the sight of God. It is composed of hate, envy, jealousy, pride. It is demonic, diabolical, fiendish, hellish, infernal, satanic, unholy, despicable, vile, worthless, wretched, and morally reprehensible. One could easily attribute one hundred such characteristics to Satan. Now can you fashion a mental picture of what this abomination represents?

It's like the mark of the beast. It's what the symbol represents that's evil. The colors red, yellow and blue are in themselves not evil but his mark is the summation of the one hundred demonic attributes I just spoke about."

Mel elaborated a little more than he should have when he said to them, "The scales on the body of this abomination contain the names of the angels that serve him, those 200 million fallen ones who left their first estate, sadly, those excommunicated from God. Their names recorded are not their original names given by God as these name have been relegated to the book of the damned, a book only God has. All names so written on this abomination are names given to these demons by Satan their deceiver."

Mel said, "As to its composition, how would you describe something indescribable? Consider the impossible for a moment. The physical attributes of their names such as hate, envy, jealousy, pride, to name only a few, all humanities' dictionaries combined would at best have only one word for this, 'abomination'."

Mel continued, "This abomination will soon be activated with full power and for now consider its composition being 200 million fallen angels. These same demons, after their allotted time, will then be bound at the Great Euphrates River and are depicted as Hell Horses. They, as Tom has recorded in his book, at the appointed time will be loosened and fly to the 200 million 'riders of death' who are the recovered 3-color zombie antichrists awaiting them in the east and when joined become the Entities of Death."

Mel looked at them saying, "Perhaps I divulged too many of the more gruesome details of the beast."

Maria and Joe responded, "Hopefully when people read of what's coming at them in Tom's book, they flee back to God."

Mel said, "And that being the case, God will have open arms for them."

"Now," Mel continued, "in short order, Satan dedicates his temple unto himself. We will watch how this abomination ceremony unfolds having his 200 million followers as its center of attraction."

Tom asked, "Where is Satan at this time?"

Mel responded, "He's manifested in the abomination along with his 200 million."

Maria said, "I now understand the true meaning of the word 'abomination'."

Mel added, "And remember when you three were discussing where this abomination is positioned? Now you will see it firsthand."

Maria then said, "This is definitely not on my happy list."

Mel said, "Now you begin to fully comprehend why this time period is call the 'Great Tribulation, time of sorrows'.

Rather than viewing from high up, let's walk upon the earth and really see what's taking place." Again, with the wave of his hand, they were walking on the narrow streets within Old Jerusalem.

People were very busy during these final days prior to the dedication of their temple. However, unknown to them, it was Satan's temple and they had no part in it.

Mel said for them to come. They were then within the temple and were watching as the finishing touches of gold were being applied to designated areas. One would have expected some type of reverence within, however, only ungodly events were happening. Certain people were there only out of fear, others for money and some for pride.

There was seating for 7,000 in the outer court and in the inner portion there were 10 thrones arranged in a circle where people would soon be seated. In their center was a portion roped off containing another circle. This circle was composed of what looked like mosaic tiles that formed three concentric circles, the outer being a sulphur gold, the middle was a blue and the center was red. To the right of the center sat a blue throne and to the left a sulphur gold throne.

The interior of the temple was constructed of precious items however it emitted a cold feeling. Mel said this was due to the fact that all materials within the temple personified only death.

Joe looked around saying, "It looks like there are trophies positioned all over the place, sort of like a hunters den of heads of killed animals."

Maria pointed out that in one far corner they could see people being whipped for some infraction.

Mel only commented that the pending slaughter is already slowly progressing.

Mel took them high up and once again they were looking down at Jerusalem and the countryside.

"See," Mel commented, "the antichrist are packed together." As far as they could see people were crowded together.

Joe said they were jammed like sardines in a can. It was very true that the Two Witnesses could not have effectively testified here due to the density of antichrist.

Mel said, "Now look. Here they come." And no sooner were his words spoken when these two supernatural beings sort of just flew past them. The sound they made was like when they moved across the earth only now it seems much louder. In seconds they were out of sight.

Maria, first to speak, said, "That was intense. Look at the people on the ground. They're all looking up to see what was happening."

Joe asked, "Why are they rejoicing and clapping?"

Mel said, "Seems like someone told them they would be spared of the looming plagues. Remember, just recently they saw the pillar of fire zoom past them and now this."

Maria asked "Why did they fly past the people making such a loud sound? Oh yea, I remember, it's the sound of the Martyrs, and as you told us, they're a rowdy lot."

Tom said, "It seems like someone's been telling lies. It must have been the unholy trinity. But what they said was a lie. We all know it."

Mel replied, "Not all. We know. The unholy trinity knows, but the antichrist don't."

Maria said, "But very soon the Flying Hell Monsters will return and attack them all.

"Remember," Mel said, "only humans get attacked, not the False Messiah, President, Prophet or the demonic angels."

Joe asked, "Won't the antichrist all complain when the attacks begin?"

Mel only said, "Do you think Satan really cares about them? Sooner or later they all die anyway. Don't forget Satan is insane. He actually delights in their sorrows, and for that matter, anyone's sorrows."

Maria asked Mel, "Now what, or where do we go?"

Mel said, "For a while let's go and follow the Two Witnesses again. Then we can come back when the temple gets dedicated."

Within seconds they were once again on the ground watching as the Two Witnesses began testifying to the people in Edom.

Tom enquired, "Was I correct when I said that Edom, Moab and Ammon are special?"

"Special?" pondered Mel. "In the past, certain events took place here that were special, not the land itself. However, I see what you mean. In bygone times the promised boundaries of Israel were very great, from Egypt on the south to the Great Euphrates River to the East and North East and to the South, part of the Mediterranean Sea. Therefore Edom, Moab and Ammon were included, in the beginning, as part of Israel. As you previously said, Tom, these lands have history attached to them whereby certain people and some of their descendants found favor before God. This is the reason we're here now. Don't forget also that Israelites are scattered all over this area."

As they watched, the pillar of fire began moving again from one area to the next. The scene was the same, some accepted, many did not and so once again on the heels of the Two Witnesses came the Flying Hell Monsters.

Now, one other variation takes place. Those who raised their hands and sparkle began following the King's Highway, only this time, it was the Two Witnesses who were corralling the people. At all times, those being attacked were always to the south of them. This created the effect sort of like when the tide comes in. Soon the dry land gets covered with water. In this picture, the dry land gets covered with the Flying Hell Monsters.

From there vantage position high up, they could see how the pillar of fire was now in the land of Moab, on the east side of the Living Sea. People accepted or rejected and the plagues moved northwards.

Soon the pillar of fire was in the land of Edom and now the pillar of fire turned from its northern direction to westward and began heading back towards the Great Domed City.

Mel said, "Look down at the land and you will see the only area yet to be testified to is that portion between the Great Domed City and Jerusalem."

Mel continued, "Very soon Satan's temple is going to be dedicated to him and then those in Judea, flee during the slaughter of the Christians."

Maria looked down at the land saying, "There are thousands of caves, smaller hills and valleys for those fleeing to travel across."

Joe commented, "Yes, but the distance is only about 20 miles so they can make good time."

Tom added, "When they flee to the hills, how far will they have to travel before they can feel safe that the antichrist will not be chasing them?"

"Remember," Mel said, "concerning the evil seeds, the antichrist will not be chasing them at all. Once they're out of the city, no one will come after them. In the confusion, some will fall, as the Christian slaughter begins."

Tom replied, "Seems like my book just got revised somewhat."

Mel commented, "A work in progress my friend."

Mel took them slowly over this area back towards Jerusalem. "Now, we come to the time when Satan's temple is dedicated, at the 1290 T/D."

"As we view the temple from high up it looks exactly like the first Temple Solomon built. Too bad something so beautiful is so evil," said Mel.

Most of the world is connected by various means. There are rows upon rows of the antichrist in concentric circles just like pebbles make when dropped into a pond. The closer to the inner temple, the higher their rank. At this time the statue of the Great Red Dragon has been positioned in the inner circle upon the red center.

Joe asked why they didn't see it being brought into Satan's temple.

Mel said, "It was not brought in, but rather it was compiled within his temple."

Maria said, "I'm not following you. Please explain."

Mel elaborated further saying, "The 200 million fallen angels, now demons recombine into the abomination. It is called a 'desolation' meaning utter ruin of its former self. These demons have fallen to their lowest caste since God created them. Now they form this abomination of desolation. They merge into one entity, for now, and give their energy to the dragon. They take on the physical, turning into evil energy that appears to have a physical dimension called life. As we said previously, their names are written and their characteristics now take on form with the beast. There is a veil covering this abomination, its color being red, yellow and blue."

Joe pointed out that this veil has 10 ropes with tassels, draping down almost to the floor.

The time of unveiling is scheduled for twelve noon and now, about one hour before noon, they begin assembling.

Mel said to them, "Listen. They think that they're not being observed. They are discussing the sacrifice that they will be offering to their god—Christians."

They now ascended upwards and it was then they saw the sacrifice soon to come. The view was sad to observe as what appeared to be an endless column of Christians were being paraded down the main street leading to the dragon's temple.

Maria said, "Look at that. The antichrist are all lined up on each side of this column and are jeering at them."

What happens next defies all human logic. All three were now inside the dragon's temple watching the events taking place for the dedication ceremony. Now the assembly was filled with those having proved evil distinctions. The entire inside of his temple were those displaying the 3-color 'Dragon's Tattoo 666'. There were 7,000 of them seated in the outer courtyard. All seated could see the veiled statue of their god as there were no walls separating them, only pillars.

Maria said, "Here it comes." And the 10 Kings who were seated around the abomination stood up and proceeded to go to and take hold of one of the golden tassels. After a silent time, they in unison pulled and the veil's shroud fell silently to the floor. All in attendance cheered.

The false prophet rose from his throne, and with extended arms pointed in the direction of the false messiah, spoke words foreign to Tom, Maria and Joe but not Mel.

When these words were spoken the abomination began to take on a resemblance of something living and soon became the personification of evil with 200 million demons now praising their god.

Mel said, "Behold the 'abomination of desolation'," and then said to them, "See where it stands on that red circle? This is where in olden times, the God of Heaven manifested Himself to the Israelites. Tom, this is the fulfilment of what was recorded in Mathew 'when you see the abomination of desolation standing in the holy place'."

Mel then asked, "Do you wish to witness the slaughter of the Christians?" They thought no, but all agreed that they must be witnesses of it for some unexplained reason.

The abomination, seemingly alive, began to speak in a very loud growling voice blaspheming the God of Heaven.

Maria with shock said, "How can he say such bad things?"

Joe then said, "It's not just him, rather he and his demons saying such evil words."

Tom then said, "Such a fall from lofty heights."

Mel said, "How sad this must feel to our God."

Maria said "Look at the floor. It's opening." And immediately, another set of large doors opened and the column of Christians began entering

Mel said, "In addition to this large abomination becoming active, there are also tens of thousands of, as you three said, mini-me statues set up in religious institutions and community centers."

Mel continued, "See, in each case the mini-me was surrounded by the 3-color antichrist who, with swords, killed with vengeance those Christians defying the false prophet."

Maria looked upon them and more specifically their eyes and into their eyes. Within their pupils she did not see her typical reflection. Rather she saw what she could only describe as God's eyes looking back at her.

Joe asked, "What feeling did this create within you?"

Maria replied, "Great joy and great sadness."

"Enough," said Mel. "Suffice it to say hundreds of millions are slaughtered. However, all received 'Holpen' which by the way, this word will be like that of 'Mary' whose holy fame forever, forever more and forever after resounds in Time and Eternity. 'Holpen' is never forgotten as it goes on eternally."

Joe asked, "What does that mean?"

Mel said, "Exactly what I said. Listen Joe, you do know of the Biblical Mary, don't you?"

Joe answered, "Yes, of course."

"See, even though she lived thousands of years ago you still know of her."

Mel continued, "The slaughter of the Christians goes on for 45 days until the 1335th day."

"This is so sad," commented Maria.

Mel sort of wrapped his arms around them saying, "Let's see something beautiful. Come, I will show you the Bride, the Wife of

God's Son." And in the twinkling of an eye Mel said, "Behold the Bride."

Maria looked at Tom and Joe in total amazement. "Whoa," she said, "now that's a most spectacular sight."

Tom said, "In my book . . ."

Mel interrupted him saying, "Really? Your book?"

Tom immediately acquiesced and corrected himself saying, "Never again will I refer to it as my book."

Mel then said, "It is recorded, that the Bride is composed of great heavenly beauty and attributes."

Maria said, "The Bride is vastly greater then we could possibly have imagined let alone comprehended."

Joe said, "Truly an uncountable multitude. With this vast community of saints, all souls will be testified to."

Maria said, "You know Joe, your mannerisms are maturing, from that of the man I loved and married, to becoming more similar to Mel."

Joe still in a transformation mode didn't know whether she was complimenting him or what.

Mel thought, "Change comes slowly at times."

"Yes," she thought, "but it's all in the right direction."

Maria asked, "What about love? Does it transform into something else?"

Mel's answer was quick and his words had a finality to them. "Love is eternal."

Her eyes radiated with joy, her question now answered.

Mel looked at her and them and said, "Here we go again," and with his signature wave, they moved ahead in time.

Chapter Forty-Seven

THUNDER MESSAGE FOUR 1400 T/D

**GET THEIR GARMENTS
NATIONS OF THE 10 KINGS**

John 10: 14-16: "I am the good shepherd and I know my sheep, and am known by my own. As the Father knows me, even so I know the Father and I lay down my life for the sheep. <u>And other sheep</u> **I have which are** <u>not of this fold</u> **them also** <u>I must bring,</u> <u>and they will hear my voice</u> **and there will be one flock and one shepherd"**.

Maria said, "Long before this Thunder Message, we were all martyred. It feels weird to now be hearing it in spirit. I can see how manipulating the time line can stir mixed emotions."

Joe said, "What do you mean?"

Mel interjected, "It would be one thing to be in Heaven and witness seeing and hearing this thunder but it's another thing entirely to be once again standing on earth hearing and feeling the thunder message."

Tom said, "It's sort of like either looking out your window and seeing it happen or being right in the middle of it."

Mel continued, "We have now arrived at the time when God's two Ambassadors begin testifying to the other sheep in different folds that His Son talked about.

'The Time of Redemption' ushered in by God's two Ambassadors now ramps up. God's Israelites have now been removed from the grasp of the evil one, the deceiver from the beginning since he was cast down from our midst. God's two Ambassadors, during their first year, moved from place to place every 24 hours. Now their agenda changes and they move every hour on the hour. This hectic schedule goes on for the next 900 days as my friends do not require rest.

During these days, those who have not taken the dragon's tattoo, and who live under the rule of the 10 kings of this earth, will hear their testimony. Some accept, most do not. Those choosing wisely are 'saved' for the Kingdom of Peace."

Joe asked Mel, "Does the Bible actually mention that the entire world will receive the testimony of the Son of God, even though they are not Christians or Israelites?"

Mel answered, "Words of God's Son recorded in John 10: 14-16 "I am the good shepherd and I know my sheep, and am known by my own. As the Father knows me, even so I know the Father and I lay down my life for the sheep. And other sheep I have which are not of this fold them also I must bring, and they will hear my voice and there will be one flock and one shepherd".

"Others will be gathered from all religions world-wide and brought into the fold and Jesus will be their shepherd. God has His eyes upon everyone and each redeemed soul is a Heavenly victory.

Read what the angel of the Son of God said to His Apostle John in Revelation 14:6 saying, "I saw another angel flying in the midst of heaven, having the everlasting gospel to preach to those who dwell on the earth — to every nation, tribe, tongue, and people."

"All religions on earth believe in a supreme being, the Christians call him God while others have various names in their own languages for him. Ancient Israelites had many names for their God. Behold an absolute, the 'God of Heaven' is 'God of all'.

The mission of God's two Ambassadors is not only to testify to all people upon the earth but to do so in a fashion that they can relate to, accept and be saved.

Remember, God's two Ambassadors have now fulfilled their first year of commission. Humans have by this time received four 'Thunder Messages' and in the lands of the 10 kings, everyone on earth has heard their 'Thunder Messages'. No one is spared, for thus it is written. The wise receive and accept their offer of salvation and obtain their 'garments of salvation'."

Tom enquired, "What about all the religions? One says this way, the other that way."

Mel said, "Those from the various religions claiming their belief is superior to their neighbor's, my answer is, 'God of Heaven is God of All'. One's opinion means nothing. Lest you forget, God has told you before, 'I am your God, have no other gods before me'."

"Heavenly Wonders of the Great God are giving hope to the people downtrodden by evil roaming the earth, these demonic fallen angels, excommunicated from God. Many people from these nations do not believe now in their so called messiah returned.

His lying and great deceptions pale in comparison to the heavenly wonders being created by God's two Ambassadors and their little helpers."

Joe commented, "You mean by my Flying Hell Monsters, and their Zombie Virus and plagues?"

Mel looked kindly saying, "Humans love clichés. I referred to them as having the curse of the damned although I must admit some found your 'weird or what' expression 'zombie', acceptable. Who says we don't have a sense of humor?"

Joe replied, "I don't see the humor in that."

"Neither do I," replied Mel, who just sailed on saying, "Even though the unholy trinity came on strong with many deceiving tactics, many people still had a firm belief in their faiths. This initially helped them through many deceptions of the unholy trinity's tactics. Satan is the father of the children of pride. He deceives most of the people using all vices known to mankind and perhaps even more. He corrupts magnificently and for some time with impunity but sooner or later payback arrives with the wrath of God.

The antichrist will, with extreme hatefulness, kill anyone that dares to challenge them or their doctrine.

The Zombie Virus and resulting Zombie Plagues have been, for the past year, taking their toll. As recorded in Revelation 16:6, where it says 'give them blood to drink', do you think it was only a mere saying? It's for real.

The two Ambassadors of God turn all water, rivers, and streams into blood. When blood is all you have to drink, then blood it is. Let me tell you a secret. The blood they drink came from the slaughter of the Christian Martyrs. Yes, it supplies nourishment, but it also metes out the wrath of God and their blood causes those partaking extreme vexation."

Tom and the others were standing on the ground watching fire issuing out of the mouths from the two Ambassadors of God killing anyone unwise enough to challenge them.

Maria commented, "This is mild compared to the plagues they unleashed. It's so amazing that the plagues issued by them in conjunction with the Flying Hell Monsters infect everyone on the planet, not having our God's Mark, with the blood-virus resulting in the undead plagues."

Mel said, "Now in Matthew 24:14 Jesus said, "This gospel of the kingdom will be preached in all the world as a witness to all the nations, and then the end will come".

"You don't have to be a rocket scientist to understand this message. Once the world has received the gospel of the two Ambassadors of God and the plagues finish, the end comes and we all know what that is. Armageddon, to use your modern word."

Mel said, "Notice this is another furtive discovery" just as Tom says, "The word 'witness' is included, and you know who these two are."

Joe answered the rhetorical question. "Yes, the Two Witnesses of God." And even Mel looked at him in amazement.

Joe, not skipping a beat asked, "Where exactly are we on earth at this time?"

Mel said, "Let's see." And immediately they found themselves perhaps ten miles upwards looking down. "What do you see?"

Maria answered, "It looks like we're in Northern Africa somewhere but without having the luxury of a global map it's impossible to tell where the country borders are."

"We are just above Egypt to be exact," replied Mel. "Salvation is now offered as recorded in Revelation 10:10-11, 'you must prophesy again about many peoples, nations, tongues, and kings'."

Maria commented, "Seems to me this message was given to the Apostle John, so either I'm not getting this message clearly or does he have some involvement with the Two Witnesses of God?'"

Tom jumped in first, "From what I understand he talks about a future time but is not physically active then."

Joe commented, "Perhaps he can time travel just like we do. If he is one of these Two Witnesses, then their baptism just got bumped up to the Baptism of the Holy Spirit."

Maria picked up his thought train saying, "Perhaps the other was, John the Baptist and he dispensed the Holy Baptism of Water for their repentance."

Tom added, "This makes sense for now. These Two Witnesses of God perform different functions."

All three looked to Mel, who was staying out of their conversation, and Maria asked, "Are we accurate or off course?"

Mel smiled saying, "When you three start rambling, I'm constantly amazed. As to your answers, how about we park that question for now?"

Maria queried, "How about a tidbit of an answer for now?"

Mel said, "My you're determined," and then said, "Consider this. If your thinking is accurate, that would mean the 'evil seeds' also have the two Baptisms, for they are shown in the wedding feast with their garments of salvation. How would you explain this?"

Maria answered, "For sure God would not allow any antichrist to receive His Holy Spirit. Now I'm confused again."

Joe added, "Who's to say the 'evil seeds' are 'antichrist'? Remember, they don't have the mark of the beast upon them. They did worship the beast, that made them bad, but perhaps they were honestly deceived by Satan."

Tom replied, "How can one be honestly deceived?"

Mel added, "Remember when Satan proclaims himself as their messiah and then all others' messiah many Israelites who have been waiting for millennia accept his words in faith."

Joe added, "Like grasping at straws, they were."

Maria thought to herself, "I really hope he's not intentionally doing his Yoda thing again."

Mel said, "Joe's correct."

Joe interjected, "See I was right," and looking perplexed said, "but just so Tom and Maria get it, please explain my answers to them." Joe thought to himself, "If he asks me to explain, I'm so busted."

"Joe, how about I explain everything for them?"

"Yes. Yes, please do," was his reply.

Mel said, "OK Maria, here's your little tidbit. Remember the Israelites only know what their leaders have taught them during these same millennia. Consider this. What if the evil seeds didn't know that they're the evil seeds, only Satan did? Perhaps and only perhaps, they are those, who only repented out of fear, when Satan's temple was destroyed?

Speaking of perhaps, perhaps I will dwell on this later on. For now, let's just park these thoughts."

Maria probed slightly, "How could one be evil and not know it?"

Mel thought, "She is so persistent. I will paraphrase the Bible's answer. 1 Timothy 6:9-10 but those who desire to be rich fall into temptation. For the love of money is a root of all kinds of evil."

"I get it," she replied. "We have a saying that some people are in it 'for all the wrong reasons'."

Mel smiled commenting, "Yes that is correct, and who else was in it 'for all the wrong reasons'?"

"Got this one," answered Tom. "Judas was one of the first 12 Apostles. He was only in it for the money and maybe power." Tom paused, "Whoa! Judas had the two Holy Baptism's and also was an Apostle of the Lord, yet he fell."

Maria said, "Got it. It's not the money, rather it's the love of money that's the root of all kinds of evil."

Tom added, "OK, we now know how these 'evil seeds' could have gotten the two Holy Baptisms."

Mel now paused and then spoke softly, "Consider this. What if some of the 'evil seeds' had all three of the Holy Sacraments? Certain Christians, of understanding, those Children of God who had the three Holy Sacraments and drifted away, you called them the Prodigal Children, not those who were martyred, rather those who didn't have the courage of martyrdom, were hated by Satan. Remember the saying, 'keep your friends close and enemies closer'? Satan turned them away from their God unto himself by catering to their ego, lust, power or whatever it took. They, for various reasons, now worshiped him as their messiah returned. Satan considered them his greatest 'trophy'. Now to them no mark was applied. They lived in his temple totally deceived. These, then, were truly his 'evil seeds', waiting to be planted for a future crop."

Maria said, "At first I thought all this 'evil seed' talk was, at best, just a handful of people. But I'm beginning to think that the scope of this topic is really huge. There are many classification that could be made concerning all of them."

"Yes" replied Mel, "however, they serve a purpose."

Maria then asked, "What about my question concerning the Two Witnesses and the Apostle John."

Now the expression on Mel's face changed.

Maria sighed, "I know that look. It seems like my question is parked for now, right?"

Mel replied, "I said 'parked' you said, 'parked for now'. We'll see."

Mel, moving forward, said, "The Apostle John is also told forget about the outer court as it's given over to the Gentiles, meaning the antichrist who desecrate it for 42 months."

Tom asked Mel, "Just to digress for a moment, a while back I wrote about the 'abomination of desolation' standing on the exact same 'spot of ground' where God once stood. Based on my understanding, then when the Bible talks about the Temple's outer court and the Gentiles desecrating it for 42 months, this means the antichrist are really defiling the same 'area of ground' that in times past was holy."

Mel replied, "Yes. It also says of them that the Two Witnesses will travel the entire world for one thousand two hundred and sixty days, clothed in sackcloth."

Maria spoke, "Yes, we all saw them leave the Great Domed City. They were very tall and were wearing these sackcloth robes."

Mel said, "This shows you two things. The antichrist and God's two Ambassadors clash head on, battling during the same time plane of 1260 days.

God gives His two Ambassadors the ability, strength, and capacity to carry out their commission. They are clothed in sackcloth, signifying humbleness and repentance, but don't let their appearances fool you. They can and will vaporize anyone and unleash thousands of plagues."

Joe commented, "Talk about zero tolerance."

Mel agreed, then said, "Their scope was global and after their death when their time of testimony has been completed the Bible says, the antichrist rejoice and send gifts to each other."

Mel continued, "I mentioned this for those who will be viewing through your eyes and thoughts. Joe, use your imagination, what must hundreds of millions of people look like to Satan, all cheering and partying. Then consider how sad this looks to Heaven."

Joe asked, "Through my thoughts?"

And Mel actually sighed, "Yes and that in itself is a miracle, Joe."

Maria, now smirking said, "Seems like we're stuck with you for eternity, Joe, and by the way, just out of curiosity Mel, how long is eternity?"

Her smiling was cut short by his strange answer. "Forever, forever more and forever after."

Joe just smirked saying, "Looks like you guys are stuck with me."

Mel was quiet. So were the others, because that was true but they didn't mind because they loved him.

Mel commented, "If I may be allowed to continue with my thoughts, I just wanted to point out the fact that they travelled and testified to the entire world excluding only those wearing the mark of the beast that no amount of testimony could redeem.

Bear in mind that the people of the Nations of the 10 Kings have up to now seen and heard the Four Fire-Thunder Messages in their respective 'Angel Halos' and now God's two Ambassadors have come to them."

Tom said, "This is so fantastic. We have discussed this happening and now we get to see it unfold first hand."

Maria exclaimed, "Look down there!"

From their vantage point, miles high in the sky, they could see God's two Ambassadors as they began to testify to the very first group of people in the lands of the 10 kings.

"Egypt," Joe interjected.

Maria just looked at him for stealing her thunder. Joe smiled at her. "Those dimples always get him out of hot water," she thought.

Tom said, "Even from up here, it's amazing how loud the roaring pillar of fire actually is."

Now the Two Witnesses begin testifying again. Joe said, "Look at the mini-dome around the pillar of fire. It's maybe 20 miles across and 5 miles high. I can see the people in its dome even from up here."

Maria said, "It seems like some are moving towards or away from the pillar of fire. I bet we know who they are, right Joe?"

"Uh, that's right Maria," came his reply. Joe had tuned her out as he watched the people attempting to flee saying, "When they reached the mini-dome's outer limits, they bounced off of it; they were trapped."

Mel said, "See there is an open space between the groups. Look at those fools. Even before they receive testimony some are firing weapons."

Mel now took them downwards to the ground saying, "Watch and listen closely as they begin to speak."

The voices of the Two Witnesses seemed to be whispering to those close by and a thundering to those at a distance. The people didn't need much time to accept what they heard partly due to the fact that they had all heard the past four thunder messages from God. Many could hardly wait for their turn to be saved, while the vast majority hated what was coming their way. After what appeared to take only ten minutes or so people were raising their hands to God of Heaven even before they were asked to. Those seeking the mercy of God wasted no time in singing praises with hands raised in prayers and supplications.

"A very touching sight indeed" commented Mel, with all nodding in complete agreement as words failed.

"Watch," said Mel as God's two Ambassadors now raised their hands and eyes to God. They themselves were drawn into the pillar of fire, yet still could visibly be seen.

Mel took them to within several feet of this massive pillar of fire and another strange happening, there was no sound now. Mel said, "The closer you get, the quieter it is."

"Peaceful," thought Tom.

Maria said, "Look, you can see within the pillar of fire some type of lightning energy that created the 'fingers of God' that were now coming out by the hundreds and touching those with hands uplifted."

Joe took Maria's hand and directed it towards some of the people facing them. "Look," he said, "when the 'finger of God' touched the people it made a sparkling and their foreheads glowed. I wish we could get closer." he thought. Immediately they found themselves standing directly in front of, however invisible to, them.

"It's beautiful," commented Maria. "Truly these are the 'fingers of God' in action that we talked about way back when."

Mel said, "See when they sparkled, the Mark of God appeared on their foreheads and this mark is very unique."

As Joe began to describe it, he was immediately cut off by Mel saying, "Seal up the things which you see. They are not for this time."

Both Tom and Maria stood at attention upon hearing his resounding words. Joe replied, "I thought people were seeing through my eyes."

"They are," said Mel, "just not in this time plane."

Joe thought, "I really don't like this time travel stuff."

Mel went on talking, "Now what do you think happens next?"

Joe blurted out, "Here they come."

"Not quite," commented Mel, "Remember those fools shooting rifles and rockets at the Two Witnesses? Here comes retribution."

Now a most thunderous lightning issued from out of their mouths. This fire was different than normal fire. It seemed like when you saw fire coming out of a dragon, like napalm, that upon contact caused the person or object to burn to ashes. This shooting flaming fire, incinerated all those that had tried to kill the Two Witnesses.

Joe said, "It looks like this hell fire could be projected for miles, whatever it took to reach those firing their weapons."

Mel looked at Joe saying, "Hell fire? Really?"

Joe asked, "What would you call it?"

Mel replied, "Avenging fire."

Tom asked, "What type of fire is that?"

"Fire of the worst type."

"I'm confused," said Maria.

Mel replied, "All in due time."

Maria commented, "With the sparkling over, there are certain people in ashes, and others, now saved, that simply began walking. Oops! I spoke too soon. They're running now to their respective homes or dwellings. I don't blame them. Run, run, run, people!"

As the Two Witnesses moved to their next zone, Mel said to Joe, "Now you can say what happens next."

Joe not wasting any time replied, "Here they come."

Immediately trailing his words as the pillar of fire disappeared, the ambient light from high up also began to darken and a thunderous sound of clattering commenced. The Zombie Plagues now started in the lands of the 10 kings at this 1400 T/D.

Maria shouted, "What happens now to those with God's Mark?"

Mel said, "Watch and see."

Now, came not millions but billions of the Flying Hell Monsters.

Joe yelled, "They're larger than I imagined."

And Maria said, "Their eyes glow in the dark. What's that high pitched screaming sound?"

Again Mel said, "Just wait and see."

It didn't take long for them to find out. Their wings clattered but from within their heads came a high pitched sound like those tree bugs that made siren sounds when it got really hot in the summer. Now imagine billions of them. The sound created is deafening.

Maria said, "Look at the saved. This sound has no effect on them. That's a reassuring scene."

The density of these flying monsters now was so great one could not move this way or that way without coming into contact with them. That alone would terrorize people.

These monsters flew rather slowly and methodically, similar to that of a bat, however at all times looking for something to attack. Their scorpion tails were always moving similar to that of a squirrel.

Now the strange part was that, as their numbers increased in magnitude, these monsters did not land nor dare touch the recently saved. The flying monsters always maneuvered around them.

"Again," thought Maria, "a comforting scene."

Tom said, "Look, when these monsters made direct eye contact with those displaying God's Mark, their eyes turned from a glowing red to a golden color."

Mel said, "That's the indicator that they were not to harm these people."

Maria said she didn't feel comfortable standing right in the path of these flying monsters, and no sooner said, these flying monsters flew directly at and through them.

Tom said, "That was eerie. Not only didn't they see us, they flew through us."

Mel said, "Don't forget, you're a spirit. You'll be able to make your presence known soon enough."

Maria replied, "I know we're spirits, but it's still scary to see them."

Mel commented, "Maria, in time you will be able to differentiate between the physical and spiritual."

Joe said, "It's one thing to say billions of them and another when you see them."

They rose in height, hundreds of feet, spreading out in every direction. The sound, even to them, was horrendous. The antichrist were holding their hands over their ears.

"That was the least of their problems," Joe said. "See, these flying monsters began with bypassing the saved, then flying through us and now they've begun their mission of attacking the antichrist."

Tom asked Mel if they could go up for a while and immediately they were up high, looking down.

"See," commented Tom. "It looks like a honey dip donut that has a hole in the center. The pillar of fire is in the center and the flying monsters are radiating outwards from it in all directions."

Joe said, "How did you get a donut out of this view?"

Mel continued saying, "Those not having the Mark of God were trying to put as much distance between themselves and the flying monsters as possible and were actually fleeing in all directions, sort of like spokes of a wheel radiating outwards. See Tom, that's how you describe them."

"Not bad," commented Maria, taking charge. "Look at these people fleeing, but to no avail as these flying monsters are very fast indeed. The people are trying to swat them and even when they connected it had no effect. If anything it only made them madder."

People were screaming in pain from their bites. Joe said that their bites were more like chunks of flesh being ripped out.

Tom said, "Look closely. These flying monsters are not eating the flesh they chunk out. They're spitting them out and keep attacking."

Joe counted the number of times one flying monster would bite and chunk out flesh. He reached 10 before the monster left that person.

While they were watching, if that weren't bad enough, other flying monsters also attacked the same person.

"Talk about bloodshed," Maria yelled.

Tom said it looked like piranha when they attacked something living in the waters in South America.

Maria asked, "How long does this attack go on for?"

Mel said "Until the next zone has been testified to and the Two Witnesses move on."

Joe said, "So they keep attacking until the hour has been fulfilled. At this fierce rate how can the people survive? They will each have many chunks of flesh missing."

Mel replied, "Remember for the first 150 days God will not let them die."

Joe said, "See. The people being attacked are dropping like flies to the ground withering in great pain. They're flopping like fish cast onto land."

After several minutes their flopping frequency began slowing down and soon they went comatose. Now the flying monsters had no further use for them.

Tom said, "Seems like they're just going to lie there for the next three days or so."

Maria said, "I don't like looking at them just lying and bleeding. It's disgusting and horrifying to see."

"OK," Mel said. "Let's move."

And the three of them were now taken by Mel to the dwellings of the people being attacked. The people slammed their doors and put objects in front of their windows. Many began hiding in crevices, caves, holes in the ground and there they hid in fear of what was coming their way.

Joe now took over saying, "Nothing can stop these flying monsters. Walls seem like the holes in Swiss cheese. They seem to be able to simply pass through material objects."

Maria said, "They even passed through us a few minutes ago," and before Joe could retort she remarked, "I know we're spirits. I was just making a point."

Joe continued, "See, these monsters are now just hopping from victim to victim restricted within their dwelling confines."

Joe moved in, really up close saying, "See, they bite them over and over again and look at the chunk of flesh they extract with their four fanged lion's teeth. They're ripping the chunks out."

Mel said to Joe to look more closely because in addition to them ripping chunks of flesh, they were also sucking blood, like a mosquito but with vastly larger fangs.

Maria said, "How do they cause the blood-virus?"

Mel waved his hand and one of these monsters alighted on it. "Look closely," he said. "See their top fangs are hollow as snakes. When they suck blood they contaminate the area with their saliva, similar to that of a malaria mosquito."

Joe said, "The only difference is that they have teeth and the mosquito has a long, pointed mouthpart used to pierce the skin. It contains two tubes; one for injecting saliva and one for drawing blood."

"That's a bit more info than needed," Maria said as she turned slightly away from all this.

Tom said, "Look at its stinger. The pointed end has a bulb on it that must be filled with venom."

Mel commented, "This venom contains the blood-virus that causes the plagues. The bulb is large so they can attack as many people as necessary in that zone."

Mel then continued, "The wound that the flying monsters create is easily contaminated with feces and other debris. This in itself leads to other diseases."

Joe was carefully observing these terrifying things due to their great numbers which seemed to cover all the land surface in that zone as their numbers were so vast.

Maria asked "When they have finished attacking everyone do they go back into the pit they first came out of?"

Mel said, "No, once released they never go back. In the land of Israel and Judea the swarms moved from zone to zone once each day. Now, as you see, they begin moving on the hour from zone to zone and their aggressiveness becomes truly mind-boggling."

Joe, zoomed over to the victims now lying helplessly upon the ground. What a bloody mess they were. He said somewhat meekly, "Hey Maria, see I can zoom around like Mel," and proceeded to do so over and over, each time looking at the mess of bloody bodies surrounding him.

Maria did not want to get too close to them. She never could handle the sight of blood very well. Joe, on the other hand, was fascinated by the attack pattern. Most attacks were on their backs, chests, arms and some on their faces.

Mel said, "There's a reason for this."

Joe replied, "Give it up."

Mel looked quizzically at Joe who almost laughed thinking that he had outfoxed Mel, only to receive the instant reply, "Tom, you answer him."

And with that, Tom replied, "Do I know the answer?"

"Sure you do," came Mel's reply. "Didn't you say they will get up and run? Tom said, "Oh yes, they need their legs to be able to do this."

Mel said, "The blood-virus will soon alter their minds, devolving into base functioning."

"I seem to recall saying that," commented Tom. "Will the pattern that we just saw repeat the same way in each zone?"

Mel said, "Every zone is unique. However, the final result will be consistent, some saved, most attacked. Don't forget, just as you used your BSW communication device and testified to the world, the antichrist will also be able to do the same."

Maria remembered talking about this very same thing. In the past they transmitted to the world, that this time would come. Then soon after, others also began replying, about skirmishes whereby two supernatural beings were testifying and offering salvation to the people of their true God of the Heavens along with the mention of some type of flying monsters.

Mel said that the unholy trinity will soon come up with their own version of the facts, only their facts will be lies.

"Why am I not surprised," Maria replied.

Tom said, "Look at the top of the continent dome. It's not static, rather it's more like fluid Northern Lights."

Maria commented, "It's very bright to look at, much more vivid than Northern Lights."

Mel said, "Each dome has its own atmosphere that is pure and free of pollutants."

Joe asked, "Why give pure air when they're all going to die anyway?"

Tom said, "Not all die Joe. Some are saved for the King's Wedding Feast."

Joe said, "Oh yeah, that's another story."

Mel thought, "Now he's already copying my mannerisms."

Joe replied, "I heard that you know."

"Really?" thought Mel.

"Yes, really," said Joe.

Maria began to ask 'how' and then changed her question to, "Why are we able to communicate telepathically?"

Mel looked and sighed. "I see this is going to tax me more than I imagined."

Joe said, "You mean we're a little much for you?" "Not the collective 'you', just the single 'you'," countered Mel.

Joe replied, "You know I'm starting to get the hang of this telepathy stuff."

Mel groaned, "Patience is a virtue."

As God's two Ambassadors left that zone, they looked back and waived. The saved were moving to their now abandoned shelters. The afflicted were unconscious, laying on the ground. Following their wave, all water sources on or under the earth in that zone, turned into actual blood.

Maria asked "Will this red blood turn dark in time, or should I park that thought?" she mused.

"Now who's emulating whom?" Mel smiled.

Tom said, "I thought they were waving at us."

Mel corrected him saying, "Their wave only triggered the blood-virus plague for that zone. Remember we are time dimension interlopers and they don't see us."

"By us," Maria asked, "does that include or exclude you?"

"Perhaps," came a somewhat cryptic reply.

Joe asked, "How can the wave of hands trigger plagues?"

Mel said, "Everyone having a function has eyes on them. Joe, do you understand this?"

"Think so," he replied and looked at Maria who had her eyes lowered meaning nobody had a clue what it meant.

Tom, seeing bewilderment in their eyes said, "Remember guys, Mel's comment a while ago about 'higher technology'. We will in due course gain knowledge at the right time."

They both sighed, then Maria asked, "What's next?"

Joe had one further question. "If all the water turns to blood, what do the saved people drink?"

"Now I've got him," thought Joe.

Mel smiled saying, "Only the water with respect to the anti-christ turned into blood. What was blood to some was still water to others."

Mel continued, "This pattern will repeat itself until all zones within that Angel Halo have been testified to. In due course, all Angel Halos residing over each of the continents or large areas of the planet will receive their opportunity for redemption or plagues.

Due to the combined effects of the Fire-Thunder messages these Heavenly Wonders will give the people great confidence to not bow to the unholy trinity. Also, remember that they will hear each Fire-Thunder message in their own language and in a fashion that will allow them to fully understand the messages that God intends them to know.

The people desiring salvation offered by God's two Ambassadors flee towards the pillar of fire while the antichrist will flee away from it."

Over and over again the antichrist tried to kill these Two Witnesses and this only resulted with them being incinerated by fire and with plagues following.

As time passed, word spread around the world as to the invincibility of God's two Ambassadors.

The antichrist now fled at the site of the Pillar of Fire as it meandered in turn throughout the Angel Halo one zone at a time.

Joe commented, "The good within each angel halo will gravitate towards the pillar of fire in the far off distance. The antichrist will flee to the most remote areas as close to its outer limits as possible."

Maria asked, "Where are you going with this?"

Joe continued, "What if, the antichrist during these 150 days flee to and congregated in great numbers at the border between them and the next angel halo?"

Joe thought for a minute and then said, "Imagine, say tens of millions, all in one location, sort of in the same last zone. When the Two Witnesses wave and leave to that next angel halo, there's going to be a lot of 1-color and 3-color zombies coming their way very soon."

Tom pondering this said, "This also means that the saved people have more food and necessities of life."

Joe added, "There seem to be many scenarios that may take place, and each one of them works."

Mel began reminiscing and said, "God's two Ambassadors' travels will take them to all countries representing all faiths. Remember Jesus said, He has other sheep which are not of this fold, not just in Christian areas, and that's exactly what it now taking place. And He further said the everlasting gospel will be preached to those who dwell on the earth to every nation, tribe, tongue, and people."

Mel began discussing the full meaning about this statement of Jesus as to who these 'other sheep' in 'other places' are. He said, "One non-Christian faith has good things to say about Jesus. They say that Jesus is considered to be a Messenger of God who will return to earth near the Day of Judgment to restore justice and to defeat the false messiah, also known as the Antichrist."

Mel continued, "The two Ambassadors of God will be accepted by them. We can see that when God speaks through his 7 Fire-Thunders and the two Ambassadors, all people will understand His special messages and then receive their 'wedding garments'. These are the sheep in other folds spoken of by Jesus as he loves them all."

Mel concluded, "No matter what the faith of a person, everyone should be respectful, love and respect one another, words easily spoken but difficult to abide by. Remember it's God's Plan of Salvation not man's. People should follow the Golden Rule 'Do unto others as you would have them do unto you'."

Maria asked, "Do God's two Ambassadors belong to a specific religion of man?"

"They are supernatural beings who are testifying to God's Plan of Salvation. It's God's Plan and His will be done on earth as it is in Heaven, so to answer the question, it's no."

Mel continued, "To understand how busy God's two Ambassadors will now be as they travel the world testifying to the people of the 10 kings, let's do some math. Using Tom's estimate for only one billion people and since there are 900 days remaining, this equates to about 1 million people each day or let's say 50,000 each hour.

God's two Ambassadors will testify to about 50,000 people each hour, 24 times each day for the balance of the 900 days and then everyone on earth would have been testified to. And remember, that's for only about 1 billion.

24 times each day the Pillar of Fire moves from zone to zone. Now those standing at a distance not actually in the zone being testified to will undoubtedly see the Pillar of Fire, fingers of God, and hear the Fire-Thunderous voices of God's two Ambassadors. This will either give them great joy or immense anger depending upon whose side they're on."

Joe said, "One can easily see how the plagues spread in a typical infection pandemic pattern. They start at point zero then expand outwards systematically and then when the infection seems to be slowing it ramps up again."

Tom asked, "How often will they hear the messages?" Mel responded, "Remember the Sabbath day and keep it holy. Do you get the analogy?"

Maria added, "OK, I get it. Each new Thunder Message takes precedence and becomes the message of importance?"

"Absolutely," replied Mel.

Joe said, "It seems like the best the people could do was to hide from the antichrist and not bow down to the thousands of abominations set up world-wide, as these horrible idols seemed to pop up everywhere, simultaneously."

Mel commented, "Remember a long time ago when you three were discussing that soldier's arm band and you said they must have been prepared for this for a long time? The same is true concerning these idols. They were in the works for a long time."

Maria asked, "Were you listening to us even back then?"

Mel replied, "Not all your thoughts."

Joe sighed, winking at Maria who was trying not to make eye contact with him. She lost, and they began howling with laughter.

Tom said, "Ok guys, you've had your laugh. Let's get back to business. Imagine skirmishes happening every hour on the hour, fire throwing, plagues turning all water to blood, along with no rain and the attack of the flying monsters and blood virus plagues. One would think that the antichrist would learn their lesson to not antagonise these two supernatural beings or you die."

Joe added, "You know it's amazing that all the people will actually hear these thunder messages in their own languages and dialects."

Maria, speaking out loud, said, "So these two supernatural beings travelled throughout the country side in defiance of the unholy trinity who up to now had ruled and killed with impunity. This must have hugely undermined the Dragon's efforts to convert his targets."

"Remember," Tom added, "every single person is a creation of God's and for God to lose but one, pains him greatly."

Joe added his two cents worth saying, "Nothing to date has been as nasty as his Flying Hell Monsters and his 'walking dead', who now can 'run like hell'."

Mel commented, "I never thought anyone would actually want to take credit for naming these vicious attackers and those pitiful humans, walking or running, who 'wished they were dead'."

Joe added, "And these vicious attackers using their lion's teeth rip out chunks of flesh the size of a person's eye."

Maria cringed, saying, "That's so gross!"

Joe was thinking and about to say something like… "eye for an eye, tooth…," but Maria, just in time covered his mumbling mouth, and looked at him, her eyes expressing, "Really?"

This was enough of a distraction as Joe was now pondering how her eyes could think.

Mel, again speaking said, "Imagine, all this takes place for the next 900 days as the spread of the Zombie Plagues continue making the same pattern as when you dropped a pebble into the water and see 'ripple rings' moving outwards from its center."

Tom commented, "When you divide the 900 days and six continent size Angel Halos, you get 150 days. Strange isn't it that it's the exact same number of days people are infected by the Flying Hell Monsters?"

Mel said, "Nothing is coincidental, my friends. During these 900 days all 6 Angel Halos which make up the entire world, receive God's testimony. They will, towards the end of their Time of Testimony, be heading from the east, travelling westward, towards the Great Euphrates River. This is reminiscent of the three wise men, who in times past also travelled this way, although for an entirely different purpose."

Joe commented, "And remember, also during their journey's wake, come the zombies and recovered zombies."

Tom added, "It's amazing that their journey ends back at the Wilderness Sanctuary, outside of Jerusalem, where they started. It's heartening that they never give up admonishing the people to repent and worship God."

Mel said, "You see within these nations there were large numbers of people who did not want to engage in war. They did not want to participate in the approaching battle of Armageddon."

Maria commented, "These people had a more tender nature who accepted their testimony and became 'saved'."

Maria asked Mel, "Is being 'saved' the same as those in Israel who 'repented'?"

"The answer is yes."

"They go into the 1000 year kingdom of peace as citizens, right?"

"Yes again," came Mel's answer. "However, they must still remain faithful or suffer Judgment Day."

Joe started to yawn after listening to Mel and the many events that that didn't include 'zombies'.

Mel smiled at Joe yawning, "Seems like I'm boring you."

"Well maybe a little bit."

Mel commented, "Thought so. OK, let's ramp things up a little."

With a wave of his hand, they watched from a slightly elevated position as the Flying Hell Monsters began attacking and infecting everyone in zone two. Joe's pattern began unfolding before their very eyes.

Perking up, Joe said, "So we're in, or rather above, Egypt and this is the first of the 900 days of zombies, still to come. Now we're getting somewhere."

Mel now lowered them to the ground, point zero. They were looking at the Flying Hell Monsters attacking the people.

"Wow!" yelled Maria. "They're really swarming that guy. Must be at least 10 on him. He's wiggling on the ground but that's not doing him any good."

Joe said, "Really chunking out flesh like a machine gun and now that's a first, after they chunk out flesh, they turn and sting the person in the same spot. Why is that?"

Mel then said, "This ensures the virus gets directly into their bloodstream."

Tom said, "It looks like the person is unconscious."

"Rightly so," piped in Joe. "Remember, we said they will lie on the ground about three days, then they get up and follow the pillar of fire. Well, the 1-color will follow the pillar of fire after three days. The 3-color will, after about 6 days follow them.

Maria said, "Let the chase begin."

Joe continued saying, "It will be some chase," and doing a little math said, "24 zones a day and a 3 days head start for the 1-colors, this means the Two Witnesses and the Pillar of Fire have about a 72 zone head start."

Tom said he never thought of it that way. "It's true, that's a lot of head start."

Joe said, "Yes, but they will still easily be able to see this pillar of fire."

Maria asked, "Do you think they have to travel in the exact same route that the Two Witnesses took?"

"I think the answer will be a work in progress," Tom replied. "Picture this, there are 72 zones of infected zombies, if all zombies rise up and follow in a straight line, this would work if they were only travelling from point A to B. The Two Witnesses don't travel in this fashion, they zigzag back and forth across the country like the pied piper."

Joe said, "I've got it. Cowboys do the same thing when corralling horses. They travel back and forth zigzagging and the end result is the horses are maneuvered into the coral."

Maria said, "That's brilliant Joe. So even if the pillar of fire keeps changing directions, the infected still follow it."

Mel added, "Yes, however you still didn't get the bigger picture. Consider this, not only are the infected following, as you said, the 'pied piper', but this corralling motion also maneuvers those who have not as of yet been infected."

Joe added, "So the 'pied piper' not only draws, he also maneuvers those in front of him. That's doubly brilliant. The infected will just lock on to the nearest fresh blood source. There will be many of them, and all having the pillar of fire in front of them."

Maria then commented, "So even after just three days there could be millions of them following the pillar of fire."

Joe said, "And then after another three days, following them the 3-color get mobile. This can also be in the millions."

Maria said, "This group does not follow the pillar of fire, right?"

Joe replied, "No, this group follows the 1-color who have a three day head start in front of them."

Maria asks, "How do they track them if they can't see them?"

Joe answered her question, "I just told you. They smell them, more precisely they smell the red blood that they've been drinking and their sources. You know, Maria, a bear's sense of smell is so sensitive that they can detect animal carcasses upwind from a distance of 20 miles away. So these zombies can easily track them. Don't forget, they leave behind a trail of debris a zombie could trip over, you know, heads, limbs,. . ."

"I get the picture, Joe."

Tom said, "It's easy to see how after a while there will be 200 million 1-color and 200 million 3-color, what about the rest of the people?"

Mel said, "There are still 200 million 3-color in Babylon the Great and you're assuming there will still be a billion people on earth at the 1400 T/D. Don't forget there are other plagues that kill many. So don't fixate on the billion number, rather what is recorded. Keep your figure of 600 million, made up of 200 million 3-color, chasing 200 million 1-color and 200 million 3-color living in Babylon the Great. The actual numbers will take care of themselves."

Joe pushing a little asked, "What about the balance, whatever it may be?"

Mel answered, "That is made up of the saved and those who died in other plagues or were eaten along the way."

Joe laughed saying, "Eaten along the way? How about a little more info on this one."

Mel just said, "The 1-color only like red blood to drink and the 3-color like red blood to drink and, 1-color to eat, so be patient grasshopper."

Joe winked at Maria saying, "I told you they like a hot meal."

Maria chuckled, "Joe, you're now our official grasshopper."

"Not impressed," replied Joe.

"That makes it even funnier," she quipped. "What's going to happen is so gross, speaking of which, this guy has the 1-color 'Dragon's Tattoo 666' on his hand." She looked around, then said, "There are lots of them scattered on the ground."

Tom, standing 20 feet or so away said, "Over here there are many with the 3-color mark on their foreheads."

Mel said, "No matter, the 1-color rise up in three days and run towards the pillar of fire, the 3-color also rise up after 6 days and follow the 1-color."

Tom asked, "When does Babylon the Great get the Two Witnesses of God?"

Mel replied, "They don't. Just like in Judea, there are only the antichrist 3-color living there. The only thing visiting these nations will be the Flying Hell Monsters coming their way soon. Then it doesn't take long for these monsters to attack and infect everyone.

How about we leave these pitiful creatures for a while. The scene repeats itself over 20,000 times before drawing to a close. Now let's look at those saved and what they are doing."

Maria asked, "Where are we going now?"

Mel said, "How about we go to New York City, Central Park to be exact?"

A second later they were there, standing on the ground.

Tom, the first to speak said, "This doesn't look like the Central Park we last saw, when the Martyrs of Understanding were still here."

Maria said, "It looks so deserted now. Where is everyone?"

Mel said, "Remember, the Two Witnesses have not yet come to this area. Right now they've left Africa and are in South America and are working their way up to us."

Tom said, "I still don't get how they can travel and cover every square inch of ground."

Mel replied, "Consider this. What if the good and the bad are drawn to certain areas within each angel halo? Similar to the antichrist migrating to the furthest area in their dome attempting to avoid the Two Witnesses. Likewise, it is possible that the good also migrate to their areas."

Mel continued, "Let's just say if the antichrist can be drawn a certain way, the good can also be drawn another certain way."

Maria said, "Something like 'pockets' of people."

Joe impatiently asked, "Are we going to see anyone here? If so, when?"

"Very soon, I reckon," replied Mel.

Maria pointed and said to them, "Look over there! All the people have the black 'Dragon's Tattoo 666' on their right hands."

Tom added, "See there are always several of the 3-color 'Dragon's Tattoo 666' snooping around, sort of making sure everyone behaved."

Mel commented, "Who do you not see?"

Maria answered, "Those with no mark. Where are they?"

"Hiding," replied Mel. "If they get caught, they get killed, no questions asked for they are deemed terrorists by the authorities."

Tom said, "The people don't seem to be doing anything. They're just milling around. I thought by having the black tattoo on their hands that they were allowed to buy and sell."

Mel said, "Correct. They're allowed to. However, they now lack the will and desire to do so. They have all heard about the plagues coming their way. As a matter of fact, other plagues have already come their way as a vast quantity of sea life and ships have been destroyed. Certain parts of the oceans have been declared 'verboten' as their waters have turned to blood like that of a dead man. It's a dark color, it smells and does not support life, but only offers death."

Joe asked, "What's the sense of living if all that you're doing is waiting for plagues to arrive?"

Mel answered, "Too bad they didn't think of the consequences sooner."

Maria asked, "So where are the people who did not take the dragon's tattoo in either color?"

Mel said, "Let's go and see," and in a flash were transported there.

"Hey," Tom said. "That looks very familiar."

They all looked at each other thinking, "You've got to be kidding."

Joe, as usual, the first to say something, most often not of particular value, said, "Home sweet home."

Mel said, "And why not? The caves served you well in your time, so why not theirs?"

Tom asked, "Are there many of these hiding in such places?"

Mel said, "Many thousands. The antichrist have their hands full with the Two Witnesses and the thousands of blood-virus plagues spreading across the earth."

"When did these people get here?" Joe asked.

"Some were on the move even before the three of you were martyred. Remember it was only a few months ago that you received 'Holpen'."

Maria said, "So these people, are they all Christians or a mix of religions?"

Mel said, "They are people who in the past were lukewarm just floating along with the tide until it turned into angry waves against them. They, for many reasons, did not agree with those in power calling themselves the government. You called them antichrist.

But, these people never turned their backs on God. They just had no interest in spiritual matters. However, they were not stupid. They all heard the Fire-Thunder messages and decided to, as you say, 'get out of Dodge'. They know that some type of salvation is coming to them."

Joe asked, "When?"

Mel's answers was, "Soon. They have all heard by now of the Two Witnesses who are more powerful than those chasing them. They also know of the Flying Hell Monsters that unleash the blood-virus plagues and this they want no part of."

Maria asked, "Will the Two Witnesses travel all throughout the USA?"

Mel said, "No. There are some places that only consist of the 1-color and 3 color antichrist. No amount of testimony would ever save them. They've made their decision and turned away from God. 'So it is written'."

Tom added, "So the Two Witnesses travel to give testimony to eligible people and not to every square foot of land."

"Correct," replied Mel, "Salvation is offered to people, not land, and as you said, eligible people not having the 1 or 3-color 'Dragon's Tattoo 666'."

Joe asked again, "When will the Two Witnesses come this way?"

Mel said, "Sooner than you think."

Joe thought, "First he says 'soon', then 'very soon', then 'sooner than you think'. He's just like Tom when he toyed with me about the zombies drinking blood."

Mel thought, "Might as well cater to him," and said, "Here they come."

Their attention was now attracted by the pulsating fire in the sky of their Angel Halo or more accurately the lack of it. As the light dimmed, they saw the pillar of fire coming directly towards them, and to say the least, it was humbling and disconcerting to see such a huge roaring pillar of fire coming their way. This pillar of fire was many times higher than their cave altitude.

Maria asked, "How will the Two Witnesses testify to people scattered all over these hundreds or thousands of caves, nooks and crannies."

Mel said, "Watch."

Now another first, this pillar of fire somehow expanded and covered many of the mountain ridges.

"This perhaps makes it about 50 miles in diameter," said Joe. "It's difficult to estimate distance in the Rockies."

Mel said, "See, the pillar of fire encompasses everyone within its walls. As the antichrist gathered elsewhere in groups so did those desiring salvation."

"That's another first," Maria said. "Imagine that, people banded together awaiting their salvation."

Tom said, "This was dangerous for them since a larger group of people could be more easily spotted."

Joe replied, "As they say, desperate times, desperate actions".

Everyone, including Mel, just went on talking. Mel said, "See how the pillar of fire now surrounds everyone? There is no possibility that anyone can now be harmed."

The Two Witnesses began testifying. Tom, the first to respond, said, "Listen to what they're saying. Their testimony is so simple, kind and loving."

Joe said, "You know, I really thought it would be like fire and brimstone, like a country preacher proclaiming heaven or hell and damnation."

Mel said, "God is always kind and loving and it's only when people turn away from Him, worshiping other gods, does he become angry."

Maria commented, "It doesn't take them long to get right down to business. See the people are already once again raising their hands in praise to God. Now we will see the 'fingers of God' touch them."

"That's strange." Maria said, "No fingers. They're just sparkling."

Mel said, "Right you are, there's no necessity since they're already in the protection of the pillar of fire."

They all now had the Mark of God upon their foreheads and then the pillar of fire moved to its next zone, once again making a tremendous sound.

Joe said, "This sound alone heralds the pillar's coming, gently admonishing people to exit the safety of their hiding places, and to come to salvation."

Maria said, "Who talks like that, my Joe? Seems like eternity is rubbing off on him."

Maria then asked, "Does everyone in these mountains become saved?"

Mel said, "No, unfortunately there still are those hiding in caves that do not desire salvation. They are lost souls, hermits of various types. They see the pillar of fire from another mountain ridge."

Joe commented, "Perhaps we could call them 'atheists' or 'agnostics'. Either way they're not going to be happy campers, that's for sure."

Joe now changed his demeanor saying to Maria and all, "Here they come, and here they came."

Maria tugged on Joe's arm. "Look," she said, "the light coming from the pillar of fire dome is fading." as it moved away to the next zone.

Joe now tugged on Maria's arm. "Look upwards." he said, as the sky from under the continent sized angel halo, reverted and began transforming back to its normal fire lightning.

Maria nestled into Joes arms as the sky began transforming into different shades of blackness descending down to pitch blackness.

The saved, not making it to their dwellings, just stood motionless as if previously instructed to do so as the Flying Hell Monsters approached and began looking everyone over. All the saved had yet another thing in common, they were not frightened of these Flying Hell Monsters. They did not run for cover, scream or panic.

Mel spoke, "Upon receiving the Mark of God, these saved souls were also instructed to observe a miracle. These flying monsters were on their side."

Soon these monsters were also staring at the three of them, with their red eyes perceiving their heavenly eyes. Now, not only did the eyes of the monsters turn golden, while in midair they paused from their quest of searching for victims, and gracefully nodded their heads for some reason.

Maria asked, "What was that all about?"

Mel replied, "It has been permitted for these few surrounding them, to be able to see you. You have no idea how you appear to them. They see in your eyes, God, their creator and their thoughts were immediately perceived by all such creatures."

Maria further asked, "Why was this allowed?"

Mel replied, "So it is written."

The three were quickly learning that not all questions are answered.

Joe looked around saying, "The swarms didn't seem to stay for more than several minutes and as quickly as they came, they left. I can't believe how loud they really are, between their wings clapping and their siren sounds, I'm surprised people don't just faint or drop dead."

Mel said, "Even if they did, they still would rise up full of bites, three days later, as death is removed for a while."

Tom said, "Look over there! That's where I was martyred."

Mel corrected him saying, "Over there you received 'Holpen'. Remember? Did you feel any pain?"

As Tom shook his head, Mel said, "Thought not."

Joe said, "See how the pillar of fire, now in the far off distance, illuminates the mountains, something like the golden sunsets we once saw when the mountain sides captured the sun's light reflected off the clouds."

Maria commented, "That was an eerily beautiful light. The sun has already gone down behind the mountain tops but sunlight bounced off of the clouds and came down to illumine the mountain sides with a very rich golden glow."

Mel said, "There are many dimensions of light. This is just one of them. Now," he continued, "would you like to say hello to the saved?"

Without them answering, immediately, the people were also allowed to see them and a few remembered them. This group believed that they would go alive into the 1000 year Kingdom of Peace.

Mel said, "They will, as part of the saved nations. They are the citizens."

Maria then commented, "You get what you believed in."

Mel expanded her statement saying, "You had to have the three prerequisites, the Holy Baptism of Water, the Holy Communion, and the Baptism with the Holy Spirit of God, and then one must have fulfilled them, to the best of their capabilities. Do you remember the parable of the 5 and the 3 talents?

"Yes," said Maria.

The people came up to Tom, Maria, and Joe and looked inquisitively at Mel, some with gladness, others somewhat sheepishly. The people asked, "Why are you glowing?"

The three hadn't noticed this effect, only mortals and others, could see it.

They began to testify to them and Mel chuckled saying, "That's not for you to do anymore." The people would not let them depart, just like Joseph in his dream would not let the angel leave without blessing him. These souls were sincere, so Mel gently began testifying to them to remain hidden and faithful, and at the 2300th day God would send his angels to gather them, so keep the faith brethren.

After a few minutes Mel said to them, "Time to move on."

This was easier said than done, as their compassion towards the saved, this human Godly quality impressed him greatly. He had to push himself forward saying, "Time to go."

Joe asked, "Now where to?"

Mel, with a slight wave of his hand, once again advanced the time line. They were atop, the Empire State Building overlooking Central Park.

Tom said, "I didn't see that one coming."

Joe commented, "It's like the King Kong movie when he's holding on to the antenna."

Maria added, "We're just floating up here. This wigs me out."

Tom pointed towards the west, and from their vantage point they saw the pillar of fire from a great distance as it zigzagged across the central states.

Joe remarked, "This is like seeing a time lapse film that shows the pillar of fire not really hopscotching, but rather powering its way through anything in its path. It's just like when we saw it make a beeline through Judea to the lands surrounding the Living Sea."

Maria looked at them and said, "To just see the enormity of this pillar of fire, even from way up here, is very humbling to us but I imagine very terrifying to others."

Mel said in a matter of a few minutes they had witnessed events that had now taken place over one week.

Joe said, "It looked like a machine gun stop action movie, as we in fact just saw the pillar of fire move over 150 times in what seemed less than two minutes."

Maria declared, "Now *that* certainly wasn't in the book. You can easily see how its route would panic the antichrist into fleeing far, far, from it."

Now the pillar of fire began slowing coming directly towards them into the zone that they were now in, making a sound that shook people to their bones.

Maria said, "Its size is phenomenally greater than we ever imagined."

"Well, will you look at that" she said. From nowhere, people were emerging out of sewers, drain pipes, manhole covers, underground exits, bridges, and overpasses, underground parking basements and other places not normally associated to living places of people. Seemingly, within only minutes, hundreds of people were running as fast as possible towards the pillar of fire.

Maria said, "I never thought of it this way. I believed that they would just stand there and wait for the pillar of fire to come to them."

Joe said, "It looks like they've been ready for some time and now they're making a run for it."

Mel said, "Look at the antichrist. They also see them running and they're firing at them. Tom, what do you see now?"

Tom startled, replied, "Those running, don't fall. It seems like not even one of them falls. Are those antichrist shooters such bad aims?"

Mel said, "How would you explain this happening Joe?"

"Either force fields or some such thing is interfering with their bullets."

"Or," Maria said, "Their bullets are not travelling in a straight line of sight. Remember Joe? That's the line from one of your favorite movies, 'Independence Day'."

Mel thought, "Humans with their clichés," and then added his own, "Perhaps this is a dimension twist."

Joe would have loved to explore this topic further, however, they were observing people rushing towards the pillar of fire, moving directly towards them.

Joe asked, "Why hasn't it stopped moving?"

Mel replied, "It hasn't reached its resting place within the zone just yet."

"This will be interesting." Maria said. "There are hundreds of buildings in its pathway. Let's see what happens next."

Mel said, "Whether in the countryside or in cities the pillar of fire moves in straight lines. Buildings in its pathway simply disintegrate."

The people by now were all on the ground, buildings were vacant. As the pillar came to a rest, all remaining antichrist fled to other areas within that zone.

"Remember" said Mel, "they see, hear and fire weapons from a distance."

The people ran into the pillar of fire, perhaps a mile or so wide and were safe.

All watched as once again the Two Witnesses did their testifying and then all sparkled and soon simply started walking either back to where they came from or to above ground homes and apartments now vacated.

"Wow! That was different. No fingers of God."

Mel said, "That's because they're already in the pillar of fire."

Still from their perch high atop the Empire State Building, Mel said, "Look in the far distance, what do you see? What do you hear?"

Joe pointed out two dust storms, the last not far behind the first, and there seems to be millions of them all headed our way. Mel said, "It's the zombies coming. They're making great dust clouds."

Tom said, "You can even hear them at this distance."

Mel said, "We're up high. Those on the ground will hear their vibrations first, then the sound will follow soon after."

Joe said, "Just like when a train is coming, you can feel something before you hear it."

Maria said, "I remember that. We could feel our home sort of resonate and at times we even commented about what was going on and then a few minutes later the low sound of a train was heard."

Mel commented, "These zombies are still three days out. Joe, do your thing."

Joe said, "Here they come!"

The sky again began darkening in the distance in degrees of gray to black to something else. This was the first time they were watching the Flying Hell Monsters attacking people in a large city.

Maria was the first to notice these flying monsters coming towards them and at first she didn't comprehend what she was seeing. Then it dawned on her, they were flying through, not around, the skyscrapers in their pathways. "That's one scary sight!" she yelled out.

Joe said, "Lights, camera, action!"

Maria said, "Really Joe? Does this seem like a movie to you?"

He replied, "Yes, it's so surreal that the only way I can fathom it is to think of it as a movie."

Maria just got trumped.

They watched as the sky turned thick black. These flying monsters were as high up as they were. Now, only the red glowing eyes of the monsters, were able to be seen.

"Truly hell on earth," she thought.

Mel moved time forward again. The three were getting used to this happening and took it all in stride. Now daylight came back as the monsters left town in pursuit of the pillar of fire and their next victims, only slightly ahead of them.

Tom commented that the devastation was horrific to look at. They saw millions of people lying on the ground, twitching and becoming comatose.

Joe looked into the distance saying, "Those dust clouds are rising higher into the sky. The two groups of zombies will be here soon."

"Three days, to be exact." commented Mel.

Mel, took them down to street level for an onsite inspection.

Maria said she had difficulty walking because the entire ground was littered with comatose victims with blood everywhere. There were bodies everywhere, in or on cars, in the gutters, in the subway tunnels. Truly, no place offered shelter once the attack of the Flying Hell Monsters began.

Joe took her arm, to steady her, then realized that they were spirits so how could they stumble? Mel answered his thought, "You can't. It just takes time for you to come to this conclusion."

Mel advanced time by three days. They watched as these zombies rose up and began staggering around for a while. Upon closer inspection, they noticed the effect of the blood-virus which caused the eyes of the zombies to turn black and shrivel within their sockets to the size of a pea. Mel said they could not see visible light but rather they perceived the ultra violet signature of the pillar of fire. They did, however, have a keen sense of smell so they could follow the pillar of fire and when blood sources came close they stampeded to and flopped into it, a most grotesque sight.

Maria asked what seemed to be a strange question, "Why don't they all just jump into the ocean since all water turns to blood during the time of the plagues?"

Mel answered saying, "The oceans turned to a different type of blood. It says in Revelation, 'then the second angel poured out his bowl on the sea, and it became <u>blood as of a dead man</u>; and every living creature in the sea died.'

The 1-color zombies don't have the capacity to even see this ocean blood. They can only smell fresh blood. The 3-color can see it, but won't go in it since it is dead blood. Both groups only desire 'red blood'."

Joe of course added, "Yea, they're 'red blooded Americans'."

Mel thought, "Of all things to say. How many of these silly slogans can he possible know? On second thought, ignorance is bliss."

"Joe!" said Maria. "Joe, look! The zombies, they're rising up, and staggering around. It certainly does not take them long to begin running after the pillar of fire." Soon this new group had stumbled over everything in their pathway and disappeared from their ground view, yet their screaming could still be heard.

Maria said, "Thank goodness that's over with. Their eyes are scary to look at and I hate their siren, screaming sounds."

Joe said, "Maria, this is only the beginning." and then spoke his line, "Here they come."

At this time, they were all still on the ground. The horde approaching them was about a mile away. Even at this distance their sound was scary. They howled and screamed like a cross between wolves and a siren. Soon their sound took on a life of its own. One could hear the crashing and breaking of objects in their pathway.

As zombies turned corners attempting to keep the pillar of fire in front of them, many stumbled and in short order were trampled.

Maria said, "Look, when they turn corners they wipe out into the sides of the buildings, just like a water surge wave would do."

Tom said, "Their bodies are beginning to pile up higher and higher, all crushed down due to the vast numbers trampling upon them."

They watched as the first several hundred thousand or so came by, a sea of zombies.

Maria was the first to complain saying, "They're running directly at us and in a few seconds will pass by or through us."

Mel sensed their fears of this happening as they were still very young in spirit. He didn't want to cause them mental trauma, and in a second they were once again atop the Empire State Building.

Maria sighed, "I'm relieved to be up here. Even though we're spirits, it's still horrifying to watch, especially when they actually run through you."

Joe not paying attention to her said, "Listen to their siren howling. I wonder if we could come up with a better name for this."

Maria said, "How about 'zombie screaming' or 'screaming zombies'?" She actually welcomed the distraction of thinking.

Joe picked 'screaming zombies'. We all know by now what this phrase entails.

Tom went on saying, "Look at their numbers. They look like a picture made up of millions of dots. There are so many of them."

Joe added, "They will number in the tens of millions, perhaps even more."

Tom gasped, "Will you look at that!" What appeared to be thousands of crushed and mangled bodies, now began to move. These things could not die for their first 150 days. They appeared to be shaking like a wet dog. Now, upright on two legs, they began running. The trampling merely slowed them down.

Joe said, "I don't know if a movie could even portray such weird events."

From their vantage perch, they watched for the next hour, then two and after watching for an extended period Maria said to Mel, that she'd had enough of this.

Mel looked at Tom and Joe saying, "Have both of you had enough, because this goes on for several days?" Both nodded, they'd had enough of this.

Mel agreed. He said, "Unfortunately, this scene is repeated over 20,000 times until its completion. I'll now really advance the time line, to the 2260 T/D. This brings us to the last 40 days before the 2300 days have been reached and to the number five fire-thunder message that admonishes everyone with God's Mark to remain faithful."

Chapter Forty-Eight
THUNDER MESSAGE FIVE 2260 T/D

KEEPS HIS GARMENTS

Revelation 16:15: "<u>Behold, I am coming</u> as a thief. <u>Blessed is he who watches</u>, and <u>keeps his garments</u>, lest he walk naked and they see his shame."

Mel said to them, "We're almost at the end of the Time of Redemption of the two Ambassadors of God and the fulfilment of Daniel's prophecy of the 2300 days at which time the 'Sanctuary is Cleansed' of the great deceiver Satan."

Tom commented, "The saved people only have 40 more days to hang in there before they're gathered by the forces of God."

Mel said, "Read carefully. This Thunder Message proclaims, "<u>Behold, I am coming</u>". The Son of God says, "<u>Blessed is he who watches</u> and <u>keeps his garments</u>."

Mel continued, "These garments are given to them upon their baptism."

Joe spotted something. "Maria," he said, "Mel referred to their garments given at their baptism. See, he didn't say 'of water'. I wonder why not?"

Maria replied, "Let's wait and see."

Joe thought, "Now she's quoting Mel. That means she doesn't know either."

Mel's voice now resounding said, "<u>Behold</u> means to keep your eyes open watching for Jesus, He is coming for you! Stand fast, stand firm, keep your garments."

Mel almost roared with such an urgency at this command. "Here's a hint! Jesus long ago in Matthew 25:6 said, "And at <u>midnight a cry was heard: 'Behold, the bridegroom is coming; go out to meet him!'</u>

The time is almost over that those who now have acquired the Mark of God have been given 'the garments of salvation' and they are being admonished to <u>keep them pure</u>."

Mel continued, "Behold, I am coming. This is a fantastic statement. Humans have a short attention span so taken literally it means, that Jesus is coming for them really soon! The Son of God also said, 'Behold I stand at the door and knock'."

Mel said, "When someone is knocking at your door, he's right there waiting to come in."

Tom said, "This also signifies that they acknowledged Him as the Son of God. This once again establishes the fact that the testimony of the two Ambassadors of God included the teaching that God's Son is Jesus."

Mel continued, "At this time, it is general knowledge that the 2300 T/D. is rapidly approaching. It's not a secret. It's recorded in the Book of Daniel. Remember, evil is not stupid, just not wise."

The hair on the necks of the 'saved' is now standing on end and the scenario, 'finger on the trigger' is being readied for a repeat. They can taste their deliverance, so to speak.

Mel continued with more insight. "At this 2260 T/D the Great Euphrates River dries up."

Tom asked, "How exactly does it dry up?"

Mel only said, "One of the many plagues did this deed."

Now he went on saying, "A while ago, you read about the three demons that come out of the unholy trinity, the false messiah who is Satan, the sea beast who is the false president and the land beast who is the false prophet. They traveled to the armies of the 10 kings, who were traumatized by the Zombie Plagues and who have only recently recovered. These 10 kings are loyal to the sea beast or the false president who controls the antichrist armies. They are those of pride wearing the 3-color 'Dragon's Tattoo 666' with blue at its top. However, due mainly to the actions of the Flying Hell Monsters unleashing the Zombie Virus, these 10 kings and their armies still require further reassurances. It seems like they need further demonstrations of the power of the 'unholy trinity' which demonstrates that they have problems in their camps and even within themselves.

Now as I just told you, these 3 demons are allowed to go out at the 2260 T/D. They are given a head start over their fellow 200 million demons still bound at the Great Euphrates dried up river."

Mel added, "You may be wondering why they are given these 40 day. Remember, we have moved again in time, and there are large numbers of saved people who accepted the Baptism unto Repentance of God's two Ambassadors when they began testifying at the Pakistan-India border 110 days ago."

Maria caught that number saying, "Mel, that's the same number of days that the Israelites were given when at the 1290 T/D they were told to flee to the hills. Now the people in this last angel halo for some reason also get the same number of days. Why is this?"

Mel said to Tom, "You answer her question."

"Oh no, not this again. Yes, I know the answer, but how about you refresh my memory."

Mel agreed, "Remember Tom, you said Jesus has other sheep in other folds. These are those sheep. They are in this last angel halo and they fully understood that Jesus will return in the future and kill the antichrist. This means that when the Two Witnesses testified to them with words they could relate to, they accepted in great numbers."

Maria said that a long time ago she remembers saying that God's Plan of Salvation is complicated, now, even more so.

Mel said, "It's really simple. The God of Heaven never gives up on His people no matter what fold or country his sheep are in."

The three watched now as these three demons flew out of the mouths of the unholy trinity, travelling eastwards.

Tom asked, "Do these 3 demons need 40 days to fly to India?"

Mel answered, "They can be there in minutes, if required."

Maria asked, "Where are the Two Witnesses at this time?"

Mel said, "They are coming from the east and still have 40 days remaining in their time of testimony."

Joe did the quick math saying, "That means they will still testify to over 960 zones."

Tom asked, "Why are these demons allowed to do this?"

Mel replied, "Remember the people have all heard the past five thunder messages and this latest one instructs them to 'Keep their garments'."

Joe asked, "But for those in these last 960 zones, they have not as of yet received the testimony of the Two Witnesses so how can they 'Keep their garments' when they haven't even got them yet?"

Maria said, "That's a good question for you Mel" who then replied, "Tom, you answer it."

"Oh great, me again!" was his response. "How am I supposed to know the answer?"

Mel replied, "You already gave it some time ago."

Joe commented, "Maria, I told you he's got to be smarter than he looks." Still, all three looked perplexed.

Mel relented saying, "Just like in Judea. Remember, great numbers of the 3-color antichrist fled from Israel to escape from the Flying Hell Monsters?"

Joe said, "But that only delayed their attack for a little while."

Tom said, "I get it. As the Two Witnesses began their testifying in this last angel halo at the border between Pakistan and India, there were many having communication devices who fled westwards seeking to escape them, only to find themselves unable to cross over the dried up Great Euphrates River." As the Two Witnesses began their testifying in this last angel halo at the border between Pakistan and India, there were many with communication devices who fled westwards seeking to escape them, only to find themselves unable to cross over the dried up Great Euphrates River."

Maria added, "So those people within these last 960 zones were the 1-color and 3-color antichrist people similar to those in Judea. No amount of testimony could help them since they had previously taken the mark of the beast."

Tom also said, "This is the area where the ancient city of Babylon was, and where the Great Red Dragon and his son will watch the zombie slaughter very soon."

Mel now said, "These three demons spend these forty days attempting to deceive the millions of saved people who are safely sequestered within their dwellings after accepting the testimony of God's two Ambassadors."

"Now picture this." Mel continued, "These three demons will be saying to everyone that soon vast numbers of their messiah's angels currently at the Great Euphrates River will be sent to his 10 kings of the east in India. They will say to everyone that 200 million 'angels' will fly to his 10 kings. Once there, they will combine with their messiah's 200 million 'soldiers'. Once combined, they form the Entities of Death'. They will then begin their path of slaughter starting at the border between Pakistan and India, travelling through the Middle East to the Great Euphrates River. Everyone not loyal to their messiah will be killed, so return and renounce your errors and be loyal to your messiah before these Entities of Death' come your way."

Joe commented, "This will certainly cause some or many to rethink their last move. Some will revert back due to fear or panic. It doesn't really matter. They chose poorly."

"Now," Mel continued, "concerning their messiah's demonic angels released at the Great Euphrates River and flying over their heads to India, their words are not a lie, they're true, but contain a lying deception. Their messiah did not release them, the God of Heaven did and ordered them to fly to India to the Soldiers of Death' awaiting them.

These 3 demons also said to the people along their route, that when you see the skies darkened by his 200 million flying angels, they should rush out and loudly renounce their former ways and return to their messiah. Some will soil their garments of salvation while others keep them clean and hold fast to their vow to God of Heaven."

Giving them a minute to absorb this information, Mel again continued. "Those who backslide to their former god Satan, and soil their garments will be seen as untrustworthy by Satan. The Entities of Death will, with malice, simply kill many of them along with others during their trek."

Maria said, "So the 3 demons went out 40 days prior to the temple being cleansed and gave it one last try to deceive the saved people living in the Middle East."

Tom added, "So this is what is meant when it says to 'keep your garments clean'. If these saved people listen to these 3 demons and backslide to their former god, Satan, they soil their garments and suffer their fate."

Maria added, "This may also mean that certain people never had the mark of the beast yet, at the last second, they backslide and turn to Satan."

Mel answered, "They chose poorly."

Joe said, "I've been thinking, the 3 demons are given 40 days and the 110 days that you mentioned a few minutes ago add up to 150 days, so once again numbers have various meanings."

Tom, also interjected, "Talking about this number 40, in the time of Noah, it rained 40 days and the waters prevailed on the earth 150 days (Genesis 7:17-24.) Do you see the numbers correlation?"

Maria replied, "I hope you were asking Joe and not me, Tom."

Joe commented, "I was listening you know, and to prove it, if you add the 3 days for Jesus to ascend to Heaven to your 150 you get 153 big fish."

Somewhere between perplexed and hysteria Maria asked, "So what does this mean, if anything?"

Joe responded, "I don't know."

Tom came to his rescue. "Joe does make an off topic point when Simon Peter went up, and drew the net to land full of great fishes, one hundred and fifty and three. It says that even though there were so many, the net was not broken."

"OK, OK, I hear you," she retorted, "but how are you going to segue this into our conversation?"

Joe continued, "Maria, we were all talking about the numbers 40, 110 and 150 if I correctly heard you, so all that I am saying is the 3 days for Jesus to ascend to Heaven plus 150 gets you 153 big fishes."

"Yes, yes," she said, "but where are you going with this?"

Joe caved, "It's just cool information, right?"

Maria sighed, "I know I'm losing this one. What does this mean?"

Tom, sighed, "I don't know. Up to now, no Bible scholar knows what the 153 great fish and the net that did not break means."

Maria sighed, "I'm so confused."

"Me too." said Tom.

Joe said he gets it, but both simultaneously gave him 'that look' before he could continue.

"Seriously guys. I get it. I think it means 153 years prior to the Rapture there will be some type of Christian leadership that like the net 'did not break' that prepares the Bride of Christ for the Rapture. They are the Holy Ones."

Both Maria and Tom were speechless since Joe's answer made perfect sense, even though they both still didn't know what it meant, or as to who these Great Christian Leaders were.

Mel seemed agitated, then said, "I always find it so fascinating that you three can take unrelated information, toss it into the air and when it lands, it gives answers to questions others dared not seek."

They laughed, except Joe, who didn't have a clue what Mel was saying.

Mel said "Let's move forward." And once again they were instantly somewhere else. Mel asked, "Do you know where you are?"

Tom said, "By the looks of those landmarks, we flew over the Taj Mahal so we're in India, the location where the 10 kings gather for their soon-to-be trek across the Middle East."

"Right you are." replied Mel.

Tom then asked. "Are we here before or after the Entities of Death leave?"

Mel asked, "Have you had enough or do you want to see how it all takes place at the border of Pakistan and India?"

They looked at each other and thought, "How could we pass up this opportunity?"

Mel pointed to the pillar of fire not far away saying, "Here it comes," as this massive tower of roaring fire came directly towards them, then through them, and into Pakistan.

Maria shouted, "Now that was intense. It actually passed right through us."

Mel said, "Now for the next 150 days the Two Witnesses testify to the people in the Middle East."

Joe said, "Look over there." Then in the distance there were once again two dust clouds making that horrible sound.

Tom added, "The zombie screaming!"

"No," replied Maria, "we decided to call it the screaming zombies."

Joe added, "Hearing you call them the screaming zombie's sort of sounds like a rock band."

Now, the ground was actually vibrating due to the vast numbers of running zombies.

Joe asked, "Where are the most recently infected and why are they not coming first?"

Mel replied, "Oh, they are coming alright. It's just that the first group has caught up to them so they're altogether now."

Mel continued, "I will make the time process speed up slightly for this happening."

What seemed like only minutes later, they saw the hordes approaching. Mel elevated them upwards for a better view. The 1-colors were rapidly approaching. Within minutes, they were passing under them.

Joe said, "I can't imagine their numbers at this time."

Mel said, "That's what 200 million 1-color zombies' looks like. And that's only half because soon after come the 3-color 200 million zombies."

Maria agreed with Joe, saying their numbers boggle their imagination.

Tom pointed out that their sounds never diminished and actually the faster they ran the louder they became.

Joe said to listen. The 'screaming zombies', even though still far off, were making a tremendous sound. It was extremely unnerving even for them.

Maria commented, "They're running faster than a race sprinter. Look at their mouths, they're wide open and are making all the screaming sounds."

Joe said, "That's strange, look at their arms hanging and flopping at their sides. Their arms are like rubber wiggling, as if they have no control over them. What used to be their eyes have been replaced with tiny black dots recessed into their sockets".

Tom said, "This will be interesting. There's a high wire fence between the two countries, more of an intimidation obstacle than a barrier."

As the front runners approached this fence they didn't seem to be able to see it. They were fixated on the pillar of fire off in the distance.

Joe said, "Here they come." They kept running at full speed closer and closer to the fence. Now what happens next is almost indescribable.

Maria gasped saying, "That's horrific!" as the front runners slammed into the fence. Those behind them slammed into them creating thousands of ricochets. Soon the fence gave way and was forced to the ground by the sheer weight of many thousands of zombies, themselves being trampled on by the millions following.

Joe, looking at the sheer number of zombies said, "We're seeing all the people on earth coming right at us in two stages, first the 1-colors and then the 3-colors."

Maria asked, "How long will it take for all to go rushing by us?"

Mel said, "Depending on how wide their column is, for now let's just say about a week. How about I speed things up?"

"Good idea," she said.

Tom said, "See, they're piling up just like ants in Africa that sacrifice themselves to form a bridge over an obstacle so the rest could pass over. Remember, I said that way back when."

Joe said, "Yuck! Thousands had been trampled on, leaving arms, body parts and a bloody mess all over the area, a most gruesome spectacle."

What seemed only minutes to them, all had crossed over the fence.

Joe commented, "That was so intense. I can't imagine watching this spectacle for a week or more."

Mel sped up the time of their running and then said, "Here comes the next group." Only minutes later, they arrived. Mel said, "Now watch this carefully."

This group also came racing towards them, screaming in the same fashion as the first group of zombies. As they approached the borders of the two countries, the only obstacle now between them and the first group was this trampled and demolished wire fence. They didn't slow down their speed as cars would do when you see brake lights in front of you that cause a chain reaction. These 200 million screaming zombies just all stopped.

Joe said, "That's so weird. We always pictured that nothing could stop zombies. Now here, they just stopped, then fell to the ground, motionless."

Mel said, "You have just witnessed 200 million 1-color fleeing into Pakistan and 200 million 3-color now, moribund, for the next 150 days until the Two Witnesses have crossed over the Great Euphrates dried up river bank."

Maria disgustedly said, "Oh no, Joe, I think even you will be aghast. Look at the fence or where it used to be."

Now a great many somehow rose up in a jerky stop motion from the ground, more accurately from within the ground, due to the fact they had been squished down into it. Some were missing arms, legs and more, but began moving towards the pillar of fire.

Joe said, "And look at that guy. His head is dangling and yet he moves. And over there, that thing has no legs, just arms and yet it moves quickly. That's so weird!"

Maria said, "Yuck! That's so gross!"

Mel said remember, "Those within their first 150 days can't die, and if you think the headless man was disgusting watch what happens now."

Maria said, "I'm going to barf!" and then realized she couldn't do this human thing anymore. Thousands of body parts started recombining into things much worse looking than the prior zombies.

Joe said, "People seeing this morphing of body parts into something that can move through my eyes would be creepy."

Tom added "How do you describe flesh crawling on the ground that recombines with other flesh and not in any specific order. Most have heads or pieces of heads, arms maybe, some only with one leg and one arm yet this thing still moves resembling a leech in motion."

Joe said, "Look at that thing go."

Tom said, "These things leech out liquids still remaining within their flesh, as they move."

They were witnessing the impossible unfolding before their very eyes. No science fiction movie ever made would come close to this scene.

Tom asked, "How far will they get in such a condition?"

Mel said, "As far as 150 days takes them. They will make for good target practise for those soon following."

Joe, taking a deep breath, realizing he doesn't need to do so anymore said, "There's nothing there for the next group to see or smell."

Mel agreed saying, "See the fallen fence and this mess are actually on the Pakistan side of the border. This is the last angel halo, so these zombies couldn't see or smell this mess. They just become inactive and mope around. Soon the 3 demons will come and stir them into a frenzy."

Mel again advanced the time line forward 150 days and said, "The Two Witnesses have now crossed over the Great Euphrates dried up river bank. The Bible tells us what happens next. To paraphrase, it says, the three unclean spirits looking like frogs coming out of the mouth of the dragon, out of the mouth of the beast, and out of the mouth of the false prophet. They are spirits of demons, performing signs, which go out to the kings of the earth and of the whole world, to gather them to the battle of that great day of God Almighty.

Tom, how about you take over since you know what takes place now."

"OK, from what I think I know, soon these 3 demons will arrive at the land of the 10 kings, slightly ahead of the 200 million Hell Horses.

They will again use deceiving partial truths to get them motivated for the soon-to-be, battle. In only a matter of days, these demonic Hell Horses will begin arriving so they have work to do. These 3 demons will have to convince the kings and soldiers to begin their 150 trek westwards to the Great Euphrates River, now void of water and starting to fill up with zombies who can't cross it. Am I right, so far?"

Mel nodded and said to them, "Look to the west. What do you see now?"

Joe said, "Some type of ball lightning, I think."

Maria said, "It looks like a ball of fire."

Tom, not to be out done, said, "It looks like a 'V' formation of three glowing globes."

All agreed whatever you called them, they were moving towards them and fast.

Maria asked, "Will they be able to see us?"

"No," was Mel's reply, "But we will be watching them, so let's follow and see what they're up to."

Now, prior to the 3 demons touching down, they did atmospheric tricks much like a 4th of July event but greater. Nevertheless, the 10 kings and their armies, who had just recently recovered from the zombie blood virus, were not impressed. Their old tricks of fire from the sky were not being well received anymore. They had to do better, much better. The Flying Hell Monsters and the Zombie Plagues had really out-shown the demons' powers. However, the demons were not phased, and they had one trick left.

Mel said, "These 3 demons have a grand finale deception that will be so spectacular, it convinces all of the invincibility of the Great Red Dragon and that they will win the next battle, Armageddon."

Joe said, "Look at those 3 demons. They're growing in size. They look like giant supermen, standing in front of the 10 kings."

These demons intend to bolster the confidence of the kings and soldiers who have during the past years been traumatised by the Zombie Plagues.

Now, they begin their greatest deception proclaiming that the angel armies of their god will soon come to them with supernatural powers and they will mount these horses and be invincible. The combination of the Hell Horses and riders of death will be called the Entities of Death. They will destroy everything standing in their way until they reach their god. They are invincible.

Mel said, "Now, they did not lie when they said that vast numbers of angels of their god are released and sent to you, mount up upon them and go forth and destroy greatly as you travel unto him for the great battle.

Their deception was in fact that the 200 million angels, depicted as demonic Hell Horses were not released by the Great Red Dragon. They were actually released from their prison by the God of Heaven who instructed them now to go to the 10 kings and their armies and to bow to humans.

Can you imagine demonic angels with monkeys on their backs? A very sorry state indeed. They were a long time ago angels God but now they had fallen from their lofty heights to kneel and allow humans to mount and ride them. A very pathetic state of affairs, to say the least."

The three demons now alongside of the 10 kings raised their hands.

Mel said, "This is actually symbolic, but it works."

The three heroes and Mel were standing on the ground. Mel said look to the west and said, "See what's coming our way?"

They saw the skies darkening and heard a very loud sound similar to horse's hoofs when running on the ground.

Maria said, "Look over at the 10 Kings. They're also raising their hands to the sky."

Joe said, "The zombie soldiers are just yelling some type of gibberish, and now also raised their hands."

Maria said, "Their deceiving tactics really work."

"Look to the sky in the west. See what is approaching?" Mel said.

The armies and the kings witness 200 million Hell Horses approaching them flying through the air with malicious intent obvious as they cast down great bombs of flames and demonstrations of their strength. With unearthly demonic power, they continued to breathe down the fire of Hell and the promise of pain and fear to all became more evident the closer they came to landing. The soldiers awaited with great anticipation. The sky illuminated in a torturing show of light that provided no relief from the impending darkness-only clearing the view of the enormity of the beasts coming towards them all. With heads like snakes upon the tails of the Hell Horses, these demons were meant for chaos and slaughter. The soldiers rejoiced upon seeing these instruments of death and will soon gladly mount, merge with and ride into battle. These entities seem invincible and bolstered by the fact that their god recently killed those two prophets that caused the Zombie Plagues they now are anxious for battle.

Mel said, "Imagine seeing such monsters wielding these tremendous powers now kneeling before them. The Soldiers of Death of the 10 kings now mount these flying Hell Horses."

Mel, with disgust, and using Tom's description, called these evil abominations, Entities of Death.

He continued, "Here comes their grand finale. These demonic fallen angel Hell Horses darken the sky as they draw near. In vast numbers they begin lowering to the surface of the earth. However, due to their vast numbers they form lines and rows. I told you before how they will stretch from north to south along the border of Pakistan. As these Hell Horses touch the earth, they have been commanded to actually bow to these Soldiers of Death who then mount."

Joe said, "Look at the 200 million Soldiers of Death, scrambling to mount the Hell Horses and arranging themselves into rows that stretch hundreds of miles, north to south, as far as the eye can see in length and depth."

Mel commented, "This landing and mounting process actually takes 3½ days start to finish as each row is successively completed because the numbers are so massive."

Maria exclaimed, "What a formidable sight! What is that flash when they combine?"

Mel replied, "The spirit of the Soldier of Death combines with the Hell Horse, a demonic demon, and the convergence of energies produces that brilliant flash. Once combined, these Entities of Death become formidable satanic forces that are earthbound and cannot fly. They are now hell-bent on destruction, and await the command to begin their spree of slaughter. This command takes place 3½ days after their arrival to the 10 kings. This corresponds to the time immediately after the Two Witnesses of God have been resurrected to Him. They will be released to begin their trek across the Middle East at the 2305.5 T/D and the countdown to Armageddon has begun. These Entities of Death at this time will be allowed to enter Pakistan when the great invisible barrier that is currently restraining them is removed."

Joe asked, "Do you mean when the force field is brought down?"

"You're right, Joe and then the 'chase is on'."

Mel said, "By now the drying of the Great Euphrates River has taken place. This is necessary due to the fact that the Entities of Death armies are now physical and require the dry river bed for access to Israel."

Tom mentioned that the now dried Great Euphrates River runs from the Persian Gulf, north-west creating a natural border between countries and this creates a barrier for armies coming from the Middle East, China, India and parts of Russia.

Maria commented, "Correct me if I'm wrong, but the people in the nations of the 10 kings during these days have heard all five of the Thunder Messages that includes this latest message 'blessed is he who watches and keeps his garments', right? So are there many saved people in India and the lands to their south?"

Mel said, "As a matter of fact, there are many safely sealed up in their dwellings with the Martyrs' Blood Mark on their doors waiting for their salvation. I didn't take you three there because you have already seen enough horrific zombie running events."

Maria asked, "What is this Martyrs' Blood Mark that you mentioned?

"Firstly, it is applied to their doors by the forces of God. I refer to it as the 'martyr's blood' because in Revelation 17:6 which deals with Babylon the great, the mother of harlots and of the abominations of the earth, the Apostle John said, 'I saw the woman, drunk with the blood of the saints and with the blood of the Martyrs of Jesus.' And again in Revelation 19:2 . . . 'and he has avenged on her the blood of His servants shed by her.' So the blood of the 'Martyrs' from times past and during the Raptures' Aftermath is sprinkled onto their doors.

The people hear the command upon receiving God's Mark to go and stay within their dwellings. Angels sprinkle the blood of the Martyrs over their entrances to their dwellings, tents or caves. They were told not to go out until the hordes of death passed them by. In the beginning this only took hours, later days, and then weeks to pass them by. This blood causes the hordes of zombies to bypass them as did the angel of death during the Exodus out of Egypt. As to how it causes the zombies to pass by, let's just say, this blood puts the 'fear of God' into them.

One last note, the blood shed when the antichrist slaughtered the Christians in times past and during these days is also the blood consumed by the zombies during their plagues lasting 1260 days. As recorded, in 'The Revelation of Jesus Christ' chapter 16:5-6.

"You are righteous, O Lord,… <u>For they have shed the blood of saints and prophets, and You have given them blood to drink for it is their just due</u>."

So to be clear, they shed the blood of the saints, these 'Under the Altar Martyrs' and 'Great Tribulation Martyrs' and 'God's Prophets', so they now must drink their blood. This drives them to distraction. The more they drink, the more they become driven in their insatiable lust for blood."

Mel continued, "In only a few days, the next Fire-Thunder Message will take place and once again all hear it. The three demons head back to the Great Red Dragon, who since his release from the 'pit' has full liberty. Now, he displays his true appearance. He is phenomenally powerful and huge.

After the Entities of Death have been released for their 150 days trek, he will go as the pied piper, to the ancient city of Babylon for this event to play out. It's going to be the bloodiest slaughter to date."

Chapter Forty-Nine

THUNDER MESSAGE SIX 2300 T/D A/C@-220

"GO AND GATHER MY PEOPLE"
SANCTUARY CLEANSED AFTER 2300 DAYS

Mel gathered the three, then said, "The 7 Year Great Tribulation 'Time of Sorrows' now has reached its 2300 T/D. From here on, the events leading to Armageddon speeds up with only 220 days remaining. At this time the Sanctuary has been Cleansed. From now on all events taking place, will be shown as countdown to Armageddon, and this date is as follows, A/C@-220 T/D.

Joe asked, "What do you mean, countdown?"

"I will begin with the chronological sequence of events. As we delve into these happenings, I'll address each as they come to pass. Now with the temple cleansed, Daniel's prophecy is fulfilled. This brings us to the Sixth Thunder Message."

Tom remembered God's Command: **Go and gather my people (the 'GOOD' guests).** He said, "Upon the command of God to 'Go and gather my people' I remember reading about this in my book, Matthew 24; 30-31[67]. Paraphrasing, he said, once again there will be wonders in the Heavens. With the sound of a great trumpet the forces of God gather the saved.

How am I doing?" he asked Mel.

Mel replied, "So far so good. Please continue."

| 471

Tom continued also in Revelation 10:4-7 and again paraphrasing said, Now another most miraculous wonder, a Heavenly trumpet, trumpeted, proclaiming in its highest ear-splitting register, a most fearsome sound. World-wide, people were immediately transfixed, motionless as if frozen in time and looked up.

Mel continued, in times past, when the call was given 'the Bridegroom comes' the trumpet heralded this call. Now upon this event to 'go and gather My people' the trumpet also heralded God's command.

Now, we come to the time that all the Baptized saved people who kept their wedding garments pure, were joyfully awaiting. Those of the unholy trinity and antichrist, did not at this time rejoice, and send gifts to each other. Many knew full well, their life existence, would soon be extinguished.

For the past 2300 days the unholy trinity and antichrist have done everything in their bag of tricks to win over as many souls as possible. They don't care about the flesh and blood person. It's their souls they desire. The more the merrier for, Armageddon the 'cull of the damned'.

Now another milestone has been reached. Daniel's prophecy of '2300 days until the sanctuary is cleansed' has arrived and been fulfilled.

When we look into the prophecy of Daniel, he saw well into the future. At this time, the effects of the original sin no longer separated souls of humans from their God. Now God will fully open His Temple and the Ark of His Covenant will be seen. The Sanctuary after 2300 days is now cleansed of the great deceiver Satan.

Now at the end of these 3½ days a great earthquake takes place and the dragon's temple crumbles into oblivion taking with it the 'abomination of desolation' that formerly stood on that invisible holy spot'.

Also the redeeming work of the 2 Ambassadors' now completed and the saved have now received white garments of salvation will soon be in God's Wedding Feast Hall, as the Good Guests."

"How did Daniel know all this?" asked Maria.

"He was told by the Archangel Gabriel, who is one of the seven Archangels."

Maria said, "Seven? There are seven archangels?"

"Yes," said Mel. "There's Michael, Uriel, Raphael, Gabriel, Raquel, Haniel and Seraqael."

Joe asked, "Where are they all recorded in the Bible?"

"They're not." was Mel's cryptic reply.

Tom commented, "An easy way to remember them is the acronym 'MURGRHS."

Maria asked, "What does it mean?"

Tom replied, "Each letter represents the first letter of their names. Then I put it into a sentence. Remember the highway traffic sign, 'M<u>urg</u> <u>r</u>ight <u>h</u>and <u>s</u>ide'?"

Maria said, "I get it, even though your spelling is wrong."

Mel asked, "May I please continue? So as I was saying, Gabriel is talking to Daniel about the 'end of days' when the sanctuary is cleansed, meaning among other things when Satan's claims are no longer valid against human souls', who now are excommunicated, from the original sin.

This now brings us to the sixth Thunder Message and to God's last 3½ days (A/C@220-216.5) of His plan of salvation of the saved people.

The command is given **"GO AND GATHER MY PEOPLE"**

The exact text is in the end notes[68] of your book Tom. Paraphrasing the text, it says that the Temple is now cleansed at this 2300 T/D. Now, the King (God) said to his servants, that the wedding reception is ready but those previously invited had rejected their invitations. Even after a second attempt by other servants, they rejected their invitation again. Some of them decided to kill His servants. When their King (God) heard of this He was furious and He <u>Sent out His armies, Destroyed those murderers and Burned up their city.</u>

This explains three events that now take place in succession.

<u>First</u> the King's Army goes out. These are God's angels.

<u>Second</u>, the murderers are destroyed. These are the antichrist that killed God's 2 Ambassadors who had been overcome by the Great Red Dragon.

<u>Third</u>, their city Jerusalem is burned to ashes.

The King said they were not worthy to attend and instructed His Servants to, go to others who were not formerly invited to His Wedding Feast for His Son.

The King then said to his servants, Thunder Message Six, "Go and Gather My People".

They are instructed to Go <u>"into" the "highways"</u>, and as many as you <u>"find"</u>, <u>"invite"</u> to the wedding.

So those servants <u>went out into the highways</u> and <u>gathered together all whom they "found", both bad</u> and <u>good. And the wedding hall was filled with guests."</u>

The guests were "gathered" together into one group of "good" saved people who had maintained their high standards and who had kept their "Garments of Salvation" clean."

Tom asked how accurate was the description in his book.

Mel answered, "Not bad," and reluctantly began speaking. Somewhere in the background, a voice was saying, "Make them understand."

Choosing his words extremely carefully he said, "Special Visitors, from the Gardens of God, now witnessed a most Heavenly and spectacular first ever event."

Mel continued, "Look at the 6 domed shaped 'Angel Halos' currently residing over the continents. Upon God's command, they become activated.

In slow motion, each begins retracting, reducing and enfolding their enormous 10 light rays that previously were extended to the outer limits of their respective areas that formed the energy barrier so the antichrist could not flee to other angel halos. These light rays slowly folded back within the embrace of their center hub tens of miles high in the sky.

"The next event is equally as impressive," he said as this center hub slowly began lowering itself down to the earth. As it touched the earth it began to make a most loud thundering and roaring sound. This brilliant 'Pillar of Fire' would soon house those saved. Soon all of these massive pillars of fire from around the world had descended to the surface of the earth.

Joe commented, "If I understand what you're I'm seeing, the angel halos fold into themselves, way up high and then descend to the earth."

Mel agreed saying, "I thought I just said that." He now continued, once settled, they began to slowly now unfold and lower their light rays or 'petals' as Maria calls them, down to the surface of the earth reaching out past the horizon. Upon touching the ground these 'petals' began emitting an 'electrical light' similar to the northern lights. I know Maria appreciates this.'

Maria commented, "Dance of the spirits."

Mel just smiled and continued. "This golden light is far denser and spread round and about the 10 light rays now upon the earth. Only those having their garments of salvation from God could bear to look into this sparkling light. All others stumbled around, then fled in great fear.

Now this golden electrical light is very strange and fulfills the parable of the King's Feast when God says, "Go and gather them." This means the 'saved' people did not have to travel. The forces of God gathered them from their dwellings and brought them into these golden light rays. Once all were safely inside, these 'petals' began to once again fold back together. Then the pillar of fire roars once again."

Maria said, "That was fantastic seeing it from our vantage point."

Joe said, "After the golden light rays unfolded, God's forces instantly went like electrical sparkings to the people who then seem to glow and in a 'twinkling of an eye' vanished."

All three were astonished.

Mel said, "These sparkings took place everywhere, in all angel halos and were the effect of the saved people who kept their garments of salvation clean when they were transported into these golden rays."

Maria asked, "Why is the pillar of fire different now? It looks like a Christian Cross surrounded by 10 petals and what looks like water waves under it."

Tom said, "Maria, remember that's how we described it when we were in the cave."

Joe pointed to the water saying that to him it appeared as three waves with the smallest at the bottom and each wave got larger and they appeared to be somewhat off the ground.

Maria said, "I never saw anything as beautiful as this. It looks like the petals are made out of golden crystal. It's so brilliant to look at."

Mel said, "Maria look closer at these the petals. They're made of transparent gold."

Maria mused, "Why does transparent gold sound familiar to me?"

Mel, without answering her, continued, "Now watch this. Another Heavenly wonder is beginning in slow motion as these Pillars of Fire, each resembling a fantastically huge fiery cross, gracefully and silently rise upwards, reaching about a mile high. Each of these glistening, gigantic star crafts could be seen from great distances. However those seeing are the antichrist, who only blasphemed.

These fiery crafts contain the 'saved' now safely out of the grasp of the unholy trinity. These crafts of light remain parked and motionless awaiting the next command of God."

Joe asked if any of the antichrist fired weapons at these fiery crafts.

Mel said, "No, they're evil, not stupid. They're waiting for their god to do so but he was strangely silent during these events."

Mel said, "Before we discuss the final thunder message number, seven more events take place during these same 3½ days. God's 2 Ambassadors have for the past 1260 days, been the scourge of the nations with their flame throwing mouths, their plagues turning waters to blood and their flying friends who attacked them resulting in the blood-virus plagues that transformed people into zombies, truly indescribable.

At the beginning of these 3½ days the Great Red Dragon was released from his confinement pit under the Gulf of Aqaba."

Maria added, "That's where the Israelites thousands of years ago crossed over. Even to this day those traveling under the surface of the water have located many of the chariot wheels from Pharaoh's soldiers along with other items, I remembered that."

Mel smiled and continued, "God has already fully described this Great Red Dragon monster in the book of Job and to say the least he is immense and extremely powerful."

"How powerful is he compared to the Angels of God?" Joe asked.

"Drop in the bucket" Mel replied, and continuing added, "Up to now he was forbidden to manifest in his true appearance to the people as this would only cause them into worshiping him out of fear of death. He desperately desires their love, praises and loyalty to be just like God, his creator, however, this eternally eludes him.

Now released the Great Red Dragon makes war with God's 2 ambassadors. Let's be clear. No power on earth is stronger than God's 2 Ambassadors.

Several days prior to their death, God's 2 Ambassadors were back in the land of Israel. Their blood-virus plagues do not repeat themselves as these events don't happen twice. However they still issue fire from their mouths killing many of the antichrist.

The Great Red Dragon, his full power now enabled, is allowed to overcome them. The definition of the word 'overcome' is, to defeat somebody or something, especially in a conflict or to make somebody incapacitated or helpless."

Tom asked, "For about how long does this battle go on?"

Mel answered, "There was much fighting that day."

"So, the Great Red Dragon overcomes the Two Witnesses, now exhausted of power, and who now lay helpless in the street, in Jerusalem." Joe summarized.

Mel nodded and continued, "Now as to who actually finish and kill these two helpless witnesses.

First a brief history of sorts. The false prophet has in the past used 7,000 guards as his personal security. Their uniforms display the three colors of the Great Red Dragon. Today there exists a 7,000-seat Cathedral and that's how many seats will be in the courtyard design of the Dragon's Temple upon its dedication, for his elite.

Now the Great Red Dragon also has 7,000 elite temple guards murder these two apparently helpless beings laying in the street. They use powerful weapons that can kill but, for reasons not known to them, cannot incinerate or disseminate their bodies. Their bodies lay in the streets of Jerusalem for these same 3½ days. The 7,000 elite cheer and the worldwide antichrist watching on devices also see and rejoice.

The Great Red Dragon knows full well that by allowing his elite 7,000 to kill God's 2 Ambassadors the army of God will very soon descend upon Jerusalem and kill these murderers. This also fulfils the parable of the King's Feast who, when he heard that his servants were murdered, sent out His Armies and destroyed them.

One may justifiably ask why does the Great Red Dragon have his 7,000 elite kill them. The answer is multiple. Again at the beginning of these 3½ days, the dragon's temple crumbles into oblivion so he has no home and plans to move to the area surrounding the Mount of Megiddo where his son the sea beast (false president) resides. His seat of military power also has 7,000 elite guards.

Now to the answer. Firstly, when his temple falls, 7,000 elite pawns are destroyed by God's forces. These murderers served a purpose and like all the rest, are expendable.

Secondly, his temple now gone, some Israelites flee into the countryside and only out of fear switch, for now, their loyalties (they are the 'BAD' guests who did not have the mark of the beast but are Satan's evil seeds. He's been saving them for the future).

Satan never loses sight of these, his future pawns. So now there are many wandering around in the Valley of Olives. God then sends his forces out to gather these evil seeds."

Maria asked, "Where were the God's 2 Ambassadors killed?"

"In the area of Golgotha, just outside the walls of the old Jerusalem, were the Son of God was crucified. People hear and see via telecommunications of this apparent victory of their god."

Displaying disgust in his voice, Mel added, "The fools actually send gifts to each other in merriment upon the death of the Two Witnesses as they have caused them much torment and were a scourge unto them during the past 1260 days during their testimony.

Once again, this is another deception proclaimed by the 3 demons who are doing their Great War dance deceiving many. To the antichrist, it appears as if Satan killed the Two Witnesses and his power is superior to the forces of God.

The death of God's 2 Ambassadors is the trigger event that releases the 200 million Hell Horses into action who then fly to the antichrist armies of the 10 kings."

Joe said, "If it weren't for the fact that they are evil, this would be an impressive sight to behold. A while back we watched as all this takes place in real time. I talked about the 3 demons previously sent out 40 days ago. They, along their way to the 10 kings, created deceiving wonders in a last effort to sway back those who have sided with the God of Heaven. They are determined to maintain the saying 'misery loves company'."

Maria said, "I find it absolutely impossible that people could make an about-face after seeing evil up close and personal."

Mel answered, "We read in the Bible, 'Behold, I am coming as a thief. Blessed is he who watches, and keeps his garments, lest he walk naked and they see his shame.

Even now, at this late date, people can partake of grace or curse, what more can be done to save them."

Maria said, "It's so amazing that at the last, seconds of time grace still exists. How magnanimous of our Heavenly Father."

Mel's smile radiated, and Maria queried,

"Why are you beaming with joy?"

Mel commented, "Did you listen to your own words?"

"I don't understand?" she replied.

"Maria you just referred to the God of the Heavens as your Heavenly Father. How magnanimous indeed!"

The three were silent as this fact dawned fully, within them.

After pausing, allowing them to regain their composure Mel went on, "Now these 3 demons are with these 10 kings and soldiers as Tom said, 'doing their dog and pony show'. In 3½ days to be exact, the 'Hell Horses' and 'Soldiers of Death' now form the 'Entities of Death' and, are released to cross over into Pakistan and begin their 150 day trek of slaughter.

Now we come to the seventh and last Thunder Message.

Just to recap—remember the saved are all now in the 6 massive hovering star crafts awaiting God's last command to bring them to Him."

Chapter Fifty

THUNDER MESSAGE SEVEN
A/C@-216.5 T/D

"COME OUT OF HER MY PEOPLE"

Mel said, "This is the seventh and final 'Thunder Message'. Now, the finality of salvation, for this phase commences, the final harvest of the earth.

All 'saved' souls are within the flaming star crafts, God has called for them as recorded in Revelation 18:4 And I heard another voice from heaven saying, <u>"come out of her, my people"</u>, lest you share in her sins, and lest you receive of her plagues.'

From the first command to <u>"go and gather My people"</u> and now this second command to <u>"come out of her My people"</u> takes 3½ days for the servants of God to accomplish their task.

See two commands given, can you imagine these words resounding throughout the 'Eyes of the Gardens of God', for all to witness.

The first command was triggered upon the Temple being Cleansed at the 2300, A/C@-220 T/D.

The second command was triggered upon the Resurrection of God's 2 Ambassadors[69] when He said for them to 'come up here', at the A/C@-216.5 T/D.

Now this, the final Thunder Message 'Come out of her my people'. Like I said, this is the trigger command.

Now, these flaming star crafts of light, currently parked and motionless, begin to move.

Your description of them is accurate. They have the appearance of giant flaming crosses and have bottoms resembling three waves of water which represent the three Holy Sacraments."

Tom asked, "What do the 10 golden rays represent?"

Mel chuckled, "The answer is currently way above your pay grades. No Jc e that was only an expression."

"Why pick on me?" he thought. Then thought, "This reading of my mind is doing me in, going to have to resort to my Vulcan mind control."

"Lots of luck" thought Maria, "How's it working for you Joe?"

Tom started laughing, then Maria, and almost Mel, as Joe was thinking "the three stooges go to Heaven".

Mel said, "Who talks like that? And who are the 'three stooges'? Strange name for a group."

Mel quizzically continued his thought train and commented that some time ago Tom had once pondered this event saying he had watched a movie that showed a similar type of star craft at its end. Its guardians were angels of light who escorted small children into it and then this cross shaped start craft slowly ascended into the sky and went off into deep space.

Mel continued, "All in all, not a bad description. The giant flaming crosses are brilliant to look upon, are vastly larger and are a sight to see, but if you see them, you're not in them and that's bad."

"Here we go," Mel whispered. "Look how these mammoth flaming star crafts begin to silently glide above the earth towards the 'Great Domed City'."

Tom asked, "Why are they silent now?"

Mel replied, "The time of sound no longer exists." They didn't pursue his answer since they were getting used to his cryptic responses.

Mel was taking them on this tour following one of the star crafts. All watched the next events.

Maria said, "See there are the other ones arriving, Mel. They seem to be parked for now," and Mel smiled.

Tom asked, "Why are there only six of them? I thought there were seven pillars of fire?"

Joe answered before Mel saying, "That's because the first one is already within the dome, and it brought the Redeemed and Repented Israelites into it a long time ago."

Mel just shook his head saying, "Seems like Joe's pay grade just went up."

Maria just looked at Joe, her dumbfounded expression, expressed it all. Joe thought her expression was actually, flummoxed.

Mel smiled at the two and said, "See. Upon their arrival, these mile-high flaming star crafts, began descending effortlessly, slowly, one by one into this Great Domed City depositing their cargo into the "King's Wedding Hall".

Mel then continued, "All flaming star crafts containing the Good and Worthy Guests are in one day transported to and into the King's Wedding Feast Hall. Tom referred to this as the Great Domed City housing the Wilderness Sanctuary. That description suit me also."

Tom said, "See, as each of these giant pillars of fire descended into the Great Domed City they combined forming even a more massive fiery sight. Their upper half displaying the cross portion still projects outwards reaching high into the sky and now merges into one massive and larger cross shaped pillar of fire."

Mel said, "Your word magnificent wouldn't even come close to describing it. This sight was seen for many hundreds of miles in all directions but the only ones seeing it were the unholy trinity and antichrists who blasphemed at its appearance.

Listen carefully. During these same 3½ days, the millions of people in Babylon the Great were actually having parties, exchanging gifts and carrying out every conceivable evil incarnation possible. The antichrist have been tormented by these Two Witnesses for the past 3½ years with their Zombie Plagues to say the least. Now events turn.

Upon the Resurrection of God's 2 Ambassadors, the antichrist will be perplexed after seeing their two bodies lying dead in the street. Now hear a tremendous voice from the Heavens saying,

'Come up here'. Immediately they come back to life, stand up and are transported to Heaven. Then comes the earthquake.

This great earthquake happens within the hour following the resurrection of God's 2 Ambassadors, His Witnesses. Again imagine the disbelief and shock of the antichrist when this takes place. There will be total pandemonium. I call this the, Resurrection Earthquake." Mel said, "Using Tom's vernacular, this is the 'finger on the trigger' and 'bang' event that commences the final countdown sequence."

Tom asked, "Do the antichrist realize this fact?"

"No but the unholy trinity does. This they keep to themselves. Now the barrier is removed and the 200 million Entities of Death begin their 150 day trek of slaughter starting from Pakistan's eastern border towards the Great Euphrates now dried river. We have already seen these events in real time."

Mel continued, "During the Resurrection earthquake a most spectacular Heavenly event unfolds. What happens now will seem like science fiction to you. The Mount of Olives in Israel actually splits in two."

Joe thought, "I never thought Mel would use such a term as science fiction, but it's correct."

Mel paused, saying, "In ancient times the Prophet Zechariah said, concerning this event, in Zechariah 14: 4-5, 'In that day, God's feet will stand on the Mount of Olives, east of Jerusalem. And the Mount of Olives shall be split in two, from east to west, making a very large valley. Half of the mountain shall move toward the north and half of it toward the south. Then you shall flee through My mountain valley.'"

Mel said, "Imagine a new valley forming in front of your eyes?"

Maria asked, "Can we see this in real time?"

"Sure. Why not?" came his reply.

Joe asked, "When you time travel us are you making the events happen there and then?"

Mel answered, "No, I'm just sliding time this way or that way allowing you three to witness the events, some in the past others in the future. Sort of either 'back to the past' or 'back to the future'."

Joe found Marias hand now over his mouth which didn't help much. "*Plagiarism!*" she thought to him.

Mel elevated them even further to the east and about 5,000 feet, so they could see the Mount of Olives and the dragon's temple behind it in the distance.

As they were talking the land began to tremble as something far below was moving, birds began alighting and took flight upwards to the sky. Dust now began rising as the Mount of Olives began splitting into two halves. Simultaneously one half moved northwards and the other southwards.

Maria commented that it all happens in slow motion with nothing violent about it.

Now there began to appear a depression in the ground as the two halves separated forming a valley that extended downwards to the Domed City.

Tom commented, "This is what we called the 'Valley of Olives'"

"That's correct." replied Mel, "You were the first human to give this valley a name and forever this will be so recorded. This new 'Valley of Olives' extends from Mt. Zion down to the northern end of the Living Sea to the Israelites and all saved people in the Great Domed City. The split occurred along the fault lines under Jerusalem and the Mount of Olives along the Kidron brook which empties into the Living Sea.'

Maria looked at this new valley commenting on how large the size of it is. Mel told them it is a mile or more in width and about 17 miles in length from top to bottom.

Tom asked Mel, "Will the slope of this new Valley of Olives be a gentle incline terminating at its highest elevation at Mount Zion?"

Joe added, "Assuming a gentle climbing rate of one mile each hour, it would take less than one day to make the entire journey considering young and old."

"Yes." Mel replied, "Its slope is gentle."

Joe looking at the valley said, "Even the ground is smooth, there's no boulders or sink holes, it's just gently sloping."

Mel finished this account by saying, "While we're up here, let's see now what happens to the dragon's temple."

Mel slid the time line back to the beginning when the valley began splitting.

"Now let's see what happens to the dragon's temple during the creation of the 'Valley of Olives'.

Jerusalem falls, now a tenth of the city falls during this great Resurrection Earthquake having its epicenter under the fault lines beneath the Mount of Olives and Jerusalem. When you look at a fault line map you can actually see that this south-east corner of Jerusalem and the Mount of Olives are adjacent to each other.

Jesus Predicted the Destruction of the Temple as recorded in Matthew 24:1-2 'Then Jesus went out and departed from the temple, and His disciples came up to show Him the buildings of the temple. And Jesus said to them, "Do you not see all these things? Assuredly, I say to you, <u>not one stone</u> shall be left here <u>upon another</u>, that shall not be <u>thrown down</u>.""

Joe responded saying, "This is an actual happening not a figurative one. It's going down big time."

Mel said, "Now, a tenth of the city falls during the Resurrection Earthquake which is exactly the site where the dragon's temple is located. The Dragon's Temple of pride now crumbles and is hurled into oblivion as the earth opens and swallows it."

Maria said, "That didn't take long, one minute it's here, the next, long gone."

Mel said, "Joe is correct, this fulfills what Jesus prophesized, not one stone shall be left here upon another that shall not be thrown down. Thrown down does not mean dismantled or crumbled, it means violently."

Maria smiled thinking, "Joe's making me jealous."

"Not possible anymore," thought Mel, also smiling.

Tom commented, "The dragon's temple is, as Mel said, hurled down. It does not crumble in slow motion. It's like an invisible hand just swatted it downwards."

Mel thought, "More accurate than you can possibly imagine, my friend."

Smiling, Mel said, "Now we come to another as Tom says a "weird or what" happening. Jerusalem has just fallen and now the forces of God destroy the 7000 Murders. We talk about Satan's pawns awhile back.

In the earthquake seven thousand people were destroyed. Reference Matthew 22:7. Remember the King's Feast, 'but when the king heard that they had killed his servants, he was furious. And he sent out his armies, destroyed those murderers.' We read that 7000 people were destroyed. The word 'destroyed' means 'slaughtered' so they were slaughtered by the King's Armies. They did not die due to the dragon's temple physically crumbling. These antichrist are destroyed by the forces of God. They are the elite 7000 temple guards or soldiers of evil. They were responsible for the murdering of God's 2 Ambassadors, His witnesses. They stood alongside of the Great Red Dragon unwittingly doing his dirty work."

Mel recapping, talked about how after Jerusalem is hurled into oblivion and 7000 are destroyed, and then the armies of God burn it to the ground.

Tom said, "Look at that these angels of God use mighty powerful slaughter weapons. They incinerate everything before them, resulting in ashes. There's nothing left of Jerusalem. Satan and his antichrist followers who have surrounded Jerusalem for the past 42 months, have moved northward to the area of the Mount of Megiddo. This was their former home until the flying monsters caused them to flee to Judea. Now they return. His son Leo, the Sea Beast resides and awaits his Father, who both know their time remaining is fleeting. This area will be the last to suffer the wrath of God's destruction.

I believe that during the destruction of the temple and city, Israelites who repented only out of fear, after their temple fell, are gathered by the forces of God for the great feast."

Maria said, "Yes, I remember, they are the evil seeds who worshiped Satan, but had no tattoo on their foreheads."

Joe added, "I remember us talking about this. These evil seeds will suffer the wrath of God at the appropriate time for they are the BAD guests."

Maria said, "They are like the weeds that crop up during the Kingdom of Peace" with Joe finishing her sentence for her with, "and they infect millions or billions of others."

Mel said, "You're right. And now another Heavenly wonder begins. All the fiery star crafts have by this time merged into one very large and brilliant fiery craft."

Joe said, "Look at the Great Dome covering the City. It's beginning its metamorphosis. All watch now, as its massive dome begins to retract folding into this fiery craft that results in an even more massive pillar of fire. The size of this new pillar of fire is tremendous, the same width at the newly created Valley of Olives."

Maria asked, "What's happening to that great dome? It's changing."

Joe replied, "Its domed roof is morphing into this massive 'pillar of fire' that looks miles high and is not the typical color of fire anymore."

Tom said to them, "Its intensity is so great a human could not look directly at it for fear of becoming blind, as it was like the Glory of God in its brilliance."

Maria, looking at these combining pillars of fire, said, "Listen guys, it's making a different sound."

Mel said, "The Martyrs are making this sound. It's their cry of victory. This is to show to the antichrist what was soon to be their end. This last group of souls saved from earth are the Redeemed, Repented, and Saved. They were all now within the brilliant pillar of fire, their numbers in the millions.

Now try and remember these two commands that begin and end the three and one half days between the death and resurrection of God's 2 Ambassadors, His Witnesses. Who remembers the first event, the trigger that begins the Armageddon Countdown?"

Tom replied, "The first command @-220 T/D. is, 'Go and gather my people.' God's servants go out and gather all the 'saved' from earth. They are brought into the pillar of fire in each of their angel halos. This all takes place in these 3½ days between the 'death and 'resurrection' of God's 2 Ambassadors."

Maria added, "And the second command is @-216.5 T/D. 'Come out of her my people'. Now these global pillars of fire containing the Good and Worthy Guests are in one day transported to and into the King's Wedding Feast Hall, the 'Great Domed City' that now has, as Joe said, morphed into this massive new pillar of fire."

Mel paused, saying, "Now another Heavenly Wonder. During their exodus, there will be a strange type of light after nightfall. Once again the Prophet Zechariah Has something to say about this. Maria, how about you tell us what it says In Zechariah 14:6-8."

"Ok, it reads: 'And it shall come to pass in that day, [that] the light shall not be clear, [nor] dark: But it shall be one day which shall be known to the LORD, not day, nor night: but it shall come to pass, [that] at evening time it shall be light."

Tom said, "A long time ago I thought this was some type of force field that protected the fleeing people. Now, we know it's this new Heavenly Pillar of Fire, projecting a special type of light, as if it were from the Glory of God's hand overshadowing them."

Maria said, "Almost as if the 10 golden light rays unfolded and made a canopy covering them."

Joe added, "Yah not like before when they stretched out hundreds of miles, now they sort of cuddled everyone."

Tom said, "This canopy could be like an energy field of some type. I sort of reminds me of that 'woman clothed with the sun' from a long time ago."

Maria replied, "I remember that. She represented all God's Children, you might say."

Mel added, "There's much more to her than people realize." He now spoke in a most majestic tone saying, "The Prophet Isaiah said in his chapter 66:8, "who has heard such a thing? Who has seen such things? Shall a land be born in one day? Shall a nation be brought forth at once'?"

Mel said to them, "Can you appreciate this miracle? Imagine in one day a Godly nation is born. The Mount of Olives splits in two and then a mass exodus. They have a unique light illuminating their pathway as they flee up and into God's Temple now located on Mount Zion."

Joe said he could very well imagine seeing these people, all having their garments of salvation, travelling up the valley slope to its top.

Mel said, "Try to picture this. A most brilliant roaring pillar of fire having a cross on top begins to glide effortlessly up the newly formed Valley of Olives. The redeemed, repented and saved in one day travel upwards through the valley of Olives fully protected by this pillar of fire. They soon arrive at God's Temple now located at the top of Mt. Zion.

Upon their arrival the glistening pillar of fire merges with and into the Temple of God."

Maria added, "I can picture it's magnificent glistening cross that is by far the highest point in the world and all outside of it must look up to it with shielded eyes."

Mel continued, "On Mount Zion, God's Temple will contain the 'Holy of Holies' which is the sanctuary that contained the Ark of His Covenant that only now was opened to them because the 'Sanctuary was now cleansed'."

Tom said, in the book we know that during the prior 'Time of Testimony' of God's 2 Ambassadors, the Temple of God upon earth was only partly accessible to them. As recorded in Revelation 11:1, 'then I was given a reed like a measuring rod. And the angel stood, saying, "Rise and measure the temple of God, the altar, and those who worship there."

"Joe how about you read what the Prophet Joel says in his chapter 12:17."

Joe read, "Let the priests, who minister to the LORD, <u>Weep between the porch and the altar</u>."

"I think this means," he continued, "during these days of sorrows the Great Domed City housing the Wilderness Sanctuary will offer the partially opened temple of God and the Israelite Redeemed priests will minister unto the Israelite Repented who make up the congregation."

Maria commented, "Joe, I'm impressed that you remember so much of what Tom taught us in the past."

Joe smiled and continued saying, "During the time of God's Two Witnesses, the Holy of Holies which is the sanctuary containing the Ark of His Covenant was not yet opened to them. God's temple now located on Mount Zion is fully opened."

Maria took over for Joe and she began, "In Revelation 11:19 it says, 'Then the temple of God was opened in heaven, and the <u>Ark</u>

of His Covenant was seen in His temple. And there were lightnings, noises, thundering's, an earthquake, and great hail.'"

Mel said, "The Ark of the Covenant recorded in Exodus 25:10–22 was the most holy object in the tabernacle. It was normally concealed from sight behind the tabernacle curtains. The revealing of this innermost object signifies that God has revealed His glory."

Joe said, "I get it. So after the 2300 days had expired the Temple of God opened in Heaven showing the Ark of His Covenant. Now, God's Temple rests upon Mount Zion on earth. 2300 days have now passed and the 'Sanctuary is Cleansed' both spiritually and naturally since the dragon's temple has crumbled into oblivion taking down with it all the evil it represented."

"That's right Mel replied, along with other things, from other times, the answers to which are sealed."

Tom asked, "Where were the 'bad' during these events?"

Mel said, "Even the 'bad' were gathered and brought in. The 'bad' were brought in first ahead of the 'good'. This all took place in the same day."

Joe commented, "This massive pillar of fire with its brilliant flaming cross can be seen for many hundreds of miles."

"True," Mel reiterated, "It's huge. The Great Red Dragon, along with his son, the beast, False Prophet and followers are making preparations for the upcoming Great War. From the Mount of Megiddo, their camp can easily see this brilliantly glowing cross of fire both in daylight and most spectacularly at night. This created great anxiety within their camps. The last thing the antichrist wanted to see was this cross as they all knew what it stood for."

Joe said, "And listen to its roaring sound. I get it. The thunders come from the seven thunders and the flaming lights come from the 7 spirits."

"Not bad, not bad at all." was Mel's reply.

"Yep! 'That's all she wrote'!"

Mel smiled, "Maria, you're so right about Joe. He's most definitely either a lump or coal or a diamond in the rough. It's difficult to tell at times. Now this brings us to a most strange time. We read in Matthew 22 'But when the king came in to see the guests, he saw a man there who did not have on a wedding garment. So he said to him, 'Friend, how did you come in here without a wedding garment? And he was speechless. Then the king said to the servants, 'Bind him hand and foot', take him away and cast him into outer darkness, there will be weeping and gnashing of teeth. 'For many are called, but few are chosen.'"

Maria asked about what kind of 'friend' gets tied up and thrown out?

Mel went on saying, "Yes, this is an interesting description, and the intruder is in the form of a man and not some other masquerade or manifestation. He is known to the King as he is referred to as 'friend'. This reference as 'friend' is used to indicate a past association.

Sometimes, we could use the word 'friend' in a pitiful way, meaning 'one who once was, but now not'. Remember, Satan before he was cast out of Heaven was the Archangel of Light and after his expulsion became an adversary so the use of 'friend' shows that God was saddened to see such a pitiful state of affairs, of his fallen Archangel of Light."

Joe asked how he had snuck in.

Mel answered, "He disguised himself as one of those who only gave glory to God out of fear, those 'evil seeds', and slips into the wedding hall."

Maria asked, "Wouldn't the angels of God be able to tell him apart?"

Mel answered, "He didn't have on the proper attire namely the 'wedding garment'. This garment was the Mark of God. This was something never to be obtained by him. This man was quiet, just sitting observing everyone. Don't feel sorry for him, since he wasn't in the wedding hall being remorseful rather he was inspecting the 'bad' his 'evil seedlings' having wedding garments on, they are his coverts. Their loyalties flip-flop and this is good because they can be bought and will serve him well during the coming Kingdom of Peace. The people he is looking at will most likely be still living upon his release from the 'bottomless pit' 1000 years from now since people don't die of natural causes during these years."

Tom asked, "Do you think Satan ever wishes he could do it over again?"

"No." was Mel's instant reply. "Remember Satan didn't rebel against God overnight as you say, this separation happened in degrees."

Maria asked, "What are those degrees?"

Mel labeled jealously as one.

Mel said, "Don't think that Satan was perplexed at seeing these 'bad' guests in the 'Wedding Hall' and wearing 'Wedding Garments'. They are still in their hearts his. Their inclinations are still evil. They are his evil seedlings that will yield a crop numbering as the sands of the sea.

Maria asked, "Why were they seated there?

Mel said, "Remember we talked about "For many are called, but few are chosen." It reveals everything and is another furtive discovery. God knows they're the evil seedlings and Satan knows that God knows, as Tom says, 'weird of what'. Satan along with the evil seeds are instruments serving a purpose as the catalyst for the next and final 'cull of the damned', Judgment Day."

Tom summing up said, "So those who repented only out of fear are these 'Bad' Israelites, the 'evil' seeds who during the past years have been worshiping the false messiah, some intentionally others in ignorance."

Maria added, "These are the evil seed Israelites who fled from Jerusalem when the dragon's temple crumbled into oblivion. They fled into the Valley of Olives. From there they were gathered and brought into the King's Wedding Feast Hall."

Joe for some reason got the last words, "Some of these 'bad' evil seeds also came from those who fled to the mountains of Judea. They both make up the evil seeds during the 1000 year Kingdom of Peace that the 'Friend' was observing.

Because this 'Friend' has no wedding garment, God commands his angels to bind and cast him into outer darkness. This is spiritual darkness away from the presence of God and all that is Holy. In a way, also back to the hell on earth." Joe finished talking, almost that is, and then added, "They have the 'morals of an alley cat and scruples of a snake'."

Maria gave a sigh saying, "Joe, that's the slogan on your old T-shirt."

Joe replied, "What's your point. It sums up everything, and you were doing so well," she said.

Tom chuckled and said, "Not bad at all".

Mel acquiesced.

Chapter Fifty-One

ARMAGEDDON COUNTDOWN A/C@-66.5

ENTITIES OF DEATH, 150 DAY TREK FINISHED

Mel was talking to them saying, "For the past 150 days these Entities of Death have been slaughtering everything unfortunate enough to have been on their route. Should a zombie for any reason get separated and lose contact with their horde, they become dormant until they hear the vibration sounds of the Entities of Death approaching. Then instinct causes them to rise up. Big mistake. The only thing left behind the horde, are ashes. Soon they arrive at the Great Euphrates River banks dry as a bone.

Joe asked, "What do these Entities of Death do as they cross the Middle East?"

Mel thought, then said, "Would you like to see?"

Maria said, "No!"

Joe said, "Sure you do. This is history in the making."

Tom agreed and she was outvoted again.

Mel said, "Within this last angel halo will be two groups consisting of the 1-color and 3-color Zombies but for all intents and purposes they are one and the same zombies. They are, as Joe once said, following the Pied Piper leading them to the river for slaughter."

Joe said, "It's only about 1500 miles from the Pakistan border to the dried up Great Euphrates River. This means they only travel about 10 miles each day. A person could walk faster than that. Why does it take 150 days?"

Mel replied, "That's a good question and volunteered no further information."

Joe pushed a little saying, "There's got to be some explanation for this."

Mel again replied, "Yes there is."

Maria started to laugh saying, "He's teasing you, right Mel?"

Mel spoke to Joe, "How we doing little buddy?" who replied, "OK, OK. Bring it on."

"Make my day."

"Remember, I'll be back."

Mel asked, "What does all that mean?"

Joe answered, "Read my mind," to which Mel replied, "I tried but the sign says 'Out to lunch'."

Joe turned to Maria for help only to hear her say, "Too bad, so sad. " She was in hysterics, but said, "That's what you get when you mess with the best."

Joe caved saying, "Seems like I've been 'out gunned'."

Mel simply said, "When it comes to a 'battle of wits, I refuse to fight an unarmed person."

Joe replied, "And what exactly does that mean?"

"Exactly", replied Mel.

Tom asked, "Mel would you please elaborate further on what happens now."

"Be glad to," was his reply as he smiled at them.

Mel began, "As recorded in Revelation 9:17-19, it says 'And thus I saw the horses in the vision: those who sat on them had breastplates of fiery red, hyacinth blue, and sulfur yellow; and the heads of the horses were like the heads of lions; and out of their mouths came fire, smoke, and brimstone.'

During their 150 day trek of destruction across the Middle East, that by the way, to answer your question, is not in a straight line, rather serpentine, winding throughout the land, they just don't make a beeline towards the dried up river bank of the Great Euphrates River. They're on a killing spree, as their name suggests. The terrain is mountainous. People hide everywhere so they must be routed out.

Now out of the mouths of these horses came, fire, smoke and brimstone. Consider your weapons of today, one is called the minigun that can fire tens of thousands of rounds in one minute. This weapon can be hand held or mounted. When you see such a device in action what do you see?"

Joe responded, "First you see fire shooting out the barrels about 10 feet, then you hear the sound it makes, then the smell of the gunpowder residue and lastly you look down range as to the destruction it caused."

"If the weapon was trained at a vehicle there would be resulting fire and explosions. So you see the description used about two thousand years ago was the only way to describe this weapon to people only having primitive swords and spears."

Mel elaborated, "Yes one third of mankind is killed by these weapons during their 150 day trek. For the sake of seeing through your eyes, millions are killed en route and 200 million are slaughtered in the dried up river banks of the once Great Euphrates River.

Even you Joe, with your vivid imagination, cannot fathom what 200 million dead bodies oozing blood looks, sounds, smells and tastes like.

With that much blood in the air, people would be able to smell and taste it, as a shark in the water does. In this case it will cause the Entities of Death to go into even more of a killing frenzy."

Maria asked, "Why are there so many roaming around? I believe you said millions of them."

"Yes," Mel replied, "however, keep in mind this is only an illustration as the numbers can fluctuate. One thing is for sure. 200 million are slaughtered. As to exactly how, it's a moot point.

Remember the 3-color follow the 1-color who chase after the pillar of fire. At this time, the pillar of fire is gone. Don't forget, these 1-color are also blind and with no guidance anymore they simply roam. They will wander the countryside seeking blood, and there's plenty of this so they travel in many directions. Also, bear in mind that there are hundreds of zones with zombies only now coming out of their comatose state. They scan, seeking the ultraviolet light from the pillar of fire that's long gone.

They wander seeking the smell of blood to drink. The 3-color seek them or the blood sources."

Joe asked, "Will the two groups of zombies sooner or later clash?"

Mel answered, "Yes, the 3-color can see but the 1-color have keen sense of hearing and smell, and it's a fair fight when the two groups converge on the blood pools".

Maria added, "As you have told us Mel, many are still in their initial 150 days so they can bite each other as much as they like and not be able to die."

Tom also added, "It seems also that the closer the Entities of Death get to the ancient city of Babylon on the dried up river bank, that the density of zombies also increases greatly because they have nowhere to exit, so the saying 'you can run but you can't hide' applies."

Mel asked, "Did I ever tell you where that saying originated?"

Joe quibbled, "Egypt's plagues perhaps?" and then smiled saying, "You give a little, you take a little."

"Exactly," replied Mel.

Joe didn't even bother to rib Mel, since he couldn't figure out why he so readily agreed with him so he acquiesced.

Maria chuckled but to herself, she said, "That's a first."

Mel said, "Let's see some of this in real time now."

He took the three firstly to Pakistan and from the ground they watched these Entities of Death in action. Mel reassured them that since they are spirits nothing can harm them. He said not to be alarmed at what they were going to sense.

Maria thought, "Strange use of the word." But it was perfectly accurate. He meant they would be using their senses, all of them, seeing, hearing, smelling, tasting, and touching.

Joe said, "Look, as they come charging through the villages, they're firing something."

Mel had told them of the weapon that was called the 'slaughter weapon'. This weapon dwarfed a mini Gatling gun. Its bullets were plasma balls that incinerated the person on the receiving end.

Mel said, "In the ancient city of Babylon they will fire other energy balls that emit shredding light, unknown to humans."

Before Joe could respond Mel elaborated. "Certain light, once emitted, resembles shards of light that shred everything it impacts with."

Joe added, "We call them photon torpedoes. In this case, photon balls, sort of a new twist of paint ball guns."

Tom said, "Now *that* I didn't see coming. Look at those Entities of Death, nothing can stop them. They look like horses but they're like tanks. See over there? One just went through a house. They just smash through walls, no matter how thick."

Mel said, "The same scenario will happen in all cities, so let's go to the mountains and see how the events unfold."

Once again Mel did his time slide thing, and they watched from an elevated outcropping of rocks, half way up the mountain side as these Entities of Death travelled through the mountain passages killing anything they came across. As they got closer to the caves, Mel lowered them down to ground level for a closer look.

Joe said, "Look at that. When they come to caves, they just charge into the opening no matter how small and begin killing everyone within."

Tom said, "These caves may have many connecting tunnels that burrow great distances in length but we have the ability to see through matter and can see the carnage taking place within."

Joe added, "They appear to take great pleasure in killing every one of them separately. They could have used their photon paint ball bullets or even their photon flame throwers."

Tom asked, "Joe, why do you refer to these things in jest?"

Joe answered, "Millions of people are watching these events through my eyes, in full color and maybe even 3-D, so I want to entertain them a little."

Tom shook his head and replied, "Joe, we're not movie stars you know."

"Speak for yourself," Joe replied. "You got the book deal, we get the movie deal."

Maria had to intervene. "All of us are spirits, brought back to help others. We're her as observers, not zombie killers, so stop all this 'bullscheisse'."

Both, Joe and Tom looked at each other. When Maria reverted to speaking German, it was time for them to 'get out of Dodge'.

Maria continued yelling, but this time for a different reason. Some of these Entities of Death came zooming past them, the riders screaming, and the horses screaming. The entire scene could only be described as insane.

The next event jolted all of them back. Joe pointed to the eyes of these horses. "Look they're glowing red, just like the Flying Hell Monsters."

Maria, having found her courage, went in front of one of the riders. "Tom, you were right, they have no face, and behind their visor is just a blackness."

Mel said, "That's because when the Soldiers of Death mounted the Hell Horses they became one entity. There was no longer any human body remaining, just spirit. The phrase 'Entity of Death' is most appropriate.

Tom commented, "Just one of these evil looking things could wipe out thousands of regular soldiers in times past. From a human standpoint, nothing could harm them. They're evil spirits unleashing energies of destruction."

Mel said, "Now we'll head to the ancient city of Babylon, and watch as the Great Red Dragon sees his Entities of Death, slaughter those restrained in the dried up river banks of the Great Euphrates River.

Tom seeing the Great Red Dragon and his son Leo, the Sea Beast actually flying and landing, said, "I pictured this beast as being very big, but nothing like this."

Joe said, "He appears to be taller than any building ever on earth. He looks like a T-rex on steroids, lots of steroids. He flies without physical wings. That's amazing."

Mel looked at them and said, "What about you three? You also fly. As a matter of fact, you are even more powerful than him. Power is not measured in physical size. That's only a human way of measuring things."

Tom spoke to Mel, "You said this is the site of the ancient city of Babylon. Where is it actually?"

Mel answered, "Exactly where the beast is standing."

Joe asked, "Why is his son, that smaller looking beast making such noises?"

Mel replied, "This is only to bolster his troops. Remember this is the first time they have seen their god. He wants to make a good first impression."

Maria said, "It seems to be working. These Entities of Death are making an extremely loud screaming sound themselves."

Joe said, "There's not much room between them and the tens of thousands of zombie bodies piling up in the old river banks."

Tom said, "Look, their bodies are growing ever higher. They are reaching hundreds of feet high."

Mel added, "This process takes several days to fully take place. Soon the pile will rise to over a thousand feet and that's only day one."

The three just stared silently as thousands of bodies grew into tens of thousands, then millions.

Joe said, "They're all fighting to get to the top of the pile and now their base is expanding outwards just like we thought, many miles in each direction. So strange to see it happening in real time."

Maria, spotted the blood first saying, "Their blood is already flowing out from the bottom of the pile. I've forgotten what's causing them to want to get over this invisible top."

Joe said, "The 200 million Entities of Death behind them and wanting to kill them, would be my guess."

Mel said, "During the last weeks these Entities of Death have been modifying their approach and are now in a pincer movement, corralling these zombies into one location for their messiah to watch the slaughter."

Tom spoke, "This picture forming is weird. We are seeing the Great Red Dragon, his son, the Sea Beast but where's the false prophet, the Land Beast?"

"Patience," Mel said, "The slaughter doesn't begin till tomorrow."

Joe said, "Tom, I think this means the remaining 100 million or whatever their total has been reduced to, have made the pyramid of zombies, and soon the slaughter begins."

Maria now said, "Look at this dragon. He's really red!"

Mel said, "The three evil colors are fiery red, hyacinth blue, and sulfur yellow."

"OK, he's fiery red then. This color looks evil to me even at this distance away from him."

Joe asked, "Why does he shoot sparks out of his nostrils?"

Mel replied, "There are many ranges of plasmas. Out of his mouth comes ionizing matter. The lightning sparks are his method of igniting this plasma that is hotter than the center of the sun, nothing on earth can withstand his blast."

Joe whispered to Maria, "Mel's really smart."

Mel fast forwarded a little, and it was the next day. The pyramid building had continued throughout the night and now reached thousands of feet into the sky.

Tom said, "The sheer weight of the number of squirming bodies is crushing those closer to the bottom. Their blood now covers the river bed from bank to bank and is flowing southwards."

Maria commented, "The blood is already flowing and the slaughter has not even begun."

Mel said, "Looking back, these Entities of Death hate everything and simply want to kill all zombies. They considered those who did not become soldiers of their god, cowards. The Hell Horses were only commanded to bow to the Soldiers of Death and to none other.

As to why these Entities of Death also killed all 3-colors that they find during their trek, simply collateral damage. They were not warriors and so served no purpose."

Joe commented, "Also, two on a horse just didn't look right."

Mel elevated them to about 10,000 feet and from there the view was most intense.

Tom went on saying, "So here we are, at the 150th day of their trek across the Middle East. These Entities of Death are forming a massive semi-circle around the screaming zombies. Their enormous pile is now 5,000 feet high and by tens of miles wide, all ready to be slaughtered.

Joe said, "Look at their base. It extends back just as high as it goes up."

Maria said, "These zombies are still trying to climb higher yet their total height isn't increasing, why is that?"

Mel said, "There comes a weight saturation point when their actual bodies, begin crushing those under them.

Did you ever imagine seeing such a site as this- the ancient city of Babylon, the Great Red Dragon, his son, the false prophet now here and 200 million Entities of Death with slaughter weapons having great power and ready for action?"

Maria asked, "How many people are still on earth?"

Mel said, "At the beginning of their 150 day trek, 600 million. 200 million Entities of Death, 200 million zombies living in this area called the Middle East, and 200 million living in Babylon the Great which totals 600 million antichrist. There will be millions killed during their trek across the Middle East."

He continued. "The 200 million Entities of Death are looking at the Great Euphrates River, waiting. Soon comes the wine-press, the wrath of God. The fire of his indignation results in the slaughter of those pathetic creatures who like ants have piled upon each other in the futile attempt to cross over this dried up river bed. Imagine living human bodies thousands of feet high and many miles in length all fighting, clawing and attempting to get over some invisible wall.

Soon, they will slaughter these sorry things that are being restrained once again, by the four angels at the Great Euphrates River. In the past these four angels restrained the demonic angels and now, once again, they restrain them again along with the zombies in front of them. Their squirming bodies pile up and spread out in the dried river bed."

Tom said he mentioned in the book that it says in Revelation about the amount of blood.

Joe said, "Yah, I remember that I compared it to filling up all the cars in the USA."

Mel said, "Let's just stick with what's recorded in the Bible. In Revelation 14:20 it says, 'And the winepress was trampled outside the city, and blood came out of the winepress, up to the horses' bridles, for one thousand six hundred furlongs.'

It was about 6 feet deep and 200 miles in length using your reckoning. The ancient city of Babylon straddled this mighty river in millennias past. It is from here that the Great Red Dragon is standing as he watches his Parade of Pride coming towards him.

Mel changed the view of the event that was now taking place. They were now slightly higher than the dragon and to the east of him.

All of a sudden a mighty flame of plasma shot out of the dragon's mouth, high over the heads of his children of pride. His troops responded with a roaring sound made up of screaming, hoof stomping and then they also fired their flame throwing weapons into the air.

Joe asked, "Will they ever run out of ammunition?"

"No," replied Mel.

Mel said, "Now it begins. The Entities of Death selected their slaughter weapons to now only fire impulse projectiles or as you call them bullets."

Maria said, "How come all the 200 million fire their weapons at the same time? Oh, I see, their forming elevated rows having the front line on the earth and each subsequent rows is slightly higher giving them a clear target."

Joe said, "See the last row is the highest, the same height as the top of the zombie pyramid."

Tom said, "I thought these Entities of Death couldn't fly?"

Mel agreed saying, "You're correct, they can't. Look more closely. They're not flying, they're elevated. Look at the dragon's son. His hand is raised. He is levitating them for this slaughter."

Maria said, "The sound of all these weapons is terrifying, even for me."

Joe said, "The fire coming out of these weapons covered all the shooters."

The picture was that of sight, sound and smell, with taste to follow soon.

The unholy trinity was enthralled with what was taking place.

Mel said, "What comes next none of you could ever have imagined."

The mile high top of the pyramid of zombies began shrinking as Mel slid time forward slightly. Soon this mile high pyramid began to draw near to the ground.

Maria looked at this saying, "They're being shredded."

Joe added, "More like minced meat."

Tom finished this thought saying, "They're being rendered down, into a gooey liquid."

Mel said, "Look at the blood now. It's 6 feet deep and now flowing outwards 200 miles as mini surge waves."

Tom said, "They just don't stop."

Joe said, "If you look carefully at these waves it seems to be filled with lopsided images, bobbing up and down. I got it. Remember the 'mummy movie' when spirits from hell, were pulling people downwards, into hell?"

Maria said, "Mel what's happening?"

Mel said, "Joe's mostly right. Truly, hell on earth in action. Remember your saying, 'misery loves company'? You're seeing it live, as human spirits are devolving into oblivion."

Maria said, "This is revolting to look at and why are we seeing it?"

Mel replied, "For a future time."

Trailing his words, what happened next caught the three of them off guard again. The Great Red Dragon now began issuing fire from his mouth directed at the river of blood. This fire was so hot it incinerated the blood into ashes and then there was only silent debris in the air.

Joe said he could still smell and taste it. They all confirmed his statement.

Mel said to them, "Look, the Great Red Dragon delights in this spectacle. Remember that God said that 'sorrow dances before him'.

Tom asked, "Why is the dragon, his son and false prophet moving out of sight? Where are they going?"

Mel said, "They don't want to stick around. What happens next causes them so much embarrassment. These Entities of Death cannot cross over the dried river bed, because the invisible barrier is still active."

Maria said, "Speaking of being active, look at that wall. It's covered with black soot of some type."

Joe furthered her comment saying, "That black stuff is changing from all the blood that previously covered it, from its top to its bottom."

Mel said, "This black wall is forbidden to them because they wanted to continue travelling to their messiah, now located at the Mount of Megiddo."

Mel looked, waved and they were now many thousands of feet high in the sky. He said, "What comes next triggers another series of events."

Immediately, they see and hear the earth quivering. Mel said that this is the most fearsome earthquake and the greatest since man was upon the earth.

While they were still looking at the black wall, simply disintegrated into a fine dust that within seconds itself dissipated.

Before these Entities of Death can react, the thought is instilled into them to hate and destroy Babylon (Rome).

Babylon, at this time has long ago fully recovered from the Zombie Plagues and the destructions going on.

Now God has put the thought into the minds of these Entities of Death that she was the reason Jerusalem along with their god's temple was destroyed. Instead of going to Jerusalem, they do some housekeeping.

They have by now slaughtered, one third of the people on earth and are anxious to continue their blood bath for the next third.

All three were now looking down at this great event and watched as the 200 million Entities of Death split into two massive columns, one went northwestward the other southwestward.

Mel said to them, "It is recorded in the Bible that Great Babylon splits into three sections during this 'greatest, since man was upon the earth', earthquake.

Mel said, "A little history for you. Babylon, the great city, is comprised of three areas. In Revelation 16:17-19 you can read, 'First the cities of the nation's fall.

Babylon (Rome) remains intact but will soon experience the wrath of God.

With another wave of Mel's hand, the three were up high, really high this time looking down at the Mediterranean Sea and the countries surrounding it.

"Babylon the great, is comprised of many countries that I described to Tom as the evil conurbation and consists of three distinct zones."

Joe not missing a beat commented, "I knew that name was too big for Tom to come up with, and use."

"Now," Mel said, "each of Babylon's three zones represent the seats of Power of the "unholy trinity", Satan, Sea Beast and Land Beast.

This evil conurbation is Rome, the interlocking central zone cities surrounding the Mediterranean Sea, Israel and Judea.

You might have forgotten what a conurbation is? It's a city that grew into mega metropolis that has merged with other such metropolises. As example, the City of New York, that has over time expanded and annexed other cities and areas that you now call New York State."

Tom said, "My thoughts exactly."

"More like Mel's thoughts and words," added Joe, somewhat cheekily.

Mel continued, "When it says that 'the great city was divided into three parts' as recorded in Revelation 16:19-20, these are the three Zones of the three beasts. Tom rightly so, dedicated a chapter in his book to further describe them."

Chapter Fifty-Two
GREAT BABYLON

Maria asked, "Why is it called Great Babylon?"
Tom replied, "It's huge in size, but it's also an absolutely vile and corrupt place."

Mel said, "We just came from the ancient city of Babylon. There's history attached to her. For now she represents evil, the unholy trinity."

Tom said, "We know that Rome is the home of the false prophet, the land beast, converter of souls. His color simply stated is, yellow, the color of commerce.

Rome, is controlled by the land beast. It consists of the 'cities of the nations'. These central zone's nations under the control of Rome, are the capitals of commerce with over 20 such cites representing the kings of commerce. Some of them are Spain, France, Monaco, Italy, Slovenia, Croatia, Bosnia, Herzegovina, Montenegro, Albania, Greece, Turkey, Morocco, Algeria, Tunisia, Libya, and Egypt, Syria, Lebanon, Palestine and the island nations Malta, and Cyprus and also include England."

Maria joined the conversation saying, "In your book, Tom you wrote that, Israel, is controlled by the Sea Beast, conqueror of souls. His northern half is the area of 'military' his color is blue, and his headquarters is the 'Mount of Megiddo'.

Tom agreed saying that around him the 10 Kings of the east have set up massive headquarters. The Bible makes reference to the 'Sea Beast' in Daniel 11:45 when it says 'He will plant the tents of his palace between the seas and the glorious holy mountain.'

Actual 'tents' are his choice for his 'seat of power'. He has no use for luxuries or women, his only lust is in the conquering of souls."

Joe asked, "I never herd of Megiddo. Whereabouts is it?"

Tom continued, "Modern Megiddo is a town approximately 25 miles southwest of the southern tip of the Sea of Galilee in the Kishon River area. Megiddo is the place where the final battle will be fought between the forces of good and evil and the Bible refers to this in Revelation 16:16, 'And they gathered them together to the place called in Hebrew, Armageddon (Megiddo).'

Tom said, "Some time ago I read that in 1964, during the visit of Pope Paul VI to the Holy Land, Megiddo was the site where he met with Israeli dignitaries, including Israeli President Zalman Shazar and Prime Minister Levi Eshkol.

Why would the Pope want to meet, at a place having such an evil connotation? This is where the Great Red Dragon, the Sea beast, Land beast, and the Entities of Death antichrist armies will gather to fight the Son of God in 'the battle called Armageddon'. Weird or what?"

Maria asked, What about Judea, the third part of Great Babylon?"

"Later," commented Mel. "Remember at this time the unholy trinity is made up of the false messiah, false president and false prophet. In the past, these last two global icons may have been sincere in their commission, however, now they're not.

Joe commented, "I remember, three spirits came out of the black sphere during their United Nations introduction. Now, we know it was the three demons up to their tricks again. These demons simply possessed the current president, religious icon and the third was the demon itself masquerading as the messiah returned."

Maria added, "Yes in the book it says that the messiah was so powerful only his manifestation could be shown to humans, to protect them from his true image. Mel," she asked, "does this spirit also possess a human being just like the other two?"

Mel answered, "He certainly could but do you think his ego would allow it?"

Joe replied, "Your answer is open-ended. Why?"

Mel answered, "Look around, as of the time of the Rapture, could you find a human being anywhere upon earth that humans could love, respect and agree upon who could fulfill this criteria? If your answer is yes, then this is possible but if your answer is no, then it's not."

Maria answered, "I think it would be next to impossible to find a human being that all world religions would find acceptable as their messiah."

Mel said, "A little correction is needed. Tom, you said the battle of Armageddon takes place at the Mount of Megiddo. Actually, what really happens is that the Great Red Dragon, his son, his false prophet and his Entities of Death all gather there and this requires a lot of ground area."

Joe said, "That's going to create a huge concentration of bodies."

Mel replied, "Yes, the unholy trinity will stand upon this mount and position their forces between themselves and Mount Zion."

Maria asked, "Do these Entities of Death understand what's really going to happen?"

"They have no clue," he answered, "and they are convinced their god is more powerful, even though they've seen numerous times, that the opposite is true."

Mel continued, "Joe is correct in his thinking. There will be 200 million Entities of Death, between the unholy trinity and the sword of Christ. This area will be saturated with evil, who will once again form a pincer movement, sort of a semicircle, focused towards Mount Zion. Satan stands behind his armies. This speaks to his nature.

Now, let's move on to the third part of Great Babylon, this is Judea, the southern half and home of the false messiah, the great red dragon.

Remember he is the collector of souls for the 'cull of the damned'. His color is red, the color Religion. This area is controlled by the 'false messiah', Satan, himself. Today this is the southern half of Israel, called Judea about 2,000 years ago. His headquarters started out in Jerusalem, in his temple. After Jerusalem falls and his temple is hurled into oblivion, he moves to his son's military camp at the Mount of Megiddo. The Great Red Dragon in full pride is now displaying his true appearance as we just saw in ancient Babylon."

Maria added, "If my thinking is accurate, we just witnessed the 200 million Entities of Death, the slaughter of the zombies, at the invisible barrier along the Great Euphrates bloody red river. Then this barrier comes tumbling down. Then lastly, these Entities of Death await a signal to cross over, one column of 100 million will then be travelling northwesterly towards Rome and the other 100 million column will be travelling southwesterly through Egypt and Northern Africa, once again killing everyone they see."

"Perfect recap," replied Mel, and using Tom's saying, 'finger on the trigger', here we go. Their signal or command to exit this now scorched and black line in the sand is very unique. The command was not verbal, rather in the form of an earthquake, remember the greatest, since men were on the earth as we just finished discussing."

Maria asked, "Some may question the enormity of their number being 200 million and where did such a fantastic figure come from."

Joe remembered. "The answer is in Revelation 9:13-21. It reads, 'now the number of the army of the horsemen was two hundred million'."

Mel said, "See, this number actually is recorded in the Bible. Some historians claim this was the great yellow horde from the east. This description is accurate since we have seen how the pillar of fire has drawn everyone to this area of the world, meaning they all came from the east."

Tom added, "It further says, 'I saw the horses in the vision and those who sat on them had breastplates of fiery red, hyacinth blue, and sulfur yellow."

Maria said, "Just as Mel told us, they were wearing the three colors of the dragon."

Tom continued, "Now look at the description of the horses. They have heads of lions, out of their mouths came, fire, smoke, and brimstone. They had tails like serpents with heads that can kill people. By these three plagues a third of mankind was killed for their power is in their mouth and in their tails."

Maria said, "You know, another interesting feature, there is no description of their faces. Since they come from the east, it would be an easy task to identify the face of Orientals however no features are given. If the riders were demonic one would think their appearance would indicate such."

Tom replied, "Since there was no mention as to their appearance, this means their faces were black having no features just the color of death."

Mel added, "Race, color or creeds meant nothing. Once they combined with the Hell Horses, these riders of death were no longer human. They were now Entities of Death. They had a face. It simply was the color of spiritual death, black."

Tom then said, "A while back we talked about the crest of England. It was very strange to look at, filled with symbolic undertones. Within its crest is a helmet on some entity, and only black is seen behind its visor. As we know, black is the color of death. When you look at the British emblem you will see a very strange emblem that embodies the 666 theme. Should I continue?"

They agreed.

"Now, the features of this emblem, a lion is depicted having its claws into the 'Rider of Death' who is wearing a golden oriental looking helmet. It has 6 vertical slits but no face, only black behind its visor slits. This 'Rider of Death' is attached to a white unicorn with a golden horn and it is chained to the earth."

Maria said while in university she took a course on this subject. "Historians claim that the unicorn originated from India and this ties India to these Entities of Death and Tom you even said its helmet looked oriental to you."

Tom took over once again saying, "Satan's son, Leo the Sea Beast, who is in charge of the military power on earth, controls these "Riders of Death" who have blue arms."

Joe commented about the rider saying, "He is coupled to a horse having a golden chain around its neck that's anchored to the earth. The rider wears a breast plate in the shape of a shield with insignias predominately red-yellow-blue, the colors of the dragon. Also attached to the rider are four tails of serpents having spots of a leopard. These four tails are the tails on the Entities of Death."

Maria commented, "We know that these horses are the demonic antichrist fallen angels but it's amazing to actually see that they are depicted as being chained and bound to the earth."

Mel interjected, "Remember, once these 'Hell Horses' join with the 'riders of death' they become the Entities of Death, the antichrist soldiers of the nations of the 10 kings from the east, and they become earthbound.

The 3-color Zombies who follow the 1-color Zombies across the earth sooner or later all wind up in India with their soldiers gathered along the way from Europe, Russia, China and India to name only a few.

Mel went on to say, "Pakistan, however, is located within the last angel halo. A great many saved people come from this area and across the Middle East as they have been waiting for the return of Jesus whom their holy writings say, will come for them and defeat the antichrist."

Maria added, "That is a great topic. Will you be teaching us on these other religions and their concept of Jesus?"

"No," came Mel's reply, "that's not within the scope of your mission."

Joe asked, the question, "Who is in command? The horses, or their riders?"

Mel answered, "These Entities of Death are actually controlled by their riders. When you compare this to, let's say a tank commander in your time, even though the tank has all the power, it's the commander within that has all the control. These Entities of Death are responsible for all the ensuing mayhem. The antichrist fallen angels being these Hell Horses having great power, but must obey their commanders as God has put this thought into their minds. In a strange way, this is humiliating for them. They are in servitude to the humans riding their backs, and must obey them."

Tom said, "The leader of these Entities of Death, their leader, the 'Sea Beast'. He is the 'conqueror of souls' and leader of the Commanders of the antichrist armies from the east and everywhere. In addition to the millions already with him, he also has a large presence of elite soldiers, previously encamped surrounding the City of Jerusalem where his father's temple was located prior to its fall."

Mel said, "You're right, Tom. Up to now these 10 kings have no geographical kingdom, however, they are the commanders of the Entities of Death, situated throughout the world, who all wind up in India. When the beast calls for them using his three demons, they receive authority for one hour as kings with the beast. They still have no geographical kingdom. They are empowered to enforce his commands and give orders for his Entities of Death.

Maria continued, "They give their loyalty to him as recorded in Revelation 17:13-17, 'these are of one mind, and they will give their power and authority to the beast.' These 10 horns on the Beast are the military leaders," she said.

Joe commented, "They also hate Rome, as God has instilled these thoughts into their minds. They will make her desolate, naked, eat her flesh, and burn her with fire."

Tom said, "The people living in these areas that the two columns are targeting are the recovered 3-colors. We know that they are the merchants of commerce, aligned to the false prophet in Rome."

Joe asked, "So during these final days all people have now encamped and surrounded Rome, that great conurbation claiming all lands bordering upon the Mediterranean Sea and then some. Aren't these areas are referred to as the 'cities of the nations'?

Maria said, "Yes, Joe." Turning to Mel, she said, "We've been discussing this topic for some time now. It's a big one."

Mel replied, "And there's still more to come. Tom, let's see how much of the book you remember. You mentioned what happens in the book. Please take over."

Tom picked up the topic saying, "These two columns of Entities of Death have the thought instilled within them to hate Rome, and they targeted her for death. Both groups first make her desolate by destroying everything in their paths. Then leave her naked as nothing remains intact. She is stripped of her pride."

Joe jumped in adding, "They also 'eat her flesh'. Remember these riders are the 3-color recovered zombies, however, they still have the taste for flesh, especially when it's fresh."

Tom replied, "OK Joe, you talk about them for a little longer."

Joe went on saying, "These Entities of Death eat the people in a vain attempt to satisfy their insatiable hunger for nourishment since all food sources are destroyed. This is very strange indeed," he said, "since they merged with the Hell Horses food was no longer necessary to sustain them."

Maria asked, "Joe, do you think they physically eat them or at this time do you consume them, with fire?"

Joe replied, "You know, I like your version better than mine, yes they will consume them with fire. And I think that's why they begin to burn her with fire."

Mel continued, "Remember the Sea Beast (false president) does not hate the Land Beast called the harlot (false prophet), only the Entities of Death do, for God has put it into their hearts to fulfill His purpose."

Maria asked, "What about their leaders, the 10 kings? Do they hate Rome, too?"

Mel replied, "Yes, until they complete their reign of mayhem and destruction the unholy trinity cannot control them."

Tom asked, "What does the Great Red Dragon think of all this?"

Mel replied, "He delights in the slaughter as 'sorrow dances before him'. Every death of a human is a victory for him and he knows his time is almost over, for now. He is more focused on the great battle soon to take place. Humans are expendable."

Maria asked, "What about these two 100 million each columns?"

Mel said, "Let's go and see them in action." And with the wave of his hand they were looking down at the column that was travelling north-west through Iraq, Turkey and into Europe.

Joe, looking downwards commented first saying, "Their attack pattern is different now, and those in the front are using their tails with the heads of snakes to bite the people, causing them to scream in great pain."

Maria asked Mel, "Why are they doing this to them?"

Mel said, "Watch what happens next," and in very short order those Entities of Death in the latter half of the column came and incinerated them from the fire out of their mouths."

Joe said, "I get it. It's like when you watched wrestling. Sometimes the wrestlers used what's called a tag team or two stage approach. By doing it this way both the front runners and those in the rear could partake in the slaughter."

Maria took a closer look at these snake heads and said, "They're pretty big, sort of like a cobra's head. Listen to the noise they make. It's a very loud hissing sound."

Joe said that he remembers reading in the book that a hissing sound would be made upon looking at them. "I thought it was only the people hissing, but now it also includes these snakeheads."

Mel now took them further north across Germany and to the countries in that area.

They watched as this massive 100 million column advanced upon each country and repeated their tactics.

Joe said, "See, sometimes they don't bite with their snake heads, they just use their fire, consuming people and objects in their path."

Mel added, "Remember the two columns of Entities of Death are travelling in a pincer fashion, one targeting these cities from the north, the other from the south."

Tom said, "These cities and people are just being annihilated. After the column has passed by, only flames remain. I remember in the book about the wrath, in Revelations it reads, 'for all the nations have drunk of the wine of the wrath of her fornication. The merchants of the earth have become rich through the abundance of her luxury.'"

Mel continued, "You are correct. These 'Kings of Wealth' are located along the coastal areas of the Mediterranean Sea referred to as the 'central zone'. They're powerful business moguls, the mega rich. Even today, in your 21st century, a new world order was emerging controlled by these world bankers who control over a quadrillion dollars."

Tom added, "You're right, of course. Before all this happened, there were about 475 billionaires that ruled earth's global economy. There were 193 nations in the world. These people have developed a network that 'wishes to remain unknown', to the people on earth at least. Their ultimate aim was to create a one-world system divided into ten economic regions which were called 'kingdoms' each having one king. The Bible refers to them as the 10 kings and today this group wants to set up 10 kingdoms. That's all now just history as they're running for their lives. As Mel or Joe says, 'you can run but you can't hide'."

Joe said he used it first. Mel just asked, "What does 'copycat' mean?" to smirking Joe.

Mel said, "These powerful cities of all the nations fell in this severe earthquake. Their dwelling places are now gone. What remains is rubble and food soon becomes nonexistent."

Joe added, "So by default, fathers will eat their children, children will eat their parents and friends will eat everyone." Then he added, "What are friends for?"

Maria, dismissing his last remark, added "What happens to all the blood sources at this time?"

Mel replied, "Remember the oceans and seas have long ago turned into the blood of a dead man making it useless to anyone. All other red blood sources, now, during this Babylon Earthquake have disappeared into the bowels of the earth."

Joe cheekily commented, "Pretty slim pickings, I'd say."

Mel just ignored him, and with the wave of his hand, took them somewhere.

Maria asked, "Where are we? I can't see the earth or the stars."

Mel replied, "In another dimension that exists between the visible and invisible. Don't dwell on this aspect, for now we come to the time when Great Babylon suffers the wrath of God. I really want you to focus on this next event."

Joe asked, "Is this how spirits always disappeared? They simply went between the visible and invisible, when people saw them, and they're gone?"

Chapter Fifty-Three

GREAT BABYLON REMEMBERED BEFORE GOD
A/C@-33.0

Mel once again ignored Joe and addressed them, saying, "Great Babylon is remembered before God. Now comes the Wrath of God upon her. These Entities of Death and their two massive 100 million each columns, by this time have destroyed what was left of life in Europe and North Africa, the outer nations surrounding Rome and the Mediterranean Sea."

Maria asked, "Are there any stragglers still on earth?"

Mel said, "There are no other people living anywhere else upon the earth. The plagues and slaughters have taken care of them."

Joe commented, "Those who died during this earthquake seemingly get off easy as they quickly go into oblivion and exist no more."

Tom said, "Such an outcome is inconceivable to me, such waste."

"Now comes the wrath of God" Mel said. "Great Babylon was remembered before God, to give her the cup of the wine of the fierceness of His wrath. Revelation 18:8 'and she will be utterly burned with fire, for strong is the Lord God who judges her.'"

Mel went on saying, "Her plagues come in one day and one hour. This is the 'one hour' portion. She will be utterly burned with fire."

Mel, now kept them high in the sky, and moved southwards to a position over the Mediterranean Sea.

Maria said, "We can easily see the massive columns coming down from the north, and upwards from the south, now converging upon Rome."

Tom said, "From up here these Entities of Death flow across the area surrounding Rome."

Joe said, "There's so many of them, they look like ants." He then said, "It doesn't take them long. In only one day, the entire lands are in flames."

Mel said, "After the 200 million Entities of Death have fulfilled their mission, they begin to exit Great Babylon, leaving in their wake, death and destruction."

Tom spotted it first, saying, "What's that large temple surrounded by smaller ones. They're not on fire."

Mel replied, "This is the building structure where the false prophet reigned. It still exists. The fire from their mouths did not consume it. It was shielded from their power."

Maria asked, "Why is the false prophet's temple not burning?"

Tom got in on this one saying, "I recall that in Revelation 17:12-17 it says that the 10 kings with their Entities of Death armies for one hour are kings with the beast. They hate the harlot Rome, make her desolate and naked, eat her flesh and burn her with fire."

Maria said, "I get it. As they leave Rome, all the above has taken place, the temple still stands, and my question still has not been answered."

"You will be amazed," Mel commented. "The destruction is described in the Bible. Zechariah 14:12 details this event. 'And this shall be the plague with which the Lord will strike all the people who fought against Jerusalem: Their flesh shall dissolve while they stand on their feet. Their eyes shall dissolve in their sockets. And their tongues shall dissolve in their mouths."

Joe commented, "That sounds like these effects are the result of a nuclear detonation."

Mel continued his answer without addressing Joe's comment.

"Secondly, in Revelation 18:9-10 it says "The kings of the earth who committed fornication and lived luxuriously with her will weep and lament for her, when they see the smoke of her burning, standing at a distance for fear of her torment, saying, 'Alas, alas, that great city Babylon, that mighty city! For in one hour your judgment has come.'"

"See," Joe added, "there's the mushroom cloud."

Again ignoring the interruption, Mel continued, "Thirdly, in Revelation 18:21 we read, 'then a mighty angel took up a stone like a great millstone and threw it into the sea, saying, 'Thus with violence' the great city Babylon shall be thrown down and shall not be found anymore.'"

Tom said he got it, this great millstone is a descriptive way of saying, and she was nuked.

Maria commented, "So as a result, all trace of Great Babylon this evil empire will not be found anymore."

Joe finished the thought saying, "Great Babylon dissolves into oblivion, into the bowels of the earth."

Mel agreed saying, "Right, so there you have it. Great Babylon was destroyed by the forces of God."

Tom extended the answer, "Just like Sodom and Gomorrah and, the dragon's temple."

They cry, when they see the great mushroom cloud ascending into the sky. They are at a safe distance and still see the smoke of her burning that all took place within in one hour.

Maria asked, "Who are these people that are doing the crying? The Entities of Death cannot cry?"

Tom replied, "They are those who wore the 10 black hooded robes and the hundreds who wore the red robes with no hoods, in the dragon's temple when it was first dedicated. They also had their own support staffs that could have numbered into the hundreds or thousands. The dragon's kings of commerce are still in human form. They along with the others weep, as everything they strove for and schemed for is now gone. Within <u>one hour</u> such great riches came to nothing."

Mel said, "See, they watched her burn from far away, not because they escaped the Entities of Death, but because these were those living in Israel around the Mount of Megiddo. Their turn was yet to come.

Joe commented, "It seems like the Entities of Death all 'got out of Dodge' 'in the nick of time'.

Mel elaborated on Joe's idiom, quoting someone from the past, 'For to these, there is annexed a clock-keeper, a grave person, as Time himself, who is to see that they all <u>keep time to a nick</u>.'"

Maria said, "I don't think you can top that one, Joe." And Joe acquiesced.

Mel, now took them to another vantage point, so they could see some of the islands, in the now dried Mediterranean Sea.

They watched, as these islands sank, and their mountains dissolved, crumbling into oblivion, sinking with them, until they were no more. As in times past, evil was now gone.

Joe said, "Kind of like, 'going, going, gone.'"

Maria commented, "Seems like Joe's 'back in the saddle'."

Mel said, "You're not the only ones to witness this event. Thousands of years ago, the Apostle John as recorded in Revelation 16, also saw them sink. And, over a thousand years before him, the Prophet Jeremiah said in chapter 4:24, 'I looked at the mountains, and they were quaking, all the hills were swaying.' The Prophet Nahum said in chapter 1:5, 'the mountains quake before him and the hills melt away. The earth trembles at his presence, the world and all who live in it.'"

Mel finished his thoughts recapping, "Great Babylon with Rome at its center, now gone. The Cities of the Nations that surrounded the Mediterranean Sea, Europe above and North Africa, now gone and the islands also, now gone.

The three of you have witnessed many wonders, and more are still to come. For the third and last part of Great Babylon, Israel still stands, awaiting her turn to be destroyed. That will occur soon, at Armageddon."

Mel repositioned them closer to Israel, saying, "Now comes the Plague of the great hail. Revelation 16 says 'and great hail from heaven fell upon men, each hailstone about the weight of a talent. Men blasphemed God because of the plague of the hail, since that plague was exceedingly great."

"I remember this," said Tom. "The weight of each of these hail boulders, not merely little hail stones, was about one hundred pounds."

Joe said, "A one pound hail stone would smash through cars and buildings. Imagine the damage a boulder sized rock of hail would do".

Tom continued saying, "I think, to put this into perspective, a man would have a difficult task, to lift a bolder this heavy."

Maria said, "Once on TV I saw hail stones the size of a golf balls, and if one were to strike a person on their head, they would easily die from it. Now imagine, an ice bolder a hundred times heavier. Somebody once said, 'you can run but you can't hide'. Very appropriate."

Mel just gave her a fleeting glance. Joe was silent for once.

Mel continued, "This plague now takes place. These are the last events of the Seventh Bowl in the book of Revelation."

They all watched, as the sky blackened over Israel, then lightnings accompanied by thunders, then the pounding of hail. Even from their height, the sounds of the hail striking buildings could be heard.

Maria then said, "I even read in the book, that the people blasphemed God, because of the plague of hail was so great. Why didn't they just repent?"

Mel answered, "Remember those in Israel were the unholy trinity, the antichrist and the Entities of Death. Did you expect anything else, from them?

Chapter Fifty-Four

MARSHALLING THE TROOPS AT MOUNT OF MEGIDDO

Mel took them, to the outskirts of Megiddo, only several thousand feet high. "Evil is doing their final battle assembly and war dance," he said.

Tom pointed to the 200 million Entities of Death returned from their killing sprees in Babylon, and gathered around the mount of Megiddo, surrounding their god, his son and his religious prophet.

Maria commented, "The area they consume for this is enormous. They are now forming vast semi circles, rows of battalions on the southern portion of the Mount of Megiddo and to its east and west. Rows upon rows, all facing towards Mount Zion. Nothing on such a massive scale like this, ever existed on earth."

"The Great Red Dragon positions himself behind his troops," Joe piped in, 'like a football quarterback'. Yes, and in front of him are his Sea Beast and Land Beast, in front of them, his Entities of Death."

Mel said, "There is a saying 'lead by example'. In this case, it doesn't apply as Satan is behind his troops. Are you surprised?"

As they shook their heads, he said, "Thought not."

"Now let me be clear," Mel continued, "all this doesn't happen overnight. Days turn into weeks, and soon the Great Red Dragon, the beast, and false prophet, have everything in order for the soon-to-take-place, Armageddon."

Mel fast forwarded time, for them to witness the coming events.

The 3 demons are not sitting idle they once again have been pumping up the 10 kings and their Entities of Death armies by shooting great fire flames upwards into the clouds.

Joe commented, "They're deceiving tactics look extremely impressive. Satan's pawns, now have the feeling that victory, is within their grasp."

Maria pointed to the huge flaming cross on top of Mount Zion. Its sheer size, brilliance and tremendous sound was intimidating to say the least.

Mel told them, "The Dragon is a master of deception. He knows that he and his forces will lose, however, as 'misery loves company', the Dragon wants to take as many of God's creations as he can into the 'cull of the damned'."

Maria added, "It seems like the Dragon somehow views this as punishment to God, for all of his misery. I can now understand why, he is void of God fear. He blames God, for being cast out of Heaven and each subsequent plague infuriates him and his own, further."

Mel said, "He calls these Entities of Death the 'caged demons'. These fallen angels are trapped on earth together with these pitiful humans controlling their actions."

Joe said, "They certainly must feel caged alright."

Tom said, "In Revelation 19:19 it says, 'and I saw the beast, the kings of the earth, and their armies, gathered together to make war against Him who sat on the horse and against His army.'

The stage is being prepared for the battle of "Armageddon". Look at their massive leader the monstrous Great Red Dragon is absolutely huge in size and power. From our perspective he's much larger than the Empire State Building."

Mel said, "Did you listen to the last line you quoted from the Bible? Also included in this scene is the Son of God sitting upon a (white) horse along with the Army of God. Everything is now ready for the command of God."

Chapter Fifty-Five
ARMAGEDDON
A/C@-00.00

Mel said, "I think a little history is warranted now. Armageddon, is the 'cull of the damned', and the dragon's prime intent was to deceive and turn as many people away from God, as possible.

Billions, are deceived or voluntarily elected to follow this 'false messiah'. Those who could not be turned were slaughtered giving him great satisfaction as 'sorrow dances before him'."

Maria commented, "Only now can I comprehend the meaning when God said, 'sorrow dances before him'. Our saying 'misery loves company', cannot even begin to come close. I can see how he is totally insane and delights in the pain and suffering of others."

Tom said, "One might say, if the Dragon has any intelligence at all, he would already know that in the long run he is going to lose to God and that he is going into this bottomless pit again."

Maria said, "This doesn't make any sense. Why go through all this if you know you have no chance of winning?"

Tom added, "The dragon knows he will not win, but, as you just said Maria, he's insane. He delights in the fact, that he is going to cause the death of billions of God's creation, since no one wants to see their creation being destroyed."

Joe commented, "Remember he has tried and failed to kill those seven groups that God has removed from earth."

Mel added, "Don't forget those from the eternal realms. There are millions of them that were taken from his grip."

Mel continued, "God has given these souls one chance after another but when they turned their back on him every time and received the 'Dragon's Tattoo 666', it sealed their fate. Just like when Sataniel (Satan) the Archangel of Light convinced 1/3 of the angels (200 million) in Heaven to follow him, it also sealed their fate.

Once they turned on God, they were expelled and their fate was sealed. Exactly the same fate awaits these souls that gave their allegiance to the Dragon. By their actions against God their fate was sealed and they now had no redemptive value."

Joe commented, "You might say that it seems like God uses the Dragon to 'cull the herd'. The Dragon has done a service and in a strange and sad way their own actions dictated their own fate. This scenario is difficult to comprehend. Simply put, the Dragon knows he will lose but has satisfaction in knowing that he will be taking with him billions of souls. 'Misery sure loves company'."

Tom commented, "Let's remember, we read in the Bible 'this earth was created for many but Heaven only for a few'. The dragon relishes this moment as it is the culmination of his efforts. He delights in witnessing the misery, even if it means his own too."

Mel said, "In 2 Peter 3:10 it indicates how horrific the outcome of Armageddon will be. It says, 'But the day of the Lord will come like a thief. The heavens will disappear with a roar, the elements will be destroyed by fire, and the earth and everything in it will be laid bare.'

There have been many earthquakes and plagues during the past but this will be different. In Isaiah 24:19-23, the Prophet Isaiah says that: The earth is violently broken. The earth is split open. The earth is shaken exceedingly. The earth shall reel to and fro like a drunkard and shall totter like a hut; its transgression shall be heavy upon it, and it will fall, and not rise again."

Mel continued, "The earth in heading for bad times. Isaiah further says, 'it shall come to pass in that day that the Lord will punish on high the host of exalted ones, and on the earth the kings of the earth.'

"See, God will punish the fallen angels with Satan being their leader, and the kings of the earth will be punished, too."

Mel said, "And finally Isaiah says, 'For the Lord of hosts will reign on Mount Zion, and in Jerusalem, and before His elders, gloriously.'

So there you have it, the Lord will reign on Mount Zion, and there is also mention of the New Jerusalem, for the previous Jerusalem has been destroyed by God's forces.

Now we come to the time just prior to the start of Armageddon, where we read of the Son of God on a White Horse."

Chapter Fifty-Six

CHRIST ON A WHITE HORSE & HEAVENLY ARMY

Mel, speaking from memory, said, "In Revelation 19:11-21, it says, 'I saw heaven opened, and behold, <u>a white horse</u>. And He who sat on him was called Faithful and True, and in righteousness He judges and makes war. His eyes were like a flame of fire, and on His head were many crowns. He had a name written that no one knew except Himself. He was clothed with a robe dipped in blood, and His name is called The Word of God. And the armies in heaven, clothed in fine linen, white and clean, followed Him on <u>white horses</u>.

Out of His mouth goes a sharp sword, that with it He should strike the nations.

And He Himself will rule them with a rod of iron. He Himself treads the winepress of the fierceness and wrath of Almighty God. And He has on His robe and on His thigh a name written: KING OF KINGS AND LORD OF LORDS.'

This is how the Bible describes Jesus, the Son of God, together with his army."

Maria was the first to respond. "I think when you said, 'And the armies in heaven, clothed in fine linen, white and clean, followed Him on white horses', the armies refer to God's Angels and the fine linen white and clean, refers to the Martyrs."

Mel smiled and said, "And much, much more."

Mel continued, "Now we also read that Jesus makes war. His eyes were like a flame of fire. Trust me, you never want to see such eyes. They only mean one thing, death."

Joe added, "His robe had His blood on it and also His Martyrs' blood."

Maria added, "And much, much more. You know what they say about payback."

Mel continued, "Out of His mouth went a sword, not of metal rather of power. And He Himself will rule them with a rod of iron, during the 1000 year Kingdom of Peace that soon follows. As a side note, in Revelation 2:27 it tells us that the Bride will also rule with a rod of iron. Do you know why" You guessed it. It's because of the evil seeds. You knew that right?"

They smiled at him.

Maria asked, "How is it that we now remember every detail of the past?"

Mel replied, "The spirit remembers everything."

Joe added, "To me, when I think of Tom's book, the pages sort of appear in my mind and either I'm reading them or their coming from my memory somehow."

Mel replied, "The Children of God are very special. You now have the ability to assimilate knowledge, by way of only one example. Merely by touching a book, you acquire its content."

"Now that's what I call speed reading," commented Joe.

Chapter Fifty-Seven

THE BEAST AND HIS ARMIES DEFEATED[70]

Mel gathered his three and positioned them upon Mount Zion to view the battle. The battle of Armageddon, if one can call it that, is one sided.

The Great Red Dragon made a strange sound. Mel whispered, watch. Maria pointed to his nostrils. They were shooting out sparks the distance of a football field. Next came sort of a gurgling sound from the belly of the beast, then some type of liquid was forcefully projected out of its mouth. The great sparks, themselves extremely brilliant, ignited. This liquid shot forth far enough to come into contact with the force field surrounding the flaming cross. It looked impressive yet had absolutely no effect on the cross.

Tom pointed to the Entities of Death. As soon as the Great Red Dragon issued his flames of fire, they also did so. The sight was very impressive, as these Entities of Death were firing everything in their arsenals. Their attack lasted less than one hour, again with the results being negative.

Joe remarked, "The three demons are flying about to and fro, yet they don't have weapons. They're just encouraging everyone to keep fighting."

Maria said, "Look! All the Entities of Death are turning around and looking back at the Great Red Dragon in complete bewilderment, They know they've lost the battle, been lied to, and know what comes next."

The next event dwarfs any Hollywood movie. Mel again whispered, "Watch!"

Two extremely powerful angels came swooping down from the Heavenly army and immediately captured the sea beast and the false prophet. At the same time a large circular portal opened in space having a rim of fire and a black swirling hole as its center. Upon closer inspection, it too had a center of fire.

Mel commented, "This is the lake of fire burning with brimstone. Into this the two beasts were cast alive. This is the point of no return. They're erased from existence."

This same portal emitted a most brilliant light, like that of the sun, yet greater. They heard a great voice commanding, "Come and gather together for the supper of the great God."

Out of the portal came strange large flying things that resembled huge birds of some type. One thing was for sure they didn't ever exist on earth.

Maria asked, "Are these flying things angels?"

Mel replied, "No, these sun portal creatures have been created to carry out many functions. One is to dispose of the flesh of creation. They will remain suspended a little while longer, until commanded to do otherwise."

Once again, Mel said for the third time, "Watch!"

Now, a most spectacular sight occurred. The Son of God, with the sword which proceeded from his mouth, in slow motion, passed through the now perplexed army of Satan and killed these Entities of Death.

Joe commented, "This sword is a brilliant flaming light of some type, as if the spark of a nuclear detonation could be extended on its edges indefinitely."

The intensity of this flaming sword didn't cut the Entities of Death in half, but rather it enveloped them, resulting in their death. When they fell to the ground, both the riders and horses turned into flesh and blood, and scattered everywhere.

Mel said, "The Bible says, 'Then I saw an angel standing in the sun and he cried with a loud voice, saying to all the birds that fly in the midst of heaven, 'Come and gather together for the supper of the great God, that you may eat,

The flesh of kings
The flesh of captains
The flesh of mighty men
The flesh of horses
The flesh of those who sit on them
The flesh of all people, free and slave, both small and great.'"

Mel ended his discussion simply by saying, "This bring us to the next happening. Satan is captured by a great Angel of God. Look closely, the angel is carrying a 'key' to the 'bottomless pit'. The science behind this is for now past your limits."

Joe quibbled, "You mean a 'black hole' with its center hollowed out, creating a seemingly bottomless void, called in layman's terms, a 'pit'?"

Mel replied, "Did you just make that up or are you're that knowledgeable?"

Joe's thought, commented, "Now 'who's the man'." "Thought so," replied Mel.

Maria commented, "Many people have in the past asked, if there really is a hell. If so, where and what is it? Now we know, where hell is."

Mel added, "And what about the key?"

Joe again, in thought, commented, "This is a seal from God locking him in and until the seal is removed by God, the Great Red Dragon is confined there."

"Not bad," replied Mel, "Humans are fast leaners."

Mel continued, "Satan now is bound for the next 1,000 years. Then comes the end, Judgment Day and the Judgment Day Books, however I will skip this topic and save it for a future time. Next I will discuss a most wonderful topic, the Book of Life."

Chapter Fifty-Eight
BOOK OF LIFE

Mel once again gathered them for a discussion. "Almost everyone has at some time or another heard the expression Judgment Day or the Judgment Day Books. These books are not good. Those whose names are recorded in them, will at the appointed time, cease to exist in any form or fashion.

Now, comes another book which is called, the Book of Life.

Before I discuss the Book of Life the question is, how did a person have their name removed from the Judgement Day Books and into this book? The answer, they were judged, each one according to their works. Does this mean if they were good people their names were automatically removed from the Judgement Day Books? No they were not. Did it mean that bad people were automatically judged and cast into the lake of fire? Not necessarily."

Maria commented, "So people had the opportunity to repent even after death. I guess an easy matter to comprehend for some, an impossibility for others. I remember the old saying 'birds of a feather flock together' meaning the good gravitated and congregated with good and evil with evil."

Joe added, "So while in their respective dwelling places in the hereafter, the good where drawn to the light of grace, accepted the offer of salvation and received garments of salvation, evil however rejected."

Maria smiled. Her Joe was maturing.

Mel now continued, "How this actually is accomplished, I'll paraphrase what is said in the Bible in 1 Peter 3-18-22[71]. The Apostle Peter talks about the people who died in the sin flood in the days of Noah many thousands of years ago. Peter says, Christ went and preached to them in their prisons, (in their realms) for they had been disobedient to God's offer of salvation while Noah was building the ark."

Maria, "Why do you think he did this, to torment them further?"

"Absolutely not. He went to these souls offering salvation. This is why the Kingdom of Peace has 1000 years. This allows for every soul ever created to be testified to just like the 'saved' from the nations of the 10 kings."

Maria queried, "I don't think I heard an answer just yet. Are you saying every soul since Adam and Eve?"

"Yes," was the reply.

Tom asked, "Will all people agree with you about this, because some believe that you must be a Christian and a good one. If you are not then when you die, you go to hell. Some Christians even go so far as to say, the other religions, not Christians, also all go to hell."

Mel displayed a look of consternation and said, "A word to the wise. If one or the other objects to souls being saved after their physical death, let me pose this question. Do you think grace is only given for you?

How many times during this Book of Thomas, did you read that God offered grace to everyone, excluded no one, their actions dictated their fate. One should be careful not to be like the Pharisee[72] who considered himself greater than the Publican. Jesus said that everyone who exalts himself will be humbled, and he who humbles himself will be exalted. You must not cast the first stone, for who is without sin? And as recorded in Matthew 7:1-2 'Judge not, that you be not judged. For with what judgment you judge, you will be judged; and with the measure you use, it will be measured back to you.'"

Whispering to his wife, Joe added, "Mel sure got riled up on this one."

Maria said, "Hush, Joe." She turned to Mel and said, "So Jesus is telling them to take heed, do not judge or your name will remain in the Judgment Day Books."

Joe added, "And that means 'you chose poorly', Christian."

"Yes, you are correct in your thinking."

Mel further said, "Even the first Apostles of Christ went to the tombs of the dead and Baptised them. We read in 1 Corinthians 15 29…32 Otherwise, what will they do who are baptized for the dead, if the dead do not rise at all? Why then are they baptized for the dead? What advantage is it to me? If the dead do not rise, "Let us eat and drink, for tomorrow we die!"

Mel said, "Now think. Why would these Apostles of Christ have Baptised those who have died, if it had no effect. It is imperative to one's salvation to have their name removed from the Judgement Day Books and entered into the Book of Life, failing which they are cast into the lake of fire. So share God's grace. You can't seek grace and deny it to the next person. Otherwise as Joe said, 'you chose poorly', Christian."

Tom asked, "Why would Christians not want to share God's grace and help all to salvation?"

Mel replied, "Part of a person's humanity is their free will. This allows them to form opinions, however, more often than not, the wrong one, 'self-righteousness'.

Now with respect to the offer of salvation for those living upon the earth during the Kingdom of Peace there are <u>two groups of people</u>, still in their human bodies.

<u>First</u>, those from the 'King's Wedding Hall' after the 'wedding feast' of His Son all wearing their wedding garments. They come from the Time of Redemption of the Two Witnesses and don't forget hidden within them, the 'evil seeds'.

<u>Second</u>, their descendants who during the 1000 year Kingdom of Peace either listened and accepted the testimony of salvation offered to them and kept their garments of salvation pure or drifted away to become once again the antichrist.

Within these two groups are those who kept their garments pure, have their names removed from the Judgement Day books and subsequently entered into the Book of Life just like those from the eternal realms."

Tom commented, "All souls exempted from Judgement Day wear the Garments of Salvation."

Mel elaborated somewhat saying, "They don't physically wear this garment. It's integral to their being. Their loyalty and love for God and His Son and Wife is, eternal."

Maria further queried, "Will their physical appearance be different than what humans looked like in the past."

Mel replied, "Yes, you'll be seeing them soon."

Maria commented, "Speaking of the Lamb's Wife. . ." Mel interjected, "Yes, let's talk about her."

Chapter Fifty-Nine
LAMB'S BOOK OF LIFE

Mel began with saying, "Now, another completely different group who are the Bride, the Lamb's Wife, spoken of by the Apostle John, as recorded in Revelation 21:9 'Then one of the seven angels who had the seven bowls filled with the seven last plagues came to me and talked with me, saying, <u>"Come, I will show you the bride, the Lamb's wife."</u>

Christianity has numerous opinions, concerning their spiritual outcome. Some merely aim for Judgment Day and hopefully enter a nice place. They don't know it, but due to their good works, they escape Judgment Day and are entered into the Book of Life."

Maria added, "If that's all they're striving for, so be it."

Mel continued, "Others have the opinion that when they die they go to Heaven and sit at the side of God or Jesus, simple thought, not accurate. Others have no clue as to what takes place.

Now, back to the Bride, the Lamb's Wife, she is comprised of special souls that I will discuss soon.

Now as to the Lamb's Wife they are recorded in yet another book called the <u>Lamb's Book of Life</u> as written in Revelation 21:27 but there shall by no means enter it anything that defiles, or causes an abomination or a lie, <u>but only those who are written in the Lamb's Book of Life.</u>

The Bride, the Lamb's Wife is not one person she consists of a hierarchy. I will be discussing her in great detail starting now.

So, what is the Bride, the Lamb's Wife? She is the highest distinction a human can achieve. "Royal Kings" and "Royal Priests" of God as recorded in 1 Peter 2:9 But you are a chosen generation, a royal priesthood, a holy nation, His own special people, that you may proclaim the praises of Him who called you out of darkness into His marvelous light.

Joe please read the next few references."

"First in, Revelation 1:6, Joe continued, and has made us kings and priests to His God. Next, Revelation 5:10 and have made us kings and priests to our God, and we shall reign on the earth."

Mel added, "We also read about them in "Revelation 21:24 concerning the New Jerusalem, but I saw no temple in it, for the Lord God Almighty and the Lamb are its temple. The city had no need of the sun or of the moon to shine in it, for the glory of God illuminated it. The Lamb is its light and the nations of those who are saved shall walk in its light, and the <u>kings of the earth bring their glory and honor into it</u>. Its gates shall not be shut at all by day (there shall be no night there).

But there shall by no means enter it anything that defiles, or causes an abomination or a lie, but only those who are written in the <u>Lamb's Book of Life</u>.

The Royal Kings of God, written in the Lamb's Book of Life, bring the praises, glory and honor of those saved, into it, what this fully entails, you will soon see.

Now, those in the Lamb's Book of Life form the hierarchy. I have briefly spoken of these Royal Kings and Royal Priests of God, the following will add more depth to my words."

Chapter Sixty

BRIDE, MARRIAGE, WIFE of GOD'S SON

"**I**, Mel, have helped guide your discovery of 'what' the Bride of Christ the Lamb's Wife are.

But now, the question everyone wants to know the answer to, 'who' is the BRIDE, the WIFE?"

"**THE BRIDE, ARE FIRSTLINGS**, not in physical stature, but rather they developed and matured into the spiritual likeness of their Lord to such an extent, they were designated as 'firstlings'. They have the 3 Holy Sacraments, and on earth matured to their absolute best, as their title suggests, they put their God and His Son first.

Of <u>The Bride</u>, we read in Revelations 19: 6-8 'And I heard, as it were, the voice of a great multitude, as the sound of many waters and as the sound of mighty thundering's, saying, "Alleluia! For the Lord God Omnipotent reigns!

Let us be glad and rejoice and give Him glory, <u>for the Marriage of the Lamb has come,</u> and <u>His Wife has made herself ready.</u>" And to her it was granted to be <u>arrayed in fine linen, clean and bright,</u> for the fine linen is the righteous acts of the saints.'

In these verses it says of the <u>BRIDE, the WIFE,</u>
She gets '<u>married</u>'.
Her Bridegroom is the <u>Lamb of God, His Son.</u>
She is called '<u>His Wife</u>'.
She has made '<u>Herself Ready</u>'.

| 543

>   She was granted to be <u>arrayed in fine linen.</u>
>   Her linen is <u>clean and bright.</u>
>   Her linen is the <u>righteous acts of the saints.</u>

> The Bride is taken to God in Heaven during the Rapture. She is attended to by her Bridegroom. The Bride is depicted as a women getting herself prepared for her Bridegroom. She radiates a special divine holiness. There is no mention of her face, rather she is a spiritual being, and one could say she is spiritually veiled. She is adorned with garlands of righteousness, is sinless, and is brilliant."

Chapter Sixty-One
HIERARCHY OF THE BRIDE

I have informed you as to 'what' and 'who' is the Bride, the Lamb's Wife. Now I will describe 'her' hierarchy.

Firstlings, they put their Lord first, during their lives. They have the 3 Holy Sacraments. They are the,

ROYAL KINGS, OF GOD
ROYAL PRIESTS, OF GOD

Overcomers, are not firstlings, however, they overcame in descending degrees, and are therefore partakers in the wedding ceremony. <u>They make up Her fine linen wedding gown, consisting of their righteous acts referred to as the saints.</u>

REFINED, CHILDREN OF GOD	WILDERNESS SANCTUARY
REFINED, CHILDREN OF GOD	MARTYRS OF UNDERSTANDING
REFINED, MARTYRS OF CHRIST	TESTIFIERS, KINGDOM OF PEACE
REFINED, MARTYRS OF CHRIST	TEMPLE PRIESTS, OF GOD
REFINED, ETERNITY REDEEMED	CHILDREN OF GOD

These are the Spiritual designations of the Bride.

Now, during the wedding ceremony that takes place as the Prophet Daniel said, "Blessed is he who waits, and comes to the one thousand three hundred and thirty-five days. Now, the Bridegroom, presents His Bride, the Firstlings clothed with the Overcomers, to His Father. She is unveiled in the presence of God.

"Behold your Wife" resounds throughout Heaven.

Chapter Sixty-Two
NEW JERUSALEM

From Mel's enlightenment to those listening, it is to be known, now, that as to the appearance of His Wife, her adornment as viewed by the Apostle John in Revelation 21:9-10 appears as a great city, the holy Jerusalem descending out of heaven from God, having the glory of God.

Mel furthered his explanation, saying, "Her light was like a most precious stone, like a jasper stone, clear as crystal.

She had a great and high wall with twelve gates and went on to describe these gates along with what was written on them."

Mel, measuring the city, concludes that it is over 1400 miles square and its height is just as high—magnificent.

He continues, "And the streets of the city were pure gold, like transparent glass or you could say transparent gold.

The Wife of the Son of God, appears as the Holy Jerusalem, descending out of heaven from God, having the Glory of God. She is most spiritually spectacular to behold, human words would fail and until all are in spirit, we'll just say: **Behold The Lamb's Wife.**"

Chapter Sixty-Three

FUNCTIONS OF THE HIERARCHY

Mel continues to enlighten Tom, Maria, and maybe even the readers who now are following along with these discoveries that leave little room to challenge, and much room for love and growth.

Mel smiles, and turns to the three heroes, and all other partakers in the feast of knowledge, and begins to explain the places and roles of the hierarchy in the Wedding Feast.

"RAPTURE PARTAKERS

THE ROYAL KINGS, or 'Firstlings' are taken in the Rapture and together with their exact counterparts in Eternity awaiting them, will rule with the 'rod of iron' and dispense the third Holy Sacrament to the saved people of the nation's currently wearing their garments of salvation. (As it says in the Parable of the talents, they increased X5 and were given the one talent taken from the wicked and lazy servant. The Royal Kings have 11 Talents). Their scope has the greatest capacity.

THE ROYAL PRIESTS, also 'Firstlings' are taken in the Rapture and together with their exact counterparts in Eternity awaiting them, will rule with the 'rod of iron' and dispense the third Holy Sacrament to the saved people of the nation's currently wearing their garments of salvation. (In the Parable of the Talents, they increased X2. The Royal Priests have 4 Talents)

REFINED, CHILDREN OF GOD, also known as 'Overcomers' come from the Great Domed City (the Wilderness Sanctuary) who needed a little more time to mature and are taken up by the Lord to Heaven at the 1260 T/D. They received special fellowship during these days allowing them to mature. Remember, not all are the first fruits. Some fruits mature later, however, they're still good.

Now, who do you think counselled them in the Wilderness Sanctuary during these days? Here's a hint. It says in Revelation 'where she is nourished for a time and times and half a time', that's 1260 days. If you said an angel counselled them, you're wrong or the Two Witnesses of God, wrong again. It says 'nourished'. Do you think this only means 'food'? Think! Why are they in the Wilderness Sanctuary in the first place? They are there for additional spiritual nourishment that will enable them to mature, so who supplies this nourishment?

Ask yourself this question, did those in the Wilderness Sanctuary have the three Holy Sacraments? Yes they did. Are they left there without any spiritual guidance? No they're not. The question is, who attends to them? The answer is the Holy Spirit."

Maria smiled and said, "So those who in the past thought, what about my husband, wife or other loved ones, what if they're not quite ready, what is their fate if I'm taken, and they're not? Now they know the other side of the story. There will be no separation, for 'love' is eternal. They will rejoin their loved ones soon enough."

Joe interjected saying, "It's just the pecking order that is different, right Mel?"

Mel nodded, "Again in Revelation we read, 'Rise and measure the temple of God, the altar, and those who worship there.' Do you believe this altar is man-made of stones? It isn't. One last tidbit of information to read carefully for it says the 'temple of God'. This altar even though on earth is linked to those in Heaven. Those in the Wilderness Sanctuary receive spiritual food and are connected to the congregation in Heaven, whom they will soon join for the wedding ceremony."

Tom commented, "I could never have fathomed such happenings. God's plan of salvation is like looking through the Hubble telescope, the deeper you see into the depths of the Universe, the more complicated it is."

Mel said, "Now we come to the next group, the

REFINED, CHILDREN OF GOD, MARTYRS OF UNDERSTANDING, the prodigal children of God who didn't fully comprehend God's Plan of Salvation or their function in it.

Their opinions lead them in many directions. Unfortunately, they sidestepped the time of grace prior to the Rapture. Later, they saw and corrected their error and came home <u>prior to the appointed time</u>.

Their intimate knowledge of their Heavenly Fathers Plan of Salvation, was now their foundation that supported their actions.

In the beginning they rallied the Christians stealthily, and commencing with the Two Witnesses of God, these Martyrs of Understanding, declared open warfare upon the unholy trinity at the 1040 T/D. Their rallying actions ramped up exponentially, and their bold actions targeted themselves for death, in the eyes of the unholy trinity, prior to the 1260 T/D.

They were the first, during these last days, to be martyred. Their time of refinement now completed, they received 'Holpen'. The Martyrs of understanding, God's prodigal children were now home. They never denied their God but they separated themselves from his love and simply lacked absolute conviction of faith.

I will give you a parable that explains them. Paraphrasing John 20:24-29 it says that after the resurrection of the Son of God, the Apostles of Christ were gathered together except the Apostle Thomas who later came to them and when they told him that Jesus was in their midst he doubted their words saying 'Unless I see in His hands the print of the nails, and put my finger into the print of the nails, and put my hand into His side, I will not believe.'

Remember, Thomas was one of them, he was an Apostle, they all loved him but his doubt was greater than his belief. For eight days he separated himself from the congregation. Later Thomas was again with them and Jesus appeared to them, and to Thomas he said, 'reach your finger here, and look at My hands; and reach your hand here, and put it into My side'.

Jesus admonished him, '<u>Do not be unbelieving</u>, <u>but believing</u>.' And Thomas answered and said to Him, 'My Lord and my God!' Jesus said to him, 'Thomas, because you have seen Me, you have believed. Blessed are those who have not seen and yet have believed.'"

Maria asked, "Why was he absent for eight days?"

Mel answered, "This is a symbolic period of time, relating to the time that the prodigal children were also absent from the congregation."

She then said, "Some hear and believe while others require more proof."

Joe said, "Those living in the Rapture's aftermath certainly now have their proof."

Tom said, "Thomas was not cast out of the congregation, he was loved. Jesus simply said, "You had to see to believe, blessed are they who have not seen, and yet have believed."

Joe asked, "So what became of Thomas?"

Mel replied, "Thomas travelled great distances and did great works in the name of Christ."

Joe said "That's reassuring to know, just like us?"

"No," Mel retorted, "when you three heard, you believed."

Curious, Maria asked, "Exactly when did we hear and believe?"

Mel smiled, "That's an answer your Bridegroom will give you, during the Wedding Ceremony."

Tom asked, "Aren't we in it now?"

Mel answered, "Yes and no. Remember you're in the time plane of God's prodigal children, Martyrs of Understanding, the Wedding Ceremony is still far ahead.

Let's finish with this group. Due to their absence, they miss the Rapture, and live during the Rapture's Aftermath, however, they go on to do great works in the name of Christ until their martyrdom. As Daniel said, it is still prior to the appointed time."

"Now we come to another group of Christians, the

REFINED, UNDER THE ALTAR MARTYRS #1 GROUP. These souls are from Dark Middle Ages. Not so long ago they were sealed with the third Holy Sacrament by our Lord Himself in the eternal realms, as Tom mentions in this book and referred to as the Commencement date, of the Fist Resurrection."

Mel pointed out, "Maria you were correct. They were not given 'palm branches, a sign of peace and reconciliation'. As recorded in Revelation 7:9, this group is ready to go into action during the Kingdom of Peace. It also says in Revelation 6:10-11 that they were crying with a loud voice, saying, 'How long, O Lord until You judge and avenge our blood on those who dwell on the earth?' Their pain of their martyrdom was now replaced with Holy Zeal and they're anxious to go forth as mighty testifiers of their Lord. They were told by Jesus to be patient for a little while until their fellow brethren were killed like they were and would come their way."

Next are the

REFINED, GREAT TRIBULATION MARTYRS, or "Great Exploit Martyrs" #2 group, 1290-1335 T/D.

They are recorded in Revelation 7:15 gathered from the sky at the sound of the great trumpet during the "Time of Refinement" Also recorded in Revelation 7:16 they are the Temple Priests who serve God. In Revelation 7:17 it says God Himself will wipe away every tear from their eyes. This is a most powerful act of love. Our Lord says, 'He who overcomes, I will make him a pillar in the temple of My God, and he shall go out no more. I will write on him the name of My God and the name of the city of My God, the New Jerusalem, which comes down out of heaven from My God. And I will write on him My new name.'

They are God's Temple Priests. In Revelation 3:8-11 it says 'I know your works. See, I have set before you an open door, and no one can shut it; <u>for you have a little strength</u>, have kept My word, and have not denied My name. Indeed I will make those of the synagogue of Satan, who say they are Jews and are not, but lie — indeed I will make them come and worship before your feet, and to know that I have loved you. Because you have kept My command to persevere, I also will keep you from the hour of trial which shall come upon the whole world, to test those who dwell on the earth. Behold, I am coming quickly! Hold fast what you have, that no one may take your crown.'"

Mel commented, "They have been persecuted by the unholy trinity and now they're exhausted both physically and spiritually, yet they stand fast.

They will soon be sealed with the third Holy Sacrament by our Lord just like their fellow brethren and this takes place in Heaven."

Maria said, "The Wedding Ceremony is much more involved than one could possibly imagine."

"Very true," replied Mel, "and speaking of involved, the next group fits that description even more so. It is the

REFINED, ETERNITY REDEEMED SOULS,
They repented after death and received the three Holy Sacraments by those commissioned by Christ to perform them, here on earth. This is called 'Baptism for the Dead', first commenced by the Apostles of Christ after their Lord's Martyrdom. Remember the Son of God went into the eternal realms to those who died during flood in Noah's time. Why did He do this? Grace. "

Maria asked, "Why are these souls taken from the billions of other souls in eternity, who only during the 1000 year Kingdom of Peace are testified unto."

Mel's answered, "Three reasons; prayers, grace, and they believed."

Chapter Sixty-Four
BLESSED IS HE WHO WAITS AND COMES TO THE 1335 T/D

Mel said, "Now, we arrive at the time prophesized in Daniel 12:12 where it says, 'Blessed is he who waits and comes to the 1335 days.' This is a most important time. Eternity has been waiting for over 6,000 years for this date. Now comes the marriage ceremony, the fully adorned Bride awaits her Bridegroom and the marriage of the Lamb now takes place. Behold the Lamb's Wife."

Maria asked, "At this time date are we included in the Wedding Ceremony?"

Mel smiling said, "Absolutely yes."

Joe commented, "Then why are we still here?"

"Really Joe, you don't think you can be two places at the same time?"

Maria smiled saying to Joe, "Ask him if you have to first answer any of his trick questions again, like 'weigh me the weight of fire'?"

"Not falling for that one again," he replied.

Tom added, "Mel we believe and have faith."

Mel smiled saying, "Now that's the perfect answer."

Joe whispered to Maria, "It seems like I missed the question."

"Me too," she replied.

Mel waved his hand as he spoke to them saying, "I'm going to park you three for a moment."

Maria chuckled, "First my thoughts and now I, get parked."

Mel said, "We read in, Revelation 20:6 'Blessed and holy is he who has part in the first resurrection. Over such the second death has no power, but they shall be priests of God and of Christ, and shall reign with Him a thousand years.'

There are many 'parts' to the first resurrection for it is a plurality of linked events as discussed in Tom's end notes of this book."

Mel commented, "It says, has 'part'. This in itself does not constitute the 'whole' of something.

The Bride is constituted with many parts having its highest part being the Royal Kings and Royal Priests of God. Now even the 'lowest part' will be spectacular. Jesus said there are the least and the greatest in the kingdom of Heaven. In Matthew 5: 19 it says 'Whoever therefore breaks one of the least of these commandments, and teaches men so, shall be called least in the kingdom of heaven; but whoever does and teaches them, he shall be called great in the kingdom of heaven.'

The Marriage Ceremony now commences and following this. All prepare for when the 'Sanctuary is Cleansed' and a new nation is born in one day when the 2300th day arrives."

Chapter Sixty-Five

SANCTUARY IS NOW CLEANSED
2300 T/D

A NEW NATION IS BORN IN ONE DAY

Mel began, "Continuing with the various groups, the next group are the <u>ISRAELITES, REDEEMED.</u> These are the Wilderness Sanctuary Temple Priests. Israelites, who accepted the Testimony of the Two Witnesses of God and received God's Mark during the 'Time of Redemption', <u>prior to</u> the 'abomination of desolation' being unveiled in the dragon's temple.

They travelled upon the King's Highway to the Great Domed City prior to the 1290 T/D, when the 'abomination of desolation' was set up. They remain in this Great Domed City until the 2300 T/D., when the Sanctuary has been cleansed."

Mel commented, "One unique feature of this group is that they are Temple Priests due to their faith in the Words of God's Two Ambassadors. They accepted their Baptism unto Repentance and they help the next group."

Mel said this next group comes later. They are the <u>ISRAELITES, REPENTED</u>. These Israelites living in Judea were instructed by Jesus to 'flee' and they did <u>after the</u> "abomination of desolation" was set up and unveiled at the 1290 T/D.

They fled to the hills, came into contact with and accepted the Testimony of the Two Witnesses of God during the 'Time of Redemption'. They are the repented congregation who remain in this

Great Domed City until the 2300 T/D., when the Sanctuary has been cleansed.

Now the next group shows how God's words were fulfilled that he wants all to be saved. Those sheep from other folds, now completed form part of the citizens of the Kingdom of Peace. They are the

SAVED NATIONS, REPENTED. Mel said these are the Good Guests in the Wedding Hall and Feast. They are the Repented people of the 'saved nations' of the 10 kings. They accepted the Testimony of the Two Witnesses of God and received their 'Baptism unto Repentance'. They were given 'Wedding Garments' and they kept them clean. They come from the 'Time of Redemption' in the Great Tribulation Time during the 1400 T/D to the fulfilment of Daniel's "2300 days, 'until the Sanctuary is Cleansed'.

They also form part of the Citizens of the Kingdom of Peace. Revelation 3:18 says, 'I counsel you to buy from Me gold refined in the fire, that you may be rich; and white garments, that you may be clothed, that the shame of your nakedness may not be revealed; and anoint your eyes with eye salve, that you may see.'"

Mel continued, "At this time, **THE WEDDING HALL** is now filled with guests. Revelation 3:5 says 'He who overcomes shall be clothed in white garments, and <u>I will not blot out his name from the Book of Life;</u> but I will confess his name before My Father and before His angels. All will be gathered for the King's (God's) Wedding Feast for His Son.

'THIS IS THE WEDDING FEAST'
2303.5 T/D

God said, "Many are <u>called</u>, few are <u>chosen,</u>' in Matthew 22:14 and we know he spoke these words to Satan. We fully understand many are called but only a few are chosen.

Mel said, Let's look at what 'called' and 'chosen' mean, and you will be surprised. A definition or synonym for 'called' is <u>Baptised or Christened</u> while a definition of 'chosen' is <u>one who is the focus of divine favor.</u>

God draws His chosen, to His Son. In John 6:44, Jesus said 'No one can come to Me unless the Father who sent Me, draws him."

Mel rhetorically said, "Who are the Bride of Christ? They are the 'holy' ones. Revelation 22:10-11 tells us 'and he said to me, 'Do not seal the words of the prophecy of this book, for the time is at hand. He who is unjust, let him be unjust still; he who is filthy, let him be filthy still; he who is righteous, let him be righteous still; he who is holy, let him be holy still."

Now after reading the above what do you think the following means when it says?

He who is unjust,	let him be unjust still
He who is filthy,	let him be filthy still
He who is righteous,	let him be righteous still
He who is holy,	let him be holy still

Maria said, "The first two are bad."

Mel answered, "Ignore them since they refer to the antichrist and now learn about the next two."

THE RIGHTEOUS, are those who live a morally correct and God fearing life."

Mel continued, "They are the 'Righteous Martyrs of Christ' from times past and the Great Tribulation time. These people were righteous and they lead a God fearing life.

THE HOLY, are those of Devine origin and have been consecrated to God.

Mel continued again, "They are the 'Holy Children of God', 'chosen' by God for the 'Bride' of His Son. You may ask why the difference between the two last groups? The 'Righteous' have 2 Sacraments and the 'Holy' have 3 Sacraments. Why? They believed.

My advice, seek the Christian denominations offering 'three sacraments'. Get them and remain faithful and become a participant in the 'Rapture' and escape every 'Time of Sorrows' event, in this book.

REWARD OF THE FAITHFUL

"You know," said Mel, "everything offers a reward; schooling, business, and professional occupations. The Rapture's Reward[73], is given to the Faithful.

In Revelations 2 & 3 the Son of God says tells the faithful about their reward. He says:

1. To him that overcometh will I give to eat of the tree of life, which is in the midst of the paradise of God.
2. He shall not be hurt by the second death and shall be given a new name.
3. I will give power over the nations. He shall rule them with a rod of iron.
4. They shall walk with Me in white, for they are worthy.
5. I will make him a pillar in the temple of My God, and he shall go out no more.
6. I will write on him the name of My God and the name of the city of My God, the New Jerusalem, which comes down out of heaven from My God. And I will write on him My new name.
7. I will grant to sit with Me on My throne, as I also overcame and sat down with My Father on His throne.

Remember, as Daniel said, 'those who are wise shall shine like the brightness of the firmament, and those who turn many to righteousness like the stars forever and ever.' And Matthew said, 'then the righteous will shine forth as the sun, in the kingdom of their Father.'

This Book of Thomas draws to a close for now. This also brings me to the end of my assistance and your time of grace. Tom, Maria and Joe once thought "Who is Mel?". The time for this answer is now at hand.

Chapter Sixty-Six
THE ORDER OF MELCHIZEDEK

Mel said, "Now I must take leave and say 'auf Wiedersehen, goodbye, until we hopefully meet again on the other side of time.

As to the question, who am I?

I exist 'without father, without mother, without genealogy', a manifestation of the Holy Spirit.

I am the priestly line through which the future king of Israel's Davidic line was ordained.

I am 'Priest forever of the Most High God'.

I am the king of Jerusalem who brought out bread and wine and blessed Abram and received his offerings many thousands of years ago.

I am the 'king of righteousness'.

I am: Melchizedek.

Welcome, God's Children to the 'Gardens of Light'.

'Come home children, it's time'.

God Bless. Amen.

EPILOGUE

Mel brought his three beloved, now once again with him, to the top of a high mountain, looking at the new Heavenly Jerusalem coming towards them.

Mel said to Maria, "Some time ago you asked if you all would be in the Wedding Ceremony. And my answer is absolutely, yes."

Mel somehow wrapped his arms around them and said, "This will be the last time you three will be in this time plain on earth. Your function is now completed."

Mel, looked at them, smiled and said "See how beautiful she is! From what seemed like thousands of miles out in space now came this glistening city. Its appearance was dazzling to say the least."

Now this huge city moved laterally and positioned itself directly in front of the sun. Due to its position, the light from the sun was blocked and the only light now came from this Heavenly city.

The closer it came to them, they all gazed at its beauty. Joe said, "This city is as bright as the sun."

Maria commented, "That's one big city!"

Joe said, "It's as high as a mountain".

Maria said, "See in the middle of it is the Lambs Wife, she is spectacular, and look, she is clothed with lovely white and bright, linen garments. These are the righteous acts of the saints, the overcomers, this is the Heavenly Jerusalem." Mel was impressed with her grasp.

Now, this Heavenly Jerusalem came even closer to them and as they looked, Joe pointed and said, "See over there, I have a twin waiving at me, so do you Maria and Tom, they're waiving at us."

Maria was astonished. "That's so weird to see yourself waving at yourself. How does this really happen?"

Mel said, "That's you over there and yes, you're waving at yourselves." They looked at each other, perplexed.

Mel, for the first time was really smiling. His face began to radiate, then glowed like the sun, yet they could look right at him without discomfort. Mel spoke softly saying, "You were always over there, remember two places at the same time, Joe?

Maria asked, "What's that sound we're hearing, it sounds like some type of bells ringing?"

"These are the bells of Heaven, Angels of God, singing" Mel explained.

"I thought that was just an expression up to now. I can hear voices singing, it's getting louder now, the words, I know them somehow." Maria whispered.

Mel said, "This is the song, only those in the New Jerusalem know and sing forever, forevermore and forever after."

Maria, then Joe, then Tom, began singing, "Jerusalem, Jerusalem, City of our God, Hosanna to our Father. . ." their countenance now filled with brilliance.

A gentle voice was whispering to them, "Come home children, its time". . . they were home, along with all their thoughts and memories.

⁂

Maria, Joseph and Thomas, their time now concluded upon earth, rejoined their brethren, all singing to their Heavenly Father, as the Marriage Ceremony, commenced.

Mel, waving to them one last time in his customary fashion, then raised his hands in praise, his countenance grew to immense brilliance, and vanished.

Finally, thought Maria looking at Tom, we're home.

Then, looking for Joe, "Oh no . . . where's Joe"?

Tom replied, "Oh no . . . here comes Mel."

"Oh no. . . What's up?" she asked.

"The Great Red Dragon's, out of his pit."

"Joe . . . Joe . . . now what did he do?"

Mel, calmed her down. "It's alright. He didn't do it, speaking of which, here he is. I need you three to come with me, to the beginning of the 1000 year Kingdom of Peace, and Judgment Day."

Joe said, "You mean 'back to the future'." All three burst into hysterics.

Mel said, "What's so funny? This is serious. You three have one last mission."

"Seems like we've heard that line before," said Maria.

Joe continued, "So we're going to the Kingdom of Peace time, and ending with Judgment Day. I've got the perfect name for another book, *DRAGON'S TATTOO 666, JUDGMENT DAY.* Mel, when this is over can you take us back, say five years, so we can get a book deal?"

Mel sighed, and said, "The things I do for 'King and Country'."

"Sure, *now* he quotes the legendary James Bond," said Joe.

Maria quipped, "Joe, James Bond is only a fictional character, just like you."

Joe didn't get it. He rubbed his hands together, ready for their next mission. "Tom, make sure you bring a pad of paper and a pen. Let's play hard ball for that book deal."

Mel's voice in the background, softly whispered,

"Give me patience Lord."

Dragon's Tattoo 666 Trilogy

Availability of this book is subject to intervention
by a Higher Power, Amen.

ENDNOTES

1. REFERENCE NOTES

During the 7 year great tribulation 'time of sorrows' 7 categories of people emerge during these two 3½ year time periods.

<u>Time of Refinement: 'first 3½ years'</u>
"Wilderness sanctuary"   Children of God "refined"
"Understanding martyrs"   Children of God "refined"
"Great exploits martyrs"   Martyrs of Christ "refined"

<u>Time of Redemption: "second 3½ years"</u>
"Redeemed Israelites"
"Repented Israelites"
"Saved Nations"

"Evil Seeds"

2. MULTITUDE FROM THE GREAT TRIBULATION

Revelation 7:9-17,
After these things I looked, and behold, a great multitude which no one could number, of all nations, tribes, peoples, and tongues ALL NATIONS, TRIBES, PEOPLES, AND TONGUES, standing before the throne and before the Lamb, clothed with white robes, with palm branches in their hands, 10, WHITE ROBES, WITH PALM BRANCHES IN THEIR HANDS and crying out with a loud voice, saying, "Salvation belongs to our God who sits on the throne, and to the Lamb!" 11, ALL the angels stood around the throne and

the elders and the four living creatures, and fell on their faces before the throne and worshiped God, 12, saying:
"Amen! Blessing and glory and wisdom,
Thanksgiving and honor and power and might,
Be to our God forever and ever.
Amen." 13, Then one of the elders answered, saying to me, "Who are these arrayed in white robes WHO ARE THESE ARRAYED IN WHITE ROBES, and where did they come from?" 14, And I said to him, "Sir, you know." So he said to me, "These are the ones who come out of the great tribulation, THESE ARE THE ONES WHO COME OUT OF THE GREAT TRIBULATION and washed their robes and made them white in the blood of the Lamb. 15, Therefore they are before the throne of God, and serve Him day and night in His temple. SERVE HIM DAY AND NIGHT IN HIS TEMPLE. And He who sits on the throne will dwell among them. 16, They shall neither hunger anymore nor thirst anymore; the sun shall not strike them, nor any heat; 17, for the Lamb who is in the midst of the throne will shepherd them and lead them to living fountains of waters. And God will wipe away every tear from their eyes." THE LAMB who is in the midst of the throne will shepherd them and lead them to living fountains of waters. God and His Son will attend to you.

3. GOD MADE MAN

Genesis 1:26-28 Then God said, "Let Us make man in our image, according to Our likeness; let them have dominion over the fish of the sea, over the birds of the air, and over the cattle, over all the earth and over every creeping thing that creeps on the earth."

So God created man in His own image; in the image of God He created him; male and female He created them. Then God blessed them, and God said to them, "Be fruitful and multiply; fill the earth and subdue it; have dominion over the fish of the sea, over the birds of the air, and over every living thing that moves on the earth."
Genesis 2:7 And the Lord God formed man of the dust of the ground, and breathed into his nostrils the breath of life; and man became a living being.

Genesis 2:21-22 And the Lord God caused a deep sleep to fall on Adam, and he slept; and He took one of his ribs, and closed up the flesh in its place. Then the rib which the Lord God had taken from man He made into a woman, and He brought her to the man.

4. THE EIGHT BEATITUDES OF JESUS

Matthew 5:3-10

Blessed are the poor in spirit, for theirs is the kingdom of heaven.
Blessed are they who mourn, for they shall be comforted.
Blessed are the meek, for they shall inherit the earth.
Blessed are they who hunger and thirst for righteousness, for they shall be satisfied.
Blessed are the merciful, for they shall obtain mercy.
Blessed are the pure of heart, for they shall see God.
Blessed are the peacemakers, for they shall be called children of God.
Blessed are they who are persecuted for the sake of righteousness, for theirs is the kingdom of heaven.

5. 4Ezra.6 (God visits earth)

11] I answered then and said, O Lord that bearest rule, if I have found favour in thy sight,

[12] I beseech thee, shew thy servant the end of thy tokens, whereof thou shewedst me part the last night.

[13] So he answered and said unto me, Stand up upon thy feet, and hear a mighty sounding voice.

[14] And it shall be as it were a great motion; but the place where thou standest shall not be moved.

[15] And therefore when it speaketh be not afraid: for the word is of the end, and the foundation of the earth is understood.

[16] And why? because the speech of these things trembleth and is moved: for it knoweth that the end of these things must be changed.

[17] And it happened, that when I had heard it I stood up upon my feet, and hearkened, and, behold, there was a voice that spake, and the sound of it was like the sound of many waters.

[18] And it said, Behold, the days come, that I will begin to draw nigh, and to visit them that dwell upon the earth,

[19] And will begin to make inquisition of them, what they be that have hurt unjustly with their unrighteousness, and when the affliction of Sion shall be fulfilled;

6. Ezekiel 1 :4-28 Ezekiel's Vision of God

4 Then I looked, and behold, a whirlwind was coming out of the north, a great cloud with raging fire engulfing itself; and brightness was all around it and radiating out of its midst like the color of amber, out of the midst of the fire. 5 Also from within it came the likeness of four living creatures. And this was their appearance: they had the likeness of a man. 6 Each one had four faces, and each one had four wings. 7 Their legs were straight, and the soles of their feet were like the soles of calves' feet. They sparkled like the color of burnished bronze. 8 The hands of a man were under their wings on their four sides; and each of the four had faces and wings. 9 Their wings touched one another. The creatures did not turn when they went, but each one went straight forward.

10 As for the likeness of their faces, each had the face of a man; each of the four had the face of a lion on the right side, each of the four had the face of an ox on the left side, and each of the four had the face of an eagle. 11 Thus were their faces. Their wings stretched upward; two wings of each one touched one another, and two covered their bodies. 12 And each one went straight forward; they went wherever the spirit wanted to go, and they did not turn when they went.

13 As for the likeness of the living creatures, their appearance was like burning coals of fire, like the appearance of torches going back and forth among the living creatures. The fire was bright, and out of the fire went lightning. 14 And the living creatures ran back and forth, in appearance like a flash of lightning.

15 Now as I looked at the living creatures, behold, a wheel was on the earth beside each living creature with its four faces. 16 The appearance of the wheels and their workings was like the color of

beryl, and all four had the same likeness. The appearance of their workings was, as it were, a wheel in the middle of a wheel. 17 When they moved, they went toward any one of four directions; they did not turn aside when they went. 18 As for their rims, they were so high they were awesome; and their rims were full of eyes, all around the four of them. 19 When the living creatures went, the wheels went beside them; and when the living creatures were lifted up from the earth, the wheels were lifted up. 20 Wherever the spirit wanted to go, they went, because there the spirit went; and the wheels were lifted together with them, for the spirit of the living creatures[c] was in the wheels. 21 When those went, these went; when those stood, these stood; and when those were lifted up from the earth, the wheels were lifted up together with them, for the spirit of the living creatures[d] was in the wheels.

22 The likeness of the firmament above the heads of the living creatures[e] was like the color of an awesome crystal, stretched out over their heads. 23 And under the firmament their wings spread out straight, one toward another. Each one had two which covered one side, and each one had two which covered the other side of the body. 24 When they went, I heard the noise of their wings, like the noise of many waters, like the voice of the Almighty, a tumult like the noise of an army; and when they stood still, they let down their wings. 25 A voice came from above the firmament that was over their heads; whenever they stood, they let down their wings.

26 And above the firmament over their heads was the likeness of a throne, in appearance like a sapphire stone; on the likeness of the throne was a likeness with the appearance of a man high above it. 27 Also from the appearance of His waist and upward I saw, as it were, the color of amber with the appearance of fire all around within it; and from the appearance of His waist and downward I saw, as it were, the appearance of fire with brightness all around. 28 Like the appearance of a rainbow in a cloud on a rainy day, so was the appearance of the brightness all around it. This was the appearance of the likeness of the glory of the Lord

7. "EYELIDS OF THE MORNING",

This is the name I have given for the Great Red Dragon's Star Craft. Described by God to Job.

Job 41 New King James Version (NKJV)
"Can you draw out Leviathan[a] with a hook,
Or snare his tongue with a line which you lower?
2 Can you put a reed through his nose,
Or pierce his jaw with a hook?
3 Will he make many supplications to you?
Will he speak softly to you?
4 WILL HE MAKE A COVENANT WITH YOU?
Will you take him as a servant forever?
5 Will you play with him as with a bird,
Or will you leash him for your maidens?
6 Will your companions make a banquet[b] of him?
Will they apportion him among the merchants?
7 Can you fill his skin with harpoons,
Or his head with fishing spears?
8 Lay your hand on him;
REMEMBER THE BATTLE—NEVER DO IT AGAIN!
9 Indeed, any hope of overcoming him is false;
Shall one not be overwhelmed at the sight of him?
10 No one is so fierce that he would dare stir him up.
Who then is able to stand against Me?
11 Who has preceded Me, that I should pay him?
Everything under heaven is Mine.
12 "I will not conceal[c] his limbs,
His mighty power, or his graceful proportions.
13 Who can remove his outer coat?
Who can approach him with a double bridle?
14 WHO CAN OPEN THE DOORS OF HIS FACE, WITH HIS TERRIBLE TEETH ALL AROUND?
15 his rows of scales are his pride,
shut up tightly as with a seal;
16 one is so near another
that no air can come between them;

17 they are joined one to another,
they stick together and cannot be parted.
18 **HIS SNEEZINGS FLASH FORTH LIGHT**,
and his eyes are like the **EYELIDS OF THE MORNING.**
19 **OUT OF HIS MOUTH GO BURNING LIGHTS; SPARKS OF FIRE SHOOT OUT.**
20 smoke goes out of his nostrils,
as from a boiling pot and burning rushes.
21 **HIS BREATH KINDLES COALS**,
and a **FLAME GOES OUT OF HIS MOUTH.**
22 Strength dwells in his neck,
AND SORROW DANCES BEFORE HIM.
23 The folds of his flesh are joined together;
They are firm on him and cannot be moved.
24 His heart is as hard as stone,
Even as hard as the lower millstone.
25 when he raises himself up, the mighty are afraid;
because of his crashings they are beside[d] themselves.
26 though the sword reaches him, it cannot avail;
Nor does spear, dart, or javelin.
27 He regards iron as straw,
And bronze as rotten wood.
28 The arrow cannot make him flee;
Sling stones become like stubble to him.
29 Darts are regarded as straw;
He laughs at the threat of javelins.
30 His undersides are like sharp potsherds;
He spreads pointed marks in the mire.
31 He makes the deep boil like a pot;
HE MAKES THE SEA LIKE A POT OF OINTMENT.
32 **HE LEAVES A SHINING WAKE BEHIND HIM; ONE WOULD THINK THE DEEP HAD WHITE HAIR.**
33 On earth there is nothing like him,
Which is made without fear.
34 He beholds every high thing;
HE IS KING OVER ALL THE CHILDREN OF PRIDE."

8. Revelation 12:3

And another sign appeared in heaven: behold, a great, fiery red dragon having seven heads and ten horns, and seven diadems on his heads.

9. (II Esdras IV 4-9)

the prophet Esdras asked God to tell him more of God's plan and the angel said to him that if he could answer three questions he would be told more. The angel Uriel asked him the following; weight me the weight of fire, measure me the blast of the wind, call me again the day that is past. Esdras responded and said "how is this possible" the angel replied "I asked you but only of the fire, and wind, and of the day wherethrough thou hast passed.

10. THE FIRST RESURRECTION TITLE, TOPIC OR COINED PHRASE?

ANALYSIS Today there are biblical titles, topics, and phrases used in conversation when discussing the contents of the Bible. Two such topics are; "The First Resurrection" and "The Rapture".

Due to the vast amount of available information being communicated via the various media, many people after hearing titles, topics, and phrases, automatically and subconsciously absorb this information as being factual.

This analysis will explore the phrase "The First Resurrection" to determine whether it is a Title, Topic, or Coined Phrase. The NKJV or AKJV Bible will be used for references.

"The First Resurrection" is this an actual Biblical Event or is it a phrase like "The Rapture" which is non-biblical and a coined phrase used to identify the coming of the Son of God?

To begin, when the words "THE FIRST RESURRECTION" were inputted into the following NKJV Bible searchable data base in search of possible biblical references as follows; http://www.biblegateway.com/quicksearch/?quicksearch=%22the+first+resurrection%22&qs_version=NKJV the following results were generated.

GREAT TRIBULATION; MARTYRS

THE FIRST RESURRECTION; This phrase is referenced in the Bible. Revelation 20:4-6 are the verses given for this reference as follows; (4) And I saw thrones, and they sat on them, and judgment was committed to them. Then I saw the souls of those who had been beheaded for their witness to Jesus and for the word of God, who had not worshiped the beast or his image, and had not received his mark on their foreheads or on their hands. And they lived and reigned with Christ for a thousand years.

But the rest of the dead did not live again until the thousand years were finished. This is the first resurrection.

Blessed and holy is he who has part in the first resurrection. Over such the second death has no power, but they shall be priests of God and of Christ, and shall reign with Him a thousand years.

Verse 4: These are the Martyrs who were beheaded for their witness to Jesus rather than worship the beast or his image. These souls will be martyred during a future event that many believe is rapidly approaching and referred to as the "Great Tribulation" time period.

Verse 5: Upon examination of this verse I noticed that the words "This is the first resurrection." were in fact, an independent sentence.

The first two words state; "This is" and when put into context they read: **"THIS IS THE FIRST RESURRECTION"**.

The reader will note that this sentence is also a conclusion statement and follows immediately after mention of the slaughter of the Martyrs. We read,

"THIS IS THE FIRST RESURRECTION"

This statement is found almost at the end of the book of Revelation.

This is a conclusion sentence/statement and indicates there is in fact a biblically referenced end to the events comprising, THE FIRST RESURRECTION. I will refer to this event as its CONCLUSION EVENT.

Since all events have a beginning it is logical to suggest that there should also be a biblically referenced beginning to the events comprising, The First Resurrection. I will refer to this event as its **COMMENCEMENT EVENT.**

The biblical reference for; The First Resurrection COMMENCEMENT EVENT is actually found within these same verses of Revelation 20: 4-5.

The reader will note a cross reference link in Revelation 20: 4 » to Revelation 6:9 identifying another group of Martyrs. http://www.biblegateway.com/passage/?search=Revelation%206:9&version=NKJV

And when He opened the fifth seal, I saw under the altar the souls of those who had been slain for the word of God and for the testimony which they held.

FIFTH SEAL;
THE CRY OF THE MARTYRS Revelation 6: 9-11

The Apostle John saw this earlier and first group of Martyrs who were shown to be under the altar of God who were a unique group of Martyrs. These souls were martyred during the past and were told to rest a little while longer until a future group of Martyrs occur.

This group comprises a vast number of souls as one source identifies possibly 70 million Martyrs have died up to now and as referenced in the article "The New Persecuted" http://www.zenit.org/article-4369?l=english

The 5th Seal depicts possibly the greatest salvation event that takes place prior to the return of the Son of God to take his own unto himself. (The Rapture Event).

During this great event we can establish that "The Son of God Himself" has returned unto this group and carried out the Holy Act of Salvation, as follows;

The Son of God, Martyrs crying out "How long O Lord, holy and true".

The Son of God, has returned to these "under the altar souls".

The Son of God gives to each of them white robes of salvation. This supports the "tarrying aspects" of the Bridegroom and the 10 virgins as it states "each of them" was given these white robes. This process takes time. (see reference # 30)

The Son of God says to them to rest a little longer. (to the group)

The Son of God says, until both the number of their fellow servants and their brethren, who would be killed as they were, was completed.

It is very interesting to note that the Last Group of Martyrs in Revelation 20:4:c link to the First Group of Martyrs in Revelation 6:9. This establishes that The First Group and the Last Group of Martyrs are biblically and directly linked.

The Son of God Himself also links the First Group to the Last Group of Martyrs when he speaks directly to them; until both the number of their fellow servants and their brethren, who would be killed as they were, was completed. Revelation 6 9-11

Revelation 6:11 the FIRST GROUP OF MARTYRS is also Biblically linked to Revelation 7:9 the LAST GROUP OF MARTYRS. A Multitude from the Great Tribulation. After these things I looked, and behold, a great multitude which no one could number, of all nations, tribes, peoples, and tongues, standing before the throne and before the Lamb, clothed with white robes, with palm branches in their hands Revelation 7:13-14 answers the question as to who they are.

13 Then one of the elders answered, saying to me, "Who are these arrayed in white robes, and where did they come from?" 14 And I said to him, "Sir, you know." So he said to me, "These are the ones who come out of the great tribulation, and washed their robes and made them white in the blood of the Lamb.

Due to the linking of the FIRST MARTYRS GROUP to the LAST MARTYRS GROUP, and vice versa, we have now biblically proven that THE FIRST RESURRECTION has both COMMENCEMENT and CONCLUSION EVENTS and that the Martyrs were involved in vast numbers in both events.

The Martyrs of the Son of God constitute the Commencement and Conclusion Events of the First Resurrection. The next question that needs to be answered is what constitutes, THE RAPTURE?

Upon searching the Bible to see if it makes any references pertaining to THE RAPTURE and if so, what does it mean?

When the phrase THE RAPTURE was inputted into the following NKJV Bible searchable data base in search of possible biblical references as follows, http://www.biblegateway.com/quicksearch/?quicksearch=%22the+rapture%22&qs_version=NKJV there are no results,

It appears, THE RAPTURE is a coined phrase not found in the Bible, however it seems to be a fitting term used to describe a single event when the Son of God comes for His Bride on earth and takes them up into the company of their counterparts, His Bride from eternity. Our Lord then takes His "collective Bride" home to God. We will now have to try a topical search as follows; http://topicalbible.org/r/rapture.htm The following TOPICS are generated each dealing with the return of the Son of God; Topicalbible.org—AKJV

For continuity I will also refer to these selected references as THE RAPTURE as follows:

SIXTH SEAL THE RAPTURE occurs during this time. Revelation 7;1-4

7 After these things I saw four angels standing at the four corners of the earth, holding the four winds of the earth, that the wind should not blow on the earth, on the sea, or on any tree. 2 Then I saw another angel ascending from the east, having the seal of the living God. And he cried with a loud voice to the four angels to whom it was granted to harm the earth and the sea, 3 saying, "Do not harm the earth, the sea, or the trees till we have sealed the servants of our God on their foreheads." 4 And I heard the number of those who were sealed. One hundred and forty-four thousand of all the tribes of the children of Israel were sealed:

1 Corinthians 15:52 In a moment, in the twinkling of an eye, at the last trump: for the trumpet shall sound, and the dead shall be raised incorruptible, and we shall be changed.

The preceding verse indicates that THE RAPTURE is an event that happens quickly.

Matthew 24: 27 also supplies information as follows: For as the lightning comes from the east and flashes to the west, so also will the coming of the Son of Man be.

Matthew 25:1-13 Then shall the kingdom of heaven be likened to ten virgins, which took their lamps, and went forth to meet the bridegroom.

These verses supply some background information and indicate that only the wise will succeed. The virgins went two times to meet the Bridegroom. The first time: there was no call from the Bridegroom or his procession to go out. This apparently had the effect as to separate the wise from the foolish since, it states prior to going out, 5 were wise and 5 were foolish. It appears their hearts attitude towards "their calling" was prior evident to the one instructing them to go out.

The second time; at midnight a cry was heard; Behold, the bridegroom is coming; go out to meet him! We now have the call from the Bridegroom's procession to go out and meet him and at the midnight hour only the wise were prepared and went to meet the Bridegroom.

Note the morality of all 10 were not in question as they were referred to as virgins. Their disposition or hearts attitude was flawed with respect to their calling. They had limited faith so when the Bridegroom tarried their faith expired. In verse 5 when we read, "But while the bridegroom was delayed", it tells us that the Bridegroom will be delayed (This delay is when the Son of God goes to His First Group of Martyrs and redeems them (as the dead in Christ will rise first) 1 Thessalonians 4:16-17

1 Thessalonians 4:16-17 For the Lord himself shall descend from heaven with a shout, with the voice of the archangel, and with

the trump of God. And the dead in Christ shall rise first. Then we which are alive and remain shall be caught up together with them in the clouds, to meet the Lord in the air: and so shall we ever be with the Lord.

The preceding verse indicates that THE RAPTURE is an event that happens quickly "with a shout" whereby the Lord takes up the faithful from earth to be forever with him and those in the clouds.

Rev. 12: 4-5 And the dragon stood before the woman who was ready to give birth, to devour her Child as soon as it was born. She bore a male Child who was to rule all nations with a rod of iron. And her Child was caught up to God and His throne.

The preceding verse again indicates that THE RAPTURE is an event that happens quickly, whereby even though Satan wants to devour her Child he fails and her Child was caught up to God and His throne.

With respect to THE RAPTURE, there seems to be an underlining urgency factor when our Lord is instructed by His Father to fetch His Bride from this earth. His Bride is depicted as the Woman giving birth to her child who upon birth is caught up to Our God in Heaven. It is interesting to note at the time of the Rapture, Satan is still at liberty in the heavens awaiting the birth of the Woman's Child and is making or preparing for war against the Son of God and the angels. Perhaps this is the reason for the urgency factor.

From the foregoing information it indicates that the topical phrase, THE RAPTURE, is a SINGULARITY EVENT and appears to consist of one great and unique event. The faithful are in a lightning flash taken up to Our Lord and along with the other faithful and are caught up to Our God in Heaven. The Rapture Event occurs in and during The First Resurrection Events along with other linked events occurring before and after it.

**THE FIRST RESURRECTION
a "PLURALITY"**

of many linked events having a commencement and conclusion

THE RAPTURE
a "SINGULARITY" event
CHRONOLOGICAL ORDER OF THE EVENTS
THE FIRST RESURRECTION COMMENCEMENT EVENT

Revelation 6:9-11

FIFTH SEAL: the Son of God comes for His First Group of Martyrs.

The Son of God goes to these Martyrs and gives them white robes
9 When He opened the fifth seal, I saw under the altar the souls of those who had been slain for the word of God and for the testimony which they held. 10 And they cried with a loud voice, saying, "How long, O Lord, holy and true, until You judge and avenge our blood on those who dwell on the earth?" 11 Then a white robe was given to each of them; and it was said to them that they should rest a little while longer, until both the number of their fellow servants and their brethren, who would be killed as they were, was completed.

THE RAPTURE
SINGULARITY EVENT

1 Corinthians 15:52

SIXTH SEAL: the Son of God comes for His Bride.

1 Thessalonians 4:16-17 For the Lord himself shall descend from heaven with a shout, with the voice of the archangel, and with the trump of God. And the dead in Christ shall rise first. Then we which are alive and remain shall be caught up together with them in the clouds, to meet the Lord in the air: and so shall we ever be with the Lord.

Revelation 7;1-4 After these things I saw four angels standing at the four corners of the earth, holding the four winds of the earth, that the wind should not blow on the earth, on the sea, or on any tree. 2 Then I saw another angel ascending from the east, having the seal of the living God. And he cried with a loud voice to the four angels to whom it was granted to harm the earth and the sea, 3 saying,

"Do not harm the earth, the sea, or the trees till we have sealed the servants of our God on their foreheads." 4 And I heard the number of those who were sealed. One hundred and forty-four thousand of all the tribes of the children of Israel were sealed:

THE FIRST RESURRECTION CONCLUSION EVENT

Revelation 20:4-6

SEVENTH SEAL: the Son of God comes for His Last Group of Martyrs.

And I saw thrones, and they sat on them, and judgment was committed to them. Then I saw the souls of those who had been beheaded for their witness to Jesus and for the word of God, who had not worshiped the beast or his image, and had not received his mark on their foreheads or on their hands. And they lived and reigned with Christ for a thousand years. But the rest of the dead did not live again until the thousand years were finished.

This is the first resurrection.

Revelation 7: 9 A Multitude from the Great Tribulation. After these things I looked, and behold, a great multitude which no one could number, of all nations, tribes, peoples, and tongues, standing before the throne and before the Lamb, clothed with white robes, with palm branches in their hands Revelation 7: 13-14 answers as to who they are.13 Then one of the elders answered, saying to me, "Who are these arrayed in white robes, and where did they come from?" 14 And I said to him, "Sir,[a] you know." So he said to me, "These are the ones who come out of the great tribulation, and washed their robes and made them white in the blood of the Lamb.

SIMPLISTIC COMPARATIVE ANALYSIS: CONCLUSION

THE FIRST RESURRECTION: BIBLICAL PHRASE

EVENT: PLURALITY: Consists of many linked events

FIFTH SEAL: Martyrs Salvation Event

BIBLICAL REFERENCE: Revelation 6:9-11

COMMENCEMENT EVENT: Group # 1 THE CRY OF THE MARTYRS

"AND THE DEAD IN CHRIST SHALL RISE FIRST"

The Son of God returned to the "under the altar souls and gave them the white garments of salvation, the First Resurrection Commenced.

COMMENCEMENT DATE: 1960 Fatima #3 prophecy.
THE RAPTURE: NON BIBLICAL COINED EXPRESSION

EVENT: SINGULARITY: One Time Event

SIXTH SEAL: Lord comes for His Bride

BIBLICAL REFERENCE: 1 Thessalonians 4:16-17

COMMENCEMENT EVENT: During "The First Resurrection" the Faithful are taken up to god in heaven. For the Lord himself shall descend from heaven with a shout, with the voice of the archangel, and with the trump of God and we which are alive and remain shall be caught up.

COMMENCEMENT DATE: So you also, when you see all these things, know that it is near—at the doors! Matthew 24;34 The Son of God is referring to "this generation"

THE FIRST RESURRECTION: BIBLICAL PHRASE

EVENT: Last of the First Resurrection Linked Events

SEVENTH SEAL: Martyrs Salvation Event during the Great Tribulation.

BIBLICAL REFERENCE: Revelation 20:4-6   CONCLUSION EVENT: Group #2 Martyrs. "This is the

First Resurrection"

CONCLUSION DATE: Mathew 24;34 Assuredly, I say to you, this generation will by no means pass away till all these things take place. This date happens a little more than 3½ years following the

Rapture. They shall be priests of God and of Christ, and shall reign with Him a thousand years

ONE FINAL QUESTION: COMMENCEMENT DATE of THE FIRST RESURRECTION: Does the Bible supply evidence as to the COMMENCEMENT DATE of THE FIRST RESURRECTION? Matthew24

http://www.biblegateway.com/passage/?search=Matthew%20 24&version=NKJV

The heading at the top of the page states: The Great Tribulation. Our lord gives many references concerning future events along with time indicators concerning the end.

The Signs of the Times and the End of the Age as spoken of by Jesus

About 10 Signs comprise:
All these are the beginning of sorrows

About 10 Signs comprise:
And then the end will come

About 10 Signs comprise:
The Coming of the Son of Man

About 5 Signs comprise:
The Parable of the Fig Tree.

The Parable of the Fig Tree.

This indicates that once the cycle starts the next event happens quickly, with respect to the fig tree not more that say 60 days. (In April and May the fig leaves develop and the fruit reaches maturity about June)

So you also, when you see all these things, know that it is near—at the doors! Matthew 24;34 Assuredly, I say to you, this generation will by no means pass away till all these things take place. Jesus is describing the events leading up to and including the "Great Tribulation" time period.

What is the definition of the word "GENERATION"? Reference: Encarta Dictionary, English (North America) "All of the people who were born at approximately the same time, considered as a group, and especially when considered as having shared interests and attitude".

With respect to a time factor, Jesus is saying that this generation will not pass away.

Here we have a reference to the generation that experience "all these things"

We do not have to assign a specific number of years for "this generation" as it means a group of people who were born at approximately the same time and having shared interests and attitude. It is sufficed to say that within this generation's life time "all these things" happen as follows;

THE FIRST RESURRECTION COMMENCEMENT EVENT: FATIMA PROPHECIES; 1960

THE RAPTURE: EXPECTED DATE; ASAP

THE GREAT TRIBULATION TIME PERIOD OF 7 YEARS

THE FIRST RESURRECTION CONCLUSION EVENT: 3½ YEARS FOLLOWING the RAPTURE.

Since the Last Group of Martyrs are connected to the First Group of Martyrs and since the Last Group of Martyrs comprise the Conclusion Event of the First Resurrection; then the First Group of Martyrs comprises the Commencement Event of the First Resurrection.

It has been established that "this generation" has lived through the commencement event of the first resurrection. In order to identify the commencement date of the first resurrection we must investigate what unique spiritual events occurred during these past recent years that would support this theory.

"This generation", as referenced by the Son of God, are currently alive on earth. During their time there has been at least one religious prophecy that has fulfilled the necessary prerequisites to indicate commencement as follows.(Note: While reviewing topics such as "Prophecies, Supernatural events Religious Predictions such as the Return of Christ and the First Resurrection data, a comprehensive search was not performed as this was not the focus of the analysis)

The FATIMA PROPHECIES upon entering the; THE FATIMA PROPHECIES into the "GOOGLE" search engine, about 1,170,000 results were displayed which indicates a very substantial amount of interest in these prophecies. http://paranormal.about.com/od/marianapparitions/a/fatimaprophecies_2.htm

1960 WAS THE YEAR designated for the third and final prophecy to be revealed. Well, **1960** came and went, and the third prophecy was not revealed because the Vatican said the world was not quite ready for it. This reluctance to disclose the secret lead to speculation among the faithful that it contained information about our future that was so horrific that the false prophet dared not reveal it. Perhaps it foretold a nuclear war... or the end of the world.

Upon reviewing the foregoing author's commentary and with hindsight being 20/20, my thoughts were that since there was no nuclear war...nor end of the world; then the contents of this prophecy must have portrayed something else equally as disturbing.

What if the prophecy slated to be introduced to the Christian World in **1960** indicated the occurrence of a most spectacular event, the commencement of **THE FIRST RESURRECTION "MARTYR COMMENCEMENT EVENT"** and if so, how would the Vatican then contend with such a message that didn't include them? If this is the case, then the vision's true contents pertaining to the third and final prophecy that was sealed and not to be opened and proclaimed to the Christian World until **1960** still remains a closely guarded secret kept within the Vatican vault.

11. CRY OF THE MARTYRS; Revelation 6:9–11

When He opened the fifth seal, I saw under the altar the souls of those who had been slain for the word of God and for the testimony which they held. And they cried with a loud voice, saying, "How long, O Lord, holy and true, until You judge and avenge our blood on those who dwell on the earth?" Then a white robe was given to each of them; and it was said to them that they should rest a little while longer, <u>until both</u> the <u>number of their fellow servants</u> and <u>their brethren, who would be killed as they were, was completed.</u>

12. THE MULTITUDE FROM THE GREAT TRIBULATION. Revelation 7:9-17

Here we have seemly millions of people consisting of all peoples of the earth clothed with white robes and with palm branches in their hands. When the Apostle John asked where did they come from he was told from the Great Tribulation. He was also informed that they will serve God in His Temple. A great multitude which no one could number, of all nations, tribes, peoples, and tongues, standing before the throne and before the Lamb, clothed with white robes, with palm branches in their hands. Then one of the elders answered, saying to me, "Who are these arrayed in white robes, and where did they come from?" "These are the ones who come out of the great tribulation, and washed their robes and made them white in the blood of the Lamb. Therefore they are before the throne of God, and serve Him day and night in His temple. And He who sits on the throne will dwell among them. They shall neither hunger anymore nor thirst anymore; the sun shall not strike them, nor any heat; for the Lamb who is in the midst of the throne will shepherd them and lead them to living fountains of waters. And God will wipe away every tear from their eyes.

13. AND I SAW THRONES, and they sat on them, and judgment was committed to them.

In Revelation 20: 4-6 it also says:
Then I saw the souls of those who had been beheaded for their witness to Jesus and for the word of God, who had not worshiped the

beast or his image, and had not received his mark on their foreheads or on their hands. And they lived and reigned with Christ for a thousand years.

But the rest of the dead did not live again until the thousand years were finished.

This is the first resurrection. Blessed and holy is he who has part in the first resurrection. Over such the second death has no power, but they shall be priests of God and of Christ, and shall reign with Him a thousand years.

14. Revelation 22: 11, it says:

He who is unjust, let him be unjust still; he who is filthy, let him be filthy still; he who is righteous, let him be righteous still; he who is holy, let him be holy still."

15. And do not grieve the Holy Spirit of God, by whom you were sealed. Do not to harm the earth, the sea, or the trees till we have sealed the servants of our God on their foreheads."

16. HOLY SEALING IN THE BIBLE

Ephesians 1:13 it reads: In Him you also trusted, after you heard the word of truth, the gospel of your salvation; in whom also, having believed, you were sealed with the Holy Spirit of promise. Ephesians 4:30 it says: And do not grieve the Holy Spirit of God, by whom you were sealed for the day of redemption"2 Corinthians 1:21-22 it further says Now He who establishes us with you in Christ and has anointed us is God, who also has sealed us and given us the Spirit in our hearts as a guarantee. 2 Corinthians 1:21-22 it further says Now He who establishes us with you in Christ and has anointed us is God, who also has sealed us and given us the Spirit in our hearts as a guarantee. Revelations 7:3" Tom said, "it says quite clearly: Do not harm the earth, the sea, or the trees till we have sealed the servants of our God on their foreheads." Acts 19 in verses 1-6 it reads: The Apostle Paul while in Ephesus came to some disciples there and said to them. "Did you receive the Holy Spirit when you believed?" They responded saying; we have not so much as heard whether there is a Holy Spirit. And the Apostle said to them, "Into what then were you baptized?" So they said, "Into John's baptism." Then the Apostle Paul said, "John indeed baptized with a "Baptism of Repentance", and then instructed the people that they should believe on Him who would come after him, that is, on Christ Jesus. When they heard this, they were baptized in the name of the Lord Jesus. AND WHEN THE APOSTLE PAUL HAD LAID HANDS ON THEM, THE HOLY SPIRIT CAME UPON THEM."

17. JESUS SEALED HIS APOSTLES

John 19:23 it says:

Then, the same day at evening, being the first day of the week, when the doors were shut where the disciples were assembled, for fear of the Jews, Jesus came and stood in the midst, and said to them, "Peace be with you." When He had said this, He showed them His hands and His side. Then the disciples were glad when they saw the Lord. So Jesus said to them again, "Peace to you! As the Father has sent Me, I also send you." And when He had said this, He breathed on them, and said to them, "Receive the Holy Spirit. If you forgive the sins of any, they are forgiven them; if you retain the sins of any, they are retained."

18. JOHN TRULY BAPTIZED WITH WATER, BUT YOU SHALL BE BAPTIZED WITH THE HOLY SPIRIT

not many days from now." But you shall receive power when the Holy Spirit has come upon you; and you shall be witnesses to Me in Jerusalem, and in all Judea and Samaria, and to the end of the earth." Acts 1:4-8 Here it tells us: for

19. THE SON OF GOD WAS TAKEN UP INTO A CLOUD AS THEY WATCHED

Now when He had spoken these things, while they watched, He was taken up, and a cloud received Him out of their sight. And while they looked steadfastly toward heaven as He went up, behold, two men stood by them in white apparel, who also said, "Men of

Galilee, why do you stand gazing up into heaven? This same Jesus, who was taken up from you into heaven, will so come in like manner as you saw Him go into heaven." Acts 1 in verses 9-11 and read excerpts from verses.

20. ONE HUNDRED AND FORTY-FOUR THOUSAND.

Revelation 7:1..4 After these things I saw four angels standing at the four corners of the earth, holding the four winds of the earth, that the wind should not blow on the earth, on the sea, or on any tree. Then I saw another angel ascending from the east, having the seal of the living God. And he cried with a loud voice to the four angels to whom it was granted to harm the earth and the sea, saying, "Do not harm the earth, the sea, or the trees till we have sealed the servants of our God on their foreheads." And I heard the number of those who were sealed. One hundred and forty-four thousand..

21. THE WOMEN CLOTHED WITH THE SUN

Revelation 12

12 Now a great sign appeared in heaven: a woman clothed with the sun, with the moon under her feet, and on her head a garland of twelve stars. 2 Then being with child, she cried out in labor and in pain to give birth.

3 And another sign appeared in heaven: behold, a great, fiery red dragon having seven heads and ten horns, and seven diadems on his heads. 4 His tail drew a third of the stars of heaven and threw them to the earth. And the dragon stood before the woman who was ready to give birth, to devour her Child as soon as it was born. 5 She bore a male Child who was to rule all nations with a rod of iron. And her Child was caught up to God and His throne. 6 Then the woman fled into the wilderness, where she has a place prepared by God, that they should feed her there one thousand two hundred and sixty days.

SATAN THROWN OUT OF HEAVEN

7 And war broke out in heaven: Michael and his angels fought with the dragon; and the dragon and his angels fought, 8 but they did

not prevail, nor was a place found for them[a] in heaven any longer. 9 So the great dragon was cast out, that serpent of old, called the Devil and Satan, who deceives the whole world; he was cast to the earth, and his angels were cast out with him.

10 Then I heard a loud voice saying in heaven, "Now salvation, and strength, and the kingdom of our God, and the power of His Christ have come, for the accuser of our brethren, who accused them before our God day and night, has been cast down. 11 And they overcame him by the blood of the Lamb and by the word of their testimony, and they did not love their lives to the death. 12 Therefore rejoice, O heavens, and you who dwell in them! Woe to the inhabitants of the earth and the sea! For the devil has come down to you, having great wrath, because he knows that he has a short time."

THE WOMAN PERSECUTED

13 Now when the dragon saw that he had been cast to the earth, he persecuted the woman who gave birth to the male *Child.* 14 But the woman was given two wings of a great eagle, that she might fly into the wilderness to her place, where she is nourished for a time and times and half a time, from the presence of the serpent. 15 So the serpent spewed water out of his mouth like a flood after the woman, that he might cause her to be carried away by the flood. 16 But the earth helped the woman, and the earth opened its mouth and swallowed up the flood which the dragon had spewed out of his mouth. 17 And the dragon was enraged with the woman, and he went to make war with the rest of her offspring, who keep the commandments of God and have the testimony of Jesus Christ.[b]

22. MARY, MARY, MARY

The first time we read of Mary John 8(NKJV)

But Jesus went to the Mount of Olives.

Now early in the morning He came again into the temple, and all the people came to Him; and He sat down and taught them. Then the scribes and Pharisees brought to Him a woman caught in adultery. And when they had set her in the midst, they said to Him,

"Teacher, this woman was caught in adultery, in the very act. Now Moses, in the law, commanded us that such should be stoned. But what do You say?" This they said, testing Him, that they might have something of which to accuse Him. But Jesus stooped down and wrote on the ground with His finger, as though He did not hear.

So when they continued asking Him, He raised Himself up and said to them, "He who is without sin among you, let him throw a stone at her first." And again He stooped down and wrote on the ground. Then those who heard it, being convicted by their conscience, went out one by one, beginning with the oldest even to the last. And Jesus was left alone, and the woman standing in the midst. When Jesus had raised Himself up and saw no one but the woman, He said to her, "Woman, where are those accusers of yours? Has no one condemned you?"

She said, "No one, Lord. "And Jesus said to her, "Neither do I condemn you; go and[k] sin no more."

THE SECOND TIME WE READ OF MARY

Luke 7: 36-50

A Sinful Woman Forgiven

Then one of the Pharisees asked Him to eat with him. And He went to the Pharisee's house, and sat down to eat. And behold, a woman in the city who was a sinner, when she knew that *Jesus* sat at the table in the Pharisee's house, brought an alabaster flask of fragrant oil, and stood at His feet behind *Him* weeping; and she began to wash His feet with her tears, and wiped *them* with the hair of her head; and she kissed His feet and anointed *them* with the fragrant oil. Now when the Pharisee who had invited Him saw *this*, he spoke to himself, saying, "This Man, if He were a prophet, would know who and what manner of woman *this is* who is touching Him, for she is a sinner." And Jesus answered and said to him, "Simon, I have something to say to you." So he said, "Teacher, say it." "There was a certain creditor who had two debtors. One owed five hundred denarii, and the other fifty. 42 And when they had nothing with which to repay, he freely forgave them both. Tell Me, therefore, which of them will love him more?" Simon answered and said, "I suppose the *one* whom he forgave more."

And He said to him, "You have rightly judged." Then He turned to the woman and said to Simon, "Do you see this woman? I entered your house; you gave Me no water for My feet, but she has washed My feet with her tears and wiped *them* with the hair of her head. You gave Me no kiss, but this woman has not ceased to kiss My feet since the time I came in. You did not anoint My head with oil, but this woman has anointed My feet with fragrant oil. 47 Therefore I say to you, her sins, which *are* many, are forgiven, for she loved much. But to whom little is forgiven, *the same* loves little."

Then He said to her, "Your sins are forgiven." And those who sat at the table with Him began to say to themselves, "Who is this who even forgives sins?" Then He said to the woman, "Your faith has saved you. Go in peace."

ALABASTER flask
Fragrant oil
Very Cost oil
Weeping
Washed Jesus feet with tears
Wiped Jesus feet with her tears and hair
Kissed Jesus feet
Anointed Jesus feet with this aromatic medicinal oil
Followed Jesus thru every city (Luke 8: 1-2)

THE THIRD TIME WE READ OF MARY

Only days prior to the Passover

The Anointing at Bethany, situated on the east slope on the Mount of Olives.

Matthew 26 6-13

And when Jesus was in Bethany at the house of Simon the leper, a woman came to Him having an alabaster flask of very costly fragrant oil, and she poured *it* on His head as He sat *at the table*. But when His disciples saw *it*, they were indignant, saying, "Why this waste? For this fragrant oil might have been sold for much and given to *the* poor." But when Jesus was aware of *it,* He said to them, "Why do you trouble the woman? For she has done a good work for Me. For you have the poor with you always, but Me you do not have always. For in pouring this fragrant oil on My body, she did *it* for My burial. Assuredly, I say to you, wherever this gospel is preached in the whole world, what this woman has done will also be told as a memorial to her."

ALABASTER flask, fragrant, oilvery, costly, she poured *it* on His head. Tom began to fit the puzzle pieces together and said, to take note:

Mary #1 She is the sinner that was to be stoned to death as the adulterous who Jesus spared and said; sin no more.

Mary #2 In the Pharisees' house she is referred to as the sinner that Jesus spared. The following are the highlights of Mary as follows;
ALABASTER FLASK (white hollow stone flask)
Fragrant oil (Spikenard medicinal oil ointment)
Very Cost oil (one flask worth one year's wages)
Weeping
Washed Jesus feet with tears
Wiped Jesus feet with her tears and hair
Kissed Jesus feet
Anointed Jesus feet with this aromatic medicinal oil

Mary #3 Sister is Martha, Brother is Lazarus and lives in Bethany and having and doing as follows:
ALABASTER FLASK (white hollow stone flask)
Fragrant oil (Spikenard medicinal oil ointment)
Very costly oil (flask containing one pound worth, this one equals one year's wages)
Anointed Jesus HEAD with this aromatic medicinal oil

This is the same Mary that when Jesus visited their home for the first time sits at his feet.

When Jesus hears that Lazarus is sick, the brother of Mary and Martha went to them. While he was a little ways out Martha went out and spoke only "words" to Jesus and then returned and said secretly to Mary Jesus is calling for you. Mary rushed to Jesus and "fell at his feet" and "weepingly said" Lord if you had been here my brother would not have died.

Jesus groaned in the spirit and troubled Jesus wept, he loved Lazarus. Jesus groaning went to the tomb and called for Lazarus to come out, he did. Mary in a act of rare devotion, gratitude and honor "STAYED" behind after the Apostles went home from the tomb, John 20:11-18 Mary (Magdalene) Sees the Risen Lord. But Mary stood outside by the tomb weeping, and as she wept she stooped down *and looked* into the tomb. And she saw two angels in white sitting, one at the head and the other at the feet, where the body of Jesus had lain. Then they said to her, "Woman, why are you weeping?" She said to them, "Because they have taken away my Lord, and I do not know where they have laid Him." Now when she had said this, she turned around and saw Jesus standing *there,* and did not know that it was Jesus. Jesus said to her, "Woman, why are you weeping? Whom are you seeking?" She, supposing Him to be the gardener, said to Him, "Sir, if You have carried Him away, tell me where You have laid Him, and I will take Him away."

Jesus said to her, "Mary!"

She turned and said to Him, "Rabboni!" (which is to say, Teacher).

Jesus said to her, "Do not cling to Me, for I have not yet ascended to My Father; but go to My brethren and say to them, 'I am ascending to My Father and your Father, and *to* My God and your God.'" Mary Magdalene came and told the disciples that she had seen the Lord, and *that* He had spoken these things to her.

John 11; Now a certain *man* was sick, Lazarus of Bethany, the town of Mary and her sister Martha. It was *that* Mary who anointed the Lord with fragrant oil and wiped His feet with her hair, whose brother Lazarus was sick. Therefore the sisters sent to Him, saying, "Lord, behold, he whom You love is sick."

Mary #1 loves her brother so much she was sinful in order to raise money to purchase a very cost aromatic oil known as Spikenard.

Spikenard? Was an expensive spice used to make perfume and had antibiotic properties. It was obtained from an Indian plant, found in the Himalaya Mountains, the *Nardostachys jatamansi*. <u>Tom said it was used on leprous wounds.</u>

So there you have it, the 3 Mary's are the same. Mary did what she thought she had to do to get money to purchase this very expensive spikenard antibiotic healing oil used in the treatment for leprosy for her brother Lazarus.

23. THE RED SEA CROSSING

Now the Lord spoke to Moses, saying: 2 "Speak to the children of Israel, that they turn and camp before Pi Hahiroth, between Migdol and the sea, opposite Baal Zephon; you shall camp before it by the sea. 3 For Pharaoh will say of the children of Israel, 'They *are* bewildered by the land; the wilderness has closed them in.' 4 Then I will harden Pharaoh's heart, so that he will pursue them; and I will gain honor over Pharaoh and over all his army, that the Egyptians may know that I *am* the Lord." And they did so.5 Now it was told the king of Egypt that the people had fled, and the heart of Pharaoh and his servants was turned against the people; and they said, "Why have we done this, that we have let Israel go from serving us?" 6 So he made ready his chariot and took his people with him. 7 Also, he took six hundred choice chariots, and all the chariots of Egypt with captains over every one of them.8 And the Lord hardened the heart of Pharaoh king of Egypt, and he pursued the children of Israel; and the children of Israel went out with boldness. 9 So the Egyptians pursued them, all the horses *and* chariots of Pharaoh, his horsemen and his army, and overtook them camping by the sea beside Pi Hahiroth, before Baal Zephon.

10 And when Pharaoh drew near, the children of Israel lifted their eyes, and behold, the Egyptians marched after them. So they were very afraid, and the children of Israel cried out to the Lord. 11 Then they said to Moses, "Because *there were* no graves in Egypt, have you taken us away to die in the wilderness? Why have you so dealt with us, to bring us up out of Egypt? 12 *Is* this not the word that we told

you in Egypt, saying, 'Let us alone that we may serve the Egyptians'? For *it would have been* better for us to serve the Egyptians than that we should die in the wilderness." 13 And Moses said to the people, "Do not be afraid. Stand still, and see the salvation of the Lord, which He will accomplish for you today. For the Egyptians whom you see today, you shall see again no more forever. 14 The Lord will fight for you, and you shall hold your peace."

15 And the Lord said to Moses, "Why do you cry to Me? Tell the children of Israel to go forward. 16 But lift up your rod, and stretch out your hand over the sea and divide it. And the children of Israel shall go on dry *ground* through the midst of the sea. 17 And I indeed will harden the hearts of the Egyptians, and they shall follow them. So I will gain honor over Pharaoh and over all his army, his chariots, and his horsemen. 18 Then the Egyptians shall know that I *am* the Lord, when I have gained honor for Myself over Pharaoh, his chariots, and his horsemen." 19 And the Angel of God, who went before the camp of Israel, moved and went behind them; and the pillar of cloud went from before them and stood behind them. 20 So it came between the camp of the Egyptians and the camp of Israel. Thus it was a cloud and darkness *to the one,* and it gave light by night *to the other,* so that the one did not come near the other all that night. 21 Then Moses stretched out his hand over the sea; and the Lord caused the sea to go *back* by a strong east wind all that night, and made the sea into dry *land,* and the waters were divided. 22 So the children of Israel went into the midst of the sea on the dry *ground,* and the waters *were* a wall to them on their right hand and on their left. 23 And the Egyptians pursued and went after them into the midst of the sea, all Pharaoh's horses, his chariots, and his horsemen. 24 Now it came to pass, in the morning watch, that the Lord looked down upon the army of the Egyptians through the pillar of fire and cloud, and He troubled the army of the Egyptians. 25 And He took off[a] their chariot wheels, so that they drove them with difficulty; and the Egyptians said, "Let us flee from the face of Israel, for the Lord fights for them against the Egyptians."

26 Then the Lord said to Moses, "Stretch out your hand over the sea, that the waters may come back upon the Egyptians, on their

chariots, and on their horsemen." 27 And Moses stretched out his hand over the sea; and when the morning appeared, the sea returned to its full depth, while the Egyptians were fleeing into it. So the Lord overthrew the Egyptians in the midst of the sea. 28 Then the waters returned and covered the chariots, the horsemen, *and* all the army of Pharaoh that came into the sea after them. Not so much as one of them remained. 29 But the children of Israel had walked on dry *land* in the midst of the sea, and the waters *were* a wall to them on their right hand and on their left.

30 So the Lord saved Israel that day out of the hand of the Egyptians, and Israel saw the Egyptians dead on the seashore. 31 Thus Israel saw the great work which the Lord had done in Egypt; so the people feared the Lord, and believed the Lord and His servant Moses.

24. ISRAELITES CROSSING PILLARS

on each side of the Gulf of Aqaba.

The Crossing site of the children of Israel is across the middle of the Gulf of Aqaba and on each side there are large stone columns with writing depicting this great event. On the one side is the city of Nuweiba (waters of Moses opening). Chariot parts and bones of humans and horses have been found. Isaiah 19 New King James Version (NKJV)

19 In that day there will be an altar to the Lord in the midst of the land of Egypt, and a pillar to the Lord at its border.

Exodus 14 (NKJV)

25. AND I SAW A BEAST RISING UP OUT OF THE SEA

APOSTLE JOHN WRITES in Revelation 13:1-10(NKJV)

Then I stood on the sand of the sea. And I saw a beast rising up out of the sea, having seven heads and ten horns, and on his horns ten crowns, and on his heads a blasphemous name. now the beast which I saw was like a leopard, his feet were like the feet of a bear, and his mouth like the mouth of a lion. The dragon gave him his power, his throne, and great authority. And I saw one of his heads as if it had been mortally wounded, and his deadly wound was healed. And all the world marveled and followed the beast. So they worshiped the dragon who gave authority to the beast; and they worshiped the beast, saying, "Who is like the beast? Who is able to make war with him?" And he was given a mouth speaking great things and blasphemies, and he was given authority to continue for forty-two months. Then he opened his mouth in blasphemy against God, to blaspheme His name, His tabernacle, and those who dwell in heaven. It was granted to him to make war with the saints and to overcome them. And authority was given him over every tribe, tongue, and nation. All who dwell on the earth will worship him, whose names have not been written in the Book of Life of the Lamb slain from the foundation of the world. If anyone has an ear, let him hear. He who leads into captivity shall go into captivity; he who kills with the sword must be killed with the sword. Here is the patience and the faith of the saints.

26. WWW.LEO.GOV

When I first accessed the FBI website about a year ago, their logo consisted of series of circles having a lion in the center along with the name LEO beside it. Their crest consisted of the colors, RED-YELLOW-BLUE, which are the colors of the dragon in my book. Included within their crest for the Federal Bureau of Investigation were the words 'Law Enforcement online'. From anywhere or anyplace they can tell who you are and where you live in the world. My publisher, requested that I get permission from them to show their logos. This I could not do since I am referring to them as the evil antichrist, and I don't think they would be in the mood to grant me a favor.

Now, in the year 2014 when I accessed their site, the crest displayed has changed and is now BLUE. I could not enter the site without an access code. Seems like someone didn't want the public to see their former colors, Red, Yellow and Blue, colors of the dragon, the armed forces of the beast.

WARNING! You are accessing a U.S. Government information system, which includes this computer, this computer network, all computers connected to this network, and all devices and/or storage media attached to this network or to a computer on this network. This information system is provided for U.S. Government-authorized use only.

WHAT IS LEO?

Law Enforcement Online (LEO) is a state-of-the-art Internet system that is accredited and approved by the FBI for sensitive but unclassified information. LEO is used to support investigative operations, send notifications and alerts, and provide an avenue to remotely access other law enforcement and intelligence systems and resources. LEO provides all levels of the law enforcement, criminal justice, and public safety communities virtual private network access to its "anytime and anywhere" system for secure electronic communications, online training, and information sharing.

LEO CAPABILITIES:

Virtual Command Center (VCC):
Provides an Internet based real-time tool that allows a LEO member to monitor the many moving parts of a complex event in a secure environment.

Law Enforcement Online Special Interest Groups (LEOSIG's):
Multi-level access areas for members to participate in communities of specialized interests to securely share information, database resources, applications, specialized training, and access to other partnering networks.

National Alert System (NAS):
The National Alert System provides a priority mechanism to notify homeland security and law Enforcement partners through their existing command, control channels, and wireless notifications to key management officials.

27. THEN I SAW ANOTHER BEAST COMING UP OUT OF THE EARTH, Apostle John wrote.

Revelation 13:11-18 as follows; and he had two horns like a lamb and spoke like a dragon. And he exercises all the authority of the first beast in his presence, and causes the earth and those who dwell in it to worship the first beast, whose deadly wound was healed. He performs great signs, so that he even makes fire come down from heaven on the earth in the sight of men. And he deceives those who dwell on the earth by those signs which he was granted to do in the sight of the beast, telling those who dwell on the earth to make an image to the beast who was wounded by the sword and lived. He was granted power to give breath to the image of the beast, that the image of the beast should both speak and cause as many as would not worship the image of the beast to be killed. He causes all, both small and great, rich and poor, free and slave, to receive a mark on their right hand or on their foreheads, and that no one may buy or sell except one who has the mark of the beast or the name of the beast, or the number of his name. Here is wisdom. Let him who has understanding calculate the number of the beast, for it is the number of a man it is, SIX HUNDRED AND SIXTY SIX.

28. Prophet Daniel wrote:

Daniel 7:21-22

As I watched, this horn was waging war against the saints and defeating them, until the Ancient of Days came and pronounced judgment in favor of the saints of the Most High, and the time came when they possessed the kingdom.

Tom said; this little horn is the Tierra worn by the Global Religious Icon.

Prophet Daniel wrote:

Daniel 7:25

<u>He shall speak pompous words</u> against the Most High, Shall <u>persecute the saints</u> of the Most High, <u>And shall intend to change times</u>

and law. Then the saints shall be given into his <u>hand for a time and times and half a time.</u>

Tom says; this also means; 1260 days or 42 months Toms said; this again shows that the beast blasphemes God, tries to change perhaps supernatural and natural happenings and he is given 1260 days.

Prophet Daniel wrote;

Daniel 8:9

<u>And out of one of them came a little horn</u> which grew exceedingly great toward the south, toward the east, and toward the Glorious Land.

Tom said this is the beginning of BABYLON THE GREAT, it will expand and encompass all the lands from Rome to Jerusalem. The nations of the 10 kings will establish their command centers in this "central zone" area that grow into cities.

Prophet Daniel writes

Daniel 8: 11-14

This beast even exalted himself as high as the Prince of the host; and by him <u>the daily sacrifices were taken away</u>, and <u>the place of His sanctuary was cast down.</u> Because of transgression, <u>an army was given over to the horn (false prophet) to oppose the daily sacrifices;</u> and he cast truth down to the ground. He did all this and prospered.

Tom said; this beast proclaims himself as great as those in Heaven and his seat of power his sanctuary was also cast down to earth and because of the evil upon earth he was able together a great army.

Prophet Daniel writes

Daniel 11:31,

And forces shall be mustered by him, and they shall defile the sanctuary fortress; <u>then they shall take away the daily sacrifices, and place there the abomination of desolation.</u>

29. RISE OF THE FALSE MESSIAH

The Apostle John writes;

Revelation 12:3-4

And another sign appeared in heaven: behold, a great, fiery red dragon having seven heads and ten horns, and seven diadems on his heads. His tail drew a third of the stars of heaven and threw them to the earth. And the dragon stood before the woman who was ready to give birth, to devour her Child as soon as it was born.

Revelation 12:7-9

And war broke out in heaven: Michael and his angels fought with the dragon; and the dragon and his angels fought, but they did not prevail, nor was a place found for them in heaven any longer. So the great dragon was cast out, that serpent of old, called the devil and Satan, who deceives the whole world; he was cast to the earth, and his angels were cast out with him.

Daniel 7:7

Fourth Beast

After this I saw in the night visions, and behold, a fourth beast, dreadful and terrible, exceedingly strong. It had huge iron teeth; it was devouring, breaking in pieces, and trampling the residue with its feet. It was different from all the beasts that were before it, and it had ten horns. is rouse.

Daniel 7:19-23

Then I wished to know the truth about the fourth beast, which was different from all the others, exceedingly dreadful, with its teeth of iron and its nails of bronze, which devoured, broke in pieces, and trampled the residue with its feet; and the ten horns that were on its head, and the other horn which came up, before which three fell, namely, that horn which had eyes and a mouth which spoke pompous words, whose appearance was greater than his fellows. "I was watching; and the same horn was making war against the saints, and prevailing against them, "Thus he said: 'The fourth beast shall be a fourth kingdom on earth, Which shall be different from all other kingdoms, And shall devour the whole earth, Trample it and break it in pieces.

Daniel 7: 24-25

<u>The ten horns are ten kings</u> Who shall arise from this kingdom. And another shall rise after them; He shall be different from the first ones, And shall subdue three kings. He shall speak pompous words against the Most High, Shall persecute the saints of the Most High, And shall intend to change times and law. Then the saints shall be given into his hand For a time and times and half a time. 1-1260 T/D

Daniel: 9:27

<u>In the middle of the week</u> 1260 T/D Tom said He shall bring an end to sacrifice and offering.

30. PROPHET EZEKIEL WRITES

Ezekiel 37:26-28

Moreover I will make a covenant of peace with them, and it shall be an everlasting covenant with them; I will establish them and multiply them, and I will set My sanctuary in their midst forevermore. My tabernacle also shall be with them; indeed I will be their God, and they shall be My people. The nations also will know that I, the Lord, sanctify Israel, when My sanctuary is in their midst forevermore.

31. ANTICHRIST SURROUND AND DESECRATE JERUSALEM, **Revelation 11:2**

But leave out the court which is outside the temple, and do not measure it, for it has been given to the Gentiles. And they will tread the holy city underfoot for forty-two months.

32. SATAN FORETOLD, 2 Thessalonians 2:3-4;

Let no one deceive you by any means; for that Day will not come unless the falling away comes first, and the man of sin is revealed, the son of perdition, who opposes and exalts himself above all that is called God or that is worshiped, so that he sits as God in the temple of God, showing himself that he is God.

33. DRAGON'S TATTOO 666

Reference: evil number of the beast "666"

Revelation 13:16-18

He causes all, both small and great, rich and poor, free and slave, to receive a mark on their right hand or on their foreheads, and that no one may buy or sell except one who has the mark or the name of the beast, or the number of his name. Here is wisdom. Let him who has understanding calculate the number of the beast, for IT IS THE NUMBER OF A MAN: His number is 666.

34. THE SEVENTY-WEEKS PROPHECY

Daniel 9: 24-27

"Seventy weeks are determined
For your people and for your holy city,
To finish the transgression,
To make an end of sins,
To make reconciliation for iniquity,
To bring in everlasting righteousness,
To seal up vision and prophecy,
And to anoint the Most Holy.
"Know therefore and understand,
That from the going forth of the command
To restore and build Jerusalem
Until Messiah the Prince,
There shall be seven weeks and sixty-two weeks;
The street shall be built again, and the wall,
Even in troublesome times.
"And after the sixty-two weeks
Messiah shall be cut off, but not for Himself;
And the people of the prince who is to come
Shall destroy the city and the sanctuary.
The end of it shall be with a flood,

And till the end of the war desolations are determined. Then he shall confirm a covenant with many for one week;
But in the middle of the week
He shall bring an end to sacrifice and offering.
And on the wing of abominations shall be one who makes desolate,
Even until the consummation, which is determined,
Is poured out on the desolate."

35. CROWN OF ENGLAND display 666, Red-yellow-blue dragon colors.

For a color version of this image, see http://commons.wikimedia.org/wiki/File:Royal_Coat_of_Arms_of_the_United_Kingdom.svg.

36. PROPHET EZEKIEL

Ezekiel 37:26-28. Satan carries out the following deceptions

He will gather all Jews back to the Land of Israel

Isaiah 43:5-6
He will usher in an era of world peace, and end all hatred, oppression, suffering and disease.

Isaiah 2:4
He will spread universal knowledge and unite humanity as one.

37. FALSE CHRIST'S AND FALSE PROPHETS

Matthew 24: 23-26

"Then if anyone says to you, 'Look, here is the Christ!' or 'There!' do not believe it. For false Christ's and false prophets will rise and show great signs and wonders to deceive, if possible, even the elect. See, I have told you beforehand. "Therefore if they say to you, 'Look, He is in the desert!' do not go out; or 'Look, He is in the inner rooms!' do not believe it.

38. HOLPEN = DIVINE HELP FROM GOD

TIME OF HOLPEN 1290-1335 WORLDWIDE (TD) Daniel says; but the people who know their God shall be strong, and carry out great exploits. 33 And those of the people who UNDERSTAND shall instruct many; yet for many days they *shall fall by sword and flame, by captivity and plundering. 34 Now when they fall, they shall be aided with a little help; but many shall join with them by INTRIGUE.

HOLPEN DEFINITIONS:

I put together a few to make one as follows;

To furnish with strength and the means of deliverance from trouble as the evil approaches; [1913 Webster]

To help on, to forward; to promote by aid.

To help out, to aid, as in delivering from a difficulty, or To aid in completing a design or task.

[1913 Webster]

To help over, to enable to surmount; as, to help one over an obstacle.

To help up, to help (one) to get up; to assist in rising, as after a fall, and the like. "A man is well holp up that trusts to you."

Syn: To aid; assist; succor; relieve; serve; support; sustain; befriend. Succor; Help for someone needing it. help given to someone who is in serious need

USAGE OF THE WORD HOLPEN: To Help, Aid, Assist. These words all agree in the idea of affording relief or support to a person under difficulties.

HELP turns attention especially to the source of relief. I call for help; and he who helps me out does it by an act of his own.

AID turns attention to the other side, and supposes co["o]peration on the part of him who is relieved

ASSIST has a primary reference to relief afforded by a person who "stands by" in order to relieve. It denotes both help and aid.

39. DANIEL'S PROPHECY OF THE END TIME

12 "At that time Michael shall stand up,

The great prince who stands watch over the sons of your people;

And there shall be a time of trouble,

Such as never was since there was a nation,

Even to that time.

And at that time your people shall be delivered,

Everyone who is found written in the book.

2 And many of those who sleep in the dust of the earth shall awake,

Some to everlasting life,

Some to shame and everlasting contempt.

3 Those who are wise shall shine

Like the brightness of the firmament,

And those who turn many to righteousness

Like the stars forever and ever.

4 "But you, Daniel, shut up the words, and seal the book until the time of the end; many shall run to and fro, and knowledge shall increase."

5 Then I, Daniel, looked; and there stood two others, one on this riverbank and the other on that riverbank. 6 And one said to the man clothed in linen, who was above the waters of the river, "How long shall the fulfillment of these wonders be?"

7 Then I heard the man clothed in linen, who was above the waters of the river, when he held up his right hand and his left hand to heaven, and swore by Him who lives forever, that it shall be for a time, times, and half a time; and when the power of the holy people has been completely shattered, all these things shall be finished.

8 Although I heard, I did not understand. Then I said, "My lord, what shall be the end of these things?"

9 And he said, "Go your way, Daniel, for the words are closed up and sealed till the time of the end. 10 Many shall be purified, made white, and refined, but the wicked shall do wickedly; and none of the wicked shall understand, but the wise shall understand.

11 "And from the time that the daily sacrifice is taken away, and the abomination of desolation is set up, there shall be one thousand two hundred and ninety days. 12 Blessed is he who waits, and comes to the one thousand three hundred and thirty-five days.

13 "But you, go your way till the end; for you shall rest, and will arise to your inheritance at the end of the days."

40. 1260 DAYS UNTIL THE POWER OF THE HOLY PEOPLE SHATTERED.

Daniel 12:5-7

Then I, Daniel, looked; and there stood two others, one on this riverbank and the other on that riverbank. And one said to the man clothed in linen, who was above the waters of the river, "How long shall the fulfillment of these wonders be?"

Then I heard the man clothed in linen, who was above the waters of the river, when he held up his right hand and his left hand to heaven, and swore by Him who lives forever, <u>that it shall be for a time, times, and half a time; and when the power of the holy people has been completely shattered, all these things shall be finished.</u>

41. SAUL'S CONVERSION TO PAUL

Acts 22:6-9

"Now it happened, as I journeyed and came near Damascus at about noon, suddenly a great light from heaven shone around me. And I fell to the ground and heard a voice saying to me, 'Saul, Saul, why are you persecuting Me?' So I answered, 'Who are You, Lord?' And He said to me, 'I am Jesus of Nazareth, whom you are persecuting.' "And those who were with me indeed saw the light and were afraid, but they did not hear the voice of Him who spoke to me.

42. 7 SPIRITS OF GOD

Revelation 1:4

John to the seven churches which are in Asia: Grace be unto you, and peace, from him which is, and which was, and which is to come; and from the seven Spirits which are before his throne;

Revelation 3:1

And unto the angel of the church in Sardis write; These things saith he that hath the seven Spirits of God, and the seven stars; I know thy works, that thou hast a name that thou livest, and art dead.

Revelation 4:5

"From the throne came flashes of lightning, rumblings and peals of thunder. Before the throne, seven lamps were blazing. These are the seven spirits of God."

Revelation 5:6

And I beheld, and, lo, in the midst of the throne and of the four beasts, and in the midst of the elders, stood a Lamb as it had been slain, having seven horns and seven eyes, which are the seven Spirits of God sent forth into all the earth.

43. 7 THUNDERS OF GOD

Revelation 10:1-4

I saw still another mighty angel coming down from heaven, clothed with a cloud. And a rainbow was on his head, his face was like the sun, and his feet like pillars of fire. He had a little book open in his hand. And he set his right foot on the sea and his left foot on the land, and cried with a loud voice, as when a lion roars.

When he cried out, seven thunders uttered their voices. Now when the seven thunders uttered their voices, I was about to write; but I heard a voice from heaven saying to me, "Seal up the things which the seven thunders uttered, and do not write them."

Revelation 4:5

"From the throne came flashes of lightning, rumblings and peals of thunder. Before the throne, seven lamps were blazing. These are the seven spirits of God."

Revelation 8:5

Then the angel took the censer, filled it with fire from the altar, and threw it to the earth. And there were noises, thunderings, lightnings, and an earthquake.

Revelation 11:19

Then the temple of God was opened in heaven, and the ark of His covenant was seen in His temple. And there were lightnings, noises, thunderings, an earthquake, and great hail.

Revelation 16:18

And there were noises and thunderings and lightnings; and there was a great earthquake, such a mighty and great earthquake as had not occurred since men were on the earth.

Psalm 18:13

The Lord thundered from heaven, And the Most High uttered His voice, Hailstones and coals of fire.

Revelation 10:4

Now when the seven thunders uttered their voices, I was about to write; but I heard a voice from heaven saying to me, "Seal up the things which the seven thunders uttered, and do not write them."

44. THE TWO WITNESSES OF GOD

Revelation 11:3-6 New King James Version (NKJV)

The Two Witnesses 11 Then I was given a reed like a measuring rod. And the angel stood,[a] saying, "Rise and measure the temple of God, the altar, and those who worship there. 2 But leave out the court which is outside the temple, and do not measure it, for it has been given to the Gentiles. And they will tread the holy city underfoot *for* forty-two months. 3 And I will give *power* to my Two Witnesses, and they will prophesy one thousand two hundred and sixty days, clothed in sackcloth."4 These are the two olive trees and the two lampstands standing before the God[b] of the earth. 5 And if anyone wants to harm them, fire proceeds from their mouth and devours their enemies. And if anyone wants to harm them, he must be killed in this manner. 6 These have power to shut heaven, so that no rain falls in the days of their prophecy; and they have power over waters to turn them to blood, and to strike the earth with all plagues, as often as they desire.

The Witnesses Killed 7 When they finish their testimony, the beast that ascends out of the bottomless pit will make war against them, overcome them, and kill them. 8 And their dead bodies *will lie* in the street of the great city which spiritually is called Sodom and Egypt, where also our[c] Lord was crucified. 9 Then *those* from the peoples, tribes, tongues, and nations will see their dead bodies three-and-a-half days, and not allow[d] their dead bodies to be put into graves. 10 And those who dwell on the earth will rejoice over them, make merry, and send gifts to one another, because these two prophets tormented those who dwell on the earth.

The Witnesses Resurrected 11 Now after the three-and-a-half days the breath of life from God entered them, and they stood on their feet, and great fear fell on those who saw them. 12 And they[e] heard a loud voice from heaven saying to them, "Come up here." And they ascended to heaven in a cloud, and their enemies saw them. 13 In the same hour there was a great earthquake, and a tenth of the city fell. In the earthquake seven thousand people were killed, and the rest were afraid and gave glory to the God of heaven. 14 The second woe is past. Behold, the third woe is coming quickly.

45. TWO WITNESSES OF GOD (additional)

Revelation 1: 1-2

The Revelation of Jesus Christ, which God gave Him to show His servants—things which must shortly take place. And He sent and signified it by His angel to His servant John, who bore witness to the Word of God, and to the testimony of Jesus Christ, to all things that he saw.

I believe that the "Word of God" and the "Testimony of Jesus Christ" can also refer to the Two Witnesses.

Also in the Bible and (Israeli Torah) we read of these Two Witnesses;

Deuteronomy 19:15

The Law Concerning Witnesses "One witness shall not rise against a man concerning any iniquity or any sin that he commits; by the mouth of two or three witnesses the matter shall be established.

The Bible requires at least "Two Witnesses" to establish any important truth.

Deuteronomy 17:6

Whoever is deserving of death shall be put to death on the testimony of two or three witnesses; he shall not be put to death on the testimony of one witness.

Roughly speaking the second half of the 7 Year Great Tribulation is for the "Israelites" and "Saved Nations" and is called the "Time of Redemption",

The Israelites relate to the Two Witnesses of God and their "Testimony unto Repentance". This infuriates the "unholy trinity" who goes from protecting Israel to persecuting her.

We read in the Old Testament the Prophet Zechariah wrote;

Reference: one lampstand & two olive trees

Zechariah 4: 1-14)

Concerning one lampstand and two olive trees. Many Israelites know of this Bible passage and some of the people refer to them as Moses and Elijah, great people of the Old Testament. In the New Testament we have references in;

Reference: two lampstand & two olive trees

Revelation 11:4

These are the two olive trees and two lampstands standing before the God of the earth.

I believe this means that there is one olive tree designated for the Old Testament and one olive tree for the New Testament, so in our time the Book of Revelation shows Two Olive Trees representing the past and future times. The Bible says;

Reference: Two Witnesses of God

Revelation 11:3

I will give power to my Two Witnesses, and they will prophesy one thousand two hundred and sixty days, clothed in sackcloth."

These are the two olive trees and the two lampstands standing before the God of the earth.

46. ONE LAMPSTAND AND TWO OLIVE TREES

Zechariah 4: 4-14

VISION OF THE LAMPSTAND AND OLIVE TREES

4 Now the angel who talked with me came back and wakened me, as a man who is wakened out of his sleep. 2 And he said to me, "What do you see?"

So I said, "I am looking, and there is a lampstand of solid gold with a bowl on top of it, and on the stand seven lamps with seven pipes to the seven lamps. 3 Two olive trees are by it, one at the right of the bowl and the other at its left." 4 So I answered and spoke to the angel who talked with me, saying, "What are these, my lord?"

5 Then the angel who talked with me answered and said to me, "Do you not know what these are?"

And I said, "No, my lord."
6 So he answered and said to me:

"This is the word of the Lord to Zerubbabel:
'Not by might nor by power, but by My Spirit,'
Says the Lord of hosts.
7 'Who are you, O great mountain?
Before Zerubbabel you shall become a plain!
And he shall bring forth the capstone
With shouts of "Grace, grace to it!"'"

8 Moreover the word of the Lord came to me, saying:
9 "The hands of Zerubbabel
Have laid the foundation of this temple;[a]
His hands shall also finish it.
Then you will know
That the Lord of hosts has sent Me to you.
10 For who has despised the day of small things?
For these seven rejoice to see
The plumb line in the hand of Zerubbabel.
They are the eyes of the Lord,
Which scan to and fro throughout the whole earth.

11 Then I answered and said to him, "What are these two olive trees—at the right of the lampstand and at its left?" 12 And I further answered and said to him, "What are these two olive branches that drip into the receptacles[b] of the two gold pipes from which the golden oil drains?"

13 Then he answered me and said, "Do you not know what these are?"

And I said, "No, my lord."

14 So he said, "These are the two anointed ones, who stand beside the Lord of the whole earth." (Reference Revelation 11:4)

47. JOHN THE BAPTIST

Matthew 3:1-5

In those days John the Baptist came preaching in the wilderness of Judea, and saying, "Repent, for the kingdom of heaven is at hand!" For this is he who was spoken of by the prophet Isaiah, saying: "The voice of one crying in the wilderness: 'Prepare the way of the Lord; Make His paths straight.' Now John himself was clothed in camel's hair, with a leather belt around his waist; and his food was locusts and wild honey. Then Jerusalem, all Judea, and all the region around the Jordan went out to him and were baptized by him in the Jordan, confessing their sins.

John the Baptist said in;

Matthew 3:11

I indeed baptize you with water unto repentance, but He who is coming after me is mightier than I, whose sandals I am not worthy to carry. He will baptize you with the Holy Spirit and fire.

48. THREE MEN IN THE FIERY FURNACE

Daniel 3: 19-25

Then Nebuchadnezzar was full of fury, and the expression on his face changed toward Shadrach, Meshach, and Abed-Nego. He spoke and commanded that they heat the furnace seven times more than it was usually heated. And he commanded certain mighty men of valor who were in his army to bind Shadrach, Meshach, and Abed-Nego, and cast them into the burning fiery furnace. Then these men were bound in their coats, their trousers, their turbans, and their other garments, and were cast into the midst of the burning fiery furnace. Therefore, because the king's command was urgent, and the furnace exceedingly hot, the flame of the fire killed those men who took up Shadrach, Meshach, and Abed-Nego. And these three men, Shadrach, Meshach, and Abed-Nego, fell down bound into the midst of the burning fiery furnace. Then King Nebuchadnezzar was astonished; and he rose in haste and spoke, saying to his counselors, "Did we not cast three men bound into the midst of the fire?" They answered and said to the king, "True, O king." "Look!" He answered, "I see four men loose, walking in the midst of the fire; and they are not hurt, and the form of the fourth is like the Son of God."

49. KINGS HIGHWAY

Isaiah 35:8

A highway will be there, a road, and it will be called The Holy Way.

Isaiah 40:3

A voice of one calling: "In the desert prepare the way for the LORD; make straight in the wilderness a highway for our God. The unclean shall not pass over it, but it will be for those who walk in the Way. Wicked fools will not go there.

Isaiah 30:21

"Whether you turn to the right or to the left, your ears will hear a voice behind you, saying, "This is the way; walk in it" guiding them along the way and only they can travel upon this highway as no evil can travel upon it.

50. FIFTH TRUMPET: THE LOCUSTS FROM THE BOTTOMLESS PIT

9 Then the fifth angel sounded: And I saw a star fallen from heaven to the earth. To him was given the key to the bottomless pit. 2 And he opened the bottomless pit, and smoke arose out of the pit like the smoke of a great furnace. So the sun and the air were darkened because of the smoke of the pit. 3 Then out of the smoke locusts came upon the earth. And to them was given power, as the scorpions of the earth have power. 4 They were commanded not to harm the grass of the earth, or any green thing, or any tree, but only those men who do not have the seal of God on their foreheads. 5 And they were not given authority to kill them, but to torment them for five months. Their torment was like the torment of a scorpion when it strikes a man. 6 In those days men will seek death and will not find it; they will desire to die, and death will flee from them.

7 The shape of the locusts was like horses prepared for battle. On their heads were crowns of something like gold, and their faces were like the faces of men. 8 They had hair like women's hair, and their teeth were like lions' teeth. 9 And they had breastplates like breastplates of iron, and the sound of their wings was like the sound of chariots with many horses running into battle. 10 They had tails like scorpions, and there were stings in their tails. Their power was to hurt men five months. 11 And they had as king over them the angel of the bottomless pit, whose name in Hebrew is Abaddon, but in Greek he has the name Apollyon.

12 One woe is past. Behold, still two more woes are coming after these things

51. FIRST BOWL: LOATHSOME SORES

Revelation 16:2

So the first went and poured out his bowl upon the earth, and a foul and loathsome sore came upon the men who had the mark of the beast and those who worshiped his image.

52. TAKE REFUGE FROM THE COMING JUDGMENT

Your dead shall live....Take Refuge from the Coming Judgment

Come, my people, enter your chambers, And shut your doors behind you; Hide yourself, as it were, for a little moment, Until the indignation is past.

53. YOUR COVENANT WITH DEATH WILL BE ANNULLED,

And your agreement with Sheol will not stand;
When the overflowing scourge passes through,
Then you will be trampled down by it.
19 As often as it goes out it will take you;
For morning by morning it will pass over,
And by day and by night;
It will be a terror just to understand the report."

54. FLESH DISSOLVING

12 And this shall be the plague with which the Lord will strike all the people who fought against Jerusalem: Their flesh shall dissolve while they stand on their feet, Their eyes shall dissolve in their sockets, And their tongues shall dissolve in their mouths. 13 It shall come to pass in that day That a great panic from the Lord will be among them. Everyone will seize the hand of his neighbor, And raise his hand against his neighbor's hand;

55. THESE HAVE POWER TO SHUT HEAVEN

Revelation 11; 6

so that no rain falls in the days of their prophecy; <u>and they have power over waters to turn them to blood, and to strike the earth with all plagues, as often as they desire.</u>

56. REAPING THE GRAPES OF WRATH

17 Then another angel came out of the temple which is in heaven, he also having a sharp sickle.

18 And another angel came out from the altar, who had power over fire, and he cried with a loud cry to him who had the sharp sickle, saying, "Thrust in your sharp sickle and gather the clusters of the vine of the earth, for her grapes are fully ripe." 19 So the angel thrust his sickle into the earth and gathered the vine of the earth, and threw it into the great winepress of the wrath of God. 20 And the winepress was trampled outside the city, and blood came out of the winepress, up to the horses' bridles, for one thousand six hundred furlongs.

57. FLESH EATING,

And I will cause them to eat the flesh of their sons, daughters and flesh of his friend.

In the Biblical book of Leviticus 26:29 you shall eat the flesh of your sons, and you shall eat the flesh of your daughters.

During my limited research of "Cannibalism in the Bible" I came across about 10 instances of the Israelites doing such gross things. They only did these abominations out of desperation that they brought on themselves because they always turned away from their God. Read more in the next foot note.

58. EZEKIEL chapter 5:9-10

And I will do among you what I have never done, and the like of which I will never do again, because of all your abominations. 10 Therefore fathers shall eat their sons in your midst, and sons shall eat their fathers; and I will execute judgments among you, and all of you who remain I will scatter to all the winds.

Deuteronomy 28:53-57

Because of the suffering that your enemy will inflict on you during the siege, you will eat the fruit of the womb, the flesh of the sons and daughters the Lord your God has given you. Even the most gentle and sensitive man among you will have no compassion on his own brother or the wife he loves or his surviving children, and he will not give to one of them any of the flesh of his children that he is eating. It will be all he has left because of the suffering your enemy will inflict on you during the siege of all your cities. The most gentle and sensitive woman among you—so sensitive and gentle that she would not venture to touch the ground with the sole of her foot—will begrudge the husband she loves and her own son or daughter the afterbirth from her womb and the children she bears. For she intends to eat them secretly during the siege and in the distress that your enemy will inflict on you in your cities.

Lev 26:29

You will eat the flesh of your sons and the flesh of your daughters.

Jeremiah 19:9

I will make them eat the flesh of their sons and daughters, and they will eat one another's flesh during the stress of the siege imposed on them by the enemies who seek their lives.

Lamentations 2:2

See, O LORD, and look! With whom have You dealt thus? Should women eat their offspring, The little ones who were born healthy? Should priest and prophet be slain In the sanctuary of the Lord?

Lamentation 4:10

With their own hands compassionate women
have cooked their own children,
who became their food
when my people were destroyed.

2 Kings 6:26-29

As the king of Israel was passing by on the wall, a woman cried to him, "Help me, my lord the king!"

The king replied, "If the Lord does not help you, where can I get help for you? From the threshing floor? From the winepress?" Then he asked her, "What's the matter?" She answered, "This woman said to me, 'Give up your son so we may eat him today, and tomorrow we'll eat my son.' So we cooked my son and ate him. The next day I said to her, 'Give up your son so we may eat him,' but she had hidden him."

59. EZEKIEL WRITES

in chapter 5:11-12 'Therefore, as I live,' says the Lord God, 'surely, because you have defiled My sanctuary with all your detestable things and with all your abominations, therefore I will also diminish you; My eye will not spare, nor will I have any pity. 12 One-third of you shall die of the pestilence, and be consumed with famine in your midst; and one-third shall fall by the sword all around you; and I will scatter another third to all the winds, and I will draw out a sword after them.

60. PILLAR OF FIRE

Exodus 14:24

Now it came to pass, in the morning watch, that the Lord looked down upon the army of the Egyptians THROUGH THE PILLAR OF FIRE and cloud, and He troubled the army of the Egyptians.

Exodus 13:21

And the Lord went before them by day in a **pillar of** cloud to lead the way, and by night in a **pillar of fire** to give them light, so as to go by day and night.

Deuteronomy 12:3

And you shall destroy their altars, break their *sacred* **pillar**s, and burn their wooden images with **fire**; you shall cut down the carved images **of** their gods and destroy their names from that place.

Nehemiah 9:12

Moreover You led them by day with a cloudy **pillar**, And by night with a **pillar of fire**, To give them light on the road Which they should travel.

Joel 2:30

"And I will show wonders in the heavens and in the earth: Blood and **fire** and **pillars of** smoke.

Revelation 10:1 this is a strange one: *The Mighty Angel with the Little Book*] I saw still another mighty angel coming down from heaven, clothed with a cloud. And a rainbow *was* on his head, his face *was* like the sun, and his feet like **pillars of fire**.

61. THE MIGHTY ANGEL WITH THE LITTLE BOOK

Revelation 10:1-4

I saw still another mighty angel coming down from heaven, clothed with a cloud. And a rainbow *was* on his head, his face *was* like the sun, and his feet like pillars of fire. 2 He had a little book open in his hand. And he set his right foot on the sea and *his* left *foot* on the land, 3 and cried with a loud voice, as *when* a lion roars. When he cried out, seven thunders uttered their voices. 4 Now when the seven thunders uttered their voices,[a] I was about to write; but I heard a voice from heaven saying to me,[b] "Seal up the things which the seven thunders uttered, and do not write them."

62. JOEL 12;17

LET THE PRIESTS, who minister to the Lord, weep between the porch and the altar, Let them say, "Spare Your people, O LORD, And do not give Your heritage to reproach, That the nations should rule over them. Why should they say among the peoples, "Where is their God?

These Redeemed Israelites worship between the porch and altar, they are allowed to be in front of the Temple however not in it. Remember that the Temple of God at this time is only partially opened. This group accepted in faith the "Testimony of the Two

Witnesses of God" prior to the "abomination of desolation" being place and activated in the "false messiah's" temple.

They become "priests" of some type in the "Wilderness Sanctuary" who are the Redeemed and who are now sanctified. Their contrite hearts attitude was acceptable to God. Let's read some Bible texts that seem to give credence to my thinking as follow, Joel 12;14..17 Blow the trumpet in Zion, Consecrate a fast, Call a sacred assembly Gather the people, Sanctify the congregation, Assemble the elders, Gather the children and nursing babes.

Tom said the following may also apply, 1 Kings 19:18 Yet I reserve seven thousand in Israel all whose knees have not bowed down to Baal and all whose mouths have not kissed him.

Tom said now another strange one, Ezekiel 9; 1-11 The Vision of Slaughter. The LORD said to him, "Go through the midst of the city, even through the midst of Jerusalem, and put a mark on the foreheads of the men who sigh and groan over all the abominations which are being com mitted in its midst."

Another future prophecy is from Isaiah 26; 20-28 edited, Take Refuge from the Coming Judgment. "Then say to them, 'Thus says the Lord God: "Surely I will take the children of Israel from among the nations, wherever they have gone, and will gather them from every side and bring them into their own land; and I will make them one nation in the land, on the mountains of Israel. Moreover I will make a covenant of peace with them, and it shall be an everlasting covenant with them; I will establish them and multiply them, and I will set My sanctuary in their midst forevermore. My tabernacle also shall be with them; indeed I will be their God, and they shall be My people. The nations also will know that I, the Lord, sanctify Israel, when My sanctuary is in their midst forevermore."

When the above passages are paraphrased we get the following; Call a sacred assembly, Gather the people, Sanctify the congregation, Assemble the elders, Gather the children and nursing babes

1 Kings 19:18 Yet I have reserved seven thousand in Israel, all whose knees have not bowed to Baal, and every mouth that has not kissed him."

Yet I have reserved seven thousand in Israel, all whose knees have not bowed to Baal, and every mouth that has not kissed him."

63. "ABOMINATION OF DESOLATION"

Matthew 24:15

"So when you see standing in the holy place 'the abomination that causes desolation,' spoken of through the prophet Daniel—let the reader understand—

Mark 13:14

"When you see 'the abomination that causes desolation' standing where it does not belong—let the reader understand—then let those who are in Judea flee to the mountains.

Ezekiel 4:6

"After you have finished this, lie down again, this time on your right side, and bear the sin of the house of Judah. I have assigned you 40 days, a day for each year.

Daniel 8:11

It set itself up to be as great as the Prince of the host; it took away the daily sacrifice from him, and the place of his sanctuary was brought low.

Daniel 8:14

He said to me, "It will take 2,300 evenings and mornings; then the sanctuary will be cleansed.

Daniel 9:27

He will confirm a covenant with many for one 'seven.' In the middle of the 'seven' he will put an end to sacrifice and offering. And on a wing [of the temple] he will set up an abomination that causes desolation, until the end that is decreed is poured out on him."

Daniel 11:31

"His armed forces will rise up to desecrate the temple fortress and will abolish the daily sacrifice. Then they will set up the abomination that causes desolation.

Daniel 12:11

New King James Version (NKJV)

11 "And from the time *that* the daily *sacrifice* is taken away, and the abomination of desolation is set up, *there shall be* one thousand two hundred and ninety days

Hosea 3:4

For the Israelites will live many days without king or prince, without sacrifice or sacred stones, without ephod or idol.

New Living Translation (©2007)

"From the time the daily sacrifice is stopped and the sacrilegious object that causes desecration is set up to be worshiped, there will be 1,290 days.

International Standard Version (©2012)

There will be 1,290 days from the time the regular burnt offering is rescinded and the destructive desolation established.

GOD'S WORD® Translation (©1995)

From the time the daily burnt offering is taken away and the disgusting thing that causes destruction is set up, there will be 1,290 days.

64. A MULTITUDE FROM THE GREAT TRIBULATION

Revelation 7:9-17 After these things I looked, and behold, a great multitude which no one could number, of all nations, tribes, peoples, and tongues, standing before the throne and before the Lamb, clothed with white robes, with palm branches in their hands, 10 and crying out with a loud voice, saying, "Salvation *belongs* to our God who sits on the throne, and to the Lamb!" 11 All the angels stood around the throne and the elders and the four living creatures, and fell on their faces before the throne and worshiped God, 12 saying:

"Amen! Blessing and glory and wisdom,
Thanksgiving and honor and power and might,
Be to our God forever and ever.
Amen."

13 Then one of the elders answered, saying to me, "Who are these arrayed in white robes, and where did they come from?"

14 And I said to him, "Sir,[b] you know." So he said to me, "These are the ones who come out of the great tribulation, and washed their robes and made them white in the blood of the Lamb. 15 Therefore they are before the throne of God, and serve Him day and night in His temple. And He who sits on the throne will dwell among them. 16 They shall neither hunger anymore nor thirst anymore; the sun shall not strike them, nor any heat; 17 for the Lamb who is in the midst of the throne will shepherd them and lead them to living fountains of waters.[c] And God will wipe away every tear from their eyes."

65. REFERENCE: A Multitude from the Great Tribulation.

Revelation 7:9-17

After these things I looked, and behold, a great multitude which no one could number, of all nations, tribes, peoples, and tongues, standing before the throne and before the Lamb, clothed with white robes, with palm branches in their hands, and crying out with a loud voice, saying, "Salvation belongs to our God who sits on the throne, and to the Lamb!"

All the angels stood around the throne and the elders and the four living creatures, and fell on their faces before the throne and worshiped God, saying: "Amen! Blessing and glory and wisdom, Thanksgiving and honor and power and might, Be to our God forever and ever. Amen."

Then one of the elders answered, saying to me, "Who are these arrayed in white robes, and where did they come from?" And I said to him, "Sir, you know." So he said to me,

"These are the ones who come out of the great tribulation, and washed their robes and made them white in the blood of the Lamb.

Therefore they are before the throne of God, and serve Him day and night in His temple. And He who sits on the throne will dwell among them. They shall neither hunger anymore nor thirst anymore; the sun shall not strike them, nor any heat; for the Lamb who is in the midst of the throne will shepherd them and lead them to living fountains of waters. And God will wipe away every tear from their eyes."

66. SOUND OF A GREAT TRUMPET, MARTYRS GATHERED FROM THE SKY

Matthew 24: 29-31

The Coming of the Son of Man

29 "Immediately after the tribulation of those days the sun will be darkened, and the moon will not give its light; the stars will fall from heaven, and the powers of the heavens will be shaken. 30 Then the sign of the Son of Man will appear in heaven, and then all the tribes of the earth will mourn, and they will see the Son of Man coming on the clouds of heaven with power and great glory. 31 And He will send His angels with a great sound of a trumpet, and they will gather together His elect from the four winds, from one end of heaven to the other.

SOUND OF A GREAT TRUMPET

1 Thessalonians 4:16 16 For the Lord Himself will descend from heaven with a shout, with the voice of an archangel, AND WITH THE TRUMPET OF GOD. And the dead in Christ will rise first. 17 Then we who are alive *and* remain shall be caught up together with them in the clouds to meet the Lord in the air. And thus we shall always be with the Lord. 18 Therefore comfort one another with these words.

67. SAVED GATHERED, 2300 T/D. Matthew 24;30-31

Then the sign of the Son of Man will appear in heaven, and then all the tribes of the earth will mourn, and they will see the Son of Man coming on the clouds of heaven with power and great glory. And He will send His angels with a great sound of a trumpet, and they will gather together His elect from the four winds, from one end of heaven to the other. Fiery star crafts are now visible to the people on earth. The 7 Thunders have uttered their voices, the mysteries of God now finished.

68. PARABLE OF THE WEDDING FEAST

And Jesus answered and spoke to them again by parables and said: 2 "The kingdom of heaven is like a certain king who arranged a marriage for his son, 3 and sent out his servants to call those who were invited to the wedding; and they were not willing to come. 4 Again, he sent out other servants, saying, 'Tell those who are invited, "See, I have prepared my dinner; my oxen and fatted cattle *are* killed, and all things *are* ready. Come to the wedding."' 5 But they made light of it and went their ways, one to his own farm, another to his business. 6 And the rest seized his servants, treated *them* spitefully, and killed *them*. 7 But when the king heard *about it,* he was furious. And he sent out his armies, destroyed those murderers, and burned up their city. 8 Then he said to his servants, 'The wedding is ready, but those who were invited were not worthy. 9 <u>Therefore go into the highways, and as many as you find, invite to the wedding.' 10 So those servants went out into the highways and gathered together all whom they found, both bad and good. And the wedding hall was filled with guests.</u>

11 "But when the king came in to see the guests, he saw a man there who did not have on a wedding garment. 12 So he said to him, 'Friend, how did you come in here without a wedding garment?' And he was speechless. 13 Then the king said to the servants, 'Bind him hand and foot, take him away, and[a] cast *him* into outer darkness; there will be weeping and gnashing of teeth.'

14 "For many are called, but few *are* chosen."

69. TWO WITNESSES OF GOD COME BACK TO LIFE

Revelation 11:13 the breath of life from God entered them, and they stood on their feet, and great fear fell on those who saw them. And they heard a loud voice from heaven saying to them, "come up here." And they ascended to heaven in a cloud, and their enemies saw them. In the same hour there was a great earthquake, and a tenth of the city fell. In the earthquake seven thousand people were killed, and the rest were afraid and gave glory to the God of heaven.

70. ARMAGEDDON

Revelation: 19: 19-21

And I saw the beast, the kings of the earth, and their armies, gathered together to make war against Him who sat on the horse and against His army. Then the beast was captured, and with him the false prophet who worked signs in his presence, by which he deceived those who received the mark of the beast and those who worshiped his image. These two were cast alive into the lake of fire burning with brimstone. And the rest were killed with the sword which proceeded from the mouth of Him who sat on the horse. And all the birds were filled with their flesh.

71. SOULS SAVED IN ETERNITY

For Christ also suffered once for sins, the just for the unjust, that He might bring us[e] to God, being put to death in the flesh but made alive by the Spirit, 19 <u>by whom also He went and preached to the spirits in prison, 20 who formerly were disobedient, when once the Divine longsuffering waited[f] in the days of Noah, while the ark was being prepared, in which a few, that is, eight souls, were saved through water.</u> 21 There is also an antitype which now saves us—baptism (not the removal of the filth of the flesh, but the answer of a good conscience toward God), through the resurrection of Jesus Christ, 22 who has gone into heaven and is at the right hand of God, angels and authorities and powers having been made subject to Him.

72. Luke, 18:9-14

The Parable of the Pharisee and the Tax Collector Also He spoke this parable to some who trusted in themselves that they were righteous, and despised others: 10 "Two men went up to the temple to pray, one a Pharisee and the other a tax collector. 11 <u>The Pharisee stood and prayed thus with himself, 'God, I thank You that I am not like other men—extortioners, unjust, adulterers, or even as this tax collector.</u> 12 I fast twice a week; I give tithes of all that I possess.'

13 <u>And the tax collector, standing afar off, would not so much as raise his eyes to heaven,</u> but beat his breast, saying, '<u>God, be merciful to me a sinner!</u>' 14 I tell you, this man went down to his house justified rather than the other; for everyone who exalts himself will be humbled, and he who humbles himself will be exalted."

73. RAPTURE'S REWARD

Revelation;

2:7 To him that overcometh will I give to eat of the tree of life, which is in the midst of the paradise of God.

2:11 He who overcomes shall not be hurt by the second death.

2:17 To him who overcomes I will give some of the hidden manna to eat. And I will give him a white stone, and on the stone a new name written which no one knows except him who receives it.

2:25-29 And he who overcomes, and keeps My works until the end, to him I will give power over the nations 'He shall rule them with a rod of iron; They shall be dashed to pieces like the potter's vessels' as I also have received from My Father; and I will give him the morning star.

3:4-5 They shall walk with Me in white, for they are worthy. He who overcomes shall be clothed in white garments, and I will not blot out his name from the Book of Life; but I will confess his name before My Father and before His angels.

3:12 He who overcomes, I will make him a pillar in the temple of My God, and he shall go out no more. I will write on him the name of My God and the name of the city of My God, the New Jerusalem, which comes down out of heaven from My God. And I will write on him My new name.

3:20-21 Behold, I stand at the door and knock. If anyone hears My voice and opens the door, I will come in to him and dine with him, and he with Me. To him who overcomes I will grant to sit with Me on My throne, as I also overcame and sat down with My Father on His throne.

THE END